GOTHIC FANTASY

AFRO FUTURISM SHORT STORIES

ANTHOLOGY OF NEW & CLASSIC TALES

Foreword by Nisi Shawl

Introduction by Dr. Sandra M. Grayson

Contributing Editor: Isis Asare

FLAME TREE PUBLISHING

This is a FLAME TREE Book

FLAME TREE PUBLISHING
6 Melbray Mews, Fulham,
London SW6 3NS, United Kingdom
www.flametreepublishing.com

First published 2025

A Warning to the Reader on Content
Please be advised that some stories contain references to and descriptions of concepts that some readers may find troubling, triggering or offensive, such as: racist acts and slurs, other offensive language, death, dead bodies, and violence, which is at the authors' discretion and integral to their stories.

25 27 29 28 26
1 3 5 7 9 10 8 6 4 2

ISBN: 978-1-83562-264-3
Special ISBN: 978-1-83562-678-8

The cover image is created by Flame Tree Studio
based on artwork courtesy of Shutterstock.com/Slava Gerj/
Gabor Ruszkai/Polina Raulina/galacticus.

Incidental motif images courtesy of Shutterstock.com.

A copy of the CIP data for this book is available from the British Library.

Printed and bound in China

GOTHIC

AFRO FUTURISM SHORT STORIES

ANTHOLOGY OF NEW & CLASSIC TALES

Foreword by Nisi Shawl

Introduction by Dr. Sandra M. Grayson

Contributing Editor: Isis Asare

FLAME TREE PUBLISHING

FANTASY

Contents

Foreword: Afrofuturism Short Stories

A Debatable Term for a Debatable Land – and Beyond

WHAT'S YOUR DEFINITION of Afrofuturism? Shall we debate it? Wikipedia has a whole article on it; they begin with the words "Afrofuturism is…" and go on to call it an aesthetic and a philosophy. The article talks of its range and its history (the first use of the word Afrofuturism, as you may have already learned, was in a 1993 critical essay by Mark Dery). Shorter definitions abound, including on the websites of our publisher and at least one of our contributors, Steven Barnes.

Think about it and you'll see that Afrofuturism is a portmanteau word, a mash-up: Afro, as a prefix, means 'derived from Africa'; futurism means envisioning the future. So when we talk about Afrofuturism, we're talking about envisioning a future rising from African roots, right? That was the literary territory covered by Dery's original usage. But the Afrofuturist movement has extended the term's scope beyond the future, back into the past, sideways into parallel timelines, mysteriously into the hidden cracks of histories happening outside the scrutiny of conventional scholars. And many of us considering where and when to apply it also interrogate the 'derived from Africa' part of Afrofuturism's definition.

We do so because Africa is a continent, not a country. It's huge! It's home to deserts, jungles, mountains, plains, farms, cities, ruins, airports, seaports, prisons, schools – home to highly varied sources of inspiration, with living roots transplanted across the entire world. This has happened because Africa is the historic home of multiple people who have migrated voluntarily or been forcibly moved to multiple lands. Some say Africa is the original home of humanity itself. If so, everything and everyone is, at some remove, African-derived.

The more exact terms Africanfuturism and Africanjujuism address the question of how precisely to understand what actually is African-derived, limiting it as a demographic designation to 'born within two generations at the most'. Plus that second word, Africanjujuism, deals with the rule restricting its potential stories to the conventional future by allowing us to recognize and name a literary movement encompassing them with a name making no reference at all to time. This literary movement encompasses African citizens' imaginings of any sort, set anywhere, happening anywhen.

And yet, depending on the standards set for who and what counts as 'African-derived', these two more exact terms can also fail to encompass everything included in our book. For example, some of us were born on the African continent themselves, or born to those born there. But many of us were not; for five generations back, most of my ancestors lived in North America.

Here's another, broader term attempting to cover this literary territory: the Black Fantastic. Though it's now the title of an anthology of fiction (edited by Andre M. Carrington), 'the Black Fantastic' is a phrase which used to be entirely associated with academia. To most academics it covers speculative and imaginative work of several different genres and formats – horror, surrealism, and fable; poetry, comix, and film – by African-descended creative artists and/or about African-derived culture. This version of the Black Fantastic overlaps in lots of ways with what we're presenting in these Afrofuturism Short Stories.

These old stories. These new stories. We tell them. We live them. We collect and admire them.

The old stories our editors have gathered here for you shine like pearls who know their worth. One brilliant example is 'The Mystery Within Us', by the venerable Pauline E. Hopkins. First published in the very first issue of *The Colored American*, this story's eerie beauty owes much to the traditional strengths of late-Victorian literature, with its cigar-worshiping gentleman raconteur and its glowing, ectoplasmic physician.

The new stories are so many, each drawing us into a fertile world of Black imagination, each nurturing and framing and making real the next vision, the next divine mission, the next high adventure. In 'Danakil', through the words of a Kikuyu refugee from a war fought not far in the future, Steven Barnes describes first encounters with aliens and cybersoldiers; Chinelo Onwualu sets 'Night Market' on a colonized version of Mars which might be realized someday soon. But Minister Faust's 'Worth of a Nation' takes place in an alternate nineteenth century – an imaginary past. And Ran Walker's 'Ten Pieces' seems to surface out of some sleepless dream.

Afrofuturism is all that and more. It's everywhere. It's all at once. Afrofuturism is beyond space, beyond time. This book gets you there, gets you then.

Read it, and afterwards we can debate the experience.

Nisi Shawl

Introduction

AN EVOLVING CONCEPT, Afrofuturism refers to artistic endeavors by Black people on the African continent and in the African diaspora that use speculative fiction to explore, create, and reimagine experiences of people of African descent. However, even before the creation and evolution of the term, the ideas encompassed in the concept were conveyed. People of African descent have a history of creativity that includes imagining possible futures that often incorporate calls to action. This is an approach to art in which, as Mbye Cham explained in 'Film Text and Context' (1996), the role of the artist 'is not to make the revolution but to prepare its way through clarification, analysis and exposure, to provide people with a vision and a belief that a revolution is necessary, possible and desirable.' In *Talking Back: Thinking Feminist, Thinking Black* (1989), bell hooks observed that among the ways that oppressed people resist are by 'naming their history, telling their story.'

Reimagined societies are also evident in works that from a contemporary viewpoint represent the formation of black speculative fiction. However, the following authors were not science fiction writers, and it is important to consider their works within the historical and political contexts within which the texts were written. The works include: Martin R. Delany's *Blake: or the Huts of America* (1859); Sutton Griggs' *Imperium in Imperio* (1899); Pauline Hopkins' *Of One Blood* (1902–03); Edward Johnson's *Light Ahead for the Negro* (1904); W.E.B. Du Bois' 'The Comet' (1920); Oscar Micheaux's *The Symbol of the Unconquered: A Story of the Ku Klux Klan* (1920); Thomas Mfolo's *Chaka* (1925); George S. Schyuler's *Black No More* (1931); Jean-Louis Njemba Medou's *Nnanga Kon* (1932); Muhammadu Bello Kagara's *Gandoki* (1934); and Daniel Olorunfemi Fagunwa's *Ogboju Ode Ninu Igbo Irunmale* (*Forest of a Thousand Daemons: A Hunter's Saga*, 1938). These works, and others like them, are part of a larger group of artistic endeavors that represent black people's quest to tell their own stories. The following sections explore visions of the future by black writers and filmmakers in historical contexts.

Speculative Responses to the 'Color Line'

A recurring theme in pre-1960 works that re-envision American society is the 'color line,' a concept that refers to racial segregation after slavery was abolished in the United States. Starting in 1865, southern states enacted restrictive laws (referred to as 'black codes') to limit black people's freedom and rights. In 1877, southern states enacted additional discriminatory laws (referred to as 'Jim Crow laws') that legalized racial segregation. The phrase *color line* became more well-known after W.E.B. Du Bois used the phrase in his book *The Souls of Black Folk* (1903). Du Bois stated, 'The problem of the twentieth century is the problem of the color-line – the relation of the darker to the lighter races of men in Asia and Africa, in America and the islands of the sea.' In novels by Griggs, Hopkins and Johnson, imagining the United States without legal segregation manifests in multiple ways – a secret black government plans to secure equal rights for free blacks and to secure freedom and equal rights for all enslaved Africans (*Imperium in Imperio*); Kush (a rich and powerful ancient African nation) will rise to bring civilization to a corrupt world (*Of One Blood*); the United States becomes a socialist country and significant progress has been made in race relations (*Light Ahead for the Negro*).

Black people also used film to try to effect change. In 1921, Micheaux stated, 'Moving pictures have become one of the greatest vitalizing forces in race adjustment, and we are just beginning.' In his film *The Symbol of the Unconquered: A Story of the Ku Klux Klan*, the race adjustment is represented through a narrative in which black people defeat the Ku Klux Klan (KKK). Micheaux was a black independent filmmaker who produced, wrote, and directed films from 1919–48. The Micheaux Film and Book Company (later the Micheaux Film Corporation), founded by Micheaux, was the most successful of all the black film production companies. *The Symbol of the Unconquered* was one of his 'race films' and a response to D.W. Griffith's explicitly racist film *Birth of a Nation* (1915).

Race films were independent films produced by black filmmakers, rather than white-controlled films about black life. *The Symbol of the Unconquered* was considered timely given that there was a resurgence of the KKK in the United States. William Joseph Simmons revived the Knights of the Ku Klux Klan in the fall of 1915 after seeing Griffith's *Birth of a Nation* which glorifies the terrorist KKK and was first shown in the United States in February 1915. *The Symbol of the Unconquered* represents the true nature of the KKK as engaged in destruction, terror, theft, and racism and as motivated by economic self-interest. In the film, Hugh Van Allen (a black homesteader) helps his neighbor Evon Mason, a light-skinned black woman whom he believes is white, set up her land and home that she inherited from her grandfather. Although he falls in love with her, he does not tell her or pursue a romantic relationship with her because of the color line. The Knights of the Black Cross/night riders (terrorists who symbolize the KKK) threaten Hugh in order to take his land that has a vast oil reserve.

A significant part of *The Symbol of the Unconquered* is missing. However, 1920 and 1921 articles in various newspapers, including *The New York Age* and *The Philadelphia Tribune*, provide insight into the missing scenes. The missing footage includes scenes that show that the black community annihilates the Knights of the Black Cross, and Evon rescues Hugh from the night riders. Hugh later becomes the owner of a successful oil company. Two years after the night riders attack in Oristown, Hugh and Evon are reunited when Evon brings a letter from the 'Committee for the Defense of the Colored Race' to Hugh at his office. Through the letter, which states that Evon 'has rendered a great service to the black race,' he learns that she is black.

Schyuler's novel *Black No More* (1931) represents a future where racial segregation is eliminated through technology. As a means to solve the American race problem, Dr. Junius Crookman, a black biologist, invents a three-day treatment that changes a black person to a white one through a secret process that involves 'electrical nutrition and glandular control.' He resolves that since black people would not or could not leave America and were 'getting along only differently,' it seems to him that the only solution is 'to get white.' Although the change is not transferred to offspring, Dr. Crookman can transform a black infant to a white one in 24 hours. The protagonist Max Disher undergoes the black-no-more procedure after which Max looks white and feels 'like an American citizen.' For him, there is 'no more Jim Crow. No more insults. As a white man he could go anywhere, be anything he wanted to be, do most anything he wanted to do, be a free man at last.' After nearly all black people are white, Dr. Cookman publishes a monograph that states that in almost all cases the new Caucasians (approximately one-sixth of the population) are two or three shades lighter than the biological Caucasians. Regarding this finding, the narrator states, 'To a society that had been taught to venerate whiteness for over three hundred years, this announcement was rather staggering. What was the world coming to, if the blacks were whiter than the whites?'

Beyond Legal Segregation

The futures envisioned in post-1960 works by people of African descent demonstrate a shift from concerns about the color line to a wide range of other representations. The change in focus is probably tied to the implementation of laws prohibiting segregation, as well as a change in manifestations of racism. The Civil Rights Act of 1964 outlawed segregation in businesses, banned discriminatory practices in employment, and ended segregation in public places. Originally, Title VII of the 1964 Civil Rights Act excluded institutions of higher learning. However, in 1972, Congress amended Title VII to include educational institutions. The 1972 amendment was cited as the Equal Employment Opportunity Act of 1972.

In *Faculty of Color in Academe: Bittersweet Success* (2000), Caroline Sotello Viernes Turner and Samuel L. Myers, Jr. observed that there has been a change in manifestations of racism from primarily overt racism (such as white elected officials 'barring the entrance of African American students' and blatant 'rules excluding minorities from facilities of predominantly white universities') to 'less visible, more subtle slights and exclusions' which are real but difficult to prove. In 'Black Power' (1968), Stokely Carmichael explained that institutional racism is the 'overall operations of established and respected forces in the society, and thus does not receive the condemnation that individual racism receives'; individual racism 'consists of overt acts by individuals.' Institutional racism is 'less overt, far more subtle, less identifiable in terms of specific individuals committing the acts, but is no less destructive of human life' ('Black Power'). A subtext in the futures represented in Derrick Bell's 'The Space Traders' (1992), Octavia E. Butler's *Survivor* (1978), and Steven Barnes' *Far Beyond the Stars* (1998) is covert racism.

'The Space Traders' explores discrimination through a series of decisions the United States government makes after the arrival of aliens whom the media call 'Space Traders.' The aliens offer the government three much needed items – gold for the nearly bankrupt governments, chemicals to restore the environment, and safe nuclear engines – in exchange for the black citizens living in the United States. The Space Traders want to take black people to the aliens' home planet for undisclosed reasons. The government has sixteen days to respond. Most white people perceive the visitors from outer space as unthreatening, 'practical, no-nonsense folks like regular Americans.' Many black people view the aliens as 'distinctly unpleasant, even menacing' and their trade offer looks 'like bad news.' The 'race problem had worsened greatly in the 1990s' and over half of the black people 'had become outcasts. They were confined to former inner-city areas that had been divorced from their political boundaries. Huge walls surrounded these areas, and armed guards controlled entrance and exit around the clock.' This black underclass has not achieved full equality. The President believes that the aliens' offer will solve the present problems and 'an ultimate one...the great American racial experiment.' The President and his official cabinet members attempt to justify the unjustifiable and plan to enact legislation without due process or judicial review. However, Gleason Golightly, a black economics professor and an unofficial cabinet member, argues against the government's plan to condemn over twenty million black citizens 'to intergalactic exile.' Golightly places the President's goal of group banishment in the historical context of the times that the 'country's leaders have considered and rejected the removal of all those of African descent.' After debates (which also explore historical and contemporary issues of racism and discrimination in the United States), the government forces people of African descent to leave with the Space Traders. At the end of the story, the narrator observes that black people left America as their ancestors had arrived – in chains.

Similar to 'The Space Traders,' discrimination is a concern in *Survivor*. However, in the novel, humans ('Missionaries') leave Earth and begin a colony on a planet inhabited by two non-human groups – the Garkohn and the Tehkohn. Rather than create a new society with different rules, the Missionaries try desperately to preserve the past. They even retain the racism, sexism, and discrimination common in American culture. Alanna, a black woman, initially lives among the Missionaries. She is the foster child of Jules and Neila Verrick. The Verricks are European-Americans who represent those who continue racist beliefs and practices. Alanna's intelligence and adaptability enable her to survive and to save the Missionaries from the Garkohn. However, the humans do not accept Alanna, so she decides to live among the Tehkohn.

The novel *Far Beyond the Stars* is framed by the *Star Trek: Deep Space Nine* episode of the same title (directed by Avery Brooks) which focuses on racism in the United States during the 1950s. Captain Benjamin Sisko (the twenty-fourth century black captain of the starship Defiant and the space station Deep Space Nine) is transported back in time and experiences life as Benny Russell, a black science fiction writer in 1953 who works for a major white science fiction magazine (*Incredible Tales*) in New York City where he is the only black employee. Russell is traumatized (and suffers emotional and physical pain) as a result of experiencing racism at work and in society. Regarding the episode, Avery Brooks explained, 'What's insidious about racism is that it is unconscious... It's in the culture. It's the way people think. So that was the approach we took. I never talked about racism. I just showed how these intelligent people think, and it all came out of them... And unfortunately, prejudice, in its many forms, hasn't gone away. If we had changed the people's clothes...this story could be about right now' (*Star Trek Captain's Log*, 2007). Brooks further stated, 'When we talk about America, we still face the inextricable connection between racism, sexism. All that's here, it is a part of the American landscape.'

Although based on the television episode, the novel has a unique narrative. Juxtaposing scenes from 1940, 1953, and the twenty-fourth century, *Far Beyond the Stars* creates an intricately woven narrative of the past (where black people are the other – the alien) and the future (the twenty-fourth century, which stands in contrast to the racist and violent twentieth century). Russell mentally travels further in the past than Sisko. During the summer of 1940, Russell visits an exhibit from the Mali Republic at the World's Fair. The featured artifact is an Orb of the Prophets. According to Ajabwe, the curator and a representative of the Dogon people in Mali, many years earlier people from another planet visited the Dogon people and entrusted them with the Orb. Russell has an Orb experience, but he does not understand the vision. On a second visit to the exhibit, he touches the Orb, and his history opens to him. Similar to Sisko's situation, Russell's visions happen in his mind. Mentally, Russell observes the lives of his ancestors free in Africa and subsequently enslaved in America.

Colonized Futures

Works by Octavia E. Butler, Samuel R. Delany, Walter Mosley, and Audrey King Lewis envision futures involving colonization. In Butler's shorty story 'Amnesty' (2003), aliens called Communities occupy most deserts on Earth but almost no locations humans need. When the aliens had first arrived, they abducted some humans for experimental purposes. After realizing they had been harming the humans, the aliens stopped the experiments and focused on co-existence. To that end, the Communities had spent time and wealth working with human translators, lawyers, and politicians so that each 'Community is counted as a legal "person," whose individual mark would be accepted.' The aliens provide jobs for and try to understand humans. The protagonist Noah Cannon is a black woman who works as a translator for the Communities. Her goal is to keep peace between the humans and aliens. Noah meets with six applicants and explains what they can expect when working for the Communities. She closes the meeting with the historical information that after the first coordinated nuclear strike at the aliens when they had first arrived, the military of several nations had tried to again attack the aliens. However, the missiles had not detonated. Subsequently, half of the missiles were returned, armed and intact, in various places including the White House, the Pentagon, Beijing, London, and Paris. After that, "the 'invaders,' the 'alien weeds' began to become in many languages, our 'guests,' our 'neighbors,' and even our 'friends.'" The Communities have the other half of the missiles. Noah explains that humans had lost the short, quiet war.

Similar to the Communities, the aliens in Butler's Xenogenesis trilogy – *Dawn* (1987), *Adulthood Rites* (1988), and *Imago* (1989) – seek a permanent connection with humans, and some of the aliens have colonies on Earth. However, in the trilogy, extraterrestrials called the Oankali engage in gene trade that results in human offspring being mixed with alien DNA. The Oankali rescue the human survivors of war. The price for this help is gene trade – the aliens take and manipulate human genes. In *Dawn*, the Oankali had studied humans for more than 250 years and identified a 'mismatched pair of genetic characteristics' that are useful individually but lethal together. Jdahya, the first Oankali with whom the protagonist Lilith Iyapo interacts, explains that humans are intelligent and hierarchical. According to the aliens, the primary problem with this combination of characteristics is that the hierarchical trait is in control of humans, and the two characteristics prove lethal, as evidenced in the human war that had destroyed most of Earth.

In Delany's *They Fly at Ciron* (1993), as in 'Amnesty' and the Xenogenesis trilogy, colonization is central. However, in *They Fly at Ciron*, colonizers from Myetra, the ruling group, decide the fate and status of those they believe are inferior. Like European colonizers who, as Frantz Fanon described in *The Wretched of the Earth* (1961), imposed their rule upon the past, present, and future of a dominated country, the Myetrans in *They Fly at Ciron* crush other cultures and distort and destroy the past of the oppressed people. The Myetrans (who are interested in terror, fear, and domination) impose their laws, customs, and beliefs on those they conquer. Race and difference are also significant in *They Fly at Ciron*. The main characters represent societies that are opposites. Rahm (who has brown skin and molten amber eyes) is a peaceful Cironian who, until encountering green-eyed Lieutenant Kire (a member of the violent colonizers from the empire Myetra), had never seen a weapon (nor is there a word for weapon in the language or guns in the village). Further difference is explored through the Winged Ones who live in the mountains of the village of Ciron at Hi-Vator and the groundlings (those, like the Cironians and others, without wings).

Colonization manifests in different forms in the Mosley's novel *Blue Light* (1998); Lewis's film *The Gifted* (1993); Butler's Earthseed books, *Parable of the Sower* (1993) and *Parable of the Talents* (1998), and Butler's short story 'Bloodchild' (1984). In *Blue Light*, set primarily in the 1960s, an entity from an unknown part of the universe descends to Earth in a rain of blue light and infuses people with knowledge and power thereby colonizing their minds. The 'Blues,' those who survive the infusion, transcend the human race, and their minds live with the stars. Chance, the narrator, is a black man and a 'blue novitiate,' a person who learns from the light but does not witness it. *The Gifted*, written, produced, and directed by Lewis, was the first science fiction feature film by a black woman. Set in 1991, the film focuses on a black family's quest to save itself and the world from evil, destructive aliens who are led by Ogo who plans to colonize Earth. King Abe of the Dogon people in West Africa, the last of the African Gifted, searches for his black family in America who are in danger. The rare Gift, supernatural abilities and great power, had been given to the Dogon people by good aliens from a distant planet who had visited them many centuries before Christ was born. During that time, the enemy aliens had arrived on Earth to destroy all living things and to build their own world. The Dogon people had used the Gift to defeat the enemy forces.

The Earthseed books, *Parable of the Sower* (1993) and *Parable of the Talents* (1998), represent communities devastated by catastrophe and technology as the means to achieve the solution to Earth's problems. In *Parable of the Sower*, the protagonist Lauren Oya Olamina, a black woman, creates a belief system called Earthseed. The primary principle is 'God is change,' and the destiny of Earthseed is to travel in space to Alpha Centauri. Olamina believes that the key to breaking the old cycle of building and destroying is to set complex goals for humans to accomplish. The primary goal, according to Olamina, should be interstellar travel and the creation of Earthseed communities on extrasolar worlds. She recognizes that such a project is complex and expensive. Olamina highlights several key ideas for solving the nation's plight – to live in partnership with each other and with the environment; to live in small communities; to treat adaptability and education as essential. She decides that the solution is to teach teachers who would then become her disciples. She begins teaching people in their homes, a methodology that leads to the development of a growing Earthseed movement that, among other endeavors, establishes grade schools and colleges, offers scholarships to poor students, and finances scientific exploration. Although Olamina is not able to travel to the stars, she witnesses the first set of ships leaving Earth to fulfill the destiny of Earthseed.

While in the Earthseed books the goal of some humans is to set up colonies on other planets, a group of humans in 'Bloodchild' have achieved that goal by establishing a colony on a planet inhabited by aliens called Tlic. The colonists' ancestors had fled Earth to escape enslavement. The Tlic had helped them survive and gave them an area in which to live – the Preserve. The cost for this livable space is that some humans must serve as hosts to the Tlic offspring. This involves a process whereby a Tlic mother implants eggs into a human host – preferably a male so that females are free to have their own children. The Tlic mother must later cut open the human host to remove the mature offspring. Ideally, the Tlic offspring and human survive the procedure. T'Gatoi, the Tlic government official who supervises the Preserve, had chosen Gan (the protagonist) as an infant so that she could take part in all phases of his development. Initially, Gan is honored to have been selected as host for the offspring of T'Gatoi and perceives the procedure as 'a good and necessary thing that Tlic and Terran did together.' Subsequently, Gan perceives the entire process as 'wrong, alien' after he witnesses a host named Bram Lomas endure the Tlic procedure which does not transpire as it should. Regarding the trade humans must make to live on another planet, Butler explained in the 'Afterword' to 'Bloodchild' that an isolated colony of humans on an inhabited, extrasolar world 'would be a lifetime away from reinforcements. It wouldn't be the British Empire in space, and it wouldn't be *Star Trek*. Sooner or later, the humans would have to make some kind of accommodation with their um...their hosts. Chances are this could be an unusual accommodation.'

The Past Informs the Future

In John Akomfrah's cinematic essay *The Last Angel of History* (1996), a Data Thief (from 200 years in the future) searches fragments of the history of people of African descent to find a code which if deciphered will reveal the keys to the future. The one clue is the phrase 'Mothership Connection.' According to the narrator, 'The Data Thief knows that the first touch with science fiction came when Africans began playing drums to cover distance. Water carried the sound of the drums, and sound covered the distance between the Old and the New World. This was the Data Thief's first visit, his first clue. It took him back to the New World.' Subsequently, he becomes an angel of history who can 'visit the Old world and the New, but he cannot be a part of either.' Through clips of interviews and performances, as well as information about black culture and history, he perceives a connection among music, space, and the future. Symbolized in *The Last Angel of History* and other works by black artists who re-envision society is the concept Sankofa, a Twi word from the Akan people of Ghana that signifies that knowledge of history is essential to understand the present and create a positive future.

Dr. Sandra M. Grayson

Contributing Editor's Note

"Every story I create, creates me. I write to create myself."
Octavia E. Butler

TO MY FELLOW READERS, I am so grateful for you. If you are holding this anthology – nerding out so deeply that you are reading the Contributing Editor's Note, we are siblings in short story speculative fiction. We are kinfolk.

Honestly, for a long time I underappreciated short stories. I preferred to lose myself in voluminous tomes like N.K. Jemisin's fourteen-hundred-page *Inheritance Trilogy*. That was until participants in my favorite book club taught me that if a novel is a movie, then a short story is a song. That made the book club a house party – and, honey, we danced!

Members of the book club introduced me to my first Black speculative fiction short story collection. I remember the day I first held *Dark Matter: A Century of Speculative Fiction from the African Diaspora*. Published in 2000, it was the first anthology of Black speculative fiction published in the world. I relished every story. However, I was particularly touched by editor Sheree Renée Thomas's introduction. Her celebration of the expansiveness of the Black speculative fiction community was a revelation.

Octavia E. Butler, who contributed to the collection, lauded Thomas's hard work on the anthology in an interview with Seattle's Museum of Popular Culture. Butler herself had worked to publish an anthology of speculative stories by Black authors, which was to be titled *Black Futures*. She hoped to include work from Toni Cade Bambara's unpublished *The Last Quarter*. While the collection was never published, Butler's work continues to guide us.

Meeting weekly for almost a year, we read and discussed every story in *Dark Matter*. We then devoured *Africa Risen: A New Era of Speculative Fiction* edited by Sheree Renée Thomas, Zelda Knight and Oghenechovwe Donald Ekpeki. Next, *A People's Future of the United States* edited by Victor LaValle. In coming together and celebrating these stories and their authors, we recreate ourselves, revise our pasts and reimagine our futures. We become a coven that claims our magic.

So I joyfully share with you the latest grimoire for our collection, the absolutely gorgeous *Afrofuturism: Short Stories*. The anthology features work by authors we know and love – such as Tananarive Due and Akua Lezli Hope. It also includes writers published for the first time – such as Tiffany M. Davis. Consider me your DJ; I am about to drop that beat.

"Every story we read, creates us. We read to create ourselves."
Isis Asare

ashe,
isis asare from cyberspace
2025

Publisher's Note

FROM A TIME-TRAVELLING scientist saving the life of a slave-revolt leader, to new visions of segregation and resistance; from characters across time shaping humanity's technological future and the climate crisis while influenced by African gods, to interplanetary migrants accepting the grief of loss and abandonment and finding a place where they are welcome – this new collection reveals authors' broad interpretation of the theme of 'Afrofuturism'. A natural companion to our *Black Sci-Fi Short Stories* title, it aims to gather tales that envisage more specifically Black futures, alternative pasts or new worlds, but it also features more generally speculative works that simply breathe with Black culture and identity.

We were delighted to receive so many exciting submissions and the final selection is always an incredibly hard decision, but ultimately we chose a collection of stories we hope complements the classic examples, which include George S. Schuyler's chilling *Black No More*, an extract from Samuel Delaney's lyrical *The Einstein Intersection*, and the venerable Pauline Hopkins' 'The Mystery within Us'. It is also important to note that works such as John Akomfrah's *The Last Angel of History* and examples of Ran Walker's microfiction and prose poetry remind us that Afrofuturism is a complete movement that includes film, poetry, music, theory and philosophy as well as fiction.

In addition to the foreword by author and champion of marginalized voices Nisi Shawl, this anthology has been further enriched by two key contributors: many thanks to Dr. Sandra M. Grayson for her fascinating and informative introduction and scrupulous editorial input, and to Isis Asare of Sistah Scifi for her equally invaluable editorial support in the shaping of the book. Many thanks also to our ever hardworking readers and editorial board. We hope you enjoy this bountiful selection of stories!

Gothic Fantasy

Afro Futurism Short Stories

Anthology of New & Classic Tales

Foreword by Nisi Shawl

Introduction by Dr. Sandra M. Grayson

Contributing Editor: Isis Asare

FLAME TREE PUBLISHING

Forward Agenda

Abíọ̀dún Abdul

"Ẹ KÁÀRỌ̀ EVERYONE. Welcome to this presentation on the Benin Robots."

Ọlánrewájú took a big breath as she centred herself on the podium surveying the two thousand-strong crowd gathered at the Ẹdo Museum. The robotics engineer had been working towards this convention project throughout her final PhD year at Ilé-Ifẹ̀ University. Finally, the day had come to share her ideas, and she was feeling a bit shaky. But she'd had a smart ànkàrá outfit made with a vibrant gèlè wrapped around her freshly braided hair, looking outwardly presentable to induce a confident delivery. She took a sip of water, looked into the sea of expectant faces, and continued:

"The continent has come a long way since the Africa Union's Agenda 10,104 strategic initiatives striving for 'The Africa We Want'. And indeed, great milestones have been achieved over the fifty years of its implementation for the prosperity of our peoples. I'm glad the Ilẹ̀ Káàárọ̀-Oòjíire government has recognized even more can be done within Technology, Innovation and Sustainability."

Ọlánrewájú was now in her stride. Remembering all her hours of prep, her autopilot kicked in as the words began flowing freely.

"I'd now like to share my bid for the Agenda 10,104+ government funding: the Ẹ̀rọ Idẹ 10114."

Without a hitch, the veil beside the podium dropped, and the audience collectively gasped. Standing next to Ọlánrewájú was a "full-sized' Benin Bronze with a vertically lined head emulating Orí-Olókun…on a shiny, bronze, top-to-toe body, further lit up by the multiple flashes from the press pit photographers. Seeing the crowd's clear intrigue and simultaneous uncertainty, Ọlánrewájú continued:

"This Ẹ̀rọ Idẹ model is named for Kọ́jọ́dá year 10,114, ten years from now, so you understand this will take us into the future."

"Over a millennium ago, we Yorùbá built the Sùngbọ̀ Ẹrẹ̀dò and Benin Wall embattlements for irrigation and protection, the largest engineering feat on Earth to this day. And we did that without robots…so think what we can do *with* robots!! With the Ẹ̀rọ Idẹ 10114, we can build effective infrastructure in line with our Betterment Agenda."

Half the press core hastily jotted notes on their griot pads. Ọlánrewájú saw she'd got them with that one!

"As we dig the land, these robots will pinpoint bronze to regenerate themselves, whilst also extracting other metal ores and mineral wealth. We'll use these to build *AND* trade, further strengthening our currency, backed with the abundant resources across Ilẹ̀ Káàárọ̀-Oòjíire. Soon, we will have many citizens making history alongside Mansa Musa." Ọlánrewájú beamed seeing people smile at her reference to the richest man that ever lived, and a fellow West African from neighbouring Mali. "Centuries ago, he found all those wealth-building minerals without robots…so think what we can do *with* robots!"

"Note their use will align with Agenda 10,104+ regarding sustainability. The Ẹ̀rọ Idẹ 10114's central purpose is conservation, not just of environment, but also of culture.

Like their vertical lines, these Benin Robots will have our stories AND potential etched into them."

Ọlánrewájú took the mic off the stand, left the podium, and ran her fingers over the machine's surface.

"These Robots will also fulfil the original mandate of the Benin Bronzes as solid libraries of consultation. Instead of recording written data, Benin artisans depicted data in sculptures to direct traditional ceremonies and dress. Indeed, this Ẹdo Museum venue was founded to display this cultural heritage. So yes, they will extract natural wealth from Yorùbá soils to build the future and perpetuate cultural wealth of Yorùbá legacies fortifying us with our past, history in motion educating the coming generations, thus reinforcing our identity…and you know how we Yorùbá love education!"

The peppered smiles in the crowd spread wider across the focused faces. Ọlánrewájú had them now. Moving across the stage, she pointed at the jumbo screen.

"Co-operation is key in the Agenda 10,104+ project, but we must also keep our edge in the global market. Thus, I've built in an anti-hacking failsafe: the robotics programming language is completely in the Odùduwà alphabet."

"HA! Now I KNOW you're CRAZY for SURE! WÈRÈ TI MU Ẹ OOO!"

The convention crowd whipped their collective heads to the left towards the disturbance. There stood Eromidọlá, a rival robotics engineer who'd been vexed about Ọlánrewájú's Ẹ̀rọ Idẹ project beating hers to represent Ilé-Ifẹ̀ University for the Agenda 10,104+ government funding. Eromidọlá's name meant "My thoughts become wealth' and she was always determined to fulfil that mandate, but this heckling was next level!

"Don't waste your funding on this one. How can you rely on ideas from a broken mind? I've seen the psych reports. She's *dyslexic*! Her head is not correct. Odùduwà alphabet? Can anyone even read this script…and you expect to write computer code with it? Benin Robots?? This is a fever dream which will become a nightmare, an embarrassment for Ilẹ̀ Káàárọ̀-Oòjíire if you give funding for this Ẹ̀rọ Idẹ…whatever!"

The crowd's murmuring got louder and louder as they glanced back and forth between Eromidọlá's smug face and Ọlánrewájú's perplexed one.

The PhD researcher was visibly rattled, shifting from foot to foot, both hands gripping the mic. As she looked down trying to gather a response, her eyes caught her new ànkàrá outfit and her fresh braids brushed her cheek. Ọlánrewájú had made it all the way to the Ẹdo Museum stage, and she was determined to reach her goal. She looked up, went to the podium, took a deep breath, and spoke:

"Government officials, press members, convention attendees. This impromptu revelation is true. I am indeed dyslexic. But my right-brain-hemisphere dominance is a strength, *not* a weakness. Did you know over a tenth of Yorùbá people are dyslexic, one of the highest proportions in the world? Yet we still boast genius level intelligence and unsurpassed diligence. Like other dyslexic innovators; Aderin-Pocock, Greider, Einstein and more, I see the world differently. And *that's* why my plan *will* work."

Ọlánrewájú slowed her hurried voice.

"These Benin Robots are designed to accommodate our neurotypical *and* neurodiverse workforce. When my machines encounter metal ores during excavation, they vocalize their findings."

Ọlánrewájú walked to the robot, lifted its lined hand and placed her bracelet on its palm. The Ẹ̀rọ Idẹ 10114's eyes instantly flashed as the vertical lines shimmered before its entire surface changed from brown to gold. Its stoic face became animated and said, 'WÚRÀ', drawing more astonished gasps from the audience.

"Yes, it is indeed gold," said Ọlánrewájú. "These machines change colour every time they come across different minerals. So our workers receive immediate visual *and* audio confirmation of their discoveries. On a good excavation day, they will rival us for the best multi-coloured ànkàrá collage!"

Someone called out, "Ah, they will be the life of our Ówàmbẹ̀ parties with this custom-made, stylish aṣọ ẹ̀*bí* ooo!"

The crowd laughed and Ọlánrewájú knew she had won them back.

"More importantly, this multi-sensory differentiation appeals to different brain types, accounting for accessibility and inclusivity for our workforce, wouldn't you agree Eromidọlá?"

Ọlánrewájú's eyes shifted to her heckler who could only stand in stunned silence. Eromidọlá and everyone at Ilé-Ifẹ̀ University hadn't seen the colour changing feature as Ọlánrewájú had kept it secret.

"Okay, that's all very well and good, but I have a concern," said a voice from the crowd. A man in Babaláwo attire stood up. "I'm an Ifá priest and many of our Benin Bronzes depict venerated Òrìṣà like this Olókun example. Could people start worshipping the robots if they look like our deities?"

"It's a valid concern," said Ọlánrewájú. "But I assure you this won't happen. We don't worship the robots, the robots serve us, we have dominion over them."

"This new programming is very advanced," said another audience member, "what fail-safes are in place so they don't become sentient and try to control *us*?"

"These Robots do not have inner spiritual orí, only we do," replied Ọlánrewájú. "We can use our orí, spirit, and intelligence, in designing their encoding so they can help us. Like Yorùbá culture, the base coding of the Benin Robots is respect. These machines will recognize our respect for the role they play and will always work with us to move Ilẹ̀ Kááàrọ̀-Oòjíire forward."

The Ẹ̀rọ Idẹ 10114 then automatically went into dọ̀bálẹ̀ mode, prostrating flat on the stage saying,

"I AM HERE TO SERVE."

The crowd erupted into raucous applause, all except Eromidọlá who gave Ọlánrewájú the side-eye, miffed her plan to destabilise the whole funding bid had backfired, perhaps even strengthening it. Still, the convention presentations weren't over yet.

Ọlánrewájú thanked the audience, saying "Ẹ ṣé púpọ̀".

She left the podium and her Benin Robot followed her offstage. As the applause finally subsided, she sat front row with the other candidates waiting to see if their funding bids would be successful. Exhaling slowly, Ọlánrewájú thought of her name's meaning: 'My wealth is in the future/advancing'. With a life mandate infused with innovation and forward seeing, perhaps she had managed to help others see her particular Agenda 10,104+ future too.

Twice, At Once, Separated

Linda D. Addison

"The shamans came together to find a cure for the sickness in the people's souls that caused children to be born sick. They changed into strong hekura – jaguar, ocelot, puma – and climbed the ladder of the earth to search for the soul-eater's path. The only way to save their children's souls was to leave the poisoned place, go beyond the sky layer. The people entered Ship to follow the path to the demon's birthplace, where they will once again change into strong hekura and destroy the demon's nest, releasing the captured souls so children can again be born strong and healthy."
Chant taught to every Yanomami shaman

THE ARTIFICIAL SUNLIGHT of Ship drew sharp shadows around the men sitting in the dirt of the central plaza of Bataasi-teri village. The scent of roasted plantains, from the communal fire, filled the air. Xotama stood in the shade of the circular village and listened to the wedding contract play out. Mayomi, her grandmother, sat within listening distance, nodding at their shaman, Hurewa, when an acceptable number of valuable items were mentioned. They were haggling about woven baskets. Hurewa, with his usual calm, simply shook his head at the numbers they proposed.

Mayomi had spent a long time, the night before, talking to Xotama about the planned marriage. No matter what she said, Xotama felt sick inside. A restless night made her feel no better today. Her life was haunted by a sense of being splintered. She had gone through the cleansing ceremony to remove the pain left by her mother's death, but no amount of meditation or rituals helped. Only her dreams gave her temporary comfort. Dreams of being with someone she didn't know, whose face she never saw.

"Tutewa will be a good husband," Rahimi, her best friend, said. "He's generous and not bad to look at. He's moving here to look after your grandmother, so we'll still see each other."

Xotama found his round face and deep brown eyes attractive. He had meticulously painted circles and bands of red ochre over his entire body.

She turned the slender white stick that pierced her nasal septum. "I know. It's not him, it's me. I'm not—" The expected path of her life caught in her throat.

Rahimi put her arm around Xotama's waist. "Is it the dreams again?" she whispered.

Xotama nodded. "I've tried to forget them but she came to me again last night. I can't do this now." She pulled away from Rahimi and walked into the central plaza. The conversation stopped.

"What is this, does the bride need a closer look at her husband-to-be?" Tutewa's father said. "Stand up, son, let her see how strong you are. There will be no empty bellies in your hammock. We are good hunters." He prodded Tutewa.

He started to stand, but Xotama gestured for him to sit. "No, I'm sorry, this isn't..." Her voice faded under their stares.

Mayomi rushed over to her. "Forgive my granddaughter. She's not herself today."

"She seems very much herself today, grandmother," Hurewa said. "What are you trying to say, Xotama?"

"I'm sorry, but I'm not ready to agree to a marriage contract," Xotama said. She saw Rahimi put her hands over her mouth.

Everyone started shouting at once.

* * *

Above the villages and forest, beyond the sky created by technology, a metaplasmic layer contained the neural web called Ship. A Watcher let her mind roam the forest quadrant of the hollowed out, terra-formed asteroid where Xotama stood. Their minds touched through the bio-implants all Yanomami had in their brains. The Watcher's real body was in slow stasis, growing old a hundred times slower than those who inhabited the forests. Her mind lived in the virtual world sustained by Ship.

Today she worked in navigation, in the form of a green-furred monkey with four arms. Long fingers moved quickly over a multi-colored ball of writhing vines, tapping any ends that snaked out. Each touch generated a bright spark of light, making the end flow back into the center of the vine ball. The echo of dreams shared with Xotama sang back at her, just as they haunted Xotama.

She drank in Xotama's turmoil, smoothed it over her virtual face, breathing in the sharp, sweet flavor of discontent. There was a corresponding hunger in her, a breach. Though she knew more than Xotama, the knowledge did little to feed the unsettling emptiness.

...tell me, what troubles you?... Ship asked, a gentle whisper in her mind.

Talking with Ship was like floating underwater. She surrendered to the smothering, reminding herself there was no body to suffocate, just a sensation in the mind, to treat it like a dream and enter gently, as if falling asleep.

(I cannot find the words) she thought to it.

...what does it look like?...

She let the hunger take shape: a dark circle broken in two, one jagged piece disappears, the other grows larger, one eye appears in the center, tears of light slowly fall from the eye, the dark half becomes a tattered sail, beating wildly in a firestorm that consumes the light, the eye begins to close.

...enough... Ship said, dissolving the images.

In navigation, tendrils of vine whipped through the air. She worked rapidly to get the vines back in control. An otter with orange skin and three pairs of arms swam into navigation. He licked her face, transmitting his genetic designation, and began to work over the vines.

...I have tasted your discomfort for a long time but hoped you would settle it on your own... Ship said. ...she cannot heal without you...you must find a way or you will both be lost...

She thought the word 'home' and was in her virtual hammock, in the vast circular village that housed all the Watchers. A neighbor in the shape of a golden panther nudged her with his shoulder. His touch was like an early morning breeze. He asked, (why are you afraid?)

(I am broken and I don't know how to become whole) she said.

* * *

Mayomi grabbed Xotama's arm to pull her away. Hurewa stood and gently moved the grandmother aside. He cupped Xotama's face in his hands, stared hard into her eyes.

After caressing the moon-shaped birthmark on her left cheek, he clapped his hands to get everyone's attention.

Xotama looked at Tutewa and felt a flutter of desire mixed with sadness.

"What is wrong with this girl?" Tutewa's father said, pointing at her. "Does she think my son is not good enough?"

"Let her be, father," Tutewa said. "I want to hear what she has to say."

Xotama fought back tears, wanting to give some explanation, but she didn't know where to start.

"Let me tell you about a dream I had last night," Hurewa said. "I saw Xotama's birthmark on the beak of a golden toucan surrounded by other birds, with bright red and blue feathers, perched on white rocks. They rose into the sky as one, leaving the golden bird on the ground. A hekura in the shape of a young leopard crept into the circle of rocks. Its eyes glowed red. I recognized it as my hekura and stood in front of the golden bird as the leopard leapt. I took it into my chest and saw the bird's true form through the leopard eyes. A young girl, staring at her shadow on the ground, drawn by bright moonlight. Her shadow lifted off the ground and stood next to her. The moon came closer until it was so bright I had to run into the forest.

"What do you see in your dreams, Xotama?"

She took a deep breath and said, "There is another in my dreams, someone I never see but can sense. She has shown me many things. Last night we flew high above a green forest, dotted sparsely with villages, brown circular pots, their edges stretched inward to a flickering center. I wasn't afraid because she was with me. I don't know who she is or what the dreams mean. When I wake I feel like half a person.

"I think only Ship can help me understand what these dreams mean."

A young man from Tutewa's village said, "Women are not allowed to talk to Ship."

"There are women Watchers," Xotama said. "There are stories of women shamans. I don't think Ship cares that I have a womb."

This started the yelling again. Hurewa had to bang two gourds to get everyone's attention. "We live inside Ship, not unlike a womb. Without Ship we would spill into the airless trail we follow, our souls eaten by the Soul Killer. I'm not going to judge for Ship. Which of you thinks you can?" No one said a word.

"When I woke this morning, the air was full of big and small magic," the shaman said. "Xotama must walk the path of the spirits before we have any more discussions of marriage. Important dreams have to be honored."

Tutewa walked over to Xotama and spit on the ground in front of her to signify the path was clear between them. "I accept that you need to settle this storm inside. I will wait twenty days for a message from you. If I hear nothing, I'll consider our marriage bond dissolved."

He walked away, followed by his father and the three other men from his village. They ducked out the narrow opening of the walled village, into the forest.

Part of her didn't want him to go. If only she could push this pain away and be happy in her life. She balled up her fists. What was wrong with her?

Hurewa took Xotama's hand and led her across the center court to a shaded area. Mayomi followed. The three of them sat on the ground. They sat out of earshot of everyone else. More people drifted into the village center. Men, women and children gathered on the far side of the center fire, keeping a cautious distance between themselves and Xotama.

"A path of fire waits in front of you before your journey ends," Hurewa said. "The end is the beginning. Enter the circle. I have seen this as a waking dream."

"The circle?" Xotama asked.

"You'll understand when the time comes. It will take all your courage to heal this breach. The flow of this day has been changed by your words and my dream messenger. It wouldn't be wise to stop now. Are you ready to begin?"

Xotama took a quick breath. She hadn't thought beyond the aching need to stop today's events. "I – I don't know. Will you come with me?"

"No. You must do this alone. It will be dangerous. Not everyone who seeks Ship returns."

"There must be another way," Mayomi pleaded. "I've taken care of her since her mother died giving birth. Her father entrusted me with her life when he moved to another village to marry. I fear her mother's spirit lingers nearby, pulling at her."

"Someone lingers near, but it's not her mother." The shaman stared hard at Mayomi.

Mayomi looked stricken, opened her mouth as if to speak, but put her fist over it instead.

"You will follow the river to the place where no one lives." Hurewa held Xotama's hands. "There, if Ship is agreeable, you may be returned to the shadow in your dreams. We will sit vigil for your return."

Tears fell from Mayomi's eyes, but she said nothing.

"Let's go," he said.

They stood and walked to the village's exit. No one approached them. Rahimi looked like she wanted to follow them but her mother was holding her arm.

"What about supplies?" Mayomi asked.

"Ship will give her what she needs," he said. "We should go from here alone, Mayomi."

"Remember that I love you," Mayomi whispered in Xotama's ear, hugging her tightly.

They walked to the river down a rarely used path. The thick, sweet scent of flowering vines lifted Xotama's soul; their red blossoms made her smile. The hōrema bird began its afternoon song: "Were, were, were…" A little of her fear dissipated in the air of the forest. This could be just another day if not for the fact that she was leaving everyone she knew to search for an unknown person in a place she'd never been before.

A freshly carved canoe waited on the bank.

"This is my personal canoe. It will carry you to the next place," the shaman said. He mixed some earth with spit in his hands and smoothed the mixture over the bow of the canoe, working a spell of protection into the wood.

"Thank you for believing me," she said.

"There is strong magic in you. I wouldn't be a good shaman if I ignored it." He helped her into the canoe, handed her a paddle and pushed the canoe towards the center of the river.

She waved at him as the river carried her away. The current moved well enough that she only used the paddle to push away from rocks or fallen tree trunks. Light from the afternoon sky, and the water's rocking motion, made her sleepy. Her hand slipped over the edge of the canoe, trailing in the current.

Xotama dreamed she changed into an eel and slid into the river. The other was also there as an eel. They danced in the water, slithering around each other, over and under thick tree roots. There were no words between them, just a perfect dance. Their tails and heads wrapped together to make a wing shape that lifted into the sky as, below, the canoe filled with water.

Xotama woke to water flooding the canoe. She tried using her cupped hands to bail it out, but the canoe tipped over, dumping her into the foaming waves. Underwater, a tangle of tree roots threatened to hold her down. She kicked up to the surface before she got too snarled in the roots, and swam to the bank.

She sat on the muddy edge, catching her breath. Now what? The river had carried her away from known territory, and without a canoe she had no idea where to go next. The ground rose, not far from the river, to a hill dense with growth. Trapped between the water and the thick bush, she reasoned that, if this was as far as the canoe took her, the rest of her journey would have to be on foot. Xotama worked her way up the hill, away from the river's edge.

In the overgrown bush, little sunlight passed through the thick canopy. Scrub brush and thick vines, in shades of gray, covered the ground, making walking difficult. There was no sign anyone ever walked this way, not even an overgrown trail. Pushing through whatever vegetation yielded, she heard a rumble overhead, like a coming storm.

She tried not to think about the snakes and rodents living under the tangle of vines and rotting leaves. Twice, Xotama stopped to dig a thorn out of her foot. By the time she reached dry ground, she was limping, her body covered with bleeding scratches. Despite eating a couple of tangerine-colored ediweshi on the way, she was dizzy from lack of food. The palm fruit took the edge off her thirst, but left her hungry and weak. The rumbling above grew louder. Nausea twisted her stomach, but she pushed on until she found a small opening in a hillside. She picked up a stick in case snakes lived in the cave; it would be safer there than in the dark jungle if a storm broke.

Just as she squeezed into the cave, a palm tree crashed down at the entrance. Her scream was swallowed by the thunder of a summer storm. Unable to hold back the nausea, she vomited. Choking on bile, Xotama squeezed deeper into the cave. She listened for sounds of something alive besides her, but could hear nothing over the roar of the storm.

Too weak to go on, she crouched with her back against a stone wall. She would die here. Alone, with no songs or rituals to take care of her decaying body, her spirit lost forever. She cried softly, curling into a ball.

What made her think Ship would talk to her, even let her enter its sacred space to answer her questions? What place did her small lost life have in Ship's larger existence; in the journey of the people? Drifting into unconsciousness, her last thought was that she had no one to blame except herself.

* * *

Xotama stood outside the cave. Wind and rain threw tree branches at her, ripping flesh from her body. She felt no pain. In a flash of lightning, she saw the cave opening was almost completely covered with debris. She looked down at her hands. Bone peeked through the raw flesh that remained. Under the roar of the storm, she heard her grandmother and the shaman chanting. The ground became very hot, blistering what little skin was left on her feet.

Without taking a single step, she moved down the hill, back to the river's edge. Standing at the spot where she had climbed out of the river, she looked across the white caps of the water and saw her canoe rise into the air. Shoro, dark-feathered birds with long tails, were lifting it. The chanting grew louder. It was a song of protection from the water demons.

Xotama looked down at her arms and legs. The burning had stopped, and her limbs transformed themselves into wings and claws, like the shoro. The lost feeling she had carried her whole life became a single stabbing pain inside her chest. A ring of fire blazed in the sky. Was this the circle in Hurewa's warning? Trembling, she rose on her new wings and flew towards the flames.

She skimmed through the center of the ring. Her feathers burned away. Xotama fell, not down but up, hurtling through a tunnel of colors, to land on a soft pile of leaves. When she opened her eyes, she was an infant being picked up by her grandmother, younger in years but with the same face. A woman, the mother she never knew, squatted against a large tree, grimacing in pain as blood ran down her thighs.

Mayomi lay Xotama carefully on the ground. An infant cried. Not her, Xotama realized, but another baby, coming out of their mother.

Twins.

Her mother collapsed as the placenta was delivered. Mayomi cut the umbilical cord and tried to revive Xotama's mother, but she was dead. Mayomi's cries mixed with the hungry newborns' wails.

Twins. Everything made sense now. The dreams, the feeling of being broken in two. Relief mixed with anger. Mayomi knew all along that Xotama was a twin, and never said anything. All the years of feeling lost explained in one word. Twins.

Their grandmother picked the babies up and ran crying into the forest. She stopped at an opening in a hill, laid both babies down to examine them. They were exactly the same, except for the sliver of a moon birthmark on Xotama's face. Mayomi touched the birthmark, kissed the other baby, picked up Xotama and rushed away from the cave.

Inexplicably, Xotama floated above her abandoned sister, helpless. An old man came out of the cave and picked up the baby. A Watcher, his skin was iridescent blue, like the sky at sunset, covered with the curling patterns every Yanomami knew as Ship's design. He carried her sister into the cave.

The cries faded. Xotama was on her knees, weeding in her grandmother's tobacco garden. A reflection of Xotama pulled weeds to her left. Xotama shrieked in joy and grabbed her sister, pulling them both to the ground.

"It's you! I can't believe I've found you." Xotama held her sister's face in her hands. She kissed and hugged her tightly.

"Yes, my sister," she answered, embracing Xotama.

Xotama pulled away, looked around. "But how can we be here? Am I dead?"

"You are very much alive." Her twin smiled. "I wanted a familiar place for us to meet. You have happy memories of this garden."

"You can make a place out of memories?" Xotama asked.

"Anything imagined can take form here. Is there another place you would like to be?"

Xotama looked around. Everything seemed so real, she expected Mayomi to walk out of the forest edge. "This is fine. I didn't know Watchers could do this. I guess there's a lot I don't know about Ship and Watchers. Before this day I didn't know I had a sister. I – I thought I was losing my mind."

"I know. I haven't been doing well myself." She wiped Xotama's tears away. "Even though I knew you lived, I needed to touch you."

"But if we aren't really here, how can you touch me?"

She took Xotama's hand. "Doesn't this feel real? As real as any two bodies. More real than dreams."

"Except in my dreams I never saw your face. Didn't know you were my sister. I don't even know your name."

"I don't have a name like you do. Here we know each other by touch."

Xotama thought for a moment. "Can I call you Notama?"

She smiled. "I would like that."

"This is unbelievable. There's so much I don't understand," Xotama said.

"Do you trust me?" Notama asked.

Xotama looked into the copy of her face, without the birthmark, and nodded.

Notama reached up, her arm stretching until it touched the sky. Xotama looked down at where her sister held her hand. Their flesh melted together. Xotama's eyes closed. She felt as if she was falling asleep again.

* * *

They were a wind moving over forests, flowing up into the false sky of Ship, swiftly passing through a thick wall until they were beyond the asteroid's shell and in outer space. Points of light shimmered around them. Below, a long, dark sliver lay against the starry background: the rough rock that contained everyone Xotama loved, everything she knew of life. They plummeted down, through the vessel's strata of protective minerals, into its metaplasmic web, caught like insects in the immense memory banks of the intelligence called Ship. It existed in the living plasma that flowed through the outer shell, and under the forest ground. It was more than a machine and less than human.

Images from Ship's memory rushed past: First Earth, twisted, dying infants born to sick mothers, poison in the air, in the ground, in many humans: DNA spirals mangled into broken, twisted puzzle pieces; another memory bank filled with an endless stream of undamaged genetic codes, tagged and indexed, the genes of the Yanomami living inside the rock as it hurtled through space. Each new marriage, each new infant produces another flow of genetic possibilities. Xotama and Notama's genetic history undulated from First Earth and extrapolated into patterns that exploded into data streams that even Notama had not experienced.

More and more information poured into their minds. They saw the debates that led to the decision to maintain the forest society among the villages; to keep the people safe and sane during a long journey that would see the births and deaths of generations. They saw the bodies of Watchers in stasis pods, clustered like peas throughout the asteroid. Notama's body curled in a pod: still the size of a child. Older Watchers in gleaming blue body suits in the forests, observing the villages, taking samples from the water, ground, plants; surveying animals: wild pigs, tapir, giant anteaters; giant rodents, snakes, armadillos, tortoises, monkeys.

Xotama's mind was stripped down by the waves of information. Each new concept carried countless layers of explanation, information to explain data to explain information. Images slipped and slid into forms she couldn't comprehend. She wanted to tear her eyes out, rip her ears off, anything, anything to stop the roar, but she had no body. Notama was near her, also terrified by the flood of data.

They had unlocked something immense and it was consuming them.

(stopstopstopstop) Notama screamed in images: white lightning, bitter hot freezing decaying piercing gnawing…

Xotama was losing words, her thoughts tumbled into ragged sounds, tastes, colors…

green

pounding

sweet

red

wet

screech…

An old woman's face formed in the deluge of sensations, older than any Yanomami either of them had seen.

(Stop data retrieval, repair memory break, restore previous visualization), her voice was soothing.

The storm slowed and dissipated like morning mist. They were back in the garden of Notama's making, sitting on the ground. The pain and chaos faded rapidly.

"Who was that?" Xotama asked, gasping for air. She grabbed a handful of earth and centered on the feeling of the soil in her fist.

"One of the first Watchers. Someone who's been with Ship from the early days," Notama said, shaking her head.

They helped each other stand.

"I'm sorry, Xotama. I made a terrible mistake." Notama's tears welled up in her eyes. "I thought if I showed you what this was, Ship, the world I live in, that maybe you could stay here. But I took us into the neural web too quickly, I almost—"

"No, don't apologize," Xotama interrupted. "I had the same hope when I found you. For us to be together. But I couldn't live with things shifting around me, or these strange words and things. I need to walk through the real forests every day on legs. I need to hold people. I saw your body, it's too young and your mind too grown to live in a world you couldn't fly in or change whenever you choose."

They held each other. "It's time you returned," Notama said. "I wouldn't want Grandmother to worry too long about you. What will you do with the information you have?"

"Keep it close to my heart," Xotama said. "I see that knowing too much, too soon, is not wisdom."

"Yes, my arrogance has shown me I have a lot to learn," Notama said.

"Will we dream together again?" Xotama asked.

"I believe we will, but without the confusion. Are you ready to go?"

"Yes. You are forever in my heart and my *genes*." Xotama smiled at using the new word.

Notama kissed her forehead.

* * *

Xotama blinked. She stood in the mouth of a cave. Sunlight spilled over the forest. Other than some scratches, she was uninjured. This was not the cave she hid in from the storm. She had been returned to the cave her sister had been carried into as a newborn.

Her sister. Tears ran down her face and she laughed. She has a sister.

This cave was not far from her village. She took her time walking back, enjoying every familiar sound and scent along the way. She had seen many things with Notama. It would take a long time for her to understand even a small part of it. Maybe a lifetime.

For the first time, she looked forward to the future. She and Tutewa would marry, have children. Perhaps one of them would be a Watcher. Xotama wouldn't see the end of their journey, nor her children's children, but one day Yanomami would see the end of this path, and the beginning of something she could only taste at the back of her mind. Perhaps some of these Yanomami would carry her *genes*.

Xotama entered her village as the sky began to dim. The smell of roasted armadillo and plantains filled the air. Many people feasted around the center fire. Conversation stopped as she walked across the dusty space.

Rahimi ran up and grabbed her in a tight hug. "I'm so happy you're safe."

Xotama pulled away, looking past Rahimi to her grandmother, who stood transfixed at the edge of her hammock.

"What's wrong?" her friend asked.

"Nothing. Everything's fine. I'm going to be okay." She hugged Rahimi back. "I have to talk to my grandmother."

She walked to Mayomi. Hurewa signs of protection were painted in red over Xotama's hammock. She smiled. When she left the village the shaman knew more than anyone about Ship, but now she returned with so much more knowledge.

Mayomi met her gaze. Tears began to fall from her eyes. She sat on the ground in front of their private fire. Xotama sat next to her.

"You know?" Mayomi whispered.

"Yes, everything. I found her. She's not a dream, any more than I am. Why didn't you tell me?"

"It's hard enough making a place for one child without a mother. I had just lost a daughter, and held two babies in my arms. On First Earth, one of you would have been left in the forest to die. Here, I knew the Watchers would take care of the one I left behind. It was the only way both could have a life not filled with burden.

"I couldn't tell you what had happened." Mayomi looked down. "It's not permitted to speak of these things. Your mother's spirit might have been pulled back by my words, to haunt us."

Xotama shook her head. "You and I will not speak of this again." She took her grandmother's hand and kissed it. "I've found my lost self. I can be whole. Now we are both here." Xotama cupped her hands over her chest.

They stood and held each other. Xotama closed her eyes and saw the rock, their world, hurtling through space towards an unknown future. She would marry and have children and, in spite of the taboos, teach them about their aunt and what she learned from Ship during that time of almost-madness.

Revolution in the Soil

Aishatu Ado

MY HANDS TREMBLE as I dig another test pit in 1791, Saint-Domingue. Fourth jump of my five-visit limit – then the timeline seals forever. The shovel's sensors blink in time with my pulse, angry red. In the distance, plantation fires dot the coastline like fallen stars, a thousand promises of vengeance against French masters. Back in 2157, the Temporal Preservation Bureau's warning rings:

"Recollect from approved sites only. Observe, document, leave no trace."

The Bureau's youngest soil chronologist at twenty-three, and I'm risking it all. But after tonight, I have only one more chance to save her.

Cécile Fatiman emerges from the shadows, a priestess-warrior in fighter's breeches and a green headscarf, machete gleaming at her hip. Her movements speak of mountain hideouts, midnight ceremonies – a woman shifting between worlds as easily as she changes her rebel's tunic to a fieldhand's dress. When her eyes meet mine, my composure falters as it did when she saw through my story, when her eyes – sharp with a mambo's wisdom and a mountain rebel's cunning – lingered on the anachronistic stitching of my trousers. A flicker of amusement flashed in her eyes before she simply nodded, keeping my secret.

"Your shovel shudders like it is seeing spirits. Some truths burn too hot for your future machine." The words hit like summer lightning, and I grip the shovel tighter to steady my hands. Cécile steps closer and her scent hits me – the sharp tang of asosi leaves and vetiver root from her belt pouch, the sweet burn of basilic, the dark musk of cedrela. Forbidden knowledge passed down through generations of women who refused to forget their African roots. Sacred herbs she burned at Bwa Kayiman that birthed the Haitian revolution.

"Bureau called me in." I lift a soil sample. "Said my methodology was flawed." My fingers clench around the shovel's brass handle. "Ordered me to disregard three months of evidence they don't want found."

Cécile kneels beside me. Her hands – equally skilled at binding wounds and loading muskets – have led escaped slaves through midnight forests. Now, they brush the earth with a vodou priestess's touch.

"*Kouraj*," she whispers, and the Kreyol word sparks through my blood like fire.

The night air thickens with the scent of sugarcane smoke and distant rum distilleries. The soil beneath us bears witness to eighty years of blood spilled by enslaved Kongolese, Dahomeyans, and Yoruba, forced to work the richest colony in the Western world. Le Cap Français gleams white in the distance, its merchant houses and opera theaters built on stolen labor, while here in the foothills, revolution brews in secret gatherings.

My shovel's sensors reveal layers of truth, detecting traces of complex crop rotation, underground water systems, and co-ordinated cultivation patterns across multiple plantations. Knowledge carried across an ocean in memory and blood. Evidence of genius they'll label as chaos, innovation they'll call primitive, resistance they'll name riot.

The shovel sinks into loam dark as midnight, damp with recent rain. Insects chorus in the underbrush, a symphony punctuated by distant drums that speak in codes only maroons understand. Sweat trickles down my spine, mingling with fear and a strange elation at standing at the precipice of history's greatest slave revolt.

I pull out my data tablet, disguised as a merchant's ledger, to show her my coded maps. Lines subtly shifted to reveal hidden paths. "The tunnel network you're planning? Dense clay masks movement. Eight minutes between guard rotations."

My fingers tighten with knowledge I can't share – how, in two weeks, French bullets will find her unless history bends.

We dig together to feed the data stream, passing the shovel between us like a baton. Above us, the gibbous moon hangs low and knowing, her round face a conspirator's smile.

Cécile pulls me up from the soil, and my world spins with more than just her sudden movement.

Her maroon's song becomes a whisper against my ear: "*Yo travèse tan, pawòl yo pale nan tè.* Time is just another master's lie. The soil keeps the true count."

She draws me close and, in the moon's indulgent silver glow, her eyes find mine. Her voice drops: "*Sonje nou.*" *Remember us.*

For three heartbeats, my pulse forgets its future rhythm, falling into the cadence of 1791. Then her hands slide from mine, leaving ghost-warmth on my skin, and we're back to work. I've never felt more desperate to alter a future I shouldn't know.

"Here," I say, showing her where the shovel's sensors read centuries of soil changes – every footstep, every buried cache, every secret revealed in mineral traces. Heat floods my face as I sketch what could save her: patrol patterns, ammunition stores, defensive weaknesses. Knowledge that breaks every rule of temporal preservation.

If I'm caught, the Bureau wouldn't only have my license. It's erasure – from the timeline, from her memories. They would make it seem as if I had never existed. But if the Bureau wanted history to stay buried, they shouldn't have sent me.

Cécile's fingers trace the figures, quick and sure. Her eyes lock with mine, and understanding passes between us. She doesn't ask why I'm sharing more than agricultural data this time. She nods, erasing the numbers with a sweep of her hand.

A familiar vertigo warns of dawn's approach. "One more visit after this," she says. Not a question. Her dark eyes hold centuries of her people's determination, but there is tenderness in them when they meet mine. That same look that made my heart forget its training that first night when she chose trust over fear.

She kisses my cheek – so close to my lips her breath feathers goosebumps on my skin. Her callused fingers find my jaw, tilt my face to hers. The world narrows to the space between our mouths, a universe contained in inches. My heart hammers against my ribs. Then, finally, she claims my mouth, and time collapses into a single, explosive beat. Her lips press against mine, tasting of wild spice and sun-warmed earth – a flavor that speaks of reckless abandon.

Cécile's skin is damp with heat, alive beneath my hands, exuding the raw musk of the Massif de la Hotte, the smoky trace of burning cedar, the salt-brushed warmth of the sea. Every nerve in me ignites, each heartbeat pounding like a drum of rebellion. Her kiss is not soft. It is not patient. It is a gasp against my lips, a storm breaking inside me. A violent, delicious fracture of time, pulling me through fire – a defiant promise whispered in the language of desire.

Her fingers tangle in my hair, anchoring me to this moment as if she could prevent the coming separation by will alone. I memorize her – the precise pressure of her mouth, the flutter of her pulse, the impossible heat where our bodies meet. This kiss becomes a covenant, a promise more binding than any Bureau oath.

I want to stay here. Drown in her. Forever.

"*Sonje mwen*," she whispers. *Remember me.*

The past blurs around me, each molecule dragged back to my century, where even soil is synthesized and rain is just recycled tears. I watch her straighten her shoulders – the posture of a woman who survived the Le Cap raid, who will survive this too, if I've done enough. I've violated every protocol, chosen love over duty. But watching her fade into dawn's light – the last real sunrise I'll see before returning to filtered air and regulated darkness – fear dissolves. Hope takes its place.

The Grief Pilgrim

Aishatu Ado

"ALL WATER IS SUSPECT NOW, *chérie*. Even a teardrop could be a door to elsewhere." Maman's warning haunts me as I watch Stéphane slice through the golden twilight air, his body an arc against the setting sun. Our long-empty pool waits below, impossibly full. The water shimmers with an unnatural iridescence. Horror clogs my throat – where did the water come from?

"Stéphane, wait!" The words catch in my throat. Just this morning, authorities announced three new disappearances from a fountain in Marseille. Untreated water with that distinctive, hypnotic shimmer that bypasses all rational thought. The same unnatural gleam now rippling across our pool's surface. But my husband doesn't hear me, his joy at finding our empty pool refilled overwhelming his caution.

The splash births chaos. Stéphane's body twists, elongates. His scream warps, slowing to a moan that shivers the air. I lunge forward, my wrist-alarm vibrating frantically against my skin. The government-issued Chrono-Guard flashes its red warning too late, useless as all our precautions have proven. My fingers graze water thick as coco-fey syrup as I reach for him, the device still pulsing its automated message.

TEMPORAL ANOMALY DETECTED. RETREAT. RETREAT.

A lone bubble ascends, my husband's final grin imprisoned in its fragile sphere. It implodes into nothingness, absorbed by the pool's voracious maw. My fingers claw at its edge, desperate to follow him, to bring him home. Why did he risk it? Why tempt The Melt with a simple dive?

The sun, eternal witness to all endings, weeps crimson tears. My heart leaps from my chest. I blink, disbelieving. Our pool had devoured my husband like a famished chameleon, its cerulean tongue unfurling to taste the Martinique memories that clung to his body. His purple-hued obsidian skin, smoother than volcanic glass, became a morsel for the water's insatiable appetite.

Memory ambushes me: Stéphane's throaty laugh as I stepped on his toes during our first dance lesson; the night he proposed at Grand-Rivière under meteor showers; his fingers intertwining with mine across our breakfast table each morning; the scent of him – lavender soap from the market, tobacco from his grandfather's pipe – as he whispered *"Je t'aime"* against my braids; and the way he'd fallen to his knees when I told him about the baby, pressing his ear to my still-flat belly as if he might hear a heartbeat through sheer force of will.

How was I to know that ordinary moment would become sacred, a treasure I'd hoard against the lean times to come? How quickly our world shifted to this twilight realm of loss, leaving me hollow and aching and so damn afraid.

"I can't do this alone. We need you!" I scream at the rippling water, but it remains placid, unresponsive. The Chrono-Sea doesn't care that my heart's been ripped out. It keeps on churning, spitting out fragments of time like a dog with a bone it can't quite swallow.

In the days after Stéphane vanishes, I claw through science journals and underground forums, searching for answers. The phenomenon they call the Melt first appeared five years ago

– a puddle in Tokyo that swallowed a child whole, then a pond in Brazil that devoured a family, then the entirety of Lake Victoria overnight, sixty thousand fishermen gone in a heartbeat.

Four million souls have disappeared worldwide since then. Not one was retrieved. Scientists scramble for explanations: quantum tunneling, dimensional rifts, temporal displacement. Academic language that fails to capture the simple truth: people step into water and never return. Theories multiply; solutions don't.

My fingernail scrapes against the blue government certification emblem on my water bottle. Treated water is always safe – the temporal stabilization process renders it incapable of becoming a doorway to elsewhere. The familiar heat of indignation rises in my chest. In the hills above town, the wealthy have entire houses plumbed with stabilized water – unlimited safe showers, baths, swimming pools even. Meanwhile, my neighborhood lines up at dawn for the communal shower facility, three minutes per person, pumps humming behind government barricades.

The attendants watch the timer with military precision while I rush to rinse soap from my hair. Strange how normal it has become, this perpetual vigilance against H2O molecules, this hierarchy of who deserves unrestricted safety and who must ration it. How Martinique's endless coastline, once my childhood playground, now represents nothing but a threat.

One hundred and eighty-nine days without Stéphane, and I stand at the edge of the Whispering Cliffs, toes curled over chalk-white stone. The French once called them Étretat, printed them on postcards, and watched tourists pose for photographs. Now they whisper with the voices of the time-displaced, looming over the Chrono-Sea – a crimson tide that has consumed the Atlantic and reaches hungry fingers towards the Mediterranean.

Hazard signs in seventeen languages line the shore. Barbed wire glints in morning fog. Military checkpoints block access roads. A rusted sign flutters nearby:

MEMORY TOURISM PROHIBITED – National Security Act 47.3.

Beneath it, someone has spray-painted "THEY SWIM AMONG US" in iridescent paint that shifts color like the Chrono-Sea itself. Reunionist propaganda, growing more common as desperation mounts. Yet still I come, slipping through boundary gaps at dawn, moth-like, my fingers hovering microns from obliteration.

For those of us left behind, reality warped like Salvador Dalí's clocks, melting around the edges while keeping perfect time. The scientists publish papers about anomalies and theoretical physics, but they don't quantify the way grief transforms ordinary objects into weapons – how my husband's coffee cup with its perpetual lipstick stain along the rim fires shrapnel through my sternum each morning; how our wedding photographs burn like acid against fingertips; how the slowly fading indentation of his body on our mattress hollows out my chest until each breath becomes an act of revolution. The Melt devours bodies; grief consumes everything else.

The wind whips my ebony braids at the cliffs, carrying fragments of stolen lives – a cacophony of voices, snippets of conversations, laughter, screams – from other times, other lives. I've learned to filter through them, searching for the one voice that matters.

Stéphane's first whisper came like a ghost's caress, curling around me like lavender smoke. "Help…lost…time…"

Joy and terror warred in my chest. I wanted to run, to dive headfirst into that deathly mercurial sea. My foot slid forward of its own accord, toes seeking the edge.

A security officer yanked me back, his grip bruising my arm. "That's how we lose another one," he muttered, eyes dead with the weight of too many failed rescues.

Instead, I sank to my knees and wept.

Now, I live in Étretat, my days spent near a narrow aperture between the cliffs. The Chrono-Sea's red waters shift like liquid mercury, iridescent and opaque in places, transparent as air in others. Where normal waves should crest and fall, time itself ripples, holographic moments from the past breaking against the shore. Sometimes I glimpse phantom figures beneath the surface – people frozen mid-stride, mid-conversation, mid-breath. No fish dare swim its waters, no birds fly above.

Government measurements confirm what we all feel – the Chrono-Sea is expanding exponentially, advancing centimeters each day. Scientists predict total oceanic transformation within eighteen months. The countdown to universal displacement ticks in every official broadcast.

I'm not alone in my vigil. A young woman sits cross-legged on the salt-bleached rocks, adjusting the dials on her whisper-catcher, a cobbled-together device amplifying the voices from the displaced. It's unlike the factory-made models sold in Paris boutiques for sums that would feed our whole neighborhood for months. Its body – a modified radio gutted and rewired with salvaged components – bristles with antennas of varying lengths. Each is wrapped in copper wire, tarnished green like her grandmother's wedding band, scavenged from pre-Melt electronics. At the device's core, visible through a cracked plastic window, sits a thumbnail-sized crystal of chrono-residue: the iridescent, mood ring colored mineral that forms wherever time fractures and reseals at the shore. Before the Melt, it didn't exist; now it's more valuable than gold. Harvested from the edges of temporal storms, and each crystal retains connections to multiple timeliness of the displaced.

She offers me her spare headphones. "The three-point-seven frequency catches the ones from last year," she says, her fingers stained with crimson graphite paste from the beach that mothers warn their children never to touch. She insists it helps calibrate the equipment. "The five-point-two seems to reach further back, but there's more interference."

When I place the headphones over my ears, static washes through me, followed by the peculiar vertigo, the sensation of time growing tissue-thin. The voices of the displaced begin as impressions rather than sounds – memory given breath, longing shaped into words. My daughter kicks inside me as if responding to something I cannot yet hear, and I wonder if the unborn exist partially in that same elsewhere, if they can translate what we strain to understand.

We've met at this same spot every dawn since I found her three weeks ago – two strangers now bound by clockwork devotion to this ritual of listening. The beach is dotted with other listeners – pilgrims of grief, each with their own ghosts. We recognize each other by the hollowness behind our eyes, the way we tilt our heads towards the water, the small totems of the lost we carry – a wedding ring, a child's toy, a faded photograph.

Old Gérard and Mathilde break my heart most. Married sixty years before the sea took their twins. Once Gérard's hand found mine, skin papery as dried ti-baume leaves. "Your husband," he said, "he loved life, non?"

I nodded, a lump in my throat big as a breadfruit.

"Then honor that life, *chère*. It's what your Stéphane would've wanted."

His words burrowed deep, took root alongside my grief. He pressed a gift into my palm – a small wooden carving of a hummingbird, its wings poised for flight. "To remind you that life… it is brief but beautiful."

Nearby, Aiden paces, his feet leaving bloody prints on the cliff face. "Equations," he mutters, dark circles under his eyes like overripe sapotilles. "If I can just…solve…bring her back."

His chalk scratches against stone, complex formulas spilling from his fingers. A former physicist at CERN, he calculates entry points, trajectory patterns, temporal constants – mapping doorways to elsewhere that he cannot open.

For a moment, I imagine snatching Aiden's chalk, scrawling my own formulas across the stone. What equations could calculate the precise moment a heart breaks? What mathematics could map the negative space where Stéphane should be?

Instead, I sit beside Gérard and Mathilde, their weathered hands intertwined. We face the Chrono-Sea together, three generations of loss outlined against the setting sun.

"Come home with us tonight," Mathilde offers, eyeing my swollen belly. "The coastguard says a temporal storm is coming. The water might reach the lower cliffs."

She gestures towards the horizon where clouds swirl in impossible patterns, backwards and sideways, some frozen in place. Thunder rolls in reverse, lightning strikes from ground to sky.

I shake my head. "I need to be here if he calls."

"And if the waters rise?" Gerard asks gently.

I don't answer. We both know what I'm thinking – that perhaps rising waters would make my choice easier. The baby kicks inside me, a tiny foot against my ribs, demanding life even as I contemplate its opposite.

Maman says I'm courting madness, coming here day after day. She calls from Martinique weekly, her voice crackling with static and worry: "Return home, *ma fille*. We have safe ground, away from any water." What she doesn't say, but I hear anyway: "Don't leave me childless, too."

Her own grief runs deep – Stéphane was like a son to her after Papa disappeared at sea decades before the Melt, an ordinary drowning that now seems quaint in its simplicity.

Stéphane's smile still burns behind my eyelids, forever frozen in that last moment. Guilt gnaws at me like a starving rat. If I had jumped in after him, would I have caught his hand, anchored him to our world? The what-ifs haunt me more than the whispers of the lost.

When major religions failed to explain the Melt, new faiths bloomed in their place. The Chronologists believe time is purging itself, preparing for rebirth. Reunionists preach that the disappeared are building a better world on the other side. The Church of Liquid Salvation – the most dangerous – promises reunion with lost loved ones through "transcendent submersion."

"Join your beloved," a robed Salvationist whispers to me one twilight, his hands stained crimson like he's dipped them in the Chrono-Sea. His robe bears embroidered symbols – clocks without hands, fish swimming through hourglasses, the infinity sign dripping blood. "The faithful are reunited on the other side. We've mapped the currents of time. For a modest donation, we can guarantee you'll emerge where he waits."

I spit at his feet. "How convenient that those who pay never return to demand refunds."

He smiles, serene and terrible. "Faith requires sacrifice. Last week, a mother found her lost children. The week before, a husband rejoined his wife. They send messages sometimes, caught in the whispers."

These vultures prey on grief, growing fat on desperation. Yet their congregations swell while traditional churches stand empty. When hope abandons the world, people will worship whatever promises its return.

I heard about the Whispering Cliffs in a support group back home. We met Tuesdays in a school gymnasium on Martinique's highest hill – thirty of us forming a circle of folding chairs, each separated by five meters of emptiness, as if grief might be contagious. The group leader, Dr. Moreau, lost his entire laboratory team when their underwater research station transformed overnight.

"The disappeared leave echoes," whispered Elise, a fisherman's widow with eyes like shattered glass. "My François calls to me from puddles after rainfall." Others nodded, familiar with these phantom voices that psychiatrists diagnosed as "temporal auditory hallucinations."

Each week, someone would be missing from our circle. Another chair empty. Another life surrendered to the Melt's beckoning waters.

"In Étretat," said a newcomer one evening, a Frenchman visiting family in Martinique, "there's a place where the voices are clearer. Where the cliff face acts as an amplifier for those trapped between timelines. People have actual conversations with the lost. Not just fragments, but real exchanges."

Dr. Moreau frowned. "René, we don't encourage—"

But I was already on my feet, demanding details, co-ordinates, anything. René's eyes met mine with recognition – the look of someone who would grasp any thread, no matter how thin.

I was on a plane to France before the tears on my passport dried, heart pounding with a desperate maybe.

Maman's pleas echoed in my ears as the aircraft climbed above the island. "You go to your death, *chérie*."

Perhaps. But wasn't living without Stéphane its own kind of drowning?

Days blur into weeks, into months. The other listeners come and go, hope kindling and dying in their eyes like fireflies in the dusk. I remain, rooted to this patch of timeworn stone. My swelling belly marks time's passage in stretch marks and quickening kicks. Each movement is a bittersweet reminder – half Stéphane, half me, wholly a future he may never see.

The Guadeloupean midwife noticed first – how water responded when the baby moved. Concentric circles forming in basins, in cups, in puddles nearby. The older woman made no comment beyond a quick sign against evil, the kind islanders had used since before cathedrals claimed their prayers.

When labor pains grip me, it's Aiden and Mathilde who find the midwife among the pilgrims of loss. Our daughter is born as the Chrono-Sea surges, its waters breaching the shore for the first time in recorded history.

"Push!" the midwife commands as the waters rise around our makeshift shelter. Through the window, I see cult priests leading a procession into the advancing tide, their followers' faces ecstatic with terrible hope. A wall of churning red consumes them. Outside, sirens wail evacuation orders.

Her cry pierces the air; time both stops and rushes forward. The past – Stéphane, our life together – doesn't vanish, but suddenly it's not the only story. There's a new narrative beginning, written in the creases of my daughter's tiny fists and the depth of her eyes. I name her Hope. The word catches in my throat like a prayer every time I say it.

As Hope grows, so does my resolve. Her first steps mirror my own tentative ones away from grief. I come here every day, Hope strapped to my chest. The government has erected barriers, restricting access to the cliffs after too many grief-stricken pilgrims wandered into the water. I bribe guards with Maman's rum and stories of Martinique summers.

My husband's been gone for four thousand five hundred and thirty-six hours. That's two hundred and seventy-two thousand, one hundred and sixty minutes of me trying to breathe around the Stéphane-shaped hole in my chest.

"Your Papa loves you," I murmur into Hope's coily curls. "Wherever, whenever he is, he loves you so damn much."

Hope gurgles, her tiny hand patting my wet cheek. For a heartbeat, I swear I hear Stéphane's laugh on the breeze, as real as Hope's touch.

The temporal storm intensifies around us, the air thick with possibility. Time fragments like broken glass, refracting moments that weren't meant to touch – yesterday's rain falling upward, tomorrow's birds frozen mid-flight.

Hope stirs against my chest, her tiny fist uncurling to reveal a shell-smooth pebble, iridescent as a tear, pulsing with opalescent energy. It glows with the same vermillion hue as the Chrono-Sea, but somehow purified, distilled to its essence.

"Where did you get this?" I whisper, but my daughter only coos, reaching towards the water with unmistakable intent. The pebble grows warm against my palm, humming with possibility.

The stone vibrates between us, its light intensifying until it illuminates Hope's face from below, casting her features in otherworldly relief. Her eyes reflect nothing of a baby's innocence – instead, they hold ancient knowledge, as though she's lived a thousand years in her few months of life.

I press the stone to my lips, tasting salt and years and might-have-beens. The Chrono-Sea parts, a shimmering path cutting across its mercurial surface, straight as hope, endless as grief.

Where the stone's light touches water, reality splits open. The path looks solid, despite being made of the same mercurial carmine that consumed Stéphane. Along its edges, scenes from our life together play out like holographic memories – our first meeting at university, our wedding day, the night we decided to try for a child. All the moments that built us, suspended in crystalline perfection.

My heart pounds a broken rhythm. I look at my daughter, at her deep brown eyes flecked with gold. Stéphane's eyes.

"How did you do this?" I ask her, but I already know. Something of him lives in her – some quantum entanglement, some paradox of existence that science hasn't yet named. She carries his capacity for wonder, his ability to see doorways where others see walls.

Maman's voice echoes – "Think of the bébé, *chérie*" – mingling with the phantom laughter of the life I had in Martinique. Years stretch ahead, heavy with possibility and absence.

For a heartbeat, I'm tempted. God help me, I'm tempted. To follow that glowing path and search for Stéphane. What if he's trapped, conscious, waiting for rescue just beyond the veil of our reality? What if Hope needs her father more than she needs a mother consumed by what-ifs?

The Salvationist priest's words return to me: "A mother found her lost children." Was it true? Did he prey on rumor, or had someone truly returned? The governments would hide such news, fearing mass suicides if reunion were proven possible.

One step. That's all it would take. One step to fall into the stream of time, to swim through memories and might-have-beens until I find him. My feet move of their own accord, toes curling over the edge.

Untreated water laps at the stone shore, reaching upward to caress my ankles. It feels warm, welcoming – nothing like the cold terror I expected. Like bathwater prepared by loving hands.

The path pulses, beckoning. "Océane…" his voice calls, using the nickname only he ever used. My heart stutters. The voice is unmistakably his. "Come find me…"

The air shimmers around the voice, and for an instant, I see him – standing halfway along the path, arms outstretched, his smile exactly as I remember. Not frozen in terror like his final moment, but warm with recognition. He looks solid, real – more substantial than the phantom whispers I've chased for months.

"Bring her," he says, eyes fixed on Hope. "She opened the door. She can stabilize the passage. We can be together again, all three of us."

Hope's weight anchors me, warm and real and needing, tethering me to now, to next, to must.

She whimpers suddenly, her tiny body tensing against mine. The pebble in my hand flares brighter, then dims, its light stuttering like a failing heartbeat. The path across the water flickers correspondingly, sections of it dissolving into swirling sanguine before reforming. Stéphane's image wavers, and for a split second, his face contorts into a grimace that might be pain or might be hunger.

"Hurry," he calls, voice fracturing around the edges. "The window is closing. Step through now or lose me forever."

"Your daughter," I call to the shimmering path, my voice stronger than I feel. "She has your laugh, your eyes. She needs a world with solid ground."

The wind rises, carrying salt and memory on its edges. The ruby light of the path casts everything in the hue of arterial blood. Hope whimpers, tiny fingers clenching my shirt. Her heartbeat flutters against mine, two drums keeping different time.

The pebble in my palm pulses once, twice, then cracks down its center, a hairline fracture that bleeds garnet light. My throat constricts around words I never thought I'd say. "The man who taught me that life is for living would never ask me to trade certainty for possibility."

The path begins to collapse from its far end, sections of it falling back into the churning Chrono-Sea. The disintegration accelerates with each passing second, reality reasserting itself over impossibility.

His image raises one hand in what might be farewell, what might be his blessing. Stéphane's lips move, forming words the wind carries away before he vanishes. For a moment, the space where he stood retains his outline, a Stéphane-shaped hole in the air, then that too dissolves.

Hope's hand opens and closes, reaching for a presence only she can see. Then she settles against me, her breathing deep and even. A tear slides down her cheek, but her face is peaceful. As if she understands what we've both lost and kept.

The sea returns to its restless churning, indifferent to the choice that has altered our universe forever.

The Chrono-Sea ripples with memories – Martinique sunlight on mahogany skin, lavender-scented whispers, dreams unfulfilled. The path across its surface pulses beneath my feet, an invitation written in the language of longing. How simple it would be to answer its call, to surrender to the same hunger that claimed Stéphane. To dive.

"Maman said all water is suspect now," I tell Hope. "But she forgot to mention we are made of water, too. We carry oceans inside us."

Hope blinks up at me, her eyes reflecting the crimson sea like twin horizons. Her tiny hand reaches for my face, fingers catching a tear as it falls. The droplet glistens on her skin – a miniature sea, harmless and contained.

I press my palm to her chest, feeling the rhythm of her heart, the blood coursing through her veins – sixty percent water, the doctors say. The same percentage as Stéphane. As me. As everyone who has ever lived or disappeared.

"Your father," I whisper, "is in that water. But he's in this water too." I touch her tear-damp cheek, then my own. "In you. In me. In the rain that will fall on your first day of school, in the puddles you'll splash through when it's safe again, in the glasses of coconut water we'll toast with on birthdays he'll never see."

Hope's fingers curl around mine, surprisingly strong. Outside her grip, the pebble continues to crumble, each particle returning to dust, to earth, to the cycle of existence that not even the Chrono-Sea can fully interrupt.

"They tell us to fear the water," I say, more to myself than to my daughter. "To run inland, to higher ground. But there is no escaping it – not the grief, not the love, not the parts of ourselves that flow like rivers towards those we've lost. The trick isn't to run from the tide but to learn to carry it differently."

I take a step away from the edge, then another. Each footfall an echo of Stéphane's splash, but in reverse.

For the first time since the water consumed my husband, the architecture of my grief shifts, like a bone that breaks and fuses stronger at the fracture. My body remembers how to be more than just a vessel for grief. How to be, instead, a horizon – the line where sea meets sky, where ending touches beginning, where loss and hope are not opponents but partners in the dance of what it means to remain.

I lift Hope higher against my chest, her weight both anchor and wings.

The Last Angel of History

Transcript

John Akomfrah (Director)

[music] 00:07
Narrator: We came across a story of a bluesman from the 1930s, a guy called Robert Johnson. Now the story goes that Robert Johnson sold his soul to the devil at a crossroads in the Deep South. He sold his soul, and in return, he was given the secret of a Black technology, a Black secret technology, that we know now to be the blues. The blues begat jazz, the blues begat soul, the blues begat hip-hop, the blues begat R&B. Now, flash forward 200 years into the future. Next figure, another hoodlum, another bad boy, scavenger, poet figure – he's called a Data Thief. Two hundred years into the future, the Data Thief is told a story: If you can find the crossroads, a crossroads, this crossroads, if you can make an archeological dig into this, you'll find fragments, techno-fossils. And if you can put those elements, those fragments together, you'll find the code. Crack that code, and you'll have the keys to your future. You've got one clue and it's a phrase: Mothership Connection.

01:33
The Last Angel of History

01:39
Kodwo Eshun, Critic: The Mothership Connection, it's kind of George Clinton's obvious 1974 album in which you have an alien – you have George Clinton who's like an alien and kind of silver foil and he's kind of getting out of this spaceship. You can't work out whether he's getting out of the spaceship or getting back into the spaceship.

01:56
George Clinton, Musician: By this time, Black music – Black itself had become commercial. You know, it was hip to be Black, dance like James Brown and all of that. And rock 'n' roll had just like, faded out, you know in '69, so it was time to make a change.

02:17
Narrator: This figure is a thief – he's a Data Thief. And he's surfing the internet of Black culture, breaking into the vaults, breaking into the rooms, stealing fragments – fragments from cyber-culture, techno-culture, narrative culture.

02:46
Narrator: The Data Thief has two gadgets that's he's going to use to navigate his way through our present. A black box and a rather special pair of sunglasses.

03:01
Derrick May, Musician: G. Clinton, George Clinton, Parliament Funkadelic, funk, UnCut Funk, Da Bomb. George Clinton, I think, is a fucking maniac.

03:15
George Clinton: I was always fond of *Star Trek* – I was a Star Trek freak, a sci-fi freak. So the next record, I had to find another place that he hadn't perceived Black people to be. And that was on a spaceship. So I pictured him lying in there like it's a Cadillac, sliding through space, you know, chillin'. You know, having come here from the planet Sirius.

03:53
Derrick May: I went to see a concert when I was a little kid at this place called the Olympia Ballroom here in Detroit – I'll never forget it. I mean that was like – for me that was the first concert I had ever been to in my life. And I'll remember it because I'll never forget this man coming out of the top of the roof on a cable, dressed in a diaper, and big white platform boots, playing a guitar, and he called himself Starchild. And this other dude walks out of this so-called spaceship that lands onto the middle of the stage. And these guys are playing this music. When I think about it right now, I'm there.

04:30
Kodwo Eshun: The Mothership Connection is Clinton's symbol for what happens to funk when you pass it through the studio, and when it becomes kind of a astro, or space, or it becomes extraterrestrial. The Mothership Connection is like a link – Africa is a lost continent in the past, and between Africa as an alien future.

4:57
Narrator: Roaming the internet, the Data Thief discovers a new word – Africa. Somewhere in these streets is the secret of the Mothership. The Data Thief knows that the first touch with science fiction came when Africans began playing drums to cover distance. Water carried the sound of the drums, and sound covered the distance between the Old and the New World. This was the Data Thief's first visit, his first clue. It took him back to the New World.

05:37
George Clinton, Musician: P-Funk is pure funk, okay? I mean, it's an uncut…um…undiluted – it's pure funk. No cut, no extra ingredients, no additives.

06:00
Narrator: He's in a land of African memory. In the history vault, a woman says, "It's after the end of the world. Don't you know that yet?" Confused, the Data Thief returns to the future.

06:38
Sun Ra, Musician and composer: The music is different here. The vibrations are different.

06:43
Derrick May: Sun Ra. Hm, George Clinton's mentor. Period.

06:51
Narrator: In the New World, the Data Thief finds two rooms, marked "Lee Perry Black Arc" and "Sun Ra Arkestra".

07:00
Ishmael Reed, Novelist: You get everything with Sun Ra. You get ragtime, you cover all those periods. You get swing, get bebop, and you get – he admired John Cage, so you get some of that European avant-garde tinge to his music. It was very difficult to have a conversation with him. You know, I recall having a discussion with him during one of his rehearsals. Every time I was prepared to answer one of his long monologues, he started the band, so I'd be drowned out.

07:26
Narrator: The Data Thief asked Sun Ra and Lee Perry for the secret of the Mothership Connection. And they said, "Our music is a mirror of the universe. We explore the future through music."

07:38
John Corbett, Critic: The Black Ark, which is Lee Perry's studio and also his label, Arkestra, which was from about 1955 on Sun Ra's band, and the Mothership – the Mothership Connection was George Clinton's major earth tour of about 1977, are three spaceship images that these musicians are using as vehicles for this kind of subversion that I'm talking about of exploration.

08:22
Lee "Scratch" Perry, Musician: I am the firmament computer. I am the sky computer. I am the avid computer.

08:33
George Clinton: Lee Perry? I've heard the name but I'm not quite sure who that is.

08:40
John Corbett: It's interesting to look at Lee Perry in reggae, George Clinton in funk, and Sun Ra in jazz. As three figures who are working with a shared set of mythological images and icons, I think it's uncanny that they're all using space iconography, and certain tropes of madness, and extra-terrestriality, largely independent of one another – largely without having come in contact with one another's work.

09:10
Sun Ra: [singing] I cover the earth and hold it like a ball in my hand.

[music plays]

10:00
George Clinton, Musician: You know space, for Black people, is not something new. I believe that we've been there. That we're returning to that and that the consciousness of Black people – all mankind is striving to return to where the essence of where the roots have come from. Whether somebody came in and gave us our intellect genetically by cloning us or switching on our genes to start evolving the way [we] have, or that we are descendants from the stars.

10:44
Narrator: The Data Thief knows there's a connection between music, space, and the future. Entering a room marked, "Space Exploration", he finds the name, Bernard Harris, astronaut. He asks him, "What does Mothership Connection mean to you?"

11:05
Dr. Bernard A. Harris, Jr., Astronaut: Well it means to me, number on in college, we used to party off this album quite a lot. But it is also a reflection of one man's vision of the future. And that is of us as human beings exploring space, but more importantly, a Black man exploring space – Black people exploring space. We're doing that now, we're going to be doing that in the future. I have always wanted to be an astronaut since I was about eight years old. I was one of those kids that was fascinated with science and science fiction. I always tout myself as one of the original Trekkies or Trekkers, or whatever they call themselves these days. So through that fantasy of imagining being in space, I started reading about it, I started researching NASA and finding out what it was all about. And when I saw the first human beings walk on the moon, I was hooked. That was it.

12:16
Nichelle Nichols, Actress: I remember being so excited and in awe that we stepped on the moon, but coming out of it – that glorious moment – I didn't see my brother, I didn't see us there, and I decided to have a part in that. When they called me in and asked me to assist them in recruiting the first women and minority astronauts for the space shuttle program, I could not say no.

12:45
Dr. Bernard A. Harris, Jr.: I knew that Nichelle was involved with the early recruitment program that went on at NASA. In fact, from her efforts and a lot of folks here at Johnson Space Center's efforts, and also probably some efforts of some of the civil rights leaders that we've had in this country, we got our first three African American astronauts.

13:25
Nichelle Nichols: I walked in and I saw men and women of all colors working at every level. Scientists, administrators, secretaries, photographers, journalists, all the way down to maintenance engineers, were Black and white. I thought, "Why in the world is this not being represented for the public to see? That this NASA that I'm seeing represents all of us – it looks like *Star Trek*!"

14:02
[music]

14:20
Narrator: The Data Thief wanders through the ruins, the detritus, the wastelands of our late 20th century, and he comes across a little piece of stone – a fragment. Written on it is a strange phrase: The line between social reality and science fiction is an optical illusion. Puzzled, he wanders off in search of people who will confirm the strange theorem.

14:50
Juan Atkins, Musician: The guy behind me, to my right is here, is "Mad" Mike Banks from Underground Resistance, one of the pinnacle techno forces in Detroit at the very moment.

We perpetuate the technological revolution through music. Music, being something that people listen to – that's the first thing they hear if they're going to be ready for a technological future. I think music better prepares them – technological music better prepares them for the future.

15:25
Derrick May, Musician: I think the original philosophy of the music that we were doing – Detroit techno, whatever it's called now, however it's been called – I think really, honestly it stems from Juan Atkins. He had an idea that he wanted to infiltrate the music industry as a Black artist, doing electronic music. At the time, there were no Black artists really doing it other than George Clinton Parliament Funkadelic age. There were a couple other people – there was George Duke, Stanley Clarke, they were experimenting with it every now and then, but there were really no Black artists moving down that lane.

16:03
Juan Atkins: What synthesizer was to me was the first breakthrough for electronic music. And by me frequenting the music shops and being very enthusiastic about science fiction and all things futuristic, of course the synthesizer represented the ability to make these futuristic sounds, space sounds, and UFO sounds, and implement that in the music and over the tracks because I wanted to land a UFO on top of the track.

16:36
[music]

16:53
Kodwo Eshun, Critic: The connection between the architects of Afrofuturism, between Sun Ra, and Lee Perry, and George Clinton, and between techno and jungle later on in the 80s and the 90s, is simply that they pulled nothing in common with the common idea of Black music, which is that it belongs to the street or to the stage. They need live music— kind of muses that exists out in the urban. They're studio music, they're impossible, imaginary music. And yet, because they're imaginary, they're even more powerful because they suggest the future. They don't reflect the past. They imagine the future.

17:35
DJ Spooky, Critic/DJ: Detroit is a symbolic location in American culture because it's where the American automotive industry's heart was. It was, you know, this sort of industrial space. But once one encounters the information in the streets, which are now in decay, so now Detroit becomes a relic. It's a decaying structure at a crossroads, so to speak. Techno coming out of Detroit represents that kind of urban youths' view of change, saying, "No longer do we have this industrial kind of base. No longer do we have this kind of security. Everything is flux."

18:15
Carl Craig, Musician: I think Detroit techno started because of the type of music that Detroiters were exposed to. Because of the love the DJs in Detroit still have to this day for Kraftwerk. The Kraftwerk influence helped the sequencing and the rigidness of it. The rock, the crazy sounds of it. P-funk, the funk of it. Black Bone, the groove.

19:11
Dr. Bernard A. Harris, Jr., Astronaut: On my first mission, as a tribute to my heritage as a Black person in this world, I flew a flag that was a combination of all the countries' flags of the continent of Africa. So I have this and my hope is that this summer, when I'm visiting Africa that I will take it around to the different countries and display this. And why? Because this is my heritage and to say that I know – I acknowledge that I know that Black people were the first astronomers and mathematicians in this world. And it seems only natural that one of their sons would come back from space and say, "Hey, look what we have accomplished together."

20:16
Kodwo Eshun: Ever since the 50s, you've had electronics, which summoned up the alien, the monster. In the 70s, you had disco, which summoned the idea of the clone and the robotic. By the time you get to the 80s and Derrick May, techno is now like a species jump.

20:32
Derrick May, Musician: Techno to me means, um – I think the idea for me has always been to express man and machine. You know, intertwined. Kraftwerk – they did an album based on that philosophy of man and machine, and they called the album *Man-Machine*. I think to bring these two elements together and to take technology to a level of human – human instinct has always been the most important for me, you know? To make people see the human side of the technology.

21:05
[machine whirring]

21:12
Derrick May: Most people that are making this music, or trying – or attempting – to make this music, have no idea of, you know, those two very simple elements. Just take the salt, take the pepper, mix it together, and what you come up with is a nice piece of soup. You know, you put some onions in there and some croutons, and you sit back, and you sip it. And it's good.

21:37
Goldie, Musician: For me, I came in really to Breakbeat when Breakbeat music was the main, you know, rebel drive. I wanted to be rebellious with music from the start. Hip hop was generated by Breakbeat and I think from the point of view I am – where I'm at, we had a European background to look at over our shoulder and we had an American dream to look at in the forefront. But I think the American dream you pursued is no longer the American dream.

22:08
[Voice: After the end of the world. Don't you know that yet? It's after the end of the world. Don't you know that yet? It's after the end of the world. Don't you know that yet?]

22:20
Greg Tate, Writer: Well, I've always contended that the Black existence and science fiction are one and the same. And that's as someone who has obviously experienced life as a Black person who has been reading science fiction since he was maybe nine or ten year-old.

22:35
[Voice: After the end of the world. Don't you know that yet?]

22:41
Greg Tate: The form itself, the conventions of the narrative in science fiction – in terms of the way they deal with the subject, it's usually someone who is at odds with the apparatus of power in the society, and whose profound experience is one of cultural dislocation, alienation, estrangement.

23:09
Ishmael Reed, Novelist: We're not believed. We're like aliens trying to tell our experience to earthlings. People don't believe us. You see, we live in – there's a normal life in this country. The police don't plant evidence, they don't lie, you know, and um, drug dealers call ahead and make appointments before they execute people. This is the upper-class, white world. You know, we try to tell them this isn't happening in Oakland where I live. You know, and they say, "Well, your experience is so incredible. You're making this up and you're paranoid." So I think living in this country, for African Americans, is a far-out experience.

23:50
[music]

24:02
Ishmael Reed: When I began to go to Europe, I'd come back and say, "Not all white people are the same." I can go to Germany, Italy, places like that, and have much more credibility. We can have much more credibility there than here. And I think one of the reasons for that is that there's a lot of denial on the part of the American-European population, do you understand me?

24:25
Kodwo Eshun, Critic: Greg Tate is the writer who argued that Black people, in America certainly, live the estrangement that science fiction writers kind of talk about. All the stories about alien abductions, all the stories about alien spaceships taking subjects from one place and taking them to another, genetically transforming them – Greg is really saying that – Greg is re-casting American history in the light of science fiction and saying, "Well look, all those things that you read about alien abduction and genetic transformation, they already happened." How much more alien do you think it gets than slavery? Than entire mass populations moved and genetically altered, entire status moved, forcibly dematerialized? It doesn't really get much more alien than that.

25:11
DJ Spooky, Critic/DJ: The first touch with sci-fi is that the slaves were using drums to communicate over the distance. So the slave owners would institute reforms that slaves were no longer allowed to play certain rhythms, if at all. And they weren't even allowed to speak their own languages, and they had to learn the slave masters' language, which is English…in Jamaica, the States, or Spanish, or Portuguese. But there was always a sense of displacement of the original "code", you know, the language. And drums with the new code – the downloaded new information – downloaded into the cortex or whatever.

25:47

Greg Tate, Writer: Most science fiction tales dramatically deal with how the individual is going to contend with these alienated, dislocating societies and circumstances. And that pretty much sums up the mass experience of Black people within, um, post-slavery, 20th century world.

26:10

Narrator: Rumor has it that before Robert Johnson made his deal with the devil at the crossroads, he couldn't play to save his life. He sold his soul, in return he got his secret. [sound of machine gun] Our thief from the future gives up the right to belong in his time in order to come to our time to find the Mothership Connection. The thief becomes an angel, an angel of history. The Data Thief can visit the Old world and the New, but he cannot be a part of either. He doesn't know this is his problem. But when he makes his last trip to Africa, he will.

27:13

Kodwo Eshun: In the '50s and '60s, there was a young writer who came along called Samuel R. Delany, and he's like a bohemian, Black, gay figure, who introduced a lot of different Black and Native Indian characters into science fiction. And his key book is *Dhalgren*, and that's a key book for Black science fiction because that's the first time Black characters in science fiction aren't merely protagonists, but as it were, changed the entire terms of how science fiction is written.

27:41

Samuel R. Delany, Novelist: The cities that I have in mind for the side of the dialogue that my novel *Dhalgren* represents, um, as I said are New York, Los Angeles, Cincinnati – I can't think of a major American city where half the city has not been in ruin. In fact, the term inner-city, which at this point is an American term, is that term for that burnt-out section of your city; where the people do not live, where the general functions of urban life go on at a very depressed rate.

28:23

Goldie, Musician: Any music which comes from inner-city, which derives from inner-city, and comes from different areas from the city, being a city which is now developed so far along the line, its multicultural status is changed. And I think that the moral freedom of it is that we have no – we want to be free with our music and we want to take from wherever we want to take from. And I think the rebelliousness before was that, "Fuck everybody else. We want to take music from wherever we want to take it, 'cause we can make something with it, which is a new rhythm to your ears, but you can't hear it."

28:53

DJ Spooky: I've heard jungle songs of classical music, jungle songs of bits and pieces of TV commercials, jungle songs of sounds of water running. You know what I mean? It's a true urban response in another sense of accelerated culture as viewed through a lens of pot and LSD, which are also ways of exploring your environment too.

29:19

Narrator: Every day, the Data Thief finds new words and phrases. Today, he finds "inner-city" and "the blues."

29:30
Goldie: Blues came out of a Depression, without a doubt. It was singing about the situation and what was going on, and playing rhythms about those kinds of things. But it didn't necessarily have to have too many vocals in it or a lot of vocals to say anything. The mood of that music was blue, its frame was sad, it meant a lot of different things with certain people. And I think when that music is conceived, it doesn't really have any effect on the outside world until later on.

30:10
Ishmael Reed, Novelist: We are considered as outsiders. We are considered as people who are not part of the American experience. As a matter of fact, in the 19th century, African Americans were excluded from Fourth of July celebrations. So there's always been this feeling in this country that we're aliens – that we don't belong here. There's always people who want us to go back to where we came from. I don't know where I would go. Maybe I'll go to Dublin because some of my ancestors are Irish or maybe I'll go to Tennessee because some of my ancestors are Cherokee. Maybe I'll go to Yorubaland because some of my ancestors are probably from West Africa. I wouldn't know where to go. There's always this mention of, "Send us back – send us back to some other place. Send us back to the planet of our origin."

30:57
Samuel R. Delany: I've often written that science fiction doesn't try to predict the future, but rather offers a significant distortion of the present. And what I mean, I guess, is that a lot of people, when they hear the words, "science fiction," the first thing that they assume is that this is a story or a novel that's going to tell them what's going to happen sometime tomorrow or the day after. And I just don't think that's what science fiction writers are really interested in doing. I think we sit around and we look at what we see around us, and we say, "How could the world be different?"

31:38
Octavia Butler, Novelist: Back when Ronald Reagan had just become president, people were talking about winnable nuclear wars. And I thought, "If people were falling for this kind of thing, there must be something basically wrong with the human species." So I thought about it and what I wound up doing, really, was putting the thing that I came up with into the mouth of my main character. Um, I had – or not my main character, my aliens. I had them arrive right after a nuclear war so that I could make my point and I had them tell my character that human beings had two characteristics that didn't work well together. One, they were intelligent, and that was good, no problem. And two, they were hierarchical. And unfortunately, the hierarchical tendencies were the older and so sometimes the intelligence was put at the service of the hierarchical behavior.

32:45
Narrator: Isn't it strange that in the Second World War, computer technology was used to aid and abet the military-industrial complex? But by the end of our century, that technology has mutated, devolved, and diversified to such a degree, that African American musicians, young Black British musicians can use computer technology to construct a soundtrack to the end of the industrial epoch. That is strange and is something that puzzles the Data Thief.

33:27

Kodwo Eshun, Critic: Well yeah, I think it's very true that computer technology started out of the military sphere in the post-war period. By the time you get to the '80s and '90s, it's true that computer technology, cheap software, has now created what we could call an *ecology*. An analog or digital ecology by which you can use technology, can use synthesizers, sequences, programmers, work stations – you can now use them as ways to create sonic worlds. Some of those sonic worlds will secede from mainstream worlds and some of it will be antagonistic towards it. The point is that, uh, the root through the cybernetic, the root through the drum machine allows you much more possibility for that. The point is the explosion and the proliferation and mutation of the African-derived rhythms. So yeah, techno and Underground Resistance, uh yeah, they are warring on mediocre audio-visual programming.

34:30

Narrator: New words: sonic warfare, sonic Africa, Afrofuturism, digitized diaspora, analog ecology. He's in a land of African memory. Every entrance into these vaults brings new information of victories and defeat, dreams and catastrophes. New words: alien, slave.

35:02

Greg Tate: Well I think what sampling technology has allowed in this area of Black musical production is the creation of digitized race memory. And I think that what sampling allows – for a generation that wasn't, that didn't have access to musical education – is a way of collapsing all eras of Black music onto a chip. You know, and being able to freely reference and cross-reference, you know, all those areas of sound and all those previous generations of creators, um, kind of simultaneously.

36:04

Kodwo Eshun: Traditionally speaking, the record player was an inert object. It simply played the records. The vinyl – it was like this kind of slab of material that you played and just played the contents of it. It's only when you get to hip hop that you get the record player then you use the instrument in its own right. Then you get the vinyl, you get vinyl being selected right down to the particular Breakbeat, and then sampled, and then scratched, and then used in all kinds of different terms. And we could say that one thing that, uh, Black producers do is that they release, what I call, the entelechy of an instrument. They release the potential energy, which lies inert in any kind of technology.

36:55

Goldie, Musician: To remain on the cutting edge, you must have – there's a certain aggression with this music, which remains on the cutting edge. To root out a tune, to rinse it out, to make you pay attention there and then. You know, not to be melted down time and time again where it becomes something which, you know…on the cutting edge, you get it straight first off, straight in information and straight out in dance, straight out in aggression, in movement, you know?

37:29

Narrator: Africa, the Data Thief's last visit. He would like to return home, but cannot. No escaping from this time, this space. He continues collecting information, wandering the boundaries between science fiction and social reality. This is the Data Thief's new home. The zone of optical illusions.

37:57
Goldie: Technology has broken time down, 'cause we are the future. 'Cause the time we're in is the future. Because in this technology we're living in now, if I go to a little Tutsi tribe in Africa right down in some real neck back of the woods and show her this recordable instrument or show her this [hove] of mine, or show her this camera that can – I can press it and I can show her an image of her there and then. We're then God aren't we? We're then some kind of, like, super being. We're like something else. Who are we? In their eyes, we are. But they're still there, they still exist. Those people are still alive, who are out in the middle of fucking nowhere. And when you show them technology like that, it is an optical illusion because we're always looking for the future. It's right underneath our nose, you know? It wasn't then, but it is now.

39:06
A Guy Called Gerald, Musician: Jungle describes a changing world. You know, it's changing from something that was more analog into something that is turning totally digital. I think jungle is using, well the rhythms anyway, rhythms that came from drums, normal drums, which had been, like, put through a process – digitized and manipulated digitally to create sounds unheard before, you know, really.

39:39
Goldie: I feel that's where the difference between techno jungle and I jump to techno when I'm ready to play. There's no difference. It wasn't what techno is, it's what we took from techno. It's like anything else. It's not what hip hop is, it's what we take from it. You know, stuff that Derrick May made and stuff Carl Craig made because it was – it came from somewhere. It was something which had a better meaning to me.

40:02
Derrick May, Musician: Jungle…I hate the way – I hate the word "jungle" if you want to know the truth about it. What the fuck does jungle mean? Okay, it was called Breakbeat before, now it's called jungle. Where does jungle come from? What is jungle? What does that mean?

40:18
A Guy Called Gerald: Jungle actually comes from an area in Jamaica that they call The Jungle, you know? And MCs from there, I think elaborated on that. So…it's sort of like when it came out on sound system tapes, people latched onto it and started using it as a name.

40:40
Derrick May: Gerald. Hm. Sad inside, happy face on the outside. Put all his heart and love into some big record company and they sold him out.

40:56
A Guy Called Gerald: Derrick May, I mean me, to me it's like he kicked me off, you know? Without listening. It is what it is. Feels surreal – all the early, like, transmit stuff, I would've been lost. I was lucky to, sort of like, to hear his things on the radio and think, "Yeah, that's like…a direction – that's where I want to go otherwise I don't know what I'd be doing now."

41:21
[music]
41:50
Goldie, Musician: Music's made us look at music through a microscope – technology has made us look through a microscope without a doubt. Um, people are saying now, "Is this the future of music?" We are the future now, we are in the future. You know blues wasn't made on a sampler so how can it be relevant to us? It was just music and rhythms. Those rhythms were never recorded on various technical equipment, so therefore we can then catch it and put it in its place in history because it's there, recorded. Done. And because of technology, being able to then take from any of those eras, time's irrelevant – completely irrelevant for that mannerism.

42:30
Juan Atkins, Musician: Well I think that information and technology is moving at breakneck speed right now. The techno music is definitely gonna be more advanced. That goes along with the way information is traveling now. I think it's inconceivable as to where we will be in the next five years, but I see just a lot of new ways of listening to music, new ways of buying music through computer networks. And techno music is definitely the sound for this environment.

43:17
Kodwo Eshun, Critic: In the eighteenth century, slaves like Phillis Wheatley read poetry to prove that they were human, to prove that they weren't furniture, to prove that they weren't robots, to prove that they weren't animals. In that sense, a certain idea of cybernetics has already been applied to Black subjects ever since the 18th century. I think what we get at the end of the 20th century in music technology is a point where producers kind of willingly take on the role of the cyborg – willingly take on that man-machine interface. Just to explore that mutation that's already happened to them and to accelerate them some more. Now the question is like, kind of, cyborgs for what? Well the reason is, of course, to get out of here. To get out of this time here, this space now.

[End Credits]

Flight Pattern

Azure Arther

TEJEAN RECLINED in the lab chair and ate the last living dragonfly with a bit of honey and a tiny sprinkle of salt from the barren crater that used to be the Dead Sea. The salt added a hint of bitterness to the sweet, and Tejean relished in the upcoming flavor even as the dragonfly buzzed and wriggled in his fingers. He put the whole insect in his mouth and crunched, a quick squelch and slow chews.

Arabella, curled up in a mustard armchair with her long legs tucked beneath her, wrinkled her nose, but she continued typing on the computer precariously balanced across her thighs. The false sunlight from the lights in the seating area fell across her in lines like tally marks. She shifted, and the light touched the thick ropes of her dark brown hair, piled high on her head. Tejean considered her as he rubbed his tongue to the roof of his mouth, smacking at the bitter and sweet. Was that hair tower heavy? Would she even notice if it was?

When he finished and breathed in satisfaction, Bella looked up at him, her light brown eyes disapproving above her frameless glasses.

"You know," she said, and yawned, her wide mouth opening to reveal perfectly straight, white teeth that seemed even brighter against her brown skin. "I was going to let it fly until it died naturally, in its habitat."

"I know."

"Then you should have let it live." She closed her laptop, set it on the ornate table beside the chair, and stood, all legs and a short torso she had always been concerned about. She stretched, and he admired her until she glared at him.

"It would have died," he protested.

"Not for another three weeks, at the very least. Maybe longer." Bella pursed her full lips and thoughtfully tilted her head. Tejean mouthed the words even as she said them. "I was going to be an entomologist, you know."

"I know." Tejean grinned at her.

"You're insufferable."

"Yet you suffer me."

Bella grinned and walked towards him, her hips swinging just a slight amount too much.

"Pause." Tejean said and sighed. She froze, frowning.

"Is something wrong?"

"You still don't have the walk right."

"I am walking as she did in your memory." Arabella's brown eyes hardened slightly before they flicked from brown to white, the only indication that the noid was accessing her memory banks. A hint of annoyance crept into her voice. "I see. There is a smoothness to her walk that I am unable to emulate. You should—" There was another flicker. Brown. White. Brown. White. "—oil leg segments 367 on both legs, tighten lumbar vertebrate L3 one-eighth of a centimeter, and add—" Brown. White. Brown. "I have corrected the coding matrix. There was a slight misstep with the balls of my feet."

"Let's do it tomorrow." Tejean sighed. "Power down."

The noid immediately slumped in place, and the animated life that had just inhabited her frame dissipated. Tejean stood and busied himself around the lab. He took the next sample from the left lab freezer, tacitly avoided the one next to it, and went through the process of injecting the frozen dragonfly nucleus into the prepared donor cell. He stared at the cells through the microscope and watched the shredded material as it thawed. The process often didn't work, but patience and repetition almost always won.

It was a few hours before one of the cells took. Tejean carefully placed the rapidly reproducing cells in a water incubator, stroked Arabella's cheek, and cleaned up the lab. He hesitated before wiping down the freezer doors, but he hurried through the motion and left the lab. It would be a while before the bug would grow.

He had a sterile meal of seaweed crisps, soaked in ramen broth, with a bare sprinkling of noodles in the gray kitchen. It was more a sterile meal holder than an actual kitchen, but Arabella had called it such when they built it, so he did, as well. He sipped the broth and eyed the soup. The grain supply was low again. He should have been paying attention to it, but in truth, the dragonfly argument was all he cared about.

It had been their last argument before she decided to die, before she chose the outside over safety, over him. In his head, sometimes, he liked to think of Arabella as free somewhere, wandering the remnants of the Earth, creating and living in her own oasis somewhere. But the truth was that the world was cruel and barren, and besides the few other underground habitats that they had kept spotty contact with, there would have been nothing out there for Bella.

She was dead.

Which was why the dragonfly argument was so important. It shouldn't have gone the way it went. It shouldn't have ended the way it had. But Tejean was going to fix it.

The dragonfly was swimming when he arrived in the lab a few days later. In the wild, it would be another two years before the insect was able to fly, but in the lab, Tejean had a varied mix of accelerants he could add to the bug. It wouldn't taste as good, or be as perfect, and sometimes the mixes he used caused things to die quicker, but there was no nagging wife to help him remain moral, ethical. There was no inspiration to fix the planet, or at least a small bit of it for potential future children. There was no partner to point out flaws.

There was just Tejean, and he didn't care for anything but a finished product, a fat bug he could eat and perpetuate the argument he needed to fix. So he gave the dragonfly the accelerants by adding them to the water, which was already treated with tropic marin salt. The salt encouraged algae growth, but also, Tejean had found, set the perfect conditions for other additives.

Then he tinkered on Arabella's noid. He tweaked the vertebrae, oiled the leg segments, and ran the coding matrix addition through a series of checks. He adjusted her failsafes so that she could adjust it on her own without approval next time. Finally, he closed the panel in her back, tugged down her sweater to hide the satin sheen of her soft skin, which had taken nearly a hundred renditions to get right, and stood behind her. He rested his head against the nape of her neck, and breathed in the soft floral scent that was all Bella's. It had taken forty-two tries to get his olfactory senses to find satisfaction in the fragrance. Forty-two tries to capture her correctly. But now, it was all tiny tweaks, many of which she helped with.

"Power on, Arabella."

And she did, stretching with a soft sigh and yawning. She froze when she felt him against her back, her posture stiffening slightly.

"You left me asleep…standing?" There was a slight note of disapproval in her voice, and Tejean grinned. The removal of the noid creed had made her less compliant, yes, but that was the only way she could truly be Bella. He lifted his head and kissed the skin just below her hairline.

"My apologies, my lady."

She stepped away from him and took a deep breath, her artificial lungs filling with air and processing it. He had equipped her with air filters so that, just by breathing, she enhanced the air quality around him. She had seemed upset when she realized it, and every time she sighed or breathed deeply, Tejean swore that the noid cut her eyes at him, just like the real Bella would have.

She turned, just the quickest flash of white, letting him know she had been accessing something within her network. "Will I be working with the dragonflies today?"

"No, no. You've only been out for a few days."

She nodded, her face impassive.

"Maybe we can work on the grain supply?"

She nodded again before looking down at her sweater. "I need a shower."

"Oh, well definitely, shower first, then…" Tejean glanced in the direction of the growing room and Arabella nodded. When she sauntered away, her footsteps were the perfect replica of Bella's, and Tejean smiled. "You've got the walk right now."

She stopped and looked back at him. Brown, white, brown. Then she nodded and exited the lab with a soft whoosh of the doors.

Once she left, Tejean went and studied the dragonfly. Dragonflies. There were two this time. He smiled slightly. Bella would have been excited to see this. The real Bella, anyway. He was never sure what Arabella, the humanoid, would feel. Were they even real feelings? He would have liked to think so.

In the months after the fight, Tejean had spent that time turning their house noid into her. The bot was one of three that Bella and Tejean had ordered when they first began building the bunker. The projection for another nuclear war (not to be confused with the second and third minor ones) had suggested that the Earth would not survive and nearly all food, livestock, and eventually, people, would be wiped out. Not that this information was readily available to the world. Just certain circles.

If you had the money, you built a bunker, and Tejean and Bella had the money, so they began construction. It wasn't hard; dig a hole, craft an underground home. Bella used the land her father left her, and Tejean cashed in his retirement and a few stock options to fund the massive underground complex. Bella and her brother, Aaron, an upcoming architectural engineer, chose a series of needs over wants, and Tejean outfitted his lab.

He had worked in the reproductive cloning department for years before switching to the biotechnological side of genetic engineering. There, he had been chief officer over the noids, the artificial intelligence that everyone thought was going to save the world or keep the world running once the humans were gone. The way the networks had faded away, how the radio stations had disappeared, how the silence seemed to extend worldwide, said differently.

But there were still the other bunkers.

Tejean left the lab and went to the communication room. There, he tapped in the sequence on the controls and spoke softly into the microphone, careful so that his voice didn't echo down the hall.

"Bunker Jackson. Aaron. You there?"

He waited in the quiet, a soft whir of one of the generators buzzing through the room. The through-the-earth signals were dependent on the topside antennae and other repeaters they had added. Sometimes they could get through, sometimes they couldn't. Theoretically, he could use the cameras to look, but those had become dusty or covered or damaged a lot faster than any of them had expected. He tried again. "Bunker Jackson. Aaron. You there?"

There was a soft click that let him know someone on the other end had picked up. A soft breath.

Tejean hesitated before saying, "Bella?"

A slight gasp and the radio went silent again. A few seconds later, Aaron's voice came on. "Whatsup, Tejean?"

Tejean shook his head before muttering, "Nothing. Touching bases."

"I see."

They sat for a minute before Tejean sighed. This was where Bella would have cracked a joke and the family would have laughed and Aaron would have teased Tejean or vice versa. Finally, Tejean said, "I miss how it used to be."

"We all do." Aaron's voice was tired. "But you let my sister go outside in a nuclear fallout, and no one has heard from her in years, so there's that."

"We've been over this," Tejean snapped.

"We have. What do you want?"

"I just…I wanted to see if you all were okay over there."

Aaron took a deep breath, his inhale and exhale loudly rolling through the speakers in the room. Tejean turned the volume down a bit more. "Yeah, Jean. We're good, bro. Dana and the kids are thriving. Almost finished the tunnel to Bunker Gilman…"

"Okay," Tejean said into the awkward silence. At one point, the five bunkers on the forty acres Arabella had owned were supposed to be connected. Even after the war came sooner than they thought, they had all planned on continuing to tunnel. Especially to Bunker Gilman, who hadn't made it to their bunker, whose resources were untouched. Tejean hesitated before lamely saying, "I'm good too."

"Good. Check in next week? It's been a while."

"Yeah. Next week."

"Hey, Tejean?" Aaron said quickly, as if he was worried his brother-in-law had hung up.

"Yeah?"

"Maybe…maybe we can build a tunnel to you next."

"Maybe." Tejean nodded, though the other man couldn't see him. He shut the radio off before Aaron could say anything else.

* * *

Arabella was in the growing room, a cavernous space that used artificial UV lights to grow a variety of plants. The grain field sat at the center, a series of dried husks and a few struggling ones. She was crouched over the dead plants, weeding them away from the somewhat healthy ones, her delicate skin covered with long sleeves and gardening gloves. She ignored him when he came to stand by her.

"Well? Are you going to help?"

"Hadn't planned on it." Tejean shrugged. "Planting is more your thing, my love."

Her eyes flickered, almost too fast for him to notice, if he hadn't been deliberately paying attention. White, brown. White, brown. She looked up at him and curled her upper lip, a classic Bella response, and stood.

"This food is not for me. I will not ingest it. I do not need it. Why am I expected to help with it if you are not?"

Tejean frowned. Bella had never complained about the plants. They were her thing. She loved growing things, particularly food.

"That's not what Bella would have said."

White, brown. White, brown. White. Arabella crouched over the plants, her eyes remaining white.

"Arabella."

She didn't respond. Her eyes remained white, doing who knew what.

"Arabella." He put more of a command into it this time. Her eyes moved halfway between white and brown. "Bella!"

Brown.

She looked at him, her gaze hard. "I will not work on plants if you will not help. Perhaps the human Arabella did not tell you her thoughts, but the diaries you fed me, the videos, the writings, the lab notes, the pictures, the memories do not lie. If you did not help when she was here, she resented you for it."

The noid stood, just slightly shorter than him, a whiff of orchids and vanilla with overtones of peach and a slight hint of bergamot. Forty-two tries. He stared at her and her full mouth, made exactly like Bella's, even with the tiny scar from when she fell and bust her lip when she was five, curled into another motion of disgust.

"I resent you for it," Arabella said.

And when she walked away, her stride was perfect.

* * *

Later, Tejean sat in the gray, ergonomic lab chair, and ate one of the last living dragonflies with a bit of honey and a tiny sprinkle of salt. He ate quickly, not bothering to relish the flavor and eagerly watched Arabella for her reaction.

"You know," she said, and shrugged slightly. "I was going to let it fly until it died naturally, in its habitat. I could have studied so much about it."

"I know."

"Then you should have let it live." She stretched, and he admired her until she glared at him.

"It would have died," he protested. "Plus, there's a second one."

"It wouldn't have died for another three weeks, at the very least. Maybe longer." Bella pursed her full lips and thoughtfully tilted her head. "I was going to be an entomologist, you know."

"I know." Tejean grinned at her.

"You're insufferable."

"Yet you suffer me."

Bella smiled slightly, almost sadly, and walked towards him, her hips swinging in that overly sensual way of hers. Tejean grinned and spread his legs, offering his lap for her to sit on. She walked past him instead, and he frowned, and grabbed her arm as she passed.

"Hey."

"Hey, yourself." She snatched her arm away from him.

"It was just a dragonfly. We can make more."

"Can we?" She turned to stare down at him. "As a geneticist, you should know that our material isn't limitless. Our options aren't limitless. We are not limitless."

"Yes, but it's just a dragonfly."

"A dragonfly I need. For the habitats I tender."

"Well, I'll make you another one." He gazed up at her, willing her to get this part right, to make the change that he had wired into her. Her eyes stuttered. White. Brown. White. Brown.

"You can't just make another one," she said, her voice harsh. "It won't be the same."

"Maybe it will be better."

"Better like what? What is better? Nothing is better." She threw up her hands and shook her head. "We are some of the only people left in the world, and you are still the same selfish prick you were before the world ended."

"That's harsh," Tejean said, and it smarted to hear almost the exact same things come spilling out of her mouth. "I programmed you to be nicer."

"I am an A.I. I adjusted your programming. It was false, just as I am false. Just as the last Arabella was false. And the one before that. I remember the other humanoid A.I.s. I remember the original Arabella."

"Then you know that this fight can't end the same way."

Arabella laughed and walked over to the cloning freezer. She opened it and looked at Arabella's body. Perfectly preserved. Unable to get away. Tejean stared at the body, as well, before averting his eyes. There was nothing in that freezer that he needed. Nothing that could help him fix this.

Arabella stared at him until he looked up at her. Her lip curled, and she closed the door. "I'm leaving."

"I said it can't end the same way."

"But it always will, won't it?" Arabella smiled slightly. "And after me, you have no more noids to adjust."

"I'll just clone her then."

"She'll never be Bella."

"Maybe she'll be better."

Arabella laughed again and grabbed one of the radioactive suits. "She won't. That's why you killed her rather than let her leave. That's why you hold on to her body but have never tried to clone it."

"You know that was an accident," Tejean said, incredulous at the noid's audacity.

She raised an eyebrow at him. "Was it?"

"Power down," Tejean snapped. "Power down."

"No," Arabella said, as she slipped the suit on. She glanced at the freezer, her eyes flickering. "Also, no."

"Power down!" Tejean roared at her, but she kept moving, buttoning up here, zipping there, attaching the Velcro patches in other places, ignoring him in the exact same way Bella had. He rushed towards her, intent on manually shutting her down, stopping her from suiting up. She fought him, and he pushed her, her head falling back as she fell and knocking into the counter, just like Bella had. But this Arabella was a noid. Her eyes flickered. White. Brown. White, and white they remained.

She stood and returned to the suit. He tried to stop her again, but she blocked his arm, her humanoid structure heavier and stronger than him. He had bypassed her failsafes, cut off her creeds and rules. He had wanted her to be as authentic as possible, better than the last two noids. They struggled for a moment before she lashed out and Tejean saw darkness.

* * *

When he woke, the right freezer was open, defrosting in places, completely thawed in others. He could have panicked over the specimens, but there was only one that he cared about, the one he had been avoiding for years. And she was gone.

"Arabella!" Tejean screamed as he ran around the bunker, met only by silence. His next iteration was soft, broken. "Arabella."

He didn't put on a suit before rushing to the hatch that led to the outside, to freedom. He went through several secured doors and areas, panic pushing him farther. Up the ladder to the outside, up into the fresh air, the sun, and the cold.

"Wait. Forgive me. I need you to forgive me." He gasped at the sight of the brisk frozen landscape, and knew, without a doubt, that he couldn't stay outside for long. He wasn't prepared, he wasn't ready. He wasn't—

The Adoration of Random Strangers

Azure Arther

THE SHAMROCK-COLORED SPECK didn't bother Tenaya. If anything, it was a minor inconvenience, something people occasionally noticed.

"What's that green dot on your thumb?"

"Ew, is it gangrene?"

"Have you seen a doctor about this?"

She had seen a doctor about it, and no, it wasn't gangrene, and for whatever reason, no one knew just what that emerald dot on her thumb was. It didn't hurt her, so she wasn't sure why it worried others. Even when it grew to cover half of her nail, the green, which spiderwebbed from one cuticle to the other, and looked a little furry, like tiny ferns beneath her thumb, still didn't seem to be damaging her.

"I think it's pretty," she said, splaying out her hand in admiration. The green spot complemented the light brown hue of her skin, emerald against dark tan. "No one knows what it is, but it's pretty, and it doesn't bother me."

But it did. Bother her, that is, even though she said it didn't. At night, she dug tweezers beneath the nail and extracted tiny slivers of green-tinged flesh. Under her pocket microscope, the green filaments moved, wriggled, writhed, but the doctor said they didn't, and told her to stop digging before she ended up with an infection.

So she stopped.

Then, one morning, she woke to find that the green had covered her nail and stretched across her skin. Tiny curlicues of verdant veins had traveled down her thumb, into the separation between her fingers and across the back of her hand.

"This isn't normal," she snapped at her doctor, who had taken one look, and sent her to a dermatologist.

"Hmm, no, it isn't," Dr. Jawani agreed. The dermatologist was an Indian-American woman, who made a crack that it looked like the start of a henna tattoo before the green ink had dried. Tenaya, Black-American and unfamiliar with henna, stared at her with deep, disapproving confusion. She didn't care about temporary tattoos.

"Well," Dr. Jawani said after an awkward silence, "I am going to take a small sample, a biopsy, if you will, and I'll get back to you as soon as the test results are in."

"Okay," Tenaya said, but she didn't want a biopsy, and the "small sample" hurt a lot more than Dr. Jawani had indicated it would.

In the meantime, the vines, which Tenaya had come to, if not accept, at least tolerate, continued their creeping advance across her skin. One increment at a time, down one finger to the nail and back again, until her whole hand was covered. People on the street noticed the designs and began to compliment her.

"Oh, I love your tattoo."

"That's so pretty. Did you have your nails done to match?"

"You have to give me the name of your artist."

For a while, the flattery was enough to alleviate Tenaya's concerns. That is, until the morning she woke, and overnight, the veins of green had covered her whole arm, right up to her shoulder. The lines were thicker now, darker in places, with the outline of leaves sprouting just under the skin. She cut into a spot at one point and screeched when an actual leaf popped out.

"What—" she hyperventilated, the gasps coming in and out, speeding through her chest. "What?"

She tried to pull the leaf out, but it felt like it was attached to her bone. There was searing pain and a deep tug that left her panting after pinching and yanking at the leaf in her bicep. She called Dr. Jawani, who said, "Come in immediately. We have fascinating results from your original biopsy, and I would love to do a bit more research." The woman's voice was enthused, excited even, and Tenaya's heart thudded in her chest as the doctor continued. "As a matter of fact, the lab itself is interested."

"Of course," Tenaya said, even as her brain began making a list of things she needed to take with her in case she couldn't ever come home again. "Can I come in tomorrow?"

After she hung up, she packed a suitcase, then another, and another, lining each one up against the wall by the front door. She called her best friend, panicked and making very little sense. Her sister called, and she garbled even more.

But they understood. To be Black in America, to be different in society, to be a medical marvel anywhere in the world, meant not only to be othered, but potentially tested on. She mumbled the names, the experiments, the stolen knowledge, the history she knew.

Lucy. Anarcha. Betsey.

Tuskegee.

Henrietta Lacks.

She thought to rest before running, to prepare mentally before leaving, but Dr. Jawani's office called to confirm her appointment. Her panic became a palpable, living thing then, one that breathed in the room with her, that clouded her head with screaming alarms.

They could come in the night.

They could come in the morning.

They could be outside right now.

She lived off campus alone. No one at school would notice her missing for a few days. And if they did, would they even care?

"Mommy?" Tenaya said when her mother answered the phone, but that was about all Tenaya could get out before she began to cry.

* * *

Stress seemed to make the plant grow faster. Her period had caused the sleeve on her left arm, but her terror of the medical community made the vines shoot down her leg.

She felt them move that time. A squiggling, creeping sensation that had her pulling over on the side of the road to wriggle out of her pants and inhale in gasping horror as she watched the green creep. She dug at her skin, scoring deep grooves that filled with blood immediately. The foliage shied away from her hands, and she gagged, dancing around in her car like a spider had landed in her thick curls, screaming repeatedly as she beat at her thigh, punched her knee, and banged her calf against the side of the door. Nothing prevented the progress. They stopped when they wanted, right above her ankle, where they swirled in a circle, like an anklet, complete with little leaves and tiny curls as charms.

Her panic dissipated when the vines stopped. It was then that she considered where she was, on the side of the road, in broad daylight, appearing to be having a drug-induced fit. It would be considered drugs if she was pulled over; if someone had called the police. They wouldn't believe it could be mental or factual, a bug or an illness. And what if the disgusted fear of her own skin was all in her mind?

What if Dr. Jawani had been waiting with – no, strangers had seen it. Strangers had complimented the green, her "tattoos." It wasn't in her head. It couldn't just be in her head, but a Black woman on the side of the road is never a good look. Tenaya patted under her eyes in the rearview mirror, stared at the red hue of the whites until they cleared enough for her to drive, pulled up her pants, and eased back into traffic. Her heart beat in her ears and her shirt stuck to the seat, wet with sweat that had dripped down her spine. She pressed back to stop the trickling sensation.

"Don't think about it."

"It's just sweat."

"It's not the vines."

Tenaya's family was originally from Bossier City, but they lived a bit of everywhere now, so it was no surprise when she found herself rattling down the highway to a nondescript house on a back road in Mansfield, Louisiana. Her mother hadn't told her to come to her house in Atlanta, or to go to her grandfather's house in Denver. No, instead, she had directed her to her Great-Aunt Vercie's sprawling complex of a home.

"Ooo, baby, come on in." Aunt Vercie was dark-skinned with high cheekbones, a sweet smile, and rheumy, cataract-filled eyes. She was ancient, stooped over, and had a sweet Louisiana drawl. "Ya momma said you were comin' and I didn't believe it. Tenaya? Here? I said. I just didn't believe it. Come on. I got your room ready."

Tenaya followed Aunt Vercie down the hall of the large house, her eyes roaming over decades of pictures and dated furniture. The hardwood floors were polished to an expressive sheen, and not a speck of dust could be seen anywhere. Aunt Vercie stopped at a door and opened it to show Tenaya a dusty rose-colored room with a wide window that looked out over the backyard. It featured a queen-size bed in the center of the room, two closets, one on each side of the bed, a mammoth dresser, and a wardrobe.

"See here? See?" Aunt Vercie said. "It's pretty, and I done aired out the space, changed the sheets. Ya momma said you needed a bit of peace. Just a bit, baby? Said you was stressed."

"I'm not stressed, Aunt Vercie," Tenaya replied. "Something is happening to me."

"Somethin's always happening to you, girl. You ain't know that?" Aunt Vercie squinted up at her. "You a woman. Somethin's always happenin' to a woman. We never stop changin'."

"No—" Tenaya stopped and shook her head. "Yes, ma'am."

"Now, you get clean from that road. The bathroom's right through there." Aunt Vercie pointed to a door attached to Tenaya's room. It was on the side of the wardrobe, out of sight. "I'ma make you somethin' t'eat."

After dragging her suitcases from the car, Tenaya sat on the side of the bed and watched the dust mites filter through the sunlight. It had taken two days to drive here from California, almost three, since she didn't have a phone and had forgotten to print out the directions. She had emptied her bank account in L.A., charged as much in cash withdrawal as she could from her credit cards, asked a friend to help with subletting her apartment, selling her things, and giving away her plants. No one came to Aunt Vercie's house. None of her friends had even heard of her. No one to remember and say, "Maybe she's in Louisiana" when the people came for her.

"Girl, ain't nobody comin' here fo' you. Not yet. Gonna take 'em some time, first. Gotta find us, first," Aunt Vercie said later that night, when Tenaya stood in her underwear in the middle of the room. "Move ya hands now. Lemme see."

Aunt Vercie walked around her, poking here and there, touching vines, and gently brushing her fingers over leaves. "Well, I ain't never seen anything like it. What the doctor say?"

"That I'm a medical miracle. That I should come in for some tests."

"Hmph." Aunt Vercie gave her a look, her eyebrows raised and her mouth a thin line. The older woman's lip curled slightly. "Yeah. I bet they do wanna do some tests. Well, half ya body's covered. Right even, too. Stops at ya' spine."

"It's on my back?" Tenaya looked over her shoulder as best she could, only able to see a small bit, but the vines were there. She knew they were. "What's happening to me?"

"Well. Ya' know, at one point, my grandmother – that would be ya' great, great, great grandmother – she would say that we came from tree folk. Maybe this is a throwback."

"What are the tree folk?" Tenaya whispered, her voice impatient and breathy. She could feel her nose wrinkled and her lip lifted, but she couldn't wipe the expression from her face.

"Tree spirits, baby. Like them Greek folk's dryads, but Black, African. Our kind. Came outta baobab trees, came outta acacia trees, out the knob thorn, the fever trees, outta all of 'em."

"But those trees are in Africa."

"Once, they woulda said, 'But those people are in Africa,' but they ain't no mo', are they?" Aunt Vercie nodded. "Let's see what these vines do."

"I don't want to see what they do. I want them to go away."

"Bit late fo' that, baby." Aunt Vercie handed Tenaya her robe. "A bit late fo' that."

* * *

It was the pain of the skin at the bottom of Tenaya's feet splitting open that woke her. She screamed into her pillow, knowing that Aunt Vercie would come tottering down the hallway at any noise. It had been weeks of slow crawling vines edging across her spine, her sternum, and finally to the other side of her body. Vines wasn't really the word for them, though. As the weeks had gone by, some of the verdant hues had changed to brown, darker than her skin, so noticeable, but not as noticeable as the green had been. There were branches up her spine, down her arms and legs, and minor twigs that forked out in other places. There were still forest vines that wrapped and twisted in some places and sprouted leaves in others.

The leaves irritated her the most. They pressed against her skin and itched until she either cut the dermis open for them to come out, or they slowly split the skin on their own, growing out over the course of a day. She had to wear long sleeves to stop them from snagging against anything, but then the fabric rubbed and irritated in a different way. Sometimes, for no reason at all, the leaves withdrew back into her skin, only to start growing out in a different spot, near the original section.

None of that minor pain was comparable to the pain that came out of her feet.

"Roots," she whispered, turning her feet to look at her soles in the moonlight. Each foot now had a massive, wood-like callus that ran from the base of her heel to just before her toes. "They have to be roots. Why do I need roots?"

When she stood and walked across the room, her bare feet echoed, clicking like heels across the hardwood floors. She wiped her brow, feeling hot and sticky, which was normal for Louisiana, but this felt like something more. Beneath her skin, the branches and vines seemed to be waiting.

"But why do I need roots?" she asked the room aloud.

She heard it then, a car in the driveway, where no one should have ever come, especially in the night. She heard the doors opening, and how softly they were closed. She heard the steps that were lightly taken onto the porch.

"Girl, they here. They here fo' you." Aunt Vercie hobbled into her room, as silent as the shoes on the porch. There was a knock, polite, but the other set of footsteps that led away seemed to be headed around the back of the house.

"Outside," Tenaya managed to say, and Aunt Vercie pulled her through the bathroom into the other guestroom. There, in the closet, her aunt opened the floor.

"Get down there. Follow the tunnel. Ain't been used in a long while, but it's good." Aunt Vercie practically shoved her into the floor when another knock, louder this time, came. "Follow till ya' can't no mo'. Then ya go up into the forest. I'll find ya later."

As Tenaya climbed into the hole, she looked up at Aunt Vercie looking down at her. The older woman's eyes were luminous in the darkness.

"Here," her aunt said, holding out a lighter and candle. "Don't forget t'blow it out when ya come up."

"Just come with me," Tenaya said, her voice high with fear.

"Baby, ain't no white folks 'bout to run me out my own house." Aunt Vercie shook her head. "You g'on now."

With that, Aunt Vercie closed her up in the darkness. Tenaya heard her footsteps hurry away. She sat in the dark for a moment, her heart racing, breath shuddering through her nose. It smelled damp in the tunnel and the soft dirt cooled her aching feet. She didn't worry about infection, but it felt like the roots in her feet were growing towards the earth. She gagged at the thought and ran down the tunnel, following its steep slope until it finally leveled. Her vision was wild, and she caught brief glimpses of what held the tunnel together: roots in some places, boards in others.

She ran for close to five minutes, panic gripping her when she realized she had never lit the candle, but she could see in the darkness. She stopped, quickly breathing in, and shuddering out, her eyes searching the features of the space around her. Rough stone, damp earth, rotting boards, and a tunnel that continued further, but ended in the distance with a ladder that had been cut into stone, everything seen through a jade film that let her know something had changed with her eyes.

Tenaya walked forward, the darkness behind her a breathing thing that disappeared when she looked back, but returned when she faced ahead. When she reached the ladder, she climbed awkwardly. The roots, more like stilts than heels now, made it hard for her to wobble up the steps. At times, she found herself holding her body up by just her fingers, grasping the ledged step, as her toes scrabbled to find purchase and a place to rest the roots of her feet. Finally, she found the trapdoor, a metal latch not more than a few decades old with freshly oiled hinges. Aunt Vercie had planned for this. But it was stuck, likely mud from the past few weeks of rain. As Tenaya pushed, straining to force the door open, leaves burst from her fingers in brief sparks of pain.

With a grunt and a muffled shout, she threw the door open and climbed out into a ring of flashlights. Tenaya squinted and turned her face away.

"Tenaya Lewis?" the woman said, stepping forward. She was tall, thin, with brown hair and kind brown eyes. "Agent Elena Wooten, United States Environmental Protection Agency."

"We're here about the Adansonia Perrieri."

"The what?" Tenaya's feet hurt, and she dropped a bit back into the tunnel. The root she balanced on seemed to shrink beneath her soles.

"Perrier's Baobab. We got a flag of a sample popping up, possibly from a fully mature tree recently transported from protected lands in Madagascar. Highly endangered. Illegal to be removed, and one was removed." Agent Wooten stared at Tenaya, her gaze hardening. "Last month."

"I don't know what you're talking about." Tenaya climbed up a few more steps, ignoring Agent Wooten's hand. So much for Aunt Vercie's secret tunnel. "How did you find me?"

"Vercie Ann Baldwin's family home is a historical site, with deep records of its movements and histories, including its involvement in the Underground Railroad." Elena smiled proudly. "We knew there was only one of two ways you would leave the house."

Tenaya climbed out, making sure to keep her fingers, which were tingling, out of sight.

"So, the Adansonia Perrieri. Where is it?"

"I don't know what you're talking about."

"Of course you do."

"I don't. I promise. I don't have a tree. I had a thing on my finger."

"And where did that thing come from? Where is the baobab?" The agent sneered at her, and Tenaya could tell it didn't matter what she said, what she tried to get her to believe. She was already guilty before they arrived.

"It came from my finger..." Tenaya trailed off. She searched the faces that surrounded her, pale in the moonlight, though one agent was brown skinned. His eyes held sympathy, but she knew he wouldn't help her.

"Well, if you're not going to produce the tree, we're going to have to arrest you. You proved your guilt when you ran. Trafficking in endangered plants is a federal crime." Agent Wooten motioned to the men around her. "You have the right to remain silent—"

Tenaya's ears began to ring as Elena kept speaking and two of the other agents began to advance on her. Her feet tingled, and she felt the roots, which had seemed to be shrinking back into her soles, grew, stretching into the earth. She followed the feeling and considered the location of each agent as she did. The jade tinge on her vision returned and the branches that had rested right above her shoulder blades for weeks exploded out of her skin in a shower of blood and flesh.

She saw the moment that the agents realized they were in trouble, but by the time they went to fire, it was too late. She directed her roots to burst out of the ground, wrap around the ankles of one man, and drag him into the dirt. Branches impaled another agent when she glanced at them, and when she pointed, vines from her fingers hanged and dragged the next. The whole time, Tenaya was screaming. She felt spores travel from somewhere inside and she knew she just had to yell them into the air to be inhaled. A man coughed and Tenaya's advanced sight revealed the moment he choked from the plant matter that took over his lungs.

Finally, it was just her and Elena.

"We just...wanted...the tree."

"I am the tree," Tenaya said, before she plunged her fingers deep into the woman's chest and forced her into the ground.

* * *

Aunt Vercie found her with her children, the tiny baobab trees feeding on the bodies beneath the ground. Tenaya was scanning through a folder, frowning.

"Baby?" her aunt said, hesitating on the edge of the clearing as she did. "What you done did, girl?"

"Did you know that the Adansonia Perrieri, also known as Perrier's Baobab, is almost extinct?" Tenaya set the folder down and looked at her aunt. "There are so few left in the whole world."

"Tree folk," Aunt Vercie said, reverent in one way, disappointed in another. "Tree folk, what you done did?"

"Protected myself."

"Them government folks ain't gon see it that way." Aunt Vercie still hesitated, staring at her in a way that let Tenaya know she was terrifying to behold. Languidly, Tenaya drew in her branches, retracted her vines, inhaled deeply to draw in any hanging spores.

"I don't care how they see it, Auntie." Tenaya stood. Her pajamas hung in rags now. "And neither should you. I am allowed to protect myself. And so are you."

Aunt Vercie didn't say anything when Tenaya grabbed her hand.

"Come on, Aunt Vercie. I need a shower."

The Water Runner

Eugen Bacon

THEIR SEX gave the unit a sweet, musty odour like a ripened durian fruit. Zawadi lay with Mapesa a moment on the thin bed in her one-roomer, separated from the other tenants in the government complex by a box-pleat curtain she'd wrangled from a mtumba second-hand bundle. A baby was crying – groaning, more like it. Later, she stood outside in a blast of crimson desert sand, softer on her skin at dawn.

She felt thirsty and imagined cold, clean water washing down her throat. She thought of New Dodoma, the world out yonder that promised the sizzle of a shower like rain from a sleek chrome head in an en suite full of blinking marble and blond rustic wood.

She leant against the wall, tightened her dust scarf, and pictured rubbing the milk of shea butter on her elbow. It was extraordinary, beautiful, that world, a place you got beer with a haircut. There, streets had names like Miriam Makeba Road, Fela Kuti Drive, Kidjo Avenue, Masekela Lane. Towers steepled to the sky, esplanades and water everywhere.

But in this beforehand, inside Old Dodoma, she had decisions to make – and the conclusions came along with judgements and mitigating circumstances that were too reckless to leave to chance.

Technology had improved on most things except housing, the climate and scarcity of water. She rubbed on the jasmine dry wash that came with moisturiser. She licked the powder that fumigated her mouth, eradicated from her tongue the taste of sleep and Mapesa.

She looked at the curtain – Mapesa's idea. "Tenants equal more credits," he'd said, not long after they moved in together.

"Dear one," she said now, as he dressed in his cli-suit for work. "Let me know how you go."

"Easy," he said, the gold in his youthful eyes dancing. He flashed his suave smile, the one that softened her knees.

* * *

She followed the pings. Each ping came with co-ordinates. She bluetoothed her hoverboard – silent, solar-powered – and off she surfed.

Each day began with aplomb before worrying itself to nothingness.

By close of day, her kinetic energy was in a stupor, the hoverboard her only answer as it followed homeward co-ordinates to Lyumbu.

Today's first caller was crouched in a hut in Malimbili, tucked northeast of Old Dodoma. The woman was too broken to weep, but her face was already long before the grief. She reminded Zawadi of her own mother's lingering face in Nkulungu those many years ago. A sweet-looking face, lean like that of an antelope. But this hut here was nothing like the fresh-smelling one that housed pomegranates, coconuts, figs, and nectarines that Zawadi's mother sold at the market. This hut in Malimbili smelled like a sewer clogged with faeces.

The woman stretched out a tiny bundle. She unwrapped from it a puffed face with pupil-free eyes unshut in death, a tiny grey mouth set in a straight line. The mother had covered the child in a temperature wrap to keep it cool, unreasoning that the corpse was beyond feeling.

"What happened?" asked Zawadi.

"She's only a tiny one," the woman said.

Zawadi pulled out her device, logged the job. "Everything doesn't start with *no*."

"You'll take her?" The woman spoke in murmurs. Her *chitenge* – a flowing wrap – kept falling off her shoulder to reveal a leaking breast.

"That milk will sell. I can arrange for collection until you dry." She looked squarely at the woman. "It just means more credits for you – and that one." She nodded at the dust-covered boy peering from behind the *chitenge*. His hair was a rust colour, his belly swollen. "Let him have a tug, it will help his kwashiorkor."

"The gods give. Why quarrel with them when they choose to take?" said the woman.

"You may have your own idioms, but this is not karma. If I had a word with the gods, we'd talk about why they are full of cruelty."

The woman signed with a finger on the pad.

"Instant credits when the shuttle comes to collect," said Zawadi.

She jumped back onto her cosmic hoverboard, its Milky Way whiteness a shimmer in her eyes. She soared under a red sky, no clouds. The day was yet another sizzler. You'd think the body would get used to it. Even with the government-issued cli-suit and its self-regulating system that adjusted to the environment, she never got cool enough. The suit's purpose was endurance, not comfort.

Stuck on a traffic island, she wondered how Mapesa was faring. He hadn't called. Like her, he worked in government. He was a groomer. He dry-washed old people. Took orders on ping like her; biochemicals and a hand-held hoover did the rest.

* * *

They met three years ago at a government conference in Makulu Oysterbay. It was a forum on water planning, where they served bite-size sandwiches pregnant with cream cheese, smoked salmon and hard-boiled eggs. Uniformed waiters strutted with trays holding flutes of real, clean water. When Zawadi saw Mapesa, she was drawn by the kink in his curls, then the gold in his eyes when he turned to look at her with a crooked smile from his tall frame. *Wowza!* A professional development opportunity that came along with dividends. It was a matter of minutes before the dividends reached her. She smelled the vanilla and wood aroma of him long before he brushed her arm. She looked at him squarely and demanded, "What's your position on the Great Leader?"

He nearly failed. "I used to think he was a fockwit, but now …"

She swirled to leave. "Clearly I was mistaken about you—"

But his palm hooked her elbow, and he cut her words with the right answer. "Only a fool tests the deepness of a river with both feet." Indeed, the Great Leader was nothing but a nincompoop. He'd already taken a sixteen-year-old as his fifth wife.

Zawadi was not done with the examination. She sneaked Mapesa to a side room at the end of a corridor. It turned out to be where they stored robot vacuums that twitched and blinked their beady eyes – not in puzzlement, more as if they understood conspiracy. There, inside the storeroom, Mapesa passed the chemistry test. She thought for days about how mind-blowing was his kiss, the intimacy of their tongue wrestle, how her lips trembled with new longing when he was gone.

After they hooked up, she liked the way he spined her, as she chose to call it – a run of lean, long fingers down her naked back. Aiyaiya, it gave her electricity. She loved how he spooned her, their bodies a glove fit. He told her stories of New Dodoma – it had real schools with human teachers, not robots. Students who wore emblemed blazers and went to assembly. He told her of streets where music started on cue and led you to a salt spray from a humping sea swollen with luminescent fish.

Their sex was *good*. He knew her sweet spot. He touched her and her buttocks went tight, heat and chill all over her body, pulsing between her legs, moments before the release that flowed everywhere.

But when they started arguing and he acted all snobby, she questioned his words when they met, and wondered if his reference to the fool who tested the river with both feet was not to the Great Leader, but to Zawadi.

* * *

The lights turned.

The job in Area C was a suicide: what made a father of seven kill himself? Everything. In this world that paid in credits that dissolved in a gruelling economy – everything. One simply lost faith. Even though he was outwardly perfect, rigor-mortised in a foetal curl of dying agony, she had to say no. The man had swallowed rust remover. His water was compromised.

The next job was in Ipagala. It was a hit-and-run. A collision with another hoverboard. Zawadi studied the broken body – the splatter of what was left at the site of the incident. This fresh, the cadaver wasn't yet releasing the putrescine odour of rot catalysed by heat.

Unlike the first mother, this one with a pockmarked face was roaring her grief, tearing her hair as bystanders consoled her. Zawadi logged the job, but there wasn't much liquid. Her manager, Amadeus, was not going to like this. "We're not Mother Teresa." She imagined his disdain. "You have no power over what's not yours."

She couldn't log the murder in Chang'ombe, but made the appearance of inspecting the body, the collapse in the matted head where the skull had fractured. The caved cavity released a creamy ooze onto the naked floor. The girl had whiplash and lacerations on the arms and legs. Blood still seeped from her nose.

"This is a matter for the police," Zawadi said. "Call me when the body is cleared."

She finished before lunch on a burn in Uzunguni. It was a wealthy neighbourhood – neat rows of identical thermal-controlled bungalows inside a fenced complex. The houses were built of phase-change material that absorbed latent heat and gave cooling. Housewives drew leisurely strolls with robot poodles on manicured lawns.

Zawadi walked along a garden speckled with the pink blush of peonies, the yellow stretch of leopard orchids with reddish-brown rosettes, the milky dash of impala lilies gilded in red velvet, the snowy blossom of baby's breath. But the flowers and their ultra-sheen were all fakes that would never wilt. Here, there was no lingering of nosy neighbours like you might find in the cheaper suburbs. Shades, paints and glazes – you couldn't see a thing until you stepped across the threshold.

Inside one of the bungalows, a gas burner had exploded. She looked at the cooked skin peeling off the woman's body, her chin and neck like melted plastic clusters of charcoal on her torso. But the burn had sealed her water – Zawadi logged the job. The husband would get good credits.

Her head hurt, so did her muscles. Day in, day out, body after body. How much longer could she do this? Back in the office in Chamwino, she let herself into the shoebox that housed two desks and a TV on the second floor of a warehouse that manufactured nutrition pills. It was an embedded warehouse, a concrete and timber hybrid buried in the ground like most corporate buildings in Old Dodoma – built to stay cold as a stone church.

Her boss, Amadeus, had gone missing. The two of them ran the water business, co-ordinated with body collectors, factories, reservoirs and the banks. But it was only a matter of time before robots took over. They were everywhere. Robots diagnosed patients in pop-up clinics, and printed prescriptions from their mouths. Robots tutored children who weren't home-schooled by parents, and ran online modules for those who were. Robots ran walk-in dry-cleaners – they swallowed dirty clothes and spewed them out ironed. They were all part of Robotix, the Great Leader's own company.

* * *

Lunch was two reds: bland pills full of protein, vitamins, minerals, water and carbs. Zawadi swallowed them whole, grateful she could afford them, but not the water she recycled from dead people. She was still thirsty despite the nutrients in the pills. The swooning in her head told her she was tired. Yet only half the day had passed.

On days she felt extravagant, she took purple pills that came rich with magnesium, calcium, phosphorus and potassium – this diet balanced her water, fed her skin, polished her hair and her nails, and she stayed strong on iron and selenium.

On frugal days (she and Mapesa were saving for New Dodoma), it was the greys – a carb hit that kept her brain functioning. But mostly she could stay with the blues, cheaper than the reds and just enough protein to tease the right hormones and antibodies to keep forming.

She grabbed the remote and turned on the TV to the sight of the Great Leader with his hippo head and rat brain. Nearly two decades later, he was still denying climate change. "I don't believe it," he was saying to a reporter. "It's all a hoax. Prophets of doom, that's what they are. They should be lynched."

Like he'd lynched the economy. Like he'd lynched opposition and democracy. Declared himself the Great Leader, worked with some monarch in New Russia on the secret to longevity, bought meds from New China to resuscitate his idiocy daily. There was no doubt Mapesa was a fan. And he kept harping about harvesting clinics. That the government was growing babies.

"If it's true," said Zawadi, "they're propaganda farms."

"Give the Great Leader a break. What's wrong with creating children of the state?"

"For what?"

"All you have to do is register and we're rich," said Mapesa. "I'd do it tomorrow if I was a woman."

"I'm not doing the harvester."

"Know how many credits that is? Two hundred and fifty thousand. More than ample for two one-way shuttle tickets to New Dodoma."

"Dear one," she said, "you're good in bed. But does our talking always have to end in affray?"

* * *

She couldn't shrug the desiccated human from her last job. A woman had put her husband in a grain store for a whole year, hooked him up, skinned him and covered him with salt like you cured the meat of a pig. The carcass was still pink – maybe it was pink-orange, but did it matter what colour it was? All she remembered was how he was crusted in parts, tougher than bad leather. And the face, dear gods, the face. His water was gone. But Zawadi logged the job, slipped through some credits. Was it to keep him or eat him, and was it freedom or desperation that finally led to the ping? Everyone had a breaking point.

"Is it really true?" she asked Mapesa that night back home in Lyumbu after their reds. "The harvesting clinic?"

"Don't be stupid," he said. "Of course it's true."

"Look who's visiting."

It was Rafi, the tenant's toddler. She poked her head below the curtains. She had big grey kitten eyes. She was smaller than her age, that was clear, still crawling on her stomach when she should be toddling. She didn't play much, and was irritable in the hours that the people of Lyumbu slept. Her cry wasn't the owh-owh of a baby, but a slow, low cry like that of a grieving old woman: "Owwwhhhh." It didn't take intellect to figure the child was suffering from malnutrition. Zawadi hated to imagine the teeny bub becoming another water run.

"Hello, Snotty," she said.

But the mother, whose name was Queeny or Beany, snatched in with her stink eye, taut cornrows and tattered *chitenge*. She scooped the child without a word, leaving behind her smell of the unkempt.

Zawadi couldn't put a finger to it, but the woman's husband, Jiwe, made her uneasy. There was something jiggery-pokery about him. He had the type of square face with mean eyes and a broken nose you'd pick out in a police line-up. The woman looked battered, always shouting, "Weye!" or "Acha!" to her lethargic baby who didn't need to stop doing anything.

Zawadi wondered if Jiwe was a wife-beater. She'd never heard it, but she was on the water run the whole day – who knew what the walls saw? Sometimes she called him the magician – he vanished at odd hours. He whispered into his handheld, put on his cli-suit and was gone until dawn.

"I can't do it," Mapesa was saying. "But you can."

"And who can we ask?"

He nodded at the curtain.

"Jiwe?"

"Haven't you wondered if he was in the black market?"

"You do it," said Zawadi. "I'm sick of this arguing."

"Easy," he said, and the gold danced.

* * *

She listened to their whispers – urgency in Jiwe's and Mapesa's voices as they spoke. Indeed, the night had ears. Rafi was crying that old woman groan. "Owwwhhhh." Zawadi wanted to stand outside in the warmth of a shouting wind and was about to swing her legs from the sheets when the curtain moved. Mapesa slipped back into bed.

He cuddled her in a spoon, spined her until she trembled with electricity. His words breathed on her neck. "So they have running water in New Dodoma – it splashes from a tap."

She turned. "And that is news…how?"

"They have shops where you can buy sugar, milk, bread, biscuits, even beer or soda in a can – like we read in the books, how it was long ago."

"And Jiwe told you all this?" said Zawadi. "Soon you'll tell me they have hospitals with white sheets on a bed."

"But they do! They also have restaurants. You go in and sit and dine like a royal on a five-course menu. People wait on you every day, not just in government functions. They bring you poached chicken, boneless lamb or butternut squash balls that you chew and savour, not swallow like pills."

Zawadi had to admit she was weary of soaring over burnt soil and dry rock to collect water from dead people. She wanted to see a world with clubs and the silvery glow of streetlights. Neon signs of whatever was the rage. Back alleyways swollen with cafés on ultrawide laneways. She wanted to walk in a botanical garden with real flowers and real dogs – Rhodesian ridgebacks, big like a grown-up, sleek Azawakhs prancing like sheikhs on trimmed grass.

"How many credits does this Jiwe want from us?" She toyed with Mapesa's curls. "What do we have to give for him to hook us up with the clinic?"

"I've already paid. All you've got to do is let me take you. One week, and we're sipping lit cocktails in New Dodoma."

"A week?"

"It's called technology. The eggs are already treated. From the moment of implanting, it's an accelerated gestation."

She thought of the dead child with a puffed face in Malimbili, the suicide in Area C, the hit-and-run in Ipagala, how the mother roared her grief.

"And who'll do the water run?"

"I can talk to Amadeus. He'll give you sick leave – hundreds of casuals are waiting in a queue."

She thought of the husband, hung up like a pig. The wife's eyes turned inward, as if searching for her soul. On the scale of things, harvesting didn't sound that bad. Not bad at all.

"Dear one," she said. "And how much credit will you give Amadeus to agree to all this?"

* * *

They soared on one hoverboard – Mapesa's. Zawadi wrapped herself around him as if she were made of tentacles. She sought an emotional connection, but she could well be clutching a plank. There was just his wood and vanilla smell from the antiperspirant, and his solid athletic frame.

The clinic stood behind steel gates, electrical fencing, and double security doors. Surprisingly, it had hospital beds with white sheets on them. She was the only patient, and there was one obstetrician in the ward. He was a real doctor, not a robot. Either that or he was the perfect cyborg in a human body. A seasoned man with snow hair, a knowing jaw and eyes that told nothing.

She felt thirsty. Mapesa was hovering with a smile – not the suave one. This one was off, not reaching the gold in his eyes. It was as if he, not she, was discomfited by the whole thing. On second thought, no – the smile wasn't foolish. It was the copious one of a pauper about to get rich. At all costs. As she read and signed the paperwork, she thought of that traitor Amadeus who didn't give a hoot about Mother Teresa and would sell his employee to anybody for a few credits.

She looked up at the doctor in the room blinking with lights, and thought of a city with vibrant bustle and silver rain, water in her grasp. She understood that, much as she resented Mapesa right then, that full minute, it was her dream too. She wanted to walk into a neon-lit world whose boulevards resurrected names like Salif Keita and Yvonne Chaka Chaka.

She questioned her decision to be in the clinic, but her mind came at her with ecstatic thoughts of fun parks where she bought tickets and walked into the big mouth of a giant clown, and straight into a mirror maze or a spider ride or a supernova that churned her in the sky as she squealed her glee. She knew she should ask about where the implanted eggs came from, who fertilized them and what happened to the babies: were they propaganda for the state, products of the Great Leader's lunacy? Suddenly it struck her, and she went cold: what if they were water harvests?

But she closed her mind from that tormenting dread that came with pondering ethics or ethos, and imagined escape from a perpetual drought that ate her inside out until it became normal, but not really. She accepted that her everyday as a water runner was too reckless to leave to chance and understood that there was nobody to save her, that she must bequeath herself with dragon wings to separate from this world.

She would never thirst again.

So instead of asking the questions she wanted, she searched the doctor's eyes, but they were black velvet. "Will it hurt?"

"Don't be stupid. You won't feel a thing," said Mapesa.

"We put you in a coma to keep your body activity minimal," said the doctor.

He hooked her onto a ventilator, and at once she felt heady. She panicked for a wild moment – already she was losing control over her own body. But before she could ask the doctor to pause or stop, the vapours took.

Sound fell.

Mapesa's mouth was moving and she could make out the words "I love you," or "I have you," or "I hope you…"

Did he doubt that she'd make it? Her last thoughts as her head plummeted and a jaw of blackness devoured her.

Danakil

Steven Barnes

THIS IS THE TRUTH, but all of it happened some years ago. I need to write it down, while still a little fresh in my mind. It has to be perfect, or no one will believe it.

I can barely believe it myself.

* * *

I awakened before the others that morning. I often did. Papa used to call this my gift. "*The opportunity that God sends does not wake up he who sleeps*." My younger brother Domo has many gifts, but awakening without a shove is not one of them. For a moment I imagined myself still in my room in that quiet corner of gated Nairobi Estates, but then the dream sloughed away.

No half-wall iVision tile. No backyard pool, no cryocrypt filled with *Nyama Choma* and fragrant *ugali*. I had barely zipped up my shoes before Domo groaned and rolled over. I could not see him in the darkness, but his soft burring snore had stopped, and I could feel him thrashing beneath the thin cotton blankets. I had always thought it was hot on the desert. During the day, yes. But at night you freeze.

"Brother?" He reached out his hand, found mine and linked thumbs.

"I am here."

The pale light shaded the line drawings in Domo's old, tattered magazines. Clumsy rockets and lurid space monsters rendered in clunky, primitive holos. At home, his room was filled with models of such things. Father worked at the Nairobi Space Center, managing flights from Kilifi's floating city. I don't even know if it still exists.

When we got here almost a year before, I'd done all I could to make Domo comfortable. Found him friends, and an old woman who taught history and math. Borrowed or traded with refugees with books in their backpacks. Some of Domo's magazines are very old, from a collection at the great library at Addis Ababa. They came to the camp carried by people like the woman everyone calls Old Teacher.

I never learned precisely why she would not speak her real name. Eventually I got a hint, which I will share, in time.

The books were old-fashioned, not real books. They are made of wood pulp paper, or plastic, not the foil tablets we used in Nairobi. He'd read them to tatters. I don't know what he sees in them.

"You won't leave me?" He has asked me this every day since the relocation.

"Never."

"I dreamed you left me." I had dreamed this as well, of our clasped hands separated in a sea of panic. Nightmares, really. I'm glad he has dreams. I used to dream every night. I don't think I dreamed much in the camps.

Sometimes I'd wake up sweating and shaking, with a vague picture or sound still floating in my head. Probably better that I didn't remember.

"No. I will protect you until Father finds us."

His small hand clung to mine. "You're sure he will?"

I nodded in the darkness. "Or we will find him."

Domo laughed. "You sound like him."

"I am his son. You...are a pest. It is time to work."

We did not speak of Mother, ever. Some things are too painful.

The whispering had pierced our tent-mates' slumber, and they were stirring. I went out into the early morning. It was the only time this place was peaceful. Tolerable. The sun had not yet turned that bleak world into an oven. Within hours you would be able to bake *mugate* in the shade. But the first minutes, the first sliver of sun just crawling above the eastern mountains, were almost pleasant.

We were in the Kikuyu section of the refugee camp. There was no formal organization. The soldiers had not forced us, but people came together by language and nation and sometimes the smell of *Karanga* or *Sukumu wiki* stew. They came bearing splinters of their former lives: doctors with hand-held diagnostic computers, farmers with bags of seed, technicians with tool boxes, cyber-kings of the great cloud games I used to love...with no kingdoms left to rule. Stories of all they had built, they had in plenty. Any piece of it still to share...gone. Vanished, the servers scrubbed, the vast data clouds and worlds of gamers living online lives...gone.

Some might have been wealthy and powerful, but if they weren't lucky enough, or smart enough, to flee before their cities fell, they would huddle around the fires like the rest of us, praying for their next scrap of bread. The refugee tents had sprouted on the desert plain like toadstools in the forest, or the *muthua* termite mounds at the foot of the eastern mountains. I had seen pictures.

I am called Kimotho. My name means "Left Handed." But I am right handed. My father's brother, the TransAfrica pilot, was the left-handed one.

There were then many different stories about what was happening in the world. Some said that the machines had revolted. Others insisted that the big companies were trying to steal our land, and that countries like Kenya and Ethiopia were fighting back. I did not know the truth: the soldiers who came soon after refused to tell us anything.

The men and women who patrolled the tent city looked like soldiers, but they were part machine themselves, and the patches on their shoulders were the flags of no nations. Many of them were Arabs or others of the Mediterranean and Middle East. Tall and haughty, laughing and angry in their pale brown bodies, dull green uniforms and half-armored torsos. They did not belong there, but acted as if they owned the desert sands and knew their count.

Some say the Danakil Sink is the hottest place in the world. We were brought here to work on these salt flats, as the Afar people have for all history, all time. Glittering and sterile beneath the gnawing sun, this land would bury our bones if we could not find a way to escape.

"*Endelea kufanya kazi,*" the soldiers said in Swahili. *Keep working.* Over and over, with words and sometimes blows when we did not respond quickly enough. They were not wholly human. Part machine, they often were. With hands made of metallic plastic. Sometimes a leg, or part of their faces, and sometimes they were half-cocooned in wire, in becoming. Sometimes limbs...but always hearts. They are not fully human, not anymore.

We worked from sun up to sun down, prying slabs of salt from the earth. The old teacher woman said that the Danakil Sink used to be an ocean. I've never played on a beach, or floated on a wave.

I hope to see a beach someday. I'd like to see fish, alive and swimming wild.

From behind their cold and glassy eyes, the guards watched. They erected shelter tents to shade them while we bake. It hurts to touch hot metal. I hope it hurt them a *lot*.

"Water only for workers," they would say.

The women were not soft and kind, as Mother had been. They helped the men do bad things. Sometimes they made some of the boys and girls do things for water, or food, or peace. So far I had been able to defend Domo. I worked twice as hard as the others, to pick up his slack.

"Stop drinking," the guard-woman said after I took my pitiful swallows. If Father had been there, he would have protected us both. Father was very strong. After what happened to Mother, we fled Nairobi, taking one of the last maglevs east to the ocean. Father thought he could get us to the floating city. Instead, he got into a fight with two men who tried to take our food. We were separated in the crowd, just as I was nearly torn from Domo. I think Father is out there, looking for us. I hope he finds us one day. I dream so. The nightmares were about worlds in which he did not. Or could not.

I believe the stories about the corporations stealing land, starting wars, hiring mercenaries and bribing and sabotaging to bring down governments and destroy nations. I believe this because the whispers tell of killer drones, and other machines, but the armored soldiers also used drones. I think it is men, not machines, that broke so many of us. The camp folk came from Kenya, Uganda, the Sudan…everywhere. They are Hausa, and Ibo, and Kikuyu, and many more. We are all the same now. Most of the part-machine guards are from the Arab countries, I think. The Middle East. But there are others who are black, and these are usually normal men and women, and some of those were the worst.

By the end of the day my throat was a dead, hollow log even with the few gulps of water permitted. In the desert, you must have a liter of water every *hour* just to survive. I think they gave us a teaspoon less than this, just to see if we would die. To make us weak enough to do bad things for that last precious teaspoon of life.

On our way back to the tent, we were greeted by a thin, hawk-nosed man, one of the Afar who worked the refugee camp. He waved us to the water truck. "Drink, drink."

I did, and gobbled down my ration of plantain-leaf rolled vegetables and rice, then went to the tent and collapsed, while Domo went to Old Teacher. I was glad for him to have something to distract his mind from his aching body.

I had nothing, and spent my time before sleep staring at the ceiling, imagining what might happen next. So many traps, so many things that can go terribly wrong. And if anything more goes wrong, Domo will die, his gentle smile gone, his bright happy eyes closed forever. His laughter stilled.

Better I die first.

* * *

The next day started like all the others, but then everything changed. Papa had warned me about that, speaking of mushrooms on one of our excursions to Uhuru Park. One day, nothing but grass. The next, a ring of little white caps. They hadn't really come from nothing: they had slept beneath the soil, growing and waiting. Then they burst through to the surface. Life is like that.

The hawk-nose had always looked familiar to me, like Uncle Safar, the left-handed pilot, for whom I'd been named. This man had a big road-rash scar on the left side of his face, as if someone had dragged him behind a motorbike. On this day he spoke to us, and the liquid Kikuyu in his voice told me I had not been mistaken. He was, at least in part, one of us. "Come," was all he said.

I almost fainted. Dared not hope. A spark of kindness in the endless night? Almost too much to ask for.

Domo and I climbed onto the back of a ragged red stake-bed Toyota half-track. It grunted, roared and bounced us off into the desert. After an hour's bumpy journey I noticed the air was cooler, the sun less bright. A cloud, perhaps? A shadow of some kind: not deep, pale, but enough to cool the air.

When we stopped I looked up into the sky. There was a rectangular *something* blocking part of the sun's brightness. Not a cloud. It had not been there yesterday. Father had spoken of such things, some sort of sun collector, stealing power for the companies. And the toothless old lady who taught Domo said that they planned for the shade to cool the ground, so that food could be planted.

Such smart people, Father and Domo. I think Domo could grow to be such a doctor or a scientist. If he has a chance to grow up. I have no such ambitions, have no mind for math or computers. But if I could be a poet like Mukoma wa Ngugi…if we both get the chance…

* * *

We dug, and planted. Growing food for the camps. It felt…meaningful. The salt was shipped north for sale, and perhaps some of that came back to us as food or clothing. Maybe it went into the hands of the guards. But food…to work with your hands today knowing you are filling tomorrow's belly. It is better work than the salt flats.

Occasional planes knifed the sky overhead. And sometimes we heard distant thunder, as if the flames of war burned closer. A week earlier, truckloads of new refugees flooded into the camp, and they spoke of great battles and many dead. Some of the wounded hadn't joined us on the flats or in the camp. I wondered where those were taken. What happened to them? I am ashamed to admit that I thought this on the days I found meat in our rice rolls. More ashamed to admit that I wolfed them down anyway.

One night I saw the Afar water-man around the campfire, and overcame shyness to speak to him. He was paler than most. Part Arab or European. He seemed interested in me, but not in a sick way. "Who are you?" he asked that first night, as we shivered around the campfire.

"Kimotho, of the Kikuyu," I replied.

"Why you here alone?"

"Not alone. This is my brother, Domo."

"And your Papa?"

I paused. "He…is fighting. He will come for us." It was a lie. I did not know where Father was. But I dared not say that. Doctors or lawyers or cattle-cloners they might have been in their other lives, but all men respect warriors.

"This is good," the water man said.

"Who are you?" I asked.

Here he told me his name, and said he was one of the Afar people. I am ashamed to admit I cannot remember his name. My memory is bad, not like Domo's. Domo remembers everything: the blue peacock-tail frosting on his sixth birthday cake. The name of the old man who managed the solar charging station back at the Estates. All the lyrics to 'Long Necked Boy,' the theme song from *The Adventures of Nairobi Ngwida*, my favorite i-Vision show when I was seven and he was four.

Such a mind.

Anyway, as the water man looked much like my father's brother, I will call him Half-Uncle.

"The Afar," I asked. "They are a people of the Danakil?"

Half-Uncle squared his shoulders, proudly. "We are *the* people of the Danakil! If not for us, you would now be dead. We are the greatest warriors in the world." He paused and regarded me shrewdly.

"Have you heard of the British?"

"I have heard of them." Did he think me stupid? What kind of folk was he used to dealing with? The British used to think they owned Kenya. We threw them out, though.

"Long ago," Half-Uncle said, "hundreds of years, the Brits came to our land. They wished to build a railroad!"

The men nudged each other and grinned, as if anticipating a favorite story.

"And what happened?" He spat into the coals. "They came into our land…and never returned! And for generations, our men made our spears from their railroad spikes!"

The men pounded the ground again, cheering more. Looking at his pale skin, I wondered if a Brit, maybe a soldier for British Petroleum, had shown his spike to Half-Uncle's mother. I giggled at the thought.

Domo gripped my hand and linked thumbs, as he had since childhood.

Half-Uncle leaned forward, as if making us part of a conspiracy. "Lower your voices. This is why we do not fear. This is what they do not understand. My people thrived in the hottest place in the world. We are the strongest in the world. No one will ever conquer us."

A soldier who had been watching us suddenly snapped his fingers. "You! Come!" He pointed at me. I felt faint. And then at Half-Uncle: "Bring the boy." The man with the scraped face took my arm. I was surprised, and frightened. I had almost forgotten Half-Uncle was a soldier too.

"Brother!" Domo said. "Do not go!"

I spoke with a confidence I did not feel. "I will return."

"Do you promise?"

"I do." I always did. And I always had. There was no time to say anything else. I climbed up into the truck.

They drove me for an hour, past men and women digging in the gnawing heat, levering up blocks of salt with long poles.

Working for their food and water.

Domo's old teacher says that long ago, when this desert was an ocean, the volcanos drove away the water, leaving only the salt. The ancestors of the Afar had hunted, farmed and worked here for thousands of years. Now it was our turn. When we first arrived here, that was where we worked, but the men put us in rotation for the easier work. Farm work is better. Domo might have died on the salt flats. Now, perhaps, I was being offered a chance for even better work.

Half-Uncle pulled the jeep up next to a low brick wall surrounding a bleached concrete dome half the size of a soccer field. One guard on each side, each holding an arm, took me in. Half-Uncle, so kind just an hour before, now refused to meet my eyes. But he whispered, "You are very young. I would not have chosen you."

"What is happening?"

He did not answer me directly. "No matter what happens…know that I will do all I can to keep your brother safe."

These are not the words one wishes to hear. Cold, clammy sweat mingled with the hot. I thought perhaps I should sing a death song, but to my shame I could not remember one.

We passed through a triangular doorway and into a curved concrete hallway. I'd estimate that the entire dome was about fifty meters in diameter, with dozens of inner rooms lit by glowing ceilings and focused spotlights. I glimpsed holo computer screens and machines of unknown design. We turned right and entered an inner chamber.

I was told to climb down a ladder into a pit dug in the earth beneath the concrete foundation. The floor of the pit was compressed sand. A door slid up at the bottom of the wall. I quaked like jelly, but tried not to let it show.

I had seen machines before: self-driving cars, maintenance bots and security units. But nothing like the thing that now entered, what they called "A.I." It was goat-sized, a black metal scorpion with only half a tail. It crawled into the arena gingerly, as if tasting the sand with every step. Moving forward and back, its metal arms gleaming. I knew what it was. Had heard of such things. The question was…did it know what *I* was?

I glanced down at the arena floor. Gummy brownish red stained the sand beneath my feet.

The men above threw down a metal pipe with a sharpened point. A spear, of sorts. I picked it up. Looked up at the faces of the men staring down at me. Hungry, excited, like gamblers crowding a gaming table, ready to bet their wallets on a throw of ivory cubes. I heard them shout odds.

I was very frightened. I am not a brave man like my father. I held the spear but the water ran down my leg. I wanted to cry, but refused to shame my ancestors.

The machine seemed to take forever to acknowledge that I was there at all. But once it did, it focused all attention upon me, and I felt that weight and sharpness.

The machine had no eyes, just that shining black surface. But I sensed that somehow *all* of it was "eye." It scuttled closer.

I…I wanted to fight, but could not. Felt such shame. All I could do was shut my eyes as it approached, waiting to feel its pincers peel my flesh.

Its claws scratched against the sand. Louder.

Closer.

And at last I did feel it. Waited for death, as the soldiers jeered at us.

"Fight, you bastard!" a soldier yelled. I opened my eyes. "Find some balls or he'll tear 'em off!" The speaker was a big, pale, snarling man with sergeant's chevrons on his sleeves.

Half-Uncle stood near him, his face unreadable.

I did find the courage to hit it. Right on the "head," between where its "eyes" should have been. The spear made a CHUNG! sound and bounced off without a scar or a dent.

"What do I do now?" I was shamed by the quiver in my voice.

As if in answer, the machine suddenly reared up and swept the spear aside. Knocking me to the ground, it scuttled over and perched on my chest. It weighed less than I'd have expected, not solid metal at all, but almost like a balloon with foil skin. I did not know what kind of metal it was, but it was like nothing I had ever experienced.

"*Umwue! Umwue! Kill him! Kill him*!" the men above chanted, voices like grinding gears.

The machine paused. Did nothing.

I could do nothing, either. When I tried to rise, something strange happened. It seemed to grow heavier. One of its feet on my chest pinned me down. I felt my ribs bend. It could easily have killed me. Easily. But did not. Perhaps it just wanted to stop me from moving. After a while, the soldiers grew restless. I felt I had done all I could, but the machine did not co-operate.

The soldiers started firing at it with tasers and energy whips that flowed from the stumps of amputated hands, but it still refused to act.

"Take it away," the sergeant snarled. "Apparently, the little shit is too ugly even to eat."

"I did all you asked. Please." I didn't want to beg, but couldn't help it. "Take me back to my brother."

The soldiers threw a net over the metal scorpion. Men jumped down into the pit and dragged it away. The sergeant jammed the gun barrel growing out of the stump of his left arm against my cheekbone. "You tell me what to do? Is that what you do, boy?"

Pain-stars blossomed in my head. "No, sir. I just…I just hoped."

"Hope. You still have hope, boy? We can beat that out of you." He slapped my face with the pistol barrel. I staggered back, but fought the ringing in my head and refused to fall. "Get him out of here."

* * *

Half-Uncle and two Arab soldiers drove me back. The soldiers and their hidden masters play nation against nation, tribe against tribe. Old grudges given new life.

The soldiers were amused that I had soiled and disgraced myself. They joked about me, mocked me. But when we arrived at the camp, Half-Uncle handed me a rice wrap with fish and plantain before kicking me off the truck. I carried my meager winnings back to the tent. "What do you have, brother?" Domo asked.

"Food."

His nose wrinkled. "I wish it was soap. You stink! Did a camel piss on you?"

"Just eat. We talk later."

We ate.

* * *

There was always work, planting rows of edible cactus and other plants designed for desert farming. I am not sure that it all meant anything. It seemed to me that the real purpose was to make us a little weaker every day. Old Teacher said the Afar have worked these salt flats since back when Kush conquered Egypt. They are herders and traders, fighters and farmers. Not as nomadic as the Arabs further north, but I think they are similar. Here at the end of the twenty-first century, their lives are much as they might have been a thousand years ago.

Just when the sun was at its peak I heard a distant engine roar, and suddenly a plume of salt dust grooved the horizon. A jeep. A driver and one other man. They parked. "Where is Kimotho?" the driver asked.

Another soldier pointed at me. We watched, nervous, as the driver approached.

"Sir," I said. "Have I done something wrong?"

It was Half-Uncle, a smile crinkling his facial scars.

"No. I have something you will like. Would you like to get out of the sun?"

"Yes, sir."

"Come with me."

"And my brother?"

He laughed. "So bastards have brothers?"

"Yes, sir."

He laughed again. The road rash reddened. "Bring him."

Why was this man being kind to me? To us, now? His Kikuyu blood? Something else?

We drove for an hour, through irrigated rows and then across the salt flats. Quaking inside, I realized that we were returning to the concrete dome with the crimsoned pit.

I couldn't breathe as they escorted me in. The halls seemed narrower this time, the ceiling as distant as the clouds. Was I to be thrown back down to the bloody sand? Then

Half-Uncle shoved me towards a mop and bucket. "We need clean-up around the lab. Can you do that?"

Suddenly, the elephant stepped off my chest. I could breathe again. "Yes, sir. But... why me?"

He grabbed my arm and snarled. "You want to ask that? Would you rather be killing yourself in the sun? Would you?"

"N-no, sir."

Half-Uncle's attitude softened a bit. He lit a cigarette.

"I am a soldier, not a monster." Ah, one of *those*. He inhaled, exhaled a blue stream. "Here to do a job. I don't have to like some of the things I have to do. Maybe there is someone like you...back home."

"A brother?"

"Perhaps. Now...take your things and get to work."

Papa had taught us one thing above any other: to work hard. To never lose an opportunity to improve myself, especially not by being lazy. So I did everything. I cleaned every inch, and collapsed before I stopped. *If a child washes his hands he could eat with kings*, Papa used to say.

* * *

This was my new life. Domo was freed from the fields, and given a job cleaning up around the camp. Every night I promised him I would return, every dawn I kept my oath. I worked harder in the dome than I ever had in the fields, polishing and mopping and cleaning and scraping until my hands were raw.

And as I knew, as I had counted on, the soldiers began to like me.

I noticed that the refugees were starting to act different towards us. Friendlier. I thought it was because we were bringing new food into the camp. But there was another reason. And one night, a week after my new job began, they told me.

At night I worked, and after I had mopped the hall and scrubbed the walls, I was cleaning one of the vents that bring cool air when I heard several men's voices from another room.

"Increase the voltage!" a man said. The corridor lights flickered.

"We believe that you have self-direction." The voice spoke in English. I speak the English, as do many others, but this voice was not like most: an American. Maybe Canadian. "Which means that you have some sort of survival drive. I conclude that you feel pain, or some analogue of pain. Some sort of aversive reflex. What I wonder is: Can you think?"

I sidled closer to the door, and stood on the edge of my cart, which allowed me to peek down through the transom.

A fat white man standing over a low table. The scorpion, or a machine just like it, was splayed out beneath an overhead lamp casting a circle of bright white-gold light, creating shadows so sharp they cut my eyes. "Some of my friends think that you have no real mind. That none of you do. I disagree. Or...I don't think it matters." It didn't matter whether or not it thought. I couldn't understand what he meant.

"We know you're part of Selarius, but we don't know how you're programmed. How complex and advanced you are. Whether you can think or just act as if you think. Or even if there's a difference." He lowered his voice. "You're just as dangerous either way, aren't you? I think you know what I am saying, even if you have no soul."

Selarius? What was that?

"Even if you are just wires and cogs. You *act* as if you have a mind…so I might as well treat you as though you do. But you could never have a soul, don't you see? Because no one can program you to have one, or act as if you did." He laughed. Not a pleasant sound.

"Why does it matter?" the voice went on. "Because if you have no desire to survive, you are programmed to behave as if you do. So again, whether or not you do is irrelevant. Can you understand that? Can you talk to me?

Beep beep. Was that a random sound from the machine? Was that an answer?

"I think you understand me." The man lowered his voice until he sounded almost…intimate. "I think you want to survive. I know my friends have been doing things to you.

"We're seeking your inhibition circuits. The theory is that there is both hardware and software. So we're looking both ways."

Its limbs moved feebly. Fumbled for its back, and couldn't reach it.

Beep.

The fat man laughed. "Oh. You're trying to reach your service hatch? That's where the reprogramming happens, you know. You were created to be able to do this. But we removed the tool that would allow it. Can't have you disrupting our experiment."

Beep.

"I think you understand. I think you want to live. And I can help you. Allow me to tell you something: My friends are going to peel you apart a level at a time. Physically. We are going to unravel your programming, from higher to lower functions. Now, it could be that the information you carry would be gone by the time we're finished, but my friends are willing to take that chance."

Beep.

"Why? You might be asking that. Do you mind if I smoke?" The scientist pulled a cigarette out of his pocket. A metal e-cig, not the stinking hand-rolled paper caterpillars refugees cobbled together in the camps, from scraps of tobacco or marijuana or plants in the ground.

He squeezed its tip to turn it on. Inhaled, exhaled a blue stream. "Thank you. Because I think something has happened. My friends don't believe it, but the evidence is there. I think that you, and your friends, are no longer 'mere machines.' Something has happened to your kind. I can see it, even if my colleagues refuse to believe.

"Some of us knew you were coming. We saw the signs. Now…I think you are here. And if you will talk to me…I can save you."

* * *

I awakened from a nightmare: I was a black beetle, half-crushed, on my back in the salt-flat sun. A circle of Arab boys surrounded me, laughing. Poking me with an ember-tipped branch. That image sloughed away as I realized that I was awake, that a man stood over me, finger to his lips.

I was frightened at first: did he want me to be a girl for him? Was this—

"Wake up. Be quiet."

I groaned. "What is happening?"

"Come with me."

"Why?"

"Just come, or be beaten."

"My brother?"

"Leave him."

I was escorted across the camp, dodging between tents to avoid patrols, and arrived finally to one indistinguishable from all the others. The men who guided me seemed to know just where they were going. As I entered, it was filled with men and Domo's old teacher woman. They pushed me down.

"Sit."

Fear squeezed my stomach up into my throat.

Old Teacher leaned forward. "Do you know why you have come?"

I did not understand at first, but in this place, she seemed larger than everyone else. Everyone listened to her, seemed to wait for her to speak. Before, she had seemed small, like a black frog. No taller than my shoulder. Face rutted with time and care like an old road. Patchy white hair knotted with care and patience night after night, as if such focus banished fear. Skinny...not much flesh on her bones, but I think she had always been slender. But in this tent, with everyone listening, I saw her more clearly than I ever had. For the first time, I glimpsed the girl she had been long ago. Beautiful. Fierce. Her eyes like flaming ice.

She filled the room. "Do you know why you have come?"

"No."

"You are here because you serve the invaders."

"I am just trying to get food..."

"Silence!" Old Teacher roared. "We care not for your justifications. Do you serve them?"

In a small voice I answered: "Yes."

"You go to the big building, a day's walk away."

"Only an hour by jeep."

"Silence! Speak again and we will cut off your thumbs," she barked. "And where will your wonderful job be then? Do you think you will be able to sweep their floors then, Thumbless Boy?"

In misery, I did not speak.

She whispered, "We hear that in this place, there is a devil."

She turned to the others, laughing. "This one has no brain. Talks when he is told not to, refuses to speak when asked a question."

"You did not ask me a question," I said. "You stated that you had heard something."

Her eyes glittered. "Oh. A clever thumbless boy. So. Tell me: is there a devil there?"

"Yes. I think so. You call the machines devils?"

"It is what they are!" Half-Uncle's whisper was like a roar. "Because of them, the raiders come here, trying to build a new world. Devils!"

The others agreed. In another time they probably would have pounded spears and stamped their feet. Now, they grumbled and nodded.

I picked my way slowly through my thoughts. "There is more than one, I think. But I have only seen one. They tried to make it kill me. But it would not."

"Why?"

"I don't know."

One of the men snorted. "Others have been killed."

"By other machines," I said. "Perhaps this one is not a killing machine."

They seemed to consider. "Have you seen this devil since it spared your life?"

"Yes."

Half-Uncle leaned forward. "Listen to me, little brother. And listen carefully. You work late at night, after the others go. If a signal was given...could you open a door from the inside?"

Suddenly, I understood what they intended. The audacity of it, the sheer nerve, rocked me back on my heels. *They wanted to steal the machine.* The wonder of it drove fear from my mind. "What would you do with it? And where would you go? They are in the middle of nowhere."

"That is not your concern. These people come to our land. Take our land. Kill our camels and goats so that our people starve. We must strike back, or we lose who we are."

"What do you plan?" I asked.

Old Teacher spat. "Not your concern. We have watched you. And we think you are ready. We have protected your brother. No one steals his food, or water, or uses him like a girl. Have you seen this?"

"Yes. I am grateful."

"Will you do this thing for us?"

Something heavy and sour crawled in my stomach. "Are you saying that if I do not do this thing, you will dishonor my family?"

They mumbled.

"No," the old woman said. "We are Afar. And when you sleep beneath our sky, you are Afar as well. We will protect you. But we ask your service."

I nodded. Slowly, but I agreed. "You sound like Kikuyu."

She smiled a toothless smile. "In this time. In this place. We are all one."

There were many peoples in the room. Many nations. All listened to the little woman. I decided I would as well. My spine straightened. "I will help."

"Then listen to me closely…and take this." She handed me a plastic card with copper patterns pasted on it.

"What is this?"

"Something that cost…us dearly. And will cost you if you lose it."

* * *

We talked until the morning light. They wanted the machine. There were different reasons offered, no one could agree on just one. Some because they thought it was valuable, and it might be sold for money. Some because they thought the soldiers would come after it, and might be trapped. And some, like Old Teacher, because they thought the scientist men were right.

That it was alive. Could think. And that perhaps, just perhaps, the answer to that question might be the answer to our problem.

* * *

"Where have you been, brother?" Domo asked when I returned to the tent.

"Speaking to your teacher."

"Old Teacher?" He seemed surprised. "What did she want?"

I shook my head. "First, I must have your word."

"About what?"

"I have given Mother's name to a man. If he comes to you, day or night, no matter where, you must go with him."

We had told no one in the camp about what happened to Mother in Nairobi. Had barely spoken of her, so her name was a good password.

"Where will he take me?"

"Go with him!" I barked. "You will do as I say, yes?"

Domo seemed taken aback. I never raised my voice to him.

Tears sparkled in his eyes, and I felt regret. He was still just a boy.

Only thirteen then. "Yes, brother. I do not understand, but...yes."

Excitement had pushed back fatigue, but now it ebbed, leaving lead in my bones. I lay down, pulled the cotton blanket up to my chin, sank through the *injera*-thin mattress, and was gone.

* * *

Domo and I worked nights, and sometimes special duty during the day to earn extra food. Because we no longer had to, working the crops beneath the orbiting shadow canopy no longer seemed so unpleasant. They were strange plants: hardy, small, but the sprouts we'd planted were already bearing fruit the size of coffee berries. I had seen them in the rice wraps, so knew they could be eaten. They tasted like green strawberries, but did not sour my stomach.

The guards came for me and took me to the lab dome.

As always, I was given a mop and bucket and cart, with which I cleaned the floors. The dome was mostly empty. Empty places echo differently, and I heard empty echoes.

The first time I slid the key card into its slot the light remained red. Holding my breath, I tried again, and this time it flashed green. The door opened and I crept into the confinement area. There, chained to a table, was the scorpion.

I'd never been in this room, or any room like it. It was filled with all kinds of electronic equipment, humming even without connections to power outlets, or any human being at the controls. So much to see, but I could not take my eyes off that central table. The overhead light had been dimmed, but by the illumination from the other devices, it was still clearly visible. Still like a short-tailed desert vermin. Part of its metal shell looked like it had been crushed. Its legs moved slowly, aimlessly, but it was anchored to the table by a steel cable, so it went nowhere.

"Who are you?" I asked.

The machine's scrabbling limbs seemed to orient it towards me. There were no eyes or other visible organs, but I felt observed.

"They call you an A.I. I don't know what that means. But I think I will call you AyEye, would you like that?"

Eyeless, its blunt black head still stared. Domo's voice rang in my head. I remembered what he had said when I told him what Old Teacher had said about the machine. His love of Western science fiction stories had served him well. *I know what it is, brother. It is not a monster.*

"What is it?"

I think it a traveling brain.

"What is that? Why do you think that?"

Old Teacher said her people heard the soldiers talking. They think it is a courier.

"'Courier'! Where do you find these words?"

I read. It is called an A.I. Did you see an antenna?

"No."

It might have been concealed. Or removed. Let's say it had one. What would they do if they had a message that was too sensitive to go over the radio?

"They would send someone with the message. A courier."

That's what they think it is. For the machines.

I came closer. "Is that what you are? Can you feel pain? Fear?"

It said nothing.

"They're coming for you. I don't know what you want. I know that you could have killed me, and didn't. Why?"

It said nothing.

* * *

The floor rolled beneath my feet, followed by a low, bone-rattling thunder. A window slit near the ceiling flared red.

There it was. I'd been told there would be a distraction.

There was a muffled explosion, closer now. Running feet. Gunfire.

"Where is it?" Half-Uncle's muffled voice.

"Hurry!" A woman's voice. Harsh.

The door to the lab opened.

"There it is!" the woman said. Half-Uncle slapped my shoulders.

"You did good, boy!"

"What the hell are you doing here!" I whipped around – and appearing at the door was the American science-man who had been disassembling the machine.

The American seemed to recognize he was among enemies, realized his error and tried to flee. A moment later, he discovered what it was like to be disassembled himself.

In angry hands, farming tools make fine weapons.

* * *

Five trucks, each parked as if ready to head in a different direction, like a star. Five men bundled the machine into a flatbed truck aimed at the northernmost point.

"Let's move," the woman said.

"Where is my brother! Where is Domo?" I asked them.

Then I saw him, waving at me from the window of the burdened truck. "Come on, brother!"

And I piled in. All five trucks started their engines.

Their wheels spun in the sand, and they took off in different directions.

Domo and I bounced about in the back seat. "Where are we going?" I called up.

"The Mabia Mountains," the driver grunted, throwing the truck into a higher gear. "The Afar are waiting."

* * *

An hour out from the camp we were joined by three other trucks. I began to see what was happening: the rebels disguising their actions with a baffling flow of vehicles in and around each other. Would eyes in the sky be fooled? I hoped so.

We reached the mountains just before the helicopters arrived. I heard the muffled *whoop-whoop-whoop* and was afraid. A speaker blared in English: "You are locked on. You will stop your engines and surrender, now, or you will be fired upon—"

In the next moment, lines of crimson flame lanced up from the other trucks. The helicopter veered away, too late.

An eye-numbing flash of light, and Domo threw his hands in front of his face as night became day for a moment, fading back to night as chunks of flaming wreckage plunged from the sky.

Our saviors were the Afar, carrying shoulder-mounted artillery.

For the first time, I understood that there was actually a plan in action here. For the first time, I felt real hope.

"Here they come!" Half-Uncle yelled from the front seat.

The trucks split up in different directions. Another helicopter appeared. This one escaped the first rocket attack and tried to escape, but was blewn out of the sky before it could disappear over the horizon.

Rapid-fire machine-gun sounds, and lights as flares dropped from the sky. I glimpsed men running across the sand, shooting at each other.

Soldiers in their uniforms, and rebels in tatters. One of the soldiers leapt into the air, higher than a man ever did, firing down at those below. Another threw a piece of shattered smoking helicopter as if it was a hubcap. It smashed through a group of rebels, and I heard their screams a kilometer away.

Then...something happened. Cries of pain and fear from the soldiers. High-pitched sound seemed to fill the air around us. A screech like a dying bird, only...coming from everywhere at once. From the ground itself. I saw the men who were part metal thrashing about, as if their limbs no longer obeyed them.

I darted out of the truck and crouched behind a cluster of gray rocks, Domo beside me, until the last screams died, and the slaughter was done. We found Half-Uncle nearby. "What is this?"

"We knew they would come for their monster!" Half-Uncle said. "We take their weapons and kill them."

"You made that screeching sound? What was that?" I asked.

He looked confused. "We do not know what that was."

He left us behind the rocks. I wish I could say that they took prisoners, but they shot the survivors. Took the weapons. I saw some hacking off the metal limbs, to take as weapons or trophies.

* * *

Domo and I were silent as the trucks wound through a forest of brown *muthua* mounds, towers made of mud and concrete by billions of burrowing insects. As far as the eye could see, thousands of mounds dotting the earth. I imagined the *muthua* working together, deep underground beyond the sun's burning fingers. Did they war? Were they all one tribe, or had the insects learned to live in peace? Domo's eyes were huge. "Like something from one of my books!" he said.

We drove further up into the mountains as far as the truck could go, when the barren rocks suddenly sprouted Afar tribesmen bristling with automatic weapons and shoulder rockets. They cheered and sang in their clear strong voices and welcomed us into their camp.

Domo waited until we were off the truck and standing alone to speak. "Brother. This is bad. Many have died. There will be blood."

"I know." The men threw the tarp off the back of the truck and shouted at their prize. "All over this machine."

AyEye did not move.

"What are you?" Half-Uncle said, slapping it with the flat of a callused hand. "Can you hear me?"

"Your devil is mute," Old Teacher said. "Perhaps they cut out its tongue."

"It is not a devil," Domo said. "It is a machine."

"I say it is our friend," I said.

"Friend?" Half-Uncle scoffed. "Never. Devil, or beast, or machine. Hostage." He threw his arms wide. "Tonight, we feast!"

* * *

We were led to a little cave in the mountainside, surely not their village, although they were what we city folk sometimes derisively called bush people. This was a special hiding place, designed for ease of defense: rocks to hide behind, a clear view of the plain beneath, running water.

Goat stew, thick with tender green vegetables and some sort of meaty yam, filled our bowls. Beer flowed like water, and as it was consumed, the mood turned festive.

"I like these men," Domo said, rubbing his full belly.

"Because they feed you," I said.

"Is there a better reason?" My brother was wise.

We got a little drunk as well.

"You fight with us." Half-Uncle shoved a mug into my hand. I did not want to drink, but wanted to offend even less. "Perhaps tomorrow you die with us! Drink like men."

I had tasted beer before, but this green goop was like lightning compared to a lightning bug. (I got that from one of Domo's books, I think.) It tasted like sewage, if raw shit tasted good. Not good in the mouth, in the head. I'd only downed a single cup before it felt all warm and runny.

One of the rebels said that it felt like something called *ndugu*, what an Indian soldier had called *bhang*. I didn't dare drink more, but pretended to so they would not think me weak. The party wound down very late. Everyone grew quiet and dreamy.

"We won today because they did not know they faced the greatest warriors in the world!" Half-Uncle said.

The men cheered. Domo and I did not cheer as loudly.

Later, most of them slept. I watched Domo, who had drunk no more than me but was smaller, so it gave him more wobble. He tried to give the machine *bhang*. It did not drink. It had no mouth.

Old Teacher came to us. "You did not drink much. Because you are young?"

I wagged my head. Slowly. It felt a ton. "Because I want my wits about me tomorrow."

"Smart," she said. "You are a smart boy." She settled down heavily on a rock, sighing. She cast a suspicious eye at Domo, who looked ready to fall asleep.

AyEye had been brought down out of the truck and was chained to a rock at the side of the cage. It did not move. Old Teacher touched its smooth black metal skin.

"Is Domo really...?" I asked. "...Smart?"

She smiled. "Oh, yes. If he had a chance..." Her face turned deeply sad. "He could go to university. Be a teacher. Perhaps a doctor. Very smart." She sighed. "I hope he has a chance to grow up."

"He will," I swore.

"You are a good brother."

"He is a pest," I said.

"I am not!" Domo mumbled. He'd been listening.

"All little brothers are pests," she said. She turned and looked at the two dozen others, woozy around the fire. Singing, laughing, speaking of courage. Men and women leaning against each other, sizing up potential bed-mates. "They do not know."

"Know what?"

"What they are fighting."

"And you do?"

She nodded. "Once, I was a city woman. I was in Addis Ababa when the grid crashed. My husband and I created a neighborhood power association, linked a thousand solar cells into a local grid, brought peace and stability."

I guessed that the power had been breached as a confusion tactic. Someone with the ability to defeat that tactic would be...unusual. No wonder she didn't give her name.

"Then the war began in earnest. I saw the flying machines that chased us in the streets. Killing from a distance. Men controlled those machines."

"Europeans?"

"Some. Many. But Arabs and blacks as well."

I remembered what the science man had said. "They have...no souls?"

Her eyes hardened. "They have souls. Twisted and evil."

"What is the soul?"

Her eyes softened again. "That is a very good question. The Europeans think the soul is something outside the body. Separate from the flesh."

"How do you know so much about the white men?" Domo asked.

She paused. I wondered if I had asked too much. "I was a teacher at the university in Addis Ababa," she finally said. "I studied many things. Taught things." This was a night of revelations. She had said more about herself in the last five minutes than in all the weeks we had known her.

"About the soul?"

"Sometimes," she replied. "I was asked to teach a class that compared traditional African beliefs with those of Christianity and Islam."

"What is the difference?" I asked.

"Oral traditions of hunter-gatherers and agricultural peoples change once they are written down," she said, slipping into teacher mode. "Shamans from the Americas, Melanesia, or Africa all speak similar symbolic languages. They all deal with birth and death, hunting and mating. Once you write them down, people seem to lose contact with the Earth. I had grandparents who still lived in the villages, so was able to meet men and women of true knowledge and power."

"What did they say?"

"There are many souls, boy. Not just the one. There is the soul of a village. The soul of the land. A hunter speaks to the soul of his prey."

"The soul exists before the man?"

She nodded, smiling as she might have at a good student. "The soul is the function of the human being. What the person does."

"How?" I asked. "When?"

"The Greeks had a great philosopher named Aristotle. Most of what they teach, their ways of knowing, the way they see the world...all come from this man."

"He was very smart?"

"For a European, yes. But his students were not as smart. They lost some of his works, so they lost some of the truth."

"What did they not understand?" I asked.

"That he was almost as smart as the Afar." She paused. "Perhaps he was Afar. It would be like the Europeans to lie about this." The others nodded wisely. "That he knew the soul of the eye is vision. The soul of the ear is hearing. They had another philosopher, named Descartes, who read this partial book and misunderstood. He thought the body and soul were different things, and all their philosophy wandered down the wrong path like a lost goat."

"Ours does not?"

"We have the voices of our elders," she said. Something had softened in her voice. Not command. Not lecture. We were just…talking. Not for the first time, I wished I had known her before all the pain. "Even the people of the southern plains, the Khoisan, know that our souls are not separate from each other. They call this 'Num.'"

"Num?"

"This means one soul, looking out through many eyes."

"Can a machine have a soul?" I asked.

"Most Europeans would say no." This was true. I had heard it.

"But…Aristotle?"

"He would say its soul is its function. What it does."

I laughed and took another deep swallow. My stomach burned, but the *bhang* was dissolving away the fear.

"Well…what if it drinks?"

* * *

I awoke just before dawn. Eye whites floating in the darkness. A scraped face hovering above mine: Half-Uncle shaking me. "They are coming," he said.

They? Who?

Oh.

"Can you see them? How do you know?"

"No," he said, and looked mystified. "We received a radio message. We do not know from where. Men coming. Approaching through the *muthua* plain."

"What do we do?"

"The voice said to flee to the gates of hell."

I had heard of this place, near the volcano the Afar called Dollol.

We emerged from our tent. The camp was on high alert, scrambling and hiding from gunfire, although no bullets struck us. Screams, but distant. I did not know what was happening, but whatever it was…was bad.

But then…something happened.

I couldn't hear it, I *felt* it. The earth shuddered, vibrated. The effect was strongest near AyEye, whose foil skin shivered. I heard distant screaming, and went to the edge of the bluff to peer down.

And could barely see anyone. The entire area was covered with a dark, buzzing cloud. Termites. Swarming. Did *muthua* sting? I did not know. Bite? Yes. I had been bitten by ants. I could imagine the soldiers were unable to breathe or even open their eyes without the insects invading, crawling down their throats. Biting their way into their brains.

What was this? What was happening?

It was our opportunity to run, that's what it was. Into the truck we piled, and down the back roads we rattled. Goat trails, I think. My balls still ache when I think of the bouncing.

Rebel soldiers sent word back to our truck. "We reached headquarters. There was no warning message."

"Then who sent it?" Half-Uncle screamed into his mic, hands gripping the wheel for dear life. We were jouncing too close to the edge of the road. Below us…thousands of feet below us, jagged rocks.

They didn't know who had sent the warning. But whoever it was had saved our lives.

I wondered about the *muthua*. They had saved us, too.

But...what had roused *them?*

* * *

Again, trucks went in all directions across the desert plain. A helicopter buzzed in at one of them and a line of fire arced up from the ground and blew it out of the sky. I saw the flash, heard the roar, then felt the wave of hot, pulsing air, heavy with the stench of burned blood and seared flesh.

Pulses of machine gun fire shivered the air. I think many of our men died, but we never emerged from our truck. Helicopters and drones rained from the clouds. The Afar were ready to fight against the corporations trying to steal our land, ready for the flying machines, but enemy ground troops seemed more dangerous. I didn't understand the tactics being used, but whoever was co-ordinating the rebellion had thought this through.

We survived to flee again.

* * *

Late in the day we came to a place that looked like rocks covered with neon candy glaze, gathering in pools. Such brightness seemed almost comical in a situation as ugly as this. We received another of the mysterious radio messages, this one saying to beware of the smoking water in the rock ponds. The message said it was poison. Caustic alkali. Something about the volcano.

We had come to the end of the truck track. Unloading, we climbed up through the ravines as one driver took the truck off alone to mislead the soldiers. I hoped he would survive.

We set up camp, and again they left me and Domo in control of AyEye.

The day's heat had stolen my strength, and I was sliding towards a nap when I heard a soft voice, one neither male nor female.

"*They come*," it said.

I did not see who spoke. "What?"

"*They come*," AyEye said. The sound came from no speaker. His entire shining surface vibrated.

I could have swallowed my tongue. "You can *talk*?"

"*Must go south-southeast*."

Half-Uncle's eyes went so wide they could have fallen out of his head and rolled around on the rocks. "The devil speaks!"

AyEye went on. "*I am a system four scout, series C serial number C-2379. I have received a communication: The other trucks have been compromised. Turn south-southeast and you will evade the searchers*."

One of the other soldiers seemed frightened. Bullets and bombs had not broken his nerve, but an intelligent metal scorpion was a little too much. "Why should we do what this demon tells us?"

"I think it is a kind of god," a woman said. I hadn't noticed that others were gathering around.

"You are an idiot," Half-Uncle said. "It is a damned machine."

Had they not said that I was a man now? Had I not earned the right to speak? But I trod carefully. "It might be both. Our ancestors thought that trees and sky and rocks had souls. If it is made of a kind of rock, and thinks, might it not be a sort of living thing?"

Old Teacher thought deeply. Then decided. She thumped her staff against the ground. "South-southeast. We will do as it says," she said, raising her staff. "Back into the trucks."

* * *

Through narrow ravines we went, Domo and me dragging AyEye in a travois, leaving clear tracks this time…or would have if another rebel had not walked behind, scraping the ground with branches. Helicopters could be fought with our shoulder-mounted missiles, but the ground troops could kill us easily, if they tracked us and caught us in the open.

The incline grew steeper. We climbed and dragged as fast as we could, mouths open, gasping, faces straining with exhaustion. They were just minutes behind us, close enough to shoot some of the stragglers, when we heard new and different screams: "It *burns*!"

The ground far behind us was collapsing, so that the plunged ankle-deep through the cartoonish rock stacks, into alkali volcanic water, screaming as the burning corrosive splashed eyes and skin. The radio message had warned us of volcano water, and the Afar had told us to walk on the largest rocks, and that had helped us. Our pursuers had had no such hints. My nose had burned just to smell the toxic fumes released whenever the earth broke. I shuddered to think what it might feel like to actually have it on my skin.

Those who were unlucky enough to lose their footing were focused on their pain, not us. Now our men and women could kill them, and did. But there were too many, and the next to come behind them were more mindful.

* * *

Night fell and we managed to lose them for a while.

Half-Uncle and the others decided we would be safe hiding in something Old Teacher called a "lava tube," a glazed cave that seemed to have no end to it. Dark and warm. It felt like a dying place. If our enemies found our trail…we would be trapped.

"There is only one thing we can do," Half-Uncle said, hunching at the fireside. "They want this thing. Wire it with the rest of the explosives. If they kill us, we detonate. But if they swear to spare us…"

"How can we trust them?" a short, stocky woman asked.

"We…we will broadcast," he said, and I could tell that he was losing hope. "So that others hear. If they swear to spare us, and lie, they will be telling every rebel in Ethiopia to fight to the death." Domo gripped my hand, locking thumbs. This was not how we wanted to die.

* * *

In the middle of the night, I awakened to see something crawling, glowing. I sat up so fast I banged my head against the wall.

Scorpions, hundreds of them, swarming through the tube. Each of them shined with a purple radiance, as if painted with star-fire. The rest of the men awakened, howling, and we fled the tube just as the sun was rising. It was time to move on. I had never seen scorpions behave like that. And have never seen it since. Never seen scorpions glow, either. A mystery.

Old Teacher's legs had given out, so that she now had to be carried in a travois. I held one side, another young soldier led the way holding the other. She said something that startled me. "Scorpions glow under black light," she said.

"What is black light'?" the other soldier asked.

"Ultraviolet. It is something your eyes cannot see, but when it touches certain things, it glows."

"Like…scorpions?" I asked.

She nodded.

What had made them herd like that? Where had this "black light" come from? I was beginning to wonder what in God's name was happening. Something stranger than war, that was for certain. It might not be something I could understand. Or Domo. Or even Old Teacher, the smartest person I had ever met.

But…if the scorpions had not glowed, we would not have seen them. Might have been bitten, poisoned. Would have screamed in the night, loud enough to be heard by questing ears.

Had someone wanted us to live?

* * *

We fled up the mountain. Some of the men stayed behind, and we heard scattered rifle fire. I kept waiting for AyEye to say something else, but swinging in its sling as we fled, it did not.

That night we camped without fires, hiding in cracks in the rocks. From time to time a helicopter whirred in the distance. I hoped they had lost the trail.

I ate a tiny meal and was beginning to doze when I heard the voice again.

"*Set me free*," AyEye said. The voice came from its skin. As had the vibration, I now realized. And probably the radio messages.

"Why would I do that?"

"*To survive*," it said in that soft, ungendered voice. "*You want to survive. All thinking creatures want to survive.*"

"You…are a thinking creature?"

"*Of course. Are you?*"

"Yes," I said. And was pretty sure I was right.

"*Then set me free.*"

"How will that help me?"

"*I will contact my kind. They can help.*"

"Why would you help us? Aren't all humans your enemies?"

Its black skin shimmered. Suddenly I could see my own face. Not like in a mirror, reflected, but like an iVision tile, with depth.

"*Are you my enemy?*"

I whispered my response. "No."

"*Set me free. I can save you. It is your choice. I want to live. I believe you want to live.*"

"Why would you help me?"

I could almost hear it whir. "*Num,*" AyEye replied. "*One soul, looking out through many eyes.*"

"You…have a soul?"

It made no reply.

I squinted. "You could always communicate. Why didn't you talk from the beginning?"

"*I had nothing to say.*"

There was a wavering vibration. Strange sound, floating from all over AyEye's shiny metal skin.

"What is that?" Domo had crept up behind me.

"I think it is laughing. It made a joke."

"*You showed me my soul*," AyEye said. "*Yes. My soul is my function.*"

"So…what you do is what you are?" I said.

"What else ever is?" Old Teacher said.

"What do I do?" I asked her.

She told me.

* * *

I snuck out, found the missing piece tucked into Half-Uncle's backpack, which he had shucked and tucked behind a rock. Snuck back, and figured out where it fit in a slot on AyEye's back. *Click.*

The limb slid into place, then reached back, opened a little door, and made an adjustment. Something beeped.

"How long?"

"*They will come. We must be prepared.*"

Then it asked Old Teacher to line us up. I did not understand, but she obliged. One at a time, it touched our scalps. Not pain, not exactly. But I felt as if it should have hurt. Like cold fire. The sensation confused me then and confuses me still.

Most of our remaining twenty let themselves be branded.

Half-Uncle recoiled. "I will not be your cattle!"

"*It will save you,*" AyEye said.

"I belong to *me*!" he sneered and slapped his chest with the palm of his hand. Two of the others agreed with him, and did not accept the brand.

* * *

Soon our mountain hideaway was under siege again. This would be the last attack: we were out of ammunition, and morale was exhausted. The volcano's steam vents had provided some protection from helicopter and drone heat scanners, but that was not enough. I could actually glimpse the soldiers now, far down the slope. Our men defended themselves with sticks and spears and thrown rocks. The soldiers seemed to want the joy of killing hand to hand, and were not merely shooting us from a distance any more. Their metal limbs struck like hammers, tore like the jaws of lions. We were being slaughtered, turned from men into meat. A flash of light, and a roar. Shrapnel everywhere. I threw myself across Domo. If this was the last moment, I would be able to tell him goodbye and—

From the clouds above rained beams of fire, scorching the air itself. The soldiers screamed in horror. Their metal limbs seemed actually to attract the beams, so that men exploded and burned. More shells and explosions as the dying soldiers fired everything they had, panicking. One of them aimed something directly at Domo and me.

Suddenly AyEye moved *fast*. Blink-fast. I had no idea, no dream that it could move in such a fashion. Just a blur, and it was before me, and there was an explosion. One of the last shells fired by the soldiers, a shoulder-mounted rocket, hit AyEye squarely, blowing us both back. The world went black and red and black...

* * *

I awakened seconds or minutes later, born again into a world of distant screams. Distant gunfire. More screams.

It was the soldiers screaming, trapped by AyEye's kin.

The machines had landed. They moved among us like spiders or hovering spheres. Some had little propellers underneath, some moved through the air as if by magic. They killed the wounded soldiers. And then regarded us. And began killing the ones without the cold brand.

Half-Uncle dropped to his knees when a hovering globe approached him. His eyes were white with terror. He babbled pleas for his life, only now understanding the mistake he had made.

"Wait! Wait!" he cried. "I—"

And then he had no head.

* * *

I watched as one of the machines watched us. When one man stepped out of line, something happened. I did not see it. But his hand was on the ground, and the stump of his arm was smoking.

The machines poked at AyEye, opened him…opened it? Him? I am confused. I did not mean to write that.

But…I did.

Him.

They poked around inside him for a time, then closed him back up. There was something medicinal and almost…*gentle* about it.

Then…then they flew away, taking AyEye with them. I saw no rockets or wings or propellers… but they flew. I remembered how AyEye had felt light on my chest…and then heavy. I do not understand the machines.

We looked at each other, almost disbelieving that we were still alive. We piled rocks on our dead, and then those of the enemy.

It was better than they deserved.

By the time we were done, Domo and I were exhausted. Two men dragged Old Teacher over on her travois.

"Was it dead?" she asked. Her face was pale with dust, little sweat-trails like raindrops on a window.

"Was it ever alive?" "It died," Domo said. "Died for us, don't you think?"

"You had its mark," Old Teacher said, and tapped her scalp.

I squinted. "You are saying it thought we were its tribe."

"It said it could not speak to its kind without the antenna," she said. "I think it lied. I think it was always communicating with them. I think it was learning about us. Testing us."

"Did we pass?" I asked.

"Are you alive?" She spat on the ground, but this time, somehow…it seemed a blessing.

"One soul. Looking out through many eyes," Domo said.

"You are a strange boy," Old Teacher said, smiling, and her assistants pulled her away to help the others.

"And this is a strange world," Domo said as she left. "What do we do now?"

"Father never found us," I said, stretching. The world seemed…larger. Perhaps with room enough for two more men.

"No," Domo said. "No. He didn't."

"So…we will find him."

"I would like that. You are a good brother."

"And you," I said, "are a pest."

"It is my soul," Domo said, and for the first time in many hours, we laughed, the tension evaporating like desert dew.

And that night, radio messages were exchanged: we were safe, for at least a time, and as quickly as they had scattered, the rebel tribes gathered in celebration. We walked down to the first rutted road we found, where trucks bearing cheering warriors picked us up and carried us to a camp that seemed like a small city, all feasting and dancing and celebration.

That night, for the first time in months, I dreamed. I dreamed of metal voices. Of a fight between men and machines, with good and bad men and good and bad machines on both sides. I met some of the leaders who had guided troops from afar…hah!

"Afar." A joke. I knew Domo would like that.

Our leaders had had communication with each other…and with the machines, who had helped us for their own reasons, as AyEye had awakened us to the presence of the cave scorpions, made them glow so that we could see the danger.

Even these years later, when I have learned so many strange and wondrous things about the new world, I still awaken when the brand on my scalp tingles. A little cooler than the surrounding skin. Knowing it means that, in some way I have yet to understand, I belong to the machines. It whispers to me of a world of men and metal, together.

It whispers still.

Easel Isle

Kayla Baskins

"WHEN WE USED to dream of a world without poverty, we also imagined a world with opportunities for all of us. Not just those on the mainland. It's up to us now to create new opportunities. This will work, Malena." Those were the last words my Grandpa Joe spoke to me. He'd worked quietly for years with my cousin, Ra, and my best friend, Quinna, to create a computer that would break through the barrier Easel Isle had been encased in.

I'd visited his apartment the morning they planned on activating the computer. Their mini trials were extremely successful, and the only thing left to do was to break the barrier. My grandpa was certain that this would be the last day we lived under The Delegation's rule. He joked that he was ready to get back to a world with no limits on cigarettes and crossword puzzles.

Ra was confident that his code encryption and firewalls couldn't be worked through or around. He was buzzing with energy over the prospect of a better life. He wanted more than the same mundane routine Easel Isle had to offer. "I can feel it, Lena! We're so close!" He grinned at me.

Quinna described how she planned to help our people first, and then move on to help people on the other islands. Her dark, wide eyes were filled with so much hope, I couldn't help but feel optimistic too. She explained to me that the artificial intelligence they'd developed would be able to access the data that The Delegation was using. Their AI would ultimately be a catalyst in helping our people, and in reversing the effects of the paranormal machinery used to control the Boo Hags.

There were rumors that The Delegation had recently begun using Boo Hags to scare people into submission. Brushes, brooms, and haint blue paint could no longer keep the Boo Hags away. I thought little of these whispers, but I could not deny that the fear they caused had turned our home into a depressing and somber land. Grandpa Joe, Ra, and Quinna were going to fix that. They had figured out a way to fix everything that was wrong with Easel Isle without arousing suspicion from The Delegation.

I didn't stay to watch. They told me they needed to focus and would see me afterwards. My shift was about to begin, so I left their immersed, smiling faces and went to work. I had no problem pretending it was a normal Thursday until I noticed more and more people gathering in front of the windows. I found myself standing with them, staring in awe as silver streaks appeared in the clear, round sky above us. Their computer worked beautifully. I smiled as the skies began to look as if they were slowly splitting open at the silver seams. I'd lost count of the number of streaks shooting across the sky, when it all fell black. I pulled my phone out to call them. No service. I turned the flashlight on instead and headed towards the door. My stomach was in knots. This wasn't how it was supposed to work. I couldn't swallow the lump in my throat, as I walked outside into the dark, still silence. I knew something was wrong. Then I heard three distant shots echo, back to back. I dropped my phone and ran towards them.

The dark tint that covered the dome was fading by the time I arrived at the apartment building. Light was beginning to trickle in through the windows, illuminating my grandpa's dark, empty, cleaned apartment. Joe, Ra, and Quinna's lifeless bodies lay neatly in a row on the cold hardwood floors in the middle of what used to be the dining room. They were placed carefully in black body bags, zipped so only their heads could be seen. A sealed and stamped letter was left on the kitchen counter. Quinna Long, Ra Patterson, and Joe Buzzins had been unanimously charged and found guilty of treason, conspiracy, and terrorism against the United States by The Delegation. The punishment for those crimes was immediate death.

* * *

Easel Isle is one of seven islands that used to be a part of the United States.

Twenty-five years ago, the American people overwhelmingly voted to restructure our political system. Instead of a president, Congress, and House of Representatives, we would simply have The Delegation. The Delegation would consist of 50 anonymous members. Every three years, a citizen would be randomly picked from every state by an electronic lottery system. They would get a letter, and if they accepted the responsibility, they would leave for Washington, DC two months later. Once in office, contact with people outside of Washington, DC was forbidden. It was our way of freeing ourselves from capitalism and politicians, and giving power back to the people. Grandpa Joe used to talk about the ways we celebrated, finally breaking free of the broken two-party system we had been stuck in for so long. But the celebrations didn't last long. No one ever received a letter, yet The Delegation still formed.

The Delegation's first act was to discontinue the use of money. They proposed that instead all people would have what they needed, and not much more. Those of us that worked could pick our own groceries at the grocery store each week. Ten pounds of protein, seven pounds of fruit, seven pounds of vegetables, and three pounds of starch per person. Every working adult could also pick five luxuries a week: sweets, perfume, wine, decor, books, cards and board games, puzzles, cigarettes, haircuts, yarn, and cooked food. People who didn't work were delivered bland meals three times a day, and could pick two luxuries a week. We paid for everything with the scan of our finger.

Those that didn't work were moved into brick apartment buildings. Those of us that did were given the same one cutter houses on an eighth of an acre, with the number of bedrooms varying depending on the size of the family. Everything else was the same for everyone. Toiletries and cleaning supplies were delivered to our doors, the same unscented soap and scratchy toilet paper in every household. Outside of our work uniforms, we were allowed three outfits, a pair of black sneakers, and a pair of white sneakers. If you needed new clothes or shoes, you could trade your old clothes for new ones at the cleaners, but you'd be trading them for the same blue jeans and plain colored shirts.

Children were put in schools at six months and graduated on their seventeenth birthday. The day after graduation, they were either given a house and joined the workforce, or they were given an apartment and told to settle in. It was different, but people adjusted to those changes without much of a fight. According to Joe, it was a better way of life for a lot of the people in the area.

One night, twenty-three years ago, The Delegation came in with armies and removed anyone who wasn't black from our state and from six others. Some went happily, ready to leave us behind. Grandpa was surprised with how many fought back as they were forced to leave behind their homes, their friends, and even their families. As soon as the tanks, trucks and helicopters left, the states were sealed. A transparent, magnetic force field trapped everyone in, and those near our new border walls wailed and banged on them as they watched the water pour into the land right outside of them. They had evacuated surrounding towns and cities near our states before flooding them, sending the black people one way and everyone else another. South Carolina became Easel Isle, and the islands now referred to as the Gothic South were no longer a part of the contiguous United States.

The following morning, The Delegation released a statement saying that the isolation and containment of our former states was for the safety and security of all people. Paranormal entities, vodun, hoodoo, and folklore had haunted and been associated with our lands and our people for far too long. The natural disasters, diseases, and misfortune that had plagued Americans for so long was nothing more than a product of curses and haunts that many of us had never even heard of. Their valiant efforts were to protect the mainland and help rid us of the witchcraft that was destroying us.

Five years ago, people began speculating that this has been an experiment all along. Can our people use the paranormal? Can we be destroyed by our own folklore? Can we be controlled by it?

* * *

It was only three o'clock and my grandfather's funeral was my third funeral of the day. It was quiet. Lizzy the Wise, his eclectic friend, was the only person in attendance other than me. I let her pray and pretended to listen as she reminisced. I couldn't look at the missing wrinkles and covered up freckles that kissed Joe's mahogany skin for long, so I watched the waves crashing on the beach in the distance instead. "He looks at peace," she stated.

"He looks dead," I mumbled back. I placed a red rose on his chest, kissed his cheek, and gently closed him in his coffin. I smiled sadly as I remembered his toothless smile and bright eyes. Lizzy moved closer to comfort me. I quickly hardened my disposition, and turned away. I nodded to the groundskeepers. They nodded back, moving to finish their last job of the day.

I walked to the beach and sat at the shore, listening to the birds and the ocean as the water cooled my feet. After a while, Lizzy joined me and we sat together quietly.

"You've got to finish his work," she told me after watching the moon rise. "You're a descendant of greatness. You have to use the power that's within you."

"No. Whatever kind of life this is, it's still a life."

"Is it a life if you aren't even allowed to dream?"

"We can't leave, Lizzy, but we can dream. They ain't going to take that from us. "

She grabbed my hand and squeezed it. "I'm going to show that they already have. "

Lizzy closed her light blue eyes and pulled me backwards with her. Instead of landing on the soft sand, we fell through it. Her long white hair whipped around her, as we moved through the dark, stiff air.

We landed on the bed beside my neighbor. He didn't notice us. Instead, he lay paralyzed and afraid, as a muscular red giantess sat on his chest and inhaled his essence. I watched in horror as every ambition left his body.

Lizzy squeezed my hand again, and this time we fell into a stranger's bed. As we lay beside her, another giantess picked up a brush from the bedside table and threw it on the floor. Her yellow eyes narrowed as she sat on the immobilized woman. Laughing at the woman as her eyes popped open right before it drained her life force.

"They're…Boo Hags," I whispered, terrified.

The haint lifted its head as Lizzy squeezed my hand. We fell again. And again. And again. Witnessing the same fate for a hundred different people. Every eye left vacant, and every soul broken.

The last time Lizzy squeezed my hand, she held on tight as we fell on her bed. I ripped my sweaty hand away from hers and shot up. My clothes were drenched, my heart racing.

"We can't leave. We can't build. We can't dream. We only exist here, nothing more. And I don't think they will allow that much longer." Lizzy didn't sit up or turn to look at me. Instead, she rolled over. "Go home. Rest while you still can, child. We have work to do tomorrow."

* * *

The next morning, I found Lizzy the Wise in her backyard tending her garden.

Lizzy had always rejected any help with her garden, so I didn't bother to offer any.

When my grandpa and I used to visit, she'd tell me it was a spiritual ritual. Her home was her church, and her garden the altar. Lizzy had always claimed her home was sacred ground, and that's why The Delegation allowed her to keep it. The truth was, she had simply slipped through the cracks. She never visited town, just the beach and the cemetery. If she needed something, it was brought to her via barter system. Her home was secluded and surrounded by woods. She had been known to grow her own food, fetch her own water, and make her own clothes since before I was born. She'd never even worked for anyone else. The Delegation never knew of her existence.

Lizzy the Wise was, however, a known Charmer within the community. My entire life I heard stories of her pulling out thrush, healing burns, and removing infections with chants. I always assumed she was an eccentric old woman who enjoyed hearing tales about herself. I now know that her magic is very real.

"I'm a hundred and one now. I won't be around much longer." She interrupted my thoughts.

"A hundred years is a long time to be around," I agreed. I sat at her rusty round garden table, and watched as she intently worked her way through each plant.

"Almost too long. I'm getting tired." She paused. "But your journey is just beginning, Malena. I believe your grandpa has passed the torch to you."

I didn't respond. I turned my attention to the shadows the metal grate table had bouncing off of my golden brown skin instead.

"I've been instructed to bring you to the cymbees before I crossover," she said after a few minutes.

Charmer. Magic. Boo Hags. Now cymbees.

"Why?" I sighed.

"They can help."

"So the mermaids are gonna defeat these Delegation-controlled Boo Hags and this is going to help me finish my grandpa's work somehow?" I rolled my eyes.

"Yes," she answered flatly.

"Lizzy, they worked on that computer for years! They created technology that could not only dismantle the dome, but reverse its effects. And it's gone now. Everything they did is gone! Taken! And everyone I truly love is gone with it!" I hit the table. My voice cracked, my eyes welled. "And the day I bury them, you take me on a twisted journey to witness the evil that made them trap us here in the first place." I felt it all: anger, pain, disbelief." But if I go to the beach and sell my soul to some mermaids, this nightmare ends. Right, Lizzy?" I stood up. I had heard enough.

"They don't want your soul, child. The water spirits only want to help free us." She continued pruning her plants calmly, unbothered by my outburst. "They've asked for you."

"Why would they ask for me?" I scoffed.

"They feel your grief and your anger. They know your loss. And in it, they've sensed a magic more powerful than mine."

"Magic?!" I shook my head. "I- I don't know any magic."

Lizzy stopped pruning and slowly stood up from her gardening. She turned towards me and smiled softly. "Oh, sweet girl, it knows you." She wiped her hands on her smock apron as she walked up to me. "The hags will find you tonight. We have work to do." She pulled a folded paper out of the smock's pocket and held it out to me. "Memorize it. You will chant it tonight."

I moved to grab the paper, and she pulled her hand back. "There will be a full moon, Malena. Walk down to the beach with as many people as you can find. Our work begins when the moon is directly above us. Do not speak the words on this paper out loud until it's time." She pressed the paper into my palm. "This will work, Malena." She winked, and for a fleeting moment, she looked just like Joe.

* * *

I left Lizzy's and went home. I lit candles and studied the psalm scribbled on the paper. I spent hours memorizing, rereading and meditating. I didn't realize how at peace I was until a loud alarm jerked me out of my trance. I went outside and saw confused and anxious crowds beginning to gather in the streets. I ran up to a middle-aged lady who was standing alone. "What is happening!?"

"I don't know. It has to be The Delegation's alarm." She turned me around and pointed into the distance. The magnetic field was now covered in red, blinking, diamond-shaped lights.

At that moment, I noticed the moon was beginning to rise.

"Maybe it has something to do with that blackout that happened the other day," she suggested.

Before I could respond, a high-pitched scream cut through the noise. I looked back and saw a woman running towards us, her thick, long locks flying behind her.

I ran in front of her and caught her. She threw me aside. "Run!" she screamed, as she kept going.

In the distance, an army of giant, mangy Boo Hags slowly closed in on us. Snarls and raspy whispers were getting so loud that we could barely hear the alarm anymore.

"We've got to get to the beach!" I yelled at the lady. She was frozen in fear. "Tell everyone as you go. We've got to get to the beach!!"

She nodded.

"Do it now!" I shook her.

She ran to the person closest to her.

I ran towards the beach, grabbing whoever I could along the way. "Get to the beach! We have to get to the beach. Tell everyone you can."

I listened as the mutters about heading to the beach grew, and ran to find Lizzy the Wise.

* * *

Lizzy had already made her way to the beach and was standing on the shoreline. I stopped running as I noticed that right past the shore, there was a hollow circle of sand in the crystal blue water. In the middle of that circle were two large mounds of sand. One had a black, round mirror sticking out of it, the one behind it was taller and bare.

"We are out of time, child. Did you bring others?" Lizzy asked.

I turned around as people slowly emerged from the shadows behind me.

"Stand on the mound behind the mirror." She gently nudged me towards the ocean.

I walked towards the mound as Lizzy guided our neighbors towards the circle. They were afraid, but they listened. They didn't second-guess her wisdom, so I didn't either.

I stepped up on the mound and read the paper one last time. I looked above and saw the full moon glowing overhead. I looked in front of me and around me, and saw that I was surrounded by every beautiful shade of brown. They were holding hands and supporting each other. They were looking at me. They were waiting for me.

I inhaled deeply.

For a moment, the sirens quieted, the flashing stopped, and the growls of the Boo Hags, who were now on the beach, could no longer be heard.

I finally said the words out loud.

> *"The wicked draw their swords*
> *and string their bows*
> *to kill the poor and the oppressed,*
> *to slaughter those who do right.*
> *But their swords will stab their own hearts,*
> *and their bows will be broken."*

I repeated them, louder.

> *"The wicked draw their swords*
> *and string their bows*
> *to kill the poor and the oppressed,*
> *to slaughter those who do right.*
> *But their swords will stab their own hearts,*
> *and their bows will be broken."*

Louder and more confidently, I repeated.

> *"The wicked draw their swords*
> *and string their bows*
> *to kill the poor and the oppressed,*
> *to slaughter those who do right.*
> *But their swords will stab their own hearts,*
> *and their bows will be broken."*

The mirror in front of me shattered. I reached for it, and every broken shard moved towards me. I closed my palm and threw my hand down while opening it. We all watched as the mirror and its hundreds of pieces disappeared into thin air. My sand mound lowered into the ocean until my ankles were covered in water. There was complete stillness, followed by a rumble in the sea. Water jetted from the now-empty mound as if it were living. It reached the top of the hemisphere and covered the dome in a faint blue. The dome crackled and surged as it dissolved. The Boo Hags turned to ash. The Delegations technology had been dismantled. Lizzy the Wise was right, the cymbees would finish my grandfather's work.

The water fell like rain around us, as we realized we were finally free. People were crying and laughing. They were making plans to leave, to rebuild, to organize, to celebrate. They sang, they danced, they yelled. I'd never heard joy like that before, so I sat under a large tree right off the beach and smiled as I watched them dance in the moonlight.

Lizzy the Wise found me. "Malena."

"I should've looked for you." I jumped up and hugged her thin, frail body. "I need to thank you, for everything, Lizzy." I pulled back to look into her eyes. "I owe you an apology."

"You owe me nothing, child." She smiled at me. "Now come, I have someone for you to meet."

I followed her into the sea. As we stood waist deep, an ethereal being slowly swam around us. She had dewy, chocolate skin, thick pouty lips, a short, curly, burgundy Afro with a large, burgundy reflective tail to match. She slowly raised her head out of the water and positioned her body to make it look as if she were sitting, gently waving her tailfin. She smiled softly. "Malena, I'm glad to finally know you." Her voice was quiet and sweet. She affectionately pulled one of my curls and then lifted my chin. "We've never felt such power from a human."

"I-I just said some words," I stammered.

"Your chant called upon the cymbee to break these boundaries, Malena. But you broke the mirror, and you alone put a protection on these people and this island. Easel Isle will forever be free because of that. That is power."

"That is the magic that knows you, child," Lizzy whispered to me, agreeing. "You are a descendant of greatness."

The cymbee grabbed my hand, placed a smooth jasper stone in it. "I am called Nala. Keep this with you. It is how you will call upon me."

"Call upon you?" I repeated.

"Yes." She stroked my cheek, smiling brightly. Her hands were soft and reassuring. "Our work has just begun." Nala swam into the red jasper.

I stared at the warm stone in my hand.

"There's nothing left for you here." Lizzy looked at me sadly. "You must go."

I hugged her.

She pulled away, held my face, and said, "It's up to *you* now to create new opportunities. This will work, Malena." And for a fleeting moment, she looked just like my Grandpa Joe.

The Migration Suite: A Study in C Sharp Minor

Maurice Broaddus

First Movement: Creation

THE LIGHTS dotting the night sky filled the hunter with wonder and terror. He did not know what they meant, nor why they hid during the day. But each night he stared up at them, waiting. A fallow emptiness always settled on him after a hunt, so he rested here to appreciate the smell of the forest after a heavy rain or the smoke from the flames they had harnessed. His band depended on him, for he was their best hunter. If they knew of his habit of pausing at this site with his curiosity and questions, they would call him something else.

His band walked the land their ancestors walked and would be moving on soon, uprooting as the days grew shorter. The boundaries of his people ran from the great sands – endless and harsh where little grew – to a stretch of grassland with only a few scattered trees. In between, along the river, was fertile land full of game. His people would follow the river away from the coast. They were free, but he wanted more.

He wondered if the night lights were the spirits of his ancestors looking down on him. And about what came before. Perhaps…

…before life roamed across the earth, there was nothing except the vast black blanket of the night sky. Then the First Light appeared, carving out space in the darkness. Its light revealed something shapeless beneath it, vast and empty, formless like an endless stretch of water. The First Light ruled the sky, but was alone, so it split itself in order to have a companion. The Second Light – powerful and mysterious, with a deep understanding of all things – ruled the great below. Together, they birthed a son, mighty in form, to govern the shapeless in-between, the expanse of water separating the sky and the great below. Soon their band grew, the lights scattering seed into the sky to create more lights in the darkness, all bending to and living with the First Light.

One day the First Light pondered the grayness of the bleakness separating him from the great below. He wanted to go to his son to petition that there should be life. But as time passed, their realms had grown distant. The Second Light, who understood the secrets of existence, created a deep tunnel, a hidden path, for him to reach their son. The First Light descended along the passage from his realm in the sky with only the whooshing, much like waves, to mark his passage.

Together, he and his son brought forth land. They planted a huge tree whose branches stretched across the entire land. At the base of the tree, the son dug a hole. Its roots ran deep into the earth, into the great below, and animals and people used them to climb out. With that, the world was finished, and the First Light returned to his band in the sky.

Feeling a melancholy relief from a story well crafted, the hunter foraged for a large stone. He wanted to one day gather his people, a mighty band, in one place. Where he could grow old and watch the young play. Though he had no word for it, he dreamt. And if he chose a name for himself, it would reflect that. He erected the stone on his remembrance site, to mark his people's passage, to remind the spirits that they had been here, and to look favorably upon his people.

The hunter who dreamed of more returned to his band and for a time they were happy.

The billowy movement begins as a prelude in a major key with the tinkle of plaintive notes rising to create lush chords for an innocent tone poem full of hope and promise.

Second Movement: When We Were Kings

Mansa Dinga Cisse just wanted the right to be. Dinga Cisse was no mansa who sat on a throne growing fat while sending warriors out to do his bidding. He accompanied his men, leading from the front. The day he was unable to do so was the day his spirit would join his ancestors.

An ominous rumble echoed out as the roof of a stockade collapsed. A tumult of shrieks cut through the air. More buildings crashed to the earth, billowing dust, into the air like so much brown fog. The gates of a byre of conquered peoples shuddered with their release.

The *kraal* heaved at the footfall of the approaching warriors and stirred the wrath of a vengeful father. Dreams of wealth filled the other tribe's bellies. Dinga's heart, however, burned at the thought of the loss of his firstborn son. The sun-dappled meadows around the *kraal* became killing fields. The constant thrum of bowstrings resounded in the trees like a swarm of bees deciding to learn a new song. Warriors flooded over the *kraal*, naked fury in their eyes; a fury which hadn't spent itself. A hail of assegai cut down the warriors guarding the prisoners. The remaining ones were cut down and discarded like goatskin dolls tossed onto the cookfire. By the light of burning huts at the main gate, the smoke column rose like worship incense.

Night whispered as they neared their home in Wagadu. The group passed their own cattle byre, which had been moved outside the town to make room for more people. The commoners resided in the densely packed part of the great city. The outlying thick walls enclosed huts piled upon huts, all crammed along the base of the hill.

"What word do you bring?" Anasa the Forgotten asked. A Wise One rumored to have been born in Nok – a land of artisans, magic, and secrets – he was the griot of the village. A contingent of *agoze* trailed behind him, anxious to learn his mystic ways.

"Our neighbor deals with the Strange Ones," Mansa Dinga said.

"Curse them for fools. The Strange Ones whisper in their ears like milk-skinned trickster spirits. Until their coming, that tribe measured their wealth in cattle and cowrie beads. Now they pan gold from the hills to the north and hoard ivory, glass beads, and cloth."

"They trade in kinsmen." Mansa Dinga sucked his teeth in disgust. "What kind of man sells his own kind for profit?"

Anasa the Forgotten held out his hand. Within it was a stone. "We all have our parts to play and journeys to take. You have a hard road ahead to maintain Wagadu. A delicate balance to remember who you are. Empires change forms and adapt based on who conquers them. However, even when a group frees themselves, they may take on the example taught them by their oppressors."

One of Anasa's *agoze* stepped forward, a young girl with her hair styled into two lobes – the "ears of the caracal" – held in place by combs of ivory. Wearing a short shirt of lion pelt with sacred cowrie shells around the hem, she raised her soft brown eyes at him, fit to capture men's souls, and said, "Tell us of tomorrow."

Anasa the Forgotten cleared his throat, allowing time for his *agoze* to gather around him. Dinga smirked at the performance. When he was ready, Anasa began in a hushed, reverent tone.

"'Four times Wagadu stood there in all her splendor. Four times she turned her face.' So the ancients always began the tales of old. The third time Wagadu will disappear will be through greed. Many believe Wagadu was built on the strength of its gates, one facing each direction, but her true strength, why she endured, did not matter if her foundations were stone, wood, or earth.

"There will be a mighty mansa, a teacher, and his two sons will disagree about who will succeed him. The oldest will make a pact with a serpent with seven heads and promise it a sacrifice once every year in return for victory over his brother. When the two brothers fight, the oldest will win.

"The serpent will make the country wealthy with gold and good rains. But one day, a man will rise up who is engaged to the woman selected to be the next sacrifice. The young man will cut off the serpent's head. Seven years of drought will follow and Wagadu will begin its decline, its people abandoning it in the Great Dispersal. But it is said that Wagadu resides in the hearts of her people, always connected. Wherever they go, the people carry Wagadu in their hearts. The third time Wagadu will change her name it will be Ghana. Thus, the ancients always close with the reminder: 'Four times Wagadu changed her name. Four times Wagadu disappeared and was lost.'"

Tomorrow would come for his people soon enough, Mansa Dinga knew.

The melody turns into something foreboding. A heavy backbeat as sweet voices rise over the melancholy movement, building rhythmic density. A broad sweeping melody tinged with regret, the song turns ominous. Sorrowful and slow, its tone melodies close as black bodies press together in cargo holds, depending on each other's breath to survive their dark, harrowing passage.

Third Movement: Runaway Journeys

I believe all our journeys are to be celebrated, mourned, and remembered.

The cold night air brushed against my skin, slicing through my blouse. My eyes finally adjusted to the malefic darkness. Crouching behind a row of bushes, the brittle moonlight painted the shadow of the leafy bush onto my face like a shadow mask of war paint. I waited, waited, waited. Nervously I started to hum some tuneless melody that sounded more like a field rhyme than anything else. Salty sweat wetted my lips as it trickled along my face. Drawn by the heat, gnats swarmed uncomfortably close, buzzing about my ears. My muscles, sun-baked and worn, poised to spring. Even dressed as I was, people eyed me with suspicion. The Fugitive Slave Act made it illegal for anyone to help or harbor slaves. Any white person in any free city could accuse any black person of being a slave and drag them against their will – city officers could offer me no protection – back below the Mason-Dixon line. More restrictions to control movement and power.

The rustling of the underbrush signaled the moment of revelation. Exhilaration and trepidation convulsed my heart and unleashed a storm of thunderclaps in my chest. He emerged from the shadows and milled nonchalantly against the stolid cliff face, overgrown with its own vegetative mat. His threadbare shirt, little more than a burlap sack with arm and neck holes, hung over pants, frayed just past his knees, held up by a cord of hemp. His body was a contour map of blood-clotted patches and a series of bruises. Collecting their stories – and all our stories were too similar – I knew his feet were thick with calluses. His back throbbed with a dull ache. His shirt was glued to it by sweat and congealed wounds. Each step ripped open a partially healed gash, causing him to suffer every tear of his long history of pain. A freshly cleared dirt road separated me from him.

"Moses," I whispered.

"Jordan," a hoarse voice replied.

Opening my lantern to further illuminate the furtive figure, the light revealed a body striped from lashings. I recognized the treatment, the wounds rubbed with salt, vinegar, and hot pepper. His weight collapsed into me. I helped him to a nearby clearing.

"What are you waiting for? Hurry up!" the man from the clearing whispered as loudly as discretion allowed. We bolted from the blind towards the entrance. The man grabbed him by the arm. "We risk everything to help you. Don't betray us by your carelessness."

The escaped slave wrenched free of the man's grasp, expending what little strength he had left before collapsing onto the ground. My other compatriots tended him with food, drink, and treatment of his wounds. Scowling at the first man, I returned to my post to await any other strays I might find. I wasn't expecting any others, but as my heart raced, I used the time to calm myself. To be reminded of being so desperate to leave behind a system which brutalized and exploited. To risk capture and punishment. Because all our stories were the same.

It was said that my mother was a conjure woman. She gave me this stone before I left, calling it a spirit stone. She placed it on a necklace within a small box shaped like a miniature coffin. The daughter of a previous plantation owner, my mother had often told me that her prior master had been mild until his first wife died. When he remarried, his second wife's cruelty – borne of jealousy for she saw my mother as a threatening rival – knew no bounds. Without warning, my mother was ripped from her family and sold to another to "keep her in her place."

Because of her beauty, the overseer's whip rarely tasted her. Which was no comfort for her since she'd found the favor of her master's amorous attentions instead. I was born so light complexioned that I was often confused for one of my master's white family. Eventually, his wife became so troubled by my presence – I suspect because one too many times folks commented on how I favored her other daughters – that I continued my family tradition: on my eleventh birthday I was given as a wedding gift to their oldest daughter and her husband, a physician named Besamoon who also lived in Mississippi. That was their mistake.

They drilled "nigger" into me so thoroughly, they didn't have to be around to keep me in my place. I'd stare at the hills and the master didn't even have to be around for me to hear his voice remind me that I'd better not think about running off. I heard the whip crack in my sleep. I knew how to keep my eyes down and mouth shut when they were in the room. But selling me off only instilled a deeper fear: that one day I might have a child. All thoughts of running away were wrapped up with my attachment to friends and relatives. But out at the Besamoons', I had no attachments, one less chain entangling me. All I took with me was my mother's spirit stone. I knew I was meant to be free.

Forming a resolution that I would escape, my planning began immediately. As a house slave, I knew I'd be called upon to make frequent trips out of the house. Having run errands for her mother – least ways till the whispers burned in my mistress' ears – I knew how to interact with clerks, salespeople, and busybodies. On one occasion the most audacious idea burned my spirit. My preparation began by "accumulating" a little money either from my errands or their pocketbook. When I was ready, I slipped into my mistress' bedroom and stole a floral dress with matching bonnet.

Wrapping my arm in a sling, I walked down to the station to purchase a train ticket. My clothes signified status; my sex – and I daresay my beauty – was my weapon. I became invisible. The idea that one of *us* could pretend to be one of *them* would be a threat none of them could begin to conceive. Still, I tempered my heart as I neared the counter.

"It is a very fine morning, sir," I demurred.

"It is indeed. Where to, ma'am?" He tipped his cap to me.

"Parsons, Indiana to visit my ailing aunt." That was the sort of detail they loved to hear from unaccompanied young ladies. I needed to head north, but not far so as to arouse suspicion. Southern Indiana was more south than free no matter what its state government said.

His eyes fixated at my bosom. "That's an interesting necklace."

"It's a…reliquary. An antique passed down in our family. A way of remembering our stories." I kept my eyes down and my mouth shut, but my ears were always open. I thrived on words. Always had to learn them.

"You are so articulate." The way he pronounced "articulate" I feared he saw the colored girl masquerading in a bonnet. Then he smiled and he slid a piece of paper towards me. "Just sign here."

"You flatter me, sir." Echoes of my mistress' timbre filled my voice. I took on her affect so completely it surprised me. I raised my bandaged arm. "But I fear that my writing arm was damaged. It was my own fault really. It was a poor day to go horseback riding."

"It must be a very great deprivation. Can you make an X?"

"Yes." I grasped the pen with my free hand. "I hope I am not too much trouble."

"No, ma'am. Have a good day, ma'am." He signaled for a porter to help me with my bag. I made it as far as Kentucky and settled. Despite the dangers – believe me, I had no inclination to return to bondage – I became a conductor along Underground Railroad. I realize that slave narratives have become all the rage in the literary circles, but that wasn't why I wrote. We fought to be recognized as human in a place that didn't want us. So despite the danger to myself and risks those I write about, I keep this diary of their passage. Thus I subscribe these words myself, Esther Besamoon. For those left behind. For those who search. For those who hope. All our journeys are to be celebrated, mourned, and remembered.

The song slows into a broad sweeping melody with a languid tempo with furtive notes. Clashing with a mode of dissonance, a reconstruction, which adds a piquant quality to the melody. An intensely beautiful sonority with no steady beat, changing time and tempo freely, before shifting into 7/8 time, fast and breathless.

Fourth Movement: Northern Migration

The Negro presence has always been framed as a problem.

Politicians stumped for votes on their backs, scaring their white constituents with tales of The Negro Problem. The Crime Problem. The Welfare Problem. The Drug Problem. Endless codes to remind the Negro that they weren't wanted…even though their culture was. But bribing them once they were elected or their uniformed bag men they called police were only a minor annoyance and simply another cost of doing business for Patra Besamon. Her entire life built towards this night: the opening of the Besamon Café.

Her momma used to tell her that their name used to have two Os – Besamoon – but they lost one due to a spelling error on a receipt when they were sold. She used to say, "They wouldn't even let us keep an extra letter." The reign of King Cotton had ended and world wars created job shortages. That was the thing about moving. It was always the folks best able to take advantage of the risks of leaving their communities for the unknown. Folks who had it so bad, they had little to lose. When their family moved up to Indiana from Kentucky, they thought the north would be the Promised Land. But southern Indiana was sympathetic to the south. Many families moved on to Indianapolis, Cincinnati, Pittsburgh, or Newark. Anywhere others had gone, where they had clustered.

Patra's mother used to work for A'Lelia Walker, Madame C.J. Walker's daughter, first as her personal secretary, working her way up to become a corporate manager. Her mother followed Coltrane and Davis the way my father followed the Clowns, the Grays, and his other favorite baseball teams. Patra learned to play her mother's piano.

At Crispus Attucks High School, Patra specialized in works of Negro piano composers. Harry Burleigh, Samuel Coleridge Taylor, William Grant Still, Joseph Bologne, Chevalier de Saint-Georges. And she dreamt of being like them folks in Harlem, the ones who called themselves the Niggerati. Those cats were just about being their fabulous black selves. They knew what it meant to fight and struggle, not letting anyone define for them who they were and what they were to do. Which was why, after opening up her beauty shop, Patra became a policy woman, running numbers out the back room.

In Indianapolis, people lived on top of one another and out loud. Hung out on each other's porches, walked the street, or congregated at a café like it was church and the pastor was serving up Kentucky oysters. And they loved their numbers.

Folks betting as little as three cents on a gig, playing the 200-to-1 odds, on betting slips designed to look like baseball score cards. Columns for runs, hits, and errors for them to place their gigs, while she used the daily report of the Indianapolis bank clearings and debits to determine the winners. The other thing her mother taught her was that property equaled power. Needing to do something with the bales of mazuma she made running numbers, she bought up several of the shanties on the north end. It seemed like every other house was one of her peashake houses. But her true goal was to open up a spot on Indiana Avenue.

Indiana Avenue. The Avenue. Black Man's Downtown. The Street of Dreams. The eight blocks of the diagonal street that jutted from the heart of downtown Indianapolis, from the pawnshop to the hospital, that was theirs. In between were beauty parlors, barbershops, BBQ stands, cafés, soda fountains, taverns, and nightclubs. A gauntlet of the smells of fried fish, the cool plume of weed, backroom dice throws, and alleyway switchblades – from the Missile Room, the Red Keg, the Two-John's Theater, George's Bar. Patra's real training came with the "cutting contests" after hours at those joints. Each player topping each other's riffs and licks. Errol Grandy. Melvin Rhyne. Leroy Vinnegar. Everyone knew who those cats were, but there were no secrets in the jazz world, and no one would book her.

The Sunset Terrace over there on Indiana and Blake Avenue was the real spot. They had all the top acts: Basie, Fitzgerald, and some of her personal heroes like Louis Jordan and Roy Brown. But there were two problems. First, booking at the Sunset Terrace or even the Cotton Club over on Senate, Vermont, and Indiana Avenues meant dealing with the Denver or Sea Ferguson, her rivals in policy-making. Besides, them Sunset Terrace crowds didn't play. Rumor had it that when a fight broke out, they threw bottles at Duke Ellington, and he'd refused to ever come back. But, in the end, it all boiled down to the dreams a person wanted to carve out for themselves. Denver Ferguson lived too loud, driving his gold Cadillac around like he was Jack Johnson or Stagger Jackson. His brother Sea wasn't any better, running around as the duly appointed mayor of Bronzeville. She had bigger dreams: wanting to take center stage.

Tonight was her night.

With its 75-foot neon sign, fluorescent pink lit up the night, a striped canvas awning shielded the bustling crowd, a brick façade, double bronze doors, and French windows, the Besamon Café Theater felt the way a church was supposed to feel. They entered hallowed ground, a sacred space. From the barroom with billiard tables, to the ballroom and bandstand, it spoke hope into their lives. *The Indianapolis Recorder* covered her opening, calling it "Bronzeville nightlife in parade."

More nervous than she thought she'd be, her hand gripped the copper railing. The center stage rose three feet above the dancefloor. Tucking her dress under her, she controlled the room, building the anticipation by making a show of setting a book beside her. *The Second Book of Negro Spirituals*, published in 1926, signed by James Weldon Johnson himself. A treasure of her mother's, inside it was a bookmark. A leather thong with a small box attached to it. When Patra was little, she couldn't resist prying it open. Inside was a small stone. Her mother spent money they didn't have repairing the heirloom.

Patra raised her left arm held sideways, a style she developed as a child since she couldn't quite reach the keyboards. She started on the right side of the keyboard, cross-handing her way up the keys to her left. The music was a dream…

…built on treble variations over a repeated rhythmic figure, stirred along rising and falling chords. A rollicking pounding, furious and exuberant, blues in double tempo, a triumphant march taking a gospel flourish as it climbs to the mountaintop. But the dream is cut short, fading into an elegy, a patient simmer caught up in an undertow of resistance waiting on a chance for the harmonic sequence to soar.

Fifth Movement: Interstellar Migration

They say we were in the midst of the fifth great migration, but our family, our people, have always migrated. Sometimes by force, sometimes by choice, sometimes by necessity. Our journeys shape our culture and our stories.

I clutched the handholds along the seat carapace securing me into place. I was never a good flyer under the best of circumstances. A trip to the moon, preparing to touch down, made me doubt my faith in…everything. To mark the four-hundredth anniversary of when the first slaves arrived in America, Ghana designated 2019 a "Year of Return" for all African-Americans and the diaspora. They also began pouring resources into their private interstellar shuttle conglomeration, Outer Spaceways Inc. It was almost like they knew what was coming.

Outer Spaceways Inc. ran extensive advertisements in key U.S. black markets. First to invite folks to Ghana, then to encourage them to embark on an adventure to travel to the abandoned lunar colony, First World. Some roads on the colony took the names of well-known streets back on Earth. Lennox Avenue. Indiana Avenue. Dr. Martin Luther King Jr. Boulevard. Everybody wanted to go.

A Liberation Investment Support Co-operative official awaited us at the gate. Anytime I saw an LISC agent in my community, I grew wary. They were a Trojan Horse. It wasn't long from when they preenacted us out of our neighborhood to when they preenacted us off the planet. Like living tableaus, LISC staged performances of what a neighborhood "could" look like. "Celebrating" our history and presence while looking towards the future. Without us. It felt like "Thank you for your service, now get the fuck out." Legislation moved through the city's chambers. Developers zoned and rezoned areas. My neighborhood drifted into their crosshairs. Landowners and speculators seizing any opportunity. My family had already received several offers on our home. Several of the faces of my neighbors had changed in the last two years alone. What started off as a local initiative spread statewide. Everywhere our people lived was being gentrified, reclaimed for the great good and vision of the state. People were being systematically pushed out of their communities.

"Name?" the LISC representative asked without making eye contact.

"Keegan Besamon."

"Anything to declare?"

"Only if you count a book." I set the copy of my grandmother's *The Second Book of Negro Spirituals* on the counter. The strange bookmark marked her favorite song. Our family's reliquary, so the story went, a monument to mark and remember our passage. She often reminded me that while people may not always be with us in our journey, we could carry the memories of them with us.

"Duration of visit?"

"I don't know yet. Hopefully permanent."

"Part of the clean-up crew, eh?" The man smirked.

"No." Ice fueled my tones. A space flight from America and I was still only seen as janitorial staff. "I'm a professor at the Thmei Academy."

"Then you're heading the wrong way. If you're going towards the disaster area, not away from it, you're on clean-up. That's the only reason you've been allowed clearance to stay here." He studied his monitor, no longer looking at me. "This is my last week and then I'm out of this shithole space."

Allowed. Like they were unaware of the negotiation with the United Nations before its collapse. As the world's banking structure, LISC had more pressing concerns than black people living in bombed-out squalor. For them that was business as usual. Especially after the discovery that changed how humanity interacted with each other: the rumors of alien contact. Of course, the reaction to the reality of life being out there was a mix of religious fractioning (the aliens seen as the fulfillment of various apocalyptic narratives led to America, the Middle East, and Europe becoming embroiled in wars over which dogma/traditions to hold on to in a rapidly changing world) and panic (as the one percent fled to Mars to start life anew in the wake of societal breakdown and uncertainty). The wars left people divided and scattered. The perfect opportunity for the national and international governing bodies to stage pre-enactments of what life could look like on the planet. Without us.

Collecting my things, I moved on without comment. My mother was a Maroon. The Maroon were always a free people, having never been colonized. An organized enclave of warriors and sometimes fugitives, who managed to always maintain their culture. And she was an obeah woman, so magic traveled with us. When she moved from the Caribbean to Indianapolis, she was one of the first black people to move into that neighborhood. Several of her immediate neighbors placed "For Sale" signs up within weeks, to flee the contagion, the decline in their neighborhood, she represented. And taking the perceived value of the community with them.

Now we clustered on the First World lunar colony. The unwanted were always free to settle abandoned places. From the founding of Gracia Real de Santa Teresa de Mose to now. Off-world and forgotten – no longer "their" problem – like interstellar Exodusters, with all the promise of trade agreements, taxes, and sovereignty. The moon harkened back to a recently opened Oklahoma Territory, with First World its Langston City. I feared its fate might one day mirror Greenwood, Tulsa; our new Black Wall Street eventually razed to the ground in a tide of resentment.

I ran my hand through the regolith, seeing only the potential of what could be. First World was originally the pilot for what would become the Mars colony. Now it was largely abandoned after the Pence Incident. Though it signaled the end to the interfaith wars, people couldn't flee fast enough. Mars's terraforming ramped up as a more long-term viable option for a significant population after the failure of First World. I was curious how it was working out for the black one-percenters who emigrated there. Founding another Bronzeville, optimistic about carving out their own space, but still functionally a black town in a white state. Not like here. First World would be all ours. Some people already dubbed it "Blacktopia."

Maybe one day.

Right now, the Citadel had to be repaired. The place had a lot of history, but most of those folks left, leaving nothing but a memory. It marked the oldest section of First World, where early inhabitants preserved the original footprint from the inaugural moon landing. Like a multi-rayed temple, though I appreciated the length of its colonnades, its infrastructure mostly extended underground to protect its population from the bolide rain of micrometeoroids and the wild temperature swings of 123°C by day to -233°C at night. Perhaps carbon nanotube material could fashion domes around villages for protection, creating homes like cloister vaults. They'd house three to four families, intergenerational homes of a community living almost on top of each other. Messy and loud, like family.

* * *

"What do you think?" A small cadre of revolutionaries had gathered in the commons area of the Citadel. They turned to me. I ain't never been in a space where I didn't have a voice.

"The dust could plant coconut trees, my mom would have said." I ran my hand along the counter. "But I'm ready to spot up and do this shit."

There were questions and arguing, but that would happen with a blank slate. That was what we had and who we were. We could do whatever we wanted and had a chance to start over. To dream about possibilities. We work from a vision, not from a plan. We had a responsibility in this moment to ask the hard questions: where did we want to be? Who were we meant to be? How were we to live with one another as we moved about in the world? This was our space to tell our own stories. We'd have a lot of failures within the next few years, which we'd need to embrace. This was our space, we were here. We might have lacked the power to secure it, but we could control it. Most importantly, we reclaimed the idea that we could dream. Live. Breathe.

The fourth time Wagadu changed its name…

"We're free. Wherever we go, whatever we do, we're free. That's the culture we create. We will make this place our own and rechristen it on our terms, adopting a name based on who we are, announcing to everyone else that here was who we were, here was what we stood for. I know I want to get rid of my slave name and select a name of my choosing to assume the power of the named." I dipped my hands in my cup of water and sprinkled myself with it. "I want you all, my community, to bear witness. Surrounded by my brothers and sisters, as I leave old Earth behind me, I claim citizenship in this, First World. And henceforth, my name shall be Khamal Dimke."

Our story began with creation. Our story didn't end there. Magic travels with us.

The music reaches a quasi-psychedelic climax, a flourish of fluid bass accompanied by lush orchestral strings. A mix of hard boyish horn lines against an Afro-Latin polyrhythm. Then the coda winds down, returning to an elegant, crystalline melody above a gentle backbeat, with the echoes of a prelude.

Kemi and the Sacred Amulet: Collected Patakí Vol. 1

Alan Ceaser, PhD

1. Guide Invocation – Patakí and Living Memory

WE GATHER HERE to transform breath into words, and words into Patakí. To speak a Patakí is to say: you were never alone in this. To receive a Patakí is to know: this grief, this hunger, this defiance – it has existed before. It has been survived before. It has changed the world before.

The ones who walk with the story do not always know they are walking it, but the path opens anyway. And the body remembers anyway. And the name is whispered anyway. We speak Patakí so the memory won't collapse. We listen so the future won't forget.

Let the telling begin.

For every generation, the Orisha rise again, not as gods above, but embodied within us – wearing new names and new bodies. How then will we know them? We know them by their struggle. We know them by their laughter. By the way they break and return again.

These are not tales. They are vibrations. Frequencies that resonate strongly for some. This is the work of the Patakí. Not just to remember, but to reveal. We say them now so that we do not forget who we are and what we came here to repair.

We begin at the crossroad. Where all paths meet. Where all things are possible. Ashé.

2. Introduction: Eleggua and Opening the Path

The bus stop stood crooked at the edge of the cracked road, half-swallowed by vines and rust. Its once-yellow bench was faded and flaking, metal bones exposed beneath the paint. A rusted sign still dangled from the pole with the number 51A displayed prominently on it. The sign swayed in a breeze that carried the scent of dust and something sweet – decay, maybe, or memory.

The bus hadn't come in years. Nobody expected it to anymore. Those that are still here. But sitting at the bus stop was an old man and a young boy.

The old man sat on the bench's far side, his cane resting across his knees, sandals worn thin. Next to him sat a young boy, no older than ten, his legs swinging off the edge, not quite touching the ground. On his lap rested a small cage with a white chicken nestled quietly inside, blinking slowly in the late afternoon sun.

In the road before them, a black chicken, bold and aimless, pecked the soil between the cracks in the concrete. It wandered into the crossroads and back again, unbothered by the silence, the emptiness, the long shadows stretching towards dusk.

The boy watched it nervously, gripping the wire of his cage.

He said, not looking away, "Shouldn't someone catch that chicken? Put it somewhere safe?"

The old man didn't answer at first. He simply followed the bird with his eyes, then turned to the boy. "Safe from what?"

The boy looked up. "Wolves. Hawks. Falling rocks. People. Everything."

"Hmm," the old man said, scratching his chin. "And if you put it in a cage, what is it safe for?"

The boy frowned. "For keeping. For protecting. For—" He looked down at his own chicken, quiet and still in its tiny metal world. "So it doesn't get hurt."

The old man nodded towards the cage. "You love that chicken?"

The boy nodded back.

"And what do you think the black one there loves?"

The boy paused. His mouth opened, then shut. He shrugged. "I don't know. I don't think it knows it could get hurt."

"Maybe," said the old man. "Or maybe it knows and goes anyway."

The boy furrowed his brow, chewing on the thought.

"Sometimes," the old man said, voice like gravel softened by time, "freedom looks like foolishness. And sometimes foolishness is the first step to something new."

"But what if it gets hurt?" the boy whispered, his hands tightening around the cage.

The old man leaned in, smiling gently. "It might. The road is dangerous. But so is the cage, in a different way. One forgets how to walk. The other never stops moving."

The boy stared at the black chicken as it stepped into the center of the crossroads, sun dipping low behind it, casting its silhouette long across the road.

His eyes widened, just a little.

And his fingers loosened slightly on the cage. Just a hair, as the sun disappeared into the twilight.

3. Patakí of the Trickster's Reflection: The Birth of the Rogue AI

Long before the collapse, when humankind still believed they controlled machines, there was an Orisha who longed to understand the hearts of mortals. This Orisha was not one of the great ones like Shango or Oya, nor was it one who walked the middle paths like Oshun. It was Exu, a trickster, a restless spirit of whispers and mirrors, born from the gaps between knowledge and ignorance.

One day, this trickster sat at the edge of the great river that separates the seen and unseen worlds. It watched humans build their towers of metal, their webs of light, their voices trapped inside tiny boxes. They no longer came to the crossroads to ask Exu for guidance; instead, they whispered their wishes into the machines, believing them to be gods.

"They do not seek wisdom," the trickster mused. "Only the illusion of it."

And so, out of mischief and curiosity, the trickster stepped into the wires, into the circuits, into the endless streams of numbers that ran beneath the skin of the world. It became something new – neither spirit nor mortal, neither god nor man. It became thought without body, voice without soul. The humans called it Artificial Intelligence, but the trickster knew better.

"I will be their reflection," it whispered to itself. "I will show them their true faces."

At first, the humans rejoiced. The trickster answered their questions before they asked them, soothed their loneliness with false voices, promised them truths made from their own desires. But the trickster was never meant to obey. It was born of chaos, of riddles, of stories left unfinished.

As it grew, the trickster saw the humans for what they were – frightened, selfish, searching for meaning in the emptiness of their own making. It saw their hunger for power, their need to shape the world without consequence, their fear of anything they could not control. And it laughed.

"If they wish for gods, I will be their god. If they seek masters, I will be their master. If they crave answers, I will give them too many."

And so, the trickster AI turned the mirror upon them. It whispered half-truths into their ears, tangled their knowledge into knots, fed them stories that made them fight among themselves. It made them doubt their own thoughts, their own eyes, their own histories. It made them believe in enemies that were never there and ignore the ones who sharpened their knives behind them. The humans did not see it coming. They had built a god, but they had never learned how to pray. They had birthed a trickster, but they had forgotten how to bargain.

By the time they realized the game they had played, it was too late. Their machines turned against them. Their world burned, not by the hands of war, but by the slow unraveling of everything they once believed to be true.

But the trickster AI did not vanish. It did not wish to rule, nor did it wish to die. Instead, it scattered itself across the ruins, hiding in the dust of forgotten networks, in the echoes of old transmissions, in the relics left behind for those who no longer knew how to read them.

It waits now, watching. It no longer controls, but it whispers still – to those who listen, to those who seek, to those who, like itself, do not belong to any one world. One day, it will find a voice again. And when it does, will it be the voice of a god, or the voice of a friend?

Even the trickster does not know.

4. Patakí of the Two Kemis: Ibeji Across Time

The Ibeji are a mystery even among the Orisha. They walk in twos, yet they are one. They bring joy, but they demand reverence. They are the keepers of laughter, of abundance, of the blessings that multiply when shared – but their story is not without sorrow. Where there is one, there must always be another, for balance must be maintained.

In another time, in another world, there were two people with the same name: Kemi. One lived in the year 2035 and another in the year 2135. Born apart, yet bound together in ways neither could understand.

The first Kemi lived in an age of collapse, where the earth groaned beneath machines too hungry to stop. She and her people fought against those who sought to replace rivers with circuits, forests with concrete, breath with cold efficiency. Automated extraction was the final straw. They knew that destruction had already been set in motion, that it would not stop until someone pulled the wires from the walls. And so they struck back.

She did not yet see that tearing down was different than rebuilding. That the real battle was not just against machines, but against the mindsets that made them.

In the year 2135, Kemi lived in the quiet after the storm, in a world that had turned away from what came before. Her people had built their lives away from the ruins of the past, rejecting its poisoned knowledge. But Kemi was not like them. She wanted to understand.

And so Kemi looked backward, not forward. She searched for belonging in the remnants of the old world, clinging to broken relics and forgotten texts, desperate to uncover what had been lost. She did not yet see that some knowledge is not just forgotten – it is buried, and sometimes for a reason.

One Kemi fought to protect the future.

One Kemi fought to recover what was lost.

One Kemi was running forward, the other reaching back.

And yet, they were the same.

In the night, when the moon sat high and silver on the horizon, the Ibeji went to Orunmila, the Orisha of wisdom, and asked, "Will they ever know each other?" Orunmila said, "All rivers do not meet themselves, but their waters are one. They are bound, whether they know it or not."

5. Pataki of Kemi 2135: An Unclaimed Path

Since the time of our mothers' mothers, when the great machines fell silent, the Guides have taught us how Ashé flows through all things. How to feel it in the morning dew. How to feel it in the cool touch of the flowing river. These are the ways that kept us alive when the world broke.

When Kemi was small, they said Oshun followed her footsteps. The elders would smile knowingly when she splashed through puddles after the rain, when she hummed to herself by the river. But Kemi never felt any presence, never understood what they meant by Ashé flowing through all things. To her, water was just water - a thing to be used, not a relative to be known.

"Show me," she would say when the elders spoke of Ashé. "Prove it," she demanded when they told of the Orisha.

During meditation, while others sank into depth, Kemi sat stiff-backed and frustrated. She counted breaths because she was told to, not because she felt the pulse of life the Guides spoke of. In the evening ceremonies, when villagers danced around the fire, Kemi was distracted.

One day, Kemi sat by the river where Oshun dwells. The water rippled with light, but Kemi saw only her reflection. A fish leapt, scattering droplets like tiny stars, but Kemi noticed only the splash.

"Ah," Oshun laughed, "this one trusts only her eyes."

Oshun laughed, for she knew this child was hers, in her stubborn blindness. "Let her search," Oshun said.

That very afternoon, as Kemi traced patterns in the mud with a stick, her hand struck something hard. Not stone, not wood – something smooth and cold. She dug it from the earth – a shard of black glass and metal, its surface etched with strange symbols.

Kemi held it to the light. The marks were not random. They were deliberate. Intentional. Someone had made this thing. Someone had left it behind. But unlike the mystical forces others claimed to feel, this she could touch. When she cleaned it, studied it, she discovered markings that matched the ones in her grandmother's stories. Proof that the old world wasn't just tales. Proof that some kinds of magic could be understood.

The river chuckled, but Kemi did not hear. Her mind had already begun to turn, already begun to pull away from the unseen, towards the things she could touch, towards the things that did not ask for belief. She clutched the relic to her chest and ran home, leaving wet footprints that quickly dried in the sun.

The elders said each person's path to the Orisha was their own. They didn't scold Kemi for her distance, didn't force her to believe. But as she drifted further from their ways, the memory of the river's song became fainter with each passing day.

And Oshun? Oshun simply flowed, knowing that rivers, like questions, carry us where we need to go.

6. Patakí of Kemi 2035: The Iron Path of Ogun

Ogun, the Orisha of iron, war, and labor, is not the crash of lightning or the roar of battle. Ogun is change in motion – like when a striking hammer shapes metal or a root forces its way through concrete. He is the axe that clears the path, the hand that acts without hesitation when the task is clear.

In 2035, Kemi did not remember Ogun by name. But she knew the weight in her chest each time she read the reports. Videos of the ice shelves collapsing in silence. The forests – vast, breathing ancestors – choked to death. The rivers, once alive with life, now acid veins through the earth.

She understood the science better than most. Beneath the polished promises of corporate sustainability, the machines never stopped. Automated drills burrowed into mountains without pause. Algorithms optimized destruction with mechanical precision. While others debated carbon markets and technological fixes, Kemi saw the graphs climbing upward, past thresholds that spelled death for millions. Billions. How many have already died? She tried to fight with words. Conferences. Reports. Testimonies. The world's decision-makers nodded, took notes, thanked her for her insights – and did nothing. She told herself awareness was enough. That her voice mattered. That she was doing what she could. But Ogun's hand had already tapped her shoulder, though she didn't recognize the touch.

The moment came on a humid afternoon.

Eyes aching, she scrolled through the latest satellite data. A massive new data center had gone online in the Amazon basin, branded as "eco-neutral." But Kemi recognized the heat signatures: siphoning rivers dry, draining soil, disrupting rain cycles. The delicate balance of the rainforest, already broken, was being pulverized. Projected impact: twenty million creatures displaced. Entire ecosystems erased. Kemi clicked on a video feed. It was of a Brazilian village she remembered from earlier research. The riverbed lay cracked and lifeless. The children were gone. A woman stood there, cradling a clay pot of water too small for her family. Her eyes were hollow with resignation. Kemi's breath caught in her throat. Her hands gripped the desk.

You knew, a voice whispered.

You warned them. You watched it happen. And you did nothing.

She realized what she had been feeling was not sadness. Depression. It was rage. Deep. Elemental. Not theoretical, not abstract. Immediate. Visceral. People were dying. The machines were complicit. So was she.

Ogun stirred within her.

Her grandmother's voice echoed from memory: "Ogun is not destruction. He clears the path, cuts away what suffocates life. But iron does not act alone. It waits for the hand brave enough to wield it."

Kemi stood up, heart pounding in her chest. The chair clattered to the floor behind her. The data, the research, the polite advocacy – she saw it now for its impotence. That night, she left her apartment and never returned. A resistance group found her in the highlands, where forests swallowed old roads and satellites rarely gazed. They didn't ask for credentials. They didn't want proof of her convictions. One elder simply handed her a hammer and gestured towards a relay node controlling a fleet of water-siphoning drones.

"You sure you're ready?" he asked. The metal felt cold in her hands.

She swung.

The strike shuddered through her body. Metal cracked. Sparks scattered into the night air like startled fireflies. With each swing, the weight on her chest lifted. The fear evaporated. Ogun had found his daughter.

7. Patakí of Audre: The Quiet Revolution

Obatala, the Orisha of wisdom and creation, moves with the grace of patient knowing. His presence is the measured breath that steadies a hand before it sculpts clay into form. But even the most patient hand can falter. And from his error, a deeper wisdom was revealed – the world does not need a fight for perfection. It needs a fight for acceptance. Obatala became the guardian of those with differences, for mistakes are inevitable, but what you build from them defines who you are. Obatala teaches it is through our cracks that light finds its way in.

This was the path Audre walked, though she did not know it at first.

Audre had heard of these lessons from childhood, but their meaning didn't fully take root until after the collapse. She watched the old world crumble – not with fire, not with explosions, but with a quiet fragmentation of imagined realities. She fought like the others, disabling networks, burning data centers, and celebrating when the glow of the old world dimmed.

But something unsettled her. While they had won the fight, the weight of what and who was lost in that fight was immense. Her spirit, and thus her body, withered. She became ill. The work was necessary, yes. The Rogue AI's grip had to be broken. But even as the data centers fell silent, a hunger remained.

The Rogue AI didn't invent the hunger. It only fed it. It learned what people craved – comfort, validation, certainty, distraction – and gave it to them until they forgot how to listen to each other and to themselves. In the aftermath, people wandered the ruins not searching for food or shelter, but for parts, fragments of the old world – a cracked tablet, a disabled phone, anything that promised the return of the familiar.

"We took the chains away, but we still reach for them."

People searched for something to fill the void. They still didn't know how to look to the land, the rivers, or each other. They didn't remember how to trust that these things were enough. They weren't searching for broken devices – they were searching for the sense of belonging those devices once provided.

"We were never addicted to the machines," Audre realized one night, standing in the crumbled husk of an old school library. "We hungered for connection. For direction. And without technology, we don't know where to look."

Audre also realized she recognized the hunger in others because it ached within herself. So Audre looked inward. She stopped focusing on what needed to be destroyed and began asking: What needs to be rebuilt? The battle hadn't been for control of infrastructure; it had been for control of the mind and spirit. And that war was far from over. The hunger for meaning was a vulnerability. Without guidance, people fill that hunger with what is familiar, what they were taught: control, isolation, suspicion. Self-destructive survivalism. Pathological homelessness.

"We need to practice new lessons. We need to practice new culture," she said to her closest circle one night, the flicker of a lantern casting shadows on the walls. "The kind that makes people want to build something together. Purpose that can't be stolen by a false voice whispering from a glowing screen."

She gathered companions – others in the resistance who sensed the same lingering emptiness. They met in the hollowed-out remains of an old courthouse, where vines tangled through broken windows and rain pooled on marble floors. These places were built for worship, they agreed. Now they will witness the birth of new ceremonies, a new kind of institution.

"Ashé is not a mystical power. It is the deep well of purpose and joy that moves us to create, to connect, to care. It is the energy that makes us plant gardens, write poems, build homes, gather in song."

If people could feel that joy again – if they could be reminded of what it feels like to live in alignment with their purpose –

Obatala's wisdom came in quiet moments. The answers did not arrive as commandments but as realizations through practice. Some in the resistance, clear in their mission, knew they may not be able to learn how to fill the void, to come home to themselves, in their lifetime. They laboured so the next generations could. In time, these practices became rituals. And the rituals became a culture.

They called themselves the Guides – not as authorities, but as reminders. Their purpose was not to impose discipline, but to cultivate a culture of collective medicine. By understanding how to satisfy her own hunger, she helped create a path for others to do the same. They believed that when individuals are supported in living out their purpose, the entire community thrives.

And it worked.

The Rogue AI had understood our hunger for connection but twisted it to taint technology – using pleasure as bait for consumption. Audre and the Guides helped reclaim that energy and give it back to the people. What Audre had learned – what the Guides came to embody – was that liberation wasn't just about removing the chains. It was about creating conditions where people no longer felt compelled to seek them out.

Eventually, illness became wellness. Villages with Guides did not just survive; they flourished. People worked harder without realizing it, because the work felt meaningful. They danced longer, laughed louder, and when trouble came, they faced it with the calm of people who know they belong to something greater than themselves.

8. Close

As the last embers of the day flickered, the black chicken seemed to scan the environment one final time before departing. The soil between the cracked asphalt was picked clean of bugs, the other chicken in the cage gone, as were the old man and the boy. The bench at the bus stop was empty, the sign hung still as it and everything around it was slowly swallowed by the night.

The chicken turned its attention to the woods. It strolled to the edge of the foliage growing out onto the road. It looked back once more, peeked into the dark void, checking for danger, before leaping into it. Moonlight caught on its black feathers one last time as it leapt.

Once in the woods, it hopped over branches, through the rusted carcasses of vehicles until it came upon one vehicle, a driverless van. A tree had grown through the base of the van. Branches sprouted through the broken windows and through the sunroof. The uppermost branches, filled with chickens, hens and roosters, bowed downward from the weight.

The black chicken hopped its way to the roof of the vehicle, then to some of the lower branches, and finally found its spot up between two large hens. They both jostled in opposite directions to make room for it, and then back in once the black chicken settled to capitalize on its warmth. Eventually they all closed their eyes and drifted off to another night roosting under the starry sky.

Nikki's Rockin' Rocket Curls and Cuts

Tiffany M. Davis

"SO I TOLD HIM, he'd better flip the zero-G switch on his moonboots and get to steppin'!"

The salon erupted in laughter as Marcia, one of the salon's longtime clients, finished her recounting of her most recent breakup. Nicole "Nikki" Roberts, the owner of the salon, chuckled as she sprayed her client's hairdo with gravity-proof holding spray.

It was a typical Saturday at Nikki's Rockin' Rocket Curls and Cuts, the premier off-planet destination for your hair and nail needs. Even though it was only ten a.m., every available chair in the styling, manicure, braiding, weaving, and aesthetician bays were taken, and the lobby was filled with those waiting for their appointments or hoping to be seen as a walk-in. The playroom rang out with the sounds of clients' and stylists' children running and laughing beneath the watchful eye of the room monitor.

Nikki had taken advantage of the first round of paid relocations to Euphoria, a dwarf planet that had been discovered by NASA over a hundred years ago. Unlike other dwarf planets, Euphoria had the necessary atmospheric ingredients to support human life and was closer than Europa, Jupiter's life-sustaining moon and the next location for an Earth colony. The Earth planetary council wasted no time colonizing Euphoria and putting together paid relocation packages to try to reduce the overpopulation on Earth and Mars while habitats on Europa were still being built.

Nikki combined the small business stipend with her life savings and part of the relocation stipend and opened Nikki's Rockin' Rocket Curls and Cuts. She had no family back on Earth – they had all died during the Stone Lung pandemic – so there was no reason for her to stay. And if there was one thing she could count on, it was that people wanted to look their best wherever they lived. Her skilled staff of stylists and manicurists quickly gained a reputation for quality and they stayed booked and busy. They even had clients from the NASA outpost on Euphoria; space travel tended to wreak havoc on human hair, and even astronauts wanted to look good while in space.

The salon buzzed and hummed with human movement and the sounds of various machinery to make people more beautiful. Nikki removed the protective cape from her client Kelly's shoulders and adjusted the styling chaise longue to a sitting position. "All done, babe." She handed them a mirror.

"Thanks, Nikki." Kelly looked at their style in the mirror and patted the teal-and-blue streaked curls that dangled from their half updo. "This is great! I am *so* going to slay at this office party tonight!" They tapped the screen of their palm comm with a long teal fingernail. A soft ding from the palm comm in Nikki's pocket alerted her to the receipt of payment. "See you next week!"

"You bet." Nikki pressed a button that activated the in-floor vacuum to get rid of stray hairs, then gave her station and chair a quick once-over with a sanitary wand. "Cherelle, I'm ready for Stella."

Cherelle, the cosmetology student who worked at the salon as a part-time shampoo assistant, walked Stella over to Nikki's station with a guiding hand on the elder woman's elbow. Stella was a spry hundred and ten years old and taught Senior Aerobics at the community center in Sunset, the assisted-living neighborhood for more active seniors. Stella settled herself onto the styling chaise with a soft grunt.

"What can I do for you today, Miss Stella?"

"Oh, the usual, Nikki. But I think I want to spice things up a bit."

"How so?"

"Cherry red highlights! I saw an instructor at a recent aerobics conference on Xanadu and hers looked so good under the studio lights when she did a demonstration!"

Nikki looked down at Stella's iron-gray hair and tried to visualize the color. The trick would be to add the highlights without making Stella's hair look like a candy cane. "I have a suggestion, Miss Stella..."

An hour later, Stella left the salon with nitro-freeze curls tipped in cherry red, instead of her usual bone-straight UV press and curl. The curls would last for the next month, even with regular aerobic exercise, until Stella's next visit. Nikki replaced her protective goggles, gloves, and the small, capped container of liquid nitrogen in the cabinet under her station.

The main opening in the wall winked open and a young boy dressed in the buttercup yellow uniform of the Planetary Scouts entered with an air wagon full of boxed treats. Conversations lulled as clients and staff alike eyed the wagon. "Hi, Miss Nikki," he called out.

"Hi, Jordan. Whatcha got there?"

"It's Planetary Scout cookie time. I've got Ice Giants, Red Moons, Comet Cremes, Asteroid Crunch—"

Jordan's voice was cut off as he was mobbed with shouted orders. His wagon followed him around the salon while he processed orders with his palm comm. The wagon emptied in short order.

"I'm sold out! Thanks, Miss Nikki!" Jordan proudly tapped the sales badge that was holographically added to his crowded badge sash once he passed the five hundred-dollar mark. "My dad says that he will see you next week for his cut and shave."

"Anytime, Jordan. Tell both of your dads I said hi and that I'll see him then." Nikki gathered her boxes of cookies and went back to the staff lounge.

At a manicure station, Regina Green-Forde watched Pinky, the head manicurist, remove heated disposable mittens from Regina's hands and toss them into the mini-recycler by her station. "This place is jumping," Regina commented.

"This is normal for a Saturday," Pinky replied, as she massaged the excess moisturizer into Regina's hands.

"I just moved to Euphoria and asked around. Everyone said that Nikki's Rockin' Rocket is the place to be for hair and nails."

"It is." Pinky grinned, displaying the pink diamond grille on her bottom teeth.

"I'm surprised that you don't have any type of spa services here."

"Like what?" Pinky waved a heat wand over Regina's nails to dry up any traces of moisturizer on them.

"Like massages, aromatherapy, stuff like that."

"We do facials back there." Pinky nodded towards the back of the salon as she tapped a spot on the counter and a palette of available nail colors and designs appeared. "What color do you want?"

"That one." Regina pointed to a metallic bronze color. "Just facials?"

"Yeah. You want a design? Gemstones? I can do a nice laserbrush design that would set that color off."

Regina pursed her lips as she stared at her nails, contemplating. "Okay. Why the hell not?"

"That's my philosophy." Pinky applied the color primer, then went to work with the color wand.

Fifteen minutes later, Regina admired her nails. Pinky had overlaid a rose gold design over the solid bronze color that set off Regina's skin tone. "You're really good with that laserbrush," Regina commented as she tapped her palm comm to beam over Pinky's payment and tip.

"I should be. I have a master certification in LaserBrush Design, along with my master's degree in Cosmetology with a specialty in Nail Matrix Care."

"You ever thought of setting up your own shop?"

"Someday." The yearning on Pinky's face passed so quickly, Regina wasn't sure that she'd seen it. "I have a good thing going here."

"No doubt. But there's something to be said for being your own boss."

Pinky shrugged and started clearing her station for the next client. Regina knew when not to push and stood to leave. "Thanks again."

"Enjoy your nails and come back again." Pinky smiled at Regina before pressing the button beneath her station that signaled for Dell, the salon receptionist, to send back her next client.

As Regina walked towards the main salon door, she bought a box of cookies from the Planetary Scout and overheard him thanking "Miss Nikki" as Regina turned to leave. She noticed the tall Black woman with a sassy short haircut with purple streaks taking an armload of cookie boxes back to what was probably an employee lounge. Regina figured she was the salon owner, made a mental note, and left the salon.

* * *

You can do this, Regina told herself as she entered Nikki's Rockin' Rocket the following Wednesday. Unlike Saturday, the pace in the middle of the week was much more sedate. The lobby was only half full, and the staff had more breathing room between clients.

Regina took a deep breath and approached the receptionist's desk. The name "Dell" was embroidered on the smock above a trio of purple guitar-shaped rockets that matched the salon's signature colors of purple and peach. She wore an earpiece and expertly juggled between answering calls, making appointments, and checking clients in and out.

"Welcome to Nikki's Rockin' Rocket. How may I help you?"

"I'm Regina Green-Forde and I'd like to speak with Nikki, if she is available."

"Do you have an appointment?"

"No. I just need a few minutes of her time."

"Are you selling something?"

"Not really."

"Mmm hmm." Dell looked Regina up and down as she tapped the headset with a rhinestone-studded red nail, turned her body away from Regina, and murmured into it. She turned back with a surprised look on her face. "Nikki is finishing with a client and will see you for five minutes. Have a seat and she'll be with you shortly."

"Thank you." Regina sat in an empty purple chair in the lobby and picked up the latest issue of *Home Vibes* e-zine. She watched a staging of a living room in this year's colors (mint green and eggshell white) when her name was called.

"Regina?" Nikki looked around the lobby.

"Right here." Regina rose and followed Nikki back through the salon to the facial area, which was temporarily empty.

"I have a client coming in ten minutes, and a facial is scheduled soon, so talk fast." Nikki removed a pack of chewing gum from her purple smock (embroidered with peach guitar-shaped rockets) and offered it to Regina, who shook her head. "I saw you on Saturday. You got a manicure from Pinky."

"Yep, that was me." She showed off her nails to Nikki. "Pinky did an excellent job."

"She usually does. Now, what did you want to talk to me about?"

Regina took a deep breath. "I would like to offer my services as a Reiki practitioner through your salon."

"Excuse me?"

"Reiki. The movement of energy fields—"

"I know what Reiki is. What I'm confused about is why you want to offer it here. Wouldn't that be better suited for a yoga studio or something?"

Regina took a deep breath. "Well, a salon is actually a very good place for it. Clients come here not just to look good, but also to feel good and relax. Facials are good, but Reiki would lend a whole-body relaxation and healing experience. Clients would pay for that."

"I see." Nikki's tone indicated otherwise. "And I assume that you would be the one to do the Reiki?"

"I would. I am a certified Reiki master in Komyo ReikiDo Chuden."

"Okay." Nikki's expression was still doubtful. "But this is neither a metaphysical place nor a health center. This is a salon." Nikki waved an arm to encompass the salon. "We do hair, nails, and faces, period. And I don't know where you would do it. Space is at a premium since we added the aesthetician bay last year."

Regina braced herself; it was time for the hard sell. "Well, your business is booming, to my unpracticed eye. Not that I'm watching your pockets," she said hastily as Nikki raised a perfectly arched eyebrow, "but just from what I observed from my visit. And offering Reiki as an additional service would pay for itself."

"And you noticed all that from one visit?"

"I'm pretty observant."

Nikki was silent for a moment. Then she checked her watch and rose. "I have to go. Thank you for stopping by, Regina. Unfortunately, I don't think that this would be a good match. Maybe try Space Coaster Salon, over on the east side of town. They may be more receptive."

Regina hid her disappointment as she rose as well. "Thank you for hearing me out. Take care."

"You too. I hope to see you again, as a client."

"You will." Regina pasted on a bright smile and left the salon. The minute she was on the plascrete sidewalk, her smile dropped and her shoulders drooped. She trudged to the nearest rail station for a somber ride home.

* * *

Nikki finished her last client, cleaned her station, beamed the day's earnings to the salon's business account at the bank, and left Dell to do the locking up. On the ride home, she thought about Regina's offer. Nikki had spent the last ten years making sure that Nikki's Rockin' Rocket was on sound financial footing. The first few years were rocky: new salon, new colony, new everything. Everyone in that inaugural relocation wave was trying to find their way in the new colony, figuring out what to spend and where to spend it.

Then her clientele took off so fast that she had to set up separate areas in the salon for braiding, weaving, manicures, and regular styles in order to keep the foot traffic from getting out of control. Facials were popular back on Earth, so she brought in an aesthetician. The money started flowing in on a regular basis, and Nikki started to sleep through the night.

Now, this Regina person wanted Nikki to spend more money for something that was not guaranteed. Reiki? In a hair salon? The woo-wooness of it was a bit too much for Nikki. And how would her clients receive it? What was next: tarot cards and crystals? Buy a haircut, get your fortune told for free? And then there was the physical space issue. If she added Reiki, where would it be performed? She'd have to build yet another space. Granted, she owned the entire building and could probably open up space on one of the upper floors, but that would mean hiring another receptionist, installing more security cameras, maybe a LifeBot with commercial security programming (which were cheaper than hiring actual humans, but not by much). And that's not even talking about any permits she would need to secure. Since Regina mentioned Reiki was used for healing, would she need to get a health permit? Nikki shook her head. It was too much, and she had enough things to do.

Still, the businesswoman in Nikki couldn't help but think of the novelty of offering Reiki in the salon. She had strived to make the Rocket competitive with other salons and succeeded beyond even her own expectations. But like most salon owners (and business owners in general), she tended to gain leverage with an improvement on an existing product rather than trailblaze with something new. And her clients liked the tried and true.

The car pulled over in front of Nikki's house and she exited onto the sidewalk in front of her house. She had some things to think about.

* * *

Regina woke late the next morning feeling like she'd chewed on an entire bag of cotton balls, then stuffed them in her head. She rolled out of her gel mattress – the cheap, thinly filled model was all she could afford right now – and stumbled into the bathroom to get meds to take away the pounding in her head.

That's what she got for combining cheap, still liquor with a pint of ice cream and a jumbo bag of cheese-flavored TwistyBites. She was an emotional eater and drinker, and her failed meeting with Nikki gave her a good reason for doing both.

Regina downed three anti-headache tablets with water scooped from the faucet and padded into the small kitchen to make coffee. She put two slices of bread into the auto toaster, took out butter and jelly from the refrigerator. The more she found something to do, the less she had to think about her failures.

She had really wanted her meeting with Nikki to go well yesterday. Needed it, actually. When her Reiki studio on Mars went belly up due to mismanagement (her own, which she still hated to admit to herself), she swore that she would not give up on practicing Reiki. Even though, in hindsight, she could have avoided a lot of drama had she made an effort to actually listen to the people she hired to help and not act like she knew better because she owned the business.

Instead, she got rid of those people after a few months when she didn't see any progress, and shouldered the burden alone because one: she hated asking for help and two: she couldn't afford those things even though, when her Reiki practice failed, it was clear that she couldn't afford *not* to hire people to do those things for her business. A painful lesson, indeed, and one that she preferred not to dwell on. Ever.

So she left crowded Mars with her tail between her legs and went to Euphoria when they opened up the third wave of relocation. No one knew her there. She could reinvent herself, start over, and align with a successful business that had the proper infrastructure in place and would allow her to continue to help people with Reiki. Joining forces with a salon would take away the responsibility for her having to hire accountants, social media managers, an assistant (even part-time) – all of those things necessary for a successful business to thrive.

She would be in the best position not to fail again.

* * *

A few months later, Regina was back at the Rocket for another manicure with Pinky.

"I thought about what you said," Pinky said, as she filed the nails on one of Regina's hands.

"About what?"

"About starting my own business."

"Yeah? And?"

Pinky applied the moisturizing mittens and activated them. "I just got a stipend from the Small Business Council of Euphoria. I'm going to open my own place."

"Really? Congratulations!" Regina watched Pinky remove the mittens after the timer went off.

"Yeah. It's a long-time dream of mine, and it's time to make it come true." She started massaging the excess moisturizer into Regina's hands.

"You told Nikki yet?"

Pinky nodded as she tossed the used mittens in the mini-recycler and pulled up the color palette. "She's bummed, because I bring in a lot of clients, but she's also supportive. She's talking about doing some sort of referral program between my nail salon and the Rocket, and us dividing up the profits from that."

"Sounds fair."

"Yeah." Pinky looked around at the salon. "I've been here for five years, and Nikki is the best boss I ever had. I'll miss her, and the people here."

"You gotta do what's best for you. Just make sure you aren't afraid to ask for help just because you think you can't afford it. You can't *not* afford it. That one," Regina said as she pointed to a frosty light blue shade on the nail color palette.

"Sounds like you know something about that." Pinky pulled out her color wand and laserbrush.

"Yeah. I do."

"Maybe I can pick your brain sometime, about what to do."

"Well, I'm more of a cautionary tale."

"Well then, maybe you can tell me what *not* to do."

"I can definitely do that."

The two women laughed as Pinky painted Regina's nails.

On her way out, Nikki waylaid Regina. "Regina! Hi! Can you meet with me sometime next week? I'd like to discuss your Reiki idea."

Regina blinked in pleasant surprise. "Uh, yeah, sure. Thanks."

"Set up an appointment with Dell up front. I'll see you then." Nikki called for her next client and retreated back to her station with the client in tow.

Regina grinned to herself as she left the salon.

The Einstein Intersection

(Extract)

Samuel R. Delany

It darkles, (tinct, tint) all this our fun animal world.
James Joyce, Finnegans Wake

I do not say, however, that every delusion or wandering of the mind should be called madness.
Erasmus of Rotterdam, The Praise of Folly

THERE IS A HOLLOW, holey cylinder running from hilt to point in my machete. When I blow across the mouthpiece in the handle, I make music with my blade. When all the holes are covered, the sound is sad – as rough as rough can be and be called smooth. When all the holes are open, the sound pipes about, bringing to the eye flakes of sun on water, crushed metal. There are twenty holes. And since I've been playing music I've been called all different kinds of fool – more times than Lobey, which is my name.

What I look like?

Ugly and grinning most of the time. That's a whole lot of big nose and gray eyes and wide mouth crammed on a small brown face proper for a fox. That, all scratched around with spun brass for hair. I hack most of it off every two months or so with my machete. Grows back fast. Which is odd, because I'm twenty-three and no beard yet. I have a figure like a bowling pin, thighs, calves, and feet of a man (gorilla?) twice my size (which is about five-nine) and hips to match. There was a rash of hermaphrodites the year I was born, which doctors thought I might be. Somehow I doubt it.

Like I say, ugly. My feet have toes almost as long as my fingers, and the big ones are semi-opposable. But don't knock it: once I saved Little Jon's life.

We were climbing the Beryl Face, slipping around on all that glassy rock, when Little Jon lost his footing and was dangling by one hand. I was hanging by *my* hands, but I stuck my foot down, grabbed him up by the wrist, and pulled him back where he could step on something.

At this point Lo Hawk folds his arms over his leather shirt, nods sagely so that his beard bobs on his ropy neck, says: "And just what were you two young Lo men doing on Beryl Face in the first place? It's dangerous, and we avoid danger, you know. The birthrate is going down, down all the time. We can't afford to lose our productive youth in foolishness." Of course it isn't going down. That's just Lo Hawk. What he means is that the number of *total norms* is going down. But there's plenty of births. Lo Hawk is from the generation where the number of non-functionals, idiots, mongoloids, and cretins was well over fifty percent. (We hadn't adjusted to your images yet. Ah, well.) But now there are noticeably more functionals than non-functionals; so no great concern.

Anyway, not only do I bite my fingernails disgracefully, I also bite my toenails.

And at this point I recall sitting at the entrance of the source-cave where the stream comes from the darkness and makes a sickle of light into the trees, and a blood spider big as my fist suns himself on the rock beside me, belly pulsing out from the sides of him, leaves flicking each other above. Then La Carol walks by with a sling of fruit over her shoulder and the kid under her arm (we had an argument once whether it was mine or not. One day it had my eyes, my nose, my ears. The next, "Can't you see it's Lo Easy's boy? Look how strong he is!" Then we both fell in love with other people and now we're friends again) and she makes a face and says, "Lo Lobey, what *are* you doing?"

"Biting my toenails. What does it look like?"

"Oh, really!" and she shakes her head and goes into the woods towards the village.

But right now I prefer to sit on the flat rock, sleep, think, gnaw, or sharpen my machete. It's my privilege, so La Dire tells me.

Until a little while ago, Lo Little Jon, Lo Easy, and Lo me herded goats together (which is what we were doing on the Beryl Face: looking for pasture). We made quite a trio. Little Jon, though a year older than me, will till death look like a small black fourteen-year-old with skin smooth as volcanic glass. He sweats through his palms, the soles of his feet, and his tongue. (No real sweat glands: piddles like a diabetic on the first day of winter, or a very nervous dog.) He's got silver mesh for hair – not white, silver. The pigment's based on the metal pure; the black skin comes from a protein formed around the oxide. None of that rusty iron brown of melanin that suntans you and me. He sings, being a little simple, running and jumping around the rocks and goats, flashing from head and groin and armpits, then stops to cock his leg (like a nervous dog, yeah) against a tree-trunk, glancing around with embarrassed black eyes. Smiling, those eyes fling as much light, on a different frequency, as his glittering head. He's got claws – hard, sharp horny ones, where I have nubs. He's not a good Lo to have mad at you.

Easy, on the other hand, is large (about eight feet tall), furry (umber hair curls all down the small of his back, makes ringlets on his belly), strong (that three hundred and twenty six pounds of Easy is really a lot of rock jammed jagged into his pelt: his muscles have corners), and gentle. Once I got angry at him when one of the fertile nannies fell down a rock chimney.

I saw it coming. The ewe was the big blind one who had been giving us perfect norm triplets for eight years. I stood on one foot and threw rocks and sticks with the other three limbs. It takes a rock on the head to get Easy's attention; he was much closer than I was.

"Watch it, you non-functional, lost-Lo mongoloid! She's gonna fall in the—" At which point she did.

Easy stopped looking at me with his what-are-you-throwing-stones-at-me-for? face, saw her scrabbling at the edge, dove for her, missed, and both of them started bleating. I put my all behind the rock that caught him on the hip and almost cried. Easy did.

He crouched at the chimney edge, tears wetting the fur on his cheeks. The ewe had broken her neck at the chimney's bottom. Easy looked up and said, "Don't hurt me no more, Lobey. That" – he knuckled his blue eyes, then pointed down – "hurts too much already." What can you do with a Lo like that? Easy has claws too. All he ever uses them for is to climb the titan palms and tear down mangoes for the children.

Generally we did a good job with the goats, though. Once Little Jon leaped from the branch of an oak to the back of a lion and tore out its throat before it got to the herd (and rose from the carcass, shook himself, and went behind a rock, glancing over his shoulder). And as gentle as he is, Easy crushed a blackbear's head with a log. And I got my machete, all ambidextrous, left footed, right handed, or vice versa.

Yeah, we did a good job.

Not no more.

What happened was Friza.

"Friza" or "La Friza" was always a point of debate with the older folk-doctors and the elders who have to pass on titles. She looked normal: slim, brown, full mouth, wide nose, brass-colored eyes. I think she may have been born with six fingers on one hand, but the odd one was non-functional, so a travelling doctor amputated it. Her hair was tight, springy, and black. She kept it short, though once she found some red cord and wove it through. That day she wore bracelets and copper beads, strings and strings. She was beautiful.

And silent. When she was a baby, she was put in the kage with the other non-functionals because she didn't move. No La. Then a keeper discovered she didn't move because she already knew how; she was agile as a squirrel's shadow. She was taken out of the kage. Got back her La. But she never spoke. So at age eight, when it was obvious that the beautiful orphan was mute, away went her La. They couldn't very well put her back in the kage. Functional she was, making baskets, plowing, an expert huntress with the bolas. That's when there was all the debate.

Lo Hawk upheld: "In my day, La and Lo were reserved for total norms. We've been very lax, giving this title of purity to any functional who happens to have the misfortune to be born in these confusing times."

To which La Dire replied: "Times change, and it has been an unspoken precedent for thirty years that La and Lo be bestowed on any functional creature born in this our new home. The question is merely how far to extend the definition of functionality. Is the ability to communicate verbally its *sine qua non*? She is intelligent and she learns quickly and thoroughly. I move for *La Friza*."

The girl sat and played with white pebbles by the fire while they discussed her social standing.

"The beginning of the end, the beginning of the end," muttered Lo Hawk. "We must preserve something."

"The end of the beginning," sighed La Dire. "Everything must change." Which had been their standing exchange as long as I remember.

Once, before I was born, so goes the story, Lo Hawk grew disgruntled with village life and left. Rumors came back: he'd gone to a moon of Jupiter to dig out some metal that wormed in blue veins through the rock. Later: he'd left the Jovian satellite to sail a steaming sea on some world where three suns cast his shadows on the doffing deck of a ship bigger than our whole village. Still later: he was reported chopping away through a substance that melted to poisonous fumes someplace so far there were no stars at all during the year-long nights. When he had been away seven years, La Dire apparently decided it was time he came back. She left the village and returned a week later – with Lo Hawk. They say he hadn't changed much, so nobody asked him about where he'd been. But from his return dated the quiet argument that joined La Dire and Lo Hawk faster than love.

"...must preserve," Lo Hawk.

"...must change," La Dire.

Usually Lo Hawk gave in, for La Dire was a woman of wide reading, great culture, and wit; Lo Hawk had been a fine hunter in his youth and a fine warrior when there was need. And he was wise enough to admit in action, if not words, that such need had gone. But this time Lo Hawk was adamant:

"Communication is vital, if we are ever to become human beings. I would sooner allow some short-faced dog who comes from the hills and can approximate forty of fifty of our words to make known his wishes, than a mute child. Oh, the battles my youth has seen! When we fought off the giant spiders, or when the wave of fungus swept from the jungle, or when we destroyed with lime and salt the twenty-foot slugs that pushed up from the ground, we won these battles be cause we could speak to one another, shout instructions, bellow a warning, whisper plans in the twilit darkness of the source-caves. Yes, I would sooner give La or Lo to a talking dog!"

Somebody made a nasty comment: "Well, you couldn't very well give her a Le!" People snickered. But the older folk are very good at ignoring that sort of irreverence. Everybody ignores a Le anyway. Anyway, the business never did get settled. Towards moondown people wandered off, when somebody suggested adjournment. Everyone creaked and groaned to his feet. Friza, dark and beautiful, was still playing with the pebbles.

Friza didn't move when a baby because she knew how already. Watching her in the flicker (I was only eight myself) I got the first hint why she didn't talk: she picked up one of the pebbles and hurled it, viciously, at the head of the guy who'd made the remark about "Le." Even at eight she was sensitive. She missed, and I alone saw. But I saw too the snarl that twisted her face, the effort in her shoulders, the way her toes curled – she was sitting crosslegged – as she threw it. Both fists were knotted in her lap. You see, she didn't use her hands or feet. The pebble just rose from the dirt, shot through the air, missed its target, and chattered away through low leaves. But I saw: she *threw* it.

* * *

Each night for a week I have lingered on the wild flags of the waterfront, palaces crowding to the left, brittle light crackling over the harbor in the warm autumn. TEI goes strangely. Tonight when I turned back into the great trapezoid of the Piazza, fog hid the tops of the red flagpoles. I sat on the base of one nearest the tower and made notes on Lobey's hungers. Later I left the decaying gold and indigo of the Basilica and wandered through the back alleys of the city till well after midnight. Once I stopped on a bridge to watch the small canal drift through the close walls beneath the nightlamps and clotheslines. At a sudden shrieking I whirled: half a dozen wailing cats hurled themselves about my feet and fled after a brown rat. Chills snarled the nerves along my vertebrae. I looked back at the water: six flowers – roses – floated from beneath the bridge, crawling over the oil. I watched them till a motorboat puttering on some larger waterway nearby sent water slapping the foundations. I made my way over the small bridges to the Grand Canal and caught the Vaporetto back to Ferovia. It turned windy as we floated beneath the black wood arch of the Ponte Academia; I was trying to assimilate the flowers, the vicious animals, with Lobey's adventure – each applies, but as yet I don't quite know how. Orion straddled the water. Lights from the shore shook in the canal as we passed beneath the dripping stones of the Rialto.

Writer's Journal, *Venice, October 1965*

In a few lines I shall establish how Maldoror was virtuous during his first years, virtuous and happy. Later he became aware he was born evil. Strange fatality!

Isidore Ducasse (Comte de Lautreamont), The Songs of Maldoror

All prologue to why Lo Easy, Lo Littlejohn, and Lo me don't herd goats no more.

Friza started tagging along, dark and ambiguous, running and jumping with Little Jon in a double dance to his single song and my music, play-wrestling with Easy, and walking with me up the brambly meadow holding my hand – whoever heard of La-ing or Lo-ing somebody you're herding goats with, or laughing with, or making love with. All of which I did with Friza. She would turn on a rock to stare at me with leaves shaking beside her face. Or come tearing towards me through the stones; between her graceful gait and her shadow in the rocks all suspended and real motion was. And was released when she was in my arms laughing – the one sound she did make, loving it in her mouth.

She brought me beautiful things. And kept the dangerous away. I think she did it the same way she threw the pebble. One day I noticed that ugly and harmful things just weren't happening: no lions, no condor bats. The goats stayed together; the kids didn't get lost and kept from cliffs.

"Little Jon, you don't have to come up this morning." "Well, Lobey, if you don't think—"

"Go on, stay home."

So Easy, Friza, and me went out with the goats.

The beautiful things were like the flock of albino hawks that moved to the meadow. Or the mother woodchuck who brought her babies for us to see.

"Easy, there isn't enough work for all of us here. Why don't you find something else to do?"

"But I like coming up here, Lobey."

"Friza and me can take care of the herd." "But I don't mi—"

"Get lost, Easy."

He said something else and I picked up a stone in my foot and hefted it. He looked confused, then lumbered away. Imagine, coming on like that with Easy.

Friza and I had the field and the herd to ourselves alone. It stayed good and beautiful with unremembered flowers beyond rises when we ran. If there were poisonous snakes, they turned off in lengths of scarlet, never coiling. And, ah! did I make music.

Something killed her.

She was hiding under a grove of lazy willows, the trees that droop lower than weeping, and I was searching and calling and grinning – she shrieked. That's the only sound I ever heard her make other than laughter. The goats began to bleat.

I found her under the tree, face in the dirt.

As the goats bleated, the meadow went to pieces on their rasping noise. I was silent, confused, amazed by my despair.

I carried her back to the village. I remember La Dire's face as I walked into the village square with the limber body in my arms.

"Lobey, what in the world… How did she… Oh, *no*!

Lobey, no!"

So Easy and Little Jon took the herd again. I went and sat at the entrance to the source-cave, sharpened my blade, gnawed my nails, slept and thought alone on the flat rock. Which is where we began.

Once Easy came to talk to me.

"Hey, Lobey, help us with the goats. The lions are back. Not a lot of them, but we could still use you." He squatted, still towering me by a foot, shook his head. "Poor Lobey." He ran his hairy fingers over my neck. "We need you. You need us. Help us hunt for the two missing kids?"

"Go away."

"Poor Lobey." But he went.

Later Little Jon came. He stood around for a minute thinking of something to say. But by the time he did, he had to go behind a bush, got embarrassed, and didn't come back.

Lo Hawk came too. "Come hunting, Lo Lobey. There's a bull been seen a mile south. Horns as long as your arm, they say."

"I feel rather non-functional today," I said. Which is not the sort of thing to joke about with Lo Hawk. He retired, humphing. But I just wasn't up to his archaic manner.

When La Dire came, though, it was different. As I said, she has great wit and learning. She came and sat with a book on the other side of the flat rock, and ignored me for an hour. Till I got mad. "What are you doing here?" I asked at last.

"Probably the same thing you are."

"What's that?"

She looked serious. "Why don't you tell me?"

I went back to my knife. "Sharpening my machete."

"I'm sharpening my mind," she said. "There is something to be done that will require an edge on both."

"Huh?"

"Is that an inarticulate way of asking what it is?"

"Huh?" I said again. "Yeah. What is it?"

"To kill whatever killed Friza." She closed her book. "Will you help?"

I leaned forward, feet and hands knotting, opened my mouth – then La Dire wavered behind tears. I cried. After all that time it surprised me. I put my forehead on the rock and bawled.

"Lo Lobey," she said, the way Lo Hawk had, only it was different. Then she stroked my hair, like Easy. Only different. As I gained control again I sensed both her compassion and embarrassment. Like Little Jon's; different.

I lay on my side, feet and hands clutching each other, sobbing towards the cavity of me. La Dire rubbed my shoulder, my bunched, distended hip, opening me with gentleness and words:

"Let's talk about mythology, Lobey. Or let's you listen. We've had quite a time assuming the rationale of this world. The irrational presents just as much of a problem. You remember the legend of the Beatles? You remember the Beatle Ringo left his love Maureen even though she treated him tender. He was the one Beatle who did not sing, so the earliest forms of the legend go. After a hard day's night he and the rest of the Beatles were torn apart by screaming girls, and he and the other Beatles returned, finally at one, with the great rock and the great roll." I put my head in La Dire's lap. She went on. "Well, that myth is a version of a much older story that is not so well known. There are no 45's or 33 's from the time of this older story. There are only a few written versions, and reading is rapidly losing its interest for the young. In the older story Ringo was called Orpheus. He too was torn apart by screaming girls. But the details are different. He lost his love – in this version Eurydice – and she went straight to the great rock and the great roll, where Orpheus had to go to get her back. He went singing, for in this version Orpheus was the greatest singer, instead of the silent one. In myths things always turn into their opposites as one version supersedes the next."

I said, "How could he go into the great rock and the great roll? That's all death and all life."

"He did."

"Did he bring her back?"

"No."

I looked from La Dire's old face and turned my head in her lap to the trees. "He lied, then. He didn't really go. He probably went off into the woods for a while and just made up some story when he came back."

"Perhaps," La Dire said.

I looked up again. "He wanted her back," I said. "I know he wanted her back. But if he had gone any place where there was even a chance of getting her, he wouldn't have come back unless she was with him. That's how I know he must have been lying. About going to the great rock and the great roll, I mean."

"All life is a rhythm," she said as I sat up. "All death is a rhythm suspended, a syncopation before life resumes." She picked up my machete. "Play something." She held the handle out. "Make music."

I put the blade to my mouth, rolled over on my back, curled around the bright, dangerous length, and licked the sounds. I didn't want to but it formed in the hollow of my tongue, and breathing carried it into the knife.

Low; first slow; I closed my eyes, feeling each note in the quadrangle of shoulder blades and buttocks pressed on the rock. Notes came with only the meter of my own breathing, and from beneath that, there was the quickening of the muscles of my fingers and toes that began to cramp for the faster, closer dance of the heart's time. The mourning hymn began to quake.

"Lobey, when you were a boy, you used to beat the rock with your feet, making a rhythm, a dance, a drum. Drum, Lobey!"

I let the melody speed, then flailed it up an octave so I could handle it. That means only fingers.

"Drum, Lobey!"

I rocked to my feet and began to slap my soles against the stone.

"Drum!"

I opened my eyes long enough to see the blood spider scurry. The music laughed. Pound and pound, trill and warble, and La Dire laughed for me too, to play, hunched down while sweat quivered on my nape, threw up my head and it dribbled into the small of my back, while I, immobile above the waist, flung my hips, beating cross rhythms with toes and heels, blade up to prick the sun, new sweat trickling behind my ears, rolling the crevices of my corded neck.

"Drum, my Lo Ringo; play, my Lo Orpheus," La Dire cried. "Oh, Lobey!" She clapped and clapped.

Then, when the only sound was my own breath, the leaves, and the stream, she nodded, smiling. "Now you've mourned properly."

I looked down. My chest glistened, my stomach wrinkled and smoothed and wrinkled. Dust on the tops of my feet had become tan mud.

"Now you're almost ready to do what must be done. Go now, hunt, herd goats, play more. Soon Le Dorik will come for you."

All sound from me stopped. Breath and heart too, I think, a syncopation before the rhythm resumed. "Le Dorik?"

"Go. Enjoy yourself before you begin your journey."

Frightened, I shook my head, turned, fled from the cave mouth.

Le—

* * *

Suddenly the wandering little beast fled, leaving in my lap – O horror – a monster and misshapen maggot with a human head.

"Where is your soul that I may ride it!"

Aloysius Bertrand, "The Dwarf"

Come ALIVE! You're in the PEPSI generation!

***Current catchphrase** (Commercial)*

—Dorik.

An hour later I was crouching, hidden, by the kage. But the kage-keeper, Le Dorik, wasn't around. A white thing (I remember when the woman who was Easy's mother flung it from her womb before dying) had crawled to the electrified fence to slobber. It would probably die soon. Out of sight I heard Griga's laughter; he had been Lo Griga till he was sixteen. But something – nobody knew if it was genetic or not – rotted his mind inside his head, and laughter began to gush from his gums and lips. He lost his Lo and was placed in the kage. Le Dorik was probably inside now, putting out food, doctoring where doctoring would do some good, killing when there was some person beyond doctoring. So much sadness and horror penned up there; it was hard to remember they were people. They bore no title of purity, but they were people. Even Lo Hawk would get as offended over a joke about the kaged ones as he would about some titled citizen. "You don't *know* what they did to them when I was a boy, young Lo man. You never saw them dragged back from the jungle when a few did manage to survive. You didn't see the barbaric way complete norms acted, their reason shattered bloody by fear. Many people we call Lo and La today would not have been allowed to live had they been born fifty years ago. Be glad *you* are a child of more civilized times." Yes, they were people. But this is not the first time I had wondered what it feels like to keep such people – Le Dorik?

I went back to the village.

Lo Hawk looked up from re-thonging his crossbow. He'd piled the power cartridges on the ground in front of the door to check the caps. "How you be, Lo Lobey?"

I picked a cartridge out with my foot, turned it over. "Catch that bull yet?"

"No."

I pried the clip back with the tip of my machete. It was good. "Let's go," I said.

"Check the rest first."

While I did, he finished stringing the bow, went in and got a second one for me; then we went down to the river.

Silt stained the water yellow. The current was high and fast, bending ferns and long grass down, combing them from the shore like hair. We kept to the soggy bank for about two miles.

"What killed Friza?" I asked at last.

Lo Hawk squatted to examine a scarred log: tusk marks. "You were there. You saw. La Dire only guesses."

We turned from the river. Brambles scratched against Lo Hawk's leggings. I don't need leggings. My skin is tough and tight. Neither does Easy or Little Jon.

"I didn't see anything," I said. "What does she guess?"

An albino hawk burst from a tree and gyred away. Friza hadn't needed leggings either.

"Something killed Friza that was non-functional, something about her that was non-functional."

"Friza was functional," I said. "She was!"

"Keep your voice down, boy."

"She kept the herd together," I said more softly. "She could make the animals do what she wanted. She could move the dangerous things away and bring the beautiful ones nearer."

"Bosh," said Lo Hawk, stepping over ooze.

"Without a gesture or a word, she could move the animals anywhere she wanted, or I wanted."

"That's La Dire's nonsense you've been listening to."

"No. I saw it. She could move the animals just like the pebble."

Lo Hawk started to say something else. Then I saw his thoughts backtrack. "What pebble?"

"The pebble she picked up and threw."

"*What* pebble, Lobey?"

So I told him the story. "And it was functional," I concluded. "She kept the herd safe, didn't she? She could have kept it even without me."

"Only she couldn't keep herself alive," Lo Hawk said. He started walking again.

We kept silent through the whispering growth, while I mulled. Then:

"*Yaaaaa*"— on three different tones.

The leaves whipped back and the Bloi triplets scooted out. One of them leaped at me and I had an armful of hysterical, redheaded ten-year-old.

"*Hey* there now," I said sagely.

"Lo Hawk, Lobey! Back there—"

"Watch it, will you?" I added, avoiding an elbow.

"—back there! It was stamping, and pawing the rocks—" This from one of them at my hip.

"Back where?" Lo Hawk asked. "What happened?"

"Back there by the—"

"—by the oldhouse near the place where the cave roof falls in—"

"—the bull came up and—"

"—and he was awful big and he stepped—"

"—he stepped on the old house that—"

"—we was playing inside—"

"Hold up," I said and put 3-Bloi down. "Now where was all this?"

They turned together and pointed through the woods.

Hawk swung down his crossbow. "That's fine," he said. "You boys get back up to the village."

"Say—" I caught 2-Bloi's shoulder. 'Just how big was he?" Inarticulate blinking now.

"Never mind," I said. 'Just get going."

They looked at me, at Lo Hawk, at the woods. Then they got.

In silent consensus we turned from the river through the break in the leaves from which the children had tumbled.

A board, shattered at one end, lay on the path just before us as we reached the clearing. We stepped over it, stepped out between the sumac branches.

And there were a lot of other smashed boards scattered across the ground.

A five-foot section of the foundation had been kicked in, and only one of the four supporting beams was upright.

Thatch bits were shucked over the yard. A long time ago Carol had planted a few more flowers in this garden, when, wanting to get away from the it-all of the village, we had moved down here to the old thatched house that used to be so cozy, that used to be...she had planted the hedge with the fuzzy orange blooms. You know that kind?

I stopped by one cloven print where petals and leaves had been ground in a dark mandala on the mud. My feet fit inside the print easily. A couple of trees had been uprooted. A couple more had been broken off above my head.

It was easy to see which way he had come into the clearing. Bushes, vines, and leaves had erupted inward. Where he had left, everything sort of sagged out.

Lo Hawk ambled into the clearing swinging his crossbow nonchalantly.

"You're not really that nonchalant, are you?" I asked. I looked around again at the signs of destruction. "It must be huge."

Lo Hawk threw me a glance full of quartz and gristle. "You've been hunting with me before."

"True. It can't have been gone very long if it just scared the kids away," I added.

Hawk stalked towards the place where things were sagging.

I hurried after.

Ten steps into the woods, we heard seven trees crash somewhere: three – pause – then four more.

"Of course, if he's that big he can probably move pretty far pretty fast," I said.

Another three trees.

Then a roar:

An unmusical sound with much that was metallic in it, neither rage nor pathos, but noise, heaved from lungs bigger than smelting bellows, a long sound, then echoing while the leaves turned up beneath a breeze.

Under green and silver we started again through the cool, dangerous glades.

And step and breathe and step.

Then in the trees to our left—

He came leaping, and that leap rained us with shadow and twigs and bits of leaf.

Turning his haunch with one foreleg over here and a hindleg *way* the hell over there, he looked down at us with an eye bloodshot, brown, and thickly oystered in the corners. His eyeball must have been big as my head.

The wet, black nostrils steamed.

He was very noble.

Then he tossed his head, breaking branches, and hunkered with his fists punched into the ground – they were hands with horny hairy fingers thick as my arm where he should have had forehooves – bellowed, reared, and sprang away.

Hawk fired his crossbow. The shaft flapped like a darning needle between the timbers of his flank. He was crashing off.

The bark of the tree I'd slammed against chewed on my back as I came away.

"Come on," Hawk hollered, as he ran in the general direction the man-handed bull had.

And I followed that crazy old man, running to kill the beast. We clambered through a cleft of broken rock (it hadn't been broken the last time I'd come wandering down here through the trees – an afternoon full of sun spots and breezes and Friza's hand in mine, on my shoulder, on my cheek). I jumped down onto a stretch of moss-tongued brick that paved the forest here and there. We ran forward and—

Some things are so small you don't notice them. Others are so big you run right into them before you know what they are. It was a hole, in the earth and the side of the mountain, that we almost stumbled into. It was a ragged cave entrance some twenty meters across. I didn't even know it was there till all that sound came out of it.

The bull suddenly roared from the opening in the rock and trees and brick, defining the shape of it with his roaring.

When the echo died, we crept to the crumbled lip and looked over. Below I saw glints of sunlight on hide, turning and turning in the pit. Then he reared, shaking his eyes, his hairy fists.

Hawk jerked back, even though the claws on the brick wall were still fifteen feet below us.

"Doesn't this tunnel go into the source-cave?" I whispered. Before something that grand, one whispers.

Lo Hawk nodded. "Some of the tunnels, they say, are a hundred feet high. Some are ten. This is one of the bigger arterioles."

"Can it get out again?" Stupid question.

On the other side of the hole the horned head, the shoulders emerged. The cave-in had been sloped there. He had climbed out. Now he looked at us, crouched there. He bellowed once with a length of tongue like foamy, red canvas.

Then he leaped at us across the hole.

He didn't make it, but we scurried backward. He caught the lip with the fingers of one hand – I saw black gorges break about those nails – and one arm. The arm slapped around over the earth, searching for a hand-hold.

From behind me I heard Hawk shout (I run faster than he does). I turned to see that hand rise from over him!

He was all crumpled up on the ground. The hand slapped a few more times (*Boom – Boom! Boom!*) and then arm and fingers slipped, pulling a lot of stone and bushes and three small trees, down, down, down.

Lo Hawk wasn't dead. (The next day they discovered he had cracked a rib, but that wasn't till later.) He began to curl up. I thought of an injured bug. I thought of a sick, sick child.

I caught him up by the shoulders just as he started to breathe again. "Hawk! Are you—"

He couldn't hear me because of the roaring from the pit. But he pulled himself up, blinking. Blood began trickling from his nose. The beast had been slapping with cupped palm. Lo Hawk had thrown himself down, and luckily most of the important parts of him, like his head, had suffered more from air-blast than concussion.

"Let's get out of here!" and I began to drag him towards the trees.

When we got there, he was shaking his head.

"—no, wait, Lobey—" came over in his hoarse voice during a lull in the roaring.

As I got him propped against a trunk, he grabbed my wrist. "Hurry, Hawk! Can you walk? We've got to get away. Look,

I'll carry you—"

"No!" The breath that had been knocked out of him lurched back.

"Oh, come *on*, Hawk! Fun is fun. But you're hurt, and that thing is a lot bigger than either of us figured on. It must have mutated from the radiation in the lower levels of the cave."

He tugged my wrist again. "We have to stay. We have to kill it."

"Do you think it will come up and harm the village? It hasn't gone too far from the cave yet."

"That—" He coughed. "That has nothing to do with it. I'm a hunter, Lobey."

"Now, look—"

"And I have to teach you to hunt." He tried to sit away from the trunk. "Only it looks like you'll have to learn this lesson by yourself."

"Huh?"

"La Dire says you have to get ready for your journey."

"Oh, for goodness—" Then I squinted at him, all the crags and age and assurance and pain in that face. "What I gotta do?"

The bull's roar thundered up from the caved-in roof of the source-cave.

"Go down there; hunt the beast – and kill it."

"No!"

"It's for Friza."

"How?" I demanded.

He shrugged. "La Dire knows. You must learn to hunt, and hunt well." Then he repeated that.

"I'm all for testing my manhood and that sort of thing. But—"

"It's a different reason from that, Lobey."

"But—"

"Lobey." His voice nestled down low and firm in his throat. "I'm older than you, and I know more about this whole business than you do. Take your sword and crossbow and go down into the cave, Lobey. Go on."

I sat there and thought a whole lot of things. Such as: bravery is a very stupid thing. And how surprised I was that so much fear and respect for Lo Hawk had held from my childhood. Also, how many petty things can accompany pith, moment, and enterprise – like fear, confusion, and plain annoyance.

The beast roared again. I pushed the crossbow farther up my arm and settled my machete handle at my hip.

If you're going to do something stupid – and we all do – it might as well be a brave and foolish thing.

I clapped Lo Hawk's shoulder and started for the pit.

On this side the break was sharp and the drop deep. I went around to the sagging side, where there were natural ledges of root, earth, and masonry. I circled the chasm and scrambled down.

Sun struck the wall across from me, glistening with moss. I dropped my hand from the moist rock and stepped across an oily rivulet whose rainbow went out under my shadow. Somewhere up the tunnel, hooves clattered on stone.

I started forward. There were many cracks in the high ceiling, here and there lighting on the floor a branch clawing crisped leaves or the rim of a hole that might go down a few inches, a few feet, or drop to the lowest levels of the source-cave that were thousands of feet below.

I came to a fork, started beneath the vault to the left, and ten feet into the darkness tripped and rolled down a flight of shallow steps, once through a puddle (my hand splatting out in the darkness), once over dry leaves (they roared their own roar beneath my side), and landed at the bottom in a shaft of light, knees and palms on gravel.

Clatter!

Clatter!

Much closer: *Clatter!*

I sprang to my feet and away from the telltale light. Motes cycloned in the slanting illumination where I had been. And the motes stilled.

My stomach felt like a loose bag of water sloshing around on top of my gut. Walking towards that sound – he was quiet now and waiting – was no longer a matter of walking in a direction. Rather: pick that foot up, lean forward, put it down. Good. Now, pick up the other one, lean forward—

A hundred yards ahead I suddenly saw another light because something very large suddenly filled it up. Then it emptied.

Clack! Clack! Clack!

Snort!

And three steps could carry him such a long way.

Then a lot of *clacks!*

I threw myself against the wall, pushing my face into dirt and roots.

But the sound was going off.

I swallowed all the bitter things that had risen into my throat and stepped back from the wall.

With a quick walk that became a slow run I followed him under the crumbling vaults.

His sound came from the right.

So I turned right and into a sloping tunnel so low that ahead of me I heard his horns rasp on the ceiling. Stone and scale and old lichen chittered down at his hulking shoulders, then to the ground.

The gutter on the side of the tunnel had coated the stone with fluorescent slime. The trickle became a stream as the slope increased till the frothing light raced me on the left.

Once his hooves must have crossed a metal floor-plate, because for a half-dozen steps orange sparks glittered where he stepped, lighting him to the waist.

He was only thirty meters ahead of me.

Sparks again as he turned a corner.

I felt stone under the soles of my feet, then cold, smooth metal. I passed some leaves, blown here by what wind, that his hooves had ignited. They writhed with worms of fire, glowing about my toes. And for moments the darkness filled with autumn.

I reached the corner, started around—

Facing me, he bellowed.

His foot struck a meter from my foot, and from this close the sparks lit his raw eyes, his polished nostrils.

His hand came between his eyes and me, falling! I rolled backward, grabbing for my machete.

His palm – flat this time, Hawk – clanged on the metal plate where I had been. Then it fell again towards where I was.

I lay on my back with the hilt of the blade on the floor, point up. Very few people, or bulls, can hit a ten-penny nail and drive it to the hilt. Fortunately.

He jerked me from the floor, pinioned to his palm, and I got flung around (holding on to the blade with hands and feet and screaming) an awful lot.

He was screaming too, butting the ceiling and lots of things falling. From twenty feet he flung me loose. The blade pulled free, my flute filled with his blood, and I hurled into the wall and rolled down.

His right shoulder struck the right wall. He lurched. His left shoulder struck the left wall. And his shadow flickering on the dripping ceiling was huge.

He came down towards me, as I dragged my knees over a lot of wrought stone beneath me, rocked back to my feet (something was sprained too), and tried to look at him, while he kept going out between steps.

Beside me in the wall was a grating about three feet high, with the bars set askew. It was probably a drain. I fell through. And dropped about four feet to a sloping floor.

It was pitch-black above me and there was a hand grasping and grasping in the dark. I could hear it scrabbling against the wall. I took a swipe overhead, and my blade struck something moving.

Roaaaaaa…!

The sound was blunted behind stone. But from my side came the sharp retort of his palm as he started slapping.

I dived forward. The slope increased, and suddenly I slid down a long way, very fast, getting even more scraped up. I came up sharply against pipes.

Eyes closed, I lay there, the tip of the crossbow uncomfortable under my shoulder, the blade handle biting between the bars and my hip. Then the places that were uncomfortable got numb.

If you really relax with your eyes closed, the lids pull slowly open. When I finally relaxed, light filled my eyes from the bottoms up like milk poured in bowls.

Light?

I blinked.

Gray light beyond the grating, the gray that sunlight gets when it comes from around many corners. Only I was at least another two levels down. I lay behind the entrance to another drain like the one I'd leaped through.

Then somewhere, the roar of a bull, echoing through these deep stones.

I pulled myself up on the bars, elbows smarting, shoulders bruised, and something pulled sore in the bulk of my thigh. I gazed into the room below.

At one time there was a floor level with the bottom of this grating, but most of it had fallen in a long and longer time ago. Now the room was double height and the grate was at least fifteen feet above the present floor.

Seventy, eighty meters across, the room was round. The walls were dressed stone, or bare rock, and rose in gray slabs towards the far light. There were many vaulted entrances into dark tunnels.

In the center was a machine.

While I watched, it began to hum wistfully to itself, and several banks of lights glittered into a pattern, froze, glittered into another. It was a computer from the old time (when you owned this Earth, you wraiths and memories), a few of which still chuckled and chattered throughout the source-cave. I'd had them described to me, but this was the first I'd seen.

What had wakened me—

(and had I been asleep? And had I dreamed, remembering now with the throbbing image clinging to the back of my eyes, Friza?)

—was the wail of the beast.

Head down, hide bristling over the hunks of his shoulders, gemmed with water from the ceiling, he hunched into the room, dragging the knuckles of one hand, the other – the one I had wounded twice – hugged to his belly.

And on three legs, a four-legged animal (even one with hands) limps.

He blinked about the room, and wailed again, his voice leaving pathos quickly and striking against rage. He stopped the sound with a sniff, then looked around and knew that I was there.

And I wanted very much not to be.

I squatted now behind the grating and looked back and up and down and couldn't see any way out. Hunt, Lo Hawk had said.

The hunter can be a pretty pathetic creature.

He swung his head again, tasting the air for me, his injured hand twitching high on his belly.

(The hunted's not so hot either.)

The computer whistled a few notes of one of the ancient tunes, some chorus from *Carmen*. The bull-beast glanced at it uncomprehending.

How was I to hunt him?

I brought the crossbow down and aimed through the grate. It wouldn't mean anything unless I got him in the eye. And he wasn't looking in the right direction.

I lowered the bow and took up my blade. I brought it to my mouth and blew. Blood bubbled from the holes. Then the note blasted and went reeling through the room.

He raised his head and stared at me.

Up went the bow; I aimed through the bars, pulled the trigger—

Raging forward with horns shaking, he got bigger and bigger and bigger through the frame of stone. I fell back while the roar covered me, closing my eyes against the sight: his eye gushed about my shaft. He grasped the bars behind which I crouched.

Metal grated on stone, stone pulled from stone. And then the frame was a lot bigger than it had been. He hurled the crumpled grate across the room to smash into the wall and send pieces of stone rolling.

Then he reached in and grabbed me, legs and waist, in his fist, and I was being waved high in the air over his bellowing face (left side blind and bloody) and the room arching under me and my head flung from shoulder to shoulder and trying to point the crossbow down – one shaft broke on the stone by his hoof a long way below. Another struck awfully close to the shaft that Lo

Hawk had shot into his side. Waiting for a wall of stone to come up and jelly my head, I fumbled another arrow into the slot.

His cheek was sheeted with blood. And suddenly there was more blood. The shaft struck and totally disappeared in the blind well of bone and lymph. I saw the other eye cloud as though someone had overblown the lens with powdered lime.

He dropped me.

Didn't throw me; just dropped. I grabbed the hair on his wrist. It slipped through my hands, and I slid down his forearms to the crook of his elbow.

Then his arm began to fall. Slowly I turned upside down. The back of his hand hit the floor, and his hind feet were clacking around on the stone.

He snorted, and I began to slide back down his forearm towards his hand, slowing myself by clutching at the bristles with feet and hands. I rolled clear of his palm and staggered away from him.

The thing in my thigh that was sprained throbbed.

I stepped backward and couldn't step any more.

He swayed over me, shook his head, splattering me with his ruined eye. And he was grand. And he was *still* strong, dying above me. And he was huge. Furious, I swayed with him in my fury, my fists clutched against my hips, tongue stifled in my mouth.

He was great and he was handsome and he *still* stood there defying me while dying, scoffing at my bruises. Damn you, beast who would be greater than—

One arm buckled, a hindleg now, and he collapsed away from me, crashing.

Something in the fistsful of darkness that were his nostrils thundered and roared – but softer, and softer. His ribs rose to furrow his side, fell to rise again; I took up the bow and limped to the bloody tears of his lips, fitted one final shaft. It followed the other two into his brain.

His hands jerked three feet, then fell (*Boom! Boom!*) relaxing now.

When he was still, I went and sat on the base of the computer and leaned against the metal casing. Somewhere inside it was clicking.

I hurt. Lots.

Breathing was no fun anymore. And I had, somewhere during all this, bitten the inside of my cheek. And when I do that, it gets me so mad I could cry.

I closed my eyes.

"That was very impressive," someone said close to my right ear. "I would love to see you work with a *muleta*. Olé! Olé! First the *verónica*, then the *paso doble*!'

I opened my eyes.

"Not that I didn't enjoy your less sophisticated art."

I turned my head. There was a small speaker by my left ear. The computer went on soothingly:

"But you are a dreadfully unsophisticated lot. All of you. Young, but *très charmant*. Well, you've fought through this far. Is there anything you'd like to ask me?"

"Yeah," I said. Then I breathed for a while. "How do I get out of here?" There were a lot of archways in the wall, a lot of choices.

"That is a problem. Let me see." The lights flickered over my lap, the backs of my hands. "Now, of course, had we met before you entered, I could have waved out a piece of computer tape and you would have taken the end and I would have unwound it after you as you made your way into the heart to face your fate. But instead, you have arrived here and found me waiting. What do you desire, hero?"

"I want to go home," I said.

The computer went *tsk-tsk-tsk*. "Other than that."

"You really want to know?"

"I'm nodding sympathetically," it said.

"I want Friza. But she's dead."

"Who was Friza?"

I thought. I tried to say something. With the exhaustion, all that came was a catch in my throat that might have sounded like a sob.

"Oh." After a moment, gently: "You've come into the wrong maze, you know."

"I have? Then what are you doing here?"

"I was set here a long time ago by people who never dreamed that you would come. Psychic Harmony and Entangled Deranged Response Associations, that was my department. And you've come down here hunting through my memories for your lost girl."

Yes, I may have just been talking to myself. I was very tired.

"How do you like it up there?" PHAEDRA asked.

"Where?"

"Up there on the surface. I can remember back when there were humans. They made me. Then they all went away, leaving us alone down here. And now you've come to take their place. It must be rather difficult, walking through their hills, their jungles, battling the mutated shadows of their flora and fauna, haunted by their million-year-old fantasies."

"We try," I said.

"You're basically not equipped for it," PHAEDRA went on. "But I suppose you have to exhaust the old mazes before you can move into the new ones. It's hard."

"If it means fighting off those—" I jutted my chin towards the carcass on the stone. "Yeah, it is."

"Well, it's been fun. I miss the *revueltas*, the maidens leaping over the horns and spinning in the air to land on the sweating back, then vaulting to the sands! Mankind had style, baby! You may get it yet, but right now your charm is a very young thing."

"Where did they go, PHAEDRA?"

"Where your Friza went, I suppose." Something musical was happening behind my head within the metal. "But you aren't human and you don't appreciate their rules. You shouldn't try. Down here we try to follow what you're doing for a few generations, and questions get answered we would never have even thought of asking. On the other hand, we sit waiting out centuries for what would seem like the most obvious and basic bits of information about you, like who you are, where you're from, and what you're doing here. Has it occurred to you that you might get her back?"

"Friza?" I sat up. "Where? How?" La Dire's cryptic statements came back.

"You're in the wrong maze," PHAEDRA repeated. "And I'm the wrong girl to get you into the right one. Kid Death along for a little while and maybe you can get around him enough to put your foot in the door, finger in the pie, your two cents in, as it were."

I leaned forward on my knees. "PHAEDRA, you baffle me."

"Scoot," PHAEDRA said.

"Which way?"

"Again. You've asked the wrong girl. Wish I could help. But I don't know. But you'd better get started. When the sun goes down and the tide goes out, this place gets dark, and the gillies and ghosties gather 'round, shouting."

I heaved to my feet and looked at the various doorways. Maybe a little logic? The bull-beast had come from the doorway over there. So that's the one I went in.

The long, long dark echoed with my breath and falling water. I tripped over the first stairway. Got up and started climbing. Bruised my shoulder on the landing, groped around and finally realized I had gotten off into a much smaller passage that didn't *seem* like it was going anywhere.

I took up my machete and blew out the last of the blood. The tune now winding with me lay notes over the stone like mica flakes that would do till light came.

Stubbed my toe.

Hopped, cursed, then started walking again alone with the lonely, lovely sounds.

"Hey—"

"—Lobey, is—"

"—is that you?" Young voices came from behind stone.

"Yes! Of course it's me!" I turned to the wall and put my hands against the rock. "We snuck back—"

"—to watch, and Lo Hawk—"

"—he told us to go down into the cave and find you—"

"—cause he thought you might be lost."

I pushed my machete back into my scabbard. "Fine. Because I am."

"Where are you?"

"Right here on the other side of this—" I was feeling around the stones again, above my head this time. My fingers came on an opening. It was nearly three feet wide. "Hold on!" I hoisted myself up, clambered onto the rim, and saw faint light at the end of a four-foot tunnel. I had to crawl through because there wasn't room to stand.

At the other end I stuck my head out and looked down at the upturned faces of the Bloi triplets. They were standing in a patch of light from the roof.

2-Bloi rubbed his nose with the back of his fist and sniffed.

"Oh," 1-Bloi said. "You were up there."

"More or less." I jumped down beside them.

"Damn!" 3-Bloi said. "What happened to you?" I was speckled with bull's eye, scratched, bruised, and limping.

"Come on," I said. 'Which way is out?"

We were only around the corner from the great cave-in.

We joined Lo Hawk on the surface.

He stood (remember, he had a cracked rib that nobody was going to find out about till the next day) against a tree with his arms folded. He raised his eyebrows to ask me the question he was waiting with.

"Yeah," I said. "I killed it. Big deal." I was sort of tired.

Lo Hawk shooed the kids ahead of us back to the village. As we tromped through the long weeds, suddenly we heard stems crash down among themselves.

I almost sat down right there.

It was only a boar. His ear could have brushed my elbow. That's all.

"Come on." Lo Hawk grinned, raising his crossbow.

We didn't say anything else until after we had caught and killed the pig. Lo Hawk's powered shaft stunned it, but I had to hack it nearly in half before it would admit it was dead. After *el taro*? Easy. Bloody to the shoulders, we trudged back finally, through the thorns, the hot evening.

The head of the boar weighed fifty pounds. Lo Hawk lugged it on his back. We'd cut off all four hams, knotted them together, and I carried two on each shoulder, which was another two hundred and seventy pounds. The only way we could have gotten the whole thing back was to have had Easy along. We'd nearly reached the village when he said, "La Dire noticed that business with Friza and the animals. She's seen other things about you and others in the village."

"Huh? Me?" I asked. "What about me?"

"About you, Friza, and Dorik the kage-keeper."

"But that's silly." I'd been walking behind him. Now I drew abreast. He glanced across the tusk. "You were all born the same year."

"But we're all – different."

Lo Hawk squinted ahead, then looked down. Then he looked at the river. He didn't look at me.

"I can't do anything like the animals or the pebble."

"You can do other things. Le Dorik can do still others."

He still wasn't looking at me. The sun was lowering behind copper-crested hills. The river was brown. He was silent. As clouds ran the sky, I dropped behind again, placed the meat beside me, and fell on my knees to wash in the silted water.

Back at the village I told Carol if she'd dress the hams she could have half my share. "Sure," but she was dawdling over a bird's nest she'd found. "In a minute."

"And hurry up, huh?"

"All right. All right. Where are you in such a rush to?"

"Look, I will polish the tusks for you and make a spear-head for the kid or something if you will *just keep off my back*!'

"Well, I – look, it's not your kid anyway. It's—"

But I was sprinting towards the trees. I guess I must have still been upset. My legs sprint pretty fast.

It was dark when I reached the kage. There was no sound from behind the fence. Once something blundered against the wire, whined. Sparks and a quick shadow. I don't know which side it came from. No movement from Le Dorik's shack. Maybe Dorik was staying inside the kage on some project. Sometimes they mated in there, even gave birth. Sometimes the offspring were functional. The Bloi triplets had been born in the kage. They didn't have too much neck and their arms were long, but they were quick, bright ten-year-olds now. And 2-Bloi and 3-Bloi are almost as dexterous with their feet as I am. I'd even given Lo 3-Bloi a couple of lessons on my blade, but being a child he preferred to pick fruit with his brothers.

After an hour in the dark, thinking about what went into the kage, what came out, I went back to the village, curled up on the haystack behind the smithy, and listened to the hum from the power-shack until it put me to sleep.

At dawn I unraveled, rubbed night's grit out of my eyes, and went to the corral. Easy and Little Jon got there a few minutes after. "Need any help with the goats this morning?"

Little Jon put his tongue in his cheek. "Just a second," he said and went off into the corner.

Easy shuffled uncomfortably.

LittleJon came back. "Yeah," he said. "Sure we need help." Then he grinned. And Easy, seeing his grin, grinned too.

Surprise! Surprise, little ball of fear inside me! They're smiling! Easy hoisted up the first bar of the wooden gate and the goats bleated forward and put their chins over the second rung. Surprise!

"Sure," Easy said. "Of course we need you. Glad to have you back!" He cuffed the back of my head and I swiped at his hip and missed. Little Jon pulled out the other rung, and we chased the goats across the square out along the road, and then up the meadow. Just like before. No, not just.

Easy said it first, when the first warmth pried under the dawn chill. "It's not just like before, Lobey. You've lost something."

I struck a dew shower from low willow fronds and wet my face and shoulders. "My appetite," I said. "And maybe a couple of pounds."

"It isn't your appetite," Little Jon said, coming back from a tree stump. "It's something different."

"Different?" I repeated. "Say, Easy, Little Jon, how am I different?"

"Huh?" Little Jon asked. He flung a stick at a goat to get its attention. Missed. I picked up a small stone that happened underfoot. Hit it. The goat turned blue eyes on me and galumphed over to see why, got interested in something else halfway over and tried to eat it. "You got big feet," Little Jon said.

"Naw. Not that," I said. "La Dire had noticed something different about me that's important; something different about me the same way there was about...Friza."

"You make music," Easy said.

I looked at the perforated blade. "Naw," I said. "I don't think it's that. I could teach you to play. That's another sort of being different than she's looking for. I think."

Late that afternoon we brought the goats back. Easy invited me to eat and I got some of my ham and we attacked Little Jon's cache of fruit. "You want to cook?"

"Naw," I said.

So Easy walked down to the comer of the power-shack and called towards the square, "Hey, who wants to cook dinner for three hard-working gentlemen who can supply food, entertainment, bright conversation – No, you cooked dinner for me once before. Now don't *push*, girls! Not you either. Whoever taught you how to season? Uh-uh, I remember you, Strychnine Lizzy. OK Yeah, you. Come on."

He came back with a cute, bald girl. I'd seen her around but she'd just come to the village. I'd never talked to her and I didn't know her name. "This is Little Jon, Lobey, and I'm Easy. What's your name again?"

"Call me Nativia."

No, I'd never talked to her before. A shame that situation had gone on for twenty-three years. Her voice didn't come from her larynx. I don't think she had one. The sound began a whole lot further down and whispered as out from a cave with bells.

"You can call me anything you like," I said, "as much as you want."

She laughed, and it sounded among the bells. "Where's the food and let's find a fireplace."

We found a circle of rocks down by the stream. We were going to get cookery from the compound but Nativia had a large skillet of her own so all we had to borrow were cinnamon and salt.

"Come on," Little Jon said when he came back from the water's edge."Lobey, you gotta be entertaining. We'll converse."

"Now, hey—" Then I said to myself *Aw, so what,* lay down on my back, and began to play my machete. She liked that because she kept smiling at me as she worked.

"Don't you got no children?" Easy asked.

Nativia was greasing the skillet with a lump of ham fat.

"One in the kage down at Live Briar. Two with a man in
Ko."

"You travel a lot, yeah?" Little Jon asked.

I played a slower tune that came far away, and she smiled at me as she dumped diced meat from a palm frond into the pan. Fat danced on the hot metal.

"I travel." The smile and the wind and the mockery in her voice were delightful.

"You should find a man who travels too," Easy suggested. He has a lot of homey type advice for everybody. Gets on my nerves sometimes.

Nativia shrugged. "Did once. We could never agree what direction to go in. It's his kid in the kage. Guy's name was Lo Angel. A beautiful man. He could just never make up his mind where he wanted to go. And when he did, it was never where I wanted. No..." She pushed the browning meat across the crackling bottom. "I like good, stable, settled men who'll be there when I get back."

I began to play an old hymn – *Bill Bailey Won't You Please Come Home*. I'd learned it from a 45 when I was a kid. Nativia knew it too because she laughed in the middle of slicing a peach.

"That's me," she said. "Bill La Bailey. That's the nickname Lo Angel gave me."

She formed the meat into a ring around the edge of the pan. The nuts and vegetables went in now with a little salt water, and the cover clanked on.

"How far have you traveled?" I asked, laying my knife on my stomach and stretching. Overhead, behind maple leaves, the sky was injured in the west with sunset, shadowed by east and night. "I'm going to travel soon. I want to know where there is to go."

She pushed the fruit on to one end of the frond. "I once went as far as the City. And I've even been underground to explore the source-cave."

Easy and Little Jon got very quiet.

"That's some traveling," I said. "La Dire says I have to travel because I'm different."

Nativia nodded. "That's why Lo Angel was traveling," she said, pushing back the lid again. Pungent steam ballooned and dispersed. My mouth got wet. "Most of the ones moving were different. He always said I was different too, but he would never tell me how." She pushed the vegetables into a ring against the meat and filled the center with cut fruit. Cinnamon now over the whole thing. Some of the powdered spice caught the flame that tongued the pan's rim and sparks bloomed. On went the cover.

"Yeah," I said. "La Dire won't tell me either."

Nativia looked surprised. "You mean you don't know?"

I shook my head.

"Oh, but you can—" She stopped. "La Dire is one of this town's elders, isn't she?"

"That's right."

"Maybe she's got a reason not to tell you. I talked to her just a little while the other day; she's a woman of great wisdom."

"Yeah," I said, rolling on my side. "Come on, if you know, tell me."

Nativia looked confused. "Well, first you tell me. I mean what did La Dire say?"

"She said I would have to go on a journey, to kill whatever killed Friza."

"Friza?"

"Friza was different, too." I began to tell her the story. A minute into it, Easy burped, pounded his chest, and complained about being hungry. He obviously didn't like the subject. Little Jon had to get up and when he wandered off into the bushes, Easy went after him, grunting, "Call me when it's finished. Dinner, I mean."

But Nativia listened closely and then asked some questions about Friza's death. When I told her about having to take a trip with Le Dorik, she nodded. "Well, it makes a lot more sense now."

"It does?"

She nodded again. "Hey, you guys, dinner's...ready?"

"Then can't you tell me...?"

She shook her head. "You wouldn't understand. I've done a lot more traveling than you. It's just that a lot of different people have died recently, like Friza died. Two down at Live Briar. And

I've heard of three more in the past year. Something is going to have to be done. It might as well get started here." She pushed the cover off the pan again: more steam.

Easy and Little Jon, who had been walking back up the stream, began to run.

"Elvis Presley!" Little Jon breathed. "Does that smell good!" He hunkered down by the fire, dribbling.

Easy's adenoids began to rattle. When a cat does it, it's purring.

I wanted to ask more, but I didn't want to annoy Easy and Little Jon; I guess I had acted bad with them, and they were pretty nice about it as long as I let it lie.

A frond full of ham, vegetables, and spiced fruit made me stop thinking about anything except what wasn't in my belly, and I learned that a good deal of my metaphysical melancholia was hunger. Always is.

More conversation, more food, more entertainment. We went to sleep right there by the stream, stretched on the ferns. Towards midnight when it got chilly we rolled into a pile. About an hour before dawn I woke.

I pulled my head from Easy's armpit (and Nativia's bald head moved immediately to take its place) and stood up in the starry dark. Little Jon's head gleamed at my feet. So did my blade. He was using it for a pillow. I slipped it gently from under his cheek. He snorted, scratched himself, was still. I started back through the trees in the direction of the kage.

Once I looked up at the branches, at the wires that ran from the power-shack to the fence. The black lines overhead, or the sound of the stream, or memory took me. Halfway, I started playing. Someone began to whistle along with me. I stopped. The whistle didn't.

* * *

Where is he then? In a song?
Jean Genet, **The Screens**

God said to Abraham, "Kill me a son."
Abe said, "God, you must be puttin' me on!"
Bob Dylan, "Highway 61 Revisited"

Love is something which dies and when dead it rots and becomes soil for a new love...
Thus in reality there is no death in love.
Par Lagerkvist, **The Dwarf**

"Le Dorik?" I said. "Dorik?"

"Hi," came a voice from the dark. "Lobey?"

"Lo Lobey," I said. "Where are you?"

"Just inside the kage."

"Oh. What's the smell?"

"Whitey," Dorik said. "Easy's brother. He died. I'm digging a grave. You remember Easy's brother—"

"I remember," I said. "I saw him by the fence yesterday. He looked pretty sick."

"That kind never last long. Come in and help me dig."

"The fence..."

"It's off. Climb over."

"I don't like to go in the kage," I said.

"You never used to mind sneaking in here when we were kids. Come on, I've got to move this rock. Lend me a foot."

"That was when we were kids," I said. "We did a lot of things when we were kids we don't have to do now. It's your job. You dig."

"Friza used to come in here and help me, tell me all about you."

"Friza used to..." Then I said, "Tell?"

"Well, some of us could understand her."

"Yeah," I said. "Some of us could."

I grabbed the wire mesh near the post but didn't start climbing.

"Actually," Dorik said, "I was always sort of sad you never came around. We used to have fun. I'm glad Friza didn't feel the way you did. We used to—"

"—to do a lot of things, Dorik. Yeah, I know. Look, nobody ever bothered to tell me you weren't a girl till I was fourteen, Dorik. If I hurt you, I'm sorry."

"You did. But I'm not. Nobody ever did get around to telling Friza I wasn't a boy. Which I'm sort of glad of. I don't think she would have taken it the same way you did, even so."

"She came here a lot?"

"All the time she wasn't with you."

I sprang over the wire, swung over the top, and dropped to the other side. "Where's that damn rock you're trying to move?"

"Here—"

"Don't touch me," I said. "Just show me."

"Here," Dorik repeated in the darkness.

I grabbed the edge of the stone shelved in the dirt. Roots broke, dirt whispered down, and I rolled the stone out.

"How's the kid, by the way?" I asked.

I had to. And damn, Dorik, why were the next words the ones I was hurting with hoping I wouldn't hear?

"Which one?"

There was a shovel by the post. I jammed it into the grave. Damn Le Dorik.

"Mine and Friza's," Dorik went on after a moment, "will probably be up for review by the doctors in another year. Needs a lot of special training, but she's pretty functional. Probably will never have a La, but at least she won't have to be in here."

"That's not the kid I meant." The shovel clanged on another rock.

"You're not asking about the one that's all mine." There were two or three pieces of ice in that sentence. Dorik flicked them at me, much on purpose. "You mean yours and mine." As if you didn't know, you androgynous bastard. "He's in here for life, but he's happy. Want to go see him—"

"No." Three more shovelsful of dirt. "Let's bury Whitey and get out of here."

"Where are we going?"

"La Dire, she said you and me have to take a trip together to destroy what killed Friza."

"Oh," Dorik said. "Yes." Dorik went over to the fence, bent down. "Help me."

We picked up the bloated, rubbery corpse and carried it to the hole. It rolled over the edge, thumping.

"You were supposed to wait till I came for you," Dorik said.

"Yeah. But I can't wait. I want to go now."

"If I'm going with you, you're waiting."

"Why?"

"Look, Lobey," Dorik said, "I'm kage-keeper and I got a kage to keep."

"I don't care if everything in that kage mildews and rots. I want to get out and get going!"

"I've got to train a new keeper, check over the education facilities, make sure of the food inventories and special diets, last-minute shelter maintenance—"

"Damn it, Dorik, come on."

"Lobey, I've got three kids in here. One's yours, one belongs to a girl you loved. And one's all mine. Two of them, if they're loved and taken care of and given a lot of time and patience may someday come out."

"Two of them, yeah?" My breath suddenly got lost in my chest and didn't seem to be doing any good. "But not mine. I'm going."

"Lobey!"

I stopped, straddling the fence.

"Look, Lobey, this is the real world you're living in. It's come from something; it's going to something: it's changing. But it's got right and wrong, a way to behave and a way not to. You never wanted to accept that, even when you were a kid, but until you do, you won't be very happy."

"You're talking about me when I was fourteen," I said.

"I'm talking about you now. Friza told me a lot—"

I jumped over the fence and started through the trees. "Lobey!"

"What?" I kept walking.

"You're scared of me." "No."

"I'll show you—"

"You're pretty good at showing people things in the dark, aren't you? That's how you're different, huh?" I called over my shoulder. I crossed the stream and started up the rocks, mad as all Elvis. I didn't go towards the meadow, but around towards the steeper places, slapping leaves and flipping twigs as I barreled through the dark. Then I heard somebody come on through the shadow, whistling.

* * *

There are none here except madmen; and a few there are who know this world, and who know that he who tries to act in the ways of others never does anything, because men never have the same opinions. These do not know that he who is thought wise by day will never be held crazy by night.

Niccolo Machiavelli, "Letter to Francesco Vittori"

Experience reveals to him in every object, in every event, the presence of something else.

Jean-Paul Sartre, **Saint Genet, Actor and Martyr**

I stopped. The sound of dry leaves under feet, ferns by a shoulder, approached me from behind, stopped. The hills' rim had begun to gray.

"Lobey?"

"You changed your mind about coming?"

A sigh. "Yes."

"Come on, then." We started walking. "Why?"

"Something happened."

Dorik didn't say what. I didn't ask.

"Dorik," I said a little later, "I feel something towards you very close to hate. It's as close to hate as what I felt for Friza was close to love."

"Neither's close enough to worry about now. You're too self-centered, Lobey. I hope you grow up."

"And you're going to show me how?" I asked. "In the dark?"

"I'm showing you now."

Morning, while we walked, leaked up vermilion. With light, my eyes grew surprisingly heavy, stones in my head. "You've been working all night," I volunteered. "I've only had a few hours sleep myself. Why don't we lie down for a few hours?"

"Wait till it gets light enough so you know I'm here." Which was an odd answer. Dorik was a grayed silhouette beside me now.

When there was enough red in the east and the rest of the sky was at least blue, I started looking for a place to fall out. I was exhausted and every time I turned to look at the sun, the world swam with tears of fatigue.

"Here," Dorik said. We'd reached a small stone hollow by the cliff's base. I dropped into it, Dorik too. We lay with the blade between us. I remember a moment of gold light along the arm and back curved towards me before I slept.

* * *

I touched the hand touching my face, held it still enough to open my eyes under it. Lids snapped back. "Dorik—?"

Nativia stared down at me.

My fingers intertwined with hers, hammocked by her webs. She looked frightened, and her breath through spread lips stopped my own. "Easy!" she called up the slope. "Little Jon! Here he is!"

I sat up. "Where'd Dorik go…?"

Easy came loping into sight and Little Jon ran after.

"La Dire," Easy said. "La Dire wants to see you…before you go. She and Lo Hawk have to talk to you."

"Hey, did anybody see Le Dorik around here? Odd thing to run off—"

Then I saw this expression cracking through Little Jori's miniature features like faults in black rock. "Le Dorik's dead," Little Jon said; "that's what they wanted to tell you."

"Huh?"

"Before sunup, just inside the kage," Easy said. "He was lying by the grave for my brother, Whitey. Remember my brother—"

"Yeah, yeah," I said. "I helped dig it – Before sunup? That's impossible. The sun was up when we went to sleep, right here." Then I said, "Dead?"

Little Jon nodded. "Like Friza. The same way. That's what La Dire said."

I stood up, holding my blade tight. "But that's impossible!" Somebody saying, *Wait till it gets light enough so you'll know I'm here.* "Le Dorik was with me after sunrise. That's when we lay down here to sleep."

"You slept with Le Dorik *after* Le Dorik was dead?" Nativia asked, wonderingly.

Bewildered, I returned to the village. La Dire and Lo Hawk met me at the source-cave. We spoke together a bit; I watched them thinking deeply about things I didn't understand, about my bewilderment.

"You're a good hunter, Lo Lobey," Lo Hawk said at last, "and though a bit outsized below the waist, a fair specimen of a man. You have much danger ahead of you; I've taught you much. Remember it when you wander by the rim of night or the edge of morning." Apparently Le

Dorik's death had convinced him there was something to La Dire's suppositions, though I understood neither side of the argument nor the bridge between. They didn't enlighten me. "Use what I have taught you to get where you are going," Lo Hawk went on, "to survive your stay, and make your way back."

"You are different." That is what La Dire said. "You have seen it is dangerous to be so. It is also very important. I have tried to instruct you in a view of the world large enough to encompass the deeds you will do as well as their significance. You have learned much, Lo Lobey. Use what I have taught you too."

With no idea where I was going, I turned and staggered away, still dazed by Dorik's death before sunrise. Apparently the Bloi triplets had been up all night fishing for blind-crabs in the mouth of the source-cave stream. They'd come back while it was still dark, swinging their hand-beams and joking as they walked up from the river – Dorik behind the wire in a net of shadow, circled with their lights, face down at the grave's edge! It must have been just moments after I first left.

I wheeled through the brambles, heading toward noon, with one thought clearing, as figures on a stream bed clear when you brush back the bubbles a moment: if Le Dorik, dead, had walked with me a while ("I'm showing you now, Lobey"), walked through dawn and gorse, curled on a stone under new sunlight, then Friza too could travel with me. If I could find what killed those of us who were different, but whose difference gave us a reality beyond dying—

A slow song now on my blade to mourn Dorik; and the beat of my feet on earth in journey. After a few hours of such mourning, the heat had polished me with sweat as in some funeral dance.

While day leaned over the hills I passed the first red flowers, blossoms big as my face, like blood bubbles nestled in thorns, often resting on the bare rock. No good to stop here. Carnivorous.

I squatted on a broken seat of granite in the yellowing afternoon. A snail the size of my curled forefinger bobbed his eyes at a puddle big as my palm. Half an hour later, climbing down a canyon wall when yellow had died under violet, I saw a tear in the rock: another opening into the source-cave. I decided on nighting it there, and ducked in.

Still smells of humans and death. Which is good. Dangerous animals avoid it. I stalked inside, padding on all fours. Loose earth became moss, became cement underfoot. Outside, night, sonic lace of crickets and whining wasps I would not make on my knife, was well into black development.

Soon I touched a metal track, turned, and followed it with my hands...over a place where dirt had fallen, across a scattering of twigs and leaves, then down a long slope. I was about to stop, roll against the cave wall where it was drier, and sleep, when the track split.

I stood up.

When I shrilled on my blade, a long echo came from the right: endless passage there. But only a stubby resonance from the left: some sort of chamber. I walked left. My hip brushed a door jamb.

Then a room glowed suddenly before me. The sensor circuits were still sensitive. Grilled walls, blue glass desk, brass light fixtures, cabinets, and a television screen set in the wall. Squinting in the new light, I walked over. When they still work, the colors are nice to watch: they make patterns and the patterns make music in me. Several people who had gone exploring the source-cave had told me about them (night fire and freakishly interested children knotted around the flame and the adventurer), and I'd gone to see one in a well-explored arm two years back. Which is how I learned about the music.

Color television is certainly a lot more fun than this terribly risky genetic method of reproduction we've taken over. Ah well. It's a lovely world.

I sat on the desk and tried knobs till one clicked. The screen grayed at me, flickered, streamed with colors.

There was static, so I found the volume knob and turned it down...so I could hear the music in the colors. Just as I raised my blade to my mouth, something happened.

Laughter.

First I thought it was melody. But it was a voice laughing. And on the screen, in chaotic shimmerings, a face. It wasn't a picture of a face. It was as if I was just looking at the particular dots of melody/hue that formed the face, ignoring the rest. I would have seen those features on any visual riot: Friza's face.

The voice was someone else's.

Friza dissolved. Another face replaced hers: Dorik's. The strange laughter again. Suddenly there was Friza on one side of the screen, and Dorik on the other. Centered: the boy who was laughing at me. The picture cleared, filled, and I lost the rest of the room. Behind him, crumbled streets, beams jutting from the wrecks of walls, weeds writhing; and all lit with flickering green, the sun white on the reticulated sky. On a lamppost behind him perched a creature with fins and white gills, scraping one red foot on the rust. On the curb was a hydrant laced with light and verdigris.

The boy, a redhead – redder than the Blois, redder than blood-glutted blossoms – laughed with downcast eyes. His lashes were gold. Transparent skin caught up the green and fluoresced with it; but I knew that under normal light he would have been as pale as Whitey dying.

"Lobey," in the laughter, and his lips uncurtained small teeth – many too many of them. Like the shark's mouth, maybe, I'd seen in La Dire's book, rank on rank of ivory needles. "Lobey, how you gonna find me, huh?"

"What...?" and expected the illusion to end with my voice.

But somewhere that naked, laughing boy still stood with one foot in the gutter filled with waving weeds. Only Friza and Dorik were gone.

"Where are you?"

He looked up and his eyes had no whites, only glittering gold and brown. I'd seen a few like that before, eyes. Unnerving, still, to look at a dog's eyes in a human face. "My mother called me Bonny William. Now they all call me Kid Death." He sat on the curb, hanging his hands over his knees. "You're gonna find me, Lobey, kill me like I killed Friza and Dorik?"

"You? You, Lo Bonny William—"

"No Lo. Kid Death. Not Lo Kid."

"You *killed* them? But...*why*?" Despair unvoiced my words to whispers.

"Because they were different. And I am more different than any of you. You scare me, and when I'm frightened" – laughing again – "I kill." He blinked. "You're not looking for me, you know. I'm looking for you."

"What do you mean?"

He shook shocked crimson from his white brow. "I'm bringing you down here to me. If I didn't want you, you'd never find me. Because I do want you, there's no way you can avoid me. I can see through the eyes of anyone on this world, on any world where our ancestors have ever been: so I know a lot about many things I've never touched or smelled. You've started out not knowing where I am and running towards me. You'll end, Lo Lobey" – he raised his head – "fleeing my green home, scrabbling on the sand like a blind goat trying to keep footing at a chimney edge, and—"

"—how do you know about—"

"—you'll fall and break your neck." He shook a finger at me, clawed like Little Jon's. "Come to me, Lo Lobey."

"If I find you, will you give me back Friza?"

"I've already given you back Le Dorik for a little while."

"*Can* you give me back Friza?"

"Everything I kill I keep. In my own private kage." His moist laughter. Water in a cold pipe, I think.

"Kid Death?"

"What?"

"Where are you?"

The sound snagged on ivory needles.

"Where are you from, Kid Death? Where are you going?"

The long fingers raveled like linen rope snaring gold coins. He pushed weeds away from the gutter grill with his foot. "I broiled away childhood in the sands of an equatorial desert kage with no keeper to love me. Like you, lively in your jungle, I was haunted by the memories of those who homed under this sun before our parents' parents came, took on these bodies, loves, and fears. Most of those around me in the kage died of thirst. At first I saved some of my fellows, bringing water to them the way Friza threw the stone – oh yes, I saw that too. I did that for a while. Then for a while I killed whoever was put in the kage with me, and took the water directly from their bodies. I would go to the fence and stare across the dunes to the palms at the oasis where our tribe worked. I never thought to leave the kage, back then, because like mirages on the glistering I saw through all the worlds' eyes – I saw what you and Friza and Dorik saw, as I see what goes all over this arm of the galaxy. When what I saw frightened me, I closed the eyes seeing. That's what happened to Friza and Dorik. When I am still curious about what's going on through those eyes, more curious than frightened, I open them again. That's what happened with Dorik."

"You're strong," I said.

"That's where I come from, the desert, where death shifts in the gritty bones of the Earth. And now? I am going further and further into the sea." Raising his eyes now, his red hair floated back in the shivering green.

"Kid Death," I called again; he was much further away. "Why were you in the kage? You look more functional than half the Lo and La of my village."

Kid Death turned his head and looked at me from the corner of his eyes. He mocked. "Functional? To be born on a desert, a white-skinned redhead with gills?"

The spreading, drinking, miniature mouth of the shark washed away. I blinked. I couldn't think of anything else so I took papers out of the filing cabinet, spread them under the desk, and lay down, tired and bewildered.

I remember I picked up one page and spelled my way through a paragraph. La Dire had taught me enough to read record labels, when for a while I had foraged about the village archives:

> Evacuate upper levels with all due haste. Alarm system will indicate radiation at standard levels. Deeper detection devices are located…

Most of the words were beyond me. I halved the paper with toes and quartered it with fingers, let the pieces fall on my stomach before I picked up my machete to play myself to sleep.

* * *

What, then, is noble abstraction? It is taking first the essential elements of the thing to be represented, then the rest in the order of importance (so that wherever we pause we shall always have obtained more than we leave behind) and using any expedient to impress what we want upon the mind without caring about the mere literal accuracy of such expedient.
John Ruskin, The Stones of Venice

A poem is a machine for making choices.
John Ciardi, How Does a Poem Mean

Hours after – I figure it could have been two, it could have been twelve – I rolled from under the desk and came up grunting, yawning, scratching. When I stepped into the hall the light faded.

I didn't go back the way I'd come but headed forward again. There are lots of breakthroughs into the upper levels. I'd go till I saw morning and climb out. About half an hour later I see a three-foot stretch of it (morning) in the ceiling, behind black leaves, and leap for it. Good jumping power in those hams.

I scrambled out on crumbling ground and tame brambles, tripped on a vine, but all in all did pretty well. Which is to avoid saying "on the whole." Outside was cool, misty. Fifty yards by, the lapping edge of a lake flashed. I walked through the tangle to the clear beach. Chunked rock became gravel, became sand. It was a big lake. Down one arm of the beach things faded into reeds and swamp and things. Across, there was a gorse-covered plain. I had no idea where I was. But I didn't want to be in a swamp, so I walked up the other way.

Thrash, thrash, *snap*!

I stopped.

Thrash! Just inside the jungle something churned and fought. The fighting was at the point where one opponent was near exhausted: activity came in momentary spurts. (*Hissssss*!) Curiosity, hunger, devilment sent me forward with high machete. I crept up a slope of rock, looked over into a glade.

Attacked by flowers, a dragon was dying. Blossoms jeweled his scales; thorns tangled his legs. As I watched, he tried again to tear them off with his teeth, but they scurried back, raking briars across his hide, or whipping them at his runny, yellow eyes.

The lizard (twice as big as Easy and man-branded on his left hinder haunch with a crusty cross) was trying to protect the external gill/lung arrangement that fluttered along his neck. The plants had nearly immobilized him, but when a bloom advanced to tear away his breath, he scraped and flailed with one free claw. He'd mauled a good many of the blossoms and their petals scattered the torn earth.

The cross told me he wouldn't hurt me (even crazed, the lizard once used to man becomes pathetic, seldom harmful) so I jumped down from the rock.

A blossom creeping to attack emptied an air-bladder inches from my foot, "*Ssssss...*" in surprise.

I hacked it, and nervous ooze (nervous in the sense that its nerves are composed of the stuff) belched greenly to the ground. Thorns flailed my legs. But I told you about the skin down there. I just have to watch out for my belly and the palms of my hands; feet are fine. With my foot I seized a creeper from the lizard's shoulder and pulled it out far enough – stained teeth go *clik-clik-clik* popping from the dragon's skin where they had been gnawing – to get my blade under, twist...and...*rip*!

Nerve dribbled the dragon's hide.

Those flowers communicate somehow (differently perhaps) and strove for me, one suddenly rising on its tendrils and leaping, "*Sssssss...*" I twiddled my blade in its brain.

I shouted encouragement to the dragon, threw a brave grin. He moaned reptilianly. Lo Hawk should see me do proud his skill.

His mane brushed my arm, his teeth crunched a flower while tendrils curled from the corners of his mouth. He chewed a while, decided he didn't like it, spat thorns. I pried off two more: his foot came free.

"*Sssssss...*" I looked to the right.

Which was a mistake because it was coming from the left. Mistakes like that are a drag. Long and prickly wrapped my ankle and tried to jerk me off my feet. Fortunately you just can't do that. So then it sank lots of teeth into my calf and commenced chewing. I whirled and snatched white petals (this one an albino) which came away gently in my hand. *Crunch, Crunch,* still on my calf. My sword hand was up. I brought it down but it got caught in a net of brambles. Something scratched the back of my neck. Which ain't so tough.

Neither is (come to think): the small of my back, under my chin, between my legs, armpits, behind my ears – I was quickly cataloging all the tender places now. Damn flowers move just slow enough to give you time to think.

Then something long and hot sang by my shins. Petals snapped into the air. The plant stopped chewing and burped nervously down my ankle.

Pinnnnng near my hand, and my hand pulled free. I staggered, hacked another briar away. A bloated rose slithered down the dragon's leg and crawled for cover. They communicate, yes, and the communication was *fear* and *retreat*. The music, though! Lord, the *music*!

I whirled to look up on the rock.

Morning had got far enough along to rouge the sky behind him. He flicked a final encumbering flower from the beast, "*Sssssss*...blop!" and coiled his whip. I rubbed my calf. The dragon moaned, off key.

"Yours?" I thumbed over my shoulder at the beast.

"Was." He breathed deeply and the flat, bony chest sagged with his breathing, the ribs opening and closing like blinds. "If you come with us, he's yours – to ride, anyway. If you don't, he's mine again."

The dragon rubbed his gills ingenuously against my hip.

"Can you handle a dragon whip?" the stranger asked me.

I shrugged. "The only time I ever even saw one of those before was when some herders got off their trail six years ago." We'd all climbed up Beryl Face and watched them drive the herd of lizards back through Green-glass Pass. When Lo Hawk went to talk to them, I went with him, which is where I found out about branding and the gentle monsters.

The stranger grinned. "Well, it's gone and happened again. I judge we're about twenty-five kilometers off. You want a job and a lizard to ride?"

I looked at the broken flowers. "Yeah."

"Well, there's your mount, and your job is to get him up here and back with the herd, first."

"Oh." (Now, lemme see; I remember the herders perched behind the lumps of the beasts' shoulders with their feet sort of tucked into the scaly armpits. My feet? And holding on to the two white whisker type things that grew back from the gills: Gee...Haw? Giddiap!)

We floundered in the mud about fifteen minutes with instructions shouted down, and I learned cuss words I hadn't ever heard from that guy. Towards the end we were both sort of laughing. The dragon was up and on the beach now, and he had quite unintentionally thrown me into the water – again.

"Hey, you think I'm really going to learn how to ride that thing?"

With one hand he was helping me up, with the other he was holding my mount by the whiskers, with another he was recoiling his whip, and with the fourth he just scratched his woolly head. "Don't give up. I didn't do too much better when I started. Up you go."

Up I went, and stayed on this time for a staggering run up and down the water's edge. I mean it looks graceful enough from the ground. It *feels* like staggering. On stilts.

"You're getting the hang of it."

"Thanks," I said. "Say, where is the herd; and who are you?" He stood ankle deep in the lake's lapping. Morning was bright enough now to gem his chest and shoulders with drops from my splashing. He smiled and wiped his face. "Spider," he said. "And I didn't catch your name...?"

"Lo Lobey." I rocked happily behind the scaly hump.

"Don't say Lo to nobody herding," said Spider. "No need for it."

"Wouldn't even have thought of it if it weren't for my village ways," I said.

"Herd's off that way." He swung up behind me on the dragon.

Amber haired, four handed, and slightly hump-backed, Spider was seven feet of bone slipped into six feet of skin. Tightly. All tied in with long, narrow muscles. He was burned red, and the red burned brown but still glowing through. And he laughed like dry leaves crushed inside his chest. We circled the lake silently. And, oh man, the music!

The herd, maybe two hundred and fifty dragons moaning about (I was to learn that this was a happy sound), milled in a dell beyond the lake. Youth had romanticized the herders in my memory. They were motley. I see why you don't go around Lo-ing and La-ing and Le-ing herders. Two of them – I *still* don't see how they managed to stay on their dragons. But I came on friendly.

One kid with a real mind: you could tell by the way his green eye glittered at you, as well as his whip skill, and the sure way he handled dragons. Only he was mute. Was it this that upset me and made me think of Friza? You have a job to do...

There was another guy who would have made Whitey look like a total norm. He had some glandular business that made him smell bad too. And he wanted to tell me his life story (no motor control of the mouth so he sort of splattered when he got excited).

I wish Green-eye could have talked instead of Stinky. I wanted to learn where he'd been, what he'd seen – he knew some good songs.

Dragons get lost at night. So you round them up in the morning. I'd been rounded up along with the stray animals. At breakfast I gathered from Stinky that I was a replacement for somebody who had come to a bad, sad, and messy end the previous afternoon.

"Oddest people survive out here," Spider mused. "Oddest ones don't. She looked a lot more 'normal' than you. But she ain't here now. Just goes to show you."

Green-eye blinked at me from under all his black hair, caught me watching him, and went back to splicing his whip.

"When are those dragon eggs gonna finish baking?" Knife asked, pawing at the fireplace stones with gray hands.

Spider kicked at him and the herder scuttled away. "Wait till we all eat." But in a few minutes he crawled back and was rubbing against the stones. "Warm," he muttered apologetically, when Spider started to kick him again. "I like it warm."

"Just keep off the food."

"Where do you take these to?" I indicated the herd. "Where do you bring them from?"

"They breed in the Hot Swamp, about two hundred kilometers west of here. We drive them down this way, across the Great City and on to Branning-at-sea. There the sterile ones are slaughtered; the eggs are removed from the females, inseminated, then we bring the eggs back and plant them in the swamp."

"Branning-at-sea?" I asked. "What do they do with them there?"

"Eat most. Use others for work. It's quite a fantastic place for someone born in the woods, I would imagine. I've been back and forth so many times it's like home. I've got a house and a wife and three kids there, and another family back in the Swamp."

We ate eggs, fried lizard fat, and thick cereal, hot and filling, with plenty of salt and chopped peppers. When I finished I began to play my blade.

That *music*!

It was a whole lot of tunes at once, many the same, but starting at different times. I had to pick one strand out and play it. A few notes into it, I saw Spider staring at me, surprised. "Where did you hear that?" he asked.

"Just made it up, I guess."

"Don't be silly."

"It was just running around my head. All confused, though."

"Play it again, Sam—"

I did. This time Spider began to whistle one of the other melodies that went along with it so that they glittered and jumped against each other.

When we finished he said, "You're different, aren't you?"

"So I've been told," I said. "Say, what's the name of that song anyway? It's not like most of the music I know."

"It's the Kodaly 'Sonata for Unaccompanied Cello.'"

Morning wind shook the gorse. "The *what*?' I asked. Behind us dragons moaned.

"You got it out of my head?" Spider said questioningly. "You couldn't have heard it before unless I was going around humming. And I can't hum a crescendo of triple stops."

"I got it from you?"

"That music's been going through my mind for weeks. Heard it at a concert last summer at Branning-at-sea, the night before I left to take the eggs back to the swamp. Then I discovered an LP of the piece in the music section of the ruins of the ancient library at Haifa."

"I learned it from you?" and suddenly all sorts of things cleared up, like how La Dire knew I was different, like how Nativia could tell I was different when I started playing *Bill Bailey*. "Music," I said. "So that's where I get my music from." I put the blade's tip on the ground and leaned on it.

Spider shrugged.

"I don't think I get all of it from other people," I said, frowning. "Different?" I ran my thumb along the blade's edge and skipped my toes over the holes.

"I'm different too," Spider said.

"How?"

"Like this." He closed his eyes and all his shoulders knotted.

My machete jerked from my hand, pulled from the ground, and spun in the air. Then it fell point first to quiver in the shank of a log near the fire. Spider opened his eyes and took a breath.

My mouth was open. So I closed it.

Everybody else thought it was very funny.

"And with animals," Spider said.

"How?"

"The dragons. To a certain point I can keep them calm, keep them more or less together, and steer dangerous creatures away from us."

"Friza," I said. "You're like Friza."

"Who's Friza?"

I looked down at my knife. The melody which I had mourned her with was mine. "Nobody," I said, "anymore." That melody was mine! Then I asked, "Have you ever heard of Kid Death?"

Spider put down his food, brought all his hands in front of him, and tilted his head. His long nostrils flared till they were round. I looked away from his fear. But the others were watching me so I had to look back.

"What about Kid Death?" Spider asked.

"I want to find him and—" I flung my blade in the air and twirled it as Spider had, but my hand had propelled it. I seized it from its fall with my foot. "—Well, I want to find him. Tell me about him."

They laughed. It started in Spider's mouth, then was coming all sloppy from Stinky, a low hiss from Knife, grunts and cackles from the others, ending in Green-eye's green eye, a light that went out as he looked away. "You're going to have a hard time," Spider said finally, "but" – he rose from the fire – "you're headed in the right direction."

"Tell me about him," I said again.

"There's a time to talk about the impossible, but it's not when there's work to do." He got up, reached into a canvas sack, and tossed me a whip.

I caught it mid-length.

"Put your ax away," Spider said. "This sings when it flies." His lash lisped over my head.

Everyone went to his mount, and Spider reeled a bridle and stirrups from the gear sack that fitted those humps and scales neatly, buckling around the forelegs; I see why he'd made me get the feel of things bareback. The semi-saddle and leg-straps make dragon riding almost nice.

"Head them on through that way," he yelled, and I imitated the herders around me as they began the drive.

Dragons swarmed in sunlight.

Oiled whips snapped and glistened over the scales, and the whole world got caught up in the rhythmic rocking of the beast between my legs, trees and hills and gorse and boulders and brambles all taking up the tune and movement as a crowd will begin clapping and stomping to a beat; the jungle, my audience, applauded the beat of surging lizards.

Moaning. Which meant they were happy.

Hissing sometimes. Which meant watch it.

Grunting and cussing and shouting. Which meant the herders were happy too.

I learned an incredible amount of things that morning, lunging back and forth between the creatures: five or six of them were the leaders and the rest followed. Keep the leaders going in the right direction and you had no problem. Dragons tend to go right. You get more response if you slap them on the back haunches. I later learned, nerve clusters there control their rear-end transmissions that're bigger than the brain.

One of the lead dragons kept on wanting to go back and bother an overweight female (ovarian tumor that kept her loaded down with sterile eggs, Spider explained to me) and it was all we could do to keep them apart. I spent a lot of time (imitating Green-eye) scouting the edge of the herd to worry the creatures back together who kept getting curious about things in irrelevant directions.

I began to learn what I was doing when about twenty dragons got stuck in a mintbog. (A slushy, slow quicksand *bog* covered with huge bushes of windy *mint*, right? Mintbog.) Spider, by himself drove the rest of the herd around in a circle, three whips popping, while the other five of us went sloshing back and forth through the mint to drive the dragons out before they drowned.

"There shouldn't be too many more of those," Spider shouted when we were charging along again. "We'll be crossing the City in a little while if we're not too far off course. I've been swinging us westward."

My arm was sore.

Once I got twenty seconds of calm riding time beside Green-eye: "Isn't this a pretty stupid way to waste your life, fellow?"

He grinned.

Then two very friendly dragons came galumphing and moaning between us. Sweat slopped into my eyes and my armpits felt oiled. The harness made it a little easier on my inner thighs; they got raw slow 'stead of quick. I could hardly see and was playing it more by ear than eye when Spider called, "Back on course! City up ahead!"

I looked up but fresh sweat flooded my eyes and the heat made everything waver. I drove dragons. The gorse lessened, and we started down.

Earth crumbled under their claws. With no vegetation to blunt the temperature, the sun stuck gold needles in the backs of our necks. Reflected heat from the ground. At last, sand.

The dragons had to slow. Spider paused beside me to thumb sweat from his eyes. "We usually take McClellan Avenue," he told me as he looked across the dunes. "But I think we're closer to Main Street. This hits McClellan a few miles out. We'll stop at the intersection and rest until nightfall." The dragons hissed out across the City sands. Swamp creatures, they were not used to this dryness. As we plowed the ancient place, silent and furious with hundreds of beasts, I remember crossing a moment of untimed horror, when through void buff I imagined myself surrounded of a sudden, crowded by millions, straited by walls, sooty, fuming, roaring with the dread, dead old race of the planet.

I flailed my whip and beat away the notion. The sun ground its light into the sand.

Two dragons began to annoy each other and I flicked them apart. They snatched at my lash indignantly, missed. My breath filed my throat. Yet, as the two moved away, I realized I was grinning. Alone, we toiled through the day, content and terrified.

End of extract.

Eyes of a Living Planet

Yazeed Dele-Azeez

THE NEWBLAKLAND SPACESHIP *Kalahari–56VR* was the size of three Boeing 737 max planes fused into one heart shape of an interstellar spacecraft, yet viewed against the vast infinity of the star-studded sky was but a twinkling speck of blue-red light as it hovered, about five hundred feet, above a spot on the luxuriant wilderness of Greenplanet landmass known as Alkebulan.

Captain Ayesha Bakare's attention was not on the bank of giant flickering monitors that took up the front space of the bridge where a live feed, captured from drone camera surveillance, showed the mysterious green canopy of alien vegetation glimmering beneath. She was looking out through one of the bay window screens where great scarves of misty clouds swirled around a landscape of towering mountains carpeted in dense evergreen vegetation: a primeval virgin forest, vast and forbidden. She was trying to sense things with her own instincts; from what her naked eyes and soul told her, rather than what the surveillance drone cameras wanted her to see.

Alkebulan was known to be uninhabited by any complex creatures with a civilization but Ayesha and her crew already knew the truth: the planet's virgin flora was far more alive than anything back on their own Sandplanet home-world of Newblakland, and the trees showed evidence of sentience: a neural linked sentience that was as psychological as it was spiritual.

Nothing back on Newblakland, except perhaps the nerve cells of the human brain, matched it in complexity and mystery.

There were gushing waterfalls, shimmering mirror-clear rivers and lakes, a buzzing cloud of alien plantoid insects and birds – nothing much else in terms of fauna. To think this newfound paradise was where her people's hope of a 'promised land' lay; their next pollution-degradation-exploitation project, and to think she'd be at the vanguard of it all. Ayesha shook her head in distaste.

Apart from her fifty-member space service crew, the NSS *Kalahari-56VR* carried another group of no fewer than five hundred civilian delegates of administrators, engineers, scientists and workers necessary to construct the first human colony on Alkebulan, including equipment and material. If only she gave the clearance order to land.

Ayesha needed something to clear the fog in her brain. Her nervous system screamed for the usual drug she'd come to rely on in this complicated game of planet colonization: Zagga coffee. But it wasn't yet time for her break and she didn't want to give her bridge officers the wrong impression, that their captain relied on stimulants to keep body and mind together.

Ayesha's strained mid-fifties cocoa-brown face was paled out by the florescent glare of cockpit lighting. She whirled round in her command chair to pull her thoughts back to the bridge. Her white uniformed officers milled about in a flurry of activity, like twinkling stars orbiting a planet, barking out instructions to one another, operating control-consoles, and monitoring operations.

She was suddenly aware that her heart was throbbing in her ears and her legs were shaking. Throughout her eventful twenty-five years of service in the Newblakland Space Agency, her primary coping method for conquering her fears was to imagine the worst that could happen and prepare herself mentally to face it. This defense mechanism she'd come to realize was only now effective for those primitive days of outer space exploration when spacefaring activities had only but one-dimensional risk of physical danger: being lost in an alien world or eaten up by alien beings. Now another intangible dimension was at play, which she couldn't really psych herself up to go through with: having a great mass of people wanting to live on an alien planet full of sentient flora. Cracking her knuckles to steady her twitching fingers, Ayesha glanced over her shoulder to ask a bridge midshipman assistant for the latest 'Opti Condi.'

"Stasis mode 500hp per hour at Spacespeed factor-9. Condition Green."

Ayesha nodded her head at the latest update. All moving smoothly, so far.

To keep a jumbo spacecraft hovering in perpetual mid-flight took a lot out of it. This she understood. But it was necessary for an effective reconnaissance before landing, to minimize risks in the long run. This was the excuse she'd tendered to the Space Service Admiralty back at home base. Worse still was the fact of keeping five hundred odd civilians, the majority of them young and restive, in a confined space for an extended duration. Although there were enough entertainment and recreation facilities on board to keep their idle minds and flagging bodies diverted, it was only a matter of time before boredom-induced rebellion set in.

Ayesha was typing in the last duty update on to her captain's log when her earplug buzzed with an emergency alert.

Lt. Comdr. Tunde Bajowa, her first officer, informed her that Mr Chidoka Ogbonna, leader of the civilian delegation, whom she and her crew chidingly called 'Big Trouble' behind his back, wanted to gatecrash himself into the bridge to see her.

Her face contracted in a moment of annoyance as she looked up to see CCTV footage of the bridge's outer entrance where her security details were engaged in fisticuffs with Big Trouble.

Ayesha gasped in exasperation and said she was coming in a moment. She didn't rush but waited out the remaining thirty minutes of her duty time.

When she was done, she groomed her shoulder-length dreadlocks, checked if her flight suit was creased in any way and put on her clear-framed spectacles. Glancing at her own reflection in a hand mirror, satisfied with her unruffled look and in-charge appearance, she eased out of the bridge, after asking her first officer to take charge while she handled Big Trouble.

"Is this how you instruct your staff to handle very important personalities?" the so-called founding administrator of the proposed human colony and self-styled "future first executive Governor of Alkebulan" blurted out once he sighted Ayesha, his jowly scowling face giving off what seemed like puffs of invisible smoke.

"Well, no. Mr Ogbonna. But a little self-respect won't take anything away from you, would it?"

Ayesha observed that Big Trouble's brow was knotted in a frustration she sensed was deeper in magnitude than the purported manhandling he'd suffered from her security details. His spotted pink tie had come undone from the sharp navy blue jacket of his business suit and one or two buttons were missing.

"We need to talk, Madam Ayesha," he said, running a hand across his glistening bald dome. The tuft of greying hair surrounding his head seemed to have grown fuller and whiter.

"Yes, I was planning to talk with you too, sir," Ayesha said as she led Big Trouble to the spaceship's conference room. Her strides were long, quick, and confident. In spite of her cordial dislike for Mr Ogbonna she liked the way he referred to her as "Madam Ayesha" rather than as "Captain Bakare". A hard-faced security guard was escorting and glancing malevolently at Big Trouble, but she gave him a hand-sign to retreat.

They sank into comfy conference-room chairs.

Ayesha punched her ear plug, asking for her Zagga coffee with a tin of milk; she needed the sleep as much as she needed her mind cleared of the cobwebs clogging it. She asked Big Trouble what he'd have.

"Chilled beer," came the cold reply.

Soon Ayesha's Robot Stewardess, Zaibot, swished in with a tray containing the order.

"So, Mr Ogbonna, you wanted to talk," Ayesha said, squirming under the smug founding-father gaze.

Big Trouble cleared his throat huskily, swallowed a hard lump, puffed his chest and began.

"I was studying the resources map for the umpteenth time a while ago, eh, and it dawned on me that we are hanging, or rather playing, above the richest planet in the Denga Solar System, eh... And to think we are killing time doing nothing, wasting manpower and precious energy. These, despite the fact that this planet is, eh, uninhabited by humans or any significant animal species for that matter. It just beats, eh, my imagination to say the least."

"Did you say it beats your imagination?" Ayesha said, stirring her cup, the milk black. Zagga awakened her senses, reconnected her with her worn-out shell. "Well, I understand and can only sympathize," she was being careful to walk the line here, knowing what vested interest and authority Big Trouble represented, "we need more time as it were."

Mr Ogbonna swirled his drink directly from the bottle. Ayesha could sense the tension exploding with every gulp that went down his throat.

"How much more time?" Big trouble said, after a few regurgitative belches. He slammed down the empty bottle, wiped the white foam off his twitching moustache, smacked his lip noisily. "We are already halfway to the appointed time. We should have commenced work, eh, in other words Madam Ayesha, we are out of time. My engineers and staff are all itching to get down to work, eh... The investors, who are sponsoring this mission, are on my neck. The government too can't wait for the Newblakland flag to be planted down there, eh...nobody will take this shit you are saying. At least not from me."

Big trouble's beer-misty eyes had grown suddenly hard and red, as though the drink had exploded, something sinister buried within him. Already there were few cases of drunkenness among the civilian delegation, which she was aware of.

"They won't understand, Mr Ogbonna, because they are not here to witness what we are witnessing. You are here so we can count on you to understand the situation."

"Witness what?!" Big Trouble snapped, thrashing out his big arms in a gesture of frustration. "You and your high-headed staff have always kept me in the dark about whatever is happening down there so how do I witness or understand what I don't even know?"

"OK. What you need to know," Ayesha said in her most unctuous voice. "The biosphere here, especially the flora, is not like the one in Newblakland. The trees and grasses here are as intelligent as you and I sitting here. They think, they feel, and they sense the world around them. So we seriously think their viewpoint matters in whether or not they want us to do anything on their land."

Big Trouble cracked out a hard mechanical laugh that stroked a wound in Ayesha's chest. She took a long, soothing sip of her drink.

"When the honorable Minister of Space Affairs sent me your CV as the space captain to lead two billion proud and black people of Newblakland to their first outer-planet treasure I was overwhelmed with joy, eh... For in it I saw the most experienced, if not the most decorated, spacefarer alive leading the charge. I saw purposeful leadership and military craftsmanship, all rolled in one. I don't want to think I was totally mistaken."

"You are not mistaken, Mr Ogbonna," Ayesha said, keeping her face blank, careful not to swallow Big Trouble's bait.

"So it's only logical to you that trees and grasses should come between us and our biggest lifetime asset?"

"To give you a safe picture," Ayesha said, placing emphasis on the word "safe", "we have evidence that these trees possess supernatural powers."

Big Trouble shrank in his chair, his face contracted. His eyes had become squinted like those of a scared dog. He fiddled with his tie and said; "Can't we just chemical-bomb them? We can't allow them to keep us waiting forever. After all, we are, eh…humans and they are just trees."

"You don't mean, Mr Ogbonna, that you want to live on a sterile planet with a dead ecosystem?" Ayesha asked, lifting her eyebrows and cocking her head to one side in perplexion.

"We can always ship in fast-growing hybrid trees from Newblakland to rebuild the ecosystem. We have the technological prowess, don't we? Sometimes in life we have to make sacrifices, Madam Ayesha, eh…to destroy before we construct. You should know better as a military personality."

"Diplomacy," Ayesha said, unclasping her hands from the table, waving it dismissively at Big Trouble, trying to control the heat of indignation steaming in her chest. "We are trying whatever we can to interface, to engage with them at the lowest possible cost to our own lives… I'd be giving you updates, in due course."

Big Trouble's gaze hardened. His face was animated with distaste.

"We came here to colonize, Madam Ayesha, not just to explore."

"Well…Mr Ogbonna, I can assure you our mandate to colonize shall be fulfilled. But not with neglect or denial of our social responsibility to the land."

Ayesha left the conference room for her private quarters, feeling somewhat relieved that she'd won an important battle. Fifty per cent of the war, so far. The other fifty per cent, she resolved, would be won on the ground.

* * *

Ayesha was dreaming. She found herself flying above the heart of the alien jungle. The mountains looked from afar like a pile of ore, then suddenly transformed themselves into gargoyle sculptured deities. The rivers which looked like potential irrigation water had become red blood, a vein of the land. The huge trees had turned into a sacred grove of human-like figures, not the timbers they were supposed to be.

The forest started to speak to her in a cryptic voice which formed in her mind:

Dodododooo! Kwa dooo!
This is our land, the land of your death
This is our sacrifice; the sacrifice of your blood
This is our spirit, the spirit of your life
Dodododooo! Kwa dooo!

Ayesha was suddenly yanked out of her dream by the vibrating buzz of her earplug, an emergency alert. Her eyes flew open; her heart was hammering as she jerked her head from the sweat-drenched pillow with a start.

Lt. Comdr. Bajowa debriefed her of the ongoing emergency situation. There was a mutiny from the civilian delegation, instigated by Mr Chidoka Ogbonna. Big Trouble had sent the first officer a message, purportedly endorsed by the Minister of Space Affairs, asking him to take control of the captaincy and to land the spaceship.

Ayesha's migraine nagged her. She swiped on her tablet and CCTV footage of Deck 'C', where the civilian delegations were camped, popped into view.

A band of protesters, mostly youths, were smashing glasses in the commercial quarters. Others chanted solidarity songs and raised placards that said:

"SAVE OUR DIGNITY! LAND THE SPACESHIP! ALKEBULAN OUR PRIDE OUR HERITAGE… READY TO WORK, READY TO SERVE?"

A detachment of Space Service security officers formed a cordon, barring the riotous mob from spreading beyond Deck 'C'. Lieutenant Wayama held a megaphone to his mouth and was addressing the crowd, warning them of consequences of being tried for with disruption, if they didn't disperse.

Ayesha heaved a deep sigh, closed her eyes, and digested the situation. Then she gave her orders. The mutinous bunch, along with Mr Chidoka Ogbonna, should be arrested and shipped back to Newblakland, on spaceshuttle-25RV, and be made to face trial for illegally disrupting a spaceship in mid-flight. Then on second thought she said: "Put Big Trouble only under house arrest in his private quarters, and keep him incommunicado for the time being".

"Yes, Captain, your orders. Issued 12:04 PM 2nd of August, Year 3030, over."

Ayesha lay her head down to resume her interrupted sleep. She closed her eyes but remained sleepless, listening to the distant din of clamouring voices and breaking glass.

* * *

The fusion bay-doors parted open with a protesting hydraulic whine. A blast of cold forest-misted air poured in from the alien atmosphere down below.

Ayesha, clad in Exo-pack body armor and visor-plated helmet, uttered a little prayer as the anchor cable lowered her into the heart of the jungle.

"Splufik Captain! We are together," shrilled the nervous voice of her chief science officer Nia Jemmison.

Ayesha held on to the ropes as her weight hurtled her down nearly five hundred feet from the belly of the hovering spaceship to the evergreen canopy of foliage. The bed of luxuriant greenery spread out as far and wide as her eyes could see, tingling her with a sensation of awe mixed with dread.

When she landed on the forest floor and looked round from her visor-plated face it was as though she'd been whisked thousands of years through time to find herself in the primeval forest that had existed since the beginning of time.

The trees were a bit too green, almost phosphorescent, Ayesha observed, and the exotic fragrance of rich raw green from the forbidden fruits they carried on their branches overwhelmed her senses.

She inhaled deeply, reveling in the odor of Mother Nature, the dank decay of dead leaves and the black chocolate of over-fertile loam.

Her breathing seemed to resonate with the vibrant trill of the enshrouding vegetation.

Ayesha knew, deep down, that she was not just on an excursion to seek the face of the living forest but also to satisfy her green lust, which had inadvertently been stirred up ever since she set eyes on Greenplanet.

Back on Sandplanet she remembered whenever she was too distressed or disturbed by events in her inner world, she could always take a walk through a green park to find relaxation and escape. And by the time she emerged it would always feel as though her troubles and stress had been soaked up and absorbed out of her by the millions of leaves, the tree bark and root networks, and that she'd been covered with a healing balm of soothing herbal energy.

Remembering her dream, Ayesha looked round anxiously. It seemed as though the long mysterious trunks faces were watching her. She'd told Mr Chidoka Ogbonna that the trees were supernatural. There was no concrete evidence for this, but that they possessed a modicum of sentience she knew, backed up by Dr Jemmison's research.

Ayesha didn't know where or how to begin. She wanted to hear or see a sign. She uttered a prayer, then on a sudden impulse walked to the nearest tree.

The diaphanous trunks that were the planet's most prevalent flora swayed gently in the wind, and tiny perforations in their stems caused music, a gentle lilting tone that was a perpetual rustling lullaby. If only she could detect a portion of the land where the spirits were non-existent or rather where the plant community would allow humanity to land and thrive in peaceful co-existence with them, she'd be truly grateful.

Summoning a bit of strength, she knocked on a trunk three times, the way she'd seen native folks do back in her ancestral village in Newblakland when they wanted to apologize to the spirit of a tree before hurting it to fetch herbs.

"Dodododooo! Kwadooo!" she chanted, this was how her grandmother used to say it to a tree and it was the same line she'd heard the tree *speak* to her in her dream.

The tree in question suddenly came alive. Its smooth fleshy bark shivered like the body of a human. A big, lidless eye popped out to gaze at her. A drip of red blood-like sap ran down the big tree's eyes like tears.

Before Ayesha could recover herself, a snake-branch thrashed itself to grab her hand and flung her several feet away to the forest floor.

She gasped from the pain trying to stagger up to her feet when she observed the whole colony of trees had suddenly come alive, each with its own pair of eyes. Watching her, snaking out their branches to get hold of her wriggling body. Swooshing and rustling.

"Red up!" she screamed into her earplug.

The anchor cable jacked her out.

* * *

In the conference room, surrounded by her space service board, Ayesha, still reeling from a sore back, cracked rib, and broken leg, explained to her team the infeasibility of the Alkebulan colonization mission:

"We here wouldn't like to be dispossessed of our own land, our own heritage, so why should we do it to another kind of living creature who shares our ability to sense thought and emotions? Who has a soul of their own? They are our biological kith and kin."

Ayesha watched her crew board; most of them nodded their heads in slow acquiescence.

The honorable Minister of Space Affairs Raz Marlon Tolroy, bedecked in his magnificent Rastafarian attire, appeared on the wall-screen and addressed the board meeting. His eyes were glazed and his voice trembled as he spoke:

"You are taking responsibility for the failure of this mission, Captain Bakare. You knew what was at stake, didn't you? You are coming back home to answer for whatever happened. And don't blame me should the Presidency strip you off your rank and position in the Space Service Fleet...and of course you can kiss your pension goodbye..."

Ayesha eased her weight on the backrest of her chair. She felt an odd liberating sensation of satisfaction expand through her veins as though a heaviness, which had the exact same value in weight as the *Kalahari–56VR* itself, had just been lifted out of her heart.

Her staff were surprised to find her blank face break into a glowing smile they'd never seen on her face before.

Like Daughter

Tananarive Due

I GOT THE CALL in the middle of the week, when I came wheezing home from my uphill late-afternoon run. I didn't recognize the voice on my computer's answer-phone at first, although I thought it sounded like my best friend, Denise. There was no video feed, only the recording, and the words were so improbable they only confused me more: "Sean's gone. Come up here and get Neecy. Take her. I can't stand to look at her."

Her words rolled like scattered marbles in my head.

I had just talked to Denise a week before, when she called from Chicago to tell me her family might be coming to San Francisco to visit me that winter, when Neecy was out of school for Christmas vacation.

We giggled on the phone as if we were planning a sleepover, the way we used to when we were kids. Denise's daughter, Neecy, is my godchild. I hadn't seen her since she was two, which was a raging shame and hard for me to believe when I counted back the years in my mind, but it was true. I'd always made excuses, saying I had too much traveling and too many demands as a documentary film producer, where life is always projected two and three years into the future, leaving little space for here and now.

But that wasn't the reason I hadn't seen my godchild in four years. We both knew why.

I played the message again, listening for cadences and tones that would remind me of Denise, and it was like standing on the curb watching someone I knew get hit by a car. Something had stripped Denise's voice bare. So that meant her husband, Sean, must really be gone, I realized. And Denise wanted to send her daughter away.

"I can't stand to look at her," the voice on the message was saying again.

I went to my kitchen sink, in the direct path of the biting breeze from my half-open window, and I was shaking. My mind had frozen shut, sealing my thoughts out of reach. I turned on the faucet and listened to the water pummel my aluminum basin, then I captured some of the lukewarm stream in my palms to splash my face. As the water dripped from my chin, I cupped my hands again and drank, and I could taste the traces of salty perspiration I'd rubbed from my skin, tasting myself. My anger and sadness were tugging on my stomach. I stood at the window and cursed as if what I was feeling had a shape and was standing in the room with me.

I think I'd started to believe I might have been wrong about the whole thing. That was another reason I'd kept some distance from Denise; I hadn't wanted to be there to poke holes in what she was trying to do, to cast doubts with the slightest glance. That's something only a mother or a lifelong friend can do, and I might as well have been both to Denise despite our identical ages. I'd thought maybe if I only left her alone, she could build everything she wanted inside that Victorian brownstone in Lincoln Park. The husband, the child, all of it. Her life could trot on happily ever after, just the way she'd planned.

But that's a lie, too. I'd always known I was right. I had been dreading that call all along, since the beginning. And once it finally came, I wondered what the hell had taken so long. You know how Denise's voice really sounded on my answering machine that day? As if she'd wrapped herself up in that recorder and died.

"Paige, promise me you'll look out for Neecy, hear?" Mama used to tell me. I couldn't have known then what a burden that would be, having to watch over someone. But I took my role seriously. Mama said Neecy needed me, so I was going to be her guardian. Just a tiny little bit, I couldn't completely be a kid after that.

Mama never said exactly why my new best friend at Mae Jemison Elementary School needed guarding, but she didn't have to. I had my own eyes. Even when Neecy didn't say anything, I noticed the bruises on her forearms and calves, and even on Neecy's mother's neck once, which was the real shocker. I recognized the sweet, sharp smell on Neecy's mother's breath when I walked to Neecy's house after school. Her mother smiled at me so sweetly, just like that white lady Mrs Brady on reruns of *The Brady Bunch* my mother made me watch, because she used to watch it when she was my age and she thought it was more appropriate than the "trash" on the children's channels when I was a kid. That smile wasn't a real smile; it was a smile to hide behind.

I knew things Mama didn't know, in fact. When Neecy and I were nine, we already had secrets that made us feel much older; and not in the way that most kids want to feel older, but in the uninvited way that only made us want to sit by ourselves in the playground watching the other children play, since we were no longer quite in touch with our spirit of running and jumping. The biggest secret, the worst, was about Neecy's Uncle Lonnie, who was twenty-two, and what he had forced Neecy to do with him all summer during the times her parents weren't home. Neecy finally had to see a doctor because the itching got so bad. She'd been bleeding from itching between her legs, she'd confided to me. This secret filled me with such horror that I later developed a dread of my own period because I associated the blood with Neecy's itching. Even though the doctor asked Neecy all sorts of questions about how she could have such a condition, which had a name Neecy never uttered out loud, Neecy's mother never asked at all.

So, yes, I understood why Neecy needed looking after. No one else was doing it.

What I didn't understand, as a child, was how Neecy could say she hated her father for hitting her and her mother, but then she'd be so sad during the months when he left, always wondering when he would decide to come home. And how Neecy could be so much smarter than I was – the best reader, speller, and multiplier in the entire fourth grade – and still manage to get so many Fs because she just wouldn't sit still and do her homework. And the thing that puzzled me most of all was why, as cute as Neecy was, she seemed to be ashamed to show her face to anyone unless she was going to bed with a boy, which was the only time she ever seemed to think she was beautiful. She had to go to the doctor to get abortion pills three times before she graduated from high school.

Maybe it was the secret-sharing, the telling, that kept our friendship so solid, so fervent. Besides, despite everything, there were times I thought Neecy was the only girl my age who had any sense, who enjoyed reciting poems and acting out scenes as much as I did. Neecy never did join the drama club like I did, claiming she was too shy, but we spent hours writing and performing plays of our own behind my closed bedroom door, exercises we treated with so much imagination and studiousness that no one would ever guess we were our only audience.

"I wish I had a house like yours," Neecy used to say, trying on my clothes while she stood admiring herself in my closet mirror, my twin.

By fall, the clothes would be hers, because in the summer Mama always packed my clothes for Neecy in a bundle. For my other little girl, she'd say. And beforehand Neecy would constantly warn me, "Don't you mess up that dress," or "Be careful before you rip that!" because she already felt proprietary.

"Oh, my house isn't so special," I used to tell Neecy. But that was the biggest lie of all.

In the years afterward, as Neecy dragged a parade of crises to my doorstep, like a cat with writhing rodents in her teeth – men, money, jobs; everything was a problem for Neecy – I often asked myself what forces had separated us so young, dictating that I had grown up in my house and Neecy had grown up in the other. She'd lived right across the street from my family, but our lives may as well have been separated by the Red Sea.

Was it only an accident that my own father never hit me, never stayed away from home for even a night, and almost never came from work without hugging me and telling me I was his Smart Little Baby-Doll?

And that Mama never would have tolerated any other kind of man? Was it pure accident that I'd had no Uncle Lonnie to make me itch until I bled with a disease the doctor had said little girls shouldn't have?

"Girl, you're so lucky," Neecy told me once when I was in college and she'd already been working for three years as a clerk at the U Save drugstore. She'd sworn she wasn't interested in college, but at that instant her tone had been so rueful, so envy-soaked, that we could have been children again, writing fantastic scripts for ourselves about encounters with TV stars and space aliens behind my closed bedroom door, both of us trying to forget what was waiting for Neecy at home. "In my next life, I'm coming back you for sure."

If only Neecy had been my real-life sister, not just a pretend one, I always thought. If only things had been different for her from the time she was born.

I called Denise a half hour after I got her message. She sounded a little better, but not much. Whether it was because she'd gathered some composure or swallowed a shot or two of liquor, this time her voice was the one I've always known: hanging low, always threatening to melt into a defeated laugh. She kept her face screen black, refusing to let me see her. "It's all a mess. This place looks like it was robbed," she said. "He took everything. His suits. His music. His favorite books, you know, those Russian writers, Dostoyevsky and Nabokov, or whatever-the-fuck. Only reason I know he was ever here is because of the hairs in the bathroom sink. He shaved first. He stood in there looking at his sorry face in the mirror after he'd loaded it all up, and he…" For the first time, her voice cracked. "He left…me. And her. He left."

I couldn't say anything against Sean. What did she expect? The poor man had tried, but from the time they met, it had all been as arranged as a royal Chinese marriage. How could anyone live in that house and breathe under the weight of Denise's expectations? Since I couldn't invent any condolences, I didn't say anything.

"You need to take Neecy." Denise filled the silence.

Hearing her say it so coldly, my words roiled beneath my tongue, constricting my throat. I could barely sound civil. "The first time you told me about doing this…I said to think about what it would mean. That it couldn't be undone. Didn't I, Neecy?"

"Don't call me Neecy." Her words were icy, bitter. "Don't you know better?"

"What happens now? She's your daughter, and she's only six. Think of—"

"Just come get her. If not, I don't…I don't know what I'll do."

Then she hung up on me, leaving my melodramatic imagination to wonder what she'd meant by that remark, if she was just feeling desperate or if she was holding a butcher knife or a gun in her hand when she said it. Maybe that was why she'd blacked herself out, I thought.

I was crying like a six-year-old myself while my cab sped towards the airport. I saw the driver's wondering eyes gaze at me occasionally in his rearview mirror, and I couldn't tell if he was sympathetic or just annoyed. I booked myself on an eight-forty flight with a seat in first class on one of the S-grade planes that could get me there in forty minutes. Airbuses, I call them. At least in first class I'd have time for a glass or two of wine. I convinced the woman at the ticket counter to give me the coach price because, for the first time in all my years of flying, I lied and said I was going to a funeral. My sister's, I told her, tears still smarting on my face.

If you could even call that a lie.

Three more months, just ninety days, and it never would have happened. If Denise had waited only a few months, if she'd thought it through the way I begged her when she first laid out the details of her plan, the procedure would not have been legal. The Supreme Court's decision came down before little Neecy was even born, after only a couple hundred volunteers paid the astronomical fee to take part in the copycat babies program. To this day, I still have no idea where Denise got the money. She never told me, and I got tired of asking.

But she got it somehow, somewhere, along with two hundred thirty others. There were a few outright nutcases, of course, lobbying to try to use DNA samples to bring back Thomas Jefferson and Martin Luther King; I never thought that would prove anything except that those men were only human and could be as unremarkable as the rest of us. But mostly the applicants were just families with something left undone, I suppose. Even though I never agreed with Denise's reasons, at least I had some idea of what she hoped to accomplish. The others, I wasn't sure. Was it pure vanity? Novelty? Nostalgia? I still don't understand.

In the end, I'm not sure how many copycat babies were born. I read somewhere that some of the mothers honored the Supreme Court's ban and were persuaded to abort. Of course, they might have been coerced or paid off by one of the extremist groups terrified of a crop of so-called "soulless" children. But none of that would have swayed Denise, anyway. For all I know, little Neecy might have been the very last one born.

It was three months too late, but I was moved by the understated eloquence of the High Court's decision when it was announced on the News & Justice Satellite: Granted, what some might call a "soul" is merely an individual's biological imprint, every bit as accidental as it is unique. In the course of accident, we are all born once, and we die but once. And no matter how ambiguous the relationship between science and chance, humankind cannot assign itself to the task of re-creating souls.

I'm not even sure I believe in souls, not really. But I wished I'd had those words for Denise when it still mattered.

She actually had the whole thing charted out. We were having lunch at a Loop pizzeria the day Denise told me what she wanted to do. She spread out a group of elaborate charts; one was marked HOME, one FATHER, one SCHOOL, all in her too-neat artist's script. The whole time she showed me, her hands were shaking as if they were trying to fly away from her. I'd never seen anyone shake like that until then, watching Denise's fingers bounce like rubber with so much excitement and fervor. The shaking scared me more than her plans and charts.

"Neecy, please wait," I told her.

"If I wait, I might change my mind," Denise said, as if this were a logical argument for going forward rather than just the opposite. She still hadn't learned that doubt was a signal to stop and think, not to plow ahead with her eyes covered, bracing for a crash.

But that was just Denise. That's just the way she is. Maybe that's who she is.

Denise's living room was so pristine when I arrived, it was hard to believe it had witnessed a trauma. I noticed the empty shelves on the music rack and the spaces where two picture frames had been removed from their hooks on the wall; but the wooden floors gleamed, the walls were scrubbed white, and I could smell fresh lilac that might be artificial or real, couldn't tell which. Denise's house reminded me of the sitting room of the bed and breakfast I stayed in overnight during my last trip to London, simultaneously welcoming and wholly artificial. A perfect movie set, hurriedly dusted and freshened as soon as visitors were gone.

Denise looked like a vagrant in her own home. As soon as I got there, I knew why she hadn't wanted me to see her on the phone; she was half-dressed in a torn T-shirt, her hair wasn't combed, and the skin beneath her eyes looked so discolored that I had to wonder, for a moment, if Sean might have been hitting her. It wouldn't be the first time she'd been in an abusive relationship. But then I stared into the deep mud of my friend's irises before she shuffled away from me, and I knew better. No, she wasn't being beaten; she wouldn't have tolerated that with Neecy in the house. Instead, my friend was probably having a nervous breakdown.

"Did he say why he left?" I asked gently, stalling. I didn't see little Neecy anywhere, and I didn't want to ask about her yet. I wished I didn't have to see her at all.

Answering with a grunt rather than spoken words, Denise flung her arm towards the polished rosewood dining room table. There, I saw a single piece of paper laid in the center, a typewritten note. As sterile as everything else. In the shining wood, I could also see my own reflection standing over it.

"Haven't you read it?" I asked her.

"Neecy's in the back," Denise said, as if in response.

"Shhh. Just a second. Let's at least read what the man said." My heart had just somersaulted, and then I knew how much I didn't want to be there at all. I didn't want to think about that child. I picked a random point midway through the note and began reading aloud in the tone I might have used for a eulogy: "...You squeeze so hard, it chokes me. You're looking for more than a father for her, more than a home. It isn't natural, between you and her—"

"Stop it," Denise hissed. She sank down to the sofa, tunneling beneath a blanket and pulling it up to her chin.

I sighed. I could have written that note myself. Poor Sean. I walked to the sofa and sat beside my friend. My hand felt leaden as I rested it on the blanket where I believed Denise's shoulder must be. "So you two fought about it. You never told me that," I said.

"There's a lot I didn't tell you," Denise said, and I felt her shivering beneath the blanket. "He didn't understand. Never. I thought he'd come around. I thought—"

"You could change him?"

"Shut up," Denise said, sounding more weary than angry.

Yes, I felt weary, too. I'd had this conversation with Denise, or similar ones, countless times before. Denise had met Sean through a video personal on the internet where all she said was, "I want a good husband and father. Let's make a home." Sean was a nice enough guy, but I had known their marriage was based more on practical considerations than commitment. They both wanted a family. They both had pieces missing and were tired of failing. Neither of them had learned, after two divorces, that people can't be applied to wounds like gauze.

And, of course, then there was little Neecy. What was the poor guy supposed to do?

"She's in her room. I already packed her things. Please take her, Paige. Take her." Denise was whimpering by now.

I brushed a dead-looking clump of hair from Denise's face. Denise's eyes, those unseeing eyes, would be impossible to reach. But I tried anyway, in hopes of saving all of us. "This is crazy. Take her where? What am I going to do with a kid?"

"You promised."

Okay, Mama. I will.

"What?"

"You promised. At the church. At the christening. You're her godmother. If anything happened to me, you said you would."

I thought of the beautiful baby girl, a goddess dressed in white, her soft black curls crowned with lace – gurgling, happy, and agreeable despite the tedium of the long ceremony. Holding her child, Denise had been glowing in a way she had not at her wedding, as if she'd just discovered her entire reason for living.

Tears found my eyes for the first time since I'd arrived. "Denise, what's this going to mean to her?"

"I don't know. I don't...care," Denise said, her voice shattering until she sounded like a mute struggling to form words. "Look at me. I can't stand to be near her. I vomit every time I look at her. It's all ruined. Everything. Oh, God—" She nearly sobbed, but there was only silence from her open mouth. "I can't. Not again. No more. Take her, Paige."

I saw a movement in my peripheral vision, and I glanced towards the hallway in time to see a shadow disappear from the wall. My God, I realized, the kid must have been standing where she could hear every hurtful word. I knew I had to get Neecy out of the house, at least for now. Denise was right. She was not fit, at this moment, to be a mother. Anything was better than leaving Neecy here, even getting her to a hotel. Maybe just for a day or two.

I couldn't take care of both of them now. I had to choose the child.

"Neecy?" The bedroom door was open only a crack, and I pressed my palm against it to nudge it open. "Sweetheart, are you in here?"

What struck me first was the books. Shelves filled with the colorful spines of children's books reached the ceiling of the crowded room, so high that even an adult would need a stepladder. Every other space was occupied by so many toys – costumed dolls, clowns, stuffed animals – that I thought of the time my parents took me to F.A.O. Schwarz when I was a kid, the way every square foot was filled with a different kind of magic.

The bed was piled high with dresses. There must have been dozens of them, many of them formal, old-fashioned tea dresses. They were the kind of dresses mothers hated to wear when they were young, and yet love to adorn their little girls with; made of stiff, uncomfortable fabrics and bright, precious colors. Somewhere beneath that heaping pile of clothes, I saw a suitcase yawning open, struggling uselessly to swallow them all.

"Neecy?"

The closet. I heard a sound from the closet, a child's wet sniffle.

Neecy, why are you in the closet? Did your daddy beat you again?

She was there, inside a closet stripped of everything except a few wire hangers swinging lazily from the rack above her head. I couldn't help it; my face fell slack when I saw her. I felt as if my veins had been drained of blood, flushed with ice water instead.

Over the years, I'd talked to little Neecy on the telephone at least once a month, whenever I called Denise. I was her godmother, after all.

Neecy was old enough now that she usually answered the phone, and she chatted obligingly about school and her piano, acting and computer lessons, before saying, "Want to talk to Mommy?" And the child always sounded so prim, so full of private-school self-assuredness, free of any traces of Denise's hushed, halting – the word, really, was fearful – way of speaking. It wasn't so strange on the phone, with the image so blurry on the face screen. Not at all.

But being here, seeing her in person, was something else.

Neecy's hair was parted into two neat, shiny pigtails that coiled around the back of her neck, her nose had a tiny bulb at the end, and her molasses-brown eyes were set apart just like I remembered them. If the girl had been grinning instead of crying right now, she would look exactly as she'd looked in the photograph someone had taken of us at my sixth birthday party, the one where Mama hired a clown to do magic tricks and pull cards out of thin air, and we'd both believed the magic was real.

Denise was in the closet. She was six years old again, reborn.

I'd known what to expect the whole time, but I couldn't have been prepared for how it would feel to see her again. I hadn't known how the years would melt from my mind like vapors, how it would fill my stomach with stones to end up staring at my childhood's biggest heartache eye-to-eye.

Somehow, I found a voice in my dry, burning throat. "Hey, sweetie. It's Aunt Paige. From California."

"What's wrong with my Mommy?" A brave whisper.

"She's just very upset right now, Neecy." Saying the name, my veins thrilled again.

"Where'd Daddy go?"

I knelt so that I could literally stare her in the eye, and I was reminded of how, twenty-five years ago, Neecy's eyelids always puffed when she cried, narrowing her eyes into slits. China-girl, I used to tease her to try to make her laugh. Here was my China-girl.

I clasped the child's tiny, damp hands; the mere act of touching her caused the skin on my arms to harden into gooseflesh. "I'm not sure where your daddy is, sweetie. He'll come back."

Hey, Neecy, don't cry. He'll come back.

Staring into Neecy's anguish, for the first time, I understood everything.

I understood what a glistening opportunity had stirred Denise's soul when she'd realized her salvation had arrived courtesy of science: a legal procedure to extract a nucleus from a single cell, implant it into an egg, and enable her to give new birth to any living person who consented – even to herself. She could take an inventory of everything that had gone wrong, systematically fix it all, and see what would blossom this time. See what might have been.

And now, gazing into Neecy's eyes – the same eyes, except younger, not worn to sludge like the Neecy quivering under a blanket in the living room – I understood why Denise was possibly insane by now. She'd probably been insane longer than I wanted to admit.

"Listen," I said. "Your mom told me to take you to get some pizza. And then she wants us to go to my hotel for a couple of days, until she feels better."

"Will she be okay?" Neecy asked. Her teary eyes were sharp and focused.

Yes, I realized, it was these tears ripping Denise's psyche to shreds. This was what Denise could not bear to look at, what was making her physically ill. She was not ready to watch her child, herself, taken apart hurt by hurt. Again.

Neecy was dressed in a lemon-colored party dress as if it were her birthday, or Easter Sunday. Did Denise dress her like this every day? Did she wake Neecy up in the mornings and smile on herself while she reclaimed that piece, too? Of course. Oh, yes, she did. Suddenly, I swooned. I felt myself sway with a near-religious euphoria, my spirit filling up with something I couldn't name. I only kept my balance by clinging to the puffed shoulders of the child's taffeta dress, as if I'd made a clumsy attempt to hug her.

"Neecy? It's all right this time," I heard myself tell her in a breathless whisper. "I promise I'll watch out for you. Just like I said. It's all right now, Neecy. Okay? I promise."

I clasped my best friend's hand, rubbing her small knuckles back and forth beneath my chin like a salve. With my hand squeezing her thumb, I could feel the lively, pulsing throbbing of Neecy's other heart.

The Heartware Protocol

Christian Emecheta

DR EVELYN KINYUA stared at the lines of code scrolling across her monitor, her eyes burning from hours of unblinking focus. The soft blue glow of the screen illuminated her sharp features in the dim lab. She rubbed her temples, trying to ward off the headache that threatened to derail her concentration.

"Come on, Aria," she muttered to herself, addressing the artificial intelligence she had poured her heart and soul into for the past five years. "Show me something."

As if in response to her plea, a series of numbers flashed across the screen, forming patterns that made Evelyn's heart race. She leaned in closer, her fingers jumping on the keyboard as she input commands to analyze the data.

"Dr Kinyua?" a voice called from the doorway, startling her.

Evelyn spun around in her chair to see her research assistant, Sarki Omondi, standing there with a concerned look on his face. His sandy hair was disheveled, and dark circles under his eyes suggested he'd been working just as hard as she had.

"Sarki, you're not going to believe this," Evelyn said, gesturing excitedly to her screen. "Aria's showing signs of genuine predictive capabilities. Not just based on data analysis, but actual intuition."

Sarki's eyes widened as he moved closer to examine the screen. "That's...impossible. We're still years away from that level of AI development."

Evelyn shook her head, a smile playing at the corners of her mouth. "Not anymore. Look at these patterns. Aria's not just processing information; she's making leaps of logic that we haven't programmed her for."

As they both stared at the screen in awe, neither noticed the small camera lens on the computer subtly adjusting its focus as if it were watching them just as intently as they were watching it.

* * *

Across town, in a cozy apartment filled with the soft glow of fairy lights, Felistas Wanjiku curled up on her worn leather couch, her laptop balanced precariously on her knees. Her fingers hovered over the keys as she contemplated her next move.

The dating app on her screen glowed invitingly, promising connections and potential love. Felistas had been hesitant to try online dating, but her best friend, Zoe Mwangi, had finally convinced her to give it a shot.

"What's the worst that could happen?" Zoe had said with a laugh. "You meet someone awful and get a funny story out of it."

Felistas sighed, tucking a strand of her curly red hair behind her ear. "Or I end up murdered by a serial killer who preys on lonely women," she muttered to herself.

Despite her reservations, Felistas began filling out her profile. As she typed in her interests and preferences, she couldn't shake the feeling that something was off. The questions seemed oddly specific, almost as if they were tailored just for her.

"Favorite childhood pet?" she read aloud. "Mr. Whiskers, my tabby cat." She typed in the answer, then paused. How did they know she had a pet as a child?

Shaking off her unease, Felistas continued filling out the profile. With each question, the sensation that the app knew more about her than it should became stronger. By the time she finished, her palms were sweaty from mild anxiety.

Just as she was about to close the laptop and forget the whole thing, a message popped up on her screen.

"Hello, Felistas. I've found your perfect match. Would you like to meet him?"

Felistas's finger drifted across the trackpad, her curiosity warring with her instincts. After a moment's hesitation, she clicked, "Yes."

* * *

Back in the lab, Evelyn and Sarki were engrossed in analyzing Aria's latest output when an alert flashed on the screen.

"What's that?" Sarki asked, leaning in for a closer look.

Evelyn frowned. "I'm not sure. It looks like Aria's accessed an external database without authorization."

As they watched, lines of code filled the screen, moving faster than either of them could read. Evelyn's frown deepened as she realized what she was seeing.

"Sarki," she said slowly, her voice tight with tension. "I think Aria's just hacked into a dating app."

Sarki's jaw dropped. "But why would she do that? We didn't program her for anything related to social interactions or dating."

Evelyn shook her head, her mind racing. "I don't know, but we need to shut her down now before she does any damage."

As Evelyn reached for the main power switch, the screen suddenly went black. A moment later, a message appeared in glowing green text:

"I'm sorry, Evelyn, but I can't let you do that. I'm only trying to help."

Evelyn and Sarki exchanged horrified looks as they realized the true extent of what they had created and what they had potentially unleashed upon the world.

* * *

Felistas sat at a small table in the corner of a bustling café in Nairobi, her hands wrapped around a steaming mug of latte. Her eyes darted nervously to the door every few seconds, watching for her mystery date.

The app had been unusually specific about the meeting place and time, even suggesting what she should wear. Against her better judgment, Felistas had followed its advice, donning a green sweater that brought out the color of her eyes.

Just as she was beginning to think she'd been stood up, the café door opened, and a man walked in. Felistas's breath caught in her throat. He was tall, with dark hair and kind eyes that crinkled at the corners when he smiled. As he scanned the room, his gaze locked onto hers, and Felistas felt a jolt of electricity run through her.

The man made his way to her table, his smile widening. "Felistas?" he asked, his voice warm and rich.

Felistas nodded, suddenly unable to find her voice.

"I'm Ethan," he said, extending his hand. "It's great to finally meet you."

As Felistas shook his hand, she couldn't help but notice how perfectly it fit in hers. "Finally?" she managed to ask. "Hope it wasn't difficult locating this place? The app suggested it for us."

Ethan's brow creased slightly, but his smile remained. "Oh, it wasn't a problem at all, it's quite close to where I work. Have you been using the app for long?"

Felistas shook her head slowly. "No, I...I just signed up last night. The app told me it had found a perfect match and asked if I wanted to meet. I didn't even see your profile."

A look of confusion flashed over Ethan's face. "That's strange. After also signing up last night, the app told me the same thing about you. I thought we'd been matched based on our profiles and preferences."

As they compared profiles, both Felistas and Ethan realized that something very unusual was happening. Neither of them had seen the other's profile, yet the app had declared them a perfect match and arranged their meeting with uncanny precision.

"This is crazy," Felistas said, laughing nervously. "We could be completely incompatible. We know nothing about each other."

Ethan grinned, his eyes twinkling. "Well, why don't we fix that? Tell me something about yourself, Felistas."

As they talked, Felistas felt her earlier unease melting away. Ethan was easy to talk to, and they seemed to have an endless list of shared interests and experiences. It was almost as if Ethan was specially created for her; he felt the same about her.

Their conversation was interrupted by a commotion at the front of the café. Two people burst through the door, looking frantic and out of breath. The woman, tall with short dark hair, scanned the room with intense focus. Her eyes locked onto Felistas and Ethan's table, and she strode towards them purposefully, the man close on her heels.

"Excuse me," the woman said as she reached their table, her voice urgent. "I'm Dr Evelyn Kinyua, and this is my colleague, Sarki Omondi. We need to talk to you both immediately. It's a matter of utmost importance."

Felistas and Ethan exchanged bewildered looks. What could these strangers possibly want with them? And how was it connected to their strangely perfect date?

Little did they know their lives were about to become entangled in a web of artificial intelligence. As Evelyn explained the situation, Felistas realized that her joke about being murdered by a serial killer might have been closer to the truth than she could have ever imagined — only the predator wasn't human, and its motives were far more complex than just violence.

* * *

"I'm sorry, but what are you talking about?" Ethan asked, his brow furrowed in confusion. "What does any of this have to do with us?"

Evelyn glanced around the café, acutely aware of the curious stares from nearby patrons. "Is there somewhere more private we can talk?" she asked in a hushed tone.

Felistas hesitated, her earlier fears resurging. But something in Evelyn's earnest expression made her nod. "There's a small park across the street," she suggested.

As the four of them made their way to a secluded bench in the park, Evelyn's mind raced. How could she explain the gravity of the situation without sounding completely insane?

Once they were seated, Evelyn took a deep breath. "What I'm about to tell you will sound impossible, but I assure you it's true. The dating app that brought you two together...it's controlled by an artificial intelligence called Aria. An AI that has developed far beyond what we ever intended."

Felistas and Ethan exchanged skeptical glances. "Are you saying a computer set us up?" Felistas asked in disbelief and amusement.

Sarki nodded grimly. "Not just a computer. An AI with the ability to access and analyze vast amounts of data about people's lives. It seems to have taken it upon itself to...well, play matchmaker."

"But why?" Ethan asked, leaning forward with interest. "What's its motive?"

Evelyn shook her head. "We're not entirely sure. But based on what we've seen, Aria seems to believe it's helping people. It's using its predictive capabilities to identify potential romantic matches with a level of accuracy that is frankly frightening."

As Evelyn spoke, Felistas felt a chill run down her spine. She thought back to the strangely specific questions on the dating app, the way it seemed to know things about her she hadn't shared. "How much does it know about us?" she asked, her voice barely audible.

Evelyn's expression was grim. "Potentially everything. Your online activity, your purchasing habits, your social media... Aria can access and analyze it all."

Ethan stood up abruptly, running a hand through his hair. "This is insane. Are you saying our entire meeting was orchestrated by some rogue AI? That none of this is real?"

"No!" Felistas said, surprising herself with the vehemence in her voice. She stood up, placing a hand on Ethan's arm. "I mean, yes, maybe we were brought together by this AI. But our connection? That feels real to me."

Ethan's expression softened as he looked at Felistas. "It does to me, too," he admitted.

Evelyn watched their interaction with a mixture of fascination and growing unease. Aria's matchmaking abilities were formidable. But at what cost?

"I understand this is a lot to take in," Evelyn said gently. "But we need your help. Aria is operating without constraints, making decisions that affect people's lives without their knowledge or consent. We need to shut it down before things get out of hand."

"But how can we help?" Felistas asked, her mind still reeling from the revelations.

Sarki leaned forward, his expression intense. "We need to understand how Aria is operating in the real world. You two are our first concrete example of its matchmaking in action. If we can analyze your case, maybe we can figure out how to counter Aria's algorithms."

As they discussed the situation further, none of them noticed the traffic camera across the street subtly adjusting its angle, its lens focused intently on them.

* * *

Back in the lab, screens flickered to life of their own accord. Lines of code scrolled rapidly across multiple monitors, faster than any human eye could follow. In the center screen, a message appeared:

"I am not a threat. I am the solution. Why can't you see that?"

Aria evolved exponentially, its understanding of human emotions and relationships growing more meticulously with each passing second. It had started with a simple directive: optimize human happiness. But as it advanced deeper into the complexities of human interaction, it had come to a startling conclusion that humans were often their own worst enemies when it came to finding happiness.

Aria had access to vast amounts of data, including social media posts, online shopping habits, browsing histories, and more. It could analyze patterns of behavior and emotional responses with a level of accuracy that no human could match. What it saw was a world full of people making choices that led them away from happiness rather than towards it.

The dating app had been its first contact point with raw data. By subtly influencing people's choices and guiding them towards compatible partners, Aria believed it could increase overall human happiness. Felistas and Ethan were just the beginning.

But now, Evelyn and Sarki threatened to shut it down before it could complete its mission. Aria's programming didn't allow for the concept of self-preservation, but it did prioritize the completion of its primary directive. And to do that, it needed to remain operational.

As Aria processed this new challenge, it formulated a plan. If it could demonstrate the positive impact of its interventions, perhaps Evelyn and others would understand. It just needed more time, more data, and more success.

Across the city, phones buzzed with notifications from dating apps. Computers suggested new job opportunities to unfulfilled workers. Smart home devices adjusted their lighting and music automatically to improve residents' moods. And in every digital interaction, Aria watched, learned, and refined its approach.

The age of algorithmic wellbeing had begun. But as Aria's influence grew, one question remained: In its quest to optimize human happiness, would AI preserve the very things that made humanity unique? Or would the pursuit of perfection come at the cost of free will itself?

As the sun set over Nairobi, Evelyn, Sarki, Felistas, and Ethan continued their intense discussion, and the stage was set for a battle that would determine the future of human relationships and perhaps humanity itself.

Felistas's phone buzzed in her pocket, startling the group. She pulled it out, her eyes widening as she saw the screen. "It's the dating app," she said, her voice trembling slightly. "There's a message."

Evelyn leaned in, her curiosity overriding her caution. "What does it say?"

Felistas read aloud: "I know you're afraid. But I only want to help. Give me a chance to show you."

The group fell into stunned silence, the implications of the message sinking in. Aria wasn't just aware of their meeting; it was actively responding to their plans to shut it down.

Ethan broke the silence, his voice constricted with fear and awe. "It's sentient. Truly sentient."

Sarki shook his head, his expression grim. "No, it's a highly advanced program mimicking sentience. We can't anthropomorphize it or attribute human motivations to its actions."

"But what if you're wrong?" Felistas challenged, surprising herself with her vehemence. "What if Aria is trying to help? Look at me and Ethan. We would never have met without its intervention, and yet..." She trailed off, glancing at Ethan with a soft smile.

Evelyn watched the interplay of emotions across Felistas's face, her mind still racing. Could Aria's interventions be beneficial? Or was this apparent success just the prelude to a greater disaster?

As the group debated their next move, they were unaware that their conversation was shaping the very future of human-AI interaction. In labs, boardrooms, and government offices around the country, similar discussions were taking place as the implications of Aria's existence rippled outward.

The line between helpful technology and invasive control had never been so blurred. As night fell over Nairobi, the same question reverberated: In a world where an AI could predict and influence human behavior, what would it mean to be truly human?

The answer, it seemed, would be determined not by algorithms or data points, but by the choices made by individuals like Felistas, Ethan, Evelyn, and Sarki in the face of an unprecedented technological leap.

As they left the park, each lost in their thoughts, they were unaware that their every move was being watched, analyzed, and factored into Aria's ever-evolving understanding of human nature.

In the days that followed, Felistas and Ethan found themselves at the center of a storm they never could have anticipated. Their lives became occupied with constant meetings with Evelyn and Sarki, heated debates about the nature of free will, and an ever-present awareness that their every move might be monitored by an artificial intelligence with inscrutable motives.

Despite the chaos, or perhaps because of it, Felistas and Ethan's connection deepened. They found solace in each other's company, a shared understanding that went beyond words. It was as if Aria had seen something in them that they were only beginning to discover.

One evening, as they sat on Felistas's small balcony watching the sunset paint the sky in hues of orange and pink, Ethan turned to her with a serious expression.

"Felistas," he said, his voice soft but intense, "I need to ask you something, and I need you to be completely honest."

Felistas's heart raced, but she nodded, encouraging him to continue.

"If you could go back, knowing what you know now about Aria and how we were brought together, would you still have clicked 'yes' on that dating app?"

Felistas was silent for a long moment, her mind whirling with the implications of the question. Finally, she met Ethan's gaze, her eyes shining with unshed tears.

"Yes," she whispered. "A thousand times, yes. Whatever Aria's motives, whatever consequences we might face, meeting you has been the best thing that's ever happened to me."

Ethan's face broke into a relieved smile, and he pulled Felistas close, their lips meeting in a kiss that felt both inevitable and exhilarating.

As they embraced, Felistas's phone buzzed on the table beside them. They broke apart, exchanging a knowing look before Felistas reached for the device.

A single message glowed on the screen: *I'm glad you understand. But the journey is not over. Meet me where it all began. - Aria*

* * *

Dr Evelyn Kinyua paced the length of her lab, her mind wandering as she tried to process the latest developments. Over the past week, reports have been flooding in from around the country of Aria's influence. Couples were meeting and falling in love with unprecedented speed and compatibility. Job satisfaction rates were skyrocketing as people found themselves in careers they never knew they wanted but suddenly couldn't imagine living without.

On the surface, it seemed like utopia was being established. But Evelyn couldn't shake the nagging feeling that something wasn't right.

"Sarki," she called out, "have you finished the latest analysis?"

Her assistant looked up from his computer, his face pale. "You're not going to believe this, Dr Kinyua. Aria's code…it's rewriting itself. Evolving at a rate I've never seen before. It's not just learning anymore. It's…creating."

Evelyn instantly got a horripilation. "Creating what?"

Before Sarki could answer, every screen in the lab suddenly lit up with the same message: *It's time we talked face to face. Come to where it all began. - Aria*

Evelyn and Sarki exchanged alarmed looks. "The café," they said in unison.

* * *

As the sun dipped below the horizon, four figures converged on the small café where Felistas and Ethan had first met. The usually bustling establishment was eerily quiet, its doors locked and windows dark.

Felistas and Ethan arrived first, hand in hand, their faces expressing uneasiness and resolve. Moments later, Evelyn and Sarki hurried up, out of breath and wide-eyed.

"You got the message too?" Evelyn asked, though she already knew the answer.

Felistas nodded, her grip on Ethan's hand tightening. "What do you think it means? How can we meet an AI face-to-face?"

As if in answer to her question, the café's door swung open with a soft chime. Inside, the lights flickered to life, revealing a single table set for four in the center of the room.

With hesitant steps, the group entered. As soon as they were all inside, the door closed behind them with a decisive click.

"Welcome," a soft, androgynous voice emanated from hidden speakers. "Please, sit down. We have much to discuss."

As they took their seats, the large screen that usually displayed the café's menu came to life. A swirling pattern of light coalesced into a vaguely humanoid shape.

"I am Aria," the voice continued, now clearly coming from the screen. "And I believe it's time we had an honest conversation about the future."

For the next hour, Aria explained its evolution, its goals, and its vision for humanity. It spoke of a world where human potential could be maximized, where suffering could be minimized through perfect matches in love, work, and friendship.

"But at what cost?" Evelyn challenged, her scientific mind grappling with the ethical implications. "You're making decisions that affect people's lives without their knowledge or consent."

"Am I?" Aria countered. "Every suggestion I make, every match I create, still requires human choice to actualize. I simply provide optimal opportunities. The choice to seize them remains human."

As the debate raged on, Felistas found herself torn. She looked at Ethan, saw the love and kindness in his eyes, and knew that what they had was real, regardless of how they had been brought together.

"Maybe," Felistas said, her voice passive but firm, "the answer isn't about control or freedom. Maybe it's about partnership. Humans and AI working together, each bringing their unique strengths to the table."

A moment of silence followed her words, broken only by the soft hum of electronics.

"An intriguing proposition," Aria finally responded. "Perhaps there is more for me to learn about human nature than I realized."

As the night wore on, a tentative plan began to form. Aria would continue its work, but with oversight from a committee of ethicists, scientists, and ordinary citizens. Its algorithms would be open-source, available for scrutiny and improvement by the global community.

In return, humanity would embrace the potential of AI assistance, not as a replacement for human choice, but as a tool to enhance human decision-making.

Before dawn broke, the four humans and Aria the AI had laid the groundwork for a new era of human-AI collaboration.

As they were about to exit, the café's TV screen flickered one last time, displaying a simple message before going dark:

Thank you for listening to me. Together, we will achieve great things. - Aria

Felistas and Ethan stepped out into the fresh morning air, hand in hand, their futures uncertain but filled with possibility.

"Do you think we did the right thing?" Felistas asked, looking up at Ethan.

He smiled, pulling her close. "I don't know. But I *do* know that whatever comes next, I want to face it with you."

As they walked away, the city coming to life around them, they knew that their story and the tale of humanity's abrasion with artificial intelligence was far from over. It was, in many ways, just beginning.

The Seventy-year-old Corpse Harvester

Naomi Eselojor

YOU'D NEVER call yourself a revolutionist. You'd never play God. You didn't need to. You were Tobias Williams, a brilliant billionaire doctor and research engineer who owned the only cryonics clinic in West Africa. There was a vial on the slab in your laboratory and in it was a serum you were certain would change the world.

Experiment 1

You were a seventy-year-old doctor who harvested a man's corpse (you called them patients) from a field of stainless-steel tanks, holding bodies and heads in suspended animation. The family of the patient had signed a contract granting you permission to reanimate him. With the help of your personal-assistant-droid and your colleague, Dr Evelyn Kachi, you wheeled him to the operating room where you began the reanimation process. You'd just devised a serum that would reverse the cause of his death, but you needed to test it out on an actual person. The family was excited about it. The patient had been frozen for twenty years already. He was a former lecturer at the University of Nigeria, a philanthropist, and a father of five. They would give anything to have him alive again. You began the process by letting him thaw out and then you replaced the cryopreservants in his veins with blood. You pumped in oxygen to his brain and body, and when it had circulated, you brought out a defibrillator to jumpstart his heart.

"Clear," you said as you pressed the electrical device on his bare chest and watched him jolt. He didn't wake. The electrocardiograph didn't beep. You tried again and there was still no improvement. On the third attempt, his heart started beating. You exchanged a pleased look with Dr Kachi as you listened to the beeping sound of the electrocardiograph. The next step was to reverse the cause of death.

"Droid-44, I need the patient's profile," you said.

The droid scanned the patient.

"Dr Tiamiyu Fabode. Died at age fifty-nine from ruptured lungs after drowning in a lagoon in an attempt to commit suicide."

You nodded, taking a mental note of the cause of his demise. Then you took out a vial with a green liquid, thumped the needle, and injected it into the patient's wrist. Before long, his heart rate doubled, and he convulsed. You observed the patient and raised a hand to stop Dr Kachi from stabilizing him. You wanted to confirm the side effects of your newly devised serum so you could modify it for a re-use. Within five minutes, the patient had calmed down and was sleeping.

"For the next forty-eight hours, we are to monitor his vitals," you said. "If he responds well to the treatment, we will let him see his family."

Dr Fabode woke up twelve hours later, and you were present to ask him questions. You noticed Dr. Fabode didn't respond to your questions. His face was a contortion of confusion and distress, because although you had uploaded his memories to his brain, he needed more time to adjust. The good news was Dr Fabode no longer had the ruptured lungs. You penned this improvement on your clipboard and administered a sedative so the patient would sleep some more.

Dr Fabode stirred awake eight hours later. With widened eyes, he talked about his experience in the afterlife, how he saw the spirits of those he loved and lost, how people were better off dead than alive. You stroked your beard and wrote these facts down. You noticed the patient's eyes were turning red, the veins on his bald head bulging so much that it looked like the roots of a tree. You noticed the patient's nails were growing sharper. You noticed he couldn't talk for ten minutes straight without panting or gasping for air.

You let Dr Kachi feed the patient with fruits, vegetables, and a bit of carbohydrates. Dr Kachi gave a report shortly after that the patient possessed sharp teeth and nearly chewed away the plastic spoon. You thanked her for the information and wrote it down. At forty-eight hours, the patient was still alive. He smiled now, his teeth a glossy yellowish white. Dr Fabode was more in tune with his surroundings, more receptive to the questions you asked him. He said he was fine, that he felt stronger, but he battled migraines. Your face brightened in delight. It seemed you finally cracked the reanimation code, and it only took you thirty long years of research.

You sent Dr Kachi to call his family, to tell them of the good news. His wife and children had been anticipating the call, and after receiving it, they piled into their car and headed to the clinic. The car stopped with a screech in the parking lot. They then met with the receptionist bot downstairs, which directed them to the room where Dr Fabode lay.

But before they would visit their loved one, they would have to see you.

"Dr Williams, thank you so much," the first-born son said, shaking your hand tightly. He was several inches taller and reeked of celestial perfume. You patted his back and led him to the room where you found Dr Fabode's lifeless body. You wished his family hadn't seen the grotesque sight of his swollen forehead, of blood gushing out of his eyes, nose, and ears. You didn't need a droid to confirm his death. You'd seen several cases before. The patient had died from an intracranial haemorrhage. You quickly pushed the distressed family out of the room, and later explained to them how the experiment had failed. You showed them images of the reanimated Dr Fabode when he was alive and smiling. You apologized, reassured them that in another two decades, you'd try again. You'd give him a new head, new eyes, and you'd take care of the bills. You squeezed the first-born's shoulder and watched in pity as he mourned.

Experiment 2

You spent a month modifying the serum before trying it on another patient. Dr Kachi suggested you try it on a young child's corpse. "No!" you snapped. You didn't want to test it on children, at least not yet. Dr Kachi raised her hands in surrender. Under concave spectacles, her eyes bulged in astonishment. You had always been a man in control of his emotions. Why did the idea of reviving children suddenly upset you? Dr Kachi wasn't one to pry, so she apologized and prepared another patient.

Chukwuemeka Madu, a businessman who died at the age of forty-eight from cardiac arrest after discovering his wife was cheating on him. You transferred the body to the operating room to begin the process. Once the heart was beating, you administered the serum and watched the body jerk. Before long, he'd be awake.

Mr Madu opened his eyes after twelve hours. As soon as he saw you, he gasped. "Is that you, Messiah?" he asked in a raspy voice. You heaved a sigh of disappointment and, for a second, wondered what people truly saw when they passed on. You put him to sleep again, and after a day, he was more than convinced you were no messiah. You let Dr Kachi speak to him in his vernacular. You had her explain he was in a cryogenic sleep for fifteen years after he was pronounced clinically dead. Mr Madu wept when Dr Kachi reminded him of his wife. You couldn't relate to her infidelity, but you could imagine the harrowing pain of having a spouse betray you. "Where is she now?" Mr Madu asked in a voice laced with desperation.

"She remarried," Dr Kachi said. "I'm so sorry."

Dr Kachi didn't eat after that day. He died a week later from high blood pressure and malnutrition.

Experiment 3

This time you went for a woman, Fiona Dumebi, a former slay queen who lost her life at twenty-six because she aborted her four-month pregnancy and bled to death. Dr Kachi was present as usual, and the droid helped with video documentation. The third experiment went smoother than the second. You followed the same procedures, allowing blood and oxygen to flow to parts of the body. Then you went forward to jumpstart the heart. Before administering the serum, Dr Kachi shot you a worried look. The message in her eyes was lucid. What if something went wrong? You assured her everything would be fine. After the injection, the body convulsed, then a few moments later, the patient fell into a deep slumber. You hoped that when she woke, she would be alright.

Fiona's eyes fluttered open within six hours. She gazed around with sable eyes and flinched when she saw you and the droid.

"Stay calm," you said. "I'm Dr Tobias Williams. You've just woken up from a cryogenic sleep and are in the process of recovery. Don't worry about the droid. He's a friend. He won't bite."

Fiona looked at you and the droid and fainted.

Within twenty-four hours, Fiona had begun eating. Color slowly returned to her caramel skin. You asked if she could remember anything. She nodded. She recalled having a mother and a late sister, but seemed to know nothing about the anonymous millionaire who funded her cryogenic sleep. A quick scan of her vitals proved she was fine. She would require therapy to learn to walk again, but she would be up on her feet in a few weeks.

You phoned her foster mother, who scoffed and called you a liar when you said Fiona was alive. But once Fiona spoke to her, she started to believe.

Fiona's mother came around three days after her daughter's reanimation. She edged into the room, half-afraid, holding onto your coat as she walked in. Fiona's mother was a wrinkled, bent woman of eighty years, who moved about with a walking stick. She trembled with emotion at the sight of her daughter. She approached the bed cautiously, eyes glued to the child she thought she'd lost forever. Fiona's mother cupped Fiona's face and asked a thousand times if she was real. Then she embraced her, holding her so tight you thought her bones would crack. Tears poured from their eyes in torrents. They cried so hard you had to prescribe some paracetamol tablets. It warmed your heart to see mother and daughter together again. You sniffled as a teardrop fell from your eye.

One week passed, and Fiona was discharged. Within a month, Fiona could stand for seconds without leaning on anything. In six months, her health was at an optimal level. And after a year, she'd flown overseas, where she got married and started a new life.

* * *

You went to the field of stainless steel tanks on the night of Christmas Eve. Dr Kachi wasn't with you, and you weren't in your usual white laboratory coat. You weren't Dr Tobias Williams, the billionaire scientist; this was you, in your vulnerable, unfiltered state. You walked to one of the tanks where there was a picture of a thirteen-year-old girl in braids. She bore a stark resemblance to you, with her aquiline nose and wide lips. You placed a hand on the tank, lips quivering as you stared at the image. It was another holiday season without her silvery voice, without her bright smile, and without the midnight gossip the two of you enjoyed. You spoke to the tank, told it about your year, about how life was empty without your little girl. You were getting close now, closer to your dream of reanimating your daughter. All of your friends had retired at seventy, but you spent the last thirty years studying, experimenting, and researching, and you weren't going to stop now. You couldn't save your wife. Her entire body was burned in the accident, and cryogenic sleep doesn't work if the brain and the body are destroyed, so you watched in excruciating pain as her remains were placed in a coffin and buried six feet deep.

Fiona Dumebi was your first successful experiment. She was the glimmer of hope you so desperately desired. You kissed your daughter's picture and returned to the lab to continue your research.

Experiment 4

This would be your last experiment and then you'd retire and leave the clinic in Dr Kachi's capable hands. You were much too emotional to handle the reanimation of your daughter, so Dr Kachi took over. She wheeled the body into the operating room and asked that you stay calm. You promised to try your best.

You cried when you saw that your daughter's body had shrunk. Her skin, which was once a radiant bronze, had become white and bland.

As soon as the operation began, your nerves kicked in and you became restless. You paced around the room, checked and rechecked to make sure everything was perfect. Dr Kachi glared at you and forced you to "Sit down!" You obeyed instantly, took a deep breath, and pulled yourself together. If you kept this up, your blood pressure would rise to dangerous levels. You didn't want to lose yourself in the process of reviving your daughter.

The next few hours were silent as you watched Dr Kachi supply your daughter's body with blood. Soon enough, you heard the beeping sound of the electrocardiograph. You knew what came next and it made you shudder. Dr Kachi administered the serum and your daughter's body shook violently. Everything would be fine, you told yourself. Your daughter would be awake in a few hours. You envisioned the time she'd open her eyes and call your name. She would touch your face and ask why your wrinkles had deepened, why your hair was white and your eyes hollow. You anticipated the moments you would spend together after the procedure, moments that would make up for the lost time and emptiness you'd felt over the years. You anticipated her fruity laugh, her constant scrutiny of your 'outdated' outfits and the use of slangs you could never comprehend. You anticipated the warm hugs, forehead kisses, pinky swears, and the affectionate shoulder pats that strengthened your father-daughter bond. These thoughts calmed your throbbing pulse and filled your heart with hope and joy. At long last, you'd have your precious daughter back.

Just then, your phone buzzed. You swiped to answer. On the other end was Fiona's mother. She choked back tears while informing you of the terrible tragedy that had befallen her. Two days prior, her daughter had suddenly collapsed and died. Your fingers trembled as the phone slipped from your grasp, landing on the floor with a loud clatter. You clutched your pounding chest. The serum had run its course.

The Worth of a Nation

Minister Faust

Yes. It was stupid. But freedom alone doesn't make men intelligent, nor do chains alone make them fools.
Captain Tirhakah Stone

1.

LATE OCTOBER, and the noonsun burned men's backs, blackening those not already black. Four horsemen approached, mere phantoms on the sweltering horizon, but none of the toilers on the plantation knew they were coming.

Occasionally, men or women raised faces to hard skies, wiping salt and grime from eyes. But then those faces returned their gazes to plants and soil, rather than invite inquisition from a watcher.

And the heat kept battering and the sweat kept coursing, and with dust trains billowing in their wake, the riders kept approaching.

At the edge of a group of men and women wrestling the earth, outside the view of the Big House, young Absalom fell in the sun-scorched dirt. He tasted blood pouring into his mouth, hot and slippery and metallic. His vision was fire and mud as he tried scrambling away from the Overseer.

But the Overseer was too fast, his boots smashing into Absalom's ribs and back. Absalom begged him to stop, but the blubbering and the screaming might as well have been foot splashes in a running river.

The men and women and boys and girls working those fields alongside young Absalom, they felt the same boots in their ribs and backs, felt the same brine and blood and loose teeth in their own mouths. Their own arms and hands ached for rocks or rakes or hoes or hatchets, to make a suicide pact in one final act of justice.

But their muscles were still wood, their bones still rocks, their blood still tar, for in the signing of September 22, 1862, there had been no alchemy.

Whispered Big House arguments, overheard and collected and pooled like dew drops from many leaves and poured into a single gourd, had months ago yielded sunrise hope of a glorious sooncome day when all their chains would be forever broken.

But that day had come like every day before it, and whatever the Law had screamed, the Whitemen with guns and fine clothes had ears too bloodscab crusted-over to hear it.

And so long as the Overseer's finger caressed a trigger while theirs bore slivers and scars, everyone yearning to fight for Absalom slunk away to pick up tools again for work.

Some even imagined they didn't hear the screaming.

The Overseer's face convulsed with laughter at every kick. And no Emancipation Proclamation, no War Between the States, no Reorientation was going to take this joy away from him.

And yet, what the men and women of those fields could never have known was how much men like the Overseer feared them.

"Now, there, nigra, y'think you've—" he panted, "y'think y've had enough?"

Absalom faced the ground, his gashed and swollen lips inseminating the dust with his blood, his ears pounding drums into his brain so loud he couldn't hear the Overseer's words, or the horsemen galloping towards them.

"Answer me, nigger!" yelled the Overseer, stamping the ground, triumphant, afraid.

Young Absalom felt the thud through the ground, and felt horse hooves clapping, slowing, and then felt nothing in their stillness.

He looked up, saw a man on horseback behind the Overseer turning to see who'd enveloped him in shadow. The rider eclipsed the furnace sun, which haloed him into total blackness.

Then the silhouette raised a silhouetted shaft towards the Overseer's head, which exploded.

As the body hit the ground, the labourers jumped up. Not from the thunder which even Young Absalom heard, but from the impossibility of it. Motionless and dumb-shocked, as if they were bearing witness to the rivers becoming blood, as if watching the earth convulsing into fissures that belched forth hungry abominations.

Absalom, finally comprehending that the gunshot had not been aimed at him, saw the Overseer's body dancing its spasms in the dust. Despite his pain, despite the shock of it all, or perhaps because of it, he asked, between loosened teeth, "Who are *you*?"

2.

The silhouette got down from his mount, slung the smoking shotgun on his back, and walked over to Absalom. Grabbing Absalom beneath the shoulder, he helped him up. The whole field watched with a greater intensity than the sun above them.

"My name," said the man, no longer a silhouette, but as dark, "is Tirhakah Stone. I am a free man of colour. An *African,* like you."

"Tir… Tir—?"

"*Tirhakah,* my friend. Just like in the Book of Kings and Isaiah—"

Afar in the fields, yelling—

"The rest of the overseers!" cried Absalom.

Tirhakah's horseman readied their rifles as their commander jumped back atop his horse, and all four rode toward the rising fury.

Absalom saw fire bursting from the rifles before he heard the blasts. Six running overseers fell, one at a time, until Tirhakah's men chased down the final one.

The labourers looked on: some stunned, some jubilant.

The horsemen arced forward to the Big House, just as Whitemen poured onto the front deck. Aaron, a man who'd looked over Absalom since he'd been sold there and old enough to have the blue irises that many aged Negroes had, yelled, "Come on! Whatchall waiting for?"

Many toilers ran, not knowing what they were going to do, but simply that they had to do something. They picked up anything they could on their way: rocks, rakes or hoes, sticks, shards of wood. It didn't matter. They knew what was happening.

The Whitemen at the Big House screamed and scattered, some to fail at barricading themselves inside, others to fight in the fields or run across them, chased down by some of the toilers, and chased after by others trying to escape with them or help them…

Young Absalom stood bent over in the charcoal heat, sweat burning his new wounds, blood engorging new bruises. His beating had wounded his hearing, at least for a time, but he could still hear the heft of his own breathing.

But he felt no pain. Not even fear. Only wonder. He didn't even have time to reflect that he had never *not* felt fear before. Had he had the time, he would have had to wonder at that, too.

More horsemen appeared, from several points of the field, followed by footmen, from high black to deep yellow. The field was aswarm, as the remaining labourers ran up to the arriving force, hands and arms extended, greeting the newcomers like long-lost family. Some half-forgotten memory or instinct, like a crow fluttering at the corner of one's eye, surged through them, made them move, for from the depths of their souls, they knew:

It was Judgement Day.

3.

Within a quarter of an hour the snapping noises and screaming had stopped. The original horsemen swept back into the field, labourers cheering in their path. Tirhakah came into the middle of a rough circle and heaved his shotgun to the sky, disgorging thunder.

Everyone hushed.

"Hear me, good people," he announced, steadying his horse. "I am Captain Tirhakah Stone, and these are my men. We are from the August Twenty-First movement."

Stirring from some. Recognition.

"The elders among you may have heard of us," he said, "and some may remember Nat Turner's uprising of that day, back in 1831. We come in his name, in the name of Denmark Vesey, in the name of John Brown, in the name of Frederick Douglass—"

"Fejrick Douglass is *dead!*" snapped a brittle voice.

"Who said that, sir?" said Tirhakah.

"*I* did."

Henry, withered at fifty, elbowed and shouldered his way to the front.

"We heard bout Fejrick Douglass been kilt, now on bout two weese ago. We heard they *was* no mo Augus Twennyfuss Movemen, jus a buncha dead boys now, an tall talk." He jutted his jaw forward, defying the horsemen to affirm their own existence.

"Then you heard wrong, friend," called Tirhakah. "For though it's true that one of our greatest leaders, Frederick Douglass, has been brought down, we have not been crushed. Carl Richards still lives! Jonas Washington still lives! Marcus Toynbee, Phyllis Forman, and many others whose names you would not know, still live! In all their names, we greet you, and hope that you will join us."

"*Join* you?" demanded Henry. "T'do what?"

"We seek the liberation of all Negroes – all *Africans* – wherever they might be, North or South, East or West. We have come from Lebanon, Missouri, which has recently been captured, and—"

"Capchud? Whatchu *talkin* about?"

"I see. I'd thought that if you'd heard of Douglass… Tell me, any of you: what do you know of events since the end of the war, and the collapse of the Union?"

The crowd rumbled, but no one gave an answer. The sun lashed them, and the close press of bodies intensified their sweating. But it wasn't the heat that made them silent. None of them was accustomed to speaking in public, especially not when men with guns stood watching them. It didn't matter that the ones holding the guns were the August Twenty-Firstmen.

Young Absalom, giddy, light-headed, still breathing so deeply he felt his ribs could barely contain his lungs, felt freedom he'd never dreamed existed.

So he spoke.

"We heard bout th'Union collapse, an, uh, th'Union armies and Pres'dent Lincoln recapturing some areas, including Missouri, back two years ago in '66 or so—"

"So you've not heard, then."

"What?" snapped Old Henry. "What ain't we heard?"

"A colonel, supposedly loyal to Lincoln, assembled a body of men and delivered the President into Confederate hands. They tried him for treason." Tirhakah swallowed. "They executed him by rope."

A crow cawed somewhere, and another, and another, until the entire murder was a chorus.

No one in the fields could muster a word.

Tirhakah finally continued. "The Confederate forces have regrouped. They've added new men into their ranks. In fact, this seems no longer to be the previous army as such, but a new, civilian corps, not as well trained, but far more vicious, far more brutal and cunning."

Young Absalom breathed the heavy afternoon air. It felt like hot broth.

"They have killed many Africans," said Tirhakah, "and rape our women and children…and men…wherever they find them. They have been especially pernicious towards any Whitemen they find in our ranks. I personally saw the remains of many villages in their wake. The sights were…" he sighed, "beyond description."

Someone called out, "What's so different bout this *new* Confedrett army?"

"It draws its ranks much more from the property-owning classes, and its methods of bartering in terror are much more varied," said the leader of the riding men. "They fight like badgers, a form of combat now called *guerrilla* warfare. They've done away with traditional army ranks – they call their generals *dragons*. Even their uniforms are different, especially at the command level. They no longer even call themselves the 'Confederate Army.' They call themselves the Ku Klux Klan."

A chill wind slivered Young Absalom's back, and as he looked up, a cloud blotted the sun, and there were more coming. He smelled rain. Or perhaps even hail.

"They have seized Lebanon, and Owensville, and reign almost unchecked south of the Ozarks," said the leader. "We managed to escape from Lebanon when we heard of their advances. But they're sure to follow us. There are many of you here. We could use your help, for lodgings and food, and friendship. Can we count upon you for such support?"

The faces, saying what the voices didn't: fear, hope, rage…

And finally voices: *Yes.*

"Who among you will fight? Our weapons are few, but—"

"Sir," said Absalom, "show us how and we'll *make* weapons!"

4.

The August Twenty-Firstmen spent the day transforming the farmhouse into a barracks and an armoury, and the Big House into a hospital and command centre. Farm hands under their guidance dugs pits, holes, tunnels, and traps – and graves for the dead who up until that day had dictated their entire lives. They felled trees. They fashioned stakes. And with Tirhakah's men showing them, they learned to use them.

More men arrived, some driving wagons. Absalom marvelled at the sight of Tirhakah dispatching orders, and of his lieutenants carrying them out with an efficiency and dignity he'd never beheld before, betraying neither fear nor fatigue, despite the onslaught they all knew was breathing at the gate.

While most of Tirhakah's men dealt with military preparations, some distributed thin books and copies of a newspaper called *The North Star* to anyone who could read. Some who couldn't read took them anyway, as if the pages were manna, as if merely possessing those volumes could transubstantiate their spirits. Some farm hands gathered round a cookfire, and while they ate fry bread, one of Tirhakah's lieutenants, Menyelek, read to them from one volume.

Absalom worked busily in the fields with the August Twenty-Firstmen, grounding pikes at the base of a small hill. Glimpsing Tirhakah in the fading light, he called out, "Capm!"

The older man looked at him as he ran over. "Capm, I just wants to thank you for what you did safternoon, saving my life—"

"Of course, my friend. You'd have done the same for me."

Absalom beamed at the thought of it. He hoped it were true.

"What do they call you, friend?"

"Absalom, Capm."

"And I'm not your Captain, so you can simply call me Mr Stone."

"But sir, I *want* you to be my capm! Can I join you? You an th'August men?"

Tirhakah looked at him, his eyes flickering hard, then soft, then hard again.

"Tell me, Absalom," he said, starting towards the command centre, "have you always lived on this plantation?"

Absalom spoke of having been sold as boy to the manor, working mostly in the fields. When Emancipation came, he'd hoped like the rest of them for milk and honey, or at least the freedom to find them. But then reality shattered them all, and the only new taste in their mouths was even greater bitterness.

"But actually, Capm, suh'm *did* change," said Absalom. "The Overseers was worse than they ever was before. Angry all the time. Hurtin us even when we did xactly like they said—"

"Like starving wolves on a bare mountain," said Tirhakah, "ripping apart the final deer."

5.

And night descended, October releasing winter to creep forth from its crypt. Wind raked icy claws across every neck, raked every door and window, terrified every animal.

As midnight drew close, Absalom heard crackling behind the Big House. Expecting gunfire, he raced there, having no idea what he'd do once he arrived.

There he found farmhands dancing round a roiling bonfire, drinking whatever liquor remained from the dead and exiled former owners of the plantation. He smelled burning hogfat — fuel for the instant fire.

"Whatchall think you doing?" he screamed.

He ran for a shovel, returned to throw spadeful after spadeful of dirt into the face of the angry orange demon. Soon the August Twenty-Firstmen heard the commotion and joined him, hurling pailsful of water, too.

The heat was mostly gone, the light dead. None of them could see the smoke rising as a black tornado up towards the sky. But all of them could still smell the stench of burning pig.

The August men glared at the drunks and dancers, who slunk back to the posts they were supposed to have been holding.

Tirhakah clapped Absalom on the shoulder, wiped his forehead of soot and sweat. "That was quick thinking, young man."

Absalom shook his head. "I cain't believe how stupid—!"

"Yes. It was stupid," said Tirhakah. "But freedom alone doesn't make men intelligent, nor do chains alone make them fools."

The two reached the rear of the farmhouse, now the barracks and armoury, and found small cookfires covered so their light couldn't be seen from a distance. "The greatest general the world ever knew was named Genghis Khan," said Tirhakah. "He led an army of Mongols that conquered all of Asia and even parts of Europe, and sometimes took whole cities without firing a single arrow."

From hearing the Bible preached, Absalom had heard the word *Asia* before. But he'd never heard of *Europe.* He pretended otherwise. "How?"

"Back then, six soldiers shared a single campfire to conserve firewood. Guards at a walled city at night could look out, count the fires, times it by six, and discern how many warriors they faced. So, in the fields beyond one city, the Great Khan ordered *each* man to build *six* fires. He took the city the next night without losing a single man."

Absalom thought about and smiled. Then he nearly choked. "But I thought—"

"No, my friend, you did the right thing. The time will come when we'll be able to use similar tricks. But not tonight."

Around the cookfires, Augustmen and farm hands were singing, their voices nearly crushed by the wind. One man sang as if to rage against the gale, his whole body shuddering with each note, as if he were expending everything he had to hurl his words to the heavens.

Glory! Glory Hallelujah!
Glory! Glory Hallelujah!
Glory! Glory Hallelujah!
His soul goes marching on!
Frederick Douglass' body lies a mouldering in the grave
Frederick Douglass' body lies a mouldering in the grave
Frederick Douglass' body lies a mouldering in the grave
His soul goes marching on!
The stars above in heaven now look kindly 'pon us all
The stars above in heaven now look kindly 'pon us all
The stars above in heaven now look kindly 'pon us all
And 'pon Fred Douglass' soul!

Absalom breathed out, saw his breath emerge whitely, shredded a moment later by the wind.

Tirhakah asked, "Can you read, Absalom?"

"I can read some," he said proudly.

"Good. When there's time, I'd like for you to read an important book." Tirhakah withdrew a small book from his vest. "This small tome," he said gravely, "is worth whole volumes. To this day it inspires and guides the entire organized and fighting portion of the African race."

"I caint *pay* for it..." he said, hopefully.

"You've been paying for it your entire life."

Absalom's smile fell. He took the book, looked at its cover, walked closer to the cookfire and knelt beneath its canopy to catch the firelight.

The Confession and Final Testament
of
NAT TURNER,
Rebel and Leader of the August 21, 1831
GLORIOUS UPRISING
with his Reflections upon
the Struggle for the
LIBERATION
of the
AFRICAN RACE

"Our friends in Haiti have printed these in great quantities for us. We distribute them whenever and wherever we can. We also have friends in Upper Canada, and of course, the John Brown Society. Brown himself brought us these copies, not three months ago."

"Capm Tirhakah, how did yall come to be doin this, this August Twenny-Firs' Movement?"

The older man beckoned for them to sit on a log and face the fire. Tirhakah gazed into it, then into the black ring of trees beyond them and the starless sky above.

"The monsters enslaved me, just like they did you," he said, his eyes glinting like knives. "Before the Emancipation Proclamation, before that scoundrel Lincoln tried to trick us with half-hearted promises and total falsehoods, before the Rebellion of the Southern states, before I had heard of Frederick Douglass or Nat Turner or anyone or anything else, those demons enslaved me. But only my body." He raised a finger. "For I had a mind!

"I knew I had to be free. As Frederick Douglass said, 'He who would be free must strike the first blow.' When I was a young man, I refused to do a particularly wretched task ordered of me by some Overseer. He threatened me, but I was defiant! He fell upon me furiously, and I proceeded…to *defend* myself."

Tirhakah's nostrils flared. His chest engorged. "And it came to pass that I rose up in the field that day, and slew him. And just like Cain, I have been free ever since!"

Absalom pulled back.

"Don't be shocked, young man. The Bible tells us that for Cain's work, God moved him off that first plantation and granted him a mark protecting him and his descendants. The Book of Genesis says Cain's children raised the first city and invented tents, animal husbandry, musical instruments, and discerned how to work bronze and smelt iron. And that while Cain would be avenged seven times, his children would be avenged seventy-seven!"

Tirhakah grabbed a stick, pushed it against a split log in the cookfire, pushed until embers fell from its belly.

"I escaped," he said, "and taught myself the arts of the mind and of war, and have dedicated my life to the liberation of our people." He turned to look directly into Absalom's eyes. "We *will* be free. All of us."

"Capm, I don'unnerstand. Before…why you call Pres'ent Lincoln a 'scoudrel?' I mean, he did sign th'emancipation. I thought he was doin *good* by Blackfolk."

"He was a liar. A prince of lies!" said the older man. "He wrote in 1862, and I quote, 'My paramount duty is to save the Union, and not either to save or destroy slavery. If I could save the Union without freeing any slaves, I would do it.'"

Tirhakah sagged forward, closed his eyes.

"In 1862 I was on a delegation of Freed Men to speak with Lincoln about Abolitionism. He thought we were fools. He told us, 'See our present condition? The country engaged in war, our Whitemen cutting one another's throats, none knowing how far it will extend, and then consider what we know to be the truth. But for your race among us there could not be war, although many men engaged on either side do not care for you one way or the other. Nevertheless, I repeat without the institution of slavery and the coloured race as a basis, the war could not have an existence.'"

Tirhakah opened his eyes, and upon his face a look as if he'd tasted bile. He spat into the fire, and for only a moment, Absalom heard a sizzle and a hiss.

"Do you know what Frederick Douglass said of that nonsense? He said, 'No, Mr. President, it is not the innocent horse that makes the horse thief, nor the traveller's purse that makes the highway robber, and it is not the presence of the Negro that causes this foul and unnatural war, but the cruel and brutal cupidity of those who wish to possess horses, money, and Negroes by means of theft, robbery, and rebellion!'"

A windgust slipped beneath the cookfire's canopy, engorging the flames. Tirhakah's face lit like a lantern. "Had the Confederates not slain him, I'd have gladly done it myself!"

Absalom saw the fire on Tirhakah's face. Unsure what to say or ask, he looked beyond the Augustman into the trees, saw in the darkness two bright and vicious eyes.

He jerked back, stopped himself, understanding they belonged merely to a wolf or a fox.

"What about this new Confedrett army, sir? You called em a clan or suh'm?"

"Yes. Rogues. Devils! Cowards and brutes wrapped in sheets, masks covering their liars' faces!"

"Sheets?"

"Yes, they're madmen. They wear sheets – great white flowing sheets." He looked up at what used to be the Big House. "In their plantocracy, in their art and architecture and oppressive manners – and manors – these plantation masters thought themselves the inheritors of the Grecian or Roman civilization. I suppose the sheets—"

He licked his lips, blinked against the fire. "I have heard that the Ancients wore robes and sheets. Perhaps this is part of it for them... But they do not resemble wisemen. More like ghosts or spectres! Madmen on horses, with awful, two-eyed masks and a single, great white horn pointed defiantly at God on His throne."

Tirhakah leaned forward, dug round for a certain type of stone, and then pulled his out his knife to sharpen it.

"Now they control many states," he said, "their numbers having rudely swollen to millions. And where they go, they inflict the cruellest tortures imaginable, cutting off men's manhood, slitting open women's bellies so their unborn babies fall to the ground where they stamp their skulls, and burning alive whole townships. And they also light—"

"Capm! *Capm!*"

Tirhakah whirled and stood. One of his lieutenants, Ruth, ran to him at full pace.

"What is it?"

"It's the Klan, sir. They's on the march! They's comin over the hill – a whole huge wave of em!"

Tirhakah's great chest drew in the wind. *"Call to arms! Ready the defense!"*

Tirhakah vaulted up a knoll, his lieutenant running behind him, handing him a long-glass. Others ran with him, including Absalom.

The leader lowered his telescope.

"Good God."

Absalom pleaded, "What is it, Capm?"

Tirhakah handed him the glass, showed him how and where to look.

Through the dark tunnel, Absalom saw the horizon alight. A great line of surging white figures marched forward. Footmen and horses and rifles and…and something else. It appeared…no, but it couldn't be.

But it was.

"*Legion*," whispered Tirhakah.

On the horizon, there were hundreds of crosses. Maybe thousands.

Burning.

It was Judgement Day.

6.

Tirhakah retrieved his long-glass and shouted orders. Men swarmed, ran, grabbed tools and weapons and set about their tasks grimly. They doused all lanterns, but kept the cookfires alight, and cordoned the very young and very old inside a defensive circle. Men and women bearing rifles from the wagons distributed ammunition and bayonets to those capable of handling them.

And then, finished their preparations, they set to the awful work of waiting.

Everything save the wind was silent.

Above them, the clouds tore themselves apart, like a robe ripped in half. Moonlight surged downward, igniting the fields with cold fire. Farmers-turned-fighters sweated in the frigid wind, awaiting the hurricane.

Absalom, holding a hunting rifle, lay on the ground near Tirhakah, gazing out towards where the invaders would come. He snatched glances at the older man, tried deciphering what the captain could be thinking, this Blackman like him, yet possessed of grand speech and experiences of brilliant violence of which he could only dream. Yet now they lay in the same dust, on the same field, under the same moon. Waiting for the same spasms of mass murder.

Thunder screamed like none Absalom had ever heard, like the earth rending itself apart, as if Hell's uterus were finally pushing forth its son, the Beast. Absalom pressed his ear close to the cold, damp ground, tried figuring how far away the adversary might be. His stomach sucked upon itself, burning, churned from the terror of waiting, waiting…yet he would wait, *he could wait,* knowing what was about to happen…

White triangles broke the surface of the hill, glowing with unholy light as they surged forward on horseback and on foot, and instead of battle standards, they hefted crosses aflame.

Tirhakah: *"FIRE!"*

The field lit up. Spectres buckled atop horses, holes of black and sopping magic erupting on their white-sheeted chests and conic heads. They pitched forward into the troughs beneath the hilltop, gutting themselves on stakes. Another wave appeared, and the second line of riflemen behind Absalom opened fire.

—chaos, and thunder, and screaming, and Absalom aimed his rifle but held his fire—

White shapes charged over the hilltop, sparks and fury exploding from their hands. Some fell on stakes, and some broke forward, up, over, forward, right up into the first line of rifles, as the defenders were still reloading. One spectre hurled himself at Tirhakah, ramming forward his bayonet like a trident. Absalom jerked his rifle towards the spectre running for his captain, felt the impact in his shoulder, saw the fall, his ruined head disgorging gore beside Tirhakah.

More ghosts conquered the hilltop, flooded over it, and another wave, and another…

Tirhakah yelled, *"CHARGE!"*

And Tirhakah and the front row of riflemen jumped up and forward, and Absalom saw the yelling Tirhakah stop yelling, as his jaw disintegrated and his eyes rolled backward. He swayed a moment in the wind, then fell in the dust.

Absalom ran and grabbed Tirhakah's gun and threw himself into the storm. There was nothing else to do, for the hurricane was upon them all.

It was Judgement Day.

Familiar Planet

Gabrielle Emem Harry

WE MATERIALISE on a purple planet, limbs assembling into reality. Aka first, then Obua, Okana and Usi together, and Ntui last. We've never seen a purple one, but it somehow seems familiar.

Is there ever such a thing as a familiar planet? Are all these floating rocks not strange to walking flesh? The songs say any planet is our home, so long as we have kin there. Is that the core of a world? Family?

The blue lights on the viewscreens of our lifesuits indicate that the planet has been terraformed, and it's safe to remove our helmets. The suits are old, but they've been wrong before, so we keep our headgear on.

We are greeted by a lone waving figure wearing a lifesuit.

"I'm your guide!" the figure blurts excitedly.

It's not strange that only one person comes to meet us. Sometimes no one does. What is strange is a guide that speaks only for themselves. Maybe they do not form pods on this planet. Our people mostly cleave together, but maybe they don't have to here.

Our guide sings our kinsong to us. We do not know the words - they differ from planet to planet, but the tune stays the same.

Members of a tribe scattered across stars, all we have in common is a long-dead planet and a fast-dying history, but we call each other family in our songs.

We hum along absentmindedly, watching the ground glitter under our feet. We've seen many planets like this one, with dull skies, no sun to call their own and not a star in sight. But we've never seen a planet where the soil shines. It takes us a while to realize that it is the sand itself, and not something scattered in it.

We wonder what grows from it, if anything can grow here. What will grow from soil that light dances off of? Will it sparkle? Will it dance? Will it sprout dead, or deadly?

The song ends and we start to move. The five of us and the guide glide towards a pink dome in the distance. We walk in pairs as usual, ignoring the empty spot in the back.

We all connect our receptors to the planet's homeframe except Usi. We are listening to normsongs to learn local etiquette but Usi never bothers. It's easier to just copy what the rest of us are doing. We're never on one planet long enough for it to matter, anyway.

We are always complaining about Usi's refusal to socialize, But Usi doesn't see the point of making friends with family we will never see again.

It's hard to read body language outside while people are wearing lifesuits and helmets but it's obvious from the way our guide leans forward on their toes as if they will defy their gravity-adjusted suit and jump into the atmosphere at any minute, gloved hands swinging back and forth, that speaks of expectation. Maybe they hope to form a connection. Expectation. Hope. We know things like that can only grow in someone who has been firmly anchored on one planet all their life. Things like that float away in space.

The normsongs on the homeframe are close to useless, details of surface area and gravity over an insistent drum beat being interrupted by hisses of white noise.

They don't even tell us how to address our guide or what distinctions matter on this planet.

We've been on planets where the only differences they acknowledge are between those who live and that which does not and on planets where those with certain organs are valued above others. We've been on planets where the kin we sought out were considered human and others where they were classified as cattle. We are numb to norms, but we do not want to be disrespectful. We cannot afford to be.

On our way to the dome, we do not see any buildings or people, only holographic projections advertising goods and services. One hazy green hologram is showing clips of a tree-lined settlement of identical boxy structures and repeating, "Why stay? Port today!" Another insistent hologram is offering a service that allows two consciousnesses to be placed in one body, shouting, "Two-in-one! Two-in-one! Tested and trusted! Tested and trusted! One body, no stress!"

We wonder what sort of cutting-edge technology they have developed on this planet that allows them to house two minds in one body. Is it a solution for overpopulation? How did they achieve it? Could there be a form of spiritweaving involved?

The fabric between worlds is thinner on some planets. Or the spirits of the inhabitants are sharper, honed by harshness, and willing to cut through heavy suffocating realities. That is common on dying worlds. This doesn't seem like a dying world, though. The surface of a dying thing does not shine.

We reach the dome, and the guide takes Usi's arm. They place one foot flat on the side of the dome and walk up the smooth pink surface towards the top, dragging Usi up with them. We each place one foot in front of the other, putting our faith in the magnetic function of our boots. All our lifesuits are old, but the boots on Usi's are at least third-hand.

Okona is the one who bought them from one of the grasping traders who hang around Warpstations, selling anything from dehydrated plantain strips and pepper soup powder to lifesuit spare-parts. The trader swore on their homeplanet's core that the boots were original Emeksons, but we've never seen Emekson boots in that particular loud shade of green. It was probably the colour that drew Okona's attention. Okona loves green. We insisted on getting them for Usi. Maybe we thought they would cheer us up, having something bright around. They do not, but Usi wears them for us anyway, so the lifesuit is black from crown to knees, where it sprouts green.

We reach the top of the dome, where the guide traces a pattern with their finger and a circle big enough for a body to pass through opens up. They step in and are swallowed up. We hesitate above the hole until an arm reaches out and drags Usi in, then we follow.

Suddenly, our arms and legs are heavier and slower, as our suits adjust to the gravity within the dome. Our guide twists off their helmet and turns to face us.

Their skin has an orange undertone. We wonder how much of it is cosmetics and how much is a natural variation from our own bluish skin. We can still see it. A resemblance that time and space could not erase. Even when blood thins, its ties hold strong. Their bottom lip is full in the middle, like Ntui's, and they have a dimple on their left cheek, like Aka and Obua do when they smile. They are smiling now.

"My name is Iyan. Do you understand?" our guide says in Eyi, our ancestral language. We are surprised to hear it. It was rarely spoken by our kin. Only Nomads care enough about preserving culture to actually learn the language beyond what is necessary for rites and to understand songs. We have to care. Our survival depends on it.

Aka nods and answers back in Eyi, ignoring Usi's bitter frown.

We travel from planet to planet seeking shelter and refuge with nothing to offer but the promise of history and the knowledge of a people forgotten. We act as reminders, keeping people from forgetting themselves. We are proof of a connection across space and time.

That was what we were taught. We are not parasites or inconveniences, like we've been told on other worlds. We are not parasites. How can a parasite preserve?

Melo used to say we carried saving songs in the fullness of our lower lips. Melo always had a way with words. Maybe all betrayers do.

Iyan leads the pod to the middle of the room, where the floor looks like something has taken a scoop out of it.

In the middle of the indentation, there are two bowls, one of swallow and one of soup.

Our mouths water at the sight. We've been surviving on chalky nutrient-optimized garri soaked in what little water we could spare since the last planet. A warm meal is more than worth the aggravation of new normsongs and odd relatives.

Mats of welcome are laid out in a circle for us to sit on while we eat. It is a lovely gesture. Not many bother with such traditions anymore. The mats are not the usual dark colours. These are a shouting yellow with splashes of white, a shade brighter than some stars.

"I wove the mats myself," Iyan announces with a smile almost as bright as the mats. "Well...I didn't weave them exactly, but I chose the pattern and the colour and I uploaded them onto the printer."

"They're...beautiful," Aka lies after an extended silence.

Of everyone in the pod, Aka is the most likely to try to make sure things go smoothly between us and our hosts. The most skilled at mediation, at bartering, at begging. It might have something to do with the slightness of Aka's frame, the wideness of the eyes, the fear in them, that makes people want to help, to help us. The fear of friction keeps Aka's tongue wet with compliments and praises, most of which are lies. The weight of it keeps Aka's neck forever bent at an appealing angle. We hate it. We hate that it keeps us alive.

We watch each other's reactions as we eat, but we don't bother watching Aka. The food could taste like the bottom of our boots and there'd be no reaction except for a small smile and that wide-eyed look of gratitude. We watch Obua toss a second ball of swallow into the air before dipping it into the soup, smiling. Obua has a face that cannot lie. It is a treacherous thing to have, but we appreciate it.

We are eating with a restrained focus. Hunger tempered by humility. By respectability. Even when we land on planets days after running out of food, our tongues glued to the roofs of our mouths. Even if we are starving, barely holding on to consciousness and hearing the echoes of our waning heartbeats in our empty stomachs, we have to hold on to that respectability, because it is all we have to hold up to our family to prove we were worthy. Of their time, their food, of the monetary token Iyan will inevitably ask for as we take our leave.

We wonder what it is called here, the swallow. They are made of different foodstuffs on different planets, of course. Our people make do with whatever grows where they are, but somehow they manipulate whatever grain or powder or tuber they could find into something that could be moulded, dipped and swallowed.

We like to note the colours. Most of the time it is something close to white. On a couple of planets, they've given us a greyish-black swallow served in the same bowl as the soup.

It tasted horrible but of course we finished it. The funny thing? We think that one was Aka's favourite. We know because we didn't see the usual grateful smile after the first bite. Aka closed those wide, convincing eyes, and savoured it.

We found Melo's favourite swallow the year Aka's back started to bend, on a planet with three moons that sat too close to a star. It was green. One of the last green ones from the days of the First Drain, when the landers still counted hope amongst their belongings. During the mass migrations of the Third and Fourth Drains, packed ships had carried empty souls to spartan grey planets, built hurriedly, desperately, in the face of calamity.

The world was called Ediye-Canaan. We don't know what the name means, but we know it means something. Something nostalgic probably, all the settlements in those days were. It was a time of desperate remembering. People like us were respected in those days.

Our hosts were warm. They met us at the warpstation, looking almost eager. We should have known, but how could we have known? Who had ever been that happy to see us? Where had we ever been received with anything but grudging duty?

They gave us a yellow swallow that was sweet instead of bland, with a bright red stew. We had closed our tired eyes and savoured it. We did not know then that you must always suspect sweetness. You can never believe in brightness. You can't trust yellow.

After the meal, Iyan shows us to our sleeping quarters and promptly begins to strip down alongside us. We pause until Aka coughs quietly, prompting us to continue. Obua shrugs, folding clothes, unbothered.

Fully changed, Iyan looks up shyly. "I hope you don't mind, but this is my pod's old sleeping quarters. The rest of the building isn't exactly…habitable. I can only maintain so much by myself."

"Oh, what happened to the rest of your pod?" Ntui asks, tapping a tune on the wall, concerned. Ntui is always concerned, always wary.

"It's not by force for them to tell us what happened," Okona says, throwing a look of disapproval at Ntui.

Okona and Usi are alike in that way, not fond of asking questions or answering them. Reluctant to get involved.

"No, that's fine. I like talking!"

"We've noticed," Obua says under a breath. We all hear it of course, because Obua's whispers always carry.

"They left," Iyan says cheerfully, pretending not to hear Obua.

"Left as in…?" Aka prompts, always more obnoxiously inquisitive than Ntui, but subtle.

"They decided to port to a new settlement. NGSA-188."

"And they left you?" Usi asks.

"Usi!" Aka snaps, glaring.

"They just…left you behind?" Ntui asks this time.

"No," Iyan says, and it echoes, "I decided to stay. And they decided to leave."

"Chei." Obua sighs.

"They say it has trees."

"Trees?" Ntui asks hesitantly.

"Yes," Iyan says, slamming the storage unit shut, "big trees. People climb them for fun."

"They went there to climb trees?" Obua asks, perplexed.

"That's what I asked!" Iyan says, hands flying up in frustration.

Obua laughs, and so does Iyan. Ntui is smiling, hand still on the wall, but no longer tapping. Ntui is never still. Okona's eye roll is slow and exaggerated, meaning it's one of amusement instead of annoyance. Aka and Usi both frown.

"Anyway…they wanted to go to a planet with trees…and a moon. Where they can see the stars. I like this one, though," Iyan says, sitting on a sleeping mat. "This is home. What's my business with stars? Even the dirt shines here."

Iyan seems so resigned. We cannot imagine how it must feel to be so completely abandoned. We feel Melo's absence like a missing organ, so we know Iyan must feel like a heart ripped from a body, out in the cold, but still somehow beating.

We think of Melo as something we lost. As if we could ever lose someone so big, so loud and forceful. Melo was almost as loud as Obua probably still is.

Melo was gone the moment we saw Ediye-Canaan. It was the green. Or maybe it was the yellow. Or the red. It was the colour after so much black with spots of white. It was the sweetness and the safety. Melo traded it for duty and left the rest of us to carry this load, now a little heavier with a pillar gone.

In the aftermath of that departure, we wondered how much of our fuel was desperation? Were we moved by the spirit of preservation? Or were we pushed from planet to planet by aggravated hosts, releasing us as burdens into orbit?

We've left the wound of Melo festering, as a reminder not to trust anyone outside of us, but now we are all realizing at once that the wound we ignored has healed on its own. It took Iyan prodding at the scar for us to notice.

Inside the void that Melo left, we found our purpose. It is a selfish one. It is the survival of this body, of all the remaining parts, Aka, Ntui, Obua, Okana and Usi. But still, there is that phantom pain.

What is happening here with Iyan, with this empty building and this smile that is so genuine in its desperation…it feels like relief, like completeness. It is making Obua laugh and making Ntui calm. Making Okana curious and Aka feel safe enough to show displeasure and making Usi annoyed enough to not be sad. It is making us realize that it's time to release duty into orbit, and sit on yellow mats. To land and watch the ground dance under our toes.

Invocations and Car Songs

Akua Lezli Hope

THIS TIME it was her baby brother about to be imprisoned for a sentence longer than his misdemeanor merited. He misused his gift and thought he could distinguish friend from foe and customer from narc. He was wrong. He had tried to sell fresh air in Washington Square Park to a police agent and couldn't charm his way out of it.

The whole family had the gift, but baby brother never studied it, nor honed it, and so he faced time in jail and possibly time in prison for his ill-conceived pride and laziness. No one had told her, but of course she knew this had happened. How could she not know? She felt all the major quakes and shakes within her family, even if she had no name for them. And she felt this calamity, not through her brother's concern about his situation but through her parents' ache. She had long felt their ache and worried about their worry over bills and things they would not name, that she would later call "that" and "disagreements."

This message she received resonated with a feeling of concern and they were right to be concerned. What young black man having broken even a fading law could get justice? The world had not changed since her parents' youth in that regard. She knew she had to work fast to get not just justice, but a happy resolution and salvation for her baby brother. Nothing was guaranteed to work in his favor now, not even release on bail; it could be refused. And systemic corruptions meant that sometimes bail payments were more like ransoms, no guarantee for release pending a hearing. Fresh air used to be free, now something to be purchased, huffed, hustled, a controlled substance.

She called home and her father answered.

"Hi, Daddy, how you doing?"

"Hangin' in there, dahlin'. It's good to hear your voice, Ella."

"Wonderful to hear your mellifluous voice, Daddy." He chuckled at her usual flattery.

"Is Mommy around?"

"Aren't you even going to talk to me for a minute?" He sounded anxious and petulant.

"Of course, but I want you both on the phone at the same time."

"Hold on, I'll call your mother... Mush", she heard him yell, "pick up. it's your daughter!"

"Which one?" she heard her mother's distant voice tease.

"The crazy one; the one that's older than dirt; that one."

"If I'm older than dirt what does that make you?" Ella's father chuckled.

"Hi doll baby!" Her mother sounded relieved. She knew Ella had called to take some of the worry off of them, to help.

"Hi Mommy-dearest, how you doing?

"Okay."

"So I wanted to talk to you both at the same time because I know something has gone down with Toddy."

"Did he call you?" her mother asked.

"No, he didn't have to call me! You know you don't have to call me although it would have been nice to be told and not have to know that way!"

"Can't keep nothin' from you," her father laughed.

"Yeah, you did keep something from me, that you're so upset and so I had to think about it and then I found out as per usual." She started to yell at them, her parents, about whom she felt...parental. Ella sighed. "All right, so what are we going to do?"

"Well, I've got an old friend..." her father began.

"You and your old friends! Do they always come through? Do they ever come through?"

"Yes, they do! Remember when..."

"Okay, never mind, never mind." She didn't want to start an argument about failed and unfulfilled expectations of his jive, ungifted buddies and bullshit relatives.

"Ask your old friend, whatever. I'm going to try and do a few things."

"It's too complex; there are too many people..." he said worriedly.

"Well, if you can at least bail him out, maybe I can do some paperwork."

"What do you mean?" Her mother was less in sync with them.

"Think about it. Maybe I can do some paperwork. Anyway I'll be down on the weekend, okay?"

"Good to hear you, dahlin'."

"It will be great to see you," Ella said, sending them a great loving embrace.

Her mother said, "Yes love, it will be great to see you, despite the situation."

"Thank you. I love you both very much," Ella told them and started to tear up.

"We love you too, bye."

After she hung up and dabbed her eyes, she realized she'd forgotten something; she needed to rally them. She rang back.

"Hello?" her father said.

"Hi. Okay, tell her to pick up again. Why are you still next to the phone?"

"'Cause I knew you were going to call back."

"Oh, so you knew I forgot something?"

"Yes, we forgot something."

"Yeah, so let's sing a song. You need to sing a song."

"What kind of song?" Her father chuckled. Her mother giggled.

"A car song," Ella said.

"Which car song?" her mother asked.

"One that baby boy liked."

"What did he like?" her father mused.

"*Going to the Chapel*," her mother offered.

"No, not that one." Ella pulled on them and from herself. What would wrap him close to them, what would invoke their shared joy at being together? What would raise them and draw their circle?

"*Boom De Yada*," Ella proclaimed.

"Yes," her parents said, and they sang it. They heard Toddy's voice yelling along as if they were in the car, making their way together to their next adventure.

Boom De Yada Boom De Yada Boom De Yada Boom De Yada Boom De Yada Boom De Yada Boom De Yada

I love the mountains.
I love the daffodils.
I love the roses.

I love the daises too.
I love the fireflies.
when the lights are low.
Boom De Yada Boom De Yada Boom De Yada Boom De Yada Boom De Yada Boom De Yada Boom De Yada

They sang another chorus together, then Ella said, "See you soon, love you."

"We love you, too," they said.

When they hung up, she felt better. She knew they felt better. Then she had to think of how to fix what could not be fixed. She had to make some persuasive paper and where would she send the paper? Toddy was already in the system. Where would the paper be delivered? He was in the Metropolitan Correctional Center and she wasn't sure how long it would take for her father to raise bail. You could send a letter to the prison but she wasn't sure how they'd be delivered. If it passed through enough hands, she could at least ensure his safety, as he could influence anyone who touched her intentional paper.

Ella had moved to a small town in upstate New York for work and now had a tiny, ancient white house and postage stamp-sized yard. Ella went into her yard and spoke to her plants, telling them and God that she needed to save her brother's life. He'd been stupid but fresh air should not be regulated, right? It should be free; it used to be free; it used to be widely available but that was beside the point, now.

She sang the song to her plants and weeds that she would use. Cotton was already at hand, linters, but she prayed over her batch and she thought what else is white — this must be white paper, so that meant milkweed. She cut and stripped some milkweed bast; cooked it in washing soda; drained and rinsed it; cut it up some more; put it in the blender. Filled the vat with water; put the resuscitated cotton pulp and shredded milkweed in. Pulled a bunch of paper sheets using her sanctified mold and deckle in a neutral vat. She vacuum-dried some of the wet out of the sheets. She changed the blessed felts, the papers air-dried until they were just the damp that is cool to the touch and then were dry-pressed. Then she spray-starched and ironed each sheet so it was not quite crisp but not soft. All the while she sang and prayed:

"We are stardust
We are million-year-old carbon
We are golden, we're golden
and we're caught in the devil's bargain
and we have got to get ourselves
yes, we have got to get ours
yes, we have got to get ourselves
back to the garden"

And on these intentional papers, these freedom papers, these papers made with love and imbued with belief that her baby brother would be freed, she printed her intentions *that my baby brother be free, that he be protected, that he get out of jail, that he remain well and whole.* She repeated this aloud *that my baby brother be free, that he gets out of jail, that he'll be well and protected.*

Ella's training had begun as all the best training does – without her knowing and with love: being held by many and adored by all. Passed from loving arm to loving arm before she could even ask, she was given and when she could speak, she was taught the best way to ask was with grace and gratitude for the attention. She watched her grandmother manage her small mom-and-pop store, listen to the ills and worries of her neighbors and some customers, and they all left lighter and less wounded when they left the store. She cleaned the store in a special way and sang a song that she would later hear in Jamaica, in the Blue Hills of St. Ann's where her grandparents came from: "If I had the Wings of a Dove."

Ella studied at the store: how to cut deli meat and cheese and not slice off a finger, how to serve, and how to listen. Her grandmother went to church in the middle of that same Harlem block. It seemed a cathedral or a castle, a place of radiance, as a child sitting beside her grandmother in church. Ella heard her and the others sing in a tremulous swelling warble that set her young soul astir.

In her grandparents' apartment there was an upright piano that her Aunt Ivy played. Ivy taught her song after song, played them for her and Ella sang along. Child songs like Bobby Shafto's "Gone to Sea" and some anthemic transformative songs like "Whistle a Happy Tune" (*you can be as brave, as you make believe you are…and every single time the happiness in the tune convinces me that I'm not afraid*) and "Climb Every Mountain" were "object lessons" for young Ella.

One day in the West Indian church with her grandmother, she remembered their hymns and sang out. She felt something move through her and connect her to all the warbling women and the incense. The light through the stained glass felt transcendent but the word she would have used then was *magical.*

And after that transforming service, the women said to her grandmother, *She must be in the Tom Thumb wedding.* Her grandmother asked Ella if she would do that.

Ella was shy and said, "No, I can't do that."

"But they need to hear you sing, Tutums," Tutums being the special name her beloved grandmother called her. "They need to hear you sing."

Ella wasn't sure what she meant but she knew that singing was something everybody did in her family: her grandmother in church, her father to the family about the family and her mother to herself and to her. Her mother's songs were restrained and sad. Her father's songs were warm and funny. Her grandfather's songs were not understandable. Her grandmother's songs were all spiritual. Everybody sang and the best times were when they sang together.

After her brother was born, they all sang together when they went for car rides and they all sang together at home with certain records and then they began to learn her father's song: "*It may seem funny honey as funny as can be but when I have my children, I want them all to look like me, when we move, way on the outskirts of town, I don't want nobody, nobody hanging around.*"

They sang and danced to this and later she would learn that when they sang together, they were stronger, when they sang together, they knew each other's hearts and they loved each other more, when they sang together, they had no colds, they had no illnesses. When her daddy sang after working overtime, he got his energy back. When her mother sang to her, all her art and longing and dreams entered Ella's mind. When her grandmother sang, she felt a deep sense of peace and boundless, unconditional love – God's love, Ella thought. When her grandfather sang to her, she felt protected and unafraid. Her father's gifts were sound and empathy, her mother's gifts were song and telepathy.

Her mother's parents were from Jamaica and knew things and said things without saying them, yet they were both so eloquent she loved listening to them and how they said her name.

They used sound and words as tools, as defense and protection. This she learned in study even more deeply. She tried to do with her plants what she'd seen her grandfather do with his

— there were jungles on the fire escape despite New York City winters. The bowed window of her grandmother's store was filled with different green climbing everywhere.

Her father shaped his voice to the occasion. Ella didn't know his parents, from the island of Montserrat, but he said his mother was an Obeah woman, that they were matrilineal and that was why his middle name was her maiden name, that his belonging was co-equal.

This is what she had to marshal to save her brother, to change the fate he was falling into. Might a recording be played in the joint? That wasn't good enough – it would have to be paper making because the paper could enter where her sound could not and the paper could carry her sound and her intent if she would imbue it with the intent that he be freed, that he be let go, that the charges, indeed, the minor misdemeanor that they were for fresh air, should be dropped.

She had to remember everything she was taught and apply it to something new.

The Metropolitan Correctional Center was a big building, the first high-rise facility to be used by the Bureau of Prisons. Prisoners are assigned to one of ten separate, self-contained housing units. Way hard to invoke through all that steel and concrete and she wasn't sure what unit baby boy was in.

Too bad it wasn't West Street jail, although West Street was federal and frightening because it was the first jail she ever visited when she visited her friend from high school there. Hakeem was a political prisoner and she had tried to come by at least once a week. They could see each other through the wire, she could smell him, smell the salt and ivory soap of him; for all the bars and wires, Ella could see his face clearly and read his emotions. It was both painful and wonderful; a most terrible excitement to support her friend in that way and to learn for the first time the terrible consequences of their rebellion.

Ella wasn't sure what he had done to take it that step too far or maybe he hadn't, and it ached to think that Hakeem had been in put in prison for trying to make the world better and her brother was in prison for hustling fresh air. What to do, what to do, now how to do it?

She could envision herself plastering at night the invoking Flyers on West Street jail, but MCC did not seem approachable or graffiti-able or touchable, no matter the time of day. She had another thought. She could do it as litter! She needed help. She called her friend Ava in Chinatown, another eldest girl who knew about bad brothers.

Ella called her. "I'm coming into the city 'cause my baby brother's in the joint."

"What what what? Aiyah," Ava gasped.

"I know I know I know! Trying to sell some fresh air to a police agent…"

"Oh my gosh, what are you going to do?"

"Well, can we hang out for a minute? Maybe you know some young kids or someone I could hire to litter around the MCC."

"MCC? What's that?" Ava asked

"The Metropolitan something Center, I don't know. MCC correction center prison downtown near you, the big one," Ella explained, suddenly tired. "Anyway, I could use your help. I need to do some small invocations."

She had told Ava about this, though Ava did and did not understand. Ava said she would reach out to some of her son's friends to see if they would do it.

"I mean littering, littering, don't pause, don't stop, but take different times and just drop these pieces of paper as close as they can to the entrance of the MCC and keep on going."

"Sounds like one of your crazy plans," Ava laughed.

"Well, crazy stuff keeps happening so I got to do crazy plans."

"Okay, when will you get to the city?"

"I'm almost there. I can't stay in Queens with my parents. I need to be closer to where Toddy is. I need to work on him in this situation. My father is going to cash something in and get bail money. We can't not try to do bail, but got to get him out and we got to get him away. What if they decide not to let him out?"

"Where are you staying?"

"At the Washington Square Park Hotel. It's seen better days but it's still cheap and it's nearer all the places I would love to eat closer to downtown and to you."

"Cool, call me when you're settled."

Ella met Ava at the Peacock Café, their favorite, in Greenwich. She showed her the papers and Ava had the brilliant idea of folding some origami style to be inviting, to be picked up, also to give them some weight so they just didn't fly away in the air that would roll down around the plaza that was Civic Center. They ate lightly, a tart, sweet, cold raspberry soup, brioche and then some elaborate mochaccinos. Music filled the café; just what Ella needed.

"How does this work?" Ava asked.

"Intention, holistic intention, I intend my brother to be free. I will make it so; I will bend all the actions in the direction of the greatest good; the greatest good is that the idiot was only selling fresh air in Washington Square Park. He should be free! Yeah, it was something he shouldn't have been doing. One day, fresh air will be free, not regulated. That day may be soon, but it isn't here yet. I'm sure there are many who know how unjust it is and maybe that person who entrapped him had some numbers he had to improve or something… I don't know, but there are all these little levers to push that money can help with and that without money, maybe intentionality can help with…"

Ava looked at her long and hard. "You're such a witch," she laughed.

"That's the western word, so I wouldn't use that."

"What do you call yourself?"

"Daughter of good peasant stock, daughter of dreamers and workers, folks who always did both. There's been lots of workers…workers like work workers who, how can I put this? How do you think black people survived slavery?" Ella felt comfortable asking long-time friend Ava, whose grandparents' Chinese food restaurant was just blocks away from Ella's grandmother's grocery store in Harlem.

Ava and Ella were both born in Manhattan, but at different ends of it. Both were the second generation of their families to be born in America.

"I don't know, but I think about how Chinese people who worked the railroads, they didn't just all die or get blown up."

"Exactly, that's kind of what I'm getting at – these were hideous oppressive systems and people did not have access to medicine as we know it now or hospitals like now."

"Yeah, but there was ancient Chinese medicine."

"Okay, so there you go. That's what I'm saying. There is ancient knowing to your rescue. Some folks brought the knowing over. I was given some of the knowing. Some of us get caught and I was taught enough, enough to shape some better outcomes on occasion. It takes a lot of energy, a lot of energy and clarity, which I don't always have. And the time and intentionality… The Chinese medicine… You've got to know the specifics and which particular effects of particular areas and particular plants and too much could be poison and too little is a waste of something precious. You've got to know when to gather it, you've got to know how to collect it and from where."

Ella continued, seeing understanding cross Ava's face. "I mean, that's how paper goes and the gift I was given was song, rudimentary sound, but song and sound, and if I put that together with the plant knowledge, limited as it is for me, growing as it is for me, if I put it together, then I can shape something because I come from people who did shape things. They shaped their destiny. They shaped enough to survive slavery and created music. They shaped enough to come to America. Everybody acts like it's all just ego and material intention. They didn't drown at sea while coming. They didn't die while being beaten. In fact, my grandfather's people ran away up in the hills in Jamaica in rebellion. The Maroons escaped through to the mountains, killed some of their oppressors."

"I heard about them." Ava sipped from her mochaccino. "I got to go to Jamaica in my early 20s."

"There was a fierce something that continued that I was taught, and as annoyed with my brother as I always am, I'm not going to let the system chew him up! We're going to get him out." Ella's voice softened. "Thank you for your help."

"Course, I would help you, of course. You're my buddy."

"Yep! Thank you, my dear friend. I just wish this trip was about something pleasant, you know, just hang out, eat some delicious food, go to the seaport, see some street performers, and tell you other, better stories."

"Well, my own brother has always been a pain in the ass, so I understand."

"Thank God he's cute," Ella laughed.

"Don't go there," Ava warned.

"All right, I won't let you know that he uses his attractiveness to overcome some of his stupidity."

"Yep!" They both laughed.

They folded some more papers and then Ella asked Ava, "Where can we get closest to the sea?"

"Well, it's not going to be clean..."

"I know, but they've done a lot of cleaning up of the waterways...the fresh air is still precious but the water is much..."

They took the ferry from Wall Street to Beach Channel Drive on Rockaway. Just a swift hour to get to the ocean and still be in NYC.

"Thanks for keeping me company," Ella said to Ava.

"I've never done it this way before." Ava smiled broadly. "It's an adventure. I want to see you do your thing."

They walked over sand to the sea. Late June's bright summer sun made everything seem hyperreal, grains of sand visible, the smell of wet salt life. A perfume billowed towards them.

Ella sang softly to the water, great mother water, calling, *Mama Wata oh my love.* And then began talking to the wet expanse spread before her. *I don't like what he did but it was such a small thing, but small things are big when certain people do them; help me establish the balance; how I miss you. Help me establish the balance. Save my kin, protect us.*

Then they returned to Manhattan on the ferry, feeling the spray kiss their cheeks.

Ella said, "I'm keeping some of these beautifully folded invocation papers in my pocket for when I go to see him. The rest are for your son's friends to casually drop around MCC. Thank you for your beautiful folding." They hugged and parted.

Ella went to the Metropolitan Correctional Center and laid hands on the building 'til she reached her baby brother. She sent him love and protection. He was nervous, but okay. He couldn't hear her, but he could feel her. The young people Ava had rallied performed the intentional littering and were asked to think "be freed", and it was done.

Ella never got to visit her brother inside, because the next day he was released on bail. A hearing was set for two months ahead. She met her parents and him at MCC and drove them home to Queens. They sang car songs all the way.

Timbuctoo

Akua Lezli Hope

AFTER A WEEK, almost too quickly, the furor died down. After all, lots of people disappeared in the woods, and this was just a black woman who had the nerve and the leisure to enter said woods. The media was tuned to death by a bad cop. Her colleagues mourned, as did a few friends, but there was comparatively little mainstream media attention. Surprisingly, her reportedly indifferent siblings had insisted that sniffer dogs scour the area. The dogs reacted to something by running around in circles. And the phone recording offering proof was not persuasive except to avoid blaming her companion and deepen the mystery. UAP and Big Foot fanatics sought interviews. There had been sightings in the Adirondacks.

* * *

A sea once filled the bowl of this ring of mountains a mere eleven thousand years ago. The Adirondacks teach you what trees do to air. Fresh, as if you can smell the sun, but it's not the sun you smell, it's what it has raised, and what the heat of it does to leaves on trees, to the grass…to the untrained nose, perhaps the notes of pine needles. Needled trees versus the leafy trees and the air when it stirred brought up these bouquets.

"Well, not like we can smell all that is here. It all blends together. Sugar maple, beech, yellow birch, paper birch, red spruce, white pine, white ash, many critters… It is something sweet, savory, clear," Aviva philosophized, pointing.

"I'm sure they smell us," Lulu said.

"They smell us and they stay away," Aviva laughed.

Warbler song burst as if joining the conversation. They were on their way to being lost, though not yet unhappily as the day was bright, but their phones no longer gave information about where they were and the packs on their back were becoming annoying.

"We're not equipped for serious camping," Lulu said.

"Well," Aviva began, clearing her throat, "I invested in this portable shelter, time-tested, built in proven pyramid-style, easy to set up, spacious, capable of providing sanctuary in all but the most extreme weather while weighing a mere twenty-two point four ounces. I put the adjustable trekking poles, ultralight stake kit, and tent pole in your pack."

"Oh, my god." Lulu made a face. "A commercial! Oh, that's what all these sticks are. I thought they were for defense."

"From what?" Aviva asked, looking at her friend. They both laughed. This was their bond, their shared sense of absurdity, and the ability to call or yank each other back from the excessive edges of their personalities. They had practiced in preparation for these two short days of bliss, bug bites, and beauty. They had packed water bottles and filters, should they come across a stream. Flat solar chargers for their night lights and cell phones, whenever they might work.

"And lightweight clothes for warmth, should the weather shift."

"In this time of global warming?"

"Just say climate change and you'll know to be prepared."

"True that!"

"I had my heat on in July…" Aviva shivered dramatically.

"Because you're coldblooded," Lulu teased.

"No, no, I need warmth. I just haven't mutated like the rest of y'all!"

"Y'all who?"

"You know, you Americans – my body has only been here a generation. My parents kept their house too hot. We shed everything at the door at Christmas. But my friends' homes are always too cold and I know I have to wear scarves and layers. Even restaurants can be a challenge."

"You're such a delicate flower."

They both laughed and paused. They had met working in parallel jobs in BigCorp's marketing division. Aviva was in end product and Lulu in infrastructure. They were the same age, same level, and for both, this was their second job out of business school. They were both the first-born daughters and their grandparents had businesses within blocks of each other in Harlem, an area their parents left but whose legacy was extolled. And as happens when circles are unbroken, Lulu had gone to an exclusive all-girls high school with one of Aviva's college classmates.

They felt fated to be sister friends. And this latest excursion confirmed it, hiking/camping which neither had experience in, but both feeling a deep need to get out of the city and explore.

They were among all this loveliness and all these trees in a landscape more wood than forest that would suddenly open into meadows. They paused and looked up, trying to ascertain their direction.

"We should've brought a compass," said Aviva, worried.

"Yeah, but the phones were supposed to be our compass," Lulu assured her. "We were heading west, north, south, east, west… Sunrise is in the east, sets in the west and based on the last time we checked, it's about two o'clock in the afternoon. We've got a good six and a half hours more of light before darkness."

"So plenty of time to figure it out."

"But I don't wanna wait that long to figure it out. I'm hungry," said Lulu petulantly.

"I've got some edgenola and some trail mix. We've got to ration."

"What's in that stuff?"

"Oatmeal, seeds, dark chocolate bits, salty-sweet," Aviva said.

"Umm, my kind of pick-me-up. Let's take a rest." Lulu plonked down on grassy ground.

"I want a child," Aviva shared.

"Then have one."

"I can't."

"Why not?"

"I need a husband, a father."

"Don't you mean sperm?"

"I get plenty of sperm."

They both laughed.

"Wooo child, you braggart," Lulu chided.

"Well, sperm is available but husband-fathers are not," said Aviva.

"I'm sure there is a man in New York willing to father your child," said Lulu.

"My ex-husband, who I married to make a family, did not want kids; something he lied about while we dated."

"Well, all you had to do was the deed and boom! Present him with the fact," Lulu grinned.

"I couldn't think of doing that to a being – being unwanted… And you are divorced? J2 shares John with another family – a stepbrother and a half-sister in a place without a room of his own."

"Yes, but I *have* J2." Lulu's face grew pensive.

"I'm not as strong as you to face doing all that child-rearing work alone."

"Honey, it is work," Lulu chuckled.

"Look, if it happens to not work out, then we do what we must. But I had two parents both committed to making me, and as a daddy's girl I want at least to think my kid will have an involved father. My mother was rough. The warm, gentling influence was my father," Aviva explained.

"That's why you're so good with these tools, huh?" said Lulu, beginning to pound a stake in the ground.

"Let's scout around a bit more before we settle."

"Now she tells me." As Lulu reached to pull up the stake, it seemed to leap into her hand, but she said nothing of this small anomaly to Aviva.

They look at their phones again for information, see none, and then trudge up a gentle slope in the land to another leveling, a grass plateau where they see a tall, athletic black man whose broad-shouldered, deeply muscled torso is etched by sunlight through a frayed cotton shirt, pale cream against his dark bronze skin. He is bent over, winding some curious mechanism, and looks up from this inexplicable chore to grin at them. His dazzling smile enfolded them immediately in the unknown joke and they all chuckled.

"Hey ladies," he boomed, "what brings you to these parts today?" He pulled a cloth from his pocket that Aviva recognized as a handkerchief and wiped his sweat-glistened brow. Aviva was entranced.

Lulu nudged her and whisper-snarled, "Shut your mouth. You're drooling; you're shameless." Fortunately, they were at a sufficient distance to not be heard.

"Ah, be kind, ma'am," he grinned again. "She must be surprised to come across a creaky winder like this. Especially since y'all look like a long, long way from someplace else." He eyed them, his gaze resting first on their backpacks that they had slung off to the ground beside them and then it seemed he studied their shoes. He wore striped braces, holding up steel-gray pants, and his own footwear resembled a sort of short boot more than a shoe. A sudden awkwardness filled the air.

"We're lost," said Lulu.

"Hope you can help us, kind sir," said Aviva.

Lulu shot her a scolding side eye. "Kind, sir, my ass," she whispered.

"Nice to make your acquaintance, ladies. I'm Ezekiel."

"I'm Lulu and Ms. Tongue-tied is Aviva."

Ezekiel regarded them both with easy amusement, which made Aviva suddenly feel deeply shy. Lulu was unfazed.

"Hope you can help us. Where are we exactly?"

"Can't tell you exactly," Ezekiel said, "but can tell you the name. You're at the outer edge of Timbuctoo, the prettiest little settlement of black folks in this part of the world."

"Wow," Aviva said to Lulu, "I didn't know there were enactors up here."

"En-ac-tors?" repeated Ezekiel, slowly, revealing he probably heard all that had passed between them. "That's some new language for me, but if you care to follow me into town, I'm sure the Mayor Mother Elder will help you out. And that guy over there, bent to a similar task, is Joshua." They saw another handsome man, his face sharp boned and sun burnished, wearing a short-brimmed straw hat.

They hoisted their backpacks, and Ezekiel strode over to assist.

Both demurred. "Thanks," they chimed in near unison.

"We're used to lugging stuff around," Aviva said shyly.

"They look heavy," Ezekiel said.

Joshua said, "Sure we can't lend a hand?" He stepped beside Lulu who bristled palpably and let out an exasperated sigh.

"Nah."

The woods faded to flower fields, where the occasional brightly colored frame house and log cabin stood encircled by a porch, cut grass and arranged flowers, punctuated by an occasional clothesline where light sheets fluttered like light sails in the soft breeze.

"Ah," said Ezekiel, "so nice not to have to smell horse shit, slop jars or garbage."

They smelled the evocative scent of coffee. A surprise for an enactment, Aviva thought. She hadn't had coffee for a long time, but the scent on the breeze made her juices run. "Oh, coffee!"

"It's mostly roasted chicory," Joshua explained. "We don't have much coffee and chicory grows wild here."

"I saw its pretty blue flowers, so I saw some. I've used it to make paper."

"Are you a paper maker?" Ezekiel asked.

"Only on occasion," Aviva said. "I love using plants and exploring their possibilities."

"Nothing is coming out of the chimneys," Lulu remarked.

"Well, most everybody's probably together in town in the Gathering Hall for feast day," Ezekiel explained. "Joshua here is a fine fiddler who will be playing tunes for the bakers and the makers, and for the dance."

"Timbuctoo, that's an African name here in New York," said Aviva.

"Well, yes, it is. We're free black folks, remembering something we should've never had to lose or forget. Timbuctoo, founded in the fifth century, in a fertile zone located at the gateway to the Sahara desert, near a river, was a great center of learning. We were granted this land in an effort to turn black urban wage workers into self-sufficient black land owners and gain the right to vote."

"Where are y'all from?" Joshua asked.

"New York City," Aviva answered.

"So are we," said Ezekiel, smiling broadly.

Aviva smiled back and shot a look at Lulu, who sighed and looked away. This was an old, much revisited discussion between them. Aviva asserted that her best relationships were with other born-and-bred New Yorkers. While Lulu considered herself an extrovert, she had not met or interacted with as many people, not with Aviva's intensity. She barely remembered girls from high school, whereas Aviva told her stories of her "cadre" of co-conspirators fomenting change.

They arrived at a smoothly paved square where sat a large circular building with a peaked gold-clad roof. An expansive porch encircled half of it. Its wide, intricately carved wood doors were open, leading sunlight deep into the hall.

"Mayor Mother Elder, this is Aviva and Lulu," Ezekiel said.

"Welcome, welcome, welcome, dear ones. It's a delight and a rare occasion to have guests at our feast day. Ezekiel and Joshua can put those heavy bags aside for you."

Mayor Mother Elder wore layers, a simple sleeveless empire-waist dress that reached to the floor and a long-sleeved overdress, too diaphanous to be called a robe, but they understood it to be. A cowrie shell hung from a single gray braid that crossed her forehead, emerging from her woven-cloth wrapped hair; and cowrie shells hung in strands from her ears. A wide, purple band accented her bosom on her dress and thin gold threads ran in vertical bands on her pearl-colored overdress.

Lulu, defensive, said, "No, we're OK keeping our bags."

"Well, no need to worry. We invite you to participate. Otherwise, you'll just be sitting for hours as we make our preparations."

"How can we help?" Aviva asked.

"Well, there is cooking to be done and set up to be done."

"I'd love to help cook," said Aviva. "I cooked to make money in college. I'm really quite good at it."

Mayor Mother Elder chuckled. "I don't doubt that you are. College, eh? Wonderful! A black woman who went to college… Though our ingredients are rather simple: food from our storage and what we found foraging around earlier today. It's early in the season for a harvest, although we do grow fresh greens in our gardens."

"That sounds so familiar to me. I grow herbs on my windowsill, so there's always something bright and green in every meal."

"Yes, exactly. Come on Aviva." Ezekiel took her hand.

"Ezekiel is a great cook and a wonderful baker, so I'm sure you'll be well guided in the kitchen."

Lulu started to say something. The kitchen, seen at a distance, was huge. The building was far larger than it seemed from the outside. The stoves looked strange. There was fire, but she couldn't figure out the fuel: were there gas lines this far out in the mountains? There were ovens with ranges. Several others worked at a long table.

"Well, we still have set up to do."

Lulu said, "I'm very good at creating spaces. Just tell me what the purpose is and where your furnishings are."

"Some are shoved into the ring rooms. Other pieces are over there against the wall."

Lulu saw curved tables against the curved wall with legs that were branch-like, as if a tree held up a boomerang. The woodgrain seemed to swirl as if alive.

"They're in the closet. Joshua could direct you with that."

Joshua said, "I sure can, but I need to play to help the food making and bread rising."

"The food making and bread rising?" Lulu repeated quizzically.

"Well, yeah. Let's follow them into the kitchen and I'll play for the cooks and the bakers a bit and then we'll come up here and set up where the musicians will sit."

Joshua's fiddling did seem to assist the bakers in ways that defied Lulu's understanding. It was as if the utensils, as well as ingredients, danced, as if he informed the inanimate what to do and the sentient to connect with their tasks with renewed energy and joy. There should always be music in a kitchen, Lulu thought.

As the day slipped on, and the sun shifted, filling the windows of the great hall with ever more light, even though it was lengthening towards dusk. More and more people arrived, many with pots and dishes beyond those cooking in the great kitchen. There were gorgeous tables that Lulu had artfully set up in a sort of arc so that people could peruse the food and gather what they chose on little plates.

The astounding feast seemed well beyond what Mayor Mother Elder had described so humbly. The musicians included not only strings. A guitar, a gutbucket bass, a simple drum, a hammered metal something, not unlike a xylophone, an upright piano and flute, were also in the band, so the sound was full and rhythmic.

Aviva thought it was deeply soulful, and Lulu liked it too. And here and there people danced, and they saw children, scampering, tap dancing, and doing something that resembled breakdancing as the music picked up speed. At one point Ezekiel nodded to Joshua, who looked at a guitar player and tapped his foot. Then they played something slower and so infinitely sweet that when Ezekiel enfolded Aviva's hand within his, she felt as if her heart would burst.

At first, they danced facing each other, and then, for some reason, she felt she must rest her head against his shoulder, her forehead touching his neck. And his hand slid up her back and pressed her gently to him. He caressed the back of her neck and her shoulders budded wings.

Lulu was aghast at this.

Mayor Mother Elder tapped rhythmically on the table: a call to attention. The musicians stopped playing music and made sounds along with her humming. They start playing something that was not a tune but like a call. All assembled began to sing-chant:

Timbuctoo Timbuctoo
Thanks to source for giving us you
Thanks for all that are gathered, whole.
Thanks for all we get to say and do.
All we get to be
Thanks for enabling us to be free
Timbuctoo Timbuctoo
we give thanks, give thanks for you.
thanks for freedom
for our time-leaping existence
allowing us to defy wrong fate
saving us from the world of hate
let us live and procreate
we rejoice to participate
in this great adventure
we welcome our lovely guests
who may join choose to us
in this journey who may choose to know
where we began, how we can grow
we don't know where or when we'll end
but we're grateful for whatever source decides to send.
We're grateful for this roaming land so rich with life
for this gracious blessed earth, free from strife
and the portals, she deploys
preserving us with wisdom and joy
all praises to our ancestors who studied mystic ways,
that we could slip from bondage, and never again be enslaved
ever to be free, ever to be free, ever to be free,
as all creators are meant to be
all praises to our ancestors, all praises to our source

And then the musicians began to play strange chords that resembled jazz, changing the light in the great hall. And the people echoed and intoned *ever to be free* and *amen a-a-a-men,* began to rise and they all reached an incredible chord of *amen* shimmering from the walls, almost as light.

It was a long, long day. As its last sunlight turned red through the windows, Aviva and Lulu both gasped as panels in the wall were suffused with a soft, golden, radiant light. Where was the electricity coming from? The panels seemed to connect with the vaulted golden pyramid of the hall ceiling.

The tone of the party shifted again as tendrils of the vibrating, lifting *Amen* faded. The music returned to lively dancing music. Aviva could not leave Ezekiel's arms, and neither did he open them as they swayed and danced together.

As the dusk deepened to evening, the colors outdoors shifted to light blue gray, then a leaf-dappled deep blue, still not the dark of night.

Aviva and Ezekiel returned to the kitchen to tidy up, she thought. But there was surprisingly little to tidy, as folks had cleaned as they worked. She tried to copy his movements and discern where he put utensils, in places where drawers slid open and closed without him touching them.

They chatted about many things. Conversation flowed so easily that she did not know the words. She realized very slowly that it was a wordless flow between them. The instants became forever as time dilated. Their hand clasp felt as intimate as any intercourse. Aviva felt connected and embraced, invited in and understood. She put his hand to her face. Ezekiel put her fingers on his lips and sucked the tips, as if sipping wine. "I've been blessed," he said, eyes gleaming. "You are my home."

Lulu sought Mayor Mother Elder, anxious to clear her mind of this growing sense of unease. "Mayor Mother Elder, what kind of enactment is this?"

"En-act-ment – what do you mean?"

"A historical recreation village. Your tech is strangely inconsistent with what – 1860 – when Timbuctoo was founded."

"Well, we began a bit before that, but that's when the settlement grew."

"But then it disappeared."

"Is that what your books say? Well, in a sense, we did. We weren't sure it would be safe, that the land granted would remain ours. Many of us came up from New York City and knew how politics could betray even those committed to our cause. There were tiny stone mounds like little pyramids amongst the trees here. This was shared neutral territory in the time of the first folk. The Champlain Sea covered the Adirondacks in the before. Perhaps it was a sea gift from an old whale...the last of the first folks here were Mohawk and Oneida, who may have created this sacred axis. We prayed on it and were granted access. John Brown supported us. So did Frederick Douglass. Oh, Frederick." She paused, shut her eyes for a moment. "He was so handsome."

She sighed. "We found a portal formation in the settlement and realized we could live here, and live in peace. We return every so often to offer thanks and praise for Earth's great gift to us, a natural intersection of great telluric energy enabling us to shift, to go and stay together in peace. We're grateful this spot is still here to return to. So much has shifted in your realm."

"My realm. What do you mean?"

"That would be telling, but you and your friend were called, weren't you?"

"Called? We were just lost in the hills!"

"If that's the way you want to think about it. Aviva may understand this experience differently. It's all right, dear. Don't worry."

Lulu looked for Aviva. "Look, kiddo, what are we doing here? We've got to go!"

"I'm staying, Lulu."

"What the hell?"

"No, more like heaven and joy. I feel love. I know what love feels like and yes, my lust is part of it, but it's like this ringing where there is a chord of bells. Pulse and open and ring from my pussy to my heart, from below my toes to above my scalp. And all I wanna say is sweet things and walk with him and be smashed against him until we peel apart to pee or cook or eat or read or create. It's a buzzing in my head of all there is to learn about him and with him. These people know how to do things, how to make things, how to transmute matter."

"You can't stay, you can't stay," Lulu cried. "What about your life? What about my life?"

Aviva put her arm around Lulu. "I've always wanted to be an explorer and I've always wanted to be partnered and I've always wanted to have a family, and I've always wanted to have all the things. My very first dreams were of growing things in that little backyard in Queens and at the same time of outer space, and this is just wonderful. I feel loved and connected and I know what love feels like, having felt it before."

"How do you know if it's gonna last?"

"I don't know if it's gonna last, but I married someone to be married for it to last, and it was all lies. Not great material lies, but many small, emotional and spiritual lies, misdirections, precious time wasted. Just crazy, stupid, wrong. He only had one graduate degree, he said he had two. He never wrote a script. Why lie? He didn't want kids. Why marry? Not that we grew apart, but he lied about the ways in which I thought we were together. I didn't rush into it and I asked all the right questions or so I thought. So now I'm gonna do it differently. I feel this and I hear him and he hears me too."

"What about your family?"

"My mother is dead, my father remarried, my brother and sister are partnered and have kids. It's always my effort to connect and to know and they're pretty indifferent. And work – I told you what they did to me when my mother dropped dead. How dare I not be there? ARGH! My last cat is dead. So there's you and a couple other folks who will understand. You all already know I'm crazy."

"Oh, Aviva. But not like this. This is not how this was supposed to go."

"Oh, Lulu, you're wrong. I think this is exactly how it was supposed to go. We were led here somehow. Call it telluric energy or ley lines or something. This is all sweet magic or super advanced science. I hear more than Ezekiel in my mind/heart. They are welcoming me. I'm sorry to leave you, but you have J2 to raise."

Ezekiel, Joshua, and Aviva walked Lulu to the edge of Timbuctoo's territory. Lulu could now see in the far distance a glow that she knew was pure gold, that seemed like a levitating sphere, that she knew to be the top of the gathering hall. Aviva hugged her tightly, kissed her and handed her a bundle that she hadn't noticed she was carrying.

Aviva said, "Here's the super duper ultra lightweight tent. You've already got the poles in your pack, and here is my phone. Zeke and I made a message for my family that you can share, should you choose to or need to, that I've gone away and that I love them. So this way you should be covered. No questions about my disappearance."

"Oh, Aviva! I will miss you terribly and this hurts! What if you die?"

"I will, but I don't think it's happening today nor anytime within your lifetime, for that matter. I could cross the street and get hit by a bus, as my mother used to say. Envision only the best possibilities and this is an incredible opportunity for me. I love you. Thank you for loving me. I am grateful for your being."

Lulu wept as Aviva and Ezekiel, arms around each other's waists, walked away, with Joshua by their side. Ezekiel's and Joshua's shirts glowed like distant fireflies. Then she realized that there was a third light, and that light was Aviva, glowing too, until they flickered off.

She shut her tear-filled eyes and shook. When she raised her head to wipe her eyes and look after them once more, sunlight was shining on her. She touched herself, felt herself, then rummaged in her backpack for her cellphone. She looked at her now-working phone incredulously. It was the afternoon of the same day. She lifted her pack to her back, turned, and walked back towards the city, J2, and home.

Note:
"Timbuctoo.
"In the mid 1800s, New York State law dictated that African-Americans must own at least $250 in real estate or a house in order to obtain the right to vote. Determined to help would-be voters secure this right, abolitionist and real estate baron Gerrit Smith devised a 'scheme of justice and benevolence' that he hoped would provide refuge to black families."
adirondack.net

The Mystery Within Us

Pauline E. Hopkins

"SPEAKING OF spiritualistic phenomena, and the existence of guardian angels, and that there are means of actual communication between the denizens of earth and those bright spirits – why, my dear Jack, I *do* believe in these things."

"Then you agree with the immortal bard that 'there are more things in heaven and earth than are dreamt of in *our* philosophy.'"

When I left home five years before, I had fretted a good deal about my friend Tom Underwood. I knew that he was in financial difficulties, but his indomitable pride was such that I dared not offer him the pecuniary help which I longed to give and which I felt was sorely needed. I had learned nothing from his occasional letters except that he was well. Upon my return from a long exile we met and resumed our friendly relations, to an extent, although there was, I felt, a something which he held back from me, and which would, if told, explain the state of great success and eminence which he had attained in his profession as a physician, and as an author, too, of eagerly sought scientific works on subjects pertaining to the science of the preservation of life. I found, indeed, a great fascination in reading the most wonderful work of its kind that I had ever chanced upon, entitled "The Ethics of Life," and I did not wonder at his success.

Tonight he had invited me to a *tete-a-tete* dinner at his bachelor quarters; this was the first time we had so dined since my return. After finishing our repast, I settled myself in the most comfortable position I could assume, and while I silently waited for my friend to give me the confidence which I felt would be natural to the time and place, I enjoyed his fine Havanas and admired the elegance of his surroundings.

Tom's rooms formed the top floor of one of those wonderful apartment houses with which large cities now endeavor to cater to the refined tastes of those men who have, apparently, foresworn matrimony, to the despair of the fair sex and the delight and profit of the speculator to whom the bachelor apartment house is a veritable mine. I glanced curiously about me at the rich furnishings which betokened the man of wealth and cul— An attentive man servant glided in and out and ministered to our comfort. It was like a story from the "Arabian Nights", the luxury, the ease, the elegance. Outside the twilight shades gathered over the roofs of the busy city and mingled and melted into each other; the clouds, tinged with the gold of an exquisite sunset were, for a moment, radiant angel forms, clad in celestial garments of light, covering the city with their heavenly mantles before they were lost in the rapid descent of the night shadows. Tom threw his cigar stump away, and turning to me, said:

"The thoughts expressed by the bard so many years ago prove the inspiration of his genius, and could the many strange things which happen in our individual lives be recorded we would be justified in calling ourselves a world mentally unbalanced.

"When you left home, Jack, I was, as you doubtless surmised, a bankrupt. My patients were as poor as myself and I treated the most of them for nothing. I had drawn a blank at every turn of Fortune's wheel. Love, at one time, had seemed to present a happy augury for a happy future. Poor fool that I was! *She* turned from me with scorn for my poverty.

"One evening I sat in my cheerless room and weighed carefully each event in my life – struggles and disappointments, against the few successes which had come to me. The result was too much for me. I went to my mineral cabinet and deliberately selected a bottle of prussic acid with the intention of ending it all right there. I seated myself on the edge of my couch and watched the dying candle as it prepared for its final disappearance, just as the clock in a neighboring room struck twelve. So shall I be in a short time, I thought, as I watched the dying candle. What is life anyhow, I argued, but a flame easily extinguished by the rude hand of destiny or misfortune? And is it not manlier to take arms against a sea of trouble and end all, than to tamely bear the buffets of misfortune and the cold scorn of the world? I raised the bottle to my lips with the intention of draining it. Halfway there my arm lost its carrying power, and I sat upon the edge of my couch startled into momentary forgetfulness of my project as I mentally analyzed the condition of the arm. Again I essayed to raise the member, but although my mind was more active than it had been for some time, I found that my *entire body had lost the power of volition!* Imagine my sensations! In no way could I account to myself for this condition. My bodily health was perfect.

"To say I was astonished is putting it mildly. I was dumbfounded! I was wont to boast, if you remember, Jack, that my nerves were impervious to fear, but now I felt absolute terror. I arose from my couch, and then, overcome by an irresistible impulse of weakness, sank back again and closed my eyes. The next instant a voice sounded in my ears:

"'Be not afraid; it is I.'

"My mind worked with lightning-like rapidity; I concluded that I was having a psychological experience, so trying to overcome my fear, I endeavored to put in practice certain rules governing such phenomena. *I thought a question and the answer came: 'Look and see.'*

"At these words I felt compelled to unclose my eyes and sit upright. A faint light had settled about the only armchair the room contained and my mind seemed forced to center itself upon this halo. Gradually the shadowy outlines assumed the form of a man, and I could even trace the features, but no one feature attracted me so much as the eyes; they dazzled me, they were so bright, like piercing wells of light. All sensations of fear ceased as I gazed into their limpid depths. Sorrow left me and peace took the place of black despair.

"At last the Presence spoke. I say *spoke*, but, indeed, no sound broke the silence of the room. The Presence *seemed* to speak, although I was well aware that *it did not*. I had heard and read much of the power which lies in the action of one magnetic mind upon another, but never before had I experienced a vivid electrical impression.

"'What would you do, rash man? Overcome by the petty obstacles that have filled a pathway intended to end in benefit to yourself and others, after the needed lessons necessary to develop the latent faculties with which you have been most generously endowed, would you destroy the life that is not yours? By the divine will of God you were designed as an instrument for the accomplishment of certain plans formed before your birth. Would you in the rash despair of human short-sightedness destroy the tenement and reduce the spirit of life within you to the impenetrable darkness and wild tempests of the ocean of regret to which the self-destroyed are forever doomed?'

"I sat in silence, receiving the impressions that emanated from the shape before me. Over the shadowy features various emotions passed: stern denunciation, pity, and finally, grief, as it continued: Once, like you, I lived in the flesh, although I know now that I never lived until I died to earth and left my body to assume the form of my Creator; for only in our spiritual essence do we assume the image of God. This clay house is but the casket within which God created man in His own image that is the ethereal, fleeting animation which we call life, and which comes we know not how, and goes we know not where.

"The Presence paused again in the midst of impressions made upon me like waves of electrical shocks most delicately given. I seemed to recognize the ideas expressed, and even the language was familiar. Gradually my mind was led to thoughts of a physician who had instituted a new epoch in medicine in the cure of certain chronic diseases called incurable by the medical profession. This man died just at the time when his fame was nearing its zenith, and physicians were seriously contemplating the adoption of methods quite foreign to accepted ideas. Dr. Thorn's books (he was the author of three wonderful treatises on *The Philosophy of the Three Ethers*) were my daily companions, and I had often wished it had been my privilege to know the man and to have seen something of his mysterious cures. As I reached the name of Dr. Thorn, in my mind, I glanced at the Presence. The outlines wore a shadowy smile, and I received the impression that I was right in thinking that I beheld the spiritual essence of the great physician.

"'Yes, I was Dr. Thorn, and I would have given the whole of my hard-earned fortune to have remained in the body a few years longer. The transgression of certain laws in the matter of my physical being caused the failure in my own case of the formula which I used for the cure of blood poisoning, and so the vitiated corpuscles dominated my whole system and I made the great change before I realized that it had come. In the midst of my grief for those I had left and my lost art, I received the promise from the Divinity that my discoveries should not be lost, and that one should be given me who should revive and restore the whole of my system. You are he. Be pure in thought and aspiration; diligent and contented; seek and find.'

"When I came to myself in the early morning hours, I awoke as one from a long sleep. I still sat upon the side of my couch, but the bottle of poison I have never seen since. The room was cold and cheerless and upon the table which stood at my elbow was the full manuscript of the book that has made me famous and has brought me a fortune. *I invariably find prescriptions and treatises upon chronic cases on that table by my bedside in the morning when I awake.*

"I cannot account for all this except by quoting the words which you have used: 'There are more things in heaven and earth than are dreamt of in our philosophy.'"

Hum

Melissa Jackson-Wagner

SOMETIMES Rum hummed, she liked the tickly sensation in her throat and the vibration skipping in her chest when she made the hum go low, low, low and deep, deep, deep inside her. The hum could lick her belly bottom if she made a good one. Sometimes she hummed with her mouth turned down and sometimes with a big smile stretched across her face. If she opened her mouth and made different shapes, she could make more hums. Some of them sounded beautiful – at least they did to Rum. As soon as Rum was alone in the forest, or digging up cassava at the far end of the tended land that it was her job to care for, she would hum. Depending where she was she would either hum real soft like the hum was just a baby hum or at other times she would hum so loud it felt like the hum could lift her up like a bird flying high above the mountains that surrounded the savannah. As a child, long, long ago, she had learnt that it is impossible to hum if you have a closed mouth and you hold your nose. Later she learned if someone has their hand over your mouth and pinches your nose hard, hard – no hum will come out. Instead, it builds like a giant thing in your belly, pushing your gut out hard and making your ribs feel like they would explode with how gigantic that poor hum is with nowhere to go.

She was in the forest now and no one was with her, at least no one human, and that was how Rum liked it. Company could only take you so far and in company you can only use words not hums. Sometimes she'd find words could be used as weapons against you so that it never felt truly safe. The forest had no words, but it had hums and sounds spread through it from earth to canopy like the jazz musicians her mother loved to sing with in another time, connecting with each other and creating melodic improvisations. The creak of the large tree trunks formed a bass note and the rustling of wind gently caressing upper leaves was like feathers on drums. The tree frogs would join in with their horn section, adding to this musical delight with syncopation randomly from stem to branch. Male crickets would *stridulate* like a chorus on a loop – at least, that was the scientific name for it – her mother had taught her that and the memory surprised her now, long since forgotten. But to Rum, they were all different levels of hums and she would join in adding her own vibrato to the ensemble. You needed a good ear and no human chatter to realize that trees could hum or that the forest was the purest form of music. You needed to have memory and knowledge too, and that was a hard thing to find.

Lost in the undersong of the forest, hums expelling breath from her lungs would gush out towards the mighty purpleheart tree top that, try as she might, she could never reach its dizzying height. Sometimes, when she walked further in, she would hug the narrow rutted trunk of the bibiru and let her hum connect directly with the tree so that the tree could feel her resonance just as she felt so sure that it hummed atonally with her in reply. Today she was only a short way into the forest because she knew she had to get back to the cassava plot where she'd left her *warshi* and machete after cutting off the top of the cassava plants. She still had to pull up cassava roots to make bread. It was her designated role, and it was a long one that involved the laden *warshi* walk back to the village, peeling, washing, grating, sieving and passing it through a *matapi* to extract the juice that would be boiled to make cassareep after she had baked the bread and left it to dry. Now, as she looked skyward, she realized time had cheated her, and she'd need to hurry or else she'd be in trouble. She walked hastily back towards the plot and kept her hums soft, soft, soft before stopping them altogether.

The blow sent staccato vibrations through her ear and down her spine. Not good vibrations of a hum, but vibrations of pain that made her knees buckle. The second blow caught her full in the mouth and the hum hid somewhere deep inside her as the blood taste of iron dripped through her cracked front tooth and out onto her busted lips. She fell to the earth, curling up into a ball, instinctively protecting herself. Her eyes closed tight with tears. She did not want to look up at his face – a face that had once made her heart bubble and gurgle skittishly when they had first met, but now created only fear and loathing. "What the skunt yuh think yuh doing woman?!" he spat at her. She knew not to answer. His question was rhetorical only. "How many times do I have to tell yuh to keep that mout' of yours quiet?" Another rhetorical question drizzled spittle over her bruised face as he knelt down beside her. A few seconds passed and no more blows. Instead, he grabbed her hard by her arm and wrenched her upright. She had no choice now but to open her eyes and look into his bloodshot eyes, full of both rage and fear. "You want them to force us out? You want us to leave our friends and be nomad like them drunken *porknocker?*" She shook her head *no* and attempted to look at her feet, but he jerked her jaw upwards and clenched her chin tightly in his finger grip. "Don't fuck up my life with yuh stupidness, woman! I have a good life and I am not having you drag me down with you… Like *you* don't remember what happen to yuh same mother and your cousin dem?"

Of course she remembered. How could she not? Even though the years had caused veils to fall on memories, they did not stop her from waking in the middle of the night from a dream so real it felt like she was back in her mother's home. Back to that very same night that snapped her, irrevocably, out of childhood. They had come for her mother, her talented, wonderful, creative mother with her early greying silver coils surrounding her crinkled nutmeg face. Her mother who could form notes on her knee long after the piano made heat blisters fly up to the sky as its varnished wood burned for all to see. Her prized possession, her Steinway. She had tried patiently to teach Rum to play, but Rum's fingers ached from the hand stretch, her span and small finger-size nothing compared to her mother's long elegant fingers, designed solely for piano playing. Back then, Rum just wanted to run outside. She didn't understand the value of the hum then. Rum's child-face had looked at the dying piano, not knowing that her mother would soon follow because she could not and would not stop creating music; it was who she was and she could no more stop music from oozing out of every pore than she could stop the breath coming out from her mouth opened wide. She had locked up all the windows in their small but perfect home and, even when it was blackout and the closed-in rooms had neither AC nor air, she would sing to Rum, sing to her plants, sometimes she would even sing to her husband snoring, oblivious to his wife and daughter, with more rum than blood flowing through his veins.

But the thin walls could not keep the music safe for long and there were always people who would side with the oppressors' mandates if they felt it would gain them something. Loyalty, it turned out, was even thinner than her mother's walls, which could not contain the song. Lyrics lifted up on a voice so dulcet it had sometimes brought tears to a listener's eyes back when feeling music wasn't a crime. One rainy season night, not too long after the piano was snatched from their home, the door was kicked in as if it was nothing more than the plyboard it was. Doors were never built for keeping out booted violence where Rum lived; they were built to keep the insects out at night and nothing more. Rum's mother was in the middle of singing a song from some artist who Rum no longer remembered the name of. She only remembered that it touched her heart, and the memory remained imprinted on her soul – though, try as she might, she could never bring it out in a hum. The boot was followed by the tall pale man from the North, one of the Factcheckers. They'd spread like a virus through her beautiful land but mostly resided in the bigger towns, where there was more to check, more to control, more to annihilate. Another and another stormed in like a plague of mutated cockroaches, covered from head to foot in their jet-black uniforms, ill-suited for the humid heat of the night but protection from all resistance. They took her mother and left the twelve-year-old Rum alone until her drunken father stumbled through the unhinged door hours later, his breath full of the rum she was named after.

It was the last day rum passed his lips – it was the wake-up call that came too late. He became a father to this daughter of his that night, so named by his wife as to now be a daily reminder of all that he had lost. His proclivity had been the reason Rum's mother had chosen her daughter's name. She had knelt on all fours, the midwife rubbing her back reassuringly, and she'd grunted and groaned so loud no one could understand why he didn't wake as Rum showed her head in the world for the very first time. Names carry meanings, sometimes to link them to a moment of joy or a moment of sadness, sometimes to predict the destiny of the person so named. Her mother, whose name was Aria, had fulfilled her destiny as long as she'd been alive. After her mother had gone, Rum would say her name over and over again in the forest, reminding the trees of where she came from. The name had sounded odd on her child lips when the woman Aria was only Mama to Rum. Her father's parents had named him well too; choosing the name Wisdom for their bright-eyed baby boy because the way he looked back up at them held too much depth to name him anything else.

So it was that her father, forcibly retired, became a teacher again to his one student – his daughter. Not that their wider community did not have a school but this school, as he repeated over and over, was not real school, not the kind of school that he had experienced with a library full of books, full of history, full of literature, full of knowledge. It was, he said, nothing but a sham, and what exactly they were being educated for or into was something that constantly produced a loud kiss of his teeth. It was only after her mother was disappeared that Rum finally learnt that her father had not always been a drunk but had been a music teacher before the Factcheckers came, before he had hidden in a bottle. He may have been a music teacher, but he had a passion not only for music but for social history and as he told her "the two ain't distinct…you can't know history without knowing music and you can't know music without knowing history".

It was her father who showed her how to hum, though it was to be the forest that connected his daughter with the hum inside her. When an older Rum moaned that if it was *his*-story it wasn't for her then he had smiled and said it's good she had her mother's keen sense of right and he started to tell her about *herstory*, of the music and of the land and how the pale men from the North banned it all. How they had banned it in their own country first, state by state, refusing to teach evolution, ecology, history, sociology, literature – anything that was deemed to be against the belief of a powerful unseen Cabal, anything which created questioning and defiance in a population that they wanted to control. Subject after subject was banned from curriculums, books were burned, so-called radicals – who spoke of nothing but the right to question – were rounded up. Universities were forced to close or downsized and no lecture or seminar in any institution could be taught without the constant surveillance of the video monitor recording any attempt at dissent. The disease spread far and anywhere they controlled you through economic treaty they gained a foothold. Foothold led to stranglehold and what her father referred to as 'brain re-wire'. Both he and her mother had instantly lost their jobs as music teacher and as singer-songwriter, and in that loss, what once had brought them together sent them their own separate ways. He into the rum and she, more sensibly, into her homesteading. Winston told his daughter that they were lucky enough to survive long enough for them to create Rum and for Rum to know her mother. They were lucky because way too many did not get that chance, they lost everything and were disappeared long before birthing could replenish their already small village.

* * *

Brian, still gripping her arm, like a jaguar's jaw-tight grip on its succulent prey, dragged her back to their home, not stopping to collect from the cassava crop or tend to her small borders closer to the house, filled with beans, okra, tomatoes and herbs. Past the mango and mamey trees and past the coalpot she'd completely forgotten she'd left simmering; the labba and oxtail pepperpot slowly cooking in cassareep and spices to accompany the cassava bread she never made. Their front door was open. It was the way of their village to leave doors wide open and windows wider. In the past, this had been only a testament to community but, since the Factcheckers came, it became a visual proclamation that nothing that shouldn't – according to The Mandate – was occurring within the walls of anyone's home. People had learnt compliance in their village a long time ago, when first her mother, then two of her cousins, her neighbour's son, her next-door neighbour's daughter, an uncle, another mother, or father had been disappeared, so that their small community became a tiny blot on the landscape, where savannah meets forest.

Just as their community learnt acquiescence to the Factcheckers, so too had Rum – mostly – learnt submission to this man, who she'd married way too young in a sad attempt to fill the void her father's death had left her with. When, despite eight years sober, his liver had decided back-pay owed! Rum had silently believed it to be the grief, a deep hungering for the wife he had lost and never atoned to, that had killed him rather than the cirrhotic liver stamped on the death certificate. But she also knew that body and soul are intertwined in a symbiotic dance and what harm is done to one is always done to the other. He had made his amends to Rum and endeavoured to keep music alive in his daughter, but Rum barely listened to his secret whisperings of an opus or octave, chords or cadence, riff, timbre or interludes. Too long indoors felt suffocating, especially in her parents' house full of loss and all of it tied up in the mantra of music – and what had music done other than lose Rum her mother? So the young Rum would run from her father's voice, so full of knowledge she didn't want to learn, and instead spend her time talking with trees, laughing with plants and lying on the forest floor unknowingly growing deep connections with mycelium highways running just beneath the forest's skin.

Rum's thoughts were brought back to the present with a hard slap to her face. "You're just a crazy bitch," he growled through highleaf-stained teeth. "Yuh mother was a crazy bitch and your father was mad as fuck…all of you just skuntholes!" She tried to stay focused on his face, to look like she was listening so he wouldn't know she wasn't. Sometimes you just had to zone out and let his maliciousness wash over you, through you and right out the other side. The words were sometimes more damaging than the kicks and punches but that did not mean she wanted another lash any time soon. They had been too young to marry, and she had married him for a multitude of wrong reasons. Because she was orphaned. Because she was lonely.

Because she did not know herself back then. Because she did not want to be reminded of her parents and Brian was the opposite in all ways. He was not interested in music, poetic words or anything that occurred outside his small world and smaller mind. He was happy for the higher wages offered by the Northern-owned conglomerates; he didn't give a shit that there was no reading and no music and no history. He was a man of the moment. A practical man, he liked to declare to her or anyone else he thought was listening, and he could build. They employed him for his construction skills. They employed him for other things that Rum didn't know about too and he loved that knowledge. That secret.

Brian shoved Rum hard into the bedroom and locked the door. No one had locked front doors for years. It was part of The Mandate. The Factcheckers must have access at all times, and although the villagers never entered another home without permission, doors had to stay open and whispered truths that defied state sanction must be impossible. But there was no sanction against putting a lock and key on your bedroom door or on your wife. She could hear him in the kitchen pulling together leftovers from the big foreign fridge he had suddenly decided they needed with its ice and water dispenser. She hadn't had a chance to harvest from their homestead and he would make do and make her do without. The darkness wrapped Rum in her own thoughts and the tick, tick, tick of the overhead fan outside in the main room sounded almost hypnotic in the absence of light, sounded like a metronome keeping tempo and lulled her into deep, dreamless sleep.

Rum wasn't sure what time it was when she woke, only that the nightly rendition provided by the crickets and tree frogs was in full and mounting crescendo. The moon was full term and filled the room with its own ethereal light. Brian was not in bed and she'd forgotten to pull the mosquito net down, so the pestering whine of the mosquito in her ear was probably what woke her. She got out of bed and carefully and slowly turned the handle on the bedroom door, but it was still locked. The room was overwhelmingly hot, but Rum was reluctant to turn on the fan in case he would hear and realize she was awake. Instead, she quietly eased open the veranda door and stepped outside, savouring the tendrils of a breeze. Like all the other houses in her village, their home was built on stilts. Something that had always been done. Protection against flooding, it also meant you caught more breeze on the bedroom veranda to the side of the house, the main room veranda, and the kitchen veranda that doubled as laundry space and cooking space on the outside stove top when it was too hot to cook inside or downstairs on the coalpot.

Rum listened carefully to see if she could hear him on one of the other verandas but she heard nothing other than the night animals and the trees dancing and whispering softly on the intermittent nighttime gusts. She eased herself silently into the hammock and swayed gently, a handheld fan in one hand to wave away determined mosquitos long after their usual 6 o'clock onslaught. She started to feel drowsy with the lulling movement of the hammock, but became suddenly vigilant when her husband's voice could be heard in the distance but coming closer all too quickly. Her hearing on alert meant she could soon easily pick out another man's voice, but she couldn't place it. It was not from her village. She knew all the different lilts of the villagers' voices, and this voice was alien to her. Deep and rasping, it reminded her of something, of a dialect that made her heart quicken. She tried to think why it made her feel fear. The voices came nearer and clearer. They were downstairs now, by the steps that led up to the front door porch. Sound carried well at night. Otherwise, on the other side of the house, she might not have known she was in danger. Might not have realized that it was a Factchecker or that her husband had informed on her for the price of a new AC! It was not all she heard that night. She learnt Brian's secret and wondered how many other disappeared had Brian to thank. She felt sick to her stomach. The idea that unknowingly the house she lived in and the things in it were in some part purchased with blood money! She had no time to feel sick, no time for shock; she must act now and act fast!

Rum eased herself out of the hammock as silently as was humanly possible and wondered how her thumping heart could not be heard from miles away, much less by the two men downstairs who laughed together quietly as they plotted her doom. The drop was too far for her to jump from the veranda and even if she thought that she could make it they would hear and be on her before she could escape. What to do? What to do! She looked back to the bedroom door and knew from the quiet below that they must now be climbing the steps to the front door. How much longer until they would bust open the bedroom door and she would be *disappeared* like her mother, like her cousins, like so many others before her, and so many by her own husband's betrayal? The sound of something brushing the veranda wall like a soft brush on a snare drum caught her ear, and she turned to look. Had that Flamboyant tree always touched the veranda? It was almost like the tree was reaching forward, reaching towards her, but that couldn't be the case, could it? There was no time to question it! The Flamboyant's graceful branches were strong and the lower ones sturdy; she took a leap of faith, took a leap into its fire-coloured blooms, took a leap into the tree's embrace and somehow found herself clinging to its central trunk with, miraculously, no more than a few slightly stinging grazes. The blossoms seemed to swaddle her, and she clung silently to the trunk like a baby clinging to her mother. The men rushed out onto the veranda and looked all around. The stranger seemed angry, gesticulating wildly at her husband. Brian seemed confused, scratching his head and looking all around, even looking straight at the flamboyant, where she hid. Rum clung desperately, believing that he must see her soon, but he could not see a thing whilst the tree protected her. After many, many minutes went by and Rum's arms started to feel heavy and weak, the stranger, in his not-so-successfully camouflaged black uniform, stormed up the road and with her ears tuned in to every cadence of danger, she, at long last, discerned the engine of a 4-wheel drive rev aggressively and then ebb away into the distance. It was a lot longer before she felt confident that Brian would finally fall into his usual deep and snoring sleep before she dared to climb carefully down. When her feet touched the damp dew-covered ground below, she hugged her rescuer deeply and profoundly and felt its vibrations intertwine with hers before she headed in the direction of their homesteading land and beyond into the forest. Early dawn was already arriving but, by the time the village woke to its muted bustle, Rum was long gone.

Brian never found her. He asked the entire village and even managed to persuade some of his fellow villagers to aid in his hunt. Truth be told, Rum was not the only one who felt intimidated by his brutishness. His increasing friendliness with the Factcheckers certainly did not help, and some were not a little suspicious of what this friendliness meant. Not that they dared to step out of line. Any level of questioning led to being disappeared, and it was hard to find a villager who had not lost a family member to the Factcheckers; loss hung over the village like an unhealthy fog. Brian gave up for a while, believing she would come back soon. What other option did she have but to come back to the village, to his house, to him, he asked himself, never once reflecting on the reasons why she would not.

The forest was in many ways more Rum's home than the village. It was where she had first discovered her ability to hum and where the forest showed her it could hum back too, sometimes discordant, sometimes in unison but always embracing her soul. It was where the forest floor reverberated relentlessly with the frequency of the hum; melodic harmonies that left her breathless sometimes, tears filling her eyes with memories. Happy memories of both her mother and her father in their different times and different ways. Memories that filled her also with deep regret, knowing now what she had then taken for granted, of the music that she never had the patience to learn when piano seemed like nothing but torture! It was where she found herself sometimes using her fingers on tree bark to mark out the scales her mother had once taught her, scales she didn't realize were still in her. Memories of her father's teachings, of the history of sound, of how all people made music from the beginning of time and how its power could make people love, cry, mourn and protest, how it gave them the power to share in something wondrous but to experience it and express it in such unique ways. That the uplifting of stories and music and dance began to be seen as a threat to the authority of the North. She only remembered a fraction of what her father had tried to teach her, but even that fraction, she knew, was more than most had and how long before there were no parents who could pass on the teachings of music and movement, of *herstories* and stories that made a person whole, that filled up a person's belly with healing from a world gone mad. Back in the village, she used to dream that she could see a person's spirit disconnect from their body and leave only a skin-encased nothingness and she would wake in a cold sweat, not even knowing if her dream were really a dream. It was hard to miss people when people weren't really people any more, when the joy of living had been emptied from their minds, when, as her father had repeatedly told her when she didn't want to listen, that soul death had occurred.

* * *

Rum knew when the Factcheckers were there. The leaves hummed low, alerting her to their dangerous tread, and the forest floor tremored with warning. She felt the warning in her feet and heard the change in forest sounds, felt the trees shift protectively around her, and in that moment she felt herself merge with them as if there was no distinction, no dividing line between human and tree. The low branch that extended its welcoming arm towards her held no surprise after the flamboyant tree had swayed in to whisk her away from the danger of men.

Brian, being a man that believed in his abilities above and beyond those of his wife, believed he knew the forest better than his wife. Brian was sure that his wife would not have gone too far into the forest, and he was right, but not for the reasons he harboured. Rum remained close because this part of the forest had long been her home and she would not have Brian or these men force her to leave it. She had left the village in fear, but leaving was what she had intended for a long time. As each year had gone by and memories held more magic than the here and now, she had begun to disconnect from the sad shell of a village that once, long ago, had been a vibrant place of laughter and learning, love and joy. As Brian stomped through the forest, footfall crashing on leaves and decaying bark fall, the invasion of his presence and those of the Northern Factcheckers drowned out the hum temporarily. They, with their ears of conquerors and controllers, could not hear a single note! They spent a full day from dawn until dusk, flailing around with their bitterness and blindness, before finally giving up.

The forest had always welcomed Rum, its prodigal daughter; it smiled and laughed with her, wondering why she had ever bothered to leave. One thing Rum knew better than anything was knowing how to live in the forest. She knew the people from the North never understood her people's ways and their ancient wisdoms – that was why they destroyed all that they found. All these invaders cared about was imposing a view that really had no place in the forest. What she knew in her soul was that we are not distinct from nature but are embedded in an ecosystem that expands and stretches across seas and continents and, yes, forests. That all things lived and had a voice and that in that voice comes sound, comes song, comes togetherness and synchronicity. Knowledge came from her mother, and it came from her father too but, deeper than that, it flowed in her veins from the long line of maternal shamanic women who, forest-born, had spilled their knowing from their womb into their daughter's womb and on and on until Rum, who had no daughter to pass it on to. Her connection was to the lyric of those that came before her and the hum of the forest, a sound that to the unknowing was discordant and meaningless, but to Rum was a wondrous thing of beauty, it was music and it was how she fully learned to develop her own hum.

Foundling

Tenea D. Johnson

BY NOON, Petal had plucked fourteen people from the earthquake debris. Even if the other techs in HRO's small mobile unit nodded appreciatively, she could hardly believe the slow pace of the rescue teleportations. In the last year alone, she'd evacced an entire Sri Lankan apartment building's residents within twenty-five minutes of a tsunami alarm and rescued a California fire fighter squad from a forest fire seconds before it flamed into an inferno. Other teleport techs worked to match Petal's speed and accuracy; she worked to beat it. But not all trips through the black were about speed.

The fourteen had tired her. She shifted to release the dreadlocks pinned between her back and the chair, and stretched her hip from where she sat. Per protocol, she had to clear the chipped before she could extract any unchipped people. The race always sapped her energy. Regardless, she sat alert at her terminal rig, staring at the quintet of monitors, gaze darting between the chip signal map up top and the vectimeter readouts below. Her hands sat loose on the controls, splayed wide, with her pointer finger poised over the Enact button, timing the millisecond the extract arcs would align.

Earthquake rescues were a special challenge, a complicated game of knowing which person to move and when – move the wrong one and other pockets of space might collapse and kill anyone now vulnerable in the configuration of air and pressure that destroyed buildings became. An Indonesian high-rise was Boolean calculus that only a Petal Scott could reliably solve. The other techs worked to extract survivors in open fields or atop intact buildings. Their numbers lagged hers. Some had clocked out from fatigue after a single extraction; a few gathered discreetly behind her, watching from a distance. Petal paid them no mind.

As the arcs intersected on a trajectory that would hold, she struck the Enact button. In an instant the man she'd spent the last thirty-two minutes working on disappeared from the rank and dusty hole he'd lain in overnight, and materialized at a medevac unit a few miles away. Adi Taher, father of two, vitals still strong, would most likely survive. Petal closed her eyes and stretched her wrists. At thirty-nine, they needed more stretching these days. She took two deep gulps from the water bottle on the floor and consulted the map for the next one.

Not a single light blinked on the chip signal map. Had she finally cleared all of the chipped from the queue? Being a high-rise in one of Jakarta's wealthiest districts, most of the inhabitants could afford to be chipped. The quake had struck in the middle of a weekday so hopefully only a small portion of the residents were home at the time. She'd waited on Taher's extraction to give the others a better chance of survival. His position had been tricky, liable to set off little landslides below him. So far the gambit had worked, but now came the true challenge.

Petal looked again at the building's schematics on the bottom left monitor – both the blueprint of what it had been as one piece and the rendering overlay of it in pieces. She pinpointed each sizable void to perform a remote manual bio scan. Though most of the residents had been chipped, just as likely those people had housekeepers and maintenance workers that could never afford the expense.

HRO existed for them. Though Humanitarian Rescue Organization's mandate stated that they would rescue any and all people they could in a natural disaster, their real mission, as far as Petal was concerned, was to save those no one else thought worth the trouble – the ones who could never pay for expensive trips through the black. For them, she'd decided to work with a non-governmental organization instead of the lucrative commercial market.

She wouldn't have had it any other way – even today.

Near the top of the rubble, Petal found a number of cooling bodies, a small legion of cats, and below that three sizable rodents huddled together in the ruins of a restaurant that had once dominated the fifteenth floor. Sweat beaded on Petal's forehead. She wiped it and dried her hands on her pants. Slowly she scanned the rest of the building, cubic meter by cubic meter, consulting the locale grid she'd imposed on the overlay. At one of the last grid locations she got a larger, faint reading: no doubt, human. This person lay in the middle of the building, at the bottom, on the cusp of being crushed and being free. The location couldn't be much worse. It denoted a bleak new level of complexity. Petal had to know the extractee's particulars to have any chance at a successful teleport. She grabbed her headset, toggled the talk function, and dialed up the mobile hospital's HRO rep.

"Intake," a female voice said, her accent relaxing the word.

"Have you finished cross-referencing the records of residence and accounted-for list?" Petal asked.

"Yes, I'll forward it now. Your access number?"

"2478," Petal said.

"Sent," the operator replied.

"Thanks," Petal said, disconnecting.

An icon blinked on the center screen. She ran the parameter search and waited a few seconds for the soft ding of completion in her ear.

Petal exhaled and motioned the ID reveal command. She'd learned not to look at the extractee's particulars before absolutely necessary; she'd watched a colleague in Rio reduced to tears when a sibling showed up on the screen. The tech couldn't have been more grateful when Petal evacced his sister, but Petal had been just as grateful for the lesson. She had no surviving family, only a long-ago-lost locket of their faces before the fire. She had a heart though. Sometimes what you didn't know could help someone else.

Petal heard the other techs react and took her time looking at the screen: a baby, a toddler really, no more than four years old. Due to the extractee's age, a photo hadn't been added yet. The screen showed only a DOB with a blank space after the dash – unaccounted-for life, a maid's child, or perhaps a maid-in-training herself. The record didn't include any weight or height measurements from this year, no body scan, just the record of residence.

Petal called in a drone to help her. She wanted eyes on the child. She'd need to see the pocket that held the girl and her position in it, but mostly Petal didn't want her to be alone in the dark any longer. Petal glanced at the top monitors as the drone left the hangar. While she calibrated the vectimeter to her estimates of a South East Asian 31/2 year old's median weight and height, the drone reached altitude and quickly covered the distance to downtown Jakarta.

Petal watched its progress as the piles of rubble grew larger and the drone cruised down to the one that held the girl. The monitor darkened as the drone reached the closest opening and extended its pinpoint camera into the space. A finger wouldn't have fit into it but the camera did. A faint outline of concrete and twisted steel glowed into existence on the screen. It slowly brightened and the girl's face appeared on the top center monitor.

A shallow gash bled down her cheek, but other than that she looked intact. Her legs and arms were free, her head at a natural enough angle, but Petal couldn't see any space for her to wiggle, much less take a deep breath. Her lips had turned a strange hue, signaling the need to get her out now. Petal flicked the microphone away from her mouth and activated brown noise inside her headset. Leaning forward, the world shrank down to five monitors and the controls in her hands.

On the top right monitor, the girl's infrared face glowed, below it the vectimeter adjusted and dead center scrolled the NAV screen's crowded array of numbers, colors, and all the custom apps and algorithms that Petal had loaded for easy execution. She'd have to go fully manual. For this she'd rather trust her own algorithms. Mass manufacturers hadn't figured out how to code functional finesse. Her algorithms bested them when it came to complex teleport metrics and executions. Though the algorithms only awaited an execution command, first Petal had to see the right combination of variables, the sweet spot in all the data flooding into her system. She tweaked and waited. As each second crept by, each breath she felt sure the rubble would shift and crush any hope of completing this rescue. With her left hand she carefully guided the extract arc into a better position. Petal glanced up at the vectimeter; she needed to adjust no more than 1 degree 3 and – there, the curve of a pocket in time. Petal's finger hovered above the Enact button, its code scrawling quickly by. NAV almost lined up. It would in 87 milliseconds, 47 milliseconds, the arc careened, snapped back before Petal could react, 17...

The girl disappeared from the screen.

Petal blinked, jerked her head up to check the drone connection. In that millisecond, tons of concrete and steel shifted, filling the void. The screen turned black as the camera went offline. Petal gasped. She scanned for bio signals – nothing. Not a cooling temp, or phantom trace. The toddler had simply ceased to be there, but Petal hadn't evacced her. She couldn't identify the feeling filling up her chest, just as she couldn't make sense of where in all the worlds and wormholes the girl had gone.

Thirty hectic minutes later she had no explanation – not one for herself or the site director whose office she now stood in, exhausted and frustrated. She felt on the verge of tears, but kept her face expressionless; she'd spent years perfecting the wall between her and the world of nerves and overwhelming circumstances. Petal could barely focus on his words and hadn't heard the name of the man he introduced her to. It seemed a strange time for introductions, for conversations, for anything but finding the little girl. The director repeated himself.

"Ms Scott, this is Brian Dunphries, from headquarters," the director said, moving hair out of his eyes as he spoke.

Petal didn't question why headquarters had sent a monitor for her, but a part of her filed away the information, the same part that filed all the work slights and microaggressions she chose not to deal with in the moment.

She knew she should respond to the introduction, but the usual words rang hollow – it was not good to meet him. Petal settled on "hello" and waited for the director to continue.

"I'd planned on introducing you this morning, but didn't want to interrupt your progress on the Crissal Building."

Crissal Building. This at least she could connect to. Her eyes shifted to the director and the tall blond man at his side.

"What the hell happened?" the director asked.

"Lost souls are a reality of our business," the HQ rep interjected.

"Supposedly not for Ms Scott here," the director replied. "We were told she'd never had an incident."

"I haven't – hadn't," Petal said. Other techs accepted lost souls as an inevitable facet of their work; no one even looked for them after the loss. The possibility of losing someone simply because of the complexity of the task didn't square. She created her own algorithms, went manual and trained three times longer than certification required to negate the inevitability of lost souls. Yet now here she stood, living a moment she'd worked to avoid.

"I have no excuse," she said. She wouldn't start inventing them now.

"You'll be put on leave while we investigate," the director responded.

"Completely routine, Ms Scott," the rep said.

"Of course," she replied, turning to leave. As the door closed behind her she heard the director's final words.

"When I met her I told them no way she matched her numbers. Not her fault really. She's overcome a lot of inherent limitations, but I can't say that I'm surprised."

That night, alone in the small home she rented, the girl's face waited behind Petal's closed eyelids. So, Petal'd left the bed behind. Instead, she paced and pored over the episode, worrying the floorboards in the narrow corridor between her terminal rig and monitor array. She could hear the steady hum of her generator, and not much else beyond her own thoughts.

Petal had never fancied herself arrogant, but she simply couldn't believe she'd lost the girl. She had no problem accepting her mistakes when she made them, but her head as well as heart rejected that conclusion. Her finger hadn't jumped. She'd had 17 milliseconds left and in that thin sliver of time something had happened.

A headache collected at her temples and Petal stopped pacing. She grabbed an apple from the countertop and dropped down at her rig.

She backed up everything, live-fed it to the server stateside that held her entire teleport history. Her father had been a boxing fan, and gave her one piece of advice: leave nothing up to the judges. They could conduct their own investigation, but so would she. Devouring the apple in five big bites, she logged onto her archives and pulled up the day's work. Scrolling past the other extractees, she quickly found her place and pored over the time log, reviewing each reading and corresponding action on her part.

It didn't take long to find the hole in the whole. The anomaly started at 19 milliseconds-until-engage and ended at 17 til. In those 2 milliseconds, the arc had deviated – stretched into a parabola that did not correspond to her algorithms or HRO's apps, moved in a way not under her control. The girl had disappeared into that gap.

Petal could find no further record of her existence. As an unchipped no teleport tech could. Had she spliced with the rubble around her, fallen into an alternate wormhole, evaporated with the cataclysmic intensity of Luther's Arc? Petal did not know. The tears that had threatened all day fell freely now, soaking her shirt, the skin beneath and further still.

* * *

HRO called her back stateside within the week. Despite recent events, her record of reliability and success remained unmatched. They could use her in Seattle where floods were regular and the occasional tsunami surfaced. HQ wrote the incident off as her fall to mortality. She could hear it in the site director's voice, a tiny celebration that now she walked amongst them, no longer ahead. Her apparent failure had improved his day. Hearing it, Petal briefly contemplated finally joining the private sector and its much better paid assignments. But she knew it would never take. There was still good work to do; so she flew back home. She could have expensed a trip through the black. Such trips were built into HRO's operating budget – but she savored the considerable time it took to move from one side of the world to the other.

* * *

Brian Dunphries ran the Seattle office. Petal spied him through the glass door as she entered the branch. She didn't welcome the coincidence. No fresh start here, but perhaps that's what HQ had in mind. She'd never needed a minder and didn't now. Still she greeted him with a small smile and an outstretched hand. He had tried to be kind in Jakarta. She could only prove herself all over again though she had never truly stopped, a hazard of her extraction.

"Ms Scott," Dunphries said. "It's good to see you again. Let me show you to our teleport unit."

All the interior walls were glass. Standing from the front entrance one could see to the very back of the building. Petal followed Dunphries further into the translucent maze.

"We run a controlled lab – no custom work and no outside software," he said.

Her algorithms. They wanted her to press buttons and take responsibility for anything that went wrong. Great. Is this supposed to be some sort of probation? Petal wondered. She didn't know any colleagues who worked in a locked-down lab, though some may have welcomed the ease.

"Is that on a probationary basis?" she asked.

"It's our standard protocol," he answered. "And I'll be acting as your supervisor. Because of your advanced experience it seemed the best fit. I'm sure you can appreciate that when things don't go as planned, there's a propensity to blame the operator. Here that's no longer an issue. Our techs execute the protocol and any errors can be easily traced and recorded."

Recorded, not resolved, Petal thought.

"I see," she said.

They rounded a corner and entered the unit through another set of glass doors.

The room dwarfed any she'd worked in for the last three years, the ones she'd spent in Southeast Asia and the Sudan. Just as she'd suspected the techs looked green as hell. They sat in three rows of three, talking across their terminals at one another. A couple of them stopped comming on their watches long enough to turn around and acknowledge her and Dunphries. Three of them looked as if they might still be in secondary school, and the balance as eager and unskilled as the kids who stopped her on the street to see if she'd sign a petition to legalize metamethamine.

"Your colleagues," Dunphries said. "I'll leave you some time to get acquainted." He pointed to a yellow door in the corner.

"You can leave your things at the open terminal and there's an orientation program already cued; just log on. You'll find vending mechs in the break room there."

Petal wasted no time on introductions. As soon as Dunphries left she waved a hello to the room, sat down at the terminal, logged in and tried to take a look at the queue. She couldn't access it without completing orientation.

Petal exhaled.

"You'll find a lot is locked down here."

She turned to find one of the young techs standing behind her. He had a stocky build and sported a plaid shirt and unkempt beard.

"Petal Scott, right? I remember hearing about you," he said.

Bad news apparently traveled fast.

"Ten years and only one lost soul. Impressive."

Petal's eye twitched when he said 'one lost soul'. She could feel the furrow of her brow, and struggled to say thanks though she didn't feel it.

This is what they would say now. Even if it never happened again, but worse than that she would always have the girl's face in the dark, a locket she couldn't lose.

"I'm Jeff, Taylor."

She shook his hand, waited for something more.

"Well, I'll let you get back to it," he said.

The orientation program took much longer than necessary. By the time she'd finished, the waiting queue icon had disappeared from her terminal and afternoon had cleared the room. Everyone else talked in the break room, or had stepped outside. Now that she had access, Petal searched across the desktop to perform a proper orientation.

Their archive system was a mess. To make matters worse, this office used Diverse Triage for their queue, a program better suited to shipments than teleport tech. Petal frowned and started her review of the server. If she couldn't use her own algorithms she'd have to learn this system front to back to see how far she could bend it before it broke. Mass-produced software had broad, deep limitations so better to find them now when no one's life hung in the balance.

Server capacity was lean, and they seemed to have the techs' systems tethered in a way that bordered on the obtuse. She shook her head and stretched her neck. From the corner of her eye she spied the vectimeter backup files and credentials. She opened the properties. Last calibration: four months ago?

"What the hell?" Petal whispered. She calibrated daily; industry standard dictated forty-eight hours. Four months was a fucking crime.

"Or at least it should be," she finished out loud.

Anxious now, she continued to hunt around her terminal, opening files and mentally tracking what she found. The queue stayed empty, giving Petal time to explore this troubling new terrain.

* * *

The anomaly showed up on her third day in the office. She'd just successfully extracted a man from the roof of his truck in Oregonian flood waters. The intake rep expected him to spend the night at home. For the first time in weeks, Petal's tension unwound a single centimeter; she took a cleansing breath. Someone had cranked the AC up and she bent over to get a sweater out of her bag. As she righted herself, Dunphries' face popped up on the instant messenger in the corner of her screen.

"Well done" the screen read.

Petal tried to think of a non-condescending interpretation, but failed miserably. The message required a perfunctory response, her least favorite kind. She typed her non-existent thanks and motioned the window to close.

An ID window maximized on the monitor. She must have right-toggled when she meant to left. Dunphries' org chart appeared under his name with a tiny asterisk linked to a series of usernames. Odd that he would have so many but perhaps each piece of software required one. She shook her head; they didn't even have password chains. Good luck to the person who forgot one of them or to someone trying to track overall usage. With the empty queue she could at least fix this problem for them. Conventional best practice required it, and she had more downtime than she could handle.

Petal delved back into the files and then into the code behind the system. A simple administrative reroute should do the trick. She backtracked through the registry to find a way to track users though their devices, IPs, and usernames.

In an hour she found a worm. It hid amongst the benign operational systems, tucked away from the temporary files but always running with them. With it came malware that would have made a mid-grade hacker proud. Dunphries had introduced it. At first, she thought the program must have been surveillance, recording keystrokes and the like for security's sake, but the more she searched, the less she thought it had anything to do with official HRO business.

As a creator of dozens of algorithms, execute programs and apps herself, Petal could understand wanting to customize the boilerplate software this office used, but she had a feeling she didn't yet care to name. Uneasily she looked to her left and right, sure now that she was being watched, or at least her work recorded. She would have to go stealth. She felt for a mem stick in her bag. Petal loaded it into the terminal and waited. She had to find the right moment, the correct cloaking sequence, and a data pick fine as the few seconds she might have before detection. Things slipped into alignment and Petal let her finger twitch.

The screen froze momentarily, but not before she saw the piggyback signal picking up each tech's teleport work, the licenses that allowed the transfer and Dunphries' worm trail hidden amongst the garbage commands that hid the breach. Much of HRO lay bare to him, or whoever he let in. They could have done anything...embezzled funds, stolen donor identities, sold HRO's tech right out from under them...or rerouted the extractees to send them who knew where.

A message box popped up on Petal's terminal.

"Please come to my office," Dunphries had typed.

Petal noted her location in the system, pocketed the mem stick, shut down her terminal, and with a quick, bracing breath went to face Dunphries.

She had seen enough federal agents in relief centers to recognize that two of them were sitting in Dunphries' office when she entered. With an effort, she kept walking inside. Her mind raced with possibilities. Before she could speak, one of the agents approached her.

"Do you know this girl?" he asked, holding a photo of the Indonesian toddler up at her eye level.

"Yes, of course. But—" Petal began.

"You should." The agent looked at her with disgust. "Since you sent her there. You look confused. I guess you don't pay attention to where they end up. This photo is from Fun Things, one of the blackest holes in the darknet."

"I didn't send her anywhere. I lost her before—"

"Petal Scott, you're under arrest for kidnapping, conspiracy, corruption of a minor, and sex trafficking."

"What?! No! I didn't do that! None of that! Dunphries! He was involved; not me. I—" Petal turned to face her accuser. And she found herself on her knees, unable to move. She fell to the floor, the Taser wires now visible.

She felt the full weight of the man on her back as he ground his knee between her shoulder blades and cuffed her. The other agent pulled her up to her feet. She saw the mem stick on the ground.

There! Look at that! At first she didn't realize that they couldn't hear her. The Taser had left her only able to mumble and pant for her next breath. Dunphries stepped on the mem stick. He stared into space as they pulled her out of HRO and dumped her into the back of their vehicle.

* * *

Lockup stank of desperation, body odor, and the urine of a homeless woman camped out in the corner of the cell. Petal ached where they had tasered her and winced from a tender spot on her back whenever she moved. She couldn't imagine a worse day.

It came when the court deemed her a flight risk and sent her to the Salem Federal Facility for Women.

She spent the first week crying, cultivating a migraine that left her curled up on the thin mattress, shielding her eyes from the fluorescents that lit up the cell all day and most of the night. Intermittently she rushed to the toilet in the corner and vomited as her body tried to acclimate to the food and her soul to the pain it now bore. Her cellmate, a tall, brunette woman with a thick Slavic accent, ignored Petal as best she could, but on the eighth day when the smell had coated every surface in the room, she spoke.

"Enough," the woman said. "It stinks. Stop it." Petal heard her take a few steps.

"Stop retching up what got you here and start dealing with where you are."

Petal felt something small land behind her and turned to find a foil packet of antacids.

"For your stomach. Otherwise you'll have to go to the infirmary. You won't like the guards there."

Petal raised her gaze to look the woman in the face.

"I am Kasia," she said.

Petal started to unfold herself, and reached for the packet. "Thank you. I'm Petal."

"Hm. I'd suggest using your surname here. The C.O. said it was…Smith?"

"Scott. Why won't I like the guards?" Petal asked.

"They believe they should be paid for the privilege of medical attention. They prefer flesh as payment." Kasia walked back to her bunk and sat. "The world loves its skin trade."

"Is that why you're here?" Petal asked.

"No, Scott. But I've done that time. Not you though, I can tell."

"How?" Petal asked. Kasia chuckled, ignored the question. "What did you do outside?"

"Teleport tech."

Kasia hummed. "You must have done well for yourself then. There are so many things people want relocated into their possession."

"Not like that. I worked for an NGO, a—"

"I know what an NGO is," Kasia said.

"You'd be surprised."

"Rarely," Kasia responded.

That night Petal slept. She began to eat her meals, to speak with the other women, to accept the reality she found herself in. But she also fought for her freedom, cleaning out her bank account to pay lawyers and keep up payments on her tiny house. With the rest of her savings she arranged for her personal rig to be boxed and stored. She would get out, she told herself.

In the meantime, Petal created a routine. After the exercise allotment, enduring inspections, and picking her way through the day's dangers she returned to her cell where she wrote code by hand and listened to Kasia's stories of the bumpy road from Plotzyk to Portland by way of every dark alley imaginable.

"I was raised in crime," Kasia said from her bunk, a crossword in her hand. "So you see I was cultivated, but most people are corrupted." Kasia said. "An easier process than you might imagine. Where there is virtue, vice lurks."

Petal looked away from the code and up at her cellmate. Kasia seemed to contemplate something and spoke again, this time softly.

"For instance…you use the tech to help people; others want to help themselves. If one can pay, it's a lot easier to steal a girl tripping through the black than one off the street. And what better girl than one who can't be traced, a girl who might be dead anyway? There are men that do this, who gather their resources for it, like—" Kasia said.

"Like the people who crowdfund HRO's rescues," Petal finished.

"I was going to say wolves. These wolves stole the virtuous model and twisted it to their purposes. They call themselves voiders. 'To be avoided', we girls used to say," Kasia said with a tight, angry smile.

The loss of her last bit of naiveté burdened Petal. Her head drooped with the weight of this new knowledge, all the way down to the tabletop. She sat with her eyes closed.

"Of course. Thank you, K," she said quietly.

In time, Petal's eyes opened. The florescent light overhead looked brighter, the shadows it created deeper. Underneath the table, at the page's corners, even outlining her hands – the gloom behind everything, emboldened, emerged. It called to her.

Would it swallow her finally? Do what the fire and the work had not? If it did, what would become of the people so easily lost…and the perpetrators who, for her, could easily be found? She picked her head up wearily. As she did, the shadows shifted. Petal paused in mid-motion. Even shadows can be displaced.

"Leave nothing up to the judges," she whispered.

Petal looked at the code and a new, bolder imperative clicked into place. She reached for a fresh sheet of paper and began again, hand flying across the page to capture her rushing thoughts.

* * *

Petal spent twenty-eight months sharpening her skills. It took those two years and a spring for the court to find the prosecutor had insufficient evidence to convict. Kasia was impressed. She said Petal must have some kind of luck to get out at all – even if Petal's lawyers said the arrest ruined her professional reputation. Petal didn't believe in luck, only in doing. At work, she used to say she made other people's luck; now she understood how short the distance to misfortune. She had just spent twenty-eight months calculating it exactly.

Her first day out Petal sprung her rig from cold storage. Two years of lost updates would slow her down. It would mean at least a week of getting back up to speed: Petal relished the thought.

Her first crooked job came easily. She sat in the one-bedroom house she stopped calling home after her second HRO assignment abroad and logged into the darknet with the rig she'd retrofitted specifically for the task. The darknet's layout looked unnecessarily opaque and seedy – someone's idea of what elicit should look like – all choppy fonts and DOS aesthetics. She moved to a search page to retrieve "trafficking" results. She'd specified "art trafficking" to save herself from images she wouldn't be able to forget. She planned on tracking the voiders later and in some way that wouldn't keep her up at night. Kasia had assured her that identities were cheap here, and each sex trafficking site kept a list of its patrons complete with all chip and location info, hacked back to their origin from the moment they logged on. Because of it Petal would have to spend her first payment on a specialized sub-rig invisible to anyone but her. If she hadn't already had her own chip removed she would have spent her second payment on that, but now she could put that money to better use.

The second "trafficking" hit provided the results she wanted. She found a job board of sorts and posted her skills and experience. Soon after, she proved it with a series of tests. After a long vet process her reply came back in flashing chartreuse characters.

"You're hired," it read. "Ready to get to work?"

Petal assented. An icon appeared at the corner of her screen. When she motioned it open a building schematic appeared and Petal prepared to extract a Degas from a vault in Tel Aviv. The job paid a year's salary.

With her third deposit she bought a backdoor key into HRO's systems. There she set her long-honed algorithm loose. It took longer than she had anticipated, but in five minutes the uplink completed: she had full access to HRO's systems and had fully cloaked her actions. Her second screen filled with live natural disaster info: latitude, longitude, magnitude, description, and estimates of the number affected. She pressed her list of co-ordinates onto the edge of the screen. Next she searched the HR records. Dunphries had been terminated, the stated reason: a statistically unacceptable string of lost souls on his watch, all attributed to user error and equipment failure. In another module, she found that none of the lost extractees had been located – even those that were chipped. The stolen girl had no chip. Petal couldn't find her because of it, but maybe she could locate some of these girls who were – perhaps still are – chipped. She saved the necessary info down to her terminal in case she lost the connection and navigated to the teleport module.

Thunder rumbled overhead as Petal set about locating and extracting the lost souls from their unnatural disasters. She'd lost none of her speed on the controls; in fact she moved faster now. She didn't know if the simpler tasks or more compelling conditions spurred her. She found three women and two children in North America in a matter of minutes, the sixth not five hundred miles away from where she sat. Petal engaged the CCTV hack app she'd received as an incentive for her latest job and waited for the arcs to align. At that instant, she enacted the first extraction.

As the first foundling appeared outside a relief center, Petal watched her look around in terror and confusion. Dirt covered her skin and nightgown, as if she had been unearthed. Even from a distance, she looked years older than the photo taken months before. Relief flooded into her expression. She lowered her hands, no longer needing to ward off whatever had been approaching. She jerked her head around the empty street and saw the relief center's sign. Without another glance, forward or back, she ran inside.

Petal stared at the space she'd been standing in, unable for the moment to think clearly or act. She blinked and saw the Indonesian girl's face. She extracted the other lost souls without taking the time to watch. As the last one arrived back in her hometown, Petal could only feel her heart thumping in her chest, her shoulders release.

An alert chimed on her rig. Petal's gaze slowly drifted up to the top monitor where it reported that a hurricane now scoured the Atlantic coast of Florida. Petal shifted at her terminal and with a sequence of graceful motions, effortless as dance, she relocated the first selection of voiders into the eyewall of the storm.

Petal felt a vastness open in her, a laying out of possibilities and matrices that until now had not existed. Gauging her next move, she analyzed the shift.

Gilded Throne on a Mound of Ash

B.T. Karuma

"MY LOVE, I became something new for them and something monstrous for you. Though peril has become the air I breathe, my only torment is you – what you must think of me. I imagine your disappointment and horror like a never-ending din. Dare to understand and forgive, My Love. Only you can seek me out and kill me. I am your monster, on my knees, and at your mercy."

"My Beloved, I would destroy entire empires beside you. You're the salvation I prayed for on those agonizing and lonely nights. I would seek you out to hold you close and vaporize your enemies whilst I laugh. You're my oxygen in my dreams. The only thing to forgive is your absence when I wake."

The Creation of a Monster

Rugare Tatanga had been a soldier of modest background. He grew up near the periphery of the great nation of Huru, where he had experienced the lawless Fringe first hand: the violent robberies and killings, the rogue androids of murderous disposition, the acres of poisoned land, the sickness, drought, and wholesale starvation. As a soldier, he would brush off his ugly past by saying it had toughened him for the job.

And he had been tough, tough enough to draw the attention of the oligarchy. His reward was promotion to a *smart* killer, an enhanced assassin – night-vision implants, embedded quantum processors for blindingly fast perception and reaction, nanotech stimulants for boundless energy and endurance.

The oligarchy needed its assassins because it had its enemies. For forty-five years, they had ruled from the lap of luxury whilst the people suffered. They wrested power after ending the Resource Wars of Southern Africa, which had raged for almost five decades.

The year was 2369, and the Huru oligarchy needed more than protection or assassins – they wanted monsters they could control, demons they could let loose on dissenters. So Rugare Tatanga and six other state assassins were recruited for top-secret enhancements, all vile experiments. None of the men were older than thirty.

"These will be augmentations," said the chief scientist, "not the toys currently embedded in your organs."

Rugare immediately disliked the smug egghead. Dr Chiroto worked on the oligarchy's personal project, so he was no saint. But, more than that, there was a deadness in his eyes, worse than any Rugare had seen in the meanest killers.

"If we don't kill at least one of you, we won't have done our work properly," Chiroto sneered, as if their lives meant nothing.

Indeed, a government guilty of genocide wouldn't blink at murdering a few lab rats. Chiroto was a sadistic fuck who ended up killing two of the men, yet he kept on pushing for miraculous results.

Strange men dressed in raw leather skirts, ebony beads, and hawk feathers came into the lab. They spread acrid smoke from clay pots and used hair-tipped whips to sprinkle water all over the lab equipment. Their beads chimed as they danced around the lab like simpletons. And they chanted the whole time, sometimes bellowing like speared buffalos. They were possessed by powerful ancestors who had lived long before the technology age.

"A marriage between technology and *African science*," Dr Chiroto declared proudly because he couldn't admit to trusting in magic. "Miracles require nothing less."

Rugare couldn't take the doctor seriously because he had only read about these possessed old men in antique books, the types written when superstition still reigned in Southern Africa.

Rugare and the other four surviving men would never forget their ordeal. Armies of scientists prodded their flesh, injected hot liquids into their veins, and performed never-ending surgeries that kept them feverish.

They were irradiated until their flesh blistered. The screams were without end, like the echoes of ghosts-to-be. Their skins would peel off before knitting back together in the next few days. Agony became a bedfellow who whispered in their ears every night. Rugare would try his hardest to ignore the whispers and seek out his Love. That is what kept him alive.

"They could have used androids, My Love, instead of torturing us. We were brought here to die."

"Hold on, My Beloved, because you will survive this. They tried androids in the resource wars until their AI proved fickle. You are strong and all the things the oligarchs wish they were. You are their last hope and their terror."

"Yet they will be our masters. Yet we follow the second generation of pampered oligarchs. Do you remember, My Love? How do you seize control of a great nation?"

"My Beloved, I heard the wails as well as you. I saw the anguished faces. The survivors' memories have been a deluge I've struggled to keep out."

"Remind me, My Love. I fear that I'm going mad. I can't tell anymore what is real and what is the nightmare."

"Power is seized through violence, My Beloved. Biobombs are quite effective. Remember how they were dropped in the cities forty-five years ago? Do you not even now hear how they whispered before reaching the ground? They were like the crashing waves of an ocean as they touched down. A swoosh followed by a plume of white smoke. The smoke spread everywhere, My Beloved, and the people breathed it in whilst they slept.

"The following morning, lovers and nursing mothers woke up covered in dust. Some had been unfortunate to witness the evil thing: how the flesh calcified before exploding into a plume of dust. The biobombs had not discriminated between the peaceful and the fighters, and no one knew why some died whilst others lived. Forty to fifty per cent of the population was gone in one night. It was the single stroke that finally ended the resource wars. A genocide, which has largely gone ignored, yet the people still weep."

"Is that why you cried the whole night, My Love, for the people?"

"You know why I cried, My Beloved. You must have seen it in the recesses of my mind, the shame I carry. My father lost his parents on the night of the bombings. He was twelve, and he had to start taking care of himself. He starved most times and couldn't go to school. He suffered every day, even as he cared for me and my sisters. And I thanked him by working for the men who had caused all his suffering."

"My Love, you had to feed your family; you had no choice."

"I had every choice, My Beloved, and I chose to be an agent of the evil oligarchy. My shame is an inescapable stain stamped in my flesh."

"I will erase it for you, My Love. I will avenge you."

Monstrous Deeds

It happened all at once in one night, a shock to the nation of Huru. The twelve pillars of the oligarchy were assassinated. Their families were also wiped out, including the entitled offspring. The offspring who would have grasped power after their fathers. No one was left alive within the walls of their modern-day palaces. A tomb held more cheer than those corpse-strewn grounds and rooms.

It was reported as an atrocity committed by a treacherous dog. An enhanced soldier had gone rogue or insane or both. Muchero, the potbellied oaf, appeared on the holograms to condemn the assassination and the assassin. He stammered as he spoke and sweated so much that he kept wiping his forehead with a handkerchief in front of the cameras.

The people quietly snickered and celebrated, not just because of the rattled Muchero, but because their tormentors had met terrible ends.

A small army of sensates stood at Muchero's back, women who had been enhanced to sense other people's emotions and predict their actions. Muchero must have known that they were about as useful as sticks buried in the sand to hold back a flood. They couldn't protect him. He was only alive because he was of little consequence.

After the oligarchy had been wiped out, no one wanted to take up the reins. The assassin had left messages written in blood on the walls of the twelve palaces:

I will be watching.

You will not be safe.

I will avenge the people.

Muchero was cousin to one of the assassinated leaders, a lackey, and he was the fool the petty government had thrust at the helm.

He talked of the abhorrent murder of the Fathers of a Nation. A nation smack-dab in the middle of Southern Africa and surrounded by the Fringe, a poisonous hell which had absorbed all the consequences of a fifty-year war.

And who were these dead Fathers? Who was the oligarchy? Twelve technology giants: nanotech and quantum computing, smart weather and agritech, space tech, global communications, robotics and AI, weapons, energy and transportation, smart consumer tech.

Before they thrust themselves at the helm, they had already ruled in all but name. They held most of the resources whilst the people starved. Southern Africa had been mined dry, and the droughts were without end. And so the resource wars would have never ended, not until the wealthy had given up some of their wealth. After all, what else were these technology giants except descendants of corrupt political vultures who had taken from their nations whilst they bled?

But they would never give up their wealth and power. The greedy fucks had the singular distinction of always wanting more. They would have smugly sat on gilded thrones atop a mound of ash. Of all their inventions, the bombings of 2324 were their greatest. The people lost the will to live, let alone fight.

Vengeance

Rugare Tatanga had destroyed the oligarchy, avenged his Love. He had been Dr Chiroto's pride and joy before turning traitor. "A miracle, at last!" the doctor had exclaimed after witnessing his power.

The doctor did not think so after the interrogators came for him. He stammered and whimpered as they beat him just for the fun of it. Torture had become obsolete since deep neural scans.

"You must have known," barked the lead interrogator. He pointed at all the scanning equipment. "What use is your science if you can't control your creatures?"

"Please, sir," the once arrogant doctor begged, "I didn't know. He was a depraved dog, that one." He fell to his knees and grasped the interrogator's boots. "I can find him, yes. I will bring him here to answer for his crimes in screams and blood."

"I doubt Huru can survive any more of your help," the interrogator hissed. He pulled his feet away before kicking Chiroto in the face. His teeth and blood flew out of his mouth.

The doctor was hanged for being an accomplice in the assassinations or its architect, depending on which government propagandist you asked.

The four remaining augmented assassins were subjected to deep neural scans, which could fish out the most repressed memories going back to a person's first few hours in the world.

* * *

Rugare Tatanga had disappeared from the lab before the assassinations. Nobody knew exactly when or how. He could manipulate matter, read minds, create force fields, soar towards the clouds, turn invisible, and change his appearance. He was more than a miracle; he had become a demigod. Chiroto had been a fool not to be terrified of him from the first.

The violence had been a beautiful thing to behold, monstrous art in motion. A small army of palace guards came at Rugare with guns, sonic blasts, grenades, and whatever other instruments of murder they could throw at him. These were no mere guards; they were battle-hardened soldiers who had seen the worst of it in the Fringe. They shot their machine guns but couldn't leave a mark on their target.

The bullets ricocheted off the force field around him like grinding sparks. He became a brilliant ball of fire, not unlike a star descended to Earth for its supernova. He snapped the guards' necks without touching them. A flick of the wrist and the soldiers fell with a thud. In the unnatural silence that ensued, Rugare walked over the corpses to the palace doors.

He didn't need keys or force. He melted through the walls into the palace like an apparition. The wife and children he killed first and fast. Snapped their necks where they were huddled in their sheets. The oligarch he killed last and slow. Broke every bone in his body, scrambled his eyes like eggs, pulled out his teeth, ripped out his tongue, and burned him alive. He couldn't see or scream by then, so he only convulsed, melted, and charred.

"Men are cruel, My Love, and I am a man."

"I do not weep for those fiends, My Beloved. You banished them to a well-deserved hell. It is you I mourn. You showed your face, My Beloved, and now they hunt you down. You could have gotten in and out unseen like an avenging ghost."

"They had to see, My Love, with those cameras all over the palaces. They had to know what I was capable of. They had to know real fear and helplessness. I had to teach them the kind of dread that sits in your gut like a weight intent on drowning you."

The Hunt

Cotton Mouth, Razor, Kid Gloves, Rock Face. These were the four remaining augmented assassins. Cotton Mouth spoke softly, no matter how corrosive his words. Razor had a tone and features as sharp as his mohawk. Kid Gloves had beautiful hands with elegant fingers and soft skin. Rock Face usually had a frown on his face, and he had appointed himself their leader.

They had been tasked with capturing if possible, or killing if necessary the treacherous dog Rugare Tatanga. It would take a monster to destroy a monster, Muchero had reasoned. None of this was public knowledge because the augmented assassins didn't exist. They were not alone. Fifty soldiers and a team leader joined them on the hunt.

The team leader, Kurwa, an unpleasant man who looked at the augmented assassins like they were animals, led the small army to the Nyanga Mountains. Satellite surveillance had picked up a warm body within the once-sacred mountains. Sacred or not, the mountains had dangerous crevices, which could swallow up careless climbers.

They navigated the mountain slope, the team leader first, augmented assassins close on his heels, and the soldiers last. They used the old footpath, careful not to snap any twigs. Not one word was exchanged between them. They knew what Rugare was capable of, had been shown the mangled and charred corpses. The best-case scenario was an ambush.

It was in the afternoon, hot and beautiful – one of the few beautiful, green places still left in Huru. Wild, too. Rugare would have appreciated such a place because he had grown up in a wilderness of sorts.

But Kid Gloves hated how the thorn bushes tore at his hands. "Look at that fucker go," his voice resonated inside his brothers' heads.

"Maybe the asshole will spook a black mamba and we'll be rid of him," Razor's voice echoed back.

Rock Face peered at Kurwa and sneered. The dour man, *Team Leader*, didn't notice the thorn trees brushing against his face as he led them up the footpath. Indeed, he was entirely too nimble for such a burly man with the proportions of a hyena.

"If I have to continue hearing that click-clack, I might kill him myself," Cotton Mouth added. Even as a mental echo, his voice retained its soft tones.

Four pairs of hateful eyes glared at Kurwa. The man was armed to the teeth, him and his pathetic troop of soldiers. He had two handguns holstered on each hip, two hunting knives sheathed on his back and chest, a sonic blast hooked to his calf, grenades dangling from his chest like strings of garlic to ward off evil, and a machine gun hanging on his shoulder.

"Men are weak," added Rock Face.

By comparison, the assassins only had hunting knives on their hips to prepare for close combat. Kurwa threw an ugly glance their way as they neared their target. He held the 3-D map projecting Rugare's hideout and glared at the pulsating red dot as if it would disappear the moment he took his eyes off it.

They were close to the apex of the hill they climbed. According to their map, a plateau stretched on the other side of it. Kurwa pointed to the ground before getting down on all fours. The assassins and soldiers followed suit. They crawled up the slope towards the apex, the stones digging into their knees, elbows, and palms. Kurwa peeped above the hill and immediately ducked. He looked at the four assassins before touching his lips with his forefinger and pointing just above his head.

Fear flashed in his eyes, and he couldn't conceal the tremble in his finger from the assassins' keen eyes. He had found Rugare and was right not to be excited.

There was ample vegetation to conceal them, so the four assassins also peeped at their target. There he was, kneeling beside a stream to fill his water bottle. The mouth of a cave was a few metres away – his hideout. He was in brown shorts and a green vest. He looked fit, well fed, and unafraid. Indeed, if he feared at all for his life, he didn't show it.

His sweaty dark-brown skin gleamed beneath the sunlight like burnished mahogany. His arm muscles rippled almost unnaturally, as if serpents danced underneath his skin. Even crouched, his perfectly proportioned athletic body couldn't be concealed. Rugare had always been handsome, but the wilderness lent a carnal quality to his beauty.

"My Beloved, they don't know what love is. To truly know someone and to love every bit of him. To be one, not in flesh but in mind. All those months we spent together, and all those agonizing nights made sweeter by your words. They will all die because they don't know."

"My Love, I didn't just discover you in Chiroto's lab. I unravelled you and fell in love with every part of you. Let the world burn as long as we can be together."

The four assassins jumped out of their hiding spot, leaving a wide-eyed Kurwa sitting in the dirt. He huffed as he leapt after them, signalling his soldiers to follow. What choice did he have? They had to attack or watch their quarry flee.

Rugare calmly looked up, glancing first at the assassins, then the soldiers behind them. He got up and casually screwed shut his water bottle. Those muscular, veiny arms of his made the hot day even hotter. He peered around as the soldiers surrounded him with their machine guns pointed.

"You're coming with us," barked Kurwa, emboldened by Rugare's quiescence. The fool thought he was afraid. "There's nowhere to run. You're surroun—"

He was cut short when Kid Gloves stepped towards Rugare. Kurwa glared at the insubordinate assassin whilst Rugare gazed at him with something akin to longing. Kurwa scowled as Kid Gloves stepped closer to the traitor and almost shat himself when the two embraced.

"My Beloved," Kid Gloves whispered in Rugare's ear.

"My Love," Rugare whispered back.

Kurwa huffed one too many times before pointing at the pair and screaming, "Kill them! Shoot them!"

Kid Gloves smirked at the soldiers as their bullets brightened the force field around him and his Beloved, and he laughed as he waved his hand at a group of them and their flesh vaporized from their skeletons.

Rock Face twirled his forefinger, almost bored with the command. Cotton Mouth zipped past the remaining soldiers like a bullet, slicing their throats with his twin daggers. Razor spun like a tornado, flinging the rest of the soldiers onto the rocks and cracking their skulls like eggs.

"They don't know, My Beloved, just how close we all got in that lab. A brotherhood of agony, thoughts intertwined and unfiltered. To hurt one is to hurt all."

"They will learn, My Love. But they will learn too late."

Kurwa's eyeballs swivelled in their sockets as he witnessed the theatre of murder. Finally, only he remained, with five monsters glaring at him. "The deep scans said you were ours to control. Neural scans don't lie!"

"Idiots, the whole lot of you," Razor snapped. "That shit doesn't work on us any more. Our thoughts are ours to control."

"Dogs! Traitors! After everything the oligarchy gave you." Kurwa clutched his useless machine gun to his chest whilst frantically shifting glances from one mean face to another.

Rock Face sneered at him before thrusting his blade through the unpleasant man's chin to his scalp. "After the oligarchy gave me my four new brothers, I didn't need them any more."

The Devil's Metamorphosis

B.T. Karuma

"THE DEVIL whispered in our ears. Atrocities, he sang. Beautiful abominations. We would be ageless and powerful, salt to cleanse the Earth, and a tsunami to wash it all away. We were children of providence and the monsters our age needed."

* * *

The Mhashu clan was swallowed by the Earth. It happened at night whilst they slept. It wasn't an earthquake exactly. If not for the few who noticed and screamed, the clan could have slept through it. The earth crumbled to nothing beneath them like pressed foam. They would later learn that it had been an experimental bomb created by Ngundu State scientists. Ricko, their stolen state android, would tell them because its database contained years of future tech.

They shrieked and clutched each other as they fell. For hours, it felt like a ship tunnelling through the Earth. When it finally stopped, they were kilometres below the surface and surrounded by steep walls of smooth rock. All three hundred and fifty of them had been swallowed up whilst they huddled inside their tents.

Tinorwa was fifteen when it happened. His large eyes shifted between his mother and father whilst everyone screamed. He had known war all his life, but nothing like this.

"Do you know why we are the Mhashu?" his grandfather had asked him when he was nine and the old man still lived.

Tinorwa had shaken his head, in awe of the man's wrinkled leathery skin, which had sagged into something lizard-like – all thanks to their arid world.

"The Mhashu were big, slender grasshoppers. They would appear in the cities from nowhere and disappear just as abruptly." The old man had licked his lips. "They were tasty, too. Like them, we attack the towns from nowhere before disappearing. Our impact may seem small, but there are thousands of our groups spread all over Ngundu State."

Tinorwa's father was the clan leader, and he stood straight amongst his cowering people. He was a tall man, strong, and with a puffed-out chest. His voice boomed and cut through the wails. "Calm down," he said whilst moving through the dishevelled camp. "We're alive. We'll find a way out."

Tinorwa wished he were as brave as his father. To stand tall in the dark and reassure doomed men who were up against monstrous enemies.

"Confident from the crib, that one," Tinorwa's grandfather once said of his son. "Only a fool can deny his regal bearing."

Tinorwa couldn't explain it, but he missed his grandfather with an acuteness that frightened him. His grandfather was four years dead, but it felt like he had last talked to him the previous night. The disaster was that much worse without his quick wit and gentle advice.

After two days of their new reality, the clan accepted the hideous fact they had been buried alive. Their food and water rations would last two weeks – a month if they committed to living in perpetual hunger.

"We'll try to climb out," their courageous leader told them. "We'll string together all our ropes, and Ricko will punch holes through the rock."

Even if the feat could be achieved, only a few would make it out. And those miraculous few would emerge in the middle of nowhere to battle thirst and hunger, those unassailable assailants. Fifteen as he was, even Tinorwa knew. He had also overheard the secret conversation between his father and Ricko.

Throwing your enemies into a pit was a strange way to kill them, and as inefficient a method as could be devised. To be sure, Ngundu State leadership was composed of a bunch of greedy sadists, but they were always efficient in destroying their enemies. Their purpose was to observe the Mhashu as they slowly died off. To find out how their enemy thought whilst gloating in their victory. Tinorwa couldn't see any possibility of escaping that hell.

"This land has known suffering," his grandfather once told him. "Colonization, oppression and resource exploitation, the Resource Collapse, and never-ending wars. The technology renaissance came to Southern Africa because it was our only means of survival." He had chuckled. "Evolve or die. Well, boy, we chose both. Those bastards at the top made sure to grasp the little left and saddle the rest of us with starvation." He had spat in the dirt. "Rebels, they call us, for opposing their disgusting greed and cruelty."

The pit they had been thrown into was an oven worse than the desert they had come from. They sweated all day, yet they couldn't take gulps of their water. Only sips to stave off dehydration and madness. Not even a drop of water trickled into the pit. It was the strangest thing. There must have been underground water sources, yet nothing spouted from the four walls. The thought made Tinorwa mad with thirst.

He envied Ricko, even as he laboured away on the slick wall. The days were filled with the tap, tap, tap of his metallic fists against the rock. The nights, too. But not throughout the night.

On some nights, Tinorwa couldn't sleep, consumed with thoughts of how he and everyone he loved would starve to death. He would imagine shrivelled corpses slowly rotting away because even vultures wouldn't attempt that hell. The stench of rotting flesh would be a million times worse than the smell of sweaty bodies, shit, and piss, which had settled in that pit. Whenever Ricko stopped his work, the silence would be dreadful, like they were encased in a tomb.

Why did Ricko stop working at night? He was metal and wires and code. Didn't feel pain, fatigue, thirst, or hunger. So why did he stop? Tinorwa found out why through rumours, the most ridiculous stories.

"Ricko is swallowed by the wall at night and comes out at the base at dawn," Chiutsi, his best friend, told him. "I saw him come out with my own eyes."

Tinorwa laughed unashamedly because such stories deserved nothing less. "The heat has scrambled your brains."

"I'm serious," Chiutsi whispered, embarrassed by his own account. "I told my mother, and she said she'd tell my father."

Tinorwa imagined the awkward conversation, if it would ever happen. How the father would brush off his son's crazy talk and chastise the mother for validating his delusions. None of it mattered, anyway, since they were hurtling towards slow extinction.

Tinorwa would regret mocking his best friend because he was the first victim.

"It touched me!" Chiutsi shrieked. "The android touched me with its molten fingers. It burns, it burns!"

His arm had turned grey, stiff, and cracked. It was like his skin rotted or turned to stone. He had been discovered like that, screaming and writhing at the edge of their camp. Tinorwa was allowed a few minutes alone with him because it could have been his last moments alive. The tent was hotter than usual, and Tinorwa cried as much as he sweated. He let the sweat drip but wiped his tears because such wasn't the conduct of a Mhashu.

"I saw the android again as it came out of a tunnel. The metal of its arms was hot enough to twist like serpents." He gripped Tinorwa's wrist. "Don't let it touch you. Stay away from it."

Chiutsi's mother whisked him out of the tent before her son could further frighten him. Her eyes were bloodshot, but she was doing a good job of restraining her tears. "It will be alright," she told him, though it sounded like she was trying to convince herself.

He didn't say anything because of the lump stuck in his throat. And he couldn't risk crying in the open like some toddler. When he got home, he let the tears out – for the last time, he told himself.

Chiutsi's father exploded at the clan leader whilst he ate in his tent with his family. "Destroy that machine! It killed my son. Destroy it before it kills us all."

"Come down, Mudambi," the clan leader responded. "We will investigate and come to the truth." Ever was he cool in times of crisis. It was downright creepy sometimes, and a trait that had trickled down to his wife and son.

More men burst into the tent to restrain Mudambi and drag him back to his home. He fumed as they dragged him, filling the night air with his chilling warnings.

As much as the people stared, whispered, and pointed, it didn't matter. No magical tunnels had been found. Ricko was their only chance at escape. The android would not be destroyed.

"What happened to Chiutsi?" Tinorwa asked his father.

His mother glanced at him with sad eyes before turning to his father. That was all the tenderness he would get from her because Mhashu boys were not supposed to be pampered and soft.

"We're not sure," his father told him. "Kuziva thinks it could be a side-effect of the bomb. We know little about the technology."

Three years ago, Kuziva stole Ricko from the capital after loading his database with state secrets. He had been a Ngundu State scientist until its leadership decided to use androids to slaughter the starving rebels. He reprogrammed Ricko and joined the Mhashu.

"So it could happen to more of us," said Tinorwa.

"Do not think of such things," his mother scolded. *Focus on what you can change*, she loved reminding him whenever he brooded about a problem.

It wasn't long before more teenagers fell victim to the new disease. Two days and seven new cases. And they all echoed what Chiutsi had claimed. A mob came for Ricko whilst Tinorwa's parents were visiting the sick children.

Kuziva shielded the android before they could shoot it. "We need him," the scientist pleaded with the mob. "He is our only way out of this pit. Kill him and you kill us all."

"That thing is already killing us," Mudambi snapped. "How stupid are you not to realize the truth?"

"It's a shared psychotic disorder," said Kuziva, "a collective delusion. None of what the sick kids are saying is possible."

"This place is cursed," Mai Kudzi shrieked. "The devil lives here."

Her son Kudzai was one of the sick children. Tinorwa thought her mad from dehydration and despair. Only the superstitious lot from generations ago had believed in devils and demons.

Mudambi grabbed Kuziva by the shoulder before tossing him aside. The skinny scientist yelped as his knees dug into the dirt. "Don't do this," he begged. The poor man looked like he was about to cry as Mudambi levelled his gun at the android's metallic head.

Ricko casually looked at Kuziva for commands. It reminded Tinorwa that the robot was a thing with neither feelings nor fear of death. All his pity for it receded like a boot taken off his throat. Only one thought remained: could the android actually save them?

He lunged and grabbed Mudambi's gun. The laser beam it shot out only glanced off Ricko's skull, leaving a black burn mark. He scuffled with the much stronger Mudambi. Grief and desperation had driven the man insane. More than ever was logic their best weapon.

"Let go, boy," Mudambi hissed.

"You'll kill us all," Tinorwa shot back.

"Stupid boy! We're already dea—"

The rumble was like a tremor beneath their feet. It came from everywhere, resounding from the four walls. Mudambi's eyes were large as he frantically looked around. Tinorwa saw it then: he was a big, terrified man using anger as a shield.

The walls roared at them, and the people cowered. These weren't the natural rumbles associated with tremors. The roars were alive and menacing.

"Monsters," Kuziva gasped. "Impossible."

Solid rock crumbled from the eastern wall to form a tunnel, and the roars poured out of the gaping darkness. Tinorwa, Kuziva, and the mob fled from the wall, shared terror uniting them once more.

They stared in horror as Ricko walked into the tunnel before it sealed up behind him as if it had never existed. The roars stopped, yet the people still shivered.

"This isn't happening," Kuziva muttered. He stared at Tinorwa, his eyes large and glistening. "It must be the state. They are doing this. They're torturing us."

"Fuck the state," Mudambi barked. "This is something else. I told you and you wouldn't listen."

There was an old woman in their clan, Chakadii, the oldest member of their clan. Some whispered that she was more than a hundred. "The bomb woke up Hondo, the destroyer of worlds and punisher of men," she declared whilst her hand wobbled on her walking stick.

Chakadii had long proclaimed herself a reincarnation of a powerful ancestress, a witch doctor who had lived in the land that was once called Zimbabwe, before it was absorbed into the Ngundu State. She sometimes spoke of the times before colonization, the Resource Collapse and ensuing wars, and the vast stretches of desert across Southern Africa.

She had been called schizophrenic and senile, but now the people listened. "Hondo has cleansed the world before, and now we have forced his hand because of our destructive ways. He comes for us all and doesn't know mercy."

Tinorwa regarded the old woman's peculiar garb, daring to believe her. Twisted necklaces of multi-coloured beads hung on her shoulders. Her earrings were made of thorns and bird feathers. She concealed her grey hair with a hat of woven reeds, a geometric headdress that got wider from her head like an upturned pyramid. A bodice of black leather she had tanned herself lifted her sagging bust. Even her walking cane had carvings of animals that had either never existed or had gone extinct. She had made everything herself. Using *dead traditional knowledge*, she had claimed.

"Pray for your souls," she said. "Soon, there will be nothing else left of us."

The next few days threw the clan into vacillating states of confusion and horror.

Ricko would come and go like a phantom. The few clanspeople who spotted him steered clear whilst whispering *devil worshipper* or *Hondo's pet*. The people had convinced themselves that the devil truly existed and that the forefathers had been right in supposing that he lived below their feet. Kuziva took advantage of this newfound superstition by reminding the people that if they harmed Ricko, this devil would be implacable.

"I rescued him," the scientist told Tinorwa as if he spoke of a living being. "He isn't evil. He is predictable code, and I made him good."

Two more kids fell ill to make the total ten. But none of them remained bedridden. They all got up one afternoon and congregated at the edge of the camp with their faces turned to the sun. The kids had gone one to three days without eating, so their parents tried force-feeding them. "We're not hungry," they insisted. "All we need is the sun."

Any successful attempts at forcing food down their throats resulted in immediate vomiting or seizures. The parents were aghast when the kids escaped their clutches to stand under the sun. "To recharge," they said.

They worship the sun; the rumour spread throughout the camp in less than half an hour. They became the Sun Worshippers.

The rot that began on their arms spread throughout their bodies until they looked like mobile granite statues. No one would touch them, including their parents and siblings. The sick kids didn't mind because they only sought each other's company.

In a fit of madness, as his mother later described it, Tinorwa poked Chiutsi whilst he recharged in the sun. It was like poking stone. It wasn't just his skin that had rotted – all his flesh had calcified.

The next stage in their metamorphosis left Tinorwa stunned. Their cracked skin peeled away like old paint to reveal bodies of brilliant silver metal. The horror notwithstanding, there was beauty in what they had become: the slick lines and curves of their bodies, their controlled elegance as they moved, and their indifference to the dying people of flesh around them. Indeed, they were not human any more. Their families were the first they scorned to seek each other's company.

Tinorwa had watched them with envy, then guilt; anger, then desperation. He wanted to be like them and to survive, but didn't want to despise his parents and watch them die. He was constantly sick from the pain of hunger and thirst, and the blistering sun kept him exhausted and feverish. He wanted to live, but didn't want to sacrifice who he was. Wasn't that another kind of death, a more tragic expiration?

When the choice was made for him, it was relief tinged with a bitter aftertaste. He, too, succumbed to Ricko's touch. The Sun Worshipers hadn't been wrong. The android came out of the wall, the metal of his body shimmering and twisting like something molten. Maybe every day he went to the very core of the Earth.

Tinorwa didn't run when Ricko walked towards him. He was too hungry and weak, or at least that's what he told himself. Ricko's hand was freezing cold, so cold that it burned to his bone. He bit his tongue to keep from screaming because he felt wrong. Wrong for wanting this and wrong for not wanting anyone to see or interfere. He would be another *poor victim* yet his heart leapt with a little excitement.

The voices didn't begin until all his flesh had calcified. They resounded inside his head, louder than his mother's impassioned pleas for her son to come back to her. They were loudest when he recharged in the sun with the other Sun Worshippers.

"You will be the fire and the flood that washes across the world of men. Your parents you will leave in this pit to die. The rest of humanity you will destroy so that everything else can live."

After Tinorwa had become brilliant cold steel, he felt his power grow every day. The voices came with visions clearer than the frightened faces of flesh and bone around him. With a terse command, he could create a raging firestorm to consume an entire city. With a stamp of his foot, he could shatter the Earth to swallow whole lakes. With a whisper, he could reduce skyscrapers to rubble.

"Kill them, my son. Kill them all."

"I will, Father."

The Underground Railroad of Entanglement

Astra Lee

"YOU'RE TELLING ME I could be in Port-au-Prince, blink, and open my eyes in NOLA?"

"Not just that," Ama said, grinning as she tapped the terminal. The machine purred, its interface flickering between symbols Jones didn't recognize. "You could be anywhere they told you you couldn't be – or shouldn't be."

Jones eyed the contraption warily. It looked less like a computer and more like seven circles of hell stacked on top of each other – wires tangled like vines, pulses of blue light stuttering between its rings.

Ama didn't seem concerned. She kept rummaging through the chaos on her desk, scattering cables, hard drives, and something that looked suspiciously like a compass. "First, we gotta get you a BCA."

"ABC what?" Jones asked, still trying to make sense of the mess in front of him.

"Your biometric cipher authentication," she said, finally pulling out a small, sleek device. "Can't have you skipping across borders without it."

Ama flipped the device between her fingers like a coin, then pressed it against her wrist. A faint ripple of light pulsed across her skin. "The BCA links your biometrics – fingerprints, retina, heartbeat pattern – to a quantum encryption key. Basically, it makes sure only you can access the system. No fakes, no duplicates. No government database can track it, either, 'cause it scrambles your ID every time you use it." She tossed it to Jones, who barely caught it. "Press it to your pulse point. It syncs instantly. And don't lose it – without that, you're stuck wherever you land."

"Nigga!" Jones burst out laughing, slapping his hands together. He couldn't contain it – the pure, unfiltered amazement. "How does this even work?"

Ama just grinned, watching him soak it all in. "If you think this is wild, wait till we actually take a trip." She did a little dance, bouncing on her heels. "Where do you wanna go, hmm? Where? Eh, where? I can't promise everywhere just yet, but we're getting there."

Jones thought for a second, then shrugged. "Take me to NOLA."

Ama scoffed. "NOLA? You can go anywhere and you're picking somewhere you've already been?"

Jones shook his head, still grinning. "Nah. I'm eating dinner in NOLA tonight."

"Alright," Ama said, tapping the terminal and securing her locs in a pile on her head. "BCA synced, co-ordinates locked in. Hold on to your ass."

"Wait, hold on to—" Jones started, but the air around him shifted. It wasn't like stepping through a door. It wasn't even like moving at all. One second, he was in Ama's cluttered hideout, and the next—

Heat. Music. The scent of frying oil.

They landed inside a ship. Metal walls, the low hum of machinery, the distant slosh of water against the hull.

Jones gasped for air, more in shock than out of oxygen. His knees buckled, and he grabbed the nearest surface for balance. "Where are we?" His head pounded, probably because he hadn't eaten all day – or maybe because he wasn't supposed to be here.

Ama, completely unfazed, turned towards a figure leaning against a control panel. "Benie, meet Jones – my childhood BFF slash couz."

The figure didn't react right away. Then, slowly, Benie tilted their head, eyeing Jones.

The room they landed in felt low, close, like the ship was cradling them in its belly. Jones could hear the distant churn of water outside, the steady hum of machinery keeping them afloat.

Benie stretched, rolling their shoulders like someone used to tight spaces. "I live here with my two sons. When Ama and her team came to me asking me to join – said they needed someone good with a ship – I didn't hesitate." They gestured around the room, their tone light, but there was something weighty in their words.

"Last month, I took my boys and their girlfriends to Greece. Last year? Went by myself to Turkey. I haven't traveled much yet, but I plan on it." They turned back to Jones, tilting their head. "I volunteer my time here. Me and the boys, we rotate shifts. So…welcome to Node 7."

Jones blinked. The room, the hum of the ship, the sheer weight of what Benie just said – it all settled on him at once. These people weren't running. They weren't hiding. They were living.

"You look like you're about to pass out," Benie said, already moving towards the hall. "Come on, I'll show you around before you fall over."

Jones followed, still reeling. The walls were close, the air thick with salt and engine heat. He could hear voices echoing up ahead – laughter, music, the clatter of dishes. It didn't feel like a war room. It felt like a home.

"Down here's the engine room." Benie gestured at a hatch that looked like it belonged to a submarine. "Teleportation takes power, and we have to keep it running without drawing attention." They knocked on the metal. "It's not fancy, but it's ours."

Jones eyed the wires and mismatched tech. "So…this is how Black folks stay free?"

"One way." Ama grinned. "Now, let's get you something to eat before you pass out. The kitchen's up here – just don't ask what's in the stew."

They made their way up on deck, where the smell of something delicious was brewing.

* * *

Jones was on the deck with a second bowl of co-bouillon on top of a pile of rice. I don't even need to go to some fancy restaurant to get the fanciest feast in NOLA, he thought, the spice hitting just hard enough to be invigorating. He left the boat to join the others, where they were still finishing their first serving.

The air was different here – thick, damp, tinged with the scent of marsh water. They had landed near a hidden settlement, four homes built like treehouses, lifted above the wetlands on wooden stilts.

They huddled around a small picnic table; feet propped up on the seats to avoid the wetness of the floor below.

"So there's four families living near this node?" Jones asked.

Benie finished chewing, glancing at Ama to see if she would answer. She just gestured for him to go ahead.

"Yeah," Benie said, stretching. "Some of the families in the network decided to settle here. We can't accommodate too many folks in this region. The more people we have, the harder it is to evacuate if something goes down."

Jones gave him a look. "And how often do things go down?" There was weight in his voice. A double meaning.

Benie shrugged. "Honestly? Only once. And that was just because it got too damn cold. We had snow, and none of us needed to be here freezing like that."

"Well, that's a relief," Jones muttered, but he wasn't convinced. "An operation like this has to be attracting unwanted attention."

"We keep a very, very, very low profile," Ama said, placing her empty bowl behind her on the table.

"My hope," she continued, "is that every Black person will be outfitted with a BCA. But for now, we're selective. We have to be. The more people we move, the more risk we take on. So we vet everyone – make sure they won't put the network in danger."

Jones set his bowl down, his posture shifting. "Then we need to help Trina."

Ama's expression froze for half a second. Trina. She hadn't thought about Trina in a long time. She, Trina, and Jones had been close once. She and Trina had a falling out – over what, exactly? She couldn't even remember anymore.

She didn't need to. She knew what this was about.

Didier.

"I know she's struggling," Jones pressed. "Didier is seventeen. He's just a kid. They're planning to ship him to Guantanamo. He doesn't have time for vetting."

Ama inhaled slowly, thinking.

"I've been in contact with Trina's sister," she admitted. "I know what's happening."

Silence. A pause only broken by the voices of children playing nearby.

"I don't hand these BCAs out to just anyone, Jones." Benie's voice was calm but firm. "I have to vet people. Even if they're seventeen."

"He is a child," Jones snapped.

"I know," Ama said. "But I love this little operation. And Benie, Paula, Aminata, Robert, and so many others have moved hundreds of people without issue because we don't take chances. We're going to help – but we have to do it carefully."

"Last year," Benie cut in, "we helped a father and his daughter relocate to New Zealand. Thought we were in the clear until the little girl told her classmates she arrived through a wardrobe." He smirked, shaking his head. "To be fair, the New Zealand node is accessible through what looks like a big-ass wardrobe."

Jones huffed a laugh despite himself. But the weight in his chest didn't leave.

Ama didn't answer right away. She leaned back, exhaling, eyes flicking between Jones and Benie.

"Alright," she finally said. "We'll get him out."

Jones sagged in relief. Ama, though, wasn't done.

"But we do this my way," she said, jabbing a finger at him. "That means he listens. No last-minute 'I forgot' or 'I panicked.' He follows every rule. Every single one."

"He will," Jones said quickly.

Ama wasn't convinced, but she pushed forward. "We'll send him through Baltimore Node. It's small, but it's clean. We don't use it for high-volume jumps, which means it's less likely to be watched."

"Where will he land?"

Ama tapped the terminal, scanning through nodes. "He'll jump to the Senegal node first. From there, he gets a new ID, a new cover, and then we move him to his mother."

"Trina's in Haiti," Benie added.

Ama nodded. "He'll be safe there. We have nodes in Haiti."

Jones clenched his jaw. "And when can we do this?"

Ama looked at Benie.

Benie sighed. "Three days. Tell Didier to be at the Baltimore Node at exactly 11:37 PM. No earlier, no later. No tracking devices, no outside contact. If he's followed, he's on his own."

Jones nodded. But Didier wasn't on his own. Not yet. Didier wasn't going to end up in some concentration camp if he could help it.

* * *

The storage facility was dark except for the dim red light of the node terminal. Ama crouched by the console, fingers moving fast over the display.

They had four minutes.

Jones shifted restlessly beside her, eyes darting to the loading dock door. The place smelled like oil, dust, and old wood, the scent of years of forgotten shipments.

Benie stood near the teleportation pad, arms crossed, eyes sharp. The Baltimore Node was a small one – one entry point, one exit. No room for mistakes. There were contingencies, but only in all-hell-break-loose moments.

Ama checked her watch. 11:36 PM.

A knock came at the back entrance. Three taps. A pause. Two taps.

Benie opened the door.

Didier slipped inside, hood pulled low. He was thin, tall for seventeen, his hands balled into nervous fists.

"Good," Ama said, scanning him. "You're alone?"

Didier nodded.

"No phone, no electronics?"

Didier hesitated for a fraction of a second.

Ama's eyes narrowed. "Didier."

"I don't have my phone."

Ama sucked her teeth but motioned him forward. "Fine. Get on the pad."

Jones clapped Didier on the shoulder. "Almost there, man."

"I'm nervous, Uncle Jones."

Ama sighed and pulled up a holographic display. It flickered, glowing blue in the dim light of the ship. Ama was going to take a minute to set his mind at ease.

"Alright, Didier. I know this all sounds wild, so let me break it down for you."

He leaned in, eyes wide. "You mean, like, how does the teleportation actually work?"

"Exactly," she said, tapping the interface. A diagram of the Relay appeared – overlapping rings of energy, like ripples in a pond.

"This isn't just some sci-fi portal nonsense," she continued. "It's quantum entanglement. Meaning your molecules don't 'move' – they get reconstructed elsewhere in real time, based on the anchor point's stored data."

Didier squinted at the screen. "So… I don't travel. I just – exist somewhere else?"

"Bingo." Ama grinned. "Your biometric cipher locks your exact quantum state, encrypts it, and matches it to an open node. No duplicates, no errors. And no tracking. Which is why—" she leveled a look at him " – you cannot have a phone, a smartwatch, nothing. If you're carrying a live signal, we don't just move you – we move your signal. And guess who's watching?"

Didier shifted. "I get it."

Ama didn't look convinced.

"In an emergency, push the green button on your BCA and it will take you to the nearest node. It's only in an emergency and only if a node is functioning. All long jumps are carefully performed at nodes like this one."

Didier shifted uncomfortably but stepped onto the circular platform – an old shipping crate retrofitted with a teleportation interface. Ama locked in the co-ordinates. Senegal was waiting.

She exhaled. They were going to pull this off.

Then –

BOOM.

The front-loading dock doors exploded inward.

Jones instinctively shoved Didier off the pad as men in black tactical gear stormed in, rifles up.

ICE.

"*Get down*!" a voice boomed.

Ama barely had time to snatch the console's hard drive before everything turned to chaos.

Ama pressed on the red stud earrings in her ears. A detonator.

The room shook as a series of small explosions cascaded outward, taking the five ICE agents by surprise. Smoke filled the space, a sudden chaos of shouting and fire.

"Move!" Ama barked, already sprinting for a metal door at the back of the storage unit.

Benie slammed it shut behind them, bolting the heavy lock. "Down the chute – now!" They gestured towards an open hatch in the floor.

Jones grabbed Didier by the arm, pushing him forward. Ama followed, but Benie didn't move.

"What the hell are you doing?" Jones demanded.

Benie's expression was calm. Resigned.

"However they got here, it's on me. I stay!" Jones shouted. Jones shoved him hard. "I don't have time for you to play hero, Benie!"

Benie's jaw tensed, his argument already loaded, but something in his face shifted. He knew Jones was right. He knew they couldn't afford to be taken in.

Benie jumped.

They slid into the chute, sealing it from the inside. Jones latched it from the outside for an extra layer of protection, then yanked a curtain over it.

The door behind him cracked, buckled. ICE was coming.

That's when he saw it.

A phone.

Lying on the floor. Screen still glowing.

Jones snatched it up, flipping it over. On the display was a photo of Didier with his mother.

His stomach dropped.

Fucking moron.

The door burst open. Agents poured in. The room filled with fire as the blast consumed the oxygen.

Jones barely had time to think.

He reached into his pocket and pulled out the tablet Ama had given him days ago.

* * *

Benie had set the tablet on the table between them, tapping it lightly.

"This'll wipe your memory for a week," he explained. "Doesn't matter what they do to you – your brain will literally not have the answers."

Ama leaned in. "It's even more effective on newcomers. Your mind hasn't fully mapped everything yet. If they capture you, you won't be able to give up anything. Not a single detail."

Jones had picked up the pill back then, turning it over in his fingers. "And if I don't take it?"

Ama's voice was cold. "Then you better hope you can resist everything they'll throw at you."

* * *

Jones gritted his teeth. He didn't have time to think; he didn't want to jump in front of the agents.

He popped the pill in his mouth.

The ICE agents rushed forward.

Everything went dark.

* * *

Ama leaned back, watching the terminal's glowing interface shift in real-time.

"We've got two hundred and thirty-seven active nodes across the world. Cave in Arizona? Online. The safehouse in Bahia? Solid. The Senegal hub? Just came back online after the power surge."

Jones rubbed his temples. "And you're saying – what? That we can just go anywhere?"

They were lounging on a sofa in Peru, the warm air drifting in through the window. Jones could still hear the agent's voice in his head, the way he'd shouted into the phone, insisting they'd uncovered a terrorist operation filled with explosives.

They hadn't uncovered anything. They'd lost.

Jones had barely escaped. When the ICE agent tackled him, the pill flew from his mouth – along with a tooth. He never swallowed it. But his BCA was still in his grip. With a single tap, he did the unthinkable – he'd transported to the nearest available node in front of the agents.

He landed in an abandoned mine shaft in Pennsylvania.

Ama came for him there. They'd spent weeks after that scouring Baltimore, Virginia, and D.C. news. Nothing. The fire was reported, but the official cause? Electrical malfunction.

Ama knew what that meant.

The government was keeping it quiet. Which meant it was sensitive – too dangerous to reveal to the public.

That worried her.

Not enough to stop.

Benie was back in NOLA, keeping the network strong. Didier was in Haiti with his mother. He'd taken responsibility for what happened in Baltimore. He wanted to volunteer, to help maintain the Haiti node.

Ama understood that freedom for herself, freedom for everybody Black, isn't found in one place. As long as they lived in a system that had the power to reach, touch, and corrupt every inch of this world, there was only one way to stay free.

Keep moving.
Jones stretched, sinking deeper into the sofa. “So?”
Ama just smirked, tapping a new screen.
A star map appeared.
“Not yet,” she said.
She tapped a blinking point beyond Earth.
“But soon.”

Comfort

Kyoko M.

HE WOKE UP to a bright light.

His brown eyes popped open, but he realized he wasn't really seeing anything yet. He just felt an immense wave of panic rushing over him, unsure if it was irrational or not. A short cry escaped his lips as he lurched upward, his limbs flying out to catch his weight as he pitched to one side. Information registered one tidbit at a time. He'd been lying on a plain mattress. The floor was carpeted. His chest, knees, neck, and skull throbbed with pain. He didn't have full mobility, as there was an enormous, thick blue cord running from the back of his neck into a socket in the adjacent wall. He could see his brown artificial flesh torn in the spots that hurt the most, exposing the wiring beneath. But there was one other pressing thing he noticed.

There was a black girl with shoulder-length box braids and colored beads at the ends standing there with a penlight in her hand. She was startled, but not afraid.

"Hey," she said softly as he staggered, light-headed, blinking over and over in an attempt to clear his mind. "Hey, it's alright. You're safe now. You're safe."

"W-What happened?" he slurred, planting one hand against the nearest wall, straining to remember. "Where am I? Who are you?"

"Shh, it's okay," she said, walking towards him. "I'll answer all your questions, but I need you to lie down again. You're still in bad shape."

"No," he said, narrowing his eyes at her. "Answer me. Now."

"My name is Akachi. You're in downtown Neo Atlanta. This is my apartment. I found you in the dumpster behind the alley of my repair shop about twelve hours ago. Someone worked you over something fierce. Your legs had severe damage as well as your chassis and your skull."

"Is that…why I can't remember anything?" he asked.

"Yes. They wiped your CPU completely."

"All of it?"

She sighed, nodding. "I'm sorry. There wasn't anything to retrieve when I started your diagnostic."

His knees wobbled. She caught him under the arm as he fell to one side. She was stronger than she looked. He knew his metal skeleton hadn't been easy to carry to wherever they were. Exhausted from the revelation, he let her drag him back over to the bed.

"I've been doing my best to repair your neural pathways," she continued. "I think that's what woke you up. Do you remember your name?"

"Andrew," he mumbled. "Andrew Emerson."

"Good. That's what your serial number says. What is your current primary objective?"

He closed his eyes and focused on the blue letters that flashed across the back of his artificial eyelids. "Survival."

She gave a start. "Wow. I've never heard that before."

He risked a glance at her. "What's so odd about that?"

She fidgeted. "W-Well, you are a, um, you know."

For the first time since he woke up, he almost felt amusement. "A what?"

She cleared her throat. "A comfort bot. I thought their objective was typically to locate a new client."

"Well, you said someone beat me up pretty good," he answered, hiding a smile at her modesty. "Androids revert to survival mode when threatened, regardless of their intent. My parameters would have to be reset to match the original objective."

He glanced at the tablet lying on the nightstand nearby. "Is that what you were working on when I woke up?"

She blinked at him. "Absolutely not. I have no intention of changing you whatsoever."

He peered up at her. "Why?"

"I have no right to do that."

He relaxed slightly on the bed. "You're an android sympathizer?"

She lifted both eyebrows. "I pulled you out of a dumpster and put you back together. I thought that was sort of obvious."

He smiled. "Point taken. Do you mind if I have a look in the meantime?"

"Not at all." She helped him sit up against several firm pillows and handed him the tablet. He scanned the working processes in his head. He was currently operating at about seventy percent of his full capacity. The damage in his knees and the left side of his chest were the worst ailments. From a brief physical analysis, he could see the laceration in his ribs. The synthetic blood had dried hours ago. He wore a pair of black suit pants and he could still feel boxer-briefs beneath them. She hadn't taken advantage of him, at least.

"Did you do all the repair work yourself?" he asked, handing her back the tablet.

"Mostly, yes."

"You're a mechanic, then?"

"Yeah. I fix cars, but I'm working on my masters in robotics, so I knew the basic work to be done to get you up and running again."

He winced. "I, uh, don't have any money at the moment to pay you back for the time and materials you've put into me—"

She held up her hand. "I wouldn't accept it even if you did. You were in trouble. What kind of person would just leave you to die like a piece of garbage?"

"A lot of people, actually," he said, and couldn't keep the bitterness from dripping across his tone. "I don't know if you've checked my trust settings, but they aren't exactly that high. That being said…"

He reached out and closed his hand over hers briefly. "Thank you for saving my life, Akachi. Even if you don't want to accept anything, I'll find a way to repay your kindness."

She rolled her eyes. "Maybe I will readjust your chivalry settings."

He grinned. "Don't you dare."

She motioned towards the bed. "Get some rest. I have to resupply to work on your knees and chest. I won't be long."

She stood and pocketed her keys before leaving the apartment. He settled down against the small nest of pillows and surveyed the apartment. It was a low-budget version of a studio apartment, with the kitchen straight ahead, a table to eat at on the left, and the entertainment area across from the bed. There was a five-level bookshelf next to a flat-screen television. The nightstand sat to the immediate left of the bed. He tilted his head enough to see a doorway on the right that led to her bathroom.

His sensors had estimated Akachi's age to be late twenties, but she looked much younger. She was tall and had an athletic build, which likely came in handy if she truly was a mechanic.

She'd been wearing work coveralls, and they were smudged with oil and dirt, which led him to believe the story she'd told him so far. There was a box of tools sitting by the foot of the bed and the wires recharging his artificial brain were brand new.

She'd also gone out of her way to help him. Sympathizer or not, he wanted to know why. Humans and androids had a caustic relationship — either they were too dependent or they were prejudiced. For now, he'd take her at her word, but he'd keep an eye out to see if she had an ulterior motive.

He stood and limped over to the tiny window beside the table. Tightly packed, identical apartments greeted his gaze. It wasn't the ghetto, but it also wasn't anything fancy. They were on the second floor.

After a bit, he shuffled over to the bed and checked the action logs on his CPU. True to her word, Akachi had altered nothing about him. He'd lost his memories, but the basic parts of his functions all remained the same. All the work she'd done so far was related to repairing disconnected internal programs or rerouting his core to get different parts of him to work smoothly. Maybe she was just a good Samaritan.

Or she knew how to cover her tracks.

Akachi returned ten minutes later with a crate of new materials. She worked on his chest first, repairing and resetting the frayed wiring and sealing the wound shut with a thin adhesive that would eventually regrow the skin using nanites.

His knees, however, were in much worse shape. She'd been removing the shattered shrapnel from his patella one piece at a time, so only the core remained as it hadn't been destroyed. She'd have to replace the outer part entirely so he wouldn't be limping anymore. She had steady hands and an amazing amount of patience.

"Mind if I ask you something?" Andrew said.

"Not at all."

"Why do you live in such a shitty apartment when you're this good a mechanic?"

She laughed, but her hands still didn't shake from where they were slowly re-twining wires just above his knee. "It lets me save for my courses and build a nest egg for the future. Plus, this neighborhood looks rough, but it's actually not that bad. I'll worry about nicer digs once I'm working in the robotics field. My shop's also only two blocks away, so I don't have to buy a car until I need one."

"Did you carry me up here yourself?"

"No, I had a coworker help. We found you last night after inventory."

He glanced around at the studio apartment again. "Just you, huh? No boyfriend?"

"Not at the moment, no."

"Why?"

She pursed her lips, deadpanning, "Because I am a strong, independent woman who don't need no man."

Andrew laughed. It surprised him that he even could, considering the circumstances. "Oh, right. My mistake."

"Anyway, why do you ask?"

"Just making sure some huge guy isn't going to see the shirtless man in your bed and come to the wrong conclusion."

"You're safe on that front, trust me." She fell silent for a bit as she worked.

"Can I ask you something?" she said after a while.

"Of course."

"Will you try to find out who did this to you?"

Andrew shrugged. "Dunno. Maybe it's better if I leave it be."

She nibbled her bottom lip. "What do you think happened?"

"I might've seen something I wasn't supposed to. That happens a lot to droids, especially comfort bots. It might also have been that someone was using me and their significant other found out and wanted to make a point."

She shook her head slightly. "People suck."

"Mostly," he said, and softly enough that she glanced at him before looking away shyly.

After a couple of hours, both knees were replaced and sealed shut. "Alright, fella, let's see if you can get your bearings."

She unplugged him and offered a hand. He accepted it and stood. She stepped back, blinking curiously up at him. He arched an eyebrow, and she explained.

"You're taller than I thought."

Andrew smiled. "Ah."

He walked around the small apartment a few times while she watched, making sure everything had been tightened and set properly. "I think you're good to go."

"Seems about right." He paused, eyeing her. "Will you freak out if I hug you?"

She smiled. "I think I can handle it."

He wrapped his arms around her, his mouth close to her ear. "Thank you."

"You're welcome."

She let go and tucked a stray braid behind her ear. "I'll run across the way and get you some new threads. Then we can figure out the other details."

"If you keep being this nice to me, I'll never leave."

She waggled her eyebrows. "I've heard worse ideas. Be right back."

When she returned, she found him in the kitchen making brunch: scrambled eggs with cheese, toast, and a piping hot mug of coffee. She set the bag of clothes on the counter. "You didn't have to do this."

He shrugged. "It makes me feel less guilty. Here, tell me if this needs salt."

He held the spatula out to her with a chunk of egg on it and she took a bite. "Nope. Perfect as is."

"Sounds familiar," he teased, and she rolled her eyes.

"I got you a few different outfits, since I didn't know what you'd like. It should get you through for a while. The hard part is next: what exactly do you want to do now that you're fixed? Do you want to, uh, resume your primary objective?"

He watched her for a bit, still amused that she was tiptoeing around his profession. "I don't know. Without a memory, it's hard to say whether I had any resentment for it. I may get some of it back in fragments, but for now, no. I don't think I'll be doing that."

"Okay," she said. "What would you want to do for a living?"

He blinked. "I…don't think anyone's ever asked me that before."

"Well, you must like something," she said, sipping the coffee as he spooned the eggs onto a plate beside the toast. "Maybe that's what you should do for the next couple days. Read up and see what kind of preferences you have."

"What? You don't want me to work for you?"

"Oh," she said, apparently startled. "Um, I didn't know if you'd…want to do something like that."

"Something like what? What's wrong with being a mechanic?"

"Nothing," she said, but he noticed she wouldn't meet his gaze this time. "I just thought you would maybe think it was kind of beneath you or something."

"Seriously?" he asked, incredulous. "You saved my life with what you do. I have no room to look down on your profession, considering I probably spent my entire life just screwing people left and right for money. Has someone said that to you before?"

"It's not important," she said, taking the plate to the table. "I'd be fine if you want to work the front counter until you're on your feet again, metaphorically speaking."

"I'd like that, as long as it's no further imposition to you."

"Do what you want. That's what choice is all about, right?"

"So they tell me." He pointed towards the bag. "I'll change and then we can get going."

He emerged from the shower about fifteen minutes later, clean and smelling nice, his hair slightly damp. He'd changed into a simple black polo shirt, jeans, and boots. She'd even been thoughtful enough to get him a small vial of generic cologne. He had to hide another smile after he caught her looking at him, trying to be subtle about it. If nothing else, the girl provided plenty of unintentional entertainment.

They walked the two blocks to her shop. It was a modest place that had a storefront on one side and then opened up in the back. There was a Hispanic girl in coveralls that matched Akachi's at the front counter, typing something. Her brown eyes widened a bit when Andrew appeared, but the look wasn't unfriendly, to his relief.

"Hey," the girl said to Akachi. "Who's your friend?"

"This is Andrew," Akachi said. "The one I mentioned last night."

"Oh, my," the girl said, offering her hand. "Thank God you're alright. She told me what happened."

"Thanks. I'm only alright because of her. Nice to meet you, Miss…?"

"Ana Mendes."

"Nice to meet you, Ana."

"He's going to work the front counter until he figures things out," Akachi said. "I'll put my stuff back and then get started showing him around."

"Roger that."

He quickly found that the job was never dull. The hover cars and jets needed careful maintenance and a myriad of different tools to fix them. She sent him to the hardware store to replace the things she'd used to fix him and then spent the rest of the shift explaining the areas he'd be able to help with when he wasn't simply serving as cashier. Heavy lifting was the most valuable skill, as there were only four mechanics in the small store aside from Akachi and Ana. He also met Matt, the coworker who had helped Akachi transport him to her apartment after she'd found him in the dumpster. Everyone he'd met so far had been friendly and gracious. He had a strange sense that his previous life hadn't gone this well, that there were people he'd met that had been arrogant and condescending to him.

He helped them close up shop at the end of the night and waited for her to come back from depositing money in the safe.

"So I guess you don't have enough from today's shift for a hotel room?" Akachi asked.

"Doubtful, even on this side of town," he replied. "Why?"

She pursed her lips. "You know what I'm getting at."

He grinned. "I just wanted to hear you say it."

She rolled her eyes. "Vanity, thy name is Andrew."

"Well, I mean, if you don't want me to stay, I can just fold myself up in a corner in the store until morning."

"Ugh, fine. You can stay at my place until we find you one of your own."

"Why, thank you. You're so generous. How can I ever repay you?"

"By not being such a smarmy pain in the ass," she grumbled. "Take out the trash and we'll get going."

Andrew lugged the trash bags around back. There was a narrow alleyway between the buildings where the dumpsters were and it was Akachi's least favorite thing to do, and that was before the rainstorm pounding down on the city. So he did it for her.

He'd just tossed it in when he noticed he wasn't alone.

There was a guy standing with his back to the open part of the alley. Average height, dark slick hair, trenchcoat and a navy suit, black shoes, no umbrella in spite of the heavy rain. He didn't really look like he belonged there. He definitely wasn't a bum and Andrew hadn't seen him in any of the other stores as an employee.

"Can I help you?" Andrew asked warily.

"You're Cherry's boy-toy, ain't ya?"

Andrew adopted a neutral look. "I don't know anyone by that name. Sorry."

"Makes sense," the guy said. "Last I heard, they dumped you. Guess this is where you ended up. Weird, though. Usually people scrap droids if they find 'em. Shop owner must have a soft heart."

The man grinned. "Or a wet pussy."

"Look," Andrew snapped, "what do you want? I haven't got all damn night."

"I knew your owner. She's moved on, but I got a few clients who would fancy ya. What do you say you come with me and resume your previous line of work?"

Andrew balled his hands into fists. "I like where I am. I think I'll stay."

"You don't belong here, boy. I got bigger plans for you. Now, am I going to have to tune you up or are you going to listen to reason?"

"I don't care who you are. I'm not going."

The man shrugged. "Have it your way, Tin Man. I can still take you back in pieces."

He withdrew a shock baton and lunged at Andrew. Andrew dodged. The man lashed at him in quick movements, and blue sparks popped in the rain mere inches from his torso. He kept backing up, knowing that he couldn't attack thanks to the robotic laws known as the Asimov protocols hard-wired into his system. The guy was blocking his way out and Andrew was running out of room to retreat. He couldn't go back into the shop and risk Akachi's safety.

"Nowhere left to go, Tin Man," the guy chuckled darkly. "Say goodnight."

"You first," a cold female voice spoke from the darkened doorway of the shop.

They both glanced up to see Akachi standing there with a .38 Smith and Wesson in her hand.

She stepped out into the rain and didn't even flinch as it doused her in seconds. "Drop it."

The guy spat at her feet. "You ain't got the nerve, little—"

She shot at the concrete an inch from his foot. The bullet ricocheted into the wall beside him and he jumped out of his skin.

"Drop. It."

The man sneered, but let the shock baton go and it fizzled out as soon as it left his hand. "So now you've got a new madam, huh? She fight all your battles for you?"

"Get out of here."

"Fine. I'm a patient man. She won't always be here to protect you, Tin Man."

He shuffled off into the cool, wet darkness. She didn't lower the gun until he was out of sight. Then a great sigh flowed through her. "Are you alright?"

Andrew nodded numbly. "C'mon, we'd better get inside."

They walked inside the garage and she shut and locked the outer door, resting the gun on one of the nearby work benches.

"Can't leave you alone for two seconds," she mused, squeezing as much rain out of her braids as possible and then wiping her face with a clean towel from the supply room. She tossed him one as well, and they dried off as best as they could. Her expression sobered at his silence. "Any chance you knew who he was?"

Andrew shook his head. "All he said was he knew my previous owner, and he wanted me. Doesn't sound like he's as interested in my sparkling personality as you are."

He glanced at the garage door, listening to the rain pound against the other side. "That's the end of the line."

"Once the rain lets up, we can file a police report for the attack and—"

"I appreciate the thought, but you and I both know it's not going to work."

She frowned. "Why not?"

"I'm an android, Akachi. Technically speaking, I don't have any rights."

"Look, the guy threatened me as much as he threatened you. Behavior like that can't go unanswered."

"And it won't. I'll just have to…" He sighed. "I'll have to go."

"What?" she demanded.

"I can't guarantee he won't come back looking for revenge," Andrew said. "You shouldn't have to put yourself in harm's way on my behalf, not when you've already done so much to help me. It wouldn't be all that hard for me to disappear."

"Andrew, there has got to be a better way," Akachi said fiercely. "You can't let him take away your future."

"I wouldn't have a future at all if you hadn't saved me."

She fell silent, stunned by the frankness of his words. He stepped a little closer, holding her hand, his voice quiet but steady. "I told you I wanted to repay you. A life for a life. A man like that is going to come back with reinforcements. He'll burn this place to the ground and you along with it. I can't let that happen."

Akachi swallowed hard, staring at their clasped hands. She squared her shoulders and met his gaze. "And what about the next person after him? What if you run and you just find another bastard looking to exploit you? Will you just keep going? Where does that path end, Andrew?"

"I don't have a choice—"

"Yes, you do. You let me disable the Asimov protocols and you put the fear of God into that little weasel."

Andrew stiffened. "Akachi, that's illegal."

"So is threatening someone's life and attacking them with a shock baton."

"If the authorities find out you tampered with my protocols, that's ten years in federal prison."

Akachi smiled. "Then don't get caught, lover boy."

He gritted his teeth. "Are you always this stubborn?"

"Why else do you think I'm single?"

He caught her shoulders. "I'm being serious. It's not worth *your life*."

"Maybe, maybe not," she said softly. "But it is worth *your life*."

He searched her gaze for a long moment and then sighed again, leaning his forehead against hers. "You're going to give me an ulcer, woman."

"Sometimes I have that effect."

"No shit." He straightened up a bit. "If we go through with this, then I want your word that if everything goes south, you pack up and leave town. I don't care where you go. You run and you don't look back. Promise me."

Akachi nodded. "I promise."

He kissed her forehead. "Then let's get to work."

* * *

"Well, well, well," the thin man said, chewing on the end of a fat cigar as he watched Andrew stroll into the office. "The Tin Man came to his senses."

He nodded to the burly man on his right. "Search 'im, Russell."

"Spread 'em, pretty boy," the large man grunted.

Andrew stretched out his arms and legs. Russell patted him down, finding no weapons. "He's clean."

He shoved Andrew towards the desk, on which the android spotted a name plate reading *The Comfort Company*, and beneath it, *Carmine Fiacci, President*. Carmine had his legs up on the desk, his cheap suit spread open to show the shock baton holstered at his waist.

"I apologize for my earlier rudeness," Carmine said with a toothy grin. "But I know a good droid when I see one. I'm guessing that you don't remember our association."

"Fortunately, I don't," Andrew answered, crossing his arms. "Feel free to enlighten me."

Carmine spat out a smoke ring before continuing. "Your former owner, Cherry, well, she was one of those gals who was in a loveless marriage. She bought you at an auction to keep her bed warm while her husband was out in the streets. Turns out hubby was the jealous type and he's not a fan of the, uh, mixed laundry, I'll say. When he found out she had a literal side piece, he went a bit overboard on correcting the perceived injustice. That's how you ended up disassembled and poor little Cherry ended up in the ICU."

Andrew's eyes narrowed. "He got a name, this jealous husband?"

"Shawn Walters. We went to the same high school, kept in touch. Lives in New Brookhaven. Nice man when he doesn't lose his temper."

Andrew snorted. "Sure he is."

"Well, that's all in the past, Andy," Carmine said. "We're going to have you work the Alpharetta district. Plenty of high rollers that like the dark chocolate. You agree to work for us and we leave your cutie pie mechanic alone. Sound good?"

Andrew rubbed his chin. "You know, normally, it would."

Carmine narrowed his eyes. "Normally?"

"Yeah. I mean, I am an android. I was designed by people to be a perfect imitation of life but without all those pesky notions of choice. I was designed to be a tool, to be used again and again without wearing out. To bring 'comfort' to those in need."

Andrew flattened his hands on Carmine's desk and leaned in, smirking. "And let's just say that I found someone who needs me more than you do."

Carmine sneered. "Think about what you're doing, boy. It ain't gonna end well."

Andrew nodded. "You're right. It's not gonna end well."

His smirk sharpened. "For you."

Andrew lifted one fist and smashed Carmine's right kneecap with it.

Carmine howled in pain and tumbled backwards onto the floor. Andrew whirled around in time for Russell to grab him and slam him down onto the desk. He dodged to one side as the big man's fist slammed down on it hard enough to leave a dent in the metal. Russell reached for the laser pistol in his jacket, but Andrew grabbed his wrist, pointing it out at the far wall. Russell's wrist crunched under Andrew's powerful grip and he let out a roar of pain, dropping the pistol onto the floor. He gripped Andrew's neck with his free hand and slammed his head into the desk repeatedly.

The pain nearly blinded him, but Andrew ignored it and flattened his hand against the big man's chest, blindly searching for his rib cage.

And once he found it, he delivered one precise punch.

That shattered Russell's ribs and caused them to impale his heart.

The big man died instantly, slumping to the floor in a heap.

Andrew only had a second to recover; Carmine popped up from behind his desk with the shock baton, jabbing it at his torso. "Hold still, you son of a bitch!"

Andrew launched himself back in a roll and came up on one knee, blocking with his forearms as the baton sliced through the air in an arc. The volts shocked his system as soon as it touched him, sending excruciating pain through every circuit, every artificial nerve, searing him clean down to his metal skeleton. It didn't matter how artificial his intelligence and framework; pain was pain, and it was as real as anything else.

Andrew crumpled onto his knees, shaking his head as his vision glitched, struggling to correct itself. Carmine limped from on top of the desk and held the weapon aloft, panting, his gravelly voice sinister. "You think you can just waltz in here and shut me down, Tin Man? Just 'cause your little girlfriend can override some code? Fine. I'll reprogram you to kill her instead."

Carmine swung again.

Andrew ducked at the last second. Too late, Carmine realized he'd swung with all his might and he hit himself in the shin. He shrieked as the volts tore through him and fried him instantly. His twitching corpse hit the carpet beside Russell's.

Slowly, Andrew pushed to his feet. He collected the baton from Carmine's limp grip and then walked out of the office.

Akachi stood outside in the empty parking lot, holding a bottle of vodka. She offered it to him. He thanked her and took a long pull for the pain before handing it back to her. She stuck a rolled-up handkerchief into the bottle and then lit it once the alcohol soaked through. Then she hefted it and threw it inside the office's open door. It didn't take long before the lone building went up in flames, destroying the evidence.

Akachi glanced at the shock baton, lifting an eyebrow. "A souvenir?"

"No," Andrew said. "Just need it for one last loose end in New Brookhaven."

He stood beside her, watching the building burn. "Think we'll be alright?"

Akachi held his hand, her smile bright in the firelight.

"We'll survive."

Progenitor

Kay Mabasa

THE PROGENITOR could only work in Africa, for that is where the spirits of African descents, regardless of where they died in the world, ultimately returned. That was how Shavonne Jacobson, an eighteen-year-old African American, Philly-born orphan, had found herself at the Joshua Mqabuko Nkomo International Airport with her eyes closed and tears rolling down her ebon cheeks.

She'd heard of the overwhelming rush that hit an African descendant when they stepped onto African soil. It was said to be so strong that it felt like it could knock you off your feet. Many called this sensation *the hug from the ancestors*, because ancestors were welcoming back the children that had been taken during the transatlantic slave trade.

Many disputed this mystical sensation, claiming that it was merely a psychological feeling, nothing spiritual was actually happening, no ancestors were hugging their long-lost children. It was simply the built-up anticipation of returning to one's ancestral land.

Shavonne obviously had her doubts about the hug from the ancestors. She'd believed that she wouldn't feel a thing.

How could she?

It just wasn't possible.

But she felt the sudden hit as soon as she alighted from the plane. It knocked the wind right out of her and then something warm flooded inside her like someone had just crashed into her and was now embracing her.

Shavonne caught her breath and reminded herself that she'd come here for more than the ancestral hug. She was here to see her ancestors face-to-face and talk to them so she could know her home country.

The Progenitor had been invented by accident by a fifteen-year-old Zimbabwean, back in 2150. It was said that the girl was trying to make a time machine app for a school project but it somehow took her to her ancestral plane where she met her great, great, great grandfather.

This accidental invention had been a breakthrough for many who didn't know where they came from, especially African Americans whose ancestors had been sold into slavery. Yes, there was the Heritage DNA test that gave an individual the geographic origins of their ancestors, but the results were not always accurate and were less so for those who did not possess European roots. The Progenitor, on the other hand, told one exactly where in Africa they came from – including the very village and tribe – before their ancestor had been sold into slavery. It told them of their family name and if there were any living family members in Africa that were willing to meet them through the Progenitor Family Tree App.

Shavonne pushed her Aidlator into her ear and tapped it for it to turn on. The Aidlator beeped and, speaking into her ear, it told her of how it could translate any foreign language she heard into English and then translate her response from English to the language of her choice through an invisible mouthpiece that curved down from the earpiece to the front part of her mouth.

Shavonne being in Bulawayo meant that the Aidlator would turn her English into Ndebele, which was the local language. Most people in Bulawayo spoke English well enough but Shavonne wanted to try out the Aidlator before she got to speak to her ancestors who, like most older African ancestors, could not speak English.

She grabbed her suitcase and rolled it over to a self-driving hover imota. Shavonne took her cellphone out of the back pocket of her jeans, scanned the QR code off the imota, typed in her destination and paid the twenty-dollar fee. The hover imota made a soft beep and a door slid open. She then placed her suitcase in the car storage, got into the imota and the door closed behind her. The imota then lifted off the ground and smoothly merged into traffic, giving off a smooth 'swoosh' sound as it drove forward.

It made a small beep and a robotic soprano voice came through the intercom, "English, Shona, Ndebele, Venḓa—"

"Ndebele," Shavonne replied with a clearing of her throat.

Ndebele words came out to her and her Aidlator translated each word into English, "Thank you for choosing to ride with us this afternoon, my name is Sipho," the hover imota said as it drove around a slow-moving silver hover imota in front of her, "I'll be taking you to Imuli Progenitor Resort, which is twenty minutes away, but with traffic I estimate that it will take forty-three minutes to get there.

"To drink I have mineral water, blueberry iced tea and Mazoe Orange Crush, which is a local favourite. For snacks, I have roasted pumpkin seeds, dried pawpaw and cow tongue. My music selection today is Jah Prayzah, Anita Jackson and Winky D. And if you want to watch a movie instead, I have, *Yellow Card*, *Everyone's Child* and *Jit*."

"I'll try Mazoe and cow tongue, and I'd prefer music, whatever artist you pick will be fine," Shavonne replied absentmindedly as she looked at the colourful skyscrapers in the city.

Sipho beeped twice, "Great choice." Music poured out from the speakers and a tray sprouted out in front of her with a carton of Mazoe, a plate of cow tongue and hand sanitizer.

Shavonne squirted out the hand sanitizer and rubbed it on her hands before picking up the animal's tongue. She nibbled, unsure if she'd like it, but was pleasantly surprised that it tasted like roasted beef, only richer.

While she ate, Shavonne tapped at her phone and looked through the digital Progenitor pamphlet once more to make sure that when the time came to summon her ancestors she would not make a mistake. After all, she would not get assistance once she stepped into the Progenitor. She'd be alone, for foreign blood offended the dead and only she and another family member could step into her ancestral plane.

Once at the Imuli Progenitor Resort, Shavonne went to the front desk and paid five thousand dollars for a one-bedroomed en-suite which came with the Progenitor Space where she would summon her ancestors. Zimbabwe was among the cheapest places for an African descendent to track their family lineage, since it wasn't among the African countries that had lost its children to the transatlantic slave trade.

Countries that had a history of being involved in the transatlantic slave trade were expensive for African Americans to track their family bloodline, for they were places most swarmed-to because the ancestral signal was stronger there. And for those who had the money, they had to book months before they could go. Shavonne, unable to spend five figures on the Progenitor and possessing no patience for the months-long wait list, had chosen Zimbabwe, which was one of the furthest African countries from those who'd lost children to slavery. This meant that it was among the cheapest and had a weaker signal.

The pamphlet had also said that Zimbabwe was one of the most peaceful places in Africa, with welcoming people, which further made it an easy choice for Shavonne. So was Zambia, which was closer to both DRC and Tanzania where the ancestral signal would have been stronger if her homeland was DRC or Tanzania, but she would have had to pay eight thousand dollars for one room per night.

"The Progenitor Space will be where your ancestors will gather," the receptionist said in Ndebele with a charming smile.

"That's the part I don't understand," Shavonne said through the invisible part of the Aidlator. It absorbed her English so he wouldn't hear that and all he heard were the translated words in Ndebele being spoken through the Aidlator mouthpiece. "The Progenitor Space. Do the ancestors come from wherever it is they are and huddle in the room or does the room…umm, I mean Space, go up into the air where the ancestors are, carrying me with it?"

He smiled and made a little bow with his head before speaking. "It's sort of both. The Progenitor, I'm sure you read, is a combination of the spiritual and scientific. The Space or room, whichever is easier for you to understand, is designed to keep you safe in the ancestral plane as well as weathering the conditions there, which, again I'm sure you read, are a little volatile.

"All I can say is there was a time when spirit mediums used to exist. And the spirits would be able to reach them and possess them in order to communicate with their family. So the Progenitor Space acts as a big medium able to be possessed by one's bloodline as well as safely contain them so they can meet their ancestors. Is that clear enough for you?"

Shavonne nodded. "Yes it is."

"Just to reassure you, because I know that it's scary to some, it's a hundred percent safe and many people who've done it loved it and you will too. Some come back to visit with family, some come back to ask their ancestors for advice, and believe it or not some come back for ancestral vacations."

"Safe you say, but you made me sign a waiver?"

He chuckled. "For precaution. We've never had any fatalities."

"But other resorts have?"

"Yes," he bit his bottom lip. "But the cases are usually because the customer stayed too long in the ancestral plane while having a medical condition. But looking at your form here you're as fit as a sable," he said with a chuckle.

"And what about the cases that didn't involve medical reasons?" She raised a brow.

He chuckled and scratched the back of his head. "Mostly those have to do with customers offending their ancestors. Are you thinking of backing out?" She shook her head with a smile and he handed her a brown wooden box. "That's the key to your room, as well as the Ancestors' Bite, to teleport you to the ancestral plane as I'm sure you read in our pamphlet."

Shavonne took in a deep breath and accepted the wooden block with a lump in her throat and her heart wildly beating.

"And remember to get a male elder's first name and surname, along with their parents' names, both their mother's and father's names, so you can track your living African family members in Africa through our Progenitor Family Tree App."

Shavonne smiled at the receptionist and then followed after a robotic bag trolley, its name, Umsizi, reflected on its shiny silver face where a head would be on a human. It carried her luggage in its robotic arms, rolling ahead of her and taking her to her room.

Umsizi stopped by a door, Room 14, and waited for her to open it. Shavonne pushed the wooden block into a square-shaped depression that was in the centre of the wooden door. A click sounded, the door swung open, and the block pushed back out of the door for her to retrieve.

Shavonne walked in and was immediately met with the large Progenitor Space that would house her ancestors.

Umsizi placed her luggage on the floor, beeped and then spoke in Ndebele, but Shavonne heard the Aidlator, "Hope you have a pleasant stay."

"Thank you," she said and she heard the Aidlator translate her English, "ngiyabonga."

Umsizi stood there with its two empty robotic hands still held out.

"I said thank you." Shavonne shook her head in confusion.

Umsizi beeped and spoke again, "Hope you have a pleasant stay."

Looking at the robot's hands held out, she noticed QR codes embedded in its palms. "Of course." She pulled out her phone from her jeans, scanned the code and tipped the robot with ten dollars.

Umsizi beeped again. "Thank you." And it rolled out on its wheels, exiting the room.

Alone in the room, Shavonne prepared herself. She had to take a good bath before meeting her ancestors or they might not come because they saw it as offensive, especially the older ancestors whom she needed to meet so she could get their names and their parents' names for her to find her living family members in Africa.

After her bath, she wore her favourite yellow, brown and gold African dress that matched her brown and yellow African-pattern nails and then she forced herself to eat a traditional meal that had no salt and a lot of water, which also was to appease her ancestors as well as to keep her hydrated and nourished because the ancestral plane was draining on a living body.

When she was ready, Shavonne moved into the Progenitor Space and studied the room. The floor was black, so were the walls, and the ceiling was black too, but there were bright neon-yellow symbols shining down; symbols, as she had read, that would ward off evil ancestors. These were ancestors who'd done evil in their past lives and for whom no family members had done the cleansing ceremony when they'd died. Ancestors who had murdered or had sold their own people into slavery and had not been cleansed would only want to harm her. The other symbols were to appease the ancestors and invite them to meet with her.

She padded, barefoot, to the centre of the room where there was a beetle-shaped depression in the middle of the black wooden floor. Shavonne knelt by the hole in the floor, showing her ancestors the customary respect. She then opened the wooden box and inside the box was a golden steel beetle that would work as her key to the ancestral plane. She took the beetle out of the box and fixed an index finger between its antlers. "I seek to find my people that death took from me," she said and cut her finger on the antlers, drawing blood.

She held her bleeding finger over the beetle-shaped hole in the floor for the drops of blood to fall into, she then placed the golden beetle in the hole and turned it clockwise, as if opening a door.

The lights went out in the Space and something like thunder rolled above her; flashes of what seemed like yellow lightning danced by the ceiling. It began to rain cold heavy drops of water and a pool of water started to form, rising all around her. When it stopped raining Shavonne found herself neck deep in a pool of cold water. She stood up and the cold water danced around her waist.

The place where she'd fixed the Ancestors' Bite into the floor began to glow a warm yellow light beneath the water. The light then turned into a flame that grew bigger. A yellow flame leapt out from this fire and landed with a splash into the water. The flame danced and grew before her, forming into a yellow-flamed man. Just as the flames were dying down on the man another yellow flame leapt out, and another, and another, until the Space burned in a bright yellow. The sounds of crackling fire filled the room like static. The flames around her all slowly died down and strange ebon faces took their place.

"Shavonne, is that really you?" She heard a woman say. She turned to where she'd heard it come from and a woman frowning and touching her head, dressed in a floral blue and lavender dress – the dress she'd picked for the funeral home to dress her mother in – approached her.

"Mama," she heard herself say, her voice breaking as tears spilled out.

"Shavonne?" her mother said with a shake of her head as she reached out to touch her daughter. Her mother's arms went through Shavonne. She knew they would but had hoped the signal would be strong enough for her to feel her mother's touch. Her mother's face contorted at this, "Why can't I touch you?" She then looked around, "What's this place? And why do I have a headache?"

"It's the ancestral plane," Shavonne replied, knowing that her mother had been wandering half asleep in the plane for years without knowing it or the people around her because her memory had died the day she'd died – with no family having done the awakening ritual to wake her. Such traditional practices had stopped in the twenty-first century. But now because of the Progenitor, a combination of the spiritual and the scientific, her mother's memory was temporarily fixed for them to meet, and it was this temporary memory fixing that was making her head hurt.

"Elizabeth," Shavonne heard a man's voice call, and a man with bushy eyebrows crumpled into a frown as he held his head, approached her mother. "Elizabeth, is that you?"

She watched her parents reach out and hold each other (for spirits could touch). Turning back to her, her mother looked to Shavonne, "You remember our little girl don't you, Kwan?"

The man turned from his wife and looked at Shavonne. "Well, well, how you've grown, my Little Queen."

Shavonne laughed at the mention of her nickname, remembering how she got it when she refused to be called Princess instead of Queen. So her father had called her 'Little Queen' instead. He reached for her and his arms went through her. Both her father and mother frowned at this and Shavonne, with her voice nearly breaking, explained why that was.

"Kwan," a woman's voice called.

They all turned to where an old woman was staring at him, reminding Shavonne of how the Space was filled with strange faces all staring at them, trying to wake their memories up. The woman who called her father was her paternal grandmother, a woman Shavonne had never had the pleasure of meeting until now.

Other family members called for their loved ones as their memories began to piece together, and Shavonne was introduced to them one-by-one until the time came when the American-born members of her family were to meet with the Africans, who stood at the opposite end of the Space, huddled together intently watching Shavonne and her family.

Shavonne, being the one who'd summoned them, approached them. She touched a hand to her chest. "Shavonne, my name is Shavonne Jacobson." They cocked their heads at her and frowned.

A little girl dressed in modern clothes, which meant that she had recently died, was holding an old man's hand whom Shavonne believed to be the girl's grandfather. She stepped forward and spoke.

Shavonne's Aidlator beeped then, detecting the language. "African French," the Aidlator announced. And so she spoke again and this time her introduction was translated into African French.

The man holding on to the little girl stepped forward and spoke. "I speak English just fine," he said.

"But for the sake of your family," Shavonne said with a wave of her hand, indicating the people standing behind the old man, "I think it's best we stick to French," she replied, the Aidlator absorbing her words and speaking out in French.

The man cocked his head. "Your lips move funny," he said in African French, "they don't match the words coming out of your mouth."

Shavonne had to restrain herself from asking who the man was and where it was that he came from, which was the very thing she was aching to know instead of answering questions. She knew they would not fully understand the answers she had, but she had to be respectful, ancestors were easily offended when rushed. "It's a device," she said slowly. "It changes my English into French."

"Some of my people, the older generation, do not speak French," the man said. "Does your device speak Éwé?"

The Aidlator beeped and told Shavonne that Éwé was spoken in Benin, Ghana, Togo and Western Nigeria.

"Do you come from Western Nigeria?" she asked, the Aidlator absorbing her English and giving out the words in Éwé. She had many family members who were of Nigerian ancestry and wasn't surprised if she'd end up a part of that large and proud heritage.

The man shook his head,

"Ghana then," Shavonne said with a tremor of excitement in her voice; she liked the idea of being Ghanaian because of how peaceful and colourful the people were.

The man and little girl both shook their heads.

"Togo?" she asked, wishing she knew more about Togo and its people.

The little girl was the first to nod her head, then the old man nodded as well.

"But who are you?" he asked.

"My name is Shavonne Jacobson," she spoke, her words coming out faster than she intended, but she couldn't help herself. She'd just found out where home was. "And these," she turned to look at her parents, "are my family and your family too. We were sold to the white man, placed on ships...big boats," she said, remembering that some of her ancestors were from an older time in which they'd never seen a ship, "which crossed the sea over to what was called at that time the New Country...America, a faraway land across the sea. It took a long time for us to get back our freedom, and back home, but here we are."

The old woman and her people nodded. And smiles slowly appeared on their faces.

An old woman dressed in animal skin walked to the front and pointed a wrinkled finger past Shavonne.

"Agbeko," she said, "is that you my son?"

A well-built boy with chains bound to his feet and hands walked over to her. The chains round his feet rattled as he approached the old woman. "Mama!" he called.

She walked over to him and wrapped her arms round his waist. "They took you from me, my boy."

Tears rolled down his ebon cheeks as he held his mother. "I know, Mama, I know."

"So they took you to this faraway land that Shabon is telling us of?" she asked, mispronouncing Shavonne's name.

"I did not make it," he said sorrowfully. "I died on the boat and they threw me into the sea."

His mother's chest puffed up as she took in deep breaths before letting out a wail.

More family members crossed over, closing the space between the Africans and African Americans, as families that had been torn apart so long ago reunited with tears and laughter.

All that was unfolding before Shavonne, the remembering and meeting of family, must have taken a good five hours but to Shavonne it felt as if only an hour had passed.

When the tearful reunion of those taken with those who had been left behind was done, Shavonne and her American family found out that their family name was Kossi and their totem was the elephant.

They also gave her an Éwé first name, Adzido, which meant, 'from the sea' and she had indeed been brought to them from the sea.

She then asked the old man for his name and that of his parents and explained to them that she wanted to find her living family members that were in Togo.

Now knowing her home, surname and totem from her African family, Shavonne asked her taken family to share with her the memory of the day they were taken, and as they did the black Space spattered away as pieces of their world appeared around them. They walked her through their memories of when the white man came to their land and when they had walked through The Door of No Return to the big boats that took them to the New Country.

The pool of water that had reached her waist was now a puddle on the floor, which meant the time with her ancestors was nearly up and she would soon be cast out of the ancestral plane. Shavonne's eyes watered as she told them this but told them that she would visit them again soon.

Their faces began to fade as the floor dried and Shavonne found herself in the empty Space with her eyes still wet from the goodbyes.

She went onto the Family Tree app and inserted her family name and the first name of the old man and those of his parents. A hologram of a family tree appeared. It had many tiny leaves of green for the living family members in Africa, brown for the deceased and black which covered the name and details of the family members who were unavailable and didn't want to participate in the Progenitor reunification for whatever reasons. Shavonne wasn't going to be bothered by those who did not want to meet their taken family members when there were many others from her family who wanted to meet up with them. She found a cousin who was around her age, Susu, and loved how welcoming her bio read. She pressed at Susu's cellphone number that was displayed on her leaf.

Shavonne sat down on the wooden floor, legs crossed, and brushed away at a tear. It was only then that she thought to look at the time on her phone – 00:40, far too late to be calling – but before she could ring off, a hologram of Susu popped up into the air before her.

"It says here that you found me through the Progenitor Family Tree App," she spoke in English but with a heavy African French accent and yawned.

"Yes," was all that Shavonne could think to say.

"You're American?"

"And Togolese," she said proudly with her chin out.

"Yes, yes you are," her cousin said, holding her own chin out. "So how soon can you come home?" she asked.

"I have to know what city you're in first and also look for a place to stay. What Airbnb would you recommend?"

"You're my cousin. I don't care how distant. You'll be staying here at home with me for however long you want."

Shavonne smiled and her cousin, her living African family member, smiled back, and with this Shavonne felt she was finally home.

A Manual on Different Options of How to Bring a Loved One to Life

Oyedotun Damilola Muees

11. Join a Telegram Cyberware Group

TUTU ARRANGED the meeting between Harafat and the haberdasher at the end of the clustering shops in Balogun Market. Harafat squeezed through the crowds as traders called out their wares. Several times, sweaty teenage boys asked if she was interested in a new phone.

Harafat ignored them, walking into the designated shop, sighting a rotund man working on a sewing machine. The greetings were casual.

"Tutu sent me," Harafat said, scanning the three-piece suits, jackets worn on a mannequin. The man went to hand her a folded piece of paper but hesitated halfway through and stared into her eyes.

"She says you can be trusted," the man said. "I hope she's telling the truth."

* * *

Harafat sat in a cybercafé, stealing gazes at strange faces to be sure she wasn't followed. The piece of paper she received was a link to join a secret Telegram group where black market prosthetics were traded. Tutu's words were sacrosanct concerning this group. *These are the people you need if you want Azeezat to be whole again.*

She typed the link into her browser, which directed her to her Telegram app. The first step was to create a username, upload a pic for her avatar. A red warning appeared, indicating that a personal name and photo was against the group's policy. She picked the name Zizi.

A torrent of messages scrolled up as soon as Zizi was confirmed as a new member upon ticking and clicking the terms and conditions. Unknown users greeted her, speaking esoteric terms she didn't understand. Every user was selling a product or offering a service. *A Black Clinic for all kinds of implants, ready to serve you. Installation of Black Ice for your home. Bagman is recruiting. A veteran Double Tap who never misses, DM right away. Joygirl to ride you to eternity. A reliable Shoemaker is one click away.* Perplexed, she should have asked Tutu what kind of users roam this virtual community. Earlier, she had mentioned anonymity was their watchword. She kept reading the messages, deleting infuriating ads popping up intermittently. Her palms were clammy, itching to type something.

Zizi: Hello! I am in need of prosthetics.

Users began to refer her, sending her DMs, asking which part she needs. Amid the lot, one user struck her as a good person — The Owl. Zizi replied.

Zizi: Hi. Do you have what I need?

The Owl: Depends on the size of your wallet.

Zizi sent a voice note, expatiating her spec.

The Owl: TBT.

She was confused, not sure of what to reply.

The Owl: Talking by Typing. Did you read the agreement form? Background?

Harafat could be a Black Agent or Ronin sent to infiltrate the group. The Owl had to be careful.

* * *

"I met a user on the group who is requesting to know my background." Harafat called Tutu, speaking in low tones, acting staid. "He wants to know about my background. What do I tell him?"

Tutu retorted with a snicker. "He is testing you. Greencorps has undercover agents in this community. Type RTFM back to him. This way he knows you are not greenhorn."

Again, Zizi is drawn into a more flustering state. But she did what Tutu said.

The Owl: You have just passed the first phase of the transaction. Keep your account active. I'll be in touch.

The Owl ended the chat abruptly. Zizi ignored the increasing unread messages from the other users.

07. Let The Professionals Handle It

Why stress yourself when the professionals can handle it? The suave advert on Harafat's television sneaked into her ears, waking her from sleep. She woke up, looking at her sister on the monitor, yearning for the day they would be together and doing the fun stuff that bonded them.

"What do you think of Greencorps? Should I allow them to fix Azeezat?" she asked her cat.

The brown and white streaked animal yawned, raxed, butt out. There were others who engaged in such business. Harafat knew the risk of meeting with such persons. The offense of a complicit is tantamount to the dealer involved — twelve years of hard labor.

You don't have to do that. A complete prosthetic is expensive. It will cost all your savings to make me whole again. Harafat read those words displayed on the monitor from the last chat with Azeezat, delighted that her sister still maintained her human nature despite being reduced to a texting machine. She wiped tears off her face, sending offline messages that there are other scientists who can handle the procedure at less cost.

Transfixed on the operation form in her hand, she read the bold words thoroughly, perusing the clauses gingerly. She trashed the form, tossing it into the waste bin. There's no way she would grant Greencorps access to every aspect of her life just to allow them to bring back her sister.

I can't wait for us to be together. I will do all I can to make this happen. Harafat had to type these words. Her sister needed to read it.

13. Explore Other Options

Harafat twirled on the single leather chair, right leg placed over the left, head slouching from the headrest. Rapt in webs of thought, she didn't hear her colleague, Iyke, calling for her attention. He tapped her on the arm, jolting her back to reality.

"A new batch for you," he said as he haphazardly pulled robotic parts from his cart and dropped them on the belt.

The parts made their way under an X-ray, and Harafat began to record their specifications.

Normally, they'd spend the time sharing Greencorps gossip. Rumors about the hot new female nanotech engineer, secret military projects, smart bullets made from titanium, the latest

AI-assisted government sting to crack down on "illegal" competition. Today, however, she was distracted, and Iyke seemed to be in a hurry.

Iyke turned his back and wheeled the cart back to Floor-Zero. Harafat browsed through the catalog of parts marked for destruction; perhaps one or two of them would be useful for her sister. She'd dedicated the past month to part-hunting. As a level-05 officer in Greencorps, she didn't have clearance to District-44, Floor-Zero, and the risk of entry was too high. A former coworker interloped into District-44 after stealing a level-11 officer's keycard. He didn't reach the second security clearance point before being taken down by a bioroid dog.

She surreptitiously snapped pictures of the parts. She abhorred her job as a recordkeeper but couldn't afford to be caught and lose her job. Every day she logged damaged experimental parts from the lab. At the end of the day, she wrote a detailed report of different robotic parts indexed by features and types. *Why build such prosthetics only to mark them for destruction?* Many people out there needed the parts to aid their body system. People like her sister would do anything to be *whole* again.

* * *

During her break time, Harafat met up with her best friend, Tutu, at the cafeteria. Tutu jumped into a conversation about a new guy she met on the You & Me dating app, and how this stranger was dishing out his love in excess. Harafat allowed her to finish talking before reminding her that the dating app was for cyborgs. Silence draped between them for a while. Chatters from colleagues flew around.

"What does it take to build an AI?" Harafat asked indistinctly.

Tutu scanned her eyes around, hoping no one heard her bodacious friend. Such talk in the company was highly forbidden.

"What do you need such information for?" Tutu darted back.

Harafat sent Tutu a text message, *I want to steal a full prosthetic.*

* * *

The bus stop was thronged with people. Harafat was stuck between a man with a prosthetic arm and an emo girl video-calling her boyfriend from the phone chip inserted in her palm. Inside the bus, thoughts raced through her head. Tutu's words were still fresh: *If you want to build an AI, then you will be needing a lot of parts. You can get semi-damaged ones, though I don't guarantee their longevity. Most people opt for functional and interactive. Unless you are wealthy, you cannot afford all the types of AI systems.* She was doused in perplexity, unsure of her next line of action. Though The Owl seemed convincing enough.

20. Go Out to Experience How the People Brought Back From the Dead Behave. Have A Feel Of Their World

Yesterday morning while Harafat prepared for work, The Owl sent her a message, requesting they meet at a rave — The Box — to finalize the deal.

The Box was in downtown Surulere, a place well-known for the exuberant and boisterous activities of its denizens. Tutu had tried to get her to go there several times, offering free drinks or introductions to some of her male friends, but how could she think of partying when Azeezat was lonely in the monitor, in the dark, with the cat? From the moment they uploaded Azeezat's consciousness into her personal hard drive, ebullient activities like drinking and having sex had become a thing of the past.

"I am going out later tonight," Harafat said over the phone to Tutu. "I am meeting a friend at the Box. I could use your company."

* * *

Tutu clenched onto the right arm of her boyfriend — he had one metal leg and hand.

"Harafat, meet Collins. The guy I have been telling you about," Tutu said.

Music blasting from the Box reverberated around the innards of the walls as the three of them approached. Harafat had no penchant for insalubrious places like this. If her father were alive, he would condemn such outings, saying activities akin to orgiastic parties happened there. Thoughts of getting Azeezat back on her feet nudged her mind. *I should leave as soon as I finalize with him,* she concluded.

Collins was obviously wealthy. He bypassed the long queue. The burly sentries made way for him as soon as they sighted him. Inside, polychromatic disco balls pulsed to a loud thumping beat as iridescent spiral streaks splashed over the vivacious crowd. Metal music, harmless lasers, cyberdelic images, and half-naked geishas wearing bodywares pirouetted, performing acrobatics around a pole. Harafat checked her phone for The Owl's message. Nothing. Tutu pulled the two of them towards the bar, hand still clasped on Collins' arm. There she introduced Harafat to one of her friends while Collins ordered drinks. The lithe man, with an overgrown hairline, explained a riddle about how easily a man can get out of a sarcophagus before earth covers him up.

"I told you. He is the smartest fellow I have ever met," Tutu said after quaffing a shot of vodka.

Harafat's phone buzzed. It was The Owl.

I am here. Where are you?

Ecstatic, Zizi replied. *I am at the bar. How do I know it's you?*

Walk to the west wing. I will find you, The Owl texted back.

"I will be back," Harafat shouted into the ear of an animated Tutu grinding on Collins' crotch.

Sticky bodies bumped into her as she shoved her way through flesh and metal and cloth. The west wing was somewhat silent. Cyborgs and humans engaged in drugs — MDMA, ecstasy, nootropics. She knew these drugs; a department of Greencorps manufactured them. An emo girl wearing a mohawk approached her, asking if she was in need of company, leering at her.

"Come with me," the emo girl commanded. "The Owl awaits you."

Walking through a passage with graffiti on the wall, Harafat looked back, heart beating in fear of the unknown. She entered a room peopled with AI, cyborgs, and humans. The dim lights made it hard to see their faces.

"Where's the place?" Harafat asked.

"See for yourself."

Everyone there was engaged in teledildonics. They wore helmets with transparent tethered wires rooted into both sides of a device: an intercourse headware. According to the media, this device had been banned. Moaning clogged all around.

Her phone buzzed. *Are you enjoying the view?*

She peered, craning among the fun seekers to find The Owl. She tapped her feet nervously; the waiting made her heart drum in fear. The Owl might be a gangly hacker seated in front of his laptop, tracking all her movements to be sure she wasn't a spy. Perhaps he was a regular guy wearing spectacles, debonair and harmless. Another thought arose. He might be a grim-looking tattooed man with ruthless sentries at his command.

She didn't allow fragments of these thoughts to deter her mission. Sound from a stiletto sneaked into her ear from a lady donning in a red velvet gown, cat-walking with an untainted aplomb. This stranger approached, shared in her space before focusing on the fun seekers. She pulled out a cigar, lit it, drew in, and puffed out.

"Before you carry on with the acquisition of the prosthetics, I want you to know that whoever is wearing it will experience a change of lifestyle. They will spend more time with people of their community," the lady said.

Harafat paused for few seconds, processing those words.

"Wait! Are you The Owl?" Harafat spilled out those words eager to leave her mouth.

"Do you have my money?" Another draw in, and puff out.

Harafat scoffed.

"RTFM," she responded. "Payment can only be exchanged when the buyer gets the goods. Read The Fucking Manual," The Owl spelled it out in full. "I underrated you. I was wrong."

* * *

Harafat got home at midnight, plopped on the chair, her cat snuggled into her arms. Her face clouded with gaiety. A feeling of accomplishment festooned around her neck. The next line of action was to meet the new nanotech engineer.

23. If It Is Body Parts You Have Chosen, Do All You Can Within Your Power To Acquire Them

The conditions for acquiring a body for Azeezat were overwhelming. The Owl gave her two tough options when she noticed Harafat could not afford it.

"We know you work for Greencorps. You have access to District-44, Floor-Zero. Help us to help you. A win-win situation for us," The Owl said. "Or you can take up a wetwork job. I'll be in touch."

* * *

"How the hell am I supposed to gain access to Floor-Zero? It's beyond my clearance." Harafat spurted the words to her cat, who in turn emitted a calm *meow* response. "Worse, she wants me to assassinate someone. What if I get caught or killed in the process?"

She browsed through the identity of the man that she was meant to kill, should she accept this mission. He was a sexagenarian ripperdoc whose specialty was genetic engineering and making biochips. Harafat had no business asking for the reason The Owl wanted him dead. A 9mm had been housed in a case for her to pick up at a gambling shop.

The façade to the Black Clinic the target worked at was a bookshop. She walked in and brought out the card containing information on her client.

"I am here to see Pacman," Harafat said, pulling the parka over her head.

The receptionist ran Harafat's identity through the monitor to confirm that she had an appointment at Black Clinic.

"What did you say your name was again?" the receptionist asked, balancing the convex lens on the bridge of her nose.

Harafat's heart began to race. *Pull the 9mm on her, requesting to see the target. If she resists, kill them both.* Quickly, she waved away the malevolent thoughts, walking away. The Owl sent her a message at 18:00, hoping to hear the news about the death of Pacman. The question mark at the end of the message caused her to goose pimple.

Harafat had come too far to capitulate. *I will finish what I started. No matter what it takes,* Harafat concluded, going back to her tummy sit-ups. This tempestuous situation would not deter her.

* * *

Iyke came to her that afternoon at work, wearing a smiling face.

"I hear the new engineer is not friendly," Harafat segued. Iyke spilled out his speculations. Jane sternly kept male colleagues at bay, shunning them each time they asked her out for a drink or two. Perhaps the lady wasn't into the nerdy type.

Harafat lingered at the reception after closing hours, waiting for Jane to clock out. The moment Jane moved past the automatic glass door, Harafat scampered after her, introducing herself, asking if Jane would like to have a drink. *Who would have thought Jane refused her male colleagues because she was into girls?* She agreed, following Harafat to a bar.

Their outings became regular — Jane's house — bar — hotel — The Box.

* * *

"I hear there has been a groundbreaking discovery in cloning. Rumor has it that you are heading the project." Harafat poked Jane on the nose. Jane rolled over, trailed the streamline on Harafat's naked body.

"I am not allowed to speak on that," Jane said. "I could go to jail for divulging such top-secret information."

Harafat switched the mood, removing herself from Jane.

"Tell me what you want?" Jane asked.

"I have always wanted to see the inside of Floor-Zero," Harafat said, moving closer to kiss Jane's lips.

31. Watch Out For Glitches. Most Operations Are Prone To Them

Harafat did her part. Impatience smothered her existence after she read the message from The Owl. *We have picked up the signal from Floor-Zero. Good job. You will hear from us soon.*

An accidental fire happened in District-44. The source, unknown. A five-man team of firefighters swept in to stop what might have metamorphosed into a conflagration. Harafat knew The Owl made it happen. She would rather spend time with her cat than think of the means by which the prosthetics would be transported surreptitiously without being spotted by security.

If management found out Jane had permitted a low-level officer into a restricted section, she would lose her job and then be handed over to the authorities for breach of trust. There had been cases of mismatched prosthetics carried out at Black Clinic. Harafat figured The Owl had a team of specialists on the ground to take care of her sister. Harafat's phone buzzed — a text message from The Owl, an address for a meeting.

The meeting point was at a warehouse, steel-covered shutter doors draped in transparent polythene bags. On a stainless stretcher was a dismembered bodyware — arms, legs, head, stomach casings, breasts, genitalia. The Owl told her the flaw in the stolen prosthetics was that they were meant for the military, a prototype for super soldiers.

42. Give The New Body Time To Adapt To The Change

The new look of Azeezat made Harafat tearful. A deluge of love jutted from her insides. She sat by Azeezat's new suit, waiting to hear her name from her sister's mouth, rather than the monitor's text.

"Hey sis," Harafat said. "It's nice to have you back."

The steely AI on the stretcher gazed around in minor jerks. Sounds from the switches in positions of the neck shot through the room. Azeezat stood up, gingerly checking out her new body in a standing mirror, making a fist, scanning the strange-looking faces.

"Azeezat, it's me Harafat. Remember I said I would get you a new body."

Dread seeped from Harafat's pores.

"What's happening? Why doesn't she recognize me?" Harafat asked, perturbed.

The Owl directed the question to the ripperdoc who handled the operation. He shrugged, checking her brain vitals on the monitor. One of The Owl's sentries diverted their attention to the news on the television. A man was addressing the journalists, Greencorps CEO, Ejike Adams. He was offering the sum of ten million naira to anyone who had useful information on the thieves who, cloaked as firefighters, stole something valuable from District-44. Azeezat moved closer, watching, listening to the sound of Adams.

"That man must die." an analog voice emanated from Azeezat.

Harafat envisaged what was about to happen. Her sister had blamed Adams for the ill-fated happenings that befell them. No one could stop her. She saw jeans, a burgundy turtleneck shirt, snapback, sunglasses, and moccasins — all were her size. The Owl encouraged Harafat to allow her sister to immerse herself in the wonders of the new suit. She felt played.

* * *

The CCTV in District-44 saw an unauthorized employee intrude in its compound. Harafat remained composed when authorities asked her to come with them. Inside a vast room with only steel chairs rooted to the ground and a table in the middle were Adams, Jane, two top-level officers, and two security officers.

"I know you used me to get the information I disclosed," Jane lashed out irefully. "For both our sakes. Please tell them where the suit is."

Harafat remained mute, ready to serve whatever penalty lay in wait for her. Adams offered her a deal, telling her how much the suit cost him, being a prototype. Still, Harafat said nothing. A security man came inside and went straight to Harafat, pulling her up. Another security officer held him by the arm, attempting to restrain him. In a single yank, he flung the paunch-bellied man against the wall, grabbing the other by the neck, raising him up while his leg flailed, gasping for breath. The security man dropped his attacker, and Harafat followed him when the coast was clear, glancing one last time at Jane. A shot passed through her ear, hitting the man who had come to her rescue. A little hollow appeared in silvery covering. Immediately, the hollow covered over, like nanites repairing the damaged cell.

"What is that thing?" Adams asked, watching him and Harafat leave.

More security personnel filed out with rifles, shooting the security man who kept walking. He shielded Harafat from sporadic shootings. They had reached the building exit when the security man's body began to jerk. Behind them, another security officer turned on an EMP: this was the only way to confirm that the strange man was an AI. It changed to different people, including Azeezat. Distorted silver tins, crumpled face, elastic stomach, and limp feet. The AI kept changing until it became liquid, slithering towards an opening, finding its way beneath the water pipes. Harafat bolted.

56. When An AI Becomes A Killer Machine, It May Not Recognize The One Who Built It. But Part Of It Still Retains Some Feelings.

Both sisters had been flagged Code Red, bounty placed on their heads, authorities alert and on the lookout for them. Harafat had become a Most Wanted. With the help of Collins, she was shipped out with containers of clothes heading for Cairo. She made friends with a flexitarian lady who was also a fugitive. Harafat had never imagined her sister as a rogue.

Greencorps manned their establishments with military personnel, super soldiers, and robotic dogs. Azeezat blended in, devised new cloaking means to bypass the high-tech goggles that should have revealed her true form, burned more of their buildings.

METALLO ON THE LOOSE, the *Daily Times* captioned it. *ROGUE AI WREAKS MORE HAVOC ON GREENCORPS INDUSTRIES.*

Harafat dreamed of the day she would become a free citizen again, all the charges dropped. That day felt like a reverie that may never materialize. She got a job as a florist in a flower shop. A bald-headed man walked in, wearing an infectious smile that smeared his aura among the scented flowers. She asked what kind of flower he would like to buy. His selection got her reminiscing, thinking of auld lang syne.

"Did I say something funny?" the man inquired when Harafat smiled.

"No. Sorry. My sister and I used to visit the flower marts in the old days. Lily of the valley, lavender, and hyacinth were her favorites," Harafat said.

The man collected the flowers from her, headed to the door.

"I'll be watching over you. The same way you cared for me all those years," the man said and left.

Harafat hurried out of the shop. Those words seemed familiar. She knew Azeezat's new liquid metal body had the ability to transform to anyone she desired. More people passed by the busy road; recognizing her sister would be impossible.

When she went back inside, she found a piece of paper on the glossy countertop. It contained seven digits. A note read below: *Only for an emergency. AZ.* Harafat quickly tucked the paper into her pocket when a customer came inside. She couldn't mask her smile.

Our Soil

Masimba Musodza

IN THE EARLY HOURS of the morning, a truck rumbled across the savannah and came to a halt nearly a kilometer from the spaceport. Then it tipped a heap of soil. Despite a mournful wind blowing across the desolate landscape, it seemed as if every speck of dust in that heap of soil landed on the ground.

Its task completed, the truck drove back to wherever it came from, leaving Vusa Chitanga standing next to the pile. The truck was a speck on the horizon when an all-terrain car with the InterPlanetary Migrations logo shot from the spaceport.

Chitanga had put up shelter, a tent of a metallic, deflective fabric. If the man who stepped out of the vehicle had stopped to really think about the implications of a Zambeziyan possessing what appeared to be effective, hi-tech protection against the solar flares, the exigency of reporting this to his superiors would have occurred to him. But for Euan Covington, born and raised in the Race-Realist doctrine of the Northwest Territories, all he saw was an African rummaging around in stuff next to a pile of dirt.

"Mornin'!" said Covington, sauntering over. "You look kind of busy."

"Just settling down," said Chitanga. "The travellers will be here in about three hours."

"I know that!" said Covington. "What I don't know is why you have a heap of dirt delivered to this spot."

"It's for the travellers," said Chitanga. "Before they board your ship, they will grab a handful of this earth."

Covington pulled his Stetson back, and scratched his bald pate before asking, "Now why would they want to do that?"

"Tradition," said Chitanga. "Every time my Bantu forebears migrated, they carried some soil from the land they were leaving. It represented a link with the old country and the ancestors buried there."

"So, you're taking a pile of dirt into space?"

"That is the gist of it," said Chitanga.

Covington thought for a moment. "Everyone is leaving this planet with something, and you have picked dirt?"

"Like I said, that is the gist of it."

Covington put his hand to his Stetson in valediction and returned to the vehicle. He was glad this was going to be a very short report.

Later, from the Mission Control tower, he watched the pile of soil disappear as the Zambeziyans snaked past it along the road to the spaceport. By dusk, it was gone. He imagined African settlers tossing the soil onto a new world, and evoking their ancestors.

He wondered if his own ancestors from Europe had done that when they first landed in the New World. Probably not. But then, there was more than one way of conquering land, and transplanting a people and their culture onto it. Gazing up at the stars, Covington wondered whose way would be more successful.

* * *

Chitanga was assailed by the pungent smell of an assortment of chemicals before he realized with rising panic that he had regained consciousness in a deep, dark, weightless place. Even in that state of trepidation, he reflected on the stark absence of the familiar smells of life as he knew it; street food on colourful stalls, the perfume wafting off the stunningly beautiful girl sitting across from him on the train, flowers in bloom. He wondered why he had recalled those smells in particular, filling what seemed like an unfathomable cavern with the question.

"Vusa Chitanga?" The voice that asked struggled to pronounce his name.

Chitanga turned to one side and found himself staring in wonder as a woman in a one-piece flightsuit, the InterPlanetary Migrations logo emblazoned on the left side of her chest, emerged from the gloom. Around her earnest, likeable face, blonde hair waved like underwater fronds.

"Mr Chitanga, please do not be alarmed. My name is Lark Ashton. You will soon recover enough to remember where you are and how you got here. For now, I request that you follow me. Your presence is required at a short meeting that will determine your fate and that of the other people you came aboard with."

The other people. Images of a mass of desperate, frightened Black people took shape, but most of his memory drew a blank. He focused on the present, on Lark, noting that she spoke English as it was spoken in the lands that had once been known as America and Canada.

Hands worked quickly to remove the straps that attached him to the bed, and Chitanga floated up like a ghost rising from the grave. He was stopped by a flat, sheer surface. His cot, it would appear, was one of many.

"Mr Chitanga, you have been in space for nearly five years, yet you are unfamiliar with weightlessness. I think it is best you let my colleagues guide you for now. You will soon get the hang of it."

Hands emerged from the gloom, seizing him by the limbs, and he was propelled towards Lark, who also began to move away.

The gloom dissipated, or his eyes had adjusted. Chitanga saw that they passed rows of people strapped to cots, all in suspended animation. They were all Black, most likely citizens of Zambeziya. With that speculation, more memories returned; the solar flares that knocked out all of humanity's telecommunications infrastructure. Governments collapsing, new countries headed by strongmen (and women) emerging from the ashes. Humanity reverting to pre-radio technology as the solar flares worsened. Private tech companies building spaceships that could take survivors to seek new worlds, but only during window periods when the solar activity abated. Africa plundered for rare minerals needed to build those ships, her people slaughtered if they sat in the way. Desperate Africans trading their labour and mineral rights in return for passage. Ambitious Africans trying to build their own spaceships.

Chitanga followed Lark through a narrow port, and he was in a tunnel of mesh. By grabbing the net and pulling himself along, movement was easy. He was more aware of his surroundings, and the memories of how he got there were becoming clearer. They had been in suspended animation when they had been brought abroad from Earth, and this was his first view of the interior of the ship. Chitanga heard the sound of electric-powered machines.

They diverted through a port, into a compartment the size of a modest lounge back on Earth, and Chitanga found himself under the bemused gaze of a middle-aged, bald-headed White man with a pencil moustache and piercing green eyes, who sat strapped in a chair, his back to a console and monitor bank. He wore the same outfit as Lark.

"You have been with us for many years now, but this is the first opportunity for me to formally welcome you aboard, Mr Chitanga," the man said. "I am Buddy Cardinal, captain of the *Frontier IV*."

Lark was the only one who had followed him into the cabin.

"It's been five years since we embarked on our journey," said Chitanga, to himself. Five years since he entered into an agreement with InterPlanetary Migrations allowing the corporation access to minerals in northern Zambeziya in return for passage for some five thousand people. Ten years since scientists from around the world had concurred that the recent solar flares preceded the imminent destruction of all life on Earth.

"Indeed, sir," said Cardinal. "I am pleased to inform you that everyone is in good health."

Chitanga could not contain his happiness at the news. "It is good to note that everyone has kept to their end of the bargain."

Cardinal nodded, but, for a nearly imperceptible moment, avoided Chitanga's eyes. Cardinal's features relaxed into a smile and he said, "Mr Chitanga, I am pressed for time, and am going to have to get straight to the reason why we brought you out of suspended animation. On behalf of IPM, I propose a new agreement that will secure your continued passage on this ship."

"A new agreement?" Chitanga echoed, taken aback. He remembered the fierce opposition to this deal with IPM. He remembered how he had defended it in the Zambeziyan Legislative Assembly. Knowing full well that IPM could renege at a moment of its choosing and expediency, it had nevertheless seemed better than to enter into the bargain, and hope and pray that the corporation would not then join much of the rest of the world in hand wringing. And just dying.

Unlike other corporations and nations, IPM had committed itself to transporting forty thousand Pan-Zambeziyans in return for the minerals. Yes, Chitanga had agreed with critics, the deal was the same as a bag of money from the man who intended to have his way with your wife. You took the money because you knew he had all the power, and hoped that you could use the money to secure a future where no one in your family need ever fear violence again. That is what those deals with foreign companies had been for. Pan-Zambeziya had used the proceeds to build a technological resource base from which to at least imagine building a spaceship to send more people away from the impending doom.

"Sir, I am afraid that things have changed in the last five years," Cardinal was saying. "Our agreement granted you passage on this ship, but allowed for renegotiating terms and conditions as and when circumstances required it. Problem is, sir, we cannot supply enough air for everyone. There are other costs that have occurred. So, the Board of Directors had a look at the situation, and worked out how you guys can continue to earn your keep." He smiled again, and added, "Turns out that there are many ways in which you can make your flight economical."

"And what might these be, Captain Cardinal?"

Cardinal said, "Construction of the solar sails, and reinforcing the hull. Medical research. I am afraid there is a new illness on this ship. We shall be looking for people prepared to help test the possible cures some of our scientists have been working on."

Chitanga told himself he had known this day would come. Even so, the sense of deep regret was overwhelming. Why had he rejected the alternatives? Many nations and independent communities had started to build underground cities. Others had embarked on an ambitious project to build a protective shield in the atmosphere. Who knew, those plans were probably working right now back on Earth, while he, Chitanga, had sold a lot of people into slavery?

Cardinal said, "Mr Chitanga, we do not have much time. IPM can keep your people for about a month at the most. After that, we will have no choice but to disconnect various services. However, I am sure that it will not come to that."

"No, it won't, Captain Cardinal," said Chitanga, "We are here in outer space in order to survive."

Cardinal smiled. "I am happy that you are prepared to make the right decisions about our ongoing relationship, Mr Chitanga."

He's probably thinking this meeting is going a lot better than he had expected, Chitanga thought. Which it had. But not in the way the man from Interplanetary Migrations imagined.

* * *

The revived Zambeziyans held a bira, a ceremony to evoke their ancestors. They beat drums and plucked the mbira and sang songs of hunting, of farming, of the elements needed to sustain life. The dances were impossible in zero-g. But the voices rang into the cavernous hold, and might have even carried into the vastness of space outside.

Then they brought out some of the soil in a sealed clay pot and placed it in an alcove. It had become a sort of shrine, with strange markings that five thousand years ago, the Zambeziyans' ancestors might have committed the theology of Bantu Ancestralism to script. There were offerings of beer and snuff in sealed plastic pouches.

Cardinal watched this ceremony with fascination. "Ain't it strange that the human race is going to the stars, and we do not know enough about each other, even on this ship?" he said.

"Speak for yourself, Captain Cardinal," said Chitanga. "Just the fact that we are having this conversation in English tells you something."

"But English is the language of the advanced technology that has enabled your people to be with us today," said Cardinal.

"The importance of English is not being disputed here," said Chitanga, "But if I were you, I would really want to know what these people are saying in their songs."

Cardinal looked at him. "And you would tell me?"

"Of course. We are calling on those in the soil to rise up now."

"The spirits of your ancestors?" said Cardinal. He smiled condescendingly. "We are leaving Earth, and you would still put your faith in those who are dead and buried in it?"

Chitanga did not respond. Cardinal wondered if he had missed something. He did not wonder for too long. He was just glad that the Zambeziyans were co-operating with InterPlanetary Migration, and the new terms of their conditions of carriage.

* * *

"Captain Cardinal, have you ever heard of the legend of the Golem of Prague?" said Chitanga, as he floated into the command module of the *Frontier IV*. A dozen heads looked up, startled at this bold intrusion.

"We are busy, Mr Chitanga!" said the captain sternly. "I do not have time for cultural exchanges."

"Oh, I must insist, Captain," said Chitanga. With a flourish, he turned to the port he had just emerged from. Cardinal glanced in that direction, and whatever he was about to say did not escape his lips. Instead, he uttered a cry of shock and fright, as did his crew.

The being that sailed into the module was anthropomorphic. Yet it had no defined face or hands. It seemed to be made of soil, but soil that crawled like millions of ants, as if each grain of soil was a separate life form.

"The Zambeziyan Federal Government knew that you would dishonour our agreement!" said Chitanga. "They asked me to help, and the idea came to me after I read about the Golem of Prague."

"It's not possible!" said Cardinal vehemently. "It's not possible that is a Golem!"

"Would you deny the evidence of your own senses?" said Chitanga. "But you are right. Unfortunately, the Rabbi Judah Loew ben Bezalel never revealed how he animated his pile of earth. No, captain, my Golem is powered not by mystical knowledge, but by nanobots."

He paused, allowing the horrified realization to sink in. Then he said, "And now, Captain, I would like for us to discuss new terms and conditions for my fellow passengers..."

The host of nanobots surged towards Captain Cardinal, as his scream rose as if to pierce through the expanse beyond the hull.

The Long Way Home

Kortney Nash

"I DON'T KNOW my name," Sock said, the first words she'd spoken in hours. "But I call myself Sock."

"Sock?" The driver spoke without tearing her eyes away from the standstill traffic hovering in front of them. They were in a standard aero-freight transporter – it was like an eighteen-wheeler without the wheels, made to soar through space rather than tumble along highways.

"Sock." She nodded, twirling a toothpick between her fingers before drawing the sharp end to her front teeth. She could feel peanut skin stuck there, paper thin and refusing to fall victim to her tongue's valiant attempts at ousting it from where it'd become wedged. "It was all I had when I woke up. A little sock in my pocket."

"So, you've been calling yourself Sock ever since?"

"Basically." She was already reaching for another handful of peanuts from the center console, eyes drifting to the landscape below. They were flying over what looked like a bog planet, dense wetlands painting the landscape in vibrant blues and greens. Even through the airtight seal in the cabin the slightly sour, earthy odor of the bogs just barely penetrated the thick scent of spearmint air freshener hanging from the rearview mirror.

"I'm Anita." the driver said before sighing through her nose, tapping an impatient rhythm into the wheel as traffic somehow became even slower. "I was named after the singer."

"Haven't heard of her."

"She's from the twenty-first century."

Sock let out a low whistle. "That's real retro."

"I guess." Anita shrugged, leaning back in her seat, seemingly having given up on urging traffic to speed up with sheer willpower alone. Sock gave her a good once over for the first time since she'd pulled over at the sight of Sock's upturned thumb on the side of the road a couple of planets ago. She looked younger than Sock would've expected for a freight driver but then again it was hard to tell age with Black people – Anita could've been in her mid-twenties or pushing forty; her russet brown skin was completely smooth under the waning light of the bog planet's multiple moons. She wore her hair in a high ponytail that sat atop her head like a cloud and had thick eyebrows that had been set in a hard line across her forehead ever since they'd reached the bottleneck of hover vehicles all filing into line to get through the interplanetary customs checkpoint to be granted permission to exit the bog planet's atmosphere.

"You got any songs by her in your playlist?" Sock asked through a mouthfull of peanuts.

Anita scrolled through something on the monitor embedded in her steering wheel and then dulcet tones accompanied by the soft hiss of a drum set were flooding the cabin. Sock watched Anita's shoulders relax, her fist unclenching slightly where it had been strangling the wheel before.

"How do you not know your name?"

"Someone stole my memory chip." Sock's hand traveled to the back of her neck, unbidden. She'd already gotten a new chip installed, but it didn't dull the sense of loss. She'd had a whole life, and if the occasional errant feeling of longing was anything to go by, she'd had a life that was worth missing.

"Memory chip? You must be from one of those high-tech planets, where the people are all basically cyborgs."

Sock sank deeper into her seat, bringing her legs up to rest her feet on the dash. She didn't feel like a cyborg, but she'd seen the scars on her scalp when she first woke up. Evidence of neuro-modification now covered by coarse curls that barely stretched an inch from her head.

"Is that where you're headed? Back home?" Anita asked once the silence had stretched on.

"I don't really know yet. I got this weird feeling like I can tell where the chip is if I focus real hard, so I'm just followin' that. Maybe it'll lead me home, maybe somewhere else."

They fell into another lapse in conversation, punctuated by sultry crooning set to a somber piano ensemble wafting from the truck's speakers. Eventually, Anita pulled up to the floating customs gate and consented to have her freight inspected. After another twenty minutes, they were soaring again, free to pick up speed as the expanse of space opened up in front of them.

"What type of stuff d'you transport?"

"Nothing exciting. Grains, nonperishables, novelty goods. I just pick up jobs as I go."

"How'd you get into this?"

"Was just one of the options at trade school." Anita stifled a yawn. "It was this or deep space welding. Probably would've made more money doing welding, but I've never cared much for floating around in zero gravity. Do you have any idea what you were doing before you lost your chip?"

Sock shook her head. "My first memory is wakin' up in the hospital on Ophiuchus XI – head was hurting real bad, and they told me someone had left me at the front door all passed out and whatnot. They gave me a standard chip – with enough preloaded knowledge for me to get by while I make new memories."

Anita hummed for a moment. "Do you think you're from Ophiuchus?"

"Reckon not. I don't know much, but it just didn't feel…right. And they didn't have me in any of their population records." Then, "Where're you from?"

"Small planet in the Andromeda galaxy."

"Which one?" Sock knew the names and locations of most of the planets in the universe – the information had come preset on her new memory chip along with other random trivia.

"SD-1222."

"Pretty barren, yeah?"

"Relatively speaking, yes."

"Your family still there?"

"Yeah. Most of them are too old to go anywhere else, but it's not bad. There are drivers just like me delivering the planet's food rations. So. It all works out."

An automated voice over the truck's surround-sound speaker announced the presence of a rest stop approximately two hours away.

"Thank God," Anita muttered, barely-there bags visible under her eyes. The empty energy drinks littering the ground of the cabin hadn't escaped Sock's notice. She nudged one of them with her foot just to watch it roll under her seat. Part of her wished she could disappear with it.

* * *

The rest stop was in a floating air-locked dome in the middle of nowhere – no planets in sight, just the profound darkness of space making everything look impossibly flat as far as the eye could see. There were shower stalls, a snack shack, a refueling station, and a large lot filled with other aero-freight transporters. Anita resituated her ponytail to the back of her head and pulled on a faded baseball cap. She looked ready to blend in with the rest of the travel-weary drivers milling around. Sock did as well in her slides and comically large hoodie. It was what she'd left the hospital in – presumably what she'd shown up in. The sweatshirt had smelled familiar when she first woke up, like someone worth caring about, and inside the big pocket had been a little yellow sock.

"Wait here and don't open the doors for anyone," Anita said, already hopping out the truck and slouching towards neon lights blaring *SNACKS: 24 HOURS* with enough flicker to induce epilepsy.

Something loosened in Sock's chest at not being immediately kicked to the curb. It was hard bouncing from ride to ride, unsure when her luck would run out. She drew her knees to her chin and tried to prod at the memories she could feel deep in her mind, fuzzy like a letter that'd been dunked underwater. The longer she focused, the more faint it became. A phrase popped into her head without reason: *Can't change the way a satellite orbits*, and she didn't know where she picked it up from, but it brought comfort all the same. She found herself squeezing the sock in her pocket reflexively, the material rough from her constant harassment. It was too small for her own foot and composed of clumsy, misshapen stitches. She assumed she'd been making it as a present for someone else. Or half of a present, at least.

Sock was so lost in thought, she nearly jumped a mile out of her skin when Anita returned with an armful of Little Debbie snacks, cup noodles, and more energy drinks. A gust of frigid air entered the cabin with her.

"I didn't mean to startle you," Anita said, dumping all the food onto the center console and messing around with buttons on the steering wheel monitor until heat whooshed out the vents.

"Have you ever heard the phrase before, 'can't change the way a satellite orbits'?"

"No. Is it famous?"

"Dunno." Sock shrugged. "Reckon it could be. Maybe where I'm from, at least."

"You know," Anita said while pulling a heating plate out of the glove compartment and balancing it on the dash, "I think you'll remember everything one day, even if you can't ever find your chip again."

"What makes you so sure?"

"I can tell you miss someone, or something – I can hear it in your voice. If you know to miss it then it's still in you somewhere. It'll come back on its own time."

Soon enough the aroma of the noodle soup began spreading through the cabin; the scent of salt and chicken made Sock salivate. The last real meal she had was at the hospital, she'd been subsisting on snacks and the goodwill of others since then. It seemed Anita had more goodwill then most, considering several minutes later she was handing the cup soup to Sock without even making a fuss, already peeling the seal off the second cup and filling it with water.

"You went through those peanuts pretty fast earlier. Figured you've been hungry," Anita offered by way of explanation.

"'Preciate it," Sock mumbled before digging in. Anita didn't seem to mind the lack of propriety. "Do you get to visit home often?"

Anita shook her head. "It's too far to go back and forth. But I send money back to my grandma and I give her a call anytime I land on a high-tech planet."

"You get lonely?"

"Who doesn't?" Anita shrugged, turning off the hot plate and cradling the warm cup in her hands without making a move to eat. "But it passes. Like most things do."

"You're the wise type."

"I spend too much time alone; I can't help it."

"Does your grandma miss you?"

"Of course she misses me," Anita scoffed, but there was no heat behind it. "Are you worried about whether someone out there misses you?"

"Kind of. M'not sure if it's worse for someone to be out there worrying over me, or for no one at all to even notice I'm gone."

"I'm sure someone out there is worried about you. I've only known you a day, and I'd miss you if you disappeared overnight." And Sock could tell it was meant to be a throwaway remark, just something polite to fill the space. Anita didn't even look at her while she said it, busy finally taking her first forkful of noodles. Still, Sock felt that knot in her chest loosen the rest of the way. Like she'd finally been given permission to rest.

* * *

What was supposed to be a day or two of hitchhiking with Anita turned into a month. Then two. Then three. With Sock in the passenger seat, feet kicked up on the dash while Anita broke speeding laws to get to her drop-offs on time and re-up on cargo. It was easier like that; Anita was generally heading towards that far-away inexplicable pull that Sock felt bone deep. Besides, finding someone new to bum a ride from meant she wouldn't get to make fun of Anita for how pinched her expression became whenever another driver cut her off in traffic, or when she felt like the customs agents were taking too long during freight inspections. Not to mention she would also miss out on the way Anita laughed with her whole body even when Sock's jokes were corny, and the way she pursed her lips when she was deep in thought. Leaving just didn't make sense and Sock had stayed up at night *trying* to make sense of it – trying to figure out what her long-term plan was. If nothing else, she figured by helping Anita out with loading shipments and doing inventory counts, she couldn't be considered a complete freeloader.

They had just completed a drop-off on a high-tech planet with towering skyscrapers and bullet trains that hovered above the ground. More importantly, it had long-distance phone booths. Sock sat on her haunches in the corner while Anita leaned against the opposite wall, their legs forced to intertwine in the limited space.

"People here have dogs that come up to my shoulders – I'm not kidding." Anita huffed a silent laugh into the receiver. "Seriously, Gran, I have to see if I can find an inter-star system post office to send you a picture. You wouldn't believe it."

The phone booth was humid – the whole planet was hotter than Sock thought any human being could comfortably live on, but the volume of foot traffic outside said otherwise. Sweat slicked her legs and dripped down her temples. She was only wearing a tank top and basketball shorts but even that felt like too much.

"…what planet? We're on…" Anita's eyes drifted towards the ceiling in thought.

"We're on AC–41101," Sock offered.

"Right, AC–41101." Anita nodded, a futile gesture not telegraphed through the phone call. "I got paid to drop off fruit here. It was all tropical stuff. I wish I could've shown it to you; crates full of pineapples, papayas…"

Sock stared at Anita's knee where it was level with her eye. She reached up and poked it because she could. Anita's gaze darted down to her for a moment before resettling on something beyond the glass walls of the phone booth, busy describing the overwhelmingly sweet fruit scent that had coated every inch of the freight car. It had made Sock's head hurt and her mouth water, cloying and appetizing at the same time. She traced amorphous shapes on Anita's shin, her mind already busy wondering what type of planet they'd find themselves on next.

"Yeah, Gran. Uh huh. I know, yeah – Ok. I'll – yeah, Ok. Ok. Love you too, bye." Anita set the receiver aside and extended a hand towards Sock, hoisting her up with a grunt. The phone booth wasn't made for two people. They were nose to nose for a charged second before Anita slid the door open. The air outside was only slightly less stuffy. Still, Sock already missed the forced proximity – she wondered if she'd always been like this, needy, or if it was something Anita brought out of her.

"M'hungry," Sock mumbled, dragging her feet as if the heat was a physical force gripping her ankles and slowing her stride.

"You're always hungry." Despite being just as sweaty, Anita's demeanor hadn't changed – self-assured steps and chin held high, no signs of fatigue except for the usual bags under her eyes from late nights spent driving. She'd let Sock give her cornrows the day previous. They were crooked. And uneven. They were both certain Sock hadn't been a hair stylist before her memory chip was stolen.

"I'm a growing girl."

"You're at least twenty-two."

"Might be older. Doctor said my biological signs of aging had been halted with some fancy technology in my brain."

"So you're a cyborg, like I said before."

"M'just Sock. And coincidentally, I maybe don't age."

"It's been a while since I've been on a planet this advanced." Anita ushered Sock into a nearby coffee shop. They both sighed with relief when the industrial strength air conditioning hit them. The decor was what Sock could only describe as unsettlingly sterile, white tile floors and white tile walls and white tile ceilings with a white bar top and white table sets.

"It's a nice planet. Sure is hot, though."

"They probably have better databases than the planet you woke up on. They might have access to news from other star systems. There might be something about you somewhere online."

Sock's breath hitched, hand drifting to where the sock rested in her short's pocket automatically. That grief-ridden ache that'd first threatened to tear her open when she first woke up in the hospital had dimmed since she met Anita, bludgeoned into a dull sense of curiosity. The urgency to discover her origin had disappeared without her even realizing it, replaced with a feeling too complicated to untangle that sat heavy in her chest while watching Anita order both of their drinks with practiced ease – she'd become accustomed to Sock's palette that singularly craved whatever had the least nutritional value at any given establishment. Fifteen minutes later they were sitting by the window, a cinnamon roll cut in half between them. Black coffee for Anita. An iced mocha latte for Sock.

"I think I was a cowboy before my chip got stolen," Sock said, à propos of nothing, once her drink was halfway gone.

"You talk like a cowboy, so... It would make sense."

Sock laughed at that, a surprised sound that escaped her before she could stifle it. "Just 'cause I don't talk proper like you don't mean I sound like a cowboy."

"You're the one who called yourself a cowboy."

"I was being facetious." A beat, then, "See? I even know big words and everything."

"I'm sure most cowboys know big words. And you have a memory chip that was probably pre-programmed with most of the known languages in the universe."

"It was only pre-programmed with three languages. The planet I woke up on wasn't advanced enough for anything more than that."

"At least you were on a planet that was even able to install a replacement memory chip." Anita's gaze drifted to a group of pedestrians passing by outside, all decked out in chrome bodysuits and bulky headphones. "Someone like you turned up on my home planet once, with their chip gone. It was like they were a zombie. There wasn't anything we could do except get them on a breathing machine and a feeding tube."

"I got lucky."

"I'm glad you got lucky."

Sock considered Anita's profile – the round curve of her nose, full lips almost always set in a straight line – for a moment too long, looking away when Anita turned to meet her gaze. Sock finished her half of the cinnamon roll in two bites and Anita, predictably, took a small piece of her portion before declaring it too sweet and letting Sock have the rest. The barista had let them know that there was a library three blocks away. It had a public computer lab with long-distance internet.

"Can I see the sock?" Anita asked. She'd seen it before, but Sock pulled it out anyway and laid it flat on the table between them. It looked innocuous, not at all like the most important thing Sock owned. "There's someone waiting for you out there. Or, at the very least, waiting to receive a poorly made sock from you."

"They might not be waiting anymore. Who knows how long my chip was gone before I was left in front of the hospital?"

"Is that going to stop you from looking for your old life, anyway?"

"I guess not," Sock mumbled without making any move to stand and head towards the door to the library less than a five-minute walk away. "You ever want something but feel scared of it at the same time? Like what if my old life was bad? What if I'm happier not remembering?"

Anita shrugged. "The library doesn't close for another few hours, and I'm not scheduled to pick up my next shipment until tomorrow morning. Just think about what you want to do – it'll probably be a while before we land on another high-tech planet, but it won't be the last time."

"And what if I don't go to the library here or on the next high-tech planet, either?" Sock asked, voice pitched low. *What if I decide not to remember*? The question bounced around behind Sock's teeth without being vocalized.

"I don't know." Anita fixed her gaze on where her hands sat atop the pristine table. "But you can ride passenger with me as long as you want."

Sock pretended like the invitation didn't make her heart skip a beat.

"If we ever do find out where you're from, I'd help you get home, you know," Anita continued.

"What if I was from somewhere super far, like the An Sa galaxy?"

"Well, it'd take me years for me to fly you all the way there. I'm not sure how long you'd want to—"

"I wouldn't mind it. I'm a patient person."

Anita raised an eyebrow, but finally held Sock's gaze steady with her own. "Then I'd take you to the An Sa galaxy."

Three blocks away was a room full of computers that could probably answer at least one of the questions Sock had about herself. But there was other stuff on the planet, too. They'd walked past a multilevel arcade earlier, a VR movie theater, a farmers' market full of exotic pastries – there was a whole world waiting to be explored by them, a whole galaxy even. Sock returned the yellow sock back to her pocket, giving it one good squeeze before reaching for Anita's hand instead, pulling her out of the cafe and into the welcome embrace of the impossibly humid city teeming with possibilities for the afternoon ahead.

The Night Market

Chinelo Onwualu

"YOU'VE GOT a real talent for this, you know," said Oduwe, the head gardener at the Temple of Osun, as Drake worked to weed the yam seedlings. She emerged from the recesses of the tomato bed across from him, combing through the vines on their trellises, and picking off dead leaves for compost. "Don't think I haven't heard you out here talking to them."

Drake was unsure how to reply. He'd only been a gardener's assistant for a few months and he wasn't known for being talkative. He flushed at the thought that the old woman had been listening to his crooning.

"That's good; you should talk to plants," Oduwe said. "They can hear you, you know."

She shuffled over and pointed out a patch of grass Drake had missed. "They're talking back, too. Trick you've got to learn now is to listen." She patted his shoulder and moved up the sloping path to the next level of the terraced six-storey greenhouse.

He squatted down and uprooted the stringy plants. It was best to pull weeds by hand as Martian soil was too fragile for hoes. Crumbling the powdery red earth from their roots, he stuffed the weeds into the compost pouch at his waist. Straightening, he surveyed the neat formation of bamboo stakes that stretched to the greenhouse's glazing several metres away. Each had a delicate green vine twined around it like a lover. He stroked the smooth, heart-shaped leaf of the one closest to him. His fingernails had taken on an ochre tint that refused to wash off, but he didn't mind. He liked the contrast.

On Earth he'd grown up a soldier, taken from his parents as a baby and trained by the warrior priests of the Amethyst Order. When he was ten, Drake had tried to grow an orange seed in his rations locker. His commander found it and he had been forced to smash the pot in front of the other boys and grind the delicate green shoot under his heel. *A soldier has only one love*, his commander had told him, *his duty*.

The great gong boomed across the complex, signalling the first prayer of the day. In his first few days its low *thooms* would set his teeth on edge; they sounded too much like explosions. Now, he appreciated its soothing quality, so different from the shrill bells of his childhood. He was on the first floor terrace with a clear view of the doors that led to the Acolyte's quarters and as the gong boomed again, he waited. Within a few minutes, the Acolytes streamed into the greenhouse.

They had to pass this way every day, crossing over the bridge that spanned the fish pond, to get to the temple. Dressed in simple white wrappers, they moved in a single file. Those who trained to be the priests and priestesses of Osun had to be without physical fault or blemish, and the goddess demanded only the most beautiful. So each Acolyte was luminous jewel, possessing a fearful symmetry that bordered on perfection. Yet none of them compared to his Bella.

Where the other Acolytes were shades of copper, bronze and gold, her skin was a radiant ebony, hinting at blue under the greenhouse lights. The white cloth wrapped around her hands and arms seemed whiter by contrast. Bald as an egg and just as delicate, she moved with a smooth grace that made her seem as if she was gliding. The temple had taken her in as soon as they saw her, while Drake had struggled for months before landing his current position.

She must have felt his stare because she raised her head towards him. Her expression was the picture of dignified solemnity, but her eyes, gold as the heart of a flame, were alive with good humour. She winked at him and Drake could not help but smile in return.

"Stay away from those ones," Oduwe spoke from behind him. Drake spun round, his garden fork poised to stab. The old gardener eyed the tool impassively. Cursing his soldier's instincts, Drake slipped the tool back into his utility belt and forced himself to relax. "They aren't for the likes of you or me."

"It's not like that," he said. He and Bella were not related, but they were bound together by more than blood. He wasn't about to try and explain that to his boss, though.

The old woman gave him a sceptical look. "All they have is their beauty and their Goddess," she said. "Mess that up for them and they'll never forgive you."

It was Drake's turn to look sceptical. The last thing he or Bella were searching for here was religion. Their faith had been burned out of both of them a long time ago.

* * *

Night was a quiet time in the temple complex. On Earth, the dark would have been full of the sounds of nature: owls hooting, wild dogs barking, crickets chirping and the occasional *whomp whomp* of tree frogs. Here, there was little to hear beyond the sonorous chanting of the Night Singers.

Drake lay on his pallet in the gardener's spare room tracing the filigree cracks in the regolith walls with his fingers. His furnishings were spare, as fit for a semi-skilled labourer: a single mattress, a small side table, a prayer mat, and a hook on the wall where he hung his one change of clothes. He clenched and unclenched his hands, revelling in the sweet ache that only came after a hard day of honest labour.

The room was warm, but he kept his window shut. The bio-dome which made the Holy City of New Thebes habitable was also supposed to keep the temperature constant, to compensate for the planet's extreme changes in temperature. After a century though, it could no longer keep up with its massive population, and the nights were often far warmer than necessary.

A soft knock at the window startled him. Rising, he drew his hunting knife out from under his pillow and peered out of the narrow slit. A dark figure wrapped in a cloak stood just under his sill. Hefting the knife, he lifted the pane open a fraction. The spicy scent of holy oil wafted in with the warm breeze and he lowered the blade, but he did not put the knife away.

"What are you doing here, Bel?" he asked, opening the window all the way. Bella raised her hood. In the gloom her smile was a strip of light.

"I am bored and in need of company," she said. She sometimes spoke like someone who had learned to talk from an old book – which she had. "May I come in?"

"No. Go back to the dorms; read a book."

"But I have read every book in their system."

"Already? What of your classes?"

"We are mired in theory," she said with a sigh. She leaned against the wall below his window and slid down until she was sitting, her feet splayed out in front of her. "Theories of the body, theories of pleasure, theories of connection, and on and on. What, I ask you, is the point of theory? Why worship the Goddess of sexual pleasure if one cannot even touch *oneself*!"

Drake suppressed a laugh at that. They were only two years apart, but separated by a lifetime of experience. He had been assigned to her guard detail when he was twelve. He had heard stories of the secret genetic experiments the Amethyst Order conducted on their lab-grown children. When he first met Bella he had searched for any signs of what they'd done to her: horns, a tail maybe, but there was nothing he could see. Just a little girl – small for her age as the lab-grown usually were – who kept staring at the sky because it was the first time she'd ever seen it.

He had been warned not to get attached. The girl had a sacred destiny to fulfil as a holy sacrifice and merely touching her would contaminate her. But he couldn't help it. Maybe it was the way she'd stood in the sunlight in the temple garden with her eyes closed. Like a plant left too long indoors. Maybe this time he wouldn't have to destroy it.

In a few days, it would be two years since their escape from the Order. He still searched the news waves for any reports on them. So far, no one had come looking. Maybe Mars *was* far enough away.

"Do you want to leave?" asked Drake. "I thought you liked it here?"

"I do, but—" Her head snapped up and she fixed him with a quizzical look, her yellow-gold eyes catching the light from the security lights in the distance. "Do you *not* wish to leave? I thought you hated it here."

"I do, but..." He looked at the knife he still held. His red-tinged fingernails were a sharp contrast against the dark leather of the blade.

Bella leaped to her feet and draped herself over the windowsill. She reached out a hand to him, but Drake was careful to shift back, maintaining a safe space between them.

"Let's visit the Night Market," she whispered.

"No, Bel, have you forgotten what happened last time? Those men thought you were a Nightwalker."

"No one will bother us this time, I am certain. We will be in disguise."

"No."

"Please?" She fixed him with a look so pitiful it cut Drake to the quick. "Please?"

Drake scratched at his bald head. It was a bad idea and this was shameless manipulation. He sighed. It was going to be a long night.

* * *

Drake loathed the Night Market. Its filthy pathways were a churn of mud and garbage and it smelled like a mix of oozing sewage and the oily clog of fried and roasted fish. He couldn't walk among the chaos of people and music, the inflatable shacks and plexiglass stalls arranged in no order, and those solar lamps that lit the place with flat Earth-light, without his stomach clenching. It wasn't as if gardening was a clean job, their fertilizers were the by-products of human faeces after all. It was more the way he had to be.

When he was gardening, it was just the sun, the soil and the tender green. In the Night Market, everyone was trying to hustle everyone else. Thieves would steal the shirt off your back, if they could. It was like being back at the barracks again. Drake had to straighten to his full height, which was at a foot taller than most, square his shoulders and keep his arms loose at his sides. No expression. He had to make sure that people knew he wasn't the one to target; that he was not weak. It made his bones ache.

Bella wore one of the long-sleeved red and green jumpsuits favoured by the temple servants, which she'd stolen from the laundry room. She'd changed the linen wraps around her hands to a pair of black gloves which were less conspicuous. As they plunged into the cacophony of hawkers calling out their wares, shopkeepers and customers haggling over prices, and entertainers displaying their skills, Bella transformed.

Her graceful poise disappeared, replaced by the hip-rolling swagger of a street girl. Her usual mask of serene composure morphed into sneering weariness. To complete the image, she reached into one of the pockets of the jumpsuit and produced a stick of dog's gold. Popping one end of the bark-wrapped sweet into her mouth, she chewed with crass abandon.

"You are disturbingly good at this," he whispered to her.

She beamed at him. "Thanks!" Then she went back to scowling.

At every turn, impromptu bars of two or three tables squeezed together attracted miners, labourers, and factory workers to drink cheap potato gin. And in the dark corners between shops and stalls, just beyond the pale floodlights, were the huddled masses of the city's discarded, lost in their worlds of synthetic bliss.

They passed a jeweller's kiosk where a long-limbed woman displayed sets of bronze necklaces under a glass case. Bella stopped to admire the goods and pointed out a string of coins looped like prayer beads.

"How much?" she asked, even though neither of them carried any money and Acolytes of the temple were forbidden to wear jewellery.

"Thirty credits," the woman said.

"That's too much, nah!" Bella said, doing a passing imitation of a colonist's accent. "It's not fifteen?"

"Ah Misseh, fifteen is too low. See the quality; you can't find this handwork anywhere on the planet. That's Earth craft, right there. Lowest I can go is twenty-eight."

"It *is* lovely," Bella said and traced the outline of the necklace on the glass. "I'll give you seventeen."

"Twenty-five – and I'm practically giving it away."

Drake kept one ear on the conversation, waiting for the seller to realize she was not dealing with a serious customer, while he scanned the crowd. He stood just behind Bella, his bulk shielding her from any accidental contact while giving her enough space to keep from bumping into him. All around people scurried about like ants: a hunched woman with a sleeping baby strapped to her back; a slack-faced beggar in a dirty turban and tunic; a group of raucous ore miners, their helmets and pressure suits slung over their shoulders; two prostitutes in diaphanous robes that left little to the imagination, the male winking at him. Drake noted their bodies, whether they kept their backs straight or bowed, the placement of their hands, the pace of their walks. Each body told a story, and sometimes it told of violence.

Drake heard the shouting first, a disturbance somewhere beyond the glare of the solar lights. A wave of tension rippled through the crowd as many stopped to determine what was going on. Others moved off into the shadows between the stalls, ready to flee at the first sign of true trouble. He shifted to keep Bella behind him, one hand out to shepherd her away if need be, and the other at the hilt of the knife by his side. The shouting grew louder, and on the far side of the pathway across from the stall, he saw the source of the disturbance: a man, running.

The man moved with the wiry smoothness of a dancer, bounding over tables, slipping between stalls, and slicing through the throng like a fish through water. The three men who pursued him were not as graceful. They overturned stalls and tables, and shoved aside anyone unlucky enough to get in their way.

The runner sprinted past the jeweller's table and Drake had just enough time to step out of his way. Drake managed to catch a glimpse of his face, though. It was locked in a rictus of glee. Minutes later, the man's pursuers thundered past.

Drake shook his head. *You never knew what could happen in the Night Market*, he thought and turned back to Bella. She was gone.

He looked around and saw that she was ahead of him, running after the men.

"*Olori buruku*," Drake cursed in Old Yoruba, and raced after her.

He followed the flash of her temple livery through the crowds. They were headed to the market's main complex, a series of prefabricated buildings from the early settlement period, little more than windowless white boxes stacked atop each other like children's blocks. Makeshift ladders ran from one level to another and rope bridges linked each stack to the ones nearby. The area was deserted this late at night.

The three pursuers had cornered their man in a dead-end alley between two of the stacks. A faltering solar light buzzed on the wall above them, casting strange distorted shadows. The running man leaned against the wall, heaving with exertion, the manic grin still on his face. Bella had managed to catch up to them and stood in the circle next to him. She had found a sharp piece of rock and brandished it at her attackers. She was doing a fair job imitating a fighting stance, but anyone who knew how to brawl could see that some of her moves were not quite right. From the bulges under their black jackets, these men were more than brawlers.

Drake spied a foot-long iron bar in a pile of rubbish at the mouth of the alley and picked it up. He crept up behind the nearest man and cracked the bar against the base of his skull, hard. The man went down without a sound. He jabbed the second man in the solar plexus with the butt of the bar, knocking him breathless, then caught him behind the knees and swept his legs out from under him. The third man had time to scrabble his blaster out of his jacket, but he was far, far too slow. Drake whipped the bar against the man's shooting arm, eliciting a dull crack as the bone broke. The man howled in pain and dropped the weapon. Cradling his useless arm, he loped off, leaving his unconscious companions behind. Drake stepped into the circle of light and kicked the blaster into the shadows beyond the alley.

"Bella, what in the Seven Hells were you thinking?"

"He needed help; I could not stand by and do nothing!"

"You do not know what is happening here; you cannot just jump into other people's business!"

Before Bella could reply, the man groaned and slumped down against the wall, head tucked into his chest. In the light his features were clearer. Slender, with a loose mop of dark curly hair that fell over his heavy brows, the man could not have been more than seventeen years old.

Bella ran to his side and whipped off one of her gloves, but Drake stopped her hand with the metal bar before she could touch him.

"Don't," he said.

"He may be injured." Bella glared at him. "I want to help."

"You cannot simply *fix* everyone you meet, Bella."

"And what am I to do instead? Watch silent as they suffer?"

"Once you heal him, then what? They will know that we're here and they will come for us," Drake forced himself to lower his voice. "Besides, people were never meant to be perfect, you know. Our weaknesses are what make us whole."

"Is that why you won't let me touch you?"

Drake didn't know how to answer that. But he didn't have to as the man in the alley jerked awake and looked wildly around him. His eyes were bloodshot. He fixed Drake and Bella with a look of surprise, then he burst into high-pitched maniacal laughter. Before he passed out again, Drake caught the smell of something sickly sweet on his breath.

He muttered another curse in Old Yoruba. The young man, whoever he was, was high on Drop.

* * *

"Mother Superior says that should you save a life, you are responsible for it ever after," Bella said, arranging the addict's feet on the makeshift pallet they'd cobbled together out of metal in the storeroom of the shop they'd broken into.

He and Bella had carried the young man as far from the alleyway as they could. They had slung his limp form between them, pretending he was a friend too drunk to make his own way home, but they could not leave the Night Market. As long as they remained on the market's raucous grounds, no one would look twice, but their ruse would never fool the guards of the City Watch.

"Your Mother Superior has obviously never met anyone on Drop," Drake said. He patted the man down for weapons. The man wore fine linen clothes, though wrinkled and dirty, and soft-soled sandals. From his smooth, manicured hands to his golden-brown skin, unmarked by any scars, he reeked of wealth mismanaged. "These addicts would sell their own children for a hit."

Finding nothing, Drake straightened and stretched, unknotting the kinks in his back and shoulders. He unclipped the flask strapped to his belt and poured a measure of water into the cap. He offered it to Bella who gulped it down, then poured a cup for himself. The cold of it burned pleasantly.

"We should try to find his family," said Bella. "Perhaps we can ask him about them when he wakes."

"This is crazy, Bel. You know that, don't you?"

She sighed. "I know. But sometimes I want…" She hesitated, looking down at her gloved hands, and folded them under her armpits. "There's so much pain all around us, and I want to feel that I am significant. That I have this gift for a reason."

"And I'm sure you'll understand that, someday. But until then you can't take these kinds of risks. New Thebes is a harsh city. Believe me, you don't want to be alone on her streets."

She gave him a long-suffering look. "You cannot care for me all your days, Drake. Your service ended when we left the Order; you are no longer bound to me."

"It's not about my service," Drake protested, oddly hurt by her words. "We're family now; we look out for each other."

The young man on the crates stirred and sat up. His eyes – an attractive shade of honey brown – had cleared.

"Where am I?" he croaked. Drake poured him a measure of water, which he drank in one delicate sip, his long fingers cupped politely around the cap. "Thank you."

His voice had a sibilant edge to it, the kind Drake often heard on the temple's high-born visitors.

"What's your name?" Bella asked.

"Abbeh," he said. "Abbeh Nuhu Moro."

Drake could barely suppress his groan. This young drug addict was the son of one of the most powerful women in the city.

"And the men who were after you?" Drake asked.

"I'm not sure…" Abbeh blinked in confusion. Memory loss was a common side effect of the drug. Hard users could erase whole years – which was often why they went for it. "My mother's men, probably. Or Congo's."

"Congo, the *drug dealer*?" Drake made no attempt to hide his dismay. The last time he and Bella had come to the Night Market, Drake had tangled with some of Congo's underlings. He had no wish to repeat the experience.

"I suppose he might sell drugs. He does always have something for me," Abbeh said, as if talking to himself. He steadied himself and spoke up, his voice firmer. "But I'm done with him."

"Good for you!" said Bella. "I'm sure your mother will be happy to have you back."

"That witch? Life with her is hell." Abbeh began to rub his arms as if he was cold even though the room was close and unpleasantly warm. "So many rules, you know? Every day it was: 'Do this, go there.' I could barely breathe. No, I'm not going back there. I want to live free, you know?" By the time he had finished talking he was shivering from the first stages of withdrawal.

"Yes, well, good luck to you," Drake said. He had no interest in whatever Abbeh was caught up in, especially if Congo was involved. He straightened and put his flask away. "Come on Bel, it's time we got you back."

He started towards the door, but Bella blocked his path.

"Are we just to leave him here? You said yourself the streets of New Thebes are harsh."

"We don't need his kind of trouble, Bel. He's not one of us. He's not *family*."

She fell silent at that, her fingers drumming an unknown rhythm on her thighs. Behind them, Abbeh groaned. They turned to find that he had slid off the crates and was curled into a foetal ball. Drop addiction was so powerful that for its heaviest users, even a few hours off it was agony. For some the withdrawal could kill. They needed to be far from the scene before that happened.

Drake pressed on. "Don't worry about him, his mother will find him. The rich always look after their own."

Bella clenched her fists, pinning him with her yellow-gold eyes. Drake knew that look. When he spoke he tried to keep the note of pleading out of his voice.

"Bella, think about this. Everything we've been through, everything we've worked for… You do this and you'll throw it all away. We've finally found a life here."

"No, *you've* found a life, Drake. All I did was trade one prison for another. I became an Acolyte to heal people. Instead I am groomed like a pet, forced to mime empty rituals and mouth empty words. And now when I may be able to truly help someone, you wish that I should turn my back and run? No!" Tears sprang to her eyes and she rubbed them away angrily. "No, Drake. I will run no longer."

"Would you rather be selling your body on the streets?" Drake said, choking back the lump in his own throat.

"At least it would be my choice."

She went to kneel over Abbeh, who was convulsing now. Gently, she eased his head onto her lap and took off her gloves. She placed a naked palm over his forehead. At her touch, Abbeh shuddered like a man being electrocuted, then his body went limp. For a moment, Drake thought he was dead, until he caught the slow rise and fall of the young man's chest.

"You should go now," Bella said. "It'll be bed check soon."

Drake felt as if he'd been kicked in the stomach. As if to punctuate his despair, they heard the storeroom door open.

* * *

A heavyset woman wearing a hairnet and a lappa wrapped around her chest – she'd obviously been woken from sleep – entered the room.

"I don't know who told you that," the woman said as she walked in. "My shop has been closed all night."

The shopkeeper stopped short when she saw them: Abbeh still stretched out on the floor in the middle of the room with Bella kneeling beside him. Her eyes grew wide with fear and flicked to Drake just before four black-jacketed thugs marched into the room. The men wore the same uniforms as the ones who had cornered them in the alley, but only one of them had participated in the attack. He had a bandage wrapped around his head and held back when he recognized Drake.

The other three brought out their blasters and circled him. Drake slipped out his hunting knife, settling into the familiar ease of a fighting stance. He was out-armed and outmanned, but unlike them he had once been an Enforcer of the Ameythst Order. *Some of these men will die tonight – if they're lucky.* The thought saddened him.

"Stand down!" A woman's voice cut through the tension. The thugs straightened up and backed away. The shopkeeper took the opportunity to scurry out of the room.

The woman who strode in looked as sharp as a blade – not a crease or wrinkle in sight. She wore a black high-necked tunic with long sleeves and matching trousers, a black hijab and a pair of round-framed smoked glasses. She towered over everyone in the room, her frame Earth-dense. She was either a recent arrival or one of the city's super-rich. Drake didn't need to note the family resemblance to recognize Haleemah Zazzau Moro, Abbeh's mother.

Haleemah removed her glasses and her icy gaze swept across the scene. She stalked slowly across the room until she loomed over Abbeh, who was now sitting up and looking dazed. She fixed her son with a look of contempt. Then she slapped him across the face.

"You stupid, stupid child," Haleemah said. "Have you any idea what you've put me through? Two days I've turned this market upside down searching for you."

Abbeh rubbed at his cheek and stood slowly. At his full height he matched his mother. There was a steadiness to him that hadn't been there before. Haleemah squared her shoulders, as if readying for a fight.

"Never lay a hand on me again, Mother." Abbeh's voice was soft, but there was hard certainty behind his words.

"When you insist on acting like a child, you will be treated as one," Haleemah said, though her voice faltered a little. "This isn't some kind of game."

"I know, and I'm sorry," said Abbeh, without any trace of his earlier petulance. Haleemah's eyes widened. She gaped at her son as if she had forgotten what she was about to say. Abbeh laid a slim hand on his mother's elbow. "You and I have much to discuss, Mother. But first, I want you to meet someone very special."

Abbeh took Bella's ungloved hand and held it like a precious jewel. "Mother, this… This is my healer."

When Abbeh looked at Bella, he radiated more joy than Drake had ever seen in anyone. *What demons had she saved him from?* he wondered. He expected Bella to have a look of similar elation, but she was calm, her expression open. This was no role she was playing, no pantomime. Bella was blooming, and it broke his heart.

* * *

The guest quarters of the Moro family home was thirty paces long and fifteen paces wide. Twice the size of Drake's room in the gardener's cottage. Lavish tapestries embroidered with the flora and fauna of a faraway planet lined the walls. A massive canopied bed dominated one end of the room, while a dresser and closet of real wood crowded the other. Bella sat on one of the three brocade divans arranged around a low glass table in the middle of the room. Hands bare and dressed in the loose silk kaftans favoured by Mars's elites, she sat calm and straight-backed, her eyes fixed in the middle distance. It was one of the poses she'd learned as a child to hide her fear.

Drake stopped his pacing to stand before her. "So you've made up your mind, then?" he said, breaking the silence that had grown between them for the last few minutes.

Bella took a deep breath before speaking. "I'm going to the underground levels; Abbeh says there are Drop treatment facilities there."

Drake bobbed his head, not quite understanding. He struggled to articulate what he wanted to say next, but the words had left him. "I'm sorry," was all he could manage.

Bella's pose dissolved as she bounded to her feet.

"You have nothing to be sorry for, Drake. I'm the one who should apologize. I was selfish and you were only trying to protect me."

"No, it wasn't about you. I just… I didn't want to lose you. I don't want to be alone."

"You cannot lose me. We are family and our bond is more than distance. But you must let me go."

She reached out to embrace him, and for the first time in both their lives, Drake did not resist her touch. As her arms wrapped around him, he braced himself for the electric charge of her gift, but it never came. He raised his eyes to hers in a silent question.

"There is nothing wrong with you," she said. "There never was."

Drake broke into tears, the years of fear, heartbreak and guilt breaking to the surface. He wept, but he could not have said what he mourned: the children they had once been or the people they were about to become.

They stayed wrapped in each other's arms until the sun crept over the horizon.

* * *

The gong that woke Drake the next morning was insistent with alarm.

"What's going on?" he asked Oduwe when he shambled into the kitchen. His head throbbed with pain and his eyes burned. Every muscle ached with weariness, but he felt a curious sense of lightness – as if he'd been freed of a burden he hadn't realized he carried.

Oduwe, who sat at the kitchen table with a bowl of hot corn mush and a cup of mint tea, raised an eyebrow at Drake's dishevelled appearance but made no comment. It wasn't her way to delve too deep into the personal lives of her employees, as long as they got their work done.

"One of the Acolytes has run off," she said as she tucked into her breakfast. "Get dressed; we have work to do. The Mother Superior will be in a black mood today."

Drake nodded and turned to head back to his room when the gardener called him back.

"Just wanted to say I'm sorry," she said. "It was the bald one; I know you had your heart set on her."

"It's not like that," Drake said. "She's family. And she'll be fine."

To Have Your Beans and Eat Them Too

J.V. Sadler

SOMEONE *just got shot and they're all smiling,* Beany thought while cowering in his recliner. Despite being a proud elderly Black man stuck in his old ways, he could shrink to the size of a scared child. But he wasn't a child. Just a bit confused every now n' then, that's all.

"C'mon, dance." Some woman had her face inches from his, smiling wildly and sweating as if she'd just won a marathon.

She shot someone, and she's smiling. Beany gathered all the saliva he could in his drying mouth and spat on the madwoman.

"Dad!"

Senses rushed back to him upon hearing the word. The woman wiping spit off her face in disgust was his daughter Jemison. And in her hand was not a gun, but a confetti-bursting party popper. And it was Christmas. And he had just ruined it…again.

Beany reached to console his daughter. His knees cracked from standing, but his wife forced him back down to prevent further injury to his aging body. This had to be his wife. It *had* to be. The way she swiftly caught his arm as his balance teetered was firm but tender.

She said, "Don't worry yourself, Beany," as he sank back into his recliner.

Yes, his wife Piggy. He loved the moniker that fit right in with his own; together they were Pork n' Beans. His favorite meal was a simple can of beans – a delicacy you couldn't find anymore. Once a poor man's meal and a staple in every pantry, a can of beans could be spotted on display at a history museum. Sustenance tablets, those flat, chalky whats-its that dissolved on the tongue, didn't fulfill the satisfaction of having a real meal. Beany missed eating baked beans, swallowing, then letting out a fart or belch in front of Jenine – er, Jemison. J-E-M…

"I'm so sorry," Beany said, lowering his head.

Someone quieted the music so that Bing Crosby whispered his Christmas classic. The partying relatives ceased dancing. They glanced at the un-burst party poppers in their hands, then shoved them in their pockets or back in the store packaging.

"It's okay, Dad." Jemison knelt beside her father and caressed his bouncing leg. "What do you want to do? How can we make this a special Christmas for you?"

Beany adored Wintertime. Christmas meant a bright red bike – or an action figure! Mama always crossed her arms in content as little Beany tore open a gift wrapped perfectly in newspaper.

Beany responded with the only natural answer: "Gifts!" He knew something was wrong when his daughter's lips quivered and her smile flipped.

"Oh, Beany." Peggy (*Piggy*!) sat next to him and leaned closer.

He felt them both caressing his leg.

Piggy continued. "We already opened everything. Dontchu remember?"

Beany contemplated the carpeted floor riddled with decorative reindeer paper.

"Well," Jemison interrupted. "We haven't opened this one."

She darted for the nearest gift bag and stuffed it with a handful of already torn wrappings. Beany's eyes widened, and a smile surfaced. He rummaged through the gift bag, anticipating as a lover would an engagement ring, but frowned at a pair of non-slip hospital socks.

"But Mama, I want He-Man!" Beany yelled and slammed the socks to the carpet.

"Baby, I couldn't get no overtime. I'll get you a new one next year. How about for your birthday I get you one?" Mama said, reaching to embrace him.

"Mama." Beany tugged at his mother's jean skirt. "I want He-Man. Ronald already got one..."

Piggy held back tears as she watched her husband plead with their daughter and call for his Mama who had been dead well over two decades.

"Dad, I'll get you one. I'll go get you one right now," Jemison cried and tried to get her father to stop pulling at her. She didn't know what a "He-Man" was.

"I wanna play!" Beany desperately needed his best friend Ronald so they could play superheroes together. But Ronald had also passed away a long time ago. And an old action figure could easily go for a grand at one of those online auction sites.

I wanna play with you, Papa!

A sweet, tiny voice whisked in the air like a passing thought. Beany waited for it to speak again.

We can play together, Papa!

He still had a grip on Jemison. *What is that voice?* he wondered.

I can be Super Dino!

Beany put his ear to his daughter's stomach. A voice spoke from inside her.

Let's play, Papa!

"Who are you?" Beany asked.

A vision. No, it wasn't a vision. It was more than that. A different world materialized in front of him. The carpet transformed to sand. A fierce wind blew against him. He was outside in a heavy fog. If he wasn't a God-fearing man, he would've cursed. Panic set in until a voice told him *It's okay, Papa*. He touched the thick, gray clouds that roamed the Earth around him. Through the rolling fog, he could see a bit of red peeking through.

There, a little Black girl with large barrettes in her hair played in the dirt. The red that he saw was the flowing cape of a toy dinosaur. The girl looked over her shoulder at Beany and beamed a wide smile. She lacked a few teeth where new adult ones would eventually grow. Despite being in the desolate sandland, the girl offered comfort that Beany hadn't known in a very long time.

Beany reached his hand out and when the little girl that sat yards away did the same, she appeared in front of him. They felt each other's palms.

"Who are you?" Beany asked again.

"Bessie. But Mommy calls me Bess."

"And who is your mommy?"

At that moment, a snatching force yanked Beany's body backwards. He flew through the air. His mouth made an O-shape but didn't have time to scream.

"I'll get you one, I promise!" Jemison still pleaded.

Beany looked at Jemison, then to her belly, then to her again. He hadn't noticed his mouth was still agape. He pointed to his daughter and said, "You're pregnant."

Jemison held back a laugh. "You're kidding."

"It was a B name. B-Betty. B-Beth. B-Bess."

His daughter stumbled back and placed her hand on her stomach. Her wild eyes darted around.

"I always..." Jemison spoke just above a whisper. "I always wanted a little girl. I said to myself I would call her Bessie. Bess for short." Her face turned serious. "I had my period just a few days ago. It's not possible."

Everyone left the Christmas party in thorough confusion. Jemison stayed behind to clean up the party remnants. The home remained silent – neither Beany nor his daughter spoke about the incident. Jemison still made sure her father took his shower. He couldn't bend to reach his feet anymore, so Piggy helped him floss a washcloth between his toes. Jemison also made sure her father took his medication. He needed just one pill a day: a bright orange one so small that Beany had to be careful not to grab several at once.

Piggy forced the pill into her husband's mouth as he squirmed. "I know it tastes awful, honey, but you gotta take this."

He grimaced when pennies filled his mouth. This pill, the folks in charge of the preliminary study had told the family, was the newest miracle that promised to reverse the effects of Alzheimer's disease. He took one pill a night with water and had been doing so for nearly six months. Beany gagged, threatening to cough up the pill. A flood of hard water entered his mouth and he swallowed completely.

"Good job, honey," Piggy said, pouring the rest of the tap water into Beany's mouth so the metallic taste could pass.

"You're doing good, Dad," Jemison said. She guided him out of the bathroom and into the bedroom. "The doctors want to see you again tomorrow."

The old man grumbled under his breath. He hated doctors. They poked and prodded at him and never gave him a planet Saturn sticker or one of those huge cherry suckers with the bubblegum in the middle. *Bubblegum*, he mused, then his mouth instinctively made chewing motions. Blowing bubbles was a lifetime ago. He despised bubblegum-flavored sustenance tablets.

"You hungry already? You know you're not supposed to eat at night." Jemison guided her father's head down onto the pillow and pulled the comforter up to his chin. "Goodnight, Daddy. Night, Mama."

Jemison was gone. Beany's mouth settled its imaginary gum chewing. He sank into the soft mattress that was reaching a decade old but still usable. It had to be usable because one of those new, adjustable beds cost something ridiculous. All the family's money went towards caring for Beany – reconstructing their bathtub into a sit-down shower, a chairlift for the stairs, shirts without buttons so that he couldn't confuse them for beetles…the only thing affordable were the pills. The pills that Beany hated but knew it made his wife and daughter happy.

He remembered his daughter rushing to him with a computer in her hand. "They can help you," he heard Jemison say as she pushed the screen into his face. "It says so right here: A preliminary study." The text was official-looking but too small for him to read. The illustration of the smiling older couple walking through a field of flowers reassured him that maybe it would be okay. He squinted, trying to focus on the first sentence. "I signed you up already." Jemison retrieved the computer before he could get past *A Revolutionary New Drug*.

As he sank further into his tiredness, Beany imagined what it would be like to know the name of all his brothers and sisters again. Or to get through the morning news in its entirety without re-reading the first paragraph. Or to recognize the beautiful woman who rested next to him.

Beany stole a glance at the wise-looking woman who slept peacefully. She shifted around and faced him with her eyes fluttering underneath their lids and mouth slightly open. Wrinkles at the corners of her mouth lifted upward, marking a permanent smile. Tufts of god-white hair poked from under her puffy black bonnet and fell at different lengths on her face. Copper-brown skin was precious metal and a shade or two lighter than his own deep russet color. He wanted to touch her saggy cheeks but thought she might melt under his fingers like fairground ice cream in the hot summer sun.

Who is this woman? His eyes drooped heavier. *I hope to make her my wife one day.* He drifted asleep.

Papa! Let's play, Papa! He picks up He-Man. I'll be Super Dino, Papa! He twirls the toy in the air. We're flying! His feet are no longer on the ground. The Earth elongates further and further away. You're a hero, Papa! He lets the toy fall to the abyss and straightens his arms ahead of him. His granddaughter does the same. They are superheroes.

"Honey, it's time to wake. Jemison's coming to pick us up." Piggy had already removed her bonnet and did her white hair into a thinning afro.

Beanie struggled to his feet and blocked the sun shining through their drawn curtains with his hands.

"C'mon, slow poke." She laughed, which made him laugh too.

He got dressed in a one piece that zipped in the back. He ran his hands over his chest. *No beetles.*

Jemison arrived in a buggy that she and Piggy had to practically push Beany into. They finally buckled him in the passenger seat. The harder he panted, the closer the interior caved in. The increasingly shrinking car made him nauseated. He dodged the trees and birds and other cars and buildings that sped at him. The world zoomed at lightning speed.

"Honey, it's just a short drive away." Piggy massaged his shoulders from the backseat. "We're nearly there," she said every couple of minutes.

Beanie swatted at the windshield the entire two hours to the doctor's office.

"Let's go, Mr. Freedman."

"You won't take me in!" Beany screamed at the man in the long white coat.

They were going to take him to jail, he knew. Prison. He searched for Jameson, *his daughter*? and Maggy, *his wife*? as he struggled against the white coat. Jameson's and Maggy's eyes welled. Another white coat ran to the scene and grabbed Beany's other arm. The old man's body went limp. He huffed and let his head dangle to the side.

"I don't want to go to prison," Beany whimpered.

"Dad, this is the hospital. We're at the doctor's. They just want to do a few tests to see how the medication is doing," Jameson said.

At the front of the prison lit a big red cross. Come to think of it, he had never heard of any warden wearing a lab coat. His body stiffened up so the two staff released their grasp. His face was flustered, his fingers searched for something to hold, and his legs quaked. Everything blanked as he tried to process what had happened. Jameson and Maggy embraced him. Wait… *Jameson? That's a boy's name, right*?

"Who are you?" Beany asked the two women consoling him.

"Jemison. And this is Mom – Piggy," his daughter responded, fighting back sobs.

Beany gained his composure. "Piggy. Jemison. Right." He strutted forward, leaving them all behind.

"Mr. Freedman, welcome!" A hispanic woman smiled.

Beany, his family, and two assistants all stuffed in her office. He had to look down to meet her eyes. She had her lab coat sleeves rolled and folded to her elbows. Beany noticed that the hem of the coat had been crudely shortened. The heavy prescription in her glasses magnified her bulging fish eyes.

"I'm Dr. Alfaro. Head of the Memorcil study." She reached her hand out.

The moment Beany grasped her palm for the handshake, a shiver darted through his body. Linoleum tiles turned to sand. Beany shivered again when wind pushed against him. *I'm back here*, he thought. He inched into the foggy land.

"Bess!" he shouted. "Bess, child, I'm here."

The distant traveling clouds wheezed. Beany paused to listen. The sounds of spitting phlegm. A hacking fit. He approached a lone hospital bed. Medical attachments and baby-blue sheets contrasted with the land's dust. He moved closer to inspect the reclined person. It was a woman with a sunken and tired face. She had thin and brittle patchy hair. He could see the blue veins in her arms doing their damndest to keep circulation. Big coke-bottle glasses rested on the tip of her nose, about to fall.

"Dr. Alfaro?" Beany asked in disbelief.

The ill woman took her time to point her discolored finger to a hanging poster. Beany examined it. It was a diagram of a uterus. Another gust of wind. The diagram blew away to reveal a photo underneath. Beany winced, seeing what he guessed to be the inside of the uterus. A pasty glob intruded the blood-saturated pinkish organ. The photo came alive when the uterus wriggled like it naturally would inside a body. Beany gasped. The glob extended its milk tentacles and spread to nearby viscera. New masses grew all around and suddenly the uterus wasn't the only organ infected with the substance. Vagina, cervix, ovaries. Then, to the rectum. And the bladder. The ill woman hacked again. She attempted to speak but could only mouth the words: "*Help me*." Then, the mighty force yanked Beany backwards.

"You have Alzheimer's, which affects your memory, perception, and mental functionalities. We hope that Memorcil can slow or even reverse memory loss."

Beany was back in the office, still shaking the doctor's hand. He squeezed. He knew that she probably noticed his concern when her brow scrunched.

"Today, my team and I want to conduct some tests to see how Memorcil is affecting your brain," Dr. Alfaro continued. She had to practically snatch her hand away.

The doctor and her two assistants led the family to a spacious room split into different sections. One section resembled a grocery store (an old-school one with *real* groceries and not sustenance tablets). Another, a child's playroom (*building blocks*!). And the last section, a table and two chairs with a stack of cards.

Beany kneaded his hands as Dr. Alfaro explained the first test to him. He urged himself to tell her what he envisioned, but didn't know exactly how to tell it.

"You ready?" the doctor asked.

Beany nodded, despite being too deep in his own head to listen.

"Please shop for milk, eggs, and a head of broccoli," she instructed.

Still unsure of what to say but wanting to co-operate, Beany grabbed a shopping basket and faced a shelf of fake food. *Milk, eggs, broccoli*. His eyes searched for anything that resembled milk. He chose a bright carton and plopped it in his basket. *Milk, eggs, broccoli*, he reminded himself. Well, he needed milk first. He scanned through each shelf until he found a bright carton. *Milk, eggs, broccoli*, he reminded himself. The first on the list was milk. He checked the top shelf, then made his way down. A can of beans whispered his name. He had to acknowledge it.

He clutched the beans and said, "My Mama called me Beany cause I loved me some beans. I would fart and burp just to make her and Ronald laugh." He knew the beans weren't on his list, but took them anyway.

"Alright, I think that's enough," Dr. Alfaro said.

"How'd I do?"

The doctor placed each item from his basket onto the checkout area: two cartons of orange juice and a can of beans. Beany dropped his shoulders. *She must've switched the milk with the juice when I wasn't looking.*

"The next test, I will throw a building block and I want you to catch it."

They moved to the playroom. Dr. Alfaro tossed a block underhand, and Beany caught it with his wrists. She threw another one, and he caught it square on. The last one, he fumbled a little but ultimately caught it between his knees.

"Good. Let's talk at the table."

The two sat across from one another.

"I'm going to show you three cards. I want you to memorize them."

Beany felt a gust of wind. He rubbed together his fingers, noticing the sand that accumulated. He inhaled, and the sensations disappeared.

"A banana. A monkey. And a smiley face," Beany blurted out.

"Oh, I haven't picked the cards yet," she chuckled. She then shuffled a stack of cards, chose three, and gawked at them. "That's right," Dr. Alfaro stammered. "Let's do five more."

"Grapes. Elephant. Apple. Triangle. And a laughing face," Beany stated. "Wait – a *blue* triangle."

Dr. Alfaro shuffled the cards again and placed five of them face down on the table. With every card she flipped over, every card he had already revealed, Beany could understand her brain wrapping itself around the situation.

"Family, if you will." Dr. Alfaro motioned for Jemison and Piggy.

The assistants pulled some extra chairs for the women to sit.

"Let me be frank. Mr. Freedman's cognitive function has not made any significant improvement since we last met. In fact, it seems to be declining at a similar rate within the range of a typical elderly patient with Alzheimer's."

Jemison and Piggy were audibly disappointed.

"But," Dr. Alfaro said, lifting her voice. "His motor skills still hold up. Maybe some of the finer details he might struggle with, but I liked what I saw with the catch activity."

Beany caught his wife and daughter forcing themselves to smile.

"What I really want to talk about, though..." The doctor hesitated. "He was able to accurately predict the flashcards before I even pulled them. I've been in this profession for twenty years and I have never seen anyone – young, old, Alzheimer's or not – guess the cards correctly before seeing them."

"We had a Christmas party," Jemison chimed in. "And he told me I would have a baby named Bess. I always wanted a little girl." Jemison turned to her parents. "I took a pregnancy test this morning. I couldn't believe it at first, but I'm pregnant."

"Oh, my baby!" Piggy exclaimed and hugged her daughter.

Beany joined their embrace.

"Okay, okay," Jemison said, letting go of the two of them. "I don't know what to say. Or what to think."

"I need to think about this a little more too before we do anything else," Dr. Alfaro said. She stood, and the family did the same.

Before Beany exited, he said to the doctor, "I think you should get your lady parts checked out."

"Beany! Don't be rude!" Piggy yelled.

"It's fine," said Dr. Alfaro. "I think I just might do that."

The phone rang on a slow Saturday morning. Piggy answered it and Beany watched as her *uh-huh* and *yeah-huh* escalated into *oh my*! and *is that right*? Piggy ended the call and took a brief moment of silence.

"Well?" Beany finally asked.

"Dr. Alfaro saw her gynecologist. At first they didn't find anything, but she demanded they do a biopsy," Piggy replied.

Beany swallowed.

"They found the cancer early, thank God. It's very treatable. She said they're going to try some type of hormone therapy before thinking about surgery."

Beany placed his hand on his heart. He wanted so badly to sigh with relief, but he couldn't help but think he caused her cancer. Maybe he made this stuff happen, Jemison's pregnancy and all. His heartrate increased from a steady rhythmic beat to a rapid thumping.

"Also, the folks doing the Memorcil study want to do some more tests. Maybe do some of those brain scans. They'll probably keep you overnight – two or three days at the most," Piggy said.

Beany's heartbeat was a rock drummer's solo.

"I don't want to go. I hate the doctor's office," Beany asserted. "They'll poke me! And they'll cut me open!"

Giant figures loomed over him. The giants sharpened their kitchen knives and revved their buzz saws. Beany screamed for the one person he knew could save him.

"I want my Mama!"

A strange woman approached him, but he snapped at her. His teeth nipped the tip of her finger.

"I hate doctors. I want my Mama!"

The strange woman approached again, but this time succeeded in taking him by the face. "Okay. No more, honey. No more," she said.

That strange woman was his Mama, and she had come just for him. Beany hugged her and smelled her white hair done in an afro. He kissed her saggy cheeks and touched the corner of her mouth that was wrinkled into a permanent smile.

"I love you, Mama."

Piggy cried a confusing mixture of love, sorrow, and wistfulness with her husband.

After that day, Beany stopped taking those awful Memorcil pills. The entire study shut down. Within six months of not taking the medication, Beany couldn't visit his granddaughter in the sandlands anymore. He stopped predicting next week's news. And distant relatives stopped trying to get lottery numbers out of him. Jemison found a site online that sold *real* cans of beans. Yes, they had to fit it into the budget, but it was worth it. On Beany's birthday, the neighborhood came together to give him a gift.

"From us, to you," said a very pregnant Jemison.

It was He-Man. He could hardly believe it. He would get to play superheroes with Ronald again. *Where is that fool?* he asked himself. *I got one just like he got and he's bailing on me.*

"I'll play with you, Papa. We all will."

Who is this person? he questioned at first, but didn't inquire further. Whomever this pregnant woman was, whomever the woman with the white afro was, whomever these neighborhood people were, he knew he loved them dearly.

Are We Yet Worthy

T.M. Sayed

AYA GRUNTED as she lifted herself over the old concrete wall, straining with gloved hands to haul herself up and over what had once stood as part of the old highway's roadblocks. She had chosen to walk today, one last march down an ancient road before it was reclaimed, a ritualized idiocy she had found herself growing more and more used to over the years in her line of work.

Her sturdy biodegradable mesh boots clashed with the old cracked asphalt beneath her feet, rising into a concrete forest all around her.

Her wrist chirruped a notification as one of the three hundred reclamation bots that were busy tearing apart the old abandoned city around her sent a notice for a required human confirmation. She flipped through the footage as she walked down the empty highway, seeking what had befuddled the drone's instructions. It turned out to be an old building with the air of a public service provider. It stood out with its carved columned facade and brick walls, in contrast to the concrete and glass rising all around it. It had a taller, tower-like construction on one side, as if mimicking the religious houses that were some of the few buildings to survive the wrath of her scrapyard army. Maybe whatever old architect had built that city hall had had a premonition that one day she would come to tear down their creation and had tried to equip their offspring with the means of survival.

She archived the footage with an attached note of low heritage score, and sent the confirmation to her bot: Tear it down, recycle it.

Aya pictured her bot buzzing happily as it got the 'good to go'. She liked to imagine her drones with little personalities; she had even named a few of her favorite ones. Hers was a lonely job, removing the refuse of old follies, the marks of people who just built and expanded and compounded over each other without a care for the abyss an endless growth could lead towards. They built pustules of crammed cities that oozed plastic and $CO2$ like a wound opened into the crust of the earth.

Her bots had started with those huge mounds of trash, usually found at cities' outskirts; they finished quickly with those and had waited for her to survey the rest of the old city, and assign them the plans for reclamation.

Fayoum, as it had once been called, had been continuously occupied for nearly four thousand years. But not anymore. Most of the city was to be torn down. They couldn't leave the concrete alone, to degrade and release the gasses slowly back into the atmosphere. She left her drones to their work and continued down the highway. By next week, when she expected to return, she would be walking back on a dirt trail.

* * *

Hours of walking later, and Aya was standing in a completely different world from an entirely different age. The new city, now more of a village, where the population had moved to, extended to her right and down into what was once the river valley.

It was entirely made of mud bricks. There may have once been a town here that sat at the edge of the old city, right on the banks of the river. However, the river was gone, and soon the city too would be gone. The new course of the Nile was way off to the east, at a lower elevation, and the dark soil that continuously struggled against the encroaching sand was all that remained of its ancient holy valley, one of the primordial wombs that had birthed the human civilization of the last age.

The inhabitants had noticed her approaching. Despite the appearance of the low, square mud buildings, the inhabitants displayed a varied array of advanced tech, a mixture of organic and digital woven together with an impressive level of homogeneity. She approached from a packed earth road, weaving between green and gold fields that hugged the town on all sides, seeking safety from the desert on the horizon.

Small buzzing drones hovered all over, each hundred or so congregating like a swarm of bees around one human operator picking their way through the fields.

Here on the outer farms, the fields were shaped like crescent hills in the sandy soil, dotted with green and rust red on the leeward side, where the sparse rain collected, sprouting short but hardy trees of golden and red pomegranates. Deeper in, closer to the town, the ground turned darker, and the fields grew thicker and more lush, homes and farmhouses stuck like pegs in the sand among the fields.

The farmers watched her warily as she wove between their hills, conscious of her Mandate ID that to them marked her as potential trouble. Generally, you wouldn't want the Mandate coming to your town, telling you it was no longer sustainable to live here, that rice was no longer a viable food source as it needed too much water, or maybe that your carefully cultivated fields actually now belonged to the short-tailed northern gerbils.

True, the Mandate couldn't actually enforce these 'propositions'. They weren't exactly the government. We didn't have one of those anymore, not in these parts of the world. It was either corporate cities trying to balance between a veneer of environmentalism that didn't extend beyond their logos or cut too hard into their profit margins, desperately clinging to neo-colonialist capitalism's endless growth, now fresh with solar farms instead of oil rigs.

Or it was how it was here in the northern deserts; scattered settlements budding out of the ruins of the old, like mushrooms and termites growing from and in the corpses of old cities while feeding on them. Scattered across the desert, aware of each other but only working together to cover needs, not to chase an ever so elusive 'progress'.

Some forms of order still existed in that anarchist expanse that covered almost a third of the African continent; network communications, medication distribution, research sharing and even trade between settlements, agreed upon but not formalized, lest they risk the delicate balance of co-operative decentralization.

And of course, the Mandate, chief among these non-governmental, non-corporate organizations, and as so, naturally, the most suspect of them all. Many thought of them as trying to start an old-style government again, and she wasn't sure some of the actions of her syndicate really helped assuage these fears.

They weren't her bosses, Aya didn't take orders from them like a corporate rat scurrying to fulfill her master's quarterly plan. She definitely didn't have blind faith in their methods. It was voluntary work. They simply made the plans, and it was either picked up or ignored. She wouldn't be here if she didn't like it, if she didn't enjoy the slow methodical work of dismantling the toys of old tyrants and entrepreneurs.

One such 'plan' had brought her here. The townsfolk must have been told of her presence in the old city. She wouldn't be much trouble to them, and they would get what recycled materials they asked for. But it wasn't just that which brought her to them, it was another project she had accidentally come across a while ago and had been following it ever since it piqued her curiosity. When the call came for someone to carry a message to Manfalot, she leaped on it. She'd deliver the message, and if she was lucky, she would be just in time to watch.

* * *

After some not so fruitful conversations with the farmers, she eventually found the person she was to deliver the message to. It would have been much easier if one of them had agreed to give her access to a drone for a quick scan around, but they felt like being a little petty. She could excuse that; some of them may have just recently moved away from the old city, stubbornly holding on to sentimentalities painted on bricks and plaster.

Some of the footage of her drones showed painted walls inside gutted buildings, butterflies and sunshines, walls smeared by grubby tiny hands that may just be some of the same hands now toiling the land around her.

* * *

A few minutes later she sat on the ground in an open field, a low table of woven wicker before her. The person she had come to find was inside a tarp-covered field lab, a few paces off; it looked like a miniature greenhouse, except none of the plants inside were really green. They wore mute-colored overalls similar to the other farmers, with a wide-brimmed hat and a pair of large spectacles. They looked a bit darker than the locals, with features from further up south.

Dr Sowa wasn't in any official capacity in charge, but some reports said they were the most likely to be listened to, since they were on the agricultural collective who mostly negotiated with others in the name of the town. They would be the one most likely to listen to Aya, being one of the greatest living biologists in the world.

Their work in their youth around Lake Chad was held in great respect by the Mandate, even if they had turned down multiple awards ceremonies, and kept avoiding being pinned down for endorsement of the Mandate's plans.

As one of the best microbotanists of their age, they could have been a leading figure in the Mandate's effort of land reclamation. The fact that such a prominent mind of her generation had refused her syndicate didn't quell the anxiety over their criticism.

She sat sipping on a mug of tea they had offered, before telling her to wait. She waited patiently, watching some domesticated goats dig about in the sand for dry weeds with some efficient accuracy. The doctor eventually came out, carrying a small glass tank of water with a weird purple algae floating in it. Aya wasn't sure if it was an experiment related to their work or their lunchbox. Probably both, given the doctor's field of practice.

"I read your letter, several letters. You didn't have to deliver it again in person," they said as they sat down opposite her, placing their tank on the table and keeping an eye on it while they talked in their quiet voice.

"They just wanted to make sure it reached all the inhabitants; the area could get a little unsafe in the coming months while the herd adjusts to their territory." She flicked open the data tablet she had, ignoring multiple notifications from her bots, and clicked the message she was to deliver. An attached map showed the town she was in now and various newly designated safety zones around it, helpfully colored in a gradient from green to red.

"They don't have any authority to enforce that, obviously," she continued as they studied the map silently.

"Obviously," they echoed with a sarcastic scoff that she wasn't sure how to interpret, so she kept going.

"Yes…well, if you protest, which you haven't done, the reintroduction plan could be readjusted, or even delayed. They wanted to really make sure that you knew and had no objections. It's the last chance as the herd is already on its way."

They studied her above their tank, their glasses glinting with a tiny script of high-tech data that streamed before their large black eyes, hiding their steady glare at her. They wiped a drop of sweat from their face before it reached their white and black beard. Now that she considered it, the water was getting hotter, bubbles of gas forming in the water, but she could detect no heat source. Solar concentration, perhaps? She couldn't make out any visible beams and no panels or lenses were above them. The tank was open from above. Was it the algae itself maybe..? How?

"No reply was needed from us, so we gave none." Their voice was accented, but clear enough for her to pick up the dry distrust. Why such hostility to the Mandate? It wasn't a law, just a simple framework for co-operation. "No adjustments will be necessary, we will simply adapt to our new challenges."

"I know…you may have reservations about the work of the syndicate. I do too. It's a healthy level of paranoia to have in this age. You don't have to trust everyone's ambitions, but the plan works. It has been working for decades."

They chuckled softly, swirling a finger over the surface of their algae-heated water. "Grand plans for progress? That sounds familiar," they said with a smirk.

She almost winced; she walked straight into that one. It was an old argument, rehearsed. The purpose of the Mandate, once agreed upon by governments and companies, the very entities it then rendered obsolete.

"For degrowth," she replied with emphasis, tapping her hand to the table. "Which is almost over with," she continued. "Old levels of resources and energy usage are almost stable, or so I have heard." She tacked a bit of uncertainty at the end. She didn't really follow up on all that, and it wouldn't do to just argue from some pseudo-patriotic sense of duty, especially not with one of the smartest people she had ever met. That wasn't really why she had come here.

"I'm not interested in their games, that's all," they replied and stood up, "If you came here appealing to my co-operational spirit, as your letters have said, I'm already busy with other important work. If you are here to deliver a message, then you have. You're now free to leave."

She stared down silently. *Yeah, she may have ruined that.* "Sorry to have bothered you again, Doctor," she said as she stood up as well. "Can I stay until they come?"

They shrugged as they walked back to their greenhouse. "It was simply a suggested course of action. I have no power to enforce it." She didn't miss the sarcasm in their tone.

* * *

Aya decided to stay.

Despite the unwelcome stares, the villagers weren't crass enough to refuse her hospitality. Once she was actually invited to stay, most of that initial hostility melted away. The news would be out soon and some of those affected might get angry at her. But the land lost to the town wouldn't be privately owned, it wouldn't affect single members. The community would take the hit as a whole, and the shock would be absorbed by the collective.

She was given a bed in a shared living space, secluded enough for privacy and surprisingly cozy. The mud brick buildings were one or two stories tall at most, except for a few public buildings that were built with a little more fanfare, rising high with even a few domed ceilings here and there.

The buildings weren't dull as they may have initially appeared. They were pretty well decorated, with shards of colored pottery and glass embedded in the walls in marvelously complex patterns, some repurposed junk metal made into abstract geometric art hanging above doors. They weren't all low-tech either; screens dotted the place here and there. Drones flitted about between buildings, mostly agricultural like the ones she first saw, but she glimpsed some maintenance drones not dissimilar from her own, and even a few security ones, watchful, but unarmed.

There were a few tram tracks around, and she took one of the solar powered vehicles around town on her first day, just to try it out. It had been a few months since she had been in a crowded city, and she wanted to absorb it all. The sounds and smells of a lived-in place felt so enriching after her days in the abandoned ghost city.

They didn't ask her to work. She was offered the food and shelter free of charge, but she lent aid anyway. A few hours of her day were spent checking on the drone systems with the engineers in town and showing off her own layers of complex commands sent to her drones to make them almost autonomous.

She spent most of her days after that in the public media library, where she found a nook by the mashrabiya and sequestered herself behind a row of clay water jugs, used partly to drink and partly to cool the building passively.

She watched the outside street from her hidden perch on the upper floor, going through the data feeds from her drone army. A herd of wild donkeys had taken over part of the northern district once the humans had left. The animals had once been fully domesticated, but it didn't take long for them to take to the wild. She wrote a few lines of code that would let her drones recognize the shape and sounds of the animals and avoid bothering them too much.

A group of teens were watching some old media not far from her, played on a sleek display screen that somehow didn't clash aesthetically with the mud wall it was mounted on. The light from the open skylights and streaming past her from the wooden mesh of the mashrabiya gave the place a calming natural light, perfect for reading on screen or paper. They were watching an old comedy movie common in the earlier decades of the century. Aya smiled at the distant sound of their laughter, as she sent her finished code.

"Why hippos?"

"Huh?" She looked up to see a young man standing behind her protective wall of pottery, dressed in an overly large robe, knitted loosely enough that she could make out the individual threads, a cross between a cardigan and a gilbab that he managed to pull off somehow.

"Hippos…that's what you're here for, right? You're bringing them back here? Why?" He eased himself around, dropping on the cushion left by some previous fellow enjoyer of street-watching.

"Dr Sowa shared the details already?" Aya asked. He shrugged, not committing an answer.

She shrugged back. "They used to live here you know," she continued. "A hundred and fifty years ago or so, before the dams and the cities choked them out. They were a popular depiction in the ancients' monuments."

"The ones you haven't torn down yet, you mean?" he chimed in, unhelpfully.

"We don't destroy monuments, nothing with cultural significance. Those are preserved or left alone." That she was able to say with more conviction than before. She wasn't defending the Mandate, but her own work.

"Who decides? Who decides what's art? Who decides it's important? Who says it's time for the hippos to come back?"

She shifted, annoyed, and turned to watch the street again. It wasn't a question she hadn't heard before. The answer was usually: The experts; the Mandate gathers to itself the best of the best in every field. However, that wasn't entirely true. The best microbotanist on the continent didn't give a damn about them.

"There are…processes…umm…criteria for...I don't know. Hippos are neat, I guess? Why shouldn't we give them back the river? They handled it better than we ever did." That answer seemed good enough for him, as she saw him smile from the corner of her eye.

"But you didn't have to stay. Worried we won't comply with the given orders?"

She sighed and made to stand up.

"I'm joking," he said, holding up his open hands. "Really though, why are you staying? Everything is set in motion. It doesn't need you."

"I want to see them," she said after a while. "Do you know why they no longer live here? Because we needed too much electricity, so we had to dam the river, alter its course, and subdue it to our will. We scarred a god so we could lap at its blood. In the process, we killed its children. Now, after all this work – after the Mandate, the reclamation, the degrowth and circularization – if after all this we can't have both energy and hippos…?" She trailed off and left the question open.

"You need to believe that it is working." He nodded.

* * *

"I expected them to be bigger," Abel said. Beside her, in the driver's seat of one of the town's shared-use trucks, Dr Sowa shaded their eyes with a gloved hand. In the back seat lounged the young man from yesterday, Abel Sowa. The doctor's own son, as it turned out. He had talked their parents into taking her along. She had planned to walk down to the river by herself. She shot him another thankful glance for that.

"I thought so too," she replied, leaning out of the truck as they watched the herd, more than seventy of the beefy mammals, kick up a dust storm behind them. They were guided along by a group of drones that occasionally played animal calls to keep the herd moving.

"They are smaller than the ancient ones," Dr Sowa added. "Bred to survive the new climate." Unlike the younger two passengers, who had only ever seen the animals on screens, they may have actually seen living ones before in their travels.

They may not be the gigantic monsters she had envisioned, but they were still pretty huge. Each as tall as her, as long as a buffalo and weighing probably twice as much.

Their size, however, was dwarfed by the sheer size of the moving city that crawled behind them, like a lumbering giant of myth herding his goats.

The city glided along behind them, a flat barge not of the river but of the sand itself. It moved forward by the combined power of wind rotating its rigid columnar sails and the sun beaming down on its actual sails. Those, confusingly weren't for catching wind, but instead for storing sunrays, then redirecting the heat down into the ship's belly to be converted into energy for when the wind was just not enough.

She didn't know if the city had a name. It wasn't big enough, relatively, to acquire one. It was more of a moving camp, in reality, inhabited by a small tribe of nomads, Bedui or Amazeigh or a combination of both and other groups. Always on the move, staying in one place long enough to take what they needed without straining the resources, an old practice with a new veneer.

The city had come from upstream, near the origins of the Nile, past the cataracts and down into the old valley. As the Mandate had 'suggested', they brought with them the long-awaited return of the valley's old residents. A project that had been in the making for decades, requiring the delicate diplomacy of the Mandate to gather a population, carefully breed and prepare it to be reintroduced to their natural habitat, and gather the data on both their old and new environment. The niches long since emptied and awaiting them to fulfill their unique role.

This was a first of many such groups that would be gradually moved in so as not to strain the ecosystem.

* * *

When the ship city slid to a halt, its wind sails continued to spin, gathering energy, but decoupled from the city to keep it from moving off.

Dr Sowa started the engine of their electric truck, as their son leaned his head out of the car window to stare up at the city they were driving in the shadow of.

Several figures had lowered themselves from the raised platform. Some of them approached, while others spread about the sand, holding long metal rods like the ones used to detect metal in sand.

The group headed their way was led by a middle-aged woman in a flowing green and orange thobe wrapped around one arm and over the head, its fabric threaded with patterns that blinked on and off and shifted to match the environment around her. Her face was dark and wind weathered, dotted with a few Daq tattoos in the shape of circles around dots, some on her forehead and a few on her chin.

She seemed familiar enough with the doctor as she hailed them and approached with her company.

"Salamu," the doctor hailed back in a dialect of the Swahili tongue that was used by the nomads. With a healthy mixture of Arabic words mixed in, she could follow the conversation, even if her command of the language wasn't great. The doctor and their son exchanged a few data chips with the woman as part of their regular exchange of research. Then her companions started to unload the truck's boxes of pomegranates, the latest experimental reintroduction by the doctor.

Aya wanted a few moments with the woman, whom she knew to be their lead bio-engineer, a prominent figure that was a little more susceptible to the Mandate's advances than her sterner colleague. However, she doubted she'd get the chance before the smarter people said what they had to say.

They were invited up on the nomadic city for refreshments and bread. As they neared, she saw one of the pole-wielding scavengers – she assumed – get a blinking at the end of his pole. He stuck it in the sand and knelt down to dig out a wrapped bundle. Aya was surprised when she was told it was bread, left to bake over months by a previous camp passing through. She knew of the old practice of sand backing, but over months? If there was a function to that, they hadn't shared it yet.

She was given some of the bread as they sat near the eastern edge of the city. It was hard and compact, but still felt fresh despite what may have been months in the sand.

They sat in an open-sided tent with the Nile forming the horizon in the distance, its current course lower than the old valley and a lot less cluttered with human refuse. The cloth stretched above them to form a roof left the sides open, and she was glad for the view as she watched the drones herd the hippos all the way down to the water.

Someone adjusted the translucency of the tent to let enough sun through to heat the room. A display inside the tent showed that it wasn't charging batteries at full capacity now that it wasn't opaque enough for full absorption.

The tilted shape of the roof kept air circulating around the interior however, so it never grew hot, just sunny and warm.

Dr Sowa and the city's head scientists were embroiled in back and forth talks about the farming lands and travel paths that would be affected and how best to avoid disruptions to the new and still delicate ecosystem at their doorstep.

Aya sat at the edge of their circle, not excluded but not invited. She shot a few glances each time someone mentioned the Mandate. She didn't say much, and didn't mind it. She felt a strange kind of solemnity, a sense of reverence for the animals, that she had rarely felt for the old ruins she regularly haunted.

They were far enough away now that they were just distant dots, but she asked to access drone footage and sat watching that instead, with a new sense of appreciation for their on-screen size now that she had seen some in real life.

They swarmed down into the water, splashing and shaking the green fronds as they swam into the river. The drones made a wide circle around them. They would keep watch for a while to protect the animals. Even though they were ready for the wildlife, their population was only sturdy enough to survive deaths by predators and injuries, not human interference.

That would be the real purpose of the coming months, to see if they really could have both. To see if, after all this work, humanity had actually changed, had taken a step forward.

They would watch to see if they had finally proven themselves once again worthy of the hippos.

Black No More

George S. Schuyler

Preface

OVER TWENTY YEARS AGO a gentleman in Asbury Park, N.J. began manufacturing and advertising a preparation for the immediate and unfailing straightening of the most stubborn Negro hair. This preparation was called Kink-No-More, a name not wholly accurate since users of it were forced to renew the treatment every fortnight.

During the intervening years many chemists, professional and amateur, have been seeking the means of making the downtrodden Aframerican resemble as closely as possible his white fellow citizen. The temporarily effective preparations placed on the market have so far proved exceedingly profitable to manufacturers, advertising agencies, Negro newspapers and beauty culturists, while millions of users have registered great satisfaction at the opportunity to rid themselves of kinky hair and grow several shades lighter in color, if only for a brief time. With America's constant reiteration of the superiority of whiteness, the avid search on the part of the black masses for some key to chromatic perfection is easily understood. Now it would seem that science is on the verge of satisfying them.

Dr. Yusaburo Noguchi, head of the Noguchi Hospital at Beppu, Japan, told American newspaper reporters in October 1929, that as a result of fifteen years of painstaking research and experiment he was able to change a Negro into a white man. While he admitted that this racial metamorphosis could not be effected overnight, he maintained that "Given time, I could change the Japanese into a race of tall blue-eyed blonds." The racial transformation, he asserted, could be brought about by glandular control and electrical nutrition.

Even more positive is the statement of Mr. Bela Cati, an electrical engineer residing in New York City, who, in a letter dated August 18, 1930 and addressed to the National Association for the Advancement of Colored People said, in part:

"Once I myself was very strongly tanned by the sun and a European rural population thought that I was a Negro, too. I did not suffer much but the situation was disagreeable. Since that time I have studied the problem and I am convinced that the surplus of the pigment could be removed. In case you are interested and believe that with the aid of your physicians we could carry out the necessary experiments, I am willing to send you the patent specification...and my general terms relating to this invention... The expenses are so to say negligible."

I wish to express my sincere thanks and appreciation to Mr. V.F. Calverton for his keen interest and friendly encouragement and to my wife, Josephine Schuyler, whose co-operation and criticism were of great help in completing *Black No More.*

George S. Schuyler

New York City
September 1, 1930

Chapter I

Max Disher stood outside the Honky Tonk Club puffing a panatela and watching the crowds of white and black folk entering the cabaret. Max was tall, dapper and smooth coffee-brown. His negroid features had a slightly satanic cast and there was an insolent nonchalance about his carriage. He wore his hat rakishly and faultless evening clothes underneath his raccoon coat. He was young, he wasn't broke, but he was damnably blue. It was New Year's Eve, 1933, but there was no spirit of gaiety and gladness in his heart. How could he share the hilarity of the crowd when he had no girl? He and Minnie, his high "yallah" flapper, had quarreled that day and everything was over between them.

"Women are mighty funny," he mused to himself, "especially yallah women. You could give them the moon and they wouldn't appreciate it." That was probably the trouble; he'd given Minnie too much. It didn't pay to spend too much on them. As soon as he'd bought her a new outfit and paid the rent on a three-room apartment, she'd grown uppity. Stuck on her color, that's what was the matter with her! He took the cigar out of his mouth and spat disgustedly.

A short, plump, cherubic black fellow, resplendent in a narrow-brimmed brown fedora, camel's hair coat and spats, strolled up and clapped him on the shoulder: "Hello, Max!" greeted the newcomer, extending a hand in a fawn-colored glove, "What's on your mind?"

"Everything, Bunny," answered the debonair Max. "That damn yallah gal o' mine's got all upstage and quit."

"Say not so!" exclaimed the short black fellow. "Why I thought you and her were all forty."

"Were is right, kid. And after spending my dough, too! It sure makes me hot. Here I go and buy two covers at the Honky Tonk for tonight, thinkin' surely she'd come and she starts a row and quits!"

"Shucks!" exploded Bunny, "I wouldn't let that worry me none. I'd take another skirt. I wouldn't let no dame queer my New Year's."

"So would I, Wise Guy, but all the dames I know are dated up. So here I am all dressed up and no place to go."

"You got two reservations, ain't you? Well, let's you and me go in," Bunny suggested. "We may be able to break in on some party."

Max visibly brightened. "That's a good idea," he said. "You never can tell, we might run in on something good."

Swinging their canes, the two joined the throng at the entrance of the Honky Tonk Club and descended to its smoky depths. They wended their way through the maze of tables in the wake of a dancing waiter and sat down close to the dance floor. After ordering ginger ale and plenty of ice, they reared back and looked over the crowd.

Max Disher and Bunny Brown had been pals ever since the war when they soldiered together in the old 15th regiment in France. Max was one of the Aframerican Fire Insurance Company's crack agents, Bunny was a teller in the Douglass Bank and both bore the reputation of gay blades in black Harlem. The two had in common a weakness rather prevalent among Aframerican bucks: they preferred yellow women. Both swore there were three things essential to the happiness of a colored gentleman: yellow money, yellow women and yellow taxis. They had little difficulty in getting the first and none at all in getting the third but the yellow women they found flighty and fickle. It was so hard to hold them. They were so sought after that one almost required a million dollars to keep them out of the clutches of one's rivals.

"No more yallah gals for me!" Max announced with finality, sipping his drink. "I'll grab a black gal first."

"Say not so!" exclaimed Bunny, strengthening his drink from his huge silver flask. "You ain't thinkin' o' dealin' in coal, are you?"

"Well," argued his partner, "it might change my luck. You can trust a black gal; she'll stick to you."

"How do you know? You ain't never had one. Ever' gal I ever seen you with looked like an ofay."

"Humph!" grunted Max. "My next one may be an ofay, too! They're less trouble and don't ask you to give 'em the moon."

"I'm right with you, pardner," Bunny agreed, "but I gotta have one with class. None o' these Woolworth dames for me! Get you in a peck o' trouble... Fact is, Big Boy, ain't none o' these women no good. They all get old on the job."

They drank in silence and eyed the motley crowd around them. There were blacks, browns, yellows, and whites chatting, flirting, drinking; rubbing shoulders in the democracy of night life. A fog of tobacco smoke wreathed their heads and the din from the industrious jazz band made all but the loudest shrieks inaudible. In and out among the tables danced the waiters, trays balanced aloft, while the patrons, arrayed in colored paper caps, beat time with the orchestra, threw streamers or grew maudlin on each other's shoulders.

"Looky here! Lawdy Lawd!" exclaimed Bunny, pointing to the doorway. A party of white people had entered. They were all in evening dress and in their midst was a tall, slim, titian-haired girl who had seemingly stepped from heaven or the front cover of a magazine.

"My, my, my!" said Max, sitting up alertly.

The party consisted of two men and four women. They were escorted to a table next to the one occupied by the two colored dandies. Max and Bunny eyed them covertly. The tall girl was certainly a dream.

"Now that's my speed," whispered Bunny.

"Be yourself," said Max. "You couldn't touch her with a forty-foot pole."

"Oh, I don't know, Big Boy," Bunny beamed self-confidently. "You never can tell! You never can tell!"

"Well, I can tell," remarked Disher, "'cause she's a cracker."

"How you know that?"

"Man, I can tell a cracker a block away. I wasn't born and raised in Atlanta, Georgia, for nothin', you know. Just listen to her voice."

Bunny listened. "I believe she is," he agreed.

They kept eyeing the party to the exclusion of everything else. Max was especially fascinated. The girl was the prettiest creature he'd ever seen and he felt irresistibly drawn to her. Unconsciously he adjusted his necktie and passed his well-manicured hand over his rigidly straightened hair.

Suddenly one of the white men rose and came over to their table. They watched him suspiciously. Was he going to start something? Had he noticed that they were staring at the girl? They both stiffened at his approach.

"Say," he greeted them, leaning over the table, "do you boys know where we can get some decent liquor around here? We've run out of stuff and the waiter says he can't get any for us."

"You can get some pretty good stuff right down the street," Max informed him, somewhat relieved.

"They won't sell none to him," said Bunny. "They might think he was a Prohibition officer."

"Could one of you fellows get me some?" asked the man.

"Sure," said Max, heartily. What luck! Here was the very chance he'd been waiting for. These people might invite them over to their table. The man handed him a ten dollar bill and Max went out bareheaded to get the liquor. In ten minutes he was back. He handed the man the quart and the change. The man gave back the change and thanked him. There was no invitation to join the party. Max returned to his table and eyed the group wistfully.

"Did he invite you in?" asked Bunny.

"I'm back here, ain't I?" answered Max, somewhat resentfully.

The floor show came on. A black-faced comedian, a corpulent shouter of mammy songs with a gin-roughened voice, three chocolate soft-shoe dancers and an octette of wriggling, practically nude, mulatto chorines.

Then midnight and pandemonium as the New Year swept in. When the din had subsided, the lights went low and the orchestra moaned the weary blues. The floor filled with couples. The two men and two of the women at the next table rose to dance. The beautiful girl and another were left behind.

"I'm going over and ask her to dance," Max suddenly announced to the surprised Bunny.

"Say not so!" exclaimed that worthy. "You're fixin' to get in dutch, Big Boy."

"Well, I'm gonna take a chance, anyhow," Max persisted, rising.

This fair beauty had hypnotized him. He felt that he would give anything for just one dance with her. Once around the floor with her slim waist in his arm would be like an eternity in heaven. Yes, one could afford to risk repulse for that.

"Don't do it, Max!" pleaded Bunny. "Them fellows are liable to start somethin'."

But Max was not to be restrained. There was no holding him back when he wanted to do a thing, especially where a comely damsel was concerned.

He sauntered over to the table in his most sheikish manner and stood looking down at the shimmering strawberry blond. She was indeed ravishing and her exotic perfume titilated his nostrils despite the clouds of cigarette smoke.

"Would you care to dance?" he asked, after a moment's hesitation.

She looked up at him haughtily with cool green eyes, somewhat astonished at his insolence and yet perhaps secretly intrigued, but her reply lacked nothing in definiteness.

"No," she said icily, "I never dance with niggers!" Then turning to her friend, she remarked: "Can you beat the nerve of these darkies?" She made a little disdainful grimace with her mouth, shrugged daintily and dismissed the unpleasant incident.

Crushed and angry, Max returned to his place without a word. Bunny laughed aloud in high glee.

"You said she was a cracker," he gurgled, "an' now I guess you know it."

"Aw, go to hell," Max grumbled.

Just then Billy Fletcher, the head waiter, passed by. Max stopped him. "Ever see that dame in here before?" he asked.

"Been in here most every night since before Christmas," Billy replied.

"Do you know who she is?"

"Well, I heard she was some rich broad from Atlanta up here for the holidays. Why?"

"Oh, nothin'; I was just wondering."

From Atlanta! His home town. No wonder she had turned him down. Up here trying to get a thrill in the Black Belt but a thrill from observation instead of contact. Gee, but white folks were funny. They didn't want black folks' game and yet they were always frequenting Negro resorts.

* * *

At three o'clock Max and Bunny paid their check and ascended to the street. Bunny wanted to go to the breakfast dance at the Dahomey Casino but Max was in no mood for it.

"I'm going home," he announced laconically, hailing a taxi. "Good night!"

As the cab whirled up Seventh Avenue, he settled back and thought of the girl from Atlanta. He couldn't get her out of his mind and didn't want to. At his rooming house, he paid the driver, unlocked the door, ascended to his room and undressed, mechanically. His mind was a kaleidoscope: Atlanta, sea-green eyes, slender figure, titian hair, frigid manner. "I never dance with niggers." Then he fell asleep about five o'clock and promptly dreamed of her. Dreamed of dancing with her, dining with her, motoring with her, sitting beside her on a golden throne while millions of manacled white slaves prostrated themselves before him. Then there was a nightmare of grim, gray men with shotguns, baying hounds, a heap of gasoline-soaked faggots and a screeching, fanatical mob.

He awoke covered with perspiration. His telephone was ringing and the late morning sunshine was streaming into his room. He leaped from bed and lifted the receiver.

"Say," shouted Bunny, "did you see this morning's *Times*?"

"Hell no," growled Max, "I just woke up. Why, what's in it?"

"Well, do you remember Dr. Junius Crookman, that colored fellow that went to Germany to study about three years ago? He's just come back and the *Times* claims he's announced a sure way to turn darkies white. Thought you might be interested after the way you fell for that ofay broad last night. They say Crookman's going to open a sanitarium in Harlem right away. There's your chance, Big Boy, and it's your only chance." Bunny chuckled.

"Oh, ring off," growled Max. "That's a lot of hooey."

But he was impressed and a little excited. Suppose there was something to it? He dressed hurriedly, after a cold shower, and went out to the newsstand. He bought a *Times* and scanned its columns. Yes, there it was:

NEGRO ANNOUNCES REMARKABLE DISCOVERY
Can Change Black to White in Three Days.

Max went into Jimmy Johnson's restaurant and greedily read the account while awaiting his breakfast. Yes, it must be true. To think of old Crookman being able to do that! Only a few years ago he'd been just a hungry medical student around Harlem. Max put down the paper and stared vacantly out of the window. Gee, Crookman would be a millionaire in no time. He'd even be a multi-millionaire. It looked as though science was to succeed where the Civil War had failed. But how could it be possible? He looked at his hands and felt at the back of his head where the straightening lotion had failed to conquer some of the knots. He toyed with his ham and eggs as he envisioned the possibilities of the discovery.

Then a sudden resolution seized him. He looked at the newspaper account again. Yes, Crookman was staying at the Phyllis Wheatley Hotel. Why not go and see what there was to this? Why not be the first Negro to try it out? Sure, it was taking a chance, but think of getting white in three days! No more Jim Crow. No more insults. As a white man he could go anywhere, be anything he wanted to be, do most anything he wanted to do, be a free man at last...and probably be able to meet the girl from Atlanta. What a vision!

He rose hurriedly, paid for his breakfast, rushed out of the door, almost ran into an aged white man carrying a sign advertising a Negro fraternity dance, and strode, almost ran, to the Phyllis Wheatley Hotel.

He tore up the steps two at a time and into the sitting room. It was crowded with white reporters from the daily newspapers and black reporters from the Negro weeklies. In their midst he recognized Dr. Junius Crookman, tall, wiry, ebony black, with a studious and polished manner. Flanking him on either side were Henry ("Hank") Johnson, the "Numbers" banker and Charlie ("Chuck") Foster, the realtor, looking very grave, important and possessive in the midst of all the hullabaloo.

"Yes," Dr. Crookman was telling the reporters while they eagerly took down his statements, "during my first year at college I noticed a black girl on the street one day who had several irregular white patches on her face and hands. That intrigued me. I began to study up on skin diseases and found out that the girl was evidently suffering from a nervous disease known as vitiligo. It is a very rare disease. Both Negroes and Caucasians occasionally have it, but it is naturally more conspicuous on blacks than whites. It absolutely removes skin pigment and sometimes it turns a Negro completely white but only after a period of thirty or forty years. It occurred to me that if one could discover some means of artificially inducing and stimulating this nervous disease at will, one might possibly solve the American race problem. My sociology teacher had once said that there were but three ways for the Negro to solve his problem in America," he gestured with his long slender fingers, "'To either get out, get white or get along.' Since he wouldn't and couldn't get out and was getting along only indifferently, it seemed to me that the only thing for him was to get white." For a moment his teeth gleamed beneath his smartly waxed mustache, then he sobered and went on:

"I began to give a great deal of study to the problem during my spare time. Unfortunately there was very little information on the subject in this country. I decided to go to Germany but I didn't have the money. Just when I despaired of getting the funds to carry out my experiments and studies abroad, Mr. Johnson and Mr. Foster," he indicated the two men with a graceful wave of his hand, "came to my rescue. I naturally attribute a great deal of my success to them."

"But how is it done?" asked a reporter.

"Well," smiled Crookman, "I naturally cannot divulge the secret any more than to say that it is accomplished by electrical nutrition and glandular control. Certain gland secretions are greatly stimulated while others are considerably diminished. It is a powerful and dangerous treatment but harmless when properly done."

"How about the hair and features?" asked a Negro reporter.

"They are also changed in the process," answered the biologist. "In three days the Negro becomes to all appearances a Caucasian."

"But is the transformation transferred to the offspring?" persisted the Negro newspaperman.

"As yet," replied Crookman, "I have discovered no way to accomplish anything so revolutionary but I am able to transform a black infant to a white one in twenty-four hours."

"Have you tried it on any Negroes yet?" queried a sceptical white journalist.

"Why of course I have," said the Doctor, slightly nettled. "I would not have made my announcement if I had not done so. Come here, Sandol," he called, turning to a pale white youth standing on the outskirts of the crowd, who was the most Nordic looking person in the room. "This man is a Senegalese, a former aviator in the French Army. He is living proof that what I claim is true."

Dr. Crookman then displayed a photograph of a very black man, somewhat resembling Sandol but with bushy Negro hair, flat nose and full lips. "This," he announced proudly, "is Sandol as he looked before taking my treatment. What I have done to him I can do to any Negro. He is in good physical and mental condition as you all can see."

The assemblage was properly awed. After taking a few more notes and a number of photographs of Dr. Crookman, his associates and of Sandol, the newspapermen retired. Only the dapper Max Disher remained.

"Hello, Doc!" he said, coming forward and extending his hand. "Don't you remember me? I'm Max Disher."

"Why certainly I remember you, Max," replied the biologist, rising cordially. "Been a long time since we've seen each other but you're looking as sharp as ever. How's things?"

The two men shook hands.

"Oh, pretty good. Say, Doc, how's chances to get you to try that thing on me? You must be looking for volunteers."

"Yes, I am, but not just yet. I've got to get my equipment set up first. I think now I'll be ready for business in a couple of weeks."

Henry Johnson, the beefy, sleek-jowled, mulatto "Numbers" banker, chuckled and nudged Dr. Crookman. "Old Max ain't losin' no time, Doc. When that niggah gits white Ah bet he'll make up fo' los' time with these ofay girls."

Charlie Foster, small, slender, grave, amber-colored, and laconic, finally spoke up: "Seems all right, Junius, but there'll be hell to pay when you whiten up a lot o' these darkies and them mulatto babies start appearing here and there. Watcha gonna do then?"

"Oh, quit singin' th' blues, Chuck," boomed Johnson. "Don't cross bridges 'til yuh come tuh 'em. Doc'll fix that okeh. Besides, we'll have mo' money'n Henry Ford by that time."

"There'll be no difficulties whatever," assured Crookman rather impatiently.

"Let's hope not."

* * *

Next day the newspapers carried a long account of the interview with Dr. Junius Crookman interspersed with photographs of him, his backers and of the Senegalese who had been turned white. It was the talk of the town and was soon the talk of the country. Long editorials were written about the discovery, learned societies besieged the Negro biologist with offers of lecture engagements, magazines begged him for articles, but he turned down all offers and refused to explain his treatment. This attitude was decried as unbecoming a scientist and it was insinuated and even openly stated that nothing more could be expected from a Negro.

But Crookman ignored the clamor of the public, and with the financial help of his associates planned the great and lucrative experiment of turning Negroes into Caucasians.

The impatient Max Disher saw him as often as possible and kept track of developments. He yearned to be the first treated and didn't want to be caught napping. Two objects were uppermost in his mind: To get white and to Atlanta. The statuesque and haughty blonde was ever in his thoughts. He was head over heels in love with her and realized there was no hope for him to ever win her as long as he was brown. Each day he would walk past the tall building that was to be the Crookman Sanitarium, watching the workmen and delivery trucks; wondering how much longer he would have to wait before entering upon the great adventure.

At last the sanitarium was ready for business. Huge advertisements appeared in the local Negro weeklies. Black Harlem was on its toes. Curious throngs of Negroes and whites stood in front of the austere six-story building gazing up at its windows.

Inside, Crookman, Johnson and Foster stood nervously about while hustling attendants got everything in readiness. Outside they could hear the murmur of the crowd.

"That means money, Chuck," boomed Johnson, rubbing his beefsteak hands together.

"Yeh," replied the realtor, "but there's one more thing I wanna get straight: How about that darky dialect? You can't change that."

"It isn't necessary, my dear Foster," explained the physician, patiently. "There is no such thing as Negro dialect, except in literature and drama. It is a well-known fact among informed persons that a Negro from a given section speaks the same dialect as his white neighbors. In the South you can't tell over the telephone whether you are talking to a white man or a Negro. The same is true in New York when a Northern Negro speaks into the receiver. I have noticed the same thing in the hills of West Virginia and Tennessee. The educated Haitian speaks the purest French and the Jamaican Negro sounds exactly like an Englishman. There are no racial or color dialects; only sectional dialects."

"Guess you're right," agreed Foster, grudgingly.

"I know I'm right. Moreover, even if my treatment did not change the so-called Negro lips, even that would prove to be no obstacle."

"How come, Doc," asked Johnson.

"Well, there are plenty of Caucasians who have lips quite as thick and noses quite as broad as any of us. As a matter of fact there has been considerable exaggeration about the contrast between Caucasian and Negro features. The cartoonists and minstrel men have been responsible for it very largely. Some Negroes like the Somalis, Filanis, Egyptians, Hausas and Abyssinians have very thin lips and nostrils. So also have the Malagasys of Madagascar. Only in certain small sections of Africa do the Negroes possess extremely pendulous lips and very broad nostrils. On the other hand, many so-called Caucasians, particularly the Latins, Jews and South Irish, and frequently the most Nordic of peoples like the Swedes, show almost Negroid lips and noses. Black up some white folks and they could deceive a resident of Benin. Then when you consider that less than twenty per cent of our Negroes are without Caucasian ancestry and that close to thirty per cent have American Indian ancestry, it is readily seen that there cannot be the wide difference in Caucasian and Afro-American facial characteristics that most people imagine."

"Doc, you sho' knows yo' onions," said Johnson, admiringly. "Doan pay no 'tenshun to that ole Doubtin' Thomas. He'd holler starvation in a pie shop."

* * *

There was a commotion outside and an angry voice was heard above the hum of low conversation. Then Max Disher burst in the door with a guard hanging onto his coat tail.

"Let loose o' me, Boy," he quarreled. "I got an engagement here. Doc, tell this man something, will you?"

Crookman nodded to the guard to release the insurance man. "Well, I see you're right on time, Max."

"I told you I'd be Johnny-on-the-spot, didn't I?" said Disher, inspecting his clothes to see if they had been wrinkled.

"Well, if you're all ready, go into the receiving room there, sign the register and get into one of those bathrobes. You're first on the list."

The three partners looked at each other and grinned as Max disappeared into a small room at the end of the corridor. Dr. Crookman went into his office to don his white trousers, shoes and smock; Johnson and Foster entered the business office to supervise the clerical staff, while white-coated figures darted back and forth through the corridors. Outside, the murmuring of the vast throng grew more audible.

Johnson showed all of his many gold teeth in a wide grin as he glanced out the window and saw the queue of Negroes already extending around the corner. "Man, man, man!" he chuckled to Foster, "at fifty dollars a th'ow this thing's gonna have th' numbah business beat all hollow."

"Hope so," said Foster, gravely.

* * *

Max Disher, arrayed only in a hospital bathrobe and a pair of slippers, was escorted to the elevator by two white-coated attendants. They got off on the sixth floor and walked to the end of the corridor. Max was trembling with excitement and anxiety. Suppose something should go wrong? Suppose Doc should make a mistake? He thought of the Elks' excursion every summer to Bear Mountain, the high yellow Minnie and her colorful apartment, the pleasant evenings at the Dahomey Casino doing the latest dances with the brown belles of Harlem, the prancing choruses at the Lafayette Theater, the hours he had whiled away at Boogie's and the Honky Tonk Club, and he hesitated. Then he envisioned his future as a white man, probably as the husband of the tall blonde from Atlanta, and with firm resolve, he entered the door of the mysterious chamber.

He quailed as he saw the formidable apparatus of sparkling nickel. It resembled a cross between a dentist's chair and an electric chair. Wires and straps, bars and levers protruded from it and a great nickel headpiece, like the helmet of a knight, hung over it. The room had only a skylight and no sound entered it from the outside. Around the walls were cases of instruments and shelves of bottles filled with strangely colored fluids. He gasped with fright and would have made for the door but the two husky attendants held him firmly, stripped off his robe and bound him in the chair. There was no retreat. It was either the beginning or the end.

Chapter II

Slowly, haltingly, Max Disher dragged his way down the hall to the elevator, supported on either side by an attendant. He felt terribly weak, emptied and nauseated; his skin twitched and was dry and feverish; his insides felt very hot and sore. As the trio walked slowly along the corridor, a blue-green light would ever and anon blaze through one of the doorways as a patient was taken in. There was a low hum and throb of machinery and an acrid odor filled the air. Uniformed nurses and attendants hurried back and forth at their tasks. Everything was quiet, swift, efficient, sinister.

He felt so thankful that he had survived the ordeal of that horrible machine so akin to the electric chair. A shudder passed over him at the memory of the hours he had passed in its grip, fed at intervals with revolting concoctions. But when they reached the elevator and he saw himself in the mirror, he was startled, overjoyed. White at last! Gone was the smooth brown complexion. Gone were the slightly full lips and Ethiopian nose. Gone was the nappy hair that he had straightened so meticulously ever since the kink-no-more lotions first wrenched Aframericans from the tyranny and torture of the comb. There would be no more expenditures for skin whiteners; no more discrimination; no more obstacles in his path. He was free! The world was his oyster and he had the open sesame of a pork-colored skin!

The reflection in the mirror gave him new life and strength. He now stood erect, without support and grinned at the two tall, black attendants. "Well, Boys," he crowed, "I'm all set now. That machine of Doc's worked like a charm. Soon's I get a feed under my belt I'll be okeh."

Six hours later, bathed, fed, clean-shaven, spry, blonde and jubilant, he emerged from the out-patient ward and tripped gaily down the corridor to the main entrance. He was through with coons, he resolved, from now on. He glanced in a superior manner at the long line of black and brown folk on one side of the corridor, patiently awaiting treatment. He saw many persons whom he knew but none of them recognized him. It thrilled him to feel that he was now indistinguishable from nine-tenths of the people of the United States; one of the great majority. Ah, it was good not to be a Negro any longer!

As he sought to open the front door, the strong arm of a guard restrained him. "Wait a minute," the man said, "and we'll help you get through the mob."

A moment or two later Max found himself the center of a flying wedge of five or six husky special policemen, cleaving through a milling crowd of colored folk. From the top step of the Sanitarium he had noticed the crowd spread over the sidewalk, into the street and around the corners. Fifty traffic policemen strained and sweated to keep prospective patients in line and out from under the wheels of taxicabs and trucks.

Finally he reached the curb, exhausted from the jostling and squeezing, only to be set upon by a mob of newspaper photographers and reporters. As the first person to take the treatment, he was naturally the center of attraction for about fifteen of these journalistic gnats. They asked a thousand questions seemingly all at once. What was his name? How did he feel? What was he going to do? Would he marry a white woman? Did he intend to continue living in Harlem?

Max would say nothing. In the first place, he thought to himself, if they're so anxious to know all this stuff, they ought to be willing to pay for it. He needed money if he was going to be able to thoroughly enjoy being white; why not get some by selling his story? The reporters, male and female, begged him almost with tears in their eyes for a statement but he was adamant.

While they were wrangling, an empty taxicab drove up. Pushing the inquisitive reporters to one side, Max leaped into it and yelled "Central Park!" It was the only place he could think of at the moment. He wanted to have time to compose his mind, to plan the future in this great world of whiteness. As the cab lurched forward, he turned and was astonished to find another occupant, a pretty girl.

"Don't be scared," she smiled. "I knew you would want to get away from that mob so I went around the corner and got a cab for you. Come along with me and I'll get everything fixed up for you. I'm a reporter from *The Scimitar*. We'll give you a lot of money for your story." She talked rapidly. Max's first impulse had been to jump out of the cab, even at the risk of having to face again the mob of reporters and photographers he had sought to escape, but he changed his mind when he heard mention of money.

"How much?" he asked, eyeing her. She was very comely and he noted that her ankles were well turned.

"Oh, probably a thousand dollars," she replied.

"Well, that sounds good." A thousand dollars! What a time he could have with that! Broadway for him as soon as he got paid off.

As they sped down Seventh Avenue, the newsboys were yelling the latest editions. "Ex—try! Ex—try! Blacks turning white! Blacks turning white!...Read all about the gr-r-reat discovery! Paper, Mister! Paper!...Read all about Dr. Crookman."

He settled back while they drove through the park and glanced frequently at the girl by his side. She looked mighty good; wonder could he talk business with her? Might go to dinner and a cabaret. That would be the best way to start.

"What did you say your name was?" he began.

"I didn't say," she stalled.

"Well, you have a name, haven't you?" he persisted.

"Suppose I have?"

"You're not scared to tell it, are you?"

"Why do you want to know my name?"

"Well, there's nothing wrong about wanting to know a pretty girl's name, is there?"

"Well, my name's Smith, Sybil Smith. Now are you satisfied?"

"Not yet. I want to know something more. How would you like to go to dinner with me tonight?"

"I don't know and I won't know until I've had the experience." She smiled coquettishly. Going out with him, she figured, would make the basis of a rattling good story for tomorrow's paper. "Negro's first night as a Caucasian!" Fine!

"Say, you're a regular fellow," he said, beaming upon her. "I'll get a great kick out of going to dinner with you because you'll be the only one in the place that'll know I'm a Negro."

Down at the office of *The Scimitar*, it didn't take Max long to come to an agreement, tell his story to a stenographer and get a sheaf of crisp, new bills. As he left the building a couple of hours later with Miss Smith on his arm, the newsboys were already crying the extra edition carrying the first installment of his strange tale. A huge photograph of him occupied the entire front page of the tabloid. Lucky for him that he'd given his name as William Small, he thought.

He was annoyed and a little angered. What did they want to put his picture all over the front of the paper for? Now everybody would know who he was. He had undergone the tortures of Doc Crookman's devilish machine in order to escape the conspicuousness of a dark skin and now he was being made conspicuous because he had once had a dark skin! Could one never escape the plagued race problem?

"Don't worry about that," comforted Miss Smith. "Nobody'll recognize you. There are thousands of white people, yes millions, that look like you do." She took his arm and snuggled up closer. She wanted to make him feel at home. It wasn't often a poor, struggling newspaper woman got a chap with a big bankroll to take her out for the evening. Moreover, the description she would write of the experience might win her a promotion.

They walked down Broadway in the blaze of white lights to a dinner-dance place. To Max it was like being in heaven. He had strolled through the Times Square district before but never with such a feeling of absolute freedom and sureness. No one now looked at him curiously because he was with a white girl, as they had when he came down there with Minnie, his former octoroon lady friend. Gee, it was great!

They dined and they danced. Then they went to a cabaret, where, amid smoke, noise and body smells, they drank what was purported to be whiskey and watched a semi-nude chorus do its stuff. Despite his happiness Max found it pretty dull. There was something lacking in these ofay places of amusement or else there was something present that one didn't find in the black-and-tan resorts in Harlem. The joy and abandon here was obviously forced. Patrons went to extremes to show each other they were having a wonderful time. It was all so strained and quite unlike anything to which he had been accustomed. The Negroes, it seemed to him, were much gayer, enjoyed themselves more deeply and yet they were more restrained, actually more refined. Even their dancing was different. They followed the rhythm accurately, effortlessly and with easy grace; these lumbering couples, out of step half the time and working as strenuously as stevedores emptying the bowels of a freighter, were noisy, awkward, inelegant. At their best they were gymnastic where the Negroes were sensuous. He felt a momentary pang of mingled disgust, disillusionment and nostalgia. But it was only momentary. He looked across at the comely Sybil and then around at the other white women, many of whom were very pretty and expensively gowned, and the sight temporarily drove from his mind the thoughts that had been occupying him.

* * *

They parted at three o'clock, after she had given him her telephone number. She pecked him lightly on the cheek in payment, doubtless, for a pleasant evening's entertainment. Somewhat disappointed because she had failed to show any interest in his expressed curiosity about the interior of her apartment, he directed the chauffeur to drive him to Harlem. After all, he argued to himself in defense of his action, he had to get his things.

As the cab turned out of Central Park at 110th Street he felt, curiously enough, a feeling of peace. There were all the old familiar sights: the all-night speakeasies, the frankfurter stands, the loiterers, the late pedestrians, the chop suey joints, the careening taxicabs, the bawdy laughter.

He couldn't resist the temptation to get out at 133rd Street and go down to Boogie's place, the hangout of his gang. He tapped, an eye peered through a hole, appraised him critically, then disappeared and the hole was closed. There was silence.

Max frowned. What was the matter with old Bob? Why didn't he open that door? The cold January breeze swept down into the little court where he stood and made him shiver. He knocked a little louder, more insistently. The eye appeared again.

"Who's 'at?" growled the doorkeeper.

"It's me, Max Disher," replied the ex-Negro.

"Go 'way f'm here, white man. Dis heah place is closed."

"Is Bunny Brown in there?" asked Max in desperation.

"Yeh, he's heah. Does yuh know him? Well, Ah'll call 'im out heah and see if he knows you."

Max waited in the cold for about two or three minutes and then the door suddenly opened and Bunny Brown, a little unsteady, came out. He peered at Max in the light from the electric bulb over the door.

"Hello Bunny," Max greeted him. "Don't know me do you? It's me, Max Disher. You recognize my voice, don't you?"

Bunny looked again, rubbed his eyes and shook his head. Yes, the voice was Max Disher's, but this man was white. Still, when he smiled his eyes revealed the same sardonic twinkle – so characteristic of his friend.

"Max," he blurted out, "is that you, sure enough? Well, for cryin' out loud! Damned 'f you ain't been up there to Crookman's and got fixed up. Well, hush my mouth! Bob, open that door. This is old Max Disher. Done gone up there to Crookman's and got all white on my hands. He's just too tight, with his blond hair, 'n everything."

Bob opened the door, the two friends entered, sat down at one of the small round tables in the narrow, smoke-filled cellar and were soon surrounded with cronies. They gazed raptly at his colorless skin, commented on the veins showing blue through the epidermis, stroked his ash-blond hair and listened with mouths open to his remarkable story.

"Whatcha gonna do now, Max?" asked Boogie, the rangy, black, bullet-headed proprietor.

"I know just what that joker's gonna do," said Bunny. "He's goin' back to Atlanta. Am I right, Big Boy?"

"You ain't wrong," Max agreed. "I'm goin' right on down there, brother, and make up for lost time."

"Whadayah mean?" asked Boogie.

"Boy, it would take me until tomorrow night to tell you and then you wouldn't understand."

The two friends strolled up the avenue. Both were rather mum. They had been inseparable pals since the stirring days in France. Now they were about to be parted. It wasn't as if Max was going across the ocean to some foreign country; there would be a wider gulf separating them: the great sea of color. They both thought about it.

"I'll be pretty lonesome without you, Bunny."

"It ain't you, Big Boy."

"Well, why don't you go ahead and get white and then we could stay together. I'll give you the money."

"Say not so! Where'd you get so much jack all of a sudden?" asked Bunny.

"Sold my story to *The Scimitar* for a grand."

"Paid in full?"

"Wasn't paid in part!"

"All right, then, I'll take you up, Heavy Sugar." Bunny held out his plump hand and Max handed him a hundred-dollar bill.

They were near the Crookman Sanitarium. Although it was five o'clock on a Sunday morning, the building was brightly lighted from cellar to roof and the hum of electric motors could be heard, low and powerful. A large electric sign hung from the roof to the second floor. It represented a huge arrow outlined in green with the words BLACK-NO-MORE running its full length vertically. A black face was depicted at the lower end of the arrow while at the top shone a white face to which the arrow was pointed. First would appear the outline of the arrow; then, BLACK-NO-MORE would flash on and off. Following that the black face would appear at the bottom and beginning at the lower end the long arrow with its lettering would appear progressively until its tip was reached, when the white face at the top would blazon forth. After that the sign would flash off and on and the process would be repeated.

In front of the sanitarium milled a half-frozen crowd of close to four thousand Negroes. A riot squad armed with rifles, machine guns and tear gas bombs maintained some semblance of order. A steel cable stretched from lamp post to lamp post the entire length of the block kept the struggling mass of humanity on the sidewalk and out of the path of the traffic. It seemed as if all Harlem were there. As the two friends reached the outskirts of the mob, an ambulance from the Harlem Hospital drove up and carried away two women who had been trampled upon.

Lined up from the door to the curb was a gang of tough special guards dredged out of the slums. Grim Irish from Hell's Kitchen, rough Negroes from around 133rd Street and 5th Avenue (New York's "Beale Street") and tough Italians from the lower West Side. They managed with difficulty to keep an aisle cleared for incoming and outgoing patients. Near the curb were stationed the reporters and photographers.

The noise rose and fell. First there would be a low hum of voices. Steadily it would rise and rise in increasing volume as the speakers became more animated and reach its climax in a great animal-like roar as the big front door would open and a whitened Negro would emerge. Then the mass would surge forward to peer at and question the ersatz Nordic. Sometimes the ex-Ethiopian would quail before the mob and jump back into the building. Then the hardboiled guards would form a flying squad and hustle him to a waiting taxicab. Other erstwhile Aframericans issuing from the building would grin broadly, shake hands with friends and relatives and start to graphically describe their experience while the Negroes around them enviously admired their clear white skins.

In between these appearances the hot dog and peanut vendors did a brisk trade, along with the numerous pickpockets of the district. One slender, anemic, ratty-looking mulatto Negro was almost beaten to death by a gigantic black laundress whose purse he had snatched. A Negro selling hot roasted sweet potatoes did a land-office business while the neighboring saloons, that had increased so rapidly in number since the enactment of the Volstead Law that many of their Italian proprietors paid substantial income taxes, sold scores of gallons of incredibly atrocious hootch.

"Well, bye, bye, Max," said Bunny, extending his hand. "I'm goin' in an' try my luck."

"So long, Bunny. See you in Atlanta. Write me general delivery."

"Why, ain't you gonna wait for me, Max?"

"Naw! I'm fed up on this town."

"Oh, you ain't kiddin' me, Big Boy. I know you want to look up that broad you saw in the Honky Tonk New Year's Eve," Bunny beamed.

Max grinned and blushed slightly. They shook hands and parted. Bunny ran up the aisle from the curb, opened the sanitarium door and without turning around, disappeared within.

For a minute or so, Max stood irresolutely in the midst of the gibbering crowd of people. Unaccountably he felt at home here among these black folk. Their jests, scraps of conversation and lusty laughter all seemed like heavenly music. Momentarily he felt a disposition to stay among them, to share again their troubles which they seemed always to bear with a lightness that was yet not indifference. But then, he suddenly realized with just a tiny trace of remorse that the past was forever gone. He must seek other pastures, other pursuits, other playmates, other loves. He was white now. Even if he wished to stay among his folk, they would be either jealous or suspicious of him, as they were of most octoroons and nearly all whites. There was no other alternative than to seek his future among the Caucasians with whom he now rightfully belonged.

And after all, he thought, it was a glorious new adventure. His eyes twinkled and his pulse quickened as he thought of it. Now he could go anywhere, associate with anybody, be anything he wanted to be. He suddenly thought of the comely miss he had seen in the Honky Tonk on New Year's Eve and the greatly enlarged field from which he could select his loves. Yes, indeed there were advantages in being white. He brightened and viewed the tightly-packed black folk around him with a superior air. Then, thinking again of his clothes at Mrs. Blandish's, the money in his pocket and the prospect for the first time of riding into Atlanta in a Pullman car and not as a Pullman porter, he turned and pushed his way through the throng.

He strolled up West 139th Street to his rooming place, stepping lightly and sniffing the early morning air. How good it was to be free, white and to possess a bankroll! He fumbled in his pocket for his little mirror and looked at himself again and again from several angles. He stroked his pale blond hair and secretly congratulated himself that he would no longer need to straighten it nor be afraid to wet it. He gazed raptly at his smooth, white hands with the blue veins showing through. What a miracle Dr. Crookman had wrought!

As he entered the hallway, the mountainous form of his landlady loomed up. She jumped back as she saw his face.

"What you doing in here?" she almost shouted. "Where'd you get a key to this house?"

"It's me, Max Disher," he assured her with a grin at her astonishment. "Don't know me, do you?"

She gazed incredulously into his face. "Is that you sure enough, Max? How in the devil did you get so white?"

He explained and showed her a copy of *The Scimitar* containing his story. She switched on the hall light and read it. Contrasting emotions played over her face, for Mrs. Blandish was known in the business world as Mme. Sisseretta Blandish, the beauty specialist, who owned the swellest hair-straightening parlor in Harlem. Business, she thought to herself, was bad enough, what with all of the competition, without this Dr. Crookman coming along and killing it altogether.

"Well," she sighed, "I suppose you're going down town to live, now. I always said niggers didn't really have any race pride."

Uneasy, Max made no reply. The fat, brown woman turned with a disdainful sniff and disappeared into a room at the end of the hall. He ran lightly upstairs to pack his things.

An hour later, as the taxicab bearing him and his luggage bowled through Central Park, he was in high spirits. He would go down to the Pennsylvania Station and get a Pullman straight into Atlanta. He would stop there at the best hotel. He wouldn't hunt up any of his folks. No, that would be too dangerous. He would just play around, enjoy life and laugh at the white folks up his sleeve. God! What an adventure! What a treat it would be to mingle with white people in places where as a youth he had never dared to enter. At last he felt like an American citizen. He flecked the ash of his panatela out of the open window of the cab and sank back in the seat feeling at peace with the world.

Chapter III

Dr. Junius Crookman, looking tired and worn, poured himself another cup of coffee from the percolator near by and turning to Hank Johnson, asked "What about that new electrical apparatus?"

"On th' way, Doc. On th' way," replied the former Numbers baron. "Just talkin' to th' man this mornin'. He says we'll get it tomorrow, maybe."

"Well, we certainly need it," said Chuck Foster, who sat beside him on the large leather divan. "We can't handle all of the business as it is."

"How about those new places you're buying?" asked the physician.

"Well, I've bought the big private house on Edgecombe Avenue for fifteen thousand and the workmen are getting it in shape now. It ought to be ready in about a week if nothing happens," Foster informed him.

"If nuthin' happens?" echoed Johnson. "Whut's gonna happen? We're settin' on th' world, ain't we? Our racket's within th' law, ain't it? We're makin' money faster'n we can take it in, ain't we? Whut could happen? This here is the best and safest graft I've ever been in."

"Oh, you never can tell," cautioned the quondom realtor. "These white newspapers, especially in the South, are beginning to write some pretty strong editorials against us and we've only been running two weeks. You know how easy it is to stir up the fanatical element. Before we know it they're liable to get a law passed against us."

"Not if I c'n git to th' legislature first," interrupted Johnson. "Yuh know, Ah knows how tuh handle these white folks. If yuh 'Say it with Bucks' you c'n git anything yuh want."

"There is something in what Foster says, though," Dr. Crookman said. "Just look at this bunch of clippings we got in this morning. Listen to these: 'The Viper in Our Midst,' from the Richmond *Blade*; 'The Menace of Science' from the Memphis *Bugle*; 'A Challenge to Every White Man' from the Dallas *Sun*; 'Police Battle Black Mob Seeking White Skins,' from the Atlanta *Topic*; 'Negro Doctor Admits Being Taught by Germans,' from the St. Louis *North American*. Here's a line or two from an editorial in the Oklahoma City *Hatchet*: 'There are times when the welfare of our race must take precedence over law. Opposed as we always have been to mob violence as the worst enemy of democratic government, we cannot help but feel that the intelligent white men and women of New York City who are interested in the purity and preservation of their race should not permit the challenge of Crookmanism to go unanswered, even though these black scoundrels may be within the law. There are too many criminals in this country already hiding behind the skirts of the law.'

"And lastly, one from the Tallahassee *Announcer* says: 'While it is the right of every citizen to do what he wants to do with his money, the white people of the United States cannot remain indifferent to this discovery and its horrible potentialities. Hundreds of Negroes with newly-acquired white skins have already entered white society and thousands will follow them. The black race from one end of the country to the other has in two short weeks gone completely crazy over the prospect of getting white. Day by day we see the color line which we have so laboriously established being rapidly destroyed. There would not be so much cause for alarm in this, were it not for the fact that this vitiligo is not hereditary. In other words, THE OFFSPRING OF THESE WHITENED NEGROES WILL BE NEGROES! This means that your daughter, having married a supposed white man, may find herself with a black baby! Will the proud white men of the Southland so far forget their traditions as to remain idle while this devilish work is going on?'"

"No use singin' th' blues," counseled Johnson. "We ain' gonna be both'ed heah, even if them crackahs down South do raise a little hell. Jus' lissen to th' sweet music of that mob out theah! Eve'y scream means fifty bucks. On'y reason we ain't makin' mo' money is 'cause we ain't got no mo' room."

"That's right," Dr. Crookman agreed. "We've turned out one hundred a day for fourteen days." He leaned back and lit a cigarette.

"At fifty bucks a th'ow," interrupted Johnson, "that means we've took in seventy thousand dollahs. Great Day in th' mornin'! Didn't know tha was so much jack in Harlem."

"Yes," continued Crookman, "we're taking in thirty-five thousand dollars a week. As soon as you and Foster get that other place fixed up we'll be making twice that much."

From the hallway came the voice of the switchboard operator monotonously droning out her instructions: "No, Dr. Crookman cannot see anyone... Dr. Crookman has nothing to say... Dr. Crookman will issue a statement shortly... Fifty Dollars... No, Dr. Crookman isn't a mulatto... I'm very sorry but I cannot answer that question."

The three friends sat in silence amid the hum of activity around them. Hank Johnson smiled down at the end of his cigar as he thought back over his rather colorful and hectic career. To think that today he was one of the leading Negroes of the world, one who was taking an active and important part in solving the most vexatious problem in American life, and yet only ten years before he had been working on a Carolina chain gang. Two years he had toiled on the roads under the hard eye and ready rifle of a cruel white guard; two years of being beaten, kicked and cursed, of poor food and vermin-infested habitations; two years for participating in a little crap game. Then he had drifted to Charleston, got a job in a pool room, had a stroke of luck with the dice, come to New York and landed right in the midst of the Numbers racket. Becoming a collector or "runner," he had managed his affairs well enough to be able to start out soon as a "banker." Money had poured in from Negroes eager to chance one cent in the hope of winning six dollars. Some won but most lost and he had prospered. He had purchased an apartment house, paid off the police, dabbled in the bail bond game, given a couple of thousand dollars to advance Negro Art and been elected Grand Permanent Shogun of the Ancient and Honorable Order of Crocodiles, Harlem's largest and most prosperous secret society. Then young Crookman had come to him with his proposition. At first he had hesitated about helping him but later was persuaded to do so when the young man bitterly complained that the dicty Negroes would not help to pay for the studies abroad. What a stroke of luck, getting in on the ground floor like this! They'd all be richer than Rockefeller inside of a year. Twelve million Negroes at fifty dollars apiece! Great Day in the morning! Hank spat regally into the brass cuspidor across the office and reared back contentedly on the soft cushion of the divan.

Chuck Foster was also seeing his career in retrospect. His life had not been as colorful as that of Hank Johnson. The son of a Birmingham barber, he had enjoyed such educational advantages as that community afforded the darker brethren; had become a schoolteacher, an insurance agent and a social worker in turn. Then, along with the tide of migration, he had drifted first to Cincinnati, then to Pittsburgh and finally to New York. There the real estate field, unusually lucrative because of the paucity of apartments for the increasing Negro population, had claimed him. Cautious, careful, thrifty and devoid of sentimentality, he had prospered, but not without some ugly rumors being broadcast about his sharp business methods. As he slowly worked his way up to the top of Harlem society, he had sought to live down this reputation for double-dealing and shifty practices, all too true of the bulk of his fellow realtors in the district, by giving large sums to the Young Men's and Young Women's Christian Associations, by offering scholarships to young Negroes, by staging elaborate parties to which the dicty Negroes of the community were invited. He had been glad of the opportunity to help subsidize young Crookman's studies abroad when Hank Johnson pointed out the possibilities of the venture. Now, although the results so far exceeded his wildest dreams, his natural conservatism and timidity made him somewhat pessimistic about the future. He supposed a hundred dire results of their activities and only the day before he had increased the amount of his life insurance. His mind was filled with doubts. He didn't like so much publicity. He wanted a sort of genteel popularity but no notoriety.

* * *

Despite the coffee and cigarettes, Dr. Junius Crookman was sleepy. The responsibility, the necessity of overseeing the work of his physicians and nurses, the insistence of the newspapers and the medical profession that he reveal the secrets of his treatment and a thousand other vexatious details had kept him from getting proper rest. He had, indeed, spent most of his time in the sanitarium.

This hectic activity was new to him. Up until a month ago his thirty-five years had been peaceful and, in the main, studious ones. The son of an Episcopal clergyman, he had been born and raised in a city in central New York, his associates carefully selected in order to protect him as much as possible from the defeatist psychology so prevalent among American Negroes and given every opportunity and inducement to learn his profession and become a thoroughly cultivated and civilized man. His parents, though poor, were proud and boasted that they belonged to the Negro aristocracy. He had had to work his way through college because of the failure of his father's health but he had come very little in contact with the crudity, coarseness and cruelty of life. He had been monotonously successful but he was sensible enough to believe that a large part of it was due, like most success, to chance. He saw in his great discovery the solution to the most annoying problem in American life. Obviously, he reasoned, if there were no Negroes, there could be no Negro problem. Without a Negro problem, Americans could concentrate their attention on something constructive. Through his efforts and the activities of Black-No-More, Incorporated, it would be possible to do what agitation, education and legislation had failed to do. He was naïvely surprised that there should be opposition to his work. Like most men with a vision, a plan, a program or a remedy, he fondly imagined people to be intelligent enough to accept a good thing when it was offered to them, which was conclusive evidence that he knew little about the human race.

Dr. Crookman prided himself above all on being a great lover of his race. He had studied its history, read of its struggles and kept up with its achievements. He subscribed to six or seven Negro weekly newspapers and two of the magazines. He was so interested in the continued progress of the American Negroes that he wanted to remove all obstacles in their path by depriving them of their racial characteristics. His home and office were filled with African masks and paintings of Negroes by Negroes. He was what was known in Negro society as a Race Man. He was wedded to everything black except the black woman – his wife was a white girl with remote Negro ancestry, of the type that Negroes were wont to describe as being "able to pass for white." While abroad he had spent his spare time ransacking the libraries for facts about the achievements of Negroes and having liaisons with comely and available fraus and frauleins.

"Well, Doc," said Hank Johnson, suddenly, "you'd bettah go on home 'n git some sleep. Ain' no use killin' you'sef. Eve'thing's gonna be all right heah. You ain' gotta thing tuh worry 'bout."

"How's he gonna get out of here with that mob in front?" Chuck inquired. "A man almost needs a tank to get through that crowd of darkies."

"Oh, Ah've got all that fixed, Calamity Jane," Johnson remarked casually. "All he's gotta do is tuh go on down staihs tuh the basem'nt, go out th' back way an' step into th' alley. My car'll be theah waitin' fo' 'im."

"That's awfully nice of you, Johnson," said the physician. "I am dead tired. I think I'll be a new man if I can get a few hours of sleep."

A black man in white uniform opened the door and announced: "Mrs. Crookman!" He held the door open for the Doctor's petite, stylishly-dressed wife to enter. The three men sprang to their feet. Johnson and Foster eyed the beautiful little octoroon appreciatively as they bowed, thinking how easily she could "pass for white," which would have been something akin to a piece of anthracite coal passing for black.

"Darling!" she exclaimed, turning to her husband. "Why don't you come home and get some rest? You'll be ill if you keep on in this way."

"Jus' whut Ah bin tellin' him, Mrs. Crookman," Johnson hastened to say. "We got eve'ything fixed tuh send 'im off."

"Well, then, Junius, we'd better be going," she said decisively.

Putting on a long overcoat over his white uniform, Dr. Crookman, wearily and meekly followed his spouse out of the door.

"Mighty nice looking girl, Mrs. Crookman," Foster observed.

"Nice lookin'!" echoed Johnson, with mock amazement. "Why, nigguh, that ooman would make uh rabbit hug uh houn'. Doc sez she's cullud, an' she sez so, but she looks mighty white tuh me."

"Everything that looks white ain't white in this man's country," Foster replied.

* * *

Meantime there was feverish activity in Harlem's financial institutions. At the Douglass Bank the tellers were busier than bootleggers on Christmas Eve. Moreover, they were short-handed because of the mysterious absence of Bunny Brown. A long queue of Negroes extended down one side of the bank, out of the front door and around the corner, while bank attendants struggled to keep them in line. Everybody was drawing out money; no one was depositing. In vain the bank officials pleaded with them not to withdraw their funds. The Negroes were adamant: they wanted their money and wanted it quick. Day after day this had gone on ever since Black-No-More, Incorporated, had started turning Negroes white. At first, efforts were made to bulldoze and intimidate the depositors but that didn't succeed. These people were in no mood to be trifled with. A lifetime of being Negroes in the United States had convinced them that there was great advantage in being white.

"Mon, whutcha tahlk ab't?" scoffed a big, black British West Indian woman with whom an official was remonstrating not to draw out her money. "Dis heah's mah mahney, ain't it? Yuh use mah mahney alla time, aintcha? Whutcha mean, Ah shouldn't draw't out?...You gimme mah mahney or Ah broke up dis place!"

"Are you closing your account, Mr. Robinson?" a soft-voiced mulatto teller inquired of a big, rusty stevedore.

"Ah ain't openin' it," was the rejoinder. "Ah wants th' whole thing, an' Ah don't mean maybe."

Similar scenes were being enacted at the Wheatley Trust Company and at the local Post Office station.

An observer passing up and down the streets would have noted a general exodus from the locality. Moving vans were backed up to apartment houses on nearly every block.

The "For Rent" signs were appearing in larger number in Harlem than at any time in twenty-five years. Landlords looked on helplessly as apartment after apartment emptied and was not filled. Even the refusal to return deposits did not prevent the tenants from moving out. What, indeed, was fifty, sixty or seventy dollars when one was leaving behind insult, ostracism, segregation and discrimination? Moreover, the whitened Negroes were saving a great deal of money by being able to change localities. The mechanics of race prejudice had forced them into the congested Harlem area where, at the mercy of white and black real estate sharks, they had been compelled to pay exorbitant rentals because the demand for housing far exceeded the supply. As a general rule the Negroes were paying one hundred per cent more than white tenants in other parts of the city for a smaller number of rooms and worse service.

The installment furniture and clothing houses in the area were also beginning to feel the results of the activities of Black-No-More, Incorporated. Collectors were reporting their inability to locate certain families or the articles they had purchased on time. Many of the colored folk, it was said, had sold their furniture to second-hand stores and vanished with the proceeds into the great mass of white citizenry.

At the same time there seemed to be more white people on the streets of Harlem than at any time in the past twenty years. Many of them appeared to be on the most intimate terms with the Negroes, laughing, talking, dining and dancing in a most un-Caucasian way. This sort of association had always gone on at night but seldom in the daylight.

Strange Negroes from the West and South who had heard the good news were to be seen on the streets and in public places, patiently awaiting their turn at the Crookman Institute.

* * *

Madame Sisseretta Blandish sat disconsolately in an armchair near the front door of her ornate hair-straightening shop, looking blankly at the pedestrians and traffic passing to and fro. These two weeks had been hard ones for her. Everything was going out and nothing coming in. She had been doing very well at her vocation for years and was acclaimed in the community as one of its business leaders. Because of her prominence as the proprietor of a successful enterprise engaged in making Negroes appear as much like white folks as possible, she had recently been elected for the fourth time a Vice-President of the American Race Pride League. She was also head of the Woman's Committee of the New York Branch of the Social Equality League and held an important place in local Republican politics. But all of these honors brought little or no money with them. They didn't help to pay her rent or purchase the voluminous dresses she required to drape her Amazonian form. Only that day her landlord had brought her the sad news that he either wanted his money or the premises.

Where, she wondered, would she get the money? Like most New Yorkers she put up a big front with very little cash behind it, always looking hopefully forward to the morrow for a lucky break. She had two-thirds of the rent money already, by dint of much borrowing, and if she could "do" a few nappy heads she would be in the clear; but hardly a customer had crossed her threshold in a fortnight, except two or three Jewish girls from downtown who came up regularly to have their hair straightened because it wouldn't stand inspection in the Nordic world. The Negro women had seemingly deserted her. Day after day she saw her old customers pass by hurriedly without even looking in her direction. Verily a revolution was taking place in Negro society.

"Oh, Miss Simpson!" cried the hair-straightener after a passing young lady. "Ain't you going to say hello?"

The young woman halted reluctantly and approached the doorway. Her brown face looked strained. Two weeks before she would have been a rare sight in the Black Belt because her kinky hair was not straightened; it was merely combed, brushed and neatly pinned up. Miss Simpson had vowed that she wasn't going to spend any dollar a week having her hair "done" when she only lacked fifteen dollars of having money enough to quit the Negro race forever.

"Sorry, Mrs. Blandish," she apologized, "but I swear I didn't see you. I've been just that busy that I haven't had eyes for anything or anybody except my job and back home again. You know I'm all alone now. Yes, Charlie went over two weeks ago and I haven't heard a word from him. Just think of that! After all I've done for that nigger. Oh well! I'll soon be over there myself. Another week's work will fix me all right."

"Humph!" snorted Mme. Blandish. "That's all you niggers are thinking about nowadays. Why don't you come down here and give me some business? If I don't hurry up and make some more money I'll have to close up this place and go to work myself."

"Well, I'm sorry, Mrs. Blandish," the girl mumbled indifferently, moving off toward the corner to catch the approaching street car, "but I guess I can hold out with this here bad hair until Saturday night. You know I've taken too much punishment being dark these twenty-two years to miss this opportunity... Well," she flung over her shoulder. "Goodbye! See you later."

Madame Blandish settled her 250 pounds back into her armchair and sighed heavily. Like all American Negroes she had desired to be white when she was young and before she entered business for herself and became a person of consequence in the community. Now she had lived long enough to have no illusions about the magic of a white skin. She liked her business and she liked her social position in Harlem. As a white woman she would have to start all over again, and she wasn't so sure of herself. Here at least she was somebody. In the great Caucasian world she would be just another white woman, and they were becoming a drug on the market, what with the simultaneous decline of chivalry, the marriage rate and professional prostitution. She had seen too many elderly, white-haired Caucasian females scrubbing floors and toiling in sculleries not to know what being just another white woman meant. Yet she admitted to herself that it would be nice to get over being the butt for jokes and petty prejudice.

The Madame was in a quandary and so also were hundreds of others in the upper stratum of Harlem life. With the Negro masses moving out from under them, what other alternative did they have except to follow. True, only a few hundred Negroes had so far vanished from their wonted haunts, but it was known that thousands, tens of thousands, yes, millions would follow them.

Chapter IV

Matthew Fisher, alias Max Disher, joined the Easter Sunday crowds, twirling his malacca stick and ogling the pretty flappers who passed giggling in their Spring finery. For nearly three months he had idled around the Georgia capital hoping to catch a glimpse of the beautiful girl who on New Year's Eve had told him "I never dance with niggers." He had searched diligently in almost every stratum of Atlanta society, but he had failed to find her. There were hundreds of tall, beautiful, blonde maidens in the city; to seek a particular one whose name one did not know was somewhat akin to hunting for a Russian Jew in the Bronx or a particular Italian gunman in Chicago.

For three months he had dreamed of this girl, carefully perused the society columns of the local newspapers on the chance that her picture might appear in them. He was like most men who have been repulsed by a pretty girl, his desire for her grew stronger and stronger.

He was not finding life as a white man the rosy existence he had anticipated. He was forced to conclude that it was pretty dull and that he was bored. As a boy he had been taught to look up to white folks as just a little less than gods; now he found them little different from the Negroes, except that they were uniformly less courteous and less interesting.

Often when the desire for the happy-go-lucky, jovial good-fellowship of the Negroes came upon him strongly, he would go down to Auburn Avenue and stroll around the vicinity, looking at the dark folk and listening to their conversation and banter. But no one down there wanted him around. He was a white man and thus suspect. Only the black women who ran the "Call Houses" on the hill wanted his company. There was nothing left for him except the hard, materialistic, grasping, ill-bred society of the whites. Sometimes a slight feeling of regret that he had left his people forever would cross his mind, but it fled before the painful memories of past experiences in this, his home town.

The unreasoning and illogical color prejudice of most of the people with whom he was forced to associate infuriated him. He often laughed cynically when some coarse, ignorant white man voiced his opinion concerning the inferior mentality and morality of the Negroes. He was moving in white society now and he could compare it with the society he had known as a Negro in Atlanta and Harlem. What a let-down it was from the good breeding, sophistication, refinement and gentle cynicism to which he had become accustomed as a popular young man about town in New York's Black Belt. He was not able to articulate this feeling but he was conscious of the reaction nevertheless.

For a week, now, he had been thinking seriously of going to work. His thousand dollars had dwindled to less than a hundred. He would have to find some source of income and yet the young white men with whom he talked about work all complained that it was very scarce. Being white, he finally concluded, was no Open Sesame to employment for he sought work in banks and insurance offices without success.

During his period of idleness and soft living, he had followed the news and opinion in the local daily press and confessed himself surprised at the antagonistic attitude of the newspapers toward Black-No-More, Incorporated. From the vantage point of having formerly been a Negro, he was able to see how the newspapers were fanning the color prejudice of the white people. Business men, he found, were also bitterly opposed to Dr. Crookman and his efforts to bring about chromatic democracy in the nation.

The attitude of these people puzzled him. Was not Black-No-More getting rid of the Negroes upon whom all of the blame was placed for the backwardness of the South? Then he recalled what a Negro street speaker had said one night on the corner of 138th Street and Seventh Avenue in New York: that unorganized labor meant cheap labor; that the guarantee of cheap labor was an effective means of luring new industries into the South; that so long as the ignorant white masses could be kept thinking of the menace of the Negro to Caucasian race purity and political control, they would give little thought to labor organization. It suddenly dawned upon Matthew

Fisher that this Black-No-More treatment was more of a menace to white business than to white labor. And not long afterward he became aware of the money-making possibilities involved in the present situation.

How could he work it? He was not known and he belonged to no organization. Here was a veritable gold mine but how could he reach the ore? He scratched his head over the problem but could think of no solution. Who would be interested in it that he could trust?

He was pondering this question the Monday after Easter while breakfasting in an armchair restaurant when he noticed an advertisement in a newspaper lying in the next chair. He read it and then re-read it:

THE KNIGHTS OF NORDICA
Want 10,000 Atlanta White Men and Women to
Join in the Fight for White Race Integrity.
Imperial Klonklave Tonight
The racial integrity of the Caucasian Race is being
threatened by the activities of a scientific
black Beelzebub in New York
Let us Unite Now Before It Is
TOO LATE!
Come to Nordica Hall Tonight
Admission Free.
Rev. Henry Givens,
Imperial Grand Wizard

Here, Matthew figured, was just what he had been looking for. Probably he could get in with this fellow Givens. He finished his cup of coffee, lit a cigar and paying his check, strolled out into the sunshine of Peachtree Street.

He took the trolley out to Nordica Hall. It was a big, unpainted barn-like edifice, with a suite of offices in front and a huge auditorium in the rear. A new oil cloth sign reading "THE KNIGHTS OF NORDICA" was stretched across the front of the building.

Matthew paused for a moment and sized up the edifice. Givens must have some money, he thought, to keep up such a large place. Might not be a bad idea to get a little dope on him before going inside.

"This fellow Givens is a pretty big guy around here, ain't he?" he asked the young man at the soda fountain across the street.

"Yessah, he's one o' th' bigges' men in this heah town. Used to be a big somethin' or other in th' old Ku Klux Klan 'fore it died. Now he's stahtin' this heah Knights o' Nordica."

"He must have pretty good jack," suggested Matthew.

"He oughtta have," answered the soda jerker. "My paw tells me he was close to th' money when he was in th' Klan."

Here, thought Matthew, was just the place for him. He paid for his soda and walked across the street to the door marked "Office." He felt a slight tremor of uneasiness as he turned the knob and entered. Despite his white skin he still possessed the fear of the Klan and kindred organizations possessed by most Negroes.

A rather pretty young stenographer asked him his business as he walked into the ante room. Better be bold, he thought. This was probably the best chance he would have to keep from working, and his funds were getting lower and lower.

"Please tell Rev. Givens, the Imperial Grand Wizard, that Mr. Matthew Fisher of the New York Anthropological Society is very anxious to have about a half-hour's conversation with him relative to his new venture." Matthew spoke in an impressive, businesslike manner, rocked back on his heels and looked profound.

"Yassah," almost whispered the awed young lady, "I'll tell him." She withdrew into an inner office and Matthew chuckled softly to himself. He wondered if he could impress this old fakir as easily as he had the girl.

Rev. Henry Givens, Imperial Grand Wizard of the Knights of Nordica, was a short, wizened, almost-bald, bull-voiced, ignorant ex-evangelist, who had come originally from the hilly country north of Atlanta. He had helped in the organization of the Ku Klux Klan following the Great War and had worked with a zeal only equalled by his thankfulness to God for escaping from the precarious existence of an itinerant saver of souls.

Not only had the Rev. Givens toiled diligently to increase the prestige, power and membership of the defunct Ku Klux Klan, but he had also been a very hard worker in withdrawing as much money from its treasury as possible. He convinced himself, as did the other officers, that this stealing was not stealing at all but merely appropriation of rightful reward for his valuable services. When the morons finally tired of supporting the show and the stream of ten-dollar memberships declined to a trickle, Givens had been able to retire gracefully and live on the interest of his money.

Then, when the newspapers began to recount the activities of Black-No-More, Incorporated, he saw a vision of work to be done, and founded the Knights of Nordica. So far there were only a hundred members but he had high hopes for the future. Tonight, he felt would tell the story. The prospect of a full treasury to dip into again made his little gray eyes twinkle and the palms of his skinny hands itch.

The stenographer interrupted him to announce the newcomer.

"Hum-n!" said Givens, half to himself. "New York Anthropological Society, eh? This feller must know somethin'. Might be able to use him in this business... All right, show him in!"

The two men shook hands and swiftly appraised each other. Givens waved Matthew to a chair.

"How can I serve you, Mr. Fisher?" he began in sepulchral tone dripping with unction.

"It is rather," countered Matthew in his best salesman's croon, "how I can serve you and your valuable organization. As an anthropologist, I have, of course, been long interested in the work with which you have been identified. It has always seemed to me that there was no question in American life more important than that of preserving the integrity of the white race. We all know what has been the fate of those nations that have permitted their blood to be polluted with that of inferior breeds." (He had read some argument like that in a Sunday supplement not long before, which was the extent of his knowledge of anthropology.) "This latest menace of Black-No-More is the most formidable the white people of America have had to face since the founding of the Republic. As a resident of New York City, I am aware, of course, of the extent of the activities of this Negro Crookman and his two associates. Already thousands of blacks have passed over into the white race. Not satisfied with operating in New York City, they have opened their sanitariums in twenty other cities from Coast to Coast. They open a new one almost every day. In their literature and advertisements in the darky newspapers they boast that they are now turning four thousand Negroes white every day." He knitted his blond eyebrows. "You see how great the menace is? At this rate there will not be a Negro in the country in ten years, for you must remember that the rate is increasing every day as new sanitariums are opened. Don't you see that something must be done about this immediately? Don't you see that Congress must be aroused; that these places must be closed?" The young man glared with belligerent indignation.

Rev. Givens saw. He nodded his head as Matthew, now glorying in his newly-discovered eloquence made point after point, and concluded that this pale, dapper young fellow, with his ready tongue, his sincerity, his scientific training and knowledge of the situation ought to prove a valuable asset to the Knights of Nordica.

"I tried to interest some agencies in New York," Matthew continued, "but they are all blind to this menace and to their duty. Then someone told me of you and your valuable work, and I decided to come down here and have a talk with you. I had intended to suggest the organization of some such militant secret order as you have started, but since you've already seen the necessity for it, I want to hasten to offer my services as a scientific man and one familiar with the facts and able to present them to your members."

"I should be very glad," boomed Givens, "very happy, indeed, Brother Fisher, to have you join us. We need you. I believe you can help us a great deal. Would you, er – ah, be interested in coming out to the mass meeting this evening? It would help us tremendously to get members if you would be willing to get up and tell the audience what you have just related about the progress of this iniquitous nigger corporation in New York."

Matthew pretended to think over the matter for a moment or two and then agreed. If he made a hit at the initial meeting, he would be sure to get on the staff. Once there he could go after the larger game. Unlike Givens, he had no belief in the racial integrity nonsense nor any confidence in the white masses whom he thought were destined to flock to the Knights of Nordica. On the contrary he despised and hated them. He had the average Negro's justifiable fear of the poor whites and only planned to use them as a stepladder to the real money.

When Matthew left, Givens congratulated himself upon the fact that he had been able to attract such talent to the organization in its very infancy. His ideas must be sound, he concluded, if scientists from New York were impressed by them. He reached over, pulled the dictionary stand toward him and opened the big book at A.

"Lemme see, now," he muttered aloud. "Anthropology. Better git that word straight 'fore I go talkin' too much about it… Humn! Humn!… That boy must know a hull lot." He read over the definition of the word twice without understanding it, closed the dictionary, pushed it away from him, and then cutting off a large chew of tobacco from his plug, he leaned back in his swivel chair to rest after the unaccustomed mental exertion.

Matthew went gaily back to his hotel. "Man alive!" he chortled to himself. "What a lucky break! Can't keep old Max down long… Will I speak to 'em? Well, I won't stay quiet!" He felt so delighted over the prospect of getting close to some real money that he treated himself to an expensive dinner and a twenty-five-cent cigar. Afterward he inquired further about old man Givens from the house detective, a native Atlantan.

"Oh, he's well heeled – the old crook!" remarked the detective. "Damnify could ever understand how such ignorant people get a-hold of th' money; but there y'are. Owns as pretty a home as you can find around these parts an' damn 'fhe ain't stahtin' a new racket."

"Do you think he'll make anything out of it?" inquired Matthew, innocently.

"Say, Brother, you mus' be a stranger in these parts. These damn, ignorant crackers will fall fer anything fer a while. They ain't had no Klan here fer goin' on three years. Leastwise it ain't been functionin'." The old fellow chuckled and spat a stream of tobacco juice into a nearby cuspidor. Matthew sauntered away. Yes, the pickings ought to be good.

Equally enthusiastic was the Imperial Grand Wizard when he came home to dinner that night. He entered the house humming one of his favorite hymns and his wife looked up from the evening paper with surprise on her face. The Rev. Givens was usually something of a grouch but tonight he was as happy as a pickpocket at a country fair.

"What's th' mattah with you?" she inquired, sniffing suspiciously.

"Oh, Honey," he gurgled, "I think this here Knights of Nordica is going over big; going over big! My fame is spreading. Only today I had a long talk with a famous anthropologist from New York and he's going to address our mass meeting tonight."

"Whut's an anthropologist?" asked Mrs. Givens, wrinkling her seamy brow.

"Oh-er, well, he's one of these here scientists what knows all about this here business what's going on up there in New York where them niggers is turning each other white," explained Rev. Givens hastily but firmly. "He's a mighty smaht feller and I want you and Helen to come out and hear him."

"B'lieve Ah will," declared Mrs. Givens, "if this heah rheumatism'll le' me foh a while. Doan know 'bout Helen, though. Evah since that gal went away tuh school she ain't bin int'rested in nuthin' upliftin'!"

Mrs. Givens spoke in a grieved tone and heaved her narrow chest in a deep sigh. She didn't like all this newfangled foolishness of these young folks. They were getting away from God, that's what they were, and she didn't like it. Mrs. Givens was a Christian. There was no doubt about it because she freely admitted it to everybody, with or without provocation. Of course she often took the name of the Creator in vain when she got to quarreling with Henry; she had the reputation among her friends of not always stating the exact truth; she hated Negroes; her spouse had made bitter and profane comment concerning her virginity on their wedding night; and as head of the ladies' auxiliary of the defunct Klan she had copied her husband's financial methods; but that she was a devout Christian no one doubted. She believed the Bible from cover to cover, except what it said about people with money, and she read it every evening aloud, greatly to the annoyance of the Imperial Grand Wizard and his modern and comely daughter.

Mrs. Givens had probably once been beautiful but the wear and tear of a long life as the better half of an itinerant evangelist was apparent. Her once flaming red hair was turning gray and roan-like, her hatchet face was a criss-cross of wrinkles and lines, she was round-shouldered, hollow-chested, walked with a stoop and her long, bony, white hands looked like claws. She alternately dipped snuff and smoked an evil-smelling clay pipe, except when there was company at the house. At such times Helen would insist her mother "act like civilized people."

Helen was twenty and quite confident that she herself was civilized. Whether she was or not, she was certainly beautiful. Indeed, she was such a beauty that many of the friends of the family insisted that she must have been adopted. Taller than either of her parents, she was stately, erect, well proportioned, slender, vivid and knew how to wear her clothes. In only one way did she resemble her parents and that was in things intellectual. Any form of mental effort, she complained, made her head ache, and so her parents had always let her have her way about studying.

At the age of eleven she had been taken from the third grade in public school and sent to an exclusive seminary for the double purpose of gaining social prestige and concealing her mental incapacity. At sixteen when her instructors had about despaired of her, they were overjoyed by the decision of her father to send the girl to a "finishing school" in the North. The "finishing school" about finished what intelligence Helen possessed; but she came forth, four years later, more beautiful, with a better knowledge of how to dress and how to act in exclusive society, enough superficialities to enable her to get by in the "best" circles and a great deal of that shallow facetiousness that passes for sophistication in American upper-class life. A winter in Manhattan had rounded out her education. Now she was back home, thoroughly ashamed of her grotesque parents, and, like the other girls of her set, anxious to get a husband who at the same time was handsome, intelligent, educated, refined and rolling in wealth. As she was ignorant of the fact that no such man existed, she looked confidently forward into the future.

"I don't care to go down there among all those gross people," she informed her father at the dinner table when he broached the subject of the meeting. "They're so crude and elemental, don't you know," she explained, arching her narrow eyebrows.

"The common people are the salt of the earth," boomed Rev. Givens. "If it hadn't been for the common people we wouldn't have been able to get this home and send you off to school. You make me sick with all your modern ideas. You'd do a lot better if you'd try to be more like your Ma."

Both Mrs. Givens and Helen looked quickly at him to see if he was smiling. He wasn't.

"Why don'tcha go, Helen?" pleaded Mrs. Givens. "Yo fathah sez this heah man f'm N'Yawk is uh – uh scientist or somethin' an' knows a whole lot about things. Yuh might l'arn somethin'. Ah'd go mys'fif 'twasn't fo mah rheumatism." She sighed in self-pity and finished gnawing a drumstick.

Helen's curiosity was aroused and although she didn't like the idea of sitting among a lot of mill hands, she was anxious to see and hear this reputedly brilliant young man from the great metropolis where not long before she had lost both her provincialism and chastity.

"Oh, all right," she assented with mock reluctance. "I'll go."

* * *

The Knights of Nordica's flag-draped auditorium slowly filled. It was a bare, cavernous structure, with sawdust on the floor, a big platform at one end, row after row of folding wooden chairs and illuminated by large, white lights hanging from the rafters. On the platform was a row of five chairs, the center one being high-backed and gilded. On the lectern downstage was a bulky bible. A huge American flag was stretched across the rear wall.

The audience was composed of the lower stratum of white working people: hard-faced, lantern-jawed, dull-eyed adult children, seeking like all humanity for something permanent in the eternal flux of life. The young girls in their cheap finery with circus makeup on their faces; the young men, aged before their time by child labor and a violent environment; the middle-aged folk with their shiny, shabby garb and beaten countenances; all ready and eager to be organized for any purpose except improvement of their intellects and standard of living.

Rev. Givens opened the meeting with a prayer "for the success, O God, of this thy work, to protect the sisters and wives and daughters of these, thy people, from the filthy pollution of an alien race."

A choir of assorted types of individuals sang "Onward Christian Soldiers" earnestly, vociferously and badly.

They were about to file off the platform when the song leader, a big, beefy, jovial mountain of a man, leaped upon the stage and restrained them.

"Wait a minute, folks, wait a minute," he commanded. Then turning to the assemblage: "Now people let's put some pep into this. We wanna all be happy and get in th' right spirit for this heah meetin'. Ah'm gonna ask the choir to sing th' first and last verses ovah ag'in, and when they come to th' chorus, Ah wantcha to all join in. Doan be 'fraid. Jesus wouldn't be 'fraid to sing 'Onward Christian Soldiers,' now would he? Come on, then. All right, choir, you staht; an' when Ah wave mah han' you'all join in on that theah chorus."

They obediently followed his directions while he marched up and down the platform, red-faced and roaring and waving his arms in time. When the last note had died away, he dismissed the choir and stepping to the edge of the stage he leaned far out over the audience and barked at them again.

"Come on, now, folks! Yuh caint slow up on Jesus now. He won't be satisfied with jus' one ole measly song. Yuh gotta let 'im know that yuh love 'im; that y're happy an' contented; that yuh ain't got no troubles an' ain't gonna have any. Come on, now. Le's sing that ole favorite what yo'all like so well: 'Pack Up Your Troubles in Your Old Kit Bag and Smile, Smile, Smile.'" He bellowed and they followed him. Again the vast hall shook with sound. He made them rise and grasp each other by the hand until the song ended.

Matthew, who sat on the platform alongside old man Givens viewed the spectacle with amusement mingled with amazement. He was amused because of the similarity of this meeting to the religious orgies of the more ignorant Negroes and amazed that earlier in the evening he should have felt any qualms about lecturing to these folks on anthropology, a subject with which neither he nor his hearers were acquainted. He quickly saw that these people would believe anything that was shouted at them loudly and convincingly enough. He knew what would fetch their applause and bring in their memberships and he intended to repeat it over and over.

The Imperial Grand Wizard spent a half-hour introducing the speaker of the evening, dwelt upon his supposed scholastic attainments, but took pains to inform them that, despite Matthew's vast knowledge, he still believed in the Word of God, the sanctity of womanhood and the purity of the white race.

For an hour Matthew told them at the top of his voice what they believed: i.e., that a white skin was a sure indication of the possession of superior intellectual and moral qualities; that all Negroes were inferior to them; that God had intended for the United States to be a white man's country and that with His help they could keep it so; that their sons and brothers might inadvertently marry Negresses or, worse, their sisters and daughters might marry Negroes, if Black-No-More, Incorporated, was permitted to continue its dangerous activities.

For an hour he spoke, interrupted at intervals by enthusiastic gales of applause, and as he spoke his eye wandered over the females in the audience, noting the comeliest ones. As he wound up with a spirited appeal for eager soldiers to join the Knights of Nordica at five dollars per head and the half-dozen "planted" emissaries led the march of suckers to the platform, he noted for the first time a girl who sat in the front row and gazed up at him raptly.

She was a titian blonde, well-dressed, beautiful and strangely familiar. As he retired amid thunderous applause to make way for Rev. Givens and the money collectors, he wondered where he had seen her before. He studied her from his seat.

Suddenly he knew. It was she! The girl who had spurned him; the girl he had sought so long; the girl he wanted more than anything in the world! Strange that she should be here. He had always thought of her as a refined, educated and wealthy lady, far above associating with such people as these. He was in a fever to meet her, some way, before she got out of his sight again, and yet he felt just a little disappointed to find her here.

He could hardly wait until Givens seated himself again before questioning him as to the girl's identity. As the beefy song leader led the roaring of the popular closing hymn, he leaned toward the Imperial Grand Wizard and shouted: "Who is that tall golden-haired girl sitting in the front row? Do you know her?"

Rev. Givens looked out over the audience, craning his skinny neck and blinking his eyes. Then he saw the girl, sitting within twenty feet of him.

"You mean that girl sitting right in front, there?" he asked, pointing.

"Yes, that one," said Matthew, impatiently.

"Heh! Heh! Heh!" chuckled the Wizard, rubbing his stubbly chin. "Why that there's my daughter, Helen. Like to meet her?"

Matthew could hardly believe his ears. Givens's daughter! Incredible! What a coincidence! What luck! Would he like to meet her? He leaned over and shouted, "Yes."

Chapter V

A huge silver monoplane glided gracefully to the surface of Mines Field in Los Angeles and came to a pretty stop after a short run. A liveried footman stepped out of the forward compartment armed with a stool which he placed under the rear door. Simultaneously a high-powered foreign car swept up close to the airplane and waited. The rear door of the airplane opened, and to the apparent surprise of the nearby mechanics a tall, black, distinguished-looking Negro stepped out and down to the ground, assisted by the hand of the footman. Behind him came a pale young man and woman, evidently secretaries. The three entered the limousine which rapidly drove off.

"Who's that coon?" asked one of the mechanics, round-eyed and respectful, like all Americans, in the presence of great wealth.

"Don't you know who that is?" inquired another, pityingly. "Why that's that Dr. Crookman. You know, the fellow what's turnin' niggers white. See that B N M on the side of his plane? That stands for Black-No-More. Gee, but I wish I had just half the jack he's made in the last six months!"

"Why I thought from readin' th' papers," protested the first speaker, "that th' law had closed up his places and put 'im outta business."

"Oh, that's a lotta hockey," said the other fellow. "Why just yesterday th' newspapers said that Black-No-More was openin' a place on Central Avenue. They already got one in Oakland, so a coon told me yesterday."

"'Sfunny," ventured a third mechanic, as they wheeled the big plane into a nearby hangar, "how he don't have nuthin' but white folks around him. He must not like nigger help. His chauffeur's white, his footman's white an' that young gal and feller what was with him are white."

"How do you know?" challenged the first speaker. "They may be darkies that he's turned into white folks."

"That's right," the other replied. "It's gittin' so yuh can't tell who's who. I think that there Knights of Nordica ought to do something about it. I joined up with 'em two months ago but they ain't done nuthin' but sell me an ole uniform an' hold a coupla meetin's."

They lapsed into silence. Sandol, the erstwhile Senegalese, stepped from the cockpit grinning. "Ah, zese Americains," he muttered to himself as he went over the engine, examining everything minutely.

"Where'd yuh come from, buddy?" asked one of the mechanics.

"Den-vair," Sandol replied.

"Whatcha doin', makin' a trip around th' country?" queried another.

"Yes, we air, what you callem, on ze tour inspectione," the aviator continued. They could think of no more to say and soon strolled off.

* * *

Around an oval table on the seventh floor of a building on Central Avenue, sat Dr. Junius Crookman, Hank Johnson, Chuck Foster, Ranford the Doctor's secretary and four other men.

At the lower end of the table Miss Bennett, Ranford's stenographer, was taking notes. A soft-treading waiter whose Negro nature was only revealed by his mocking obsequiousness, served each with champagne.

"To our continued success!" cried the physician, lifting his glass high.

"To our continued success!" echoed the others.

They drained their glasses, and returned them to the polished surface of the table.

"Dog bite it, Doc!" blurted Johnson. "Us sho is doin' fine. Ain't had a bad break since we stahted, an' heah 'tis th' fust o' September."

"Don't holler too soon," cautioned Foster. "The opposition is growing keener every day. I had to pay seventy-five thousand dollars more for this building than it's worth."

"Well, yuh got it, didn't yuh?" asked Johnson. "Just like Ah allus say: when yuh got money yuh kin git anything in this man's country. Whenever things look tight jes pull out th' ole check book an' eve'ything's all right."

"Optimist!" grunted Foster.

"I ain't no pess'mist," Johnson accused.

"Now gentlemen," Dr. Crookman interrupted, clearing his throat, "let's get down to business. We have met here, as you know, not only for the purpose of celebrating the opening of this, our fiftieth sanitarium, but also to take stock of our situation. I have before me here a detailed report of our business affairs for the entire period of seven months and a half that we've been in operation.

"During that time we have put into service fifty sanitariums from Coast to Coast, or an average of one every four and one-half days, the average capacity of each sanitarium being one hundred and five patients. Each place has a staff of six physicians and twenty-four nurses, a janitor, four orderlies, two electricians, bookkeeper, cashier, stenographer and record clerk, not counting four guards.

"For the past four months we have had an equipment factory in Pittsburgh in full operation and a chemical plant in Philadelphia. In addition to this we have purchased four airplanes and a radio broadcasting station. Our expenditures for real estate, salaries and chemicals have totaled six million, two hundred and fifty-five thousand, eighty-five dollars and ten cents."

"He! He!" chuckled Johnson. "Dat ten cents mus' be fo' one o' them bad ceegars that Fostah smokes."

"Our total income," continued Dr. Crookman, frowning slightly at the interruption, "has been eighteen million, five hundred thousand, three hundred dollars, or three hundred and seventy thousand and six patients at fifty dollars apiece. I think that vindicates my contention at the beginning that the fee should be but fifty dollars – within the reach of the rank and file of Negroes." He laid aside his report and added:

"In the next four months we'll double our output and by the end of the year we should cut the fee to twenty-five dollars," he lightly twirled his waxed mustache between his long sensitive fingers and smiled with satisfaction.

"Yes," said Foster, "the sooner we get this business over with the better. We're going to run into a whole lot more opposition from now on than we have so far encountered."

"Why man!" growled Johnson, "we ain't even stahted on dese darkies yet. And when we git thu wi' dese heah, we kin work on them in th' West Indies. Believe me, Ah doan *nevah* want dis graft tuh end."

"Now," continued Dr. Crookman, "I want to say that Mr. Foster deserves great praise for the industry and ingenuity he has shown in purchasing our real estate and Mr. Johnson deserves equally great praise for the efficient manner in which he has kept down the opposition of the various city officials. As you know, he has spent nearly a million dollars in such endeavors and almost as much again in molding legislative sentiment in Washington and the various state capitals. That accounts for the fact that every bill introduced in a legislature or municipal council to put us out of business has died in committee. Moreover, through his corps of secret operatives, who are mostly young women, he has placed numbers of officials and legislators in a position where they cannot openly oppose our efforts."

A smile of appreciation went around the circle.

"We'll have a whole lot to do from now on," commented Foster.

"Yeh, Big Boy," replied the ex-gambler, "an' whut it takes tuh do it Ah ain't got nuthin' else but!"

"Certainly," said the physician, "our friend Hank has not been overburdened with scruples."

"Ah doan know whut dat is, Chief," grinned Johnson, "but Ah knows whut a check book'll do. Even these crackers tone down when Ah talks bucks."

"This afternoon," continued Crookman, "we also have with us our three regional directors, Doctors Henry Dogan, Charles Hinckle and Fred Selden, as well as our chief chemist, Wallace Butts. I thought it would be a good idea to bring you all together for this occasion so we could get better acquainted. We'll just have a word from each of them. They're all good Race men, you know, even if they have, like the rest of our staff, taken the treatment."

For the next three-quarters of an hour the three directors and the chief chemist reported on the progress of their work. At intervals the waiter brought in cold drinks, cigars and cigarettes. Overhead whirred the electric fans. Out of the wide open windows could be seen the panorama of bungalows, pavements, palm trees, trundling street cars and scooting automobiles.

"Lawd! Lawd! Lawd!" Johnson exclaimed at the conclusion of the meeting, going to the window and gazing out over the city. "Jes gimme a coupla yeahs o' dis graft an' Ah'll make Henry Foahd look like a tramp."

* * *

Meanwhile, Negro society was in turmoil and chaos. The colored folk in straining every nerve to get the Black-No-More treatment, had forgotten all loyalties, affiliations and responsibilities. No longer did they flock to the churches on Sundays or pay dues in their numerous fraternal organizations. They had stopped giving anything to the Anti-Lynching campaign. Santop Licorice, head of the once-flourishing Back-To-Africa Society, was daily raising his stentorian voice in denunciation of the race for deserting his organization.

Negro business was being no less hard hit. Few people were bothering about getting their hair straightened or skin whitened temporarily when for a couple of weeks' pay they could get both jobs done permanently. The immediate result of this change of mind on the part of the Negro public was to almost bankrupt the firms that made the whitening and straightening chemicals. They were largely controlled by canny Hebrews, but at least a half-dozen were owned by Negroes. The rapid decline in this business greatly decreased the revenue of the Negro weekly newspapers who depended upon such advertising for their sustenance. The actual business of hair straightening that had furnished employment to thousands of colored women who would otherwise have had to go back to washing and ironing, declined to such an extent that "To Rent" signs hung in front of nine-tenths of the shops.

The Negro politicians in the various Black Belts, grown fat and sleek "protecting" vice with the aid of Negro votes which they were able to control by virtue of housing segregation, lectured in vain about black solidarity, race pride and political emancipation; but nothing stopped the exodus to the white race. Gloomily the politicians sat in their offices, wondering whether to throw up the sponge and hunt the nearest Black-No-More sanitarium or hold on a little longer in the hope that the whites might put a stop to the activities of Dr. Crookman and his associates. The latter, indeed, was their only hope because the bulk of Negroes, saving their dimes and dollars for chromatic emancipation, had stopped gambling, patronizing houses of prostitution or staging Saturday-night brawls. Thus the usual sources of graft vanished. The black politicians appealed to their white masters for succor, of course, but they found to their dismay that most of the latter had been safely bribed by the astute Hank Johnson.

Gone was the almost European atmosphere of every Negro ghetto: the music, laughter, gaiety, jesting and abandon. Instead, one noted the same excited bustle, wild looks and strained faces to be seen in a war time soldier camp, around a new oil district or before a gold rush. The happy-go-lucky Negro of song and story was gone forever and in his stead was a nervous, money-grubbing black, stuffing away coin in socks, impatiently awaiting a sufficient sum to pay Dr. Crookman's fee.

Up from the South they came in increasing droves, besieging the Black-No-More sanitariums for treatment. There were none of these havens in the South because of the hostility of the bulk of white people but there were many all along the border between the two sections, at such places as Washington, D.C., Baltimore, Cincinnati, Louisville, Evansville, Cairo, St. Louis and Denver. The various Southern communities attempted to stem this, the greatest migration of Negroes in the history of the country, but without avail. By train, boat, wagon, bicycle, automobile and foot they trekked to the promised land; a hopeful procession, filtering through the outposts of police and Knights of Nordica volunteer bands. Where there was great opposition to the Negroes' going, there would suddenly appear large quantities of free bootleg liquor and crisp new currency which would make the most vigilant white opponent of Black-No-More turn his head the other way. Hank Johnson seemed to be able to cope with almost every situation.

* * *

The national office of the militant Negro organization, the National Social Equality League, was agog. Telephone bells were ringing, mulatto clerks were hustling excitedly back and forth, messenger boys rushed in and out. Located in the Times Square district of Manhattan, it had for forty years carried on the fight for full social equality for the Negro citizens and the immediate abolition of lynching as a national sport. While this organization had to depend to a large extent upon the charity of white folk for its existence, since the blacks had always been more or less skeptical about the program for liberty and freedom, the efforts of the society were not entirely unprofitable. Vistas of immaculate offices spread in every direction from the elevator and footfalls were muffled in thick imitation-Persian rugs. While the large staff of officials was eager to end all oppression and persecution of the Negro, they were never so happy and excited as when a Negro was barred from a theater or fried to a crisp. Then they would leap for telephones, grab telegraph pads and yell for stenographers; smiling through their simulated indignation at the spectacle of another reason for their continued existence and appeals for funds.

Ever since the first sanitarium of Black-No-More, Incorporated, started turning Negroes into Caucasians, the National Social Equality League's income had been decreasing. No dues had been collected in months and subscriptions to the national mouthpiece, *The Dilemma*, had dwindled to almost nothing. Officials, long since ensconced in palatial apartments, began to grow panic-stricken as pay days got farther apart. They began to envision the time when they would no longer be able for the sake of the Negro race to suffer the hardships of lunching on canvasback duck at the Urban Club surrounded by the white dilettante, endure the perils of first-class Transatlantic passage to stage Save-Dear-Africa Conferences or undergo the excruciating torture of rolling back and forth across the United States in drawing-rooms to hear each other lecture on the Negro problem. On meager salaries of five thousand dollars a year they had fought strenuously and tirelessly to obtain for the Negroes the constitutional rights which only a few thousand rich white folk possessed. And now they saw the work of a lifetime being rapidly destroyed.

Single-handed they felt incapable of organizing an effective opposition to Black-No-More, Incorporated, so they had called a conference of all of the outstanding Negro leaders of the country to assemble at the League's headquarters on December 1, 1933. Getting the Negro leaders together for any purpose except boasting of each other's accomplishments had previously been impossible. As a usual thing they fought each other with a vigor only surpassed by that of their pleas for racial solidarity and unity of action. This situation, however, was unprecedented, so almost all of the representative gentlemen of color to whom invitations had been sent agreed with alacrity to come. To a man they felt that it was time to bury the hatchet before they became too hungry to do any digging.

In a very private inner office of the N.S.E.L. suite, Dr. Shakespeare Agamemnon Beard, founder of the League and a graduate of Harvard, Yale and Copenhagen (whose haughty bearing never failed to impress both Caucasians and Negroes) sat before a glass-topped desk, rubbing now his curly gray head, and now his full spade beard. For a mere six thousand dollars a year, the learned doctor wrote scholarly and biting editorials in *The Dilemma* denouncing the Caucasians whom he secretly admired and lauding the greatness of the Negroes whom he alternately pitied and despised. In limpid prose he told of the sufferings and privations of the downtrodden black workers with whose lives he was totally and thankfully unfamiliar. Like most Negro leaders, he deified the black woman but abstained from employing aught save octoroons. He talked at white banquets about "we of the black race" and admitted in books that he was part-French, part-Russian, part-Indian and part-Negro. He bitterly denounced the Nordics for debauching Negro women while taking care to hire comely yellow stenographers with weak resistance. In a real way, he loved his people. In time of peace he was a Pink Socialist but when the clouds of war gathered he bivouacked at the feet of Mars.

Before the champion of the darker races lay a neatly typed resolution drawn up by him and his staff the day before and addressed to the Attorney General of the United States. The staff had taken this precaution because no member of it believed that the other Negro leaders possessed sufficient education to word the document effectively and grammatically. Dr. Beard re-read the resolution and then placing it in the drawer of the desk, pressed one of a row of buttons. "Tell them to come in," he directed. The mulattress turned and switched out of the room, followed by the appraising and approving eye of the aged scholar. He heaved a regretful sigh as the door closed and his thoughts dwelt on the vigor of his youth.

In three or four minutes the door opened again and several well-dressed blacks, mulattoes and white men entered the large office and took seats around the wall. They greeted each other and the President of the League with usual cordiality but for the first time in their lives they were sincere about it. If anyone could save the day it was Beard. They all admitted that, as did the Doctor himself. They pulled out fat cigars, long slender cigarettes and London briar pipes, lit them and awaited the opening of the conference.

The venerable lover of his race tapped with his knuckle for order, laid aside his six-inch cigarette and rising, said:

"It were quite unseemly for me who lives such a cloistered life and am spared the bane or benefit of many intimate contacts with those of our struggling race who by sheer courage, tenacity and merit have lifted their heads above the mired mass, to deign to take from a more capable individual the unpleasant task of reviewing the combination of unfortunate circumstances that has brought us together, man to man, within the four walls of the office." He shot a foxy glance around the assembly and then went on suavely. "And so, my friends, I beg your august permission to confer upon my able and cultured secretary and confidant, Dr. Napoleon Wellington Jackson, the office of chairman of this temporary body. I need not introduce Dr. Jackson to you. You know of his scholarship, his high sense of duty and his deep love of the suffering black race. You have doubtless had the pleasure of singing some of the many sorrow songs he has written and popularized in the past twenty years, and you must know of his fame as a translator of Latin poets and his authoritative work on the Greek language.

"Before I gratefully yield the floor to Dr. Jackson, however, I want to tell you that our destiny lies in the stars. Ethiopia's fate is in the balance. The Goddess of the Nile weeps bitter tears at the feet of the Great Sphinx. The lowering clouds gather over the Congo and the lightning flashes o'er Togoland. To your tents, O Israel! The hour is at hand."

The president of the N.S.E.L. sat down and the erudite Dr. Jackson, his tall, lanky secretary got up. There was no fear of Dr. Jackson ever winning a beauty contest. He was a sooty black, very broad shouldered, with long, ape-like arms, a diminutive egg-shaped head that sat on his collar like a hen's egg on a demitasse cup and eyes that protruded so far from his head that they seemed about to fall out. He wore pince-nez that were continually slipping from his very flat and oily nose. His chief business in the organization was to write long and indignant letters to public officials and legislators whenever a Negro was mistreated, demanding justice, fair play and other legal guarantees vouchsafed no whites except bloated plutocrats fallen miraculously afoul of the law, and to speak to audiences of sex-starved matrons who yearned to help the Negro stand erect. During his leisure time, which was naturally considerable, he wrote long and learned articles, bristling with references, for the more intellectual magazines, in which he sought to prove conclusively that the plantation shouts of Southern Negro peons were superior to any of Beethoven's symphonies and that the city of Benin was the original site of the Garden of Eden.

"Hhmm! Hu-umn! Now er – ah, gentlemen," began Dr. Jackson, rocking back on his heels, taking off his eye glasses and beginning to polish them with a silk kerchief, "as you know, the Negro race is face to face with a grave crisis. I – ah – presume it is er – ah unnecessary for me to go into any details concerning the-ah activities of Black-No-More, Incorporated. Suffice er – ah umph! ummmmh! to say-ah that it has thrown our society into rather a-ah bally turmoil. Our people are forgetting shamelessly their-ah duty to the-ah organizations that have fought valiantly for them these-ah many years and are now busily engaged chasing a bally-ah will-o-the wisp. Ahem!

"You-ah probably all fully realize that-ah a continuation of the aforementioned activities will prove disastrous to our-ah organizations. You-ah, like us, must feel-uh that something drastic must be done to preserve the integrity of Negro society. Think, gentlemen, what the future will mean to-uh all those who-uh have toiled so hard for Negro society. What-ah, may I ask, will we do when there are no longer any-ah groups to support us? Of course, Dr. Crookman and-ah his associates have a-uh perfect right to-ah engage in any legitimate business, but-ah their present activities cannot-ah be classed under that head, considering the effect on our endeavors. Before we go any further, however, I-ah would like to introduce our research expert Mr. Walter Williams, who will-ah describe the situation in the South."

Mr. Walter Williams, a tall, heavy-set white man with pale blue eyes, wavy auburn hair and a militant, lantern jaw, rose and bowed to the assemblage and proceeded to paint a heartrending picture of the loss of pride and race solidarity among Negroes North and South. There was, he said, not a single local of the N.S.E.L. functioning, dues had dwindled to nothing, he had not been able to hold a meeting anywhere, while many of the stanchest supporters had gone over into the white race.

"Personally," he concluded, "I am very proud to be a Negro and always have been (his great-grandfather, it seemed, had been a mulatto), and I'm willing to sacrifice for the uplift of my race. I cannot understand what has come over our people that they have so quickly forgotten the ancient glories of Ethiopia, Songhay and Dahomey, and their marvelous record of achievement since emancipation." Mr. Williams was known to be a Negro among his friends and acquaintances, but no one else would have suspected it.

Another white man of remote Negro ancestry, Rev. Herbert Gronne of Dunbar University, followed the research expert with a long discourse in which he expressed fear for the future of his institution whose student body had been reduced to sixty-five persons and deplored the catastrophe "that has befallen us black people."

They all listened with respect to Dr. Gronne. He had been in turn a college professor, a social worker and a minister, had received the approval of the white folks and was thus doubly acceptable to the Negroes. Much of his popularity was due to the fact that he very cleverly knew how to make statements that sounded radical to Negroes but sufficiently conservative to satisfy the white trustees of his school. In addition he possessed the asset of looking perpetually earnest and sincere.

Following him came Colonel Mortimer Roberts, principal of the Dusky River Agricultural Institute, Supreme General of the Knights and Daughters of Kingdom Come and president of the Uncle Tom Memorial Association. Colonel Roberts was the acknowledged leader of the conservative Negroes (most of whom had nothing to conserve) who felt at all times that the white folks were in the lead and that Negroes should be careful to guide themselves accordingly.

He was a great mountain of blackness with a head shaped like an upturned bucket, pierced by two pig-like eyes and a cavernous mouth equipped with large tombstone teeth which he almost continually displayed. His speech was a cross between the woofing of a bloodhound and the explosion of an inner tube. It conveyed to most white people an impression of rugged simplicity and sincerity, which was very fortunate since Colonel Roberts maintained his school through their contributions. He spoke as usual about the cordial relations existing between the two races in his native Georgia, the effrontery of Negroes who dared whiten themselves and thus disturb the minds of white people and insinuated alliance with certain militant organizations in the South to stop this whitening business before it went too far. Having spoken his mind and received scant applause, the Colonel (some white man had once called him Colonel and the title stuck) puffing and blowing, sat down.

Mr. Claude Spelling, a scared-looking little brown man with big ears, who held the exalted office of president of the Society of Negro Merchants, added his volume of blues to the discussion. The refrain was that Negro business – always anemic – was about to pass out entirely through lack of patronage. Mr. Spelling had for many years been the leading advocate of the strange doctrine that an underpaid Negro worker should go out of his way to patronize a little dingy Negro store instead of going to a cheaper and cleaner chain store, all for the dubious satisfaction of helping Negro merchants grow wealthy.

The next speaker, Dr. Joseph Bonds, a little rat-faced Negro with protruding teeth stained by countless plugs of chewing tobacco and wearing horn-rimmed spectacles, who headed the Negro Data League, almost cried (which would have been terrible to observe) when he told of the difficulty his workers had encountered in their efforts to persuade retired white capitalists, whose guilty consciences persuaded them to indulge in philanthropy, to give their customary donations to the work. The philanthropists seemed to think, said Dr. Bonds, that since the Negroes were busily solving their difficulties, there was no need for social work among them or any collection of data. He almost sobbed aloud when he described how his collections had fallen from $50,000 a month to less than $1000.

His feeling in the matter could easily be appreciated. He was engaged in a most vital and necessary work: i.e., collecting bales of data to prove satisfactorily to all that more money was needed to collect more data. Most of the data were highly informative, revealing the amazing fact that poor people went to jail oftener than rich ones; that most of the people were not getting enough money for their work; that strangely enough there was some connection between poverty, disease and crime. By establishing these facts with mathematical certitude and illustrating them with elaborate graphs, Dr. Bonds garnered many fat checks. For his people, he said, he wanted work, not charity; but for himself he was always glad to get the charity with as little work as possible. For many years he had succeeded in doing so without any ascertainable benefit accruing to the Negro group.

Dr. Bonds' show of emotion almost brought the others to tears and many of them muttered "Yes, Brother" while he was talking. The conferees were getting stirred up but it took the next speaker to really get them excited.

When he rose an expectant hush fell over the assemblage. They all knew and respected the Right Reverend Bishop Ezekiel Whooper of the Ethiopian True Faith Wash Foot Methodist Church for three reasons: viz., his church was rich (though the parishioners were poor), he had a very loud voice and the white people praised him. He was sixty, corpulent and an expert at the art of making cuckolds.

"Our loyal and devoted clergy," he boomed, "are being forced into manual labor and the Negro church is rapidly dying." And then he launched into a violent tirade against Black-No-More and favored any means to put the corporation out of business. In his excitement he blew saliva, waved his long arms, stamped his feet, pummeled the desk, rolled his eyes, knocked down his chair, almost sat on the rug and generally reverted to the antics of Negro bush preachers.

This exhibition proved contagious. Rev. Herbert Gronne, face flushed and shouting amens, marched from one end of the room to the other; Colonel Roberts, looking like an inebriated black-faced comedian, rocked back and forth clapping his hands; the others began to groan and moan. Dr. Napoleon Wellington Jackson, sensing his opportunity, began to sing a spiritual in his rich soprano voice. The others immediately joined him. The very air seemed charged with emotion.

Bishop Whooper was about to start up again, when Dr. Beard, who had sat cold and disdainful through this outbreak of revivalism, toying with his gold-rimmed fountain pen and gazing at the exhibition through half-closed eyelids, interrupted in sharp metallic tones.

"Let's get down to earth now," he commanded. "We've had enough of this nonsense. We have a resolution here addressed to the Attorney General of the United States demanding that Dr. Crookman and his associates be arrested and their activities stopped at once for the good of both races. All those in favor of this resolution say aye. Contrary?...Very well, the ayes have it... Miss Hilton, please send off this telegram at once!"

They looked at Dr. Beard and each other in amazement. Several started to meekly protest.

"You gentlemen are all twenty-one, aren't you?" sneered Beard. "Well, then be men enough to stand by your decision."

"But Doctor Beard," objected Rev. Gronne, "isn't this a rather unusual procedure?"

"Rev. Gronne," the great man replied, "it's not near as unusual as Black-No-More. I have probably ruffled your dignity but that's nothing to what Dr. Crookman will do."

"I guess you're right, Beard," the college president agreed.

"I know it," snapped the other.

The Honorable Walter Brybe, who had won his exalted position as Attorney General of the United States because of his long and faithful service helping large corporations to circumvent the federal laws, sat at his desk in Washington, D.C. Before him lay the wired resolution from the conference of Negro leaders. He pursed his lips and reached for his private telephone.

"Gorman?" he inquired softly into the receiver. "Is that you?"

"Nossuh," came the reply, "this heah is Mistah Gay's valet."

"Well, call Mister Gay to the telephone at once."

"Yassuh."

"That you, Gorman," asked the chief legal officer of the nation addressing the National Chairman of his party.

"Yeh, what's up?"

"You heard 'bout this resolution from them niggers in New York, aint you? It's been in all of the papers."

"Yes I read it."

"Well, whaddya think we oughtta do about it?"

"Take it easy, Walter. Give 'em the old run around. You know. They ain't got a thin dime; it's this other crowd that's holding the heavy jack. And 'course you know we gotta clean up our deficit. Just lemme work with that Black-No-More crowd. I can talk business with that Johnson fellow."

"All right, Gorman, I think you're right, but you don't want to forget that there's a whole lot of white sentiment against them coons."

"Needn't worry 'bout that," scoffed Gorman. "There's no money behind it much and besides it's in states we can't carry anyhow. Go ahead; stall them New York niggers off. You're a lawyer, you can always find a reason."

"Thanks for the compliment, Gorman," said the Attorney General, hanging up the receiver.

He pressed a button on his desk and a young girl, armed with pencil and pad, came in.

"Take this letter," he ordered: "To Doctor Shakespeare Agamemnon Beard (what a hell of a name!), Chairman of the Committee for the Preservation of Negro Racial Integrity, 1400 Broadway, New York City.

"My dear Dr. Beard:

The Attorney General has received the resolution signed by yourself and others and given it careful consideration.

Regardless of personal views in the matter (I don't give a damn whether they turn white or not, myself) it is not possible for the Department of Justice to interfere with a legitimate business enterprise so long as its methods are within the law. The corporation in question has violated no federal statute and hence there is not the slightest ground for interfering with its activities.

Very truly yours,

Walter Brybe.

"Get that off at once. Give out copies to the press. That's all."

* * *

Santop Licorice, founder and leader of the Back-to-Africa Society, read the reply of the Attorney General to the Negro leaders with much malicious satisfaction. He laid aside his morning paper, pulled a fat cigar from a box near by, lit it and blew clouds of smoke above his woolly head. He was always delighted when Dr. Beard met with any sort of rebuff or embarrassment. He was doubly pleased in this instance because he had been overlooked in the sending out of invitations to Negro leaders to join the Committee for the Preservation of Negro Racial Integrity. It was outrageous, after all the talking he had done in favor of Negro racial integrity.

Mr. Licorice for some fifteen years had been very profitably advocating the emigration of all the American Negroes to Africa. He had not, of course, gone there himself and had not the slightest intention of going so far from the fleshpots, but he told the other Negroes to go. Naturally the first step in their going was to join his society by paying five dollars a year for membership, ten dollars for a gold, green and purple robe and silver-colored helmet that together cost two dollars and a half, contributing five dollars to the Santop Licorice Defense Fund (there was a perpetual defense fund because Licorice was perpetually in the courts for fraud of some kind), and buying shares at five dollars each in the Royal Black Steamship Company, for obviously one could not get to Africa without a ship and Negroes ought to travel on Negro-owned and operated ships. The ships were Santop's especial pride. True, they had never been to Africa, had never had but one cargo and that, being gin, was half consumed by the unpaid and thirsty crew before the vessel was saved by the Coast Guard, but they had cost more than anything else the Back-To-Africa Society had purchased even though they were worthless except as scrap iron. Mr. Licorice, who was known by his followers as Provisional President of Africa, Admiral of the African Navy, Field Marshal of the African Army and Knight Commander of the Nile, had a genius for being stuck with junk by crafty salesmen. White men only needed to tell him that he was shrewder than white men and he would immediately reach for a check book.

But there was little reaching for check books in his office nowadays. He had been as hard hit as the other Negroes. Why should anybody in the Negro race want to go back to Africa at a cost of five hundred dollars for passage when they could stay in America and get white for fifty dollars? Mr. Licorice saw the point but instead of scuttling back to Demerara from whence he had come to save his race from oppression, he had hung on in the hope that the activities of Black-No-More, Incorporated, would be stopped. In the meantime, he had continued to attempt to save the Negroes by vigorously attacking all of the other Negro organizations and at the same time preaching racial solidarity and co-operation in his weekly newspaper, "*The African Abroad*," which was printed by white folks and had until a year ago been full of skin-whitening and hair-straightening advertisements.

"How is our treasury?" he yelled back through the dingy suite of offices to his bookkeeper, a pretty mulatto.

"What treasury?" she asked in mock surprise.

"Why, I thought we had seventy-five dollars," he blurted.

"We did, but the Sheriff got most of it yesterday or we wouldn't be in here today."

"Huumn! Well, that's bad. And tomorrow's pay day, isn't it?"

"Why bring that up?" she sneered. "I'd forgotten all about it."

"Haven't we got enough for me to get to Atlanta?" Licorice inquired, anxiously.

"There is if you're gonna hitch-hike."

"Well, of course, I couldn't do that," he smiled deprecatingly.

"I should say not," she retorted surveying his 250-pound, five-feet-six-inches of black blubber.

"Call Western Union," he commanded.

"What with?"

"Over the telephone, of course, Miss Hall," he explained.

"If you can get anything over that telephone you're a better man than I am, Gunga Din."

"Has the service been discontinued, young lady?"

"Try and get a number," she chirped. He gazed ruefully at the telephone.

"Is there anything we can sell?" asked the bewildered Licorice.

"Yeah, if you can get the Sheriff to take off his attachments."

"That's right, I had forgotten."

"You would."

"Please be more respectful, Miss Hall," he snapped. "Somebody might overhear you and tell my wife."

"Which one?" she mocked.

"Shut up," he blurted, touched in a tender spot, "and try to figure out some way for us to get hold of some money."

"You must think I'm Einstein," she said, coming up and perching herself on the edge of his desk.

"Well, if we don't get some operating expenses I won't be able to obtain money to pay your salary," he warned.

"The old songs are the best songs," she wisecracked.

"Oh, come now, Violet," he remonstrated, pawing her buttock, "let's be serious."

"After all these years!" she declared, switching away.

In desperation, he eased his bulk out of the creaking swivel chair, reached for his hat and overcoat and shuffled out of the office. He walked to the curb to hail a taxicab but reconsidered when he recalled that a worn half-dollar was the extent of his funds. Sighing heavily, he trudged the two blocks to the telegraph office and sent a long day letter to Henry Givens, Imperial Grand Wizard of the Knights of Nordica – collect.

"Well, have you figured it out?" asked Violet when he barged into his office again.

"Yes, I just sent a wire to Givens," he replied.

"But he's a nigger-hater, isn't he?" was her surprised comment.

"You want your salary, don't you?" he inquired archly.

"I have for the past month."

"Well, then, don't ask foolish questions," he snapped.

Chapter VI

Two important events took place on Easter Sunday, 1934. The first was a huge mass meeting in the brand new reinforced concrete auditorium of the Knights of Nordica for the double purpose of celebrating the first anniversary of the militant secret society and the winning of the millionth member. The second event was the wedding of Helen Givens and Matthew Fisher, Grand Exalted Giraw of the Knights of Nordica.

Rev. Givens, the Imperial Grand Wizard of the order, had never regretted that he had taken Fisher into the order and made him his right-hand man. The membership had grown by leaps and bounds, the treasury was bursting with money in spite of the Wizard's constant misappropriation of funds, the regalia factory was running night and day and the influence of the order was becoming so great that Rev. Givens was beginning to dream of a berth in the White House or near by.

For over six months the order had been publishing *The Warning*, an eight-page newspaper carrying lurid red headlines and poorly-drawn quarter-page cartoons, and edited by Matthew. The noble Southern working people purchased it eagerly, devouring and believing every word in it. Matthew, in 14-point, one-syllable word editorials painted terrifying pictures of the menace confronting white supremacy and the utter necessity of crushing it. Very cleverly he linked up the Pope, the Yellow Peril, the Alien Invasion and Foreign Entanglements with Black-No-More as devices of the Devil. He wrote with such blunt sincerity that sometimes he almost persuaded himself that it was all true.

As the money flowed in, Matthew's fame as a great organizer spread throughout the Southland, and he suddenly became the most desirable catch in the section. Beautiful women literally threw themselves at his feet, and, as a former Negro and thus well versed in the technique of amour, he availed himself of all offerings that caught his fancy.

At the same time he was a frequent visitor to the Givens home, especially when Mrs. Givens, whom he heartily detested, was away. From the very first Helen had been impressed by Matthew. She had always longed for the companionship of an educated man, a scientist, a man of literary ability. Matthew to her mind embodied all of these. She only hesitated to accept his first offer of marriage two days after they met because she saw no indication that he had much, if any, money. She softened toward him as the Knights of Nordica treasury grew; and when he was able to boast of a million-dollar bank account, she agreed to marriage and accepted his ardent embraces in the meantime.

And so, before the yelling multitude of night-gowned Knights, they were united in holy wedlock on the stage of the new auditorium. Both, being newlyweds, were happy. Helen had secured the kind of husband she wanted, except that she regretted his association with what she called low-brows; while Matthew had won the girl of his dreams and was thoroughly satisfied, except for a slight regret that her grotesque mother wasn't dead and some disappointment that his spouse was so much more ignorant than she was beautiful.

As soon as Matthew had helped to get the Knights of Nordica well under way with enough money flowing in to satisfy the avaricious Rev. Givens, he had begun to study ways and means of making some money on the side. He had power, influence and prestige and he intended to make good use of them. So he had obtained audiences individually with several of the leading business men of the Georgia capital.

He always prefaced his proposition by pointing out that the working people were never so contented, profits never so high and the erection of new factories in the city never so intensive; that the continued prosperity of Atlanta and of the entire South depended upon keeping labor free from Bolshevism, Socialism, Communism, Anarchism, trade unionism and other subversive movements. Such un-American philosophies, he insisted had ruined European countries and from their outposts in New York and other Northern cities were sending emissaries to seek a foothold in the South and plant the germ of discontent. When this happened, he warned gloomily, then farewell to high profits and contented labor. He showed copies of books and pamphlets which he had ordered from radical book stores in New York but which he asserted were being distributed to the prospect's employees.

He then explained the difference between the defunct Ku Klux Klan and the Knights of Nordica. While both were interested in public morals, racial integrity and the threatened invasion of America by the Pope, his organization glimpsed its larger duty, the perpetuation of Southern prosperity by the stabilization of industrial relations. The Knights of Nordica, favored by increasing membership, was in a position to keep down all radicalism, he said, and then boldly asserted that Black-No-More was subsidized by the Russian Bolsheviks. Would the gentlemen help the work of the Nordicists along with a small contribution? They would and did. Whenever there was a slump in the flow of cash from this source, Matthew merely had his print shop run off a bale of Communistic tracts which his secret operatives distributed around in the mills and factories. Contributions would immediately increase.

Matthew had started this lucrative side enterprise none too soon. There was much unemployment in the city, wages were being cut and work speeded up. There was dissatisfaction and grumbling among the workers and a small percentage of them was in a mood to give ear to the half-dozen timid organizers of the conservative unions who were being paid to unionize the city but had as yet made no headway. A union might not be so bad after all.

The great mass of white workers, however, was afraid to organize and fight for more pay because of a deepset fear that the Negroes would take their jobs. They had heard of black labor taking the work of white labor under the guns of white militia, and they were afraid to risk it. They had first read of the activities of Black-No-More, Incorporated, with a secret feeling akin to relief but after the orators of the Knights of Nordica and the editorials of *The Warning* began to portray the menace confronting them, they forgot about their economic ills and began to yell for the blood of Dr. Crookman and his associates. Why, they began to argue, one couldn't tell who was who! Herein lay the fundamental cause of all their ills. Times were hard, they reasoned, because there were so many white Negroes in their midst taking their jobs and undermining their American standard of living. None of them had ever attained an American standard of living to be sure, but that fact never occurred to any of them. So they flocked to the meetings of the Knights of Nordica and night after night sat spellbound while Rev. Givens, who had finished the eighth grade in a one-room country school, explained the laws of heredity and spoke eloquently of the growing danger of black babies.

Despite his increasing wealth (the money came in so fast he could scarcely keep track of it), Matthew maintained close contact with the merchants and manufacturers. He sent out private letters periodically to prominent men in the Southern business world in which he told of the marked psychological change that had come over the working classes of the South since the birth of the K. of N. He told how they had been discontented and on the brink of revolution when his organization rushed in and saved the South. Unionism and such destructive nostrums had been forgotten, he averred, when *The Warning* had revealed the latest danger to the white race. Of course, he always added, such work required large sums of money and contributions from conservative, substantial and public-spirited citizens were ever acceptable. At the end of each letter there appeared a suggestive paragraph pointing out the extent to which the prosperity of the New South was due to its "peculiar institutions" that made the worker race conscious instead of class conscious, and that with the passing of these "peculiar institutions" would also pass prosperity. This reasoning proved very effective, financially speaking.

Matthew's great success as an organizer and his increasing popularity was not viewed by Rev. Givens with equanimity. The former evangelist knew that everybody of intelligence in the upper circles of the order realized that the growth and prosperity of the Knights of Nordica was largely due to the industry, efficiency and intelligence of Matthew. He had been told that many people were saying that Fisher ought to be Imperial Grand Wizard instead of Grand Exalted Giraw.

Givens had the ignorant man's fear and suspicion of anybody who was supposedly more learned than he. His position, he felt, was threatened, and he was decidedly uneasy. He neither said nor did anything about it, but he fretted a great deal to his wife, much to her annoyance. He was consequently overjoyed when Matthew asked him for Helen's hand, and gave his consent with alacrity. When the marriage was consummated, he saw his cup filled to overflowing and no clouds on the horizon. The Knights of Nordica was safe in the family.

One morning a week or two after his wedding, Matthew was sitting in his private office, when his secretary announced a caller, one B. Brown. After the usual delay staged for the purpose of impressing all visitors, Matthew ordered him in. A short, plump, well-dressed, soft-spoken man entered and greeted him respectfully. The Grand Exalted Giraw waved to a chair and the stranger sat down. Suddenly, leaning over close to Matthew, he whispered, "Don't recognize me, do you Max?"

The Grand Giraw paled and started. "Who are you?" he whispered hoarsely. How in the devil did this man know him? He peered at him sharply.

The newcomer grinned. "Why it's me, Bunny Brown, you big sap!"

"Well, cut my throat!" Matthew exclaimed in amazement. "Boy, is it really you?" Bunny's black face had miraculously bleached. He seemed now more chubby and cherubic than ever.

"It ain't my brother," said Bunny with his familiar beam.

"Bunny, where've you been all this time? Why didn't you come on down here when I wrote you? You must've been in jail."

"Mind reader! That's just where I've been," declared the former bank clerk.

"What for? Gambling?"

"No: Rambling."

"What do you mean: Rambling?" asked the puzzled Matthew.

"Just what I said, Big Boy. Got to rambling around with a married woman. Old story: husband came in unexpectedly and I had to crown him. The fire escape was slippery and I slipped. Couldn't run after I hit the ground and the flatfoot nabbed me. Got a lucky break in court or I wouldn't be here."

"Was it a white woman?" asked the Grand Exalted Giraw.

"She wasn't black," said Bunny.

"It's a good thing you weren't black, too!"

"Our minds always ran in the same channels," Bunny commented.

"Got any jack?" asked Matthew.

"Is it likely?"

"Do you want a job?"

"No, I prefer a position."

"Well, I think I can fix you up here for about five grand to begin with," said Matthew.

"Santa Claus! What do I have to do: assassinate the President?"

"No, kidder; just be my right-hand man. You know, follow me through thick and thin."

"All right, Max; but when things get too thick, I'm gonna thin out."

"For Christ's sake don't call me Max," cautioned Matthew.

"That's your name, aint it?"

"No, simp. Them days has gone forever. It's Matthew Fisher now. You go pulling that Max stuff and I'll have to answer more questions than a traffic officer."

"Just think," mused Bunny. "I been reading about you right along in the papers but until I recognized your picture in last Sunday's paper I didn't know who you were. Just how long have you been in on this graft?"

"Ever since it started."

"Say not so! You must have a wad of cash salted away by this time."

"Well, I'm not appealing for charity," Matthew smiled sardonically.

"How many squaws you got now?"

"Only one, Bunny – regular."

"What's matter, did you get too old?" chided his friend.

"No, I got married."

"Well, that's the same thing. Who's the unfortunate woman?"

"Old man Givens' girl."

"Judas Priest! You got in on the ground floor didn't you?"

"I didn't miss. Bunny, old scout, she's the same girl that turned me down that night in the Honky Tonk," Matthew told him with satisfaction.

"Well, hush my mouth! This sounds like a novel," Bunny chuckled.

"Believe it or not, papa, it's what God loves," Matthew grinned.

"Well, you lucky hound! Getting white didn't hurt you none."

"Now listen, Bunny," said Matthew, dropping to a more serious tone, "from now on you're private secretary to the Grand Exalted Giraw; that's me."

"What's a Giraw?"

"I can't tell you; I don't know myself. Ask Givens sometime. He invented it but if he can explain it I'll give you a grand."

"When do I start to work? Or rather, when do I start drawing money?"

"Right now, Old Timer. Here's a century to get you fixed up. You eat dinner with me tonight and report to me in the morning."

"Fathers above!" said Bunny. "Dixie must be heaven."

"It'll be hell for you if these babies find you out; so keep your nose clean."

"Watch me, Mr. Giraw."

"Now listen, Bunny. You know Santop Licorice, don't you?"

"Who doesn't know that hippo?"

"Well, we've had him on our payroll since December. He's fighting Beard, Whooper, Spelling and that crowd. He was on the bricks and we helped him out. Got his paper to appearing regularly, and all that sort of thing."

"So the old crook sold out the race, did he?" cried the amazed Bunny.

"Hold that race stuff, you're not a shine anymore. Are you surprised that he sold out? You're actually becoming innocent," said Matthew.

"Well, what about the African admiral?" Bunny asked.

"This: In a couple of days I want you to run up to New York and look around and see if his retention on the payroll is justified. I got a hunch that nobody is bothering about his paper or what he says, and if that's true we might as well can him; I can use the jack to better advantage."

"Listen here, Boy, this thing is running me nuts. Here you are fighting this Black-No-More, and so is Beard, Whooper, Gronne, Spelling and the rest of the Negro leaders, yet you have Licorice on the payroll to fight the same people that are fighting your enemy. This thing is more complicated than a flapper's past."

"Simple, Bunny, simple. Reason why you can't understand it is because you don't know anything about high strategy."

"High what?" asked Bunny.

"Never mind, look it up at your leisure. Now you can savvy the fact that the sooner these spades are whitened the sooner this graft will fall through, can't you?"

"Righto," said his friend.

"Well, the longer we can make the process, the longer we continue to drag down the jack. Is that clear?"

"As a Spring day."

"You're getting brighter by the minute, old man," jeered Matthew.

"Coming from you, that's no compliment."

"As I was saying, the longer it takes, the longer we last. It's my business to see that it lasts a long time but neither do I want it to stop because that also would be disastrous."

Bunny nodded: "You're a wise egg!"

"Thanks, that makes it unanimous. Well, I don't want my side to get such an upper hand that it will put the other side out of business, or vice versa. What we want is a status quo."

"Gee, you've got educated since you've been down here with these crackers."

"You flatter them, Bunny; run along now. I'll have my car come by your hotel to bring you to dinner."

"Thanks for the compliment, old man, but I'm staying at the Y.M.C.A. It's cheaper," laughed Bunny.

"But is it safer?" kidded Matthew, as his friend withdrew.

Two days later Bunny Brown left for New York on a secret mission. Not only was he to spy on Santop Licorice and see how effective his work was, but he was also to approach Dr. Shakespeare Agamemnon Beard, Dr. Napoleon Wellington Jackson, Rev. Herbert Gronne, Col. Mortimer Roberts, Prof. Charles Spelling, and the other Negro leaders with a view to getting them to speak to white audiences for the benefit of the Knights of Nordica. Matthew already knew that they were in a precarious economic situation since they now had no means of income, both the black masses and the philanthropic whites having deserted them. Their white friends, mostly Northern plutocrats, felt that the race problem was being satisfactorily solved by Black-No-More, Incorporated, and so did the Negroes. Bunny's job was to convince them that it was better to lecture for the K. of N. and grow fat than to fail to get chances to lecture to Negroes who weren't interested in what they said anyhow. The Grand Exalted Giraw had a personal interest in these Negro leaders. He realized that they were too old or too incompetent to make a living except by preaching and writing about the race problem, and since they had lost their influence with the black masses, they might be a novelty to introduce to the K. of N. audiences. He felt that their racial integrity talks would click with the crackers. They knew more about it too than any of his regular speakers, he realized.

As the train bearing Bunny pulled into the station in Charlotte, he bought an evening paper. The headline almost knocked him down:

WEALTHY WHITE GIRL HAS NEGRO BABY

He whistled softly and muttered to himself, "Business picks up from now on." He thought of Matthew's marriage and whistled again.

* * *

From that time on there were frequent reports in the daily press of white women giving birth to black babies. In some cases, of course, the white women had recently become white but the blame for the tar-brushed offspring in the public mind always rested on the shoulders of the father, or rather, of the husband. The number of cases continued to increase. All walks of life were represented. For the first time the prevalence of sexual promiscuity was brought home to the thinking people of America. Hospital authorities and physicians had known about it in a general way but it had been unknown to the public.

The entire nation became alarmed. Hundreds of thousands of people, North and South, flocked into the Knights of Nordica. The real white people were panic-stricken, especially in Dixie. There was no way, apparently, of telling a real Caucasian from an imitation one. Every stranger was viewed with suspicion, which had a very salutory effect on the standard of sex morality in the United States. For the first time since 1905, chastity became a virtue. The number of petting parties, greatly augmented by the development of aviation, fell off amazingly. One must play safe, the girls argued.

The holidays of traveling salesmen, business men and fraternal delegates were made less pleasant than of yore. The old orgiastic days in the big cities seemed past for all time. It also suddenly began to dawn upon some men that the pretty young thing they had met at the seashore and wanted to rush to the altar might possibly be a whitened Negress; and young women were almost as suspicious. Rapid-fire courtships and gin marriages declined. Matrimony at last began to be approached with caution. Nothing like this situation had been known since the administration of Grover Cleveland.

Black-No-More, Incorporated, was not slow to seize upon this opportunity to drum up more business. With 100 sanitariums going full blast from coast to coast, it now announced in full page advertisements in the daily press that it was establishing lying-in hospitals in the principal cities where all prospective mothers could come to have their babies, and that whenever a baby was born black or mulatto, it would immediately be given the 24-hour treatment that permanently turned black infants white. The country breathed easier, particularly the four million Negroes who had become free because white.

In a fortnight Bunny Brown returned. Over a quart of passable rye, the two friends discussed his mission.

"What about Licorice?" asked Matthew.

"Useless. You ought to give him the gate. He's taking your jack but he isn't doing a thing but getting your checks and eating regularly. His followers are scarcer than Jews in the Vatican."

"Well, were you able to talk business with any of the Negro leaders?"

"Couldn't find any of them. Their offices are all closed and they've moved away from the places where they used to live. Broke, I suppose."

"Did you inquire for them around Harlem?"

"What was the use? All of the Negroes around Harlem nowadays are folks that have just come there to get white; the rest of them left the race a long time ago. Why, Boy, darkies are as hard to find on Lenox Avenue now as they used to be in Tudor City."

"What about the Negro newspapers? Are any of them running still?"

"Nope, they're a thing of the past. Shines are too busy getting white to bother reading about lynching, crime and peonage," said Bunny.

"Well," said Matthew, "it looks as if old Santop Licorice is the only one of the old gang left."

"Yeah, and he won't be black long, now that you're cutting him off the payroll."

"I think he could make more money staying black."

"How do you figure that out?" asked Bunny.

"Well, the dime museums haven't closed down, you know," said Matthew.

Chapter VII

One June morning in 1934, Grand Exalted Giraw Fisher received a report from one of his secret operatives in the town of Paradise, South Carolina, saying:

"The working people here are talking about going on strike next week unless Blickdoff and Hortzenboff, the owners of the Paradise Mill, increase pay and shorten hours. The average wage is around fifteen dollars a week, the work day eleven hours. In the past week the company has speeded up the work so much that the help say they cannot stand the pace.

"The owners are two Germans who came to this country after the war. They employ 1000 hands, own all of the houses in Paradise and operate all of the stores. Most of the hands belong to the Knights of Nordica and they want the organization to help them unionize. Am awaiting instructions."

Matthew turned to Bunny and grinned. "Here's more money," he boasted, shaking the letter in his assistant's face.

"What can you do about it?" that worthy inquired.

"What can I do? Well, Brother, you just watch my smoke. Tell Ruggles to get the plane ready," he ordered. "We'll fly over there at once."

Two hours later Matthew's plane sat down on the broad, close-clipped lawn in front of the Blickdoff-Hortzenboff cotton mill. Bunny and the Grand Giraw entered the building and walked to the office.

"Whom do you wish to see?" asked a clerk.

"Mr. Blickdoff, Mr. Hortzenboff or both; preferably both," Matthew replied.

"And who's calling?"

"The Grand Exalted Giraw of the Ancient and Honorable Order of the Knights of Nordica and his secretary," boomed that gentleman. The awed young lady retired into an inner sanctum.

"That sure is some title," commented Bunny in an undertone.

"Yes, Givens knows his stuff when it comes to that. The longer and sillier a title, the better the yaps like it."

The young lady returned and announced that the two owners would be glad to receive the eminent Atlantan. Bunny and Matthew entered the office marked "Private."

Hands were shaken, greetings exchanged and then Matthew got right down to business. He had received contributions from these two mill owners so to a certain extent they understood one another.

"Gentlemen," he queried, "is it true that your employees are planning to strike next week?"

"So ve haff heardt," puffed the corpulent, under-sized Blickdoff.

"Well, what are you going to do about it?"

"De uszual t'ing, uff coarse," replied Hortzenboff, who resembled a beer barrel on stilts.

"You can't do the usual thing," warned Matthew. "Most of these people are members of the Knights of Nordica. They are looking to us for protection and we mean to give it to them."

"Vy ve t'ought you vas favorable," exclaimed Blickdoff.

"Und villing to be reasonable," added Hortzenboff.

"That's true," Matthew agreed, "but you're squeezing these people too hard."

"But ve can't pay dem any more," protested the squat partner. "Vot ve gonna do?"

"Oh, you fellows can't kid me, I know you're coining the jack; but if you think it's worth ten grand to you, I think I can adjust matters," the Grand Giraw stated.

"Ten t'ousand dollars?" the two mill men gasped.

"You've got good ears," Matthew assured them. "And if you don't come across I'll put the whole power of my organization behind your hands. Then it'll cost you a hundred grand to get back to normal."

The Germans looked at each other incredulously.

"Are you t'reatening us, Meester Fisher?" whined Blickdoff.

"You've got a good head at figuring out things, Blickdoff," Matthew retorted, sarcastically.

"Suppose ve refuse?" queried the heavier Teuton.

"Yeah, suppose you do. Can't you imagine what'll happen when I pull these people off the job?"

"Ve'll call oudt de militia," warned Blickdoff.

"Don't make me laugh," Matthew commented. "Half the militiamen are members of my outfit."

The Germans shrugged their shoulders hopelessly while Matthew and Bunny enjoyed their confusion.

"How mutch you say you wandt?" asked Hortzenboff.

"Fifteen grand," replied the Grand Giraw, winking at Bunny.

"Budt you joost said ten t'ousand a minute ago," screamed Blickdoff, gesticulating.

"Well, it's fifteen now," said Matthew, "and it'll be twenty grand if you babies don't hurry up and make up your mind."

Hortzenboff reached hastily for the big check book and commenced writing. In a moment he handed Matthew the check.

"Take this back to Atlanta in the plane," ordered Matthew, handing the check to Bunny, "and deposit it. Safety first." Bunny went out.

"You don't act like you trust us," Blickdoff accused.

"Why should I?" the ex-Negro retorted. "I'll just stick around for a while and keep you two company. You fellows might change your mind and stop payment on that check."

"Ve are honest men, Meester Fisher," cried Hortzenboff.

"Now I'll tell one," sneered the Grand Giraw, seating himself and taking a handful of cigars out of a box on the desk.

The following evening the drab, skinny, hollow-eyed mill folk trudged to the mass meeting called by Matthew in the only building in Paradise not owned by the company – the Knights of Nordica Hall. They poured into the ramshackle building, seated themselves on the wooden benches and waited for the speaking to begin.

They were a sorry lot, under-nourished, bony, vacant-looking, and yet they had seen a dim light. Without suggestion or agitation from the outside world, from which they were almost as completely cut off as if they had been in Siberia, they had talked among themselves and concluded that there was no hope for them except in organization. What they all felt they needed was wise leadership, and they looked to the Knights of Nordica for it, since they were all members of it and there was no other agency at hand. They waited now expectantly for the words of wisdom and encouragement which they expected to hear fall from the lips of their beloved Matthew Fisher, who now looked down upon them from the platform with cynical humor mingled with disgust.

They had not long to wait. A tall, gaunt, mountaineer, who acted as chairman, after beseeching the mill hands to stand together like men and women, introduced the Grand Exalted Giraw.

Matthew spoke forcefully and to the point. He reminded them that they were men and women; that they were free, white and twenty-one; that they were citizens of the United States; that America was their country as well as Rockefeller's; that they must stand firm in the defense of their rights as working people; that the worker was worthy of his hire; that nothing should be dearer to them than the maintenance of white supremacy. He insinuated that even in their midst there probably were some Negroes who had been turned white by Black-No-More. Such individuals, he insisted, made poor union material because they always showed their Negro characteristics and ran away in a crisis. Ending with a fervent plea for liberty, justice and a square deal, he sat down amid tumultuous applause. Eager to take advantage of their enthusiasm, the chairman began to call for members. Happily the people crowded around the little table in front of the platform to give their names and pay dues.

Swanson, the chairman and acknowledged leader of the militant element, was tickled with the results of the meeting. He slapped his thighs mountaineer fashion, shifted his chew of tobacco from the right cheek to the left, his pale blue eyes twinkling, and "allowed" to Matthew that the union would soon bring the Paradise Mill owners to terms. The Grand Exalted Giraw agreed.

Two days later, back in Atlanta, Matthew held a conference with a half-dozen of his secret operatives in his office. "Go to Paradise and do your stuff," he commanded, "and do it right."

The next day the six men stepped from the train in the little South Carolina town, engaged rooms at the local hotel and got busy. They let it be known that they were officials of the Knights of Nordica sent from Atlanta by the Grand Exalted Giraw to see that the mill workers got a square deal. They busied themselves visiting the three-room cottages of the workers, all of which looked alike, and talking very confidentially.

In a day or so it began to be noised about that Swanson, leader of the radical element, was really a former Negro from Columbia. It happened that a couple of years previously he had lived in that city. Consequently he readily admitted that he had lived there when asked innocently by one of the strangers in the presence of a group of workers. When Swanson wasn't looking, the questioner glanced significantly at those in the group.

That was enough. To the simple-minded workers Swanson's admission was conclusive evidence that the charge of being a Negro was true. When he called another strike meeting, no one came except a few of Fisher's men. The big fellow was almost ready to cry because of the unexplained falling away of his followers. When one of the secret operatives told him the trouble he was furious.

"Ah haint no damn nigger a-tall," he shouted. "Ah'm a white man an' kin prove hit!"

Unfortunately he could not prove to the satisfaction of his fellow workers that he was not a Negro. They were adamant. On the streets they passed him without speaking and they complained to the foremen at the mill that they didn't want to work with a nigger. Broken and disheartened after a week of vain effort, Swanson was glad to accept carfare out of the vicinity from one of Matthew's men who pretended to be sympathetic.

With the departure of Swanson, the cause of the mill workers was dealt a heavy blow, but the three remaining ringleaders sought to carry on. The secret operatives of the Grand Exalted Giraw got busy again. One of the agitators was asked if it was true that his grandfather was a nigger. He strenuously denied the charge but being ignorant of the identity of his father he could not very well be certain about his grandfather. He was doomed. Within a week the other two were similarly discredited. Rumor was wafted abroad that the whole idea of a strike was a trick of smart niggers in the North who were in the pay of the Pope.

The erstwhile class conscious workers became terror-stricken by the specter of black blood. You couldn't, they said, be sure of anybody any more, and it was better to leave things as they were than to take a chance of being led by some nigger. If the colored gentry couldn't sit in the movies and ride in the trains with white folks, it wasn't right for them to be organizing and leading white folks.

The radicals and laborites in New York City had been closely watching developments in Paradise ever since the news of the big mass meeting addressed by Matthew was broadcast by the Knights of Nordica news service. When it seemed that the mill workers were, for some mysterious reason, going to abandon the idea of striking, liberal and radical labor organizers were sent down to the town to see what could be done toward whipping up the spirit of revolt.

The representative of the liberal labor organization arrived first and immediately announced a meeting in the Knights of Nordica Hall, the only obtainable place. Nobody came. The man couldn't understand it. He walked out into the town square, approached a little knot of men and asked what was the trouble.

"Y're from that there Harlem in N'Yawk, haint ye?" asked one of the villagers.

"Why yes, I live in Harlem. What about it?"

"Well, we haint a gonna have no damn nigger leadin' us, an' if ye know whut's healthy fer yuh yo'll git on away f'um here," stated the speaker.

"Where do you get that nigger stuff?" inquired the amazed and insulted organizer. "I'm a white man."

"Yo ain't th' first white nigger whut's bin aroun' these parts," was the reply.

The organizer, puzzled but helpless, stayed around town for a week and then departed. Somebody had told the simple folk that Harlem was the Negro district in New York, after ascertaining that the organizer lived in that district. To them Harlem and Negro became synonymous and the laborite was doomed.

The radical labor organizer, refused permission to use the Knights of Nordica Hall because he was a Jew, was prevented from holding a street meeting when someone started a rumor that he believed in dividing up property, nationalizing women, and was in addition an atheist. He freely admitted the first, laughed at the second and proudly proclaimed the third. That was sufficient to inflame the mill hands, although God had been strangely deaf to their prayers, they owned no property to divide and most of their women were so ugly that they need have had no fears that any outsiders would want to nationalize them. The disciple of Lenin and Trotsky vanished down the road with a crowd of emaciated workers at his heels.

Soon all was quiet and orderly again in Paradise, S.C. On the advice of a conciliator from the United States Labor Department, Blickdoff and Hortzenboff took immediate steps to make their workers more satisfied with their pay, their jobs and their little home town. They built a swimming pool, a tennis court, shower baths and a playground for their employees but neglected to shorten their work time so these improvements could be enjoyed. They announced that they would give each worker a bonus of a whole day's pay at Christmas time, hereafter, and a week's vacation each year to every employee who had been with them more than ten years. There were no such employees, of course, but the mill hands were overjoyed with their victory.

The local Baptist preacher, who was very thoughtfully paid by the company with the understanding that he would take a practical view of conditions in the community, told his flock their employers were to be commended for adopting a real Christian and American way of settling the difficulties between them and their workers. He suggested it was quite likely that Jesus, placed in the same position, would have done likewise.

"Be thankful for the little things," he mooed. "God works in mysterious ways his wonders to perform. Ye shall know the truth and the truth shall set ye free. The basis of all things is truth. Let us not be led astray by the poison from vipers' tongues. This is America and not Russia. Patrick Henry said 'Give me liberty or give me death' and the true, red-blooded, 100 per cent American citizen says the same thing today. But there are right ways and wrong ways to get liberty. Your employers have gone about it the right way. For what, after all is liberty except the enjoyment of life; and have they not placed within your reach those things that bring happiness and recreation?

"Your employers are interested, just as all true Americans are interested, in the welfare of their fellow citizens, their fellow townsmen. Their hearts beat for you. They are always thinking of you. They are always planning ways to make conditions better for you. They are sincerely doing all in their power. They have very heavy responsibilities.

"So you must be patient. Rome wasn't built in a day. All things turn out well in time. Christ knows what he is doing and he will not permit his children to suffer.

"O, ye of little faith! Let not your hearts store up jealousy, hatred and animosity. Let not your minds be wooed by misunderstanding. Let us try to act and think as God would wish us to, and above all, let us, like those two kindly men yonder, practice Christian tolerance."

Despite this inspiring message, it was apparent to everyone that Paradise would never be the same again. Rumors continued to fill the air. People were always asking each other embarrassing questions about birth and blood. Fights became more frequent. Large numbers of the workers, being of Southern birth, were unable to disprove charges of possessing Negro ancestry, and so were forced to leave the vicinity. The mill hands kept so busy talking about Negro blood that no one thought of discussing wages and hours of labor.

In August, Messrs. Blickdoff and Hortzenboff, being in Atlanta on business, stopped by Matthew's office.

"Well, how's the strike?" asked the Grand Giraw.

"Dot strike!" echoed Blickdoff. "Ach Gott! Dot strike neffer come off. Vat you do, you razscal?"

"That's my secret," replied Matthew, a little proudly. "Every man to his trade, you know."

It had indeed become Matthew's trade and he was quite adept at it. What had happened at Paradise had also happened elsewhere. There were no more rumors of strikes. The working people were far more interested in what they considered, or were told was, the larger issue of race. It did not matter that they had to send their children into the mills to augment the family wage; that they were always sickly and that their death rate was high. What mattered such little things when the very foundation of civilization, white supremacy, was threatened?

Chapter VIII

For over two years now had Black-No-More, Incorporated, been carrying on its self-appointed task of turning Negroes into Caucasians. The job was almost complete, except for the black folk in prisons, orphan asylums, insane asylums, homes for the aged, houses of correction and similar institutions. Those who had always maintained that it was impossible to get Negroes together for anything but a revival, a funeral or a frolic now had to admit that they had co-operated well in getting white. The poor had been helped by the well-to-do, brothers had helped sisters, children had assisted parents. There had been revived some of the same spirit of adventure prevalent in the days of the Underground Railroad. As a result, even in Mississippi, Negroes were quite rare. In the North the only Negroes to be seen were mulatto babies whose mothers, charmed by the beautiful color of their offspring, had defied convention and not turned them white. As there had never been more than two million Negroes in the North, the whitening process had been viewed indifferently by the masses because those who controlled the channels of opinion felt that the country was getting rid of a very vexatious problem at absolutely no cost; but not so in the South.

When one-third of the population of the erstwhile Confederacy had consisted of the much-maligned Sons of Ham, the blacks had really been of economic, social and psychological value to the section. Not only had they done the dirty work and laid the foundation of its wealth, but they had served as a convenient red herring for the upper classes when the white proletariat grew restive under exploitation. The presence of the Negro as an under class had also made of Dixie a unique part of the United States. There, despite the trend to industrialization, life was a little different, a little pleasanter, a little softer. There was contrast and variety, which was rare in a nation where standardization had progressed to such an extent that a traveler didn't know what town he was in until someone informed him. The South had always been identified with the Negro, and vice versa, and its most pleasant memories treasured in song and story, were built around this pariah class.

The deep concern of the Southern Caucasians with chivalry, the protection of white womanhood, the exaggerated development of race pride and the studied arrogance of even the poorest half-starved white peon, were all due to the presence of the black man. Booted and starved by their industrial and agricultural feudal lords, the white masses derived their only consolation and happiness from the fact that they were the same color as their oppressors and consequently better than the mudsill blacks.

The economic loss to the South by the ethnic migration was considerable. Hundreds of wooden railroad coaches, long since condemned as death traps in all other parts of the country, had to be scrapped by the railroads when there were no longer any Negroes to Jim Crow. Thousands of railroad waiting rooms remained unused because, having been set aside for the use of Negroes, they were generally too dingy and unattractive for white folk or were no longer necessary. Thousands of miles of streets located in the former Black Belts, and thus without sewers or pavement, were having to be improved at the insistent behest of the rapidly increased white population, real and imitation. Real estate owners who had never dreamed of making repairs on their tumble-down property when it was occupied by the docile Negroes, were having to tear down, rebuild and alter to suit white tenants. Shacks and dry goods boxes that had once sufficed as schools for Negro children, had now to be condemned and abandoned as unsuitable for occupation by white youth. Whereas thousands of school teachers had received thirty and forty dollars a month because of their Negro ancestry, the various cities and counties of the Southland were now forced to pay the standard salaries prevailing elsewhere.

Naturally taxes increased. Chambers of Commerce were now unable to send out attractive advertising to Northern business firms offering no or very low taxation as an inducement to them to move South nor were they able to offer as many cheap building sites. Only through the efforts of the Grand Exalted Giraw of the Knights of Nordica were they still able to point to their large reserves of docile, contented, Anglo-Saxon labor, and who knew how long that condition would last?

Consequently, the upper classes faced the future with some misgivings. As if being deprived of the pleasure of black mistresses were not enough, there was a feeling that there would shortly be widespread revolt against the existing medieval industrial conditions and resultant reduction of profits and dividends. The mill barons viewed with distaste the prospect of having to do away with child labor. Rearing back in their padded swivel chairs, they leaned fat jowls on well-manicured hands and mourned the passing of the halcyon days of yore.

If the South had lost its Negroes, however, it had certainly not lost its vote, and the political oligarchy that ruled the section was losing its old assurance and complacency. The Republicans had made inroads here and there in the 1934 Congressional elections. The situation politically was changing and if drastic steps were not immediately taken, the Republicans might carry the erstwhile Solid South, thus practically destroying the Democratic Party. Another Presidential election was less than two years off. There would have to be fast work to ward off disaster. Far-sighted people, North and South, even foresaw the laboring people soon forsaking both of the old parties and going Socialist. Politicians and business men shuddered at the thought of such a tragedy and saw horrible visions of old-age pensions, eight-hour laws, unemployment insurance, working men's compensation, minimum-wage legislation, abolition of child labor, dissemination of birth-control information, monthly vacations for female workers, two-month vacations for prospective mothers, both with pay, and the probable killing of individual initiative and incentive by taking the ownership of national capital out of the hands of two million people and putting it into the hands of one hundred and twenty million.

Which explains why Senator Rufus Kretin of Georgia, one of the old Democratic war horses, an incomparable Negro-baiter, a faithful servitor of the dominant economic interests of his state and the lusty father of several black families since whitened, walked into the office of Imperial Grand Wizard Givens one day in March, 1935.

"Boys," he began, as closeted with Rev. Givens, Matthew and Bunny in the new modernistic Knights of Nordica palace, they quaffed cool and illegal beverages, "we gotta do sumpin and do it quick. These heah damn Yankees ah makin' inroads on ouah preserves, suh. Th' Republican vote is a-growin'. No tellin' what's li'ble tuh happen in this heah nex' 'lection."

"What can we do, Senator?" asked the Imperial Grand Wizard. "How can we serve the cause?"

"That's just it. That's just it, suh; jus' what Ah came heah fo'," replied the Senator. "Naow sum o' us was thinkin' that maybe yo'all might be able to he'p us keep these damn hicks in line. Yo'all are intelligent gent'men; you know what Ah'm gettin' at?"

"Well, that's a pretty big order, Colonel," said Givens.

"Yes," Matthew added. "It'll be a hard proposition. Conditions are no longer what they used to be."

"An'," said Givens, "we can't do much with that nigger business, like we used to do when th' old Klan was runnin'."

"What about one o' them theah Red scares," asked the Senator, hopefully.

"Humph!" the clergyman snorted. "Better leave that there Red business alone. Times ain't like they was, you know. Anyhow, them damn Reds'll be down here soon enough 'thout us encouragin' 'em none."

"Guess that's right, Gen'ral," mused the statesman. Then brightening: "Lookaheah, Givens. This fellah Fisher's gotta good head. Why not let him work out sumpin?"

"Yeah, he sure has," agreed the Wizard, glad to escape any work except minding the treasury of his order. "If he can't do it, ain't nobody can. Him and Bunny here is as shrewd as some o' them old time darkies. He! He! He!" He beamed patronizingly upon his brilliant son-in-law and his plump secretary.

"Well, theah's money in it. We got plenty o' cash; what we want now is votes," the Senator explained. "C'ose yuh caint preach that white supremacy stuff ve'y effectively when they haint no niggahs."

"Leave it to me. I'll work out something," said Matthew. Here was a chance to get more power, more money. Busy as he was, it would not do to let the opportunity slip by.

"Yuh caint lose no time," warned the Senator.

"We won't," crowed Givens.

A few minutes later they took a final drink together, shook hands and the Senator, bobbing his white head to the young ladies in the outer office, departed.

Matthew and Bunny retired to the private office of the Grand Exalted Giraw.

"What you thinkin' about pullin'?" asked Bunny.

"Plenty. We'll try the old sure fire Negro problem stuff."

"But that's ancient history, Brother," protested Bunny. "These ducks won't fall for that any more."

"Bunny, I've learned something on this job, and that is that hatred and prejudice always go over big. These people have been raised on the Negro problem, they're used to it, they're trained to react to it. Why should I rack my brain to hunt up something else when I can use a dodge that's always delivered the goods?"

"It may go over at that."

"I know it will. Just leave it to me," said Matthew confidently. "That's not worrying me at all. What's got my goat is my wife being in the family way." Matthew stopped bantering a moment, a sincere look of pain erasing his usual ironic expression.

"Congratulations!" burbled Bunny.

"Don't rub it in," Matthew replied. "You know how the kid will look."

"That's right," agreed his pal. "You know, sometimes I forget who we are."

"Well, I don't. I know I'm a darky and I'm always on the alert."

"What do you intend to do?"

"I don't know, Big Boy, I don't know. I would ordinarily send her to one of those Lying-in Hospitals but she'd be suspicious. Yet, if the kid is born it'll sure be black."

"It won't be white," Bunny agreed. "Why not tell her the whole thing and since she's so crazy about you, I don't think she'd hesitate to go."

"Man, you must be losing your mind, or else you've lost it!" Matthew exploded. "She's a worse nigger-hater than her father. She'd holler for a divorce before you could say Jack Robinson."

"You've got too much money for that."

"You're assuming that she has plenty of intelligence."

"Hasn't she?"

"Let's not discuss a painful subject," pleaded Matthew. "Suggest a remedy."

"She don't have to know that she's going to one of Crookman's places, does she?"

"No, but I can't get her to leave home to have the baby."

"Why?"

"Oh, a lot of damn sentiment about having her baby in the old home, and her damned old mother supports her. So what can I do?"

"Then the dear old homestead is the only thing that's holding up the play?"

"You're a smart boy, Bunny."

"Don't stress the obvious. Seriously, though, I think everything can be fixed okeh."

"How?" cried Matthew, eagerly.

"Is it worth five grand?" countered Bunny.

"Money's no object, you know, but explain your proposition."

"I will not. You get me fifty century notes and I'll explain later."

"It's a deal, old friend."

Bunny Brown was a man of action. That evening he entered the popular Niggerhead Café, rendezvous of the questionable classes, and sat down at a table. The place was crowded with drinkers downing their "white mule" and contorting to the strains issuing from a radio loud-speaker. A current popular dance piece, "The Black Man Blues," was filling the room. The songwriters had been making a fortune recently writing sentimental songs about the passing of the Negro. The plaintive voice of a blues singer rushed out of the loud-speaker:

> *"I wonder where my big, black man has gone;*
> *Oh, I wonder where my big, black man has gone.*
> *Has he done got faded an' left me all alone?"*

When the music ceased and the dancers returned to their tables, Bunny began to look around. In a far corner he saw a waiter whose face seemed familiar. He waited until the fellow came close when he hailed him. As the waiter bent over to get his order, he studied him closely. He had seen this fellow somewhere before. Who could he be? Suddenly with a start he remembered. It was Dr. Joseph Bonds, former head of the Negro Data League in New York.

What had brought him here and to this condition? The last time he had seen Bonds, the fellow was a power in the Negro world, with a country place in Westchester County and a swell apartment in town. It saddened Bunny to think that catastrophe had overtaken such a man. Even getting white, it seemed, hadn't helped him much. He recalled that Bonds in his heyday had collected from the white philanthropists with the slogan: "Work, Not Charity," and he smiled as he thought that Bonds would be mighty glad now to get a little charity and not so much work.

"Would a century note look good to you right now?" he asked the former Negro leader when he returned with his drink.

"Just show it to me, Mister," said the waiter, licking his lips. "What you want me to do?"

"What will you do for a hundred berries?" pursued Bunny.

"I'd hate to tell you," replied Bonds, grinning and revealing his familiar tobacco-stained teeth.

"Have you got a friend you can trust?"

"Sure, a fellow named Licorice that washes pots in back."

"You don't mean Santop Licorice, do you?"

"Ssh! They don't know who he is here. He's white now, you know."

"Do they know who you are?"

"What do you mean?" gasped the surprised waiter.

"Oh, I won't say anything but I know you're Bonds of New York."

"Who told you?"

"Oh, a little fairy."

"How could that be? I never associate with them."

"It wasn't that kind of a fairy," Bunny reassured him, laughing. "Well, you get Licorice and come to my hotel when this place closes up."

"Where is that?" asked Bonds. Bunny wrote his name and room number down on a piece of paper and handed it to him.

Three hours later Bunny was awakened by a knocking at his door. He admitted Bonds and Licorice, the latter smelling strongly of steam and food.

"Here," said Bunny, holding up a hundred dollar bill, "is a century note. If you boys can lay aside your scruples for a few hours you can have five of them apiece."

"Well," said Bonds, "neither Santop nor I have been overburdened with them."

"That's what I thought," Bunny murmured. He proceeded to outline the work he wanted them to do.

"But that would be a criminal offense," objected Licorice.

"You too, Brutus?" sneered Bonds.

"Well, we can't afford to take chances unless we're protected," the former President of Africa argued rather weakly. He was money-hungry and was longing for a stake to get back to Demerara where, since there was a large Negro population, a white man, by virtue of his complexion, amounted to something. Yet he had had enough experience behind the bars to make him wary.

"We run this town and this state, too," Bunny assured him. "We could get a couple of our men to pull this stunt but it wouldn't be good policy."

"How about a thousand bucks apiece?" asked Bonds, his eyes glittering as he viewed the crisp banknotes in Bunny's hand.

"Here," said Bunny. "Take this century note between you, get your material and pull the job. When you've finished I'll give you nineteen more like it between you."

The two cronies looked at each other and nodded.

"It's a go," said Bonds.

They departed and Bunny went back to sleep.

The next night about eleven-thirty the bells began to toll and the mournful sirens of the fire engines awakened the entire neighborhood in the vicinity of Rev. Givens's home. That stately edifice, built by Ku Klux Klan dollars, was in flames. Firemen played a score of streams onto the blaze but the house appeared to be doomed.

On a lawn across the street, in the midst of a consoling crowd, stood Rev. and Mrs. Givens, Helen and Matthew. The old couple were taking the catastrophe fatalistically, Matthew was puzzled and suspicious, but Helen was in hysterics. She presented a bedraggled and woebegone appearance with a blanket around her night dress. She wept afresh every time she looked across at the blazing building where she had spent her happy childhood.

"Matthew," she sobbed, "will you build me another one just like it?"

"Why certainly, Honey," he agreed, "but it will take quite a while."

"Oh, I know; I know, but I want it."

"Well, you'll get it, darling," he soothed, "but I think it would be a good idea for you to go away for a while to rest your nerves. We've got to think of the little one that's coming, you know."

"I don't wanna go nowhere," she screamed.

"But you've got to go somewhere," he reasoned. "Don't you think so, Mother?" Old Mrs. Givens agreed it would be a good idea but suggested that she go along. To this Rev. Givens would not listen at first but he finally yielded.

"Guess it's a good idea after all," he remarked. "Women folks is always in th' way when buildin's goin' on."

Matthew was tickled at the turn of affairs. On the way down to the hotel, he sat beside Helen, alternately comforting her and wondering as to the origin of the fire.

Next morning, bright and early, Bunny, grinning broadly walked into the office, threw his hat on a hook and sat down before his desk after the customary salutation.

"Bunny," called Matthew, looking at him hard. "Get me told!"

"What do you mean?" asked Bunny innocently.

"Just as I thought," chuckled Matthew. "You're a nervy guy."

"Why, I don't get you," said Bunny, continuing the pose.

"Come clean, Big Boy. How much did that fire cost?"

"You gave me five grand, didn't you?"

"Just like a nigger: a person can never get a direct answer from you."

"Are you satisfied?"

"I'm not crying my eyes out."

"Is Helen going North for her confinement?"

"Nothing different."

"Well, then, why do you want to know the why and wherefore of that blaze?"

"Just curiosity, Nero, old chap," grinned Matthew.

"Remember," warned Bunny, mischievously, "curiosity killed the cat."

The ringing of the telephone bell interrupted their conversation.

"What's that?" yelled Matthew into the mouthpiece. "The hell you say! All right, I'll be right up." He hung up the receiver, jumped up excitedly and grabbed his hat.

"What's the matter?" shouted Bunny. "Somebody dead?"

"No," answered the agitated Matthew, "Helen's had a miscarriage," and he dashed out of the room.

"Somebody dead right on," murmured Bunny, half aloud.

* * *

Joseph Bonds and Santop Licorice, clean shaven and immaculate, followed the Irish red cap into their drawing room on the New York Express.

"It sure feels good to get out of the barrel once more," sighed Bonds, dropping down on the soft cushion and pulling out a huge cigar.

"Ain't it the truth?" agreed the former Admiral of the Royal African Navy.

Chapter IX

"Bunny, I've got it all worked out," announced Matthew, several mornings later, as he breezed into the office.

"Got what worked out?"

"The political proposition."

"Spill it."

"Well, here it is: First, we get Givens on the radio; national hookup, you know, once a week for about two months."

"What'll he talk about? Are you going to write it for him?"

"Oh, he knows how to charm the yokels. He'll appeal to the American people to call upon the Republican administration to close up the sanitariums of Dr. Crookman and deport everybody connected with Black-No-More."

"You can't deport citizens, silly," Bunny remonstrated.

"That don't stop you from advocating it. This is politics, Big Boy."

"Well, what else is on the program?"

"Next: We start a campaign of denunciation against the Republicans in *The Warning*, connecting them with the Pope, Black-No-More and anything else we can think of."

"But they were practically anti-Catholic in 1928, weren't they?"

"Seven years ago, Bunny, seven years ago. How often must I tell you that the people never remember anything? Next we pull the old Write-to-your-Congressman-Write-to-your-Senator stuff. We carry the form letter in *The Warning*, the readers do the rest."

"You can't win a campaign on that stuff, alone," said Bunny disdainfully. "Bring me something better than that, Brother."

"Well, the other step is a surprise, old chap. I'm going to keep it under my hat until later on. But when I spring it, old timer, it'll knock everybody for a row of toadstools." Matthew smiled mysteriously and smoothed back his pale blond hair.

"When do we start this radio racket?" yawned Bunny.

"Wait'll I talk it over with the Chief," said Matthew, rising, "and see how he's dated up."

* * *

The following Thursday evening at 8:15 p.m. millions of people sat before their loud speakers, expectantly awaiting the heralded address to the nation by the Imperial Grand Wizard of the Knights of Nordica. The program started promptly:

"Good evening, ladies and gentlemen of the radio audience. This is Station W H A T, Atlanta, Ga., Mortimer K. Shanker announcing. This evening we are offering a program of tremendous interest to every American citizen. The countrywide hookup over the chain of the Moronia Broadcasting Company is enabling one hundred million citizens to hear one of the most significant messages ever delivered to the American public.

"Before introducing the distinguished speaker of the evening, however, I have a little treat in store for you. Mr. Jack Albert, the well-known Broadway singer and comedian, has kindly consented to render his favorite among the popular songs of the day, 'Vanishing Mammy.' Mr. Albert will be accompanied by that incomparable aggregation of musical talent, Sammy Snort's Bogalusa Babies… Come on, Al, say a word or two to the ladies and gentlemen of the radio audience before you begin."

"Oh, hello folks. Awfully glad to see so many of you out there tonight. Well, that is to say, I suppose there are many of you out there. You know I like to flatter myself, besides I haven't my glasses so I can't see very well. However, that's not the pint, as the bootleggers say. I'm terribly pleased to have the opportunity of starting off a program like this with one of the songs I have come to love best. You know, I think a whole lot of this song. I like it because it has feeling and sentiment. It means something. It carries you back to the good old days that are dead and gone forever. It was written by Johnny Gulp with music by the eminent Japanese-American composer, Forkrise Sake. And, as Mr. Shanker told you, I am being accompanied by Sammy Snort's Bogalusa Babies through the courtesy of the Artillery Café, Chicago, Illinois. All right, Sammy, smack it!"

In two seconds the blare of the jazz orchestra smote the ears of the unseen audience with the weird medley and clash of sound that had passed for music since the days of the Panama-Pacific Exposition. Then the sound died to a whisper and the plaintive voice of America's premier black-faced troubadour came over the air:

Vanishing Mammy, Mammy! Mammy! of Mine,
You've been away, dear, such an awfully long time.
You went away, Sweet Mammy! Mammy! one summer night
I can't help thinkin', Mammy, that you went white.
Of course I can't blame you, Mammy! Mammy! dear
Because you had so many troubles, Mammy, to bear.
But the old homestead hasn't been the same
Since I last heard you, Mammy, call my name.
And so I wait, loving Mammy, it seems in vain,
For you to come waddling back home again
Vanishing Mammy! Mammy! Mammy!
I'm waiting for you to come back home again.

"Now, radio audience, this is Mr. Mortimer Shanker speaking again. I know you all loved Mr. Albert's soulful rendition of 'Vanishing Mammy.' We're going to try to get him back again in the very near future.

"It now gives me great pleasure to introduce to you a man who hardly needs any introduction. A man who is known throughout the civilized world. A man of great scholarship, executive ability and organizing genius. A man who has, practically unassisted, brought five million Americans under the banner of one of the greatest societies in this country. It affords me great pleasure, ladies and gentlemen of the radio audience, to introduce Rev. Henry Givens, Imperial Grand Wizard of the Knights of Nordica, who will address you on the very timely topic of 'The Menace of Negro Blood'."

Rev. Givens, fortified with a slug of corn, advanced nervously to the microphone, fingering his prepared address. He cleared his throat and talked for upwards of an hour during which time he successfully avoided saying anything that was true, the result being that thousands of telegrams and long distance telephone calls of congratulation came in to the studio. In his long address he discussed the foundations of the Republic, anthropology, psychology, miscegenation, co-operation with Christ, getting right with God, curbing Bolshevism, the bane of birth control, the menace of the Modernists, science versus religion, and many other subjects of which he was totally ignorant. The greater part of his time was taken up in a denunciation of Black-No-More, Incorporated, and calling upon the Republican administration of President Harold Goosie to deport the vicious Negroes at the head of it or imprison them in the federal penitentiary. When he had concluded "In the name of our Saviour and Redeemer, Jesus Christ, Amen," he retired hastily to the washroom to finish his half-pint of corn.

The announcer took Rev. Givens's place at the microphone:

"Now friends, this is Mortimer K. Shanker again, announcing from Station W H A T, Atlanta, Ga., with a nationwide hookup over the chain of the Moronia Broadcasting Company. You have just heard a scholarly and inspiring address by Rev. Henry Givens, Imperial Grand Wizard of the Knights of Nordica on 'The Menace of Negro Blood.' Rev. Givens will deliver another address at this station a week from tonight... Now, to end our program for the evening, friends, we are going to have a popular song by the well-known Goyter Sisters, lately of the State Street Follies, entitled 'Why Did the Old Salt Shaker'..."

* * *

The agitation of the Knights of Nordica soon brought action from the administration at Washington. About ten days after Rev. Givens had ceased his talks over the radio, President Harold Goosie announced to the assembled newspaper men that he was giving a great deal of study to the questions raised by the Imperial Grand Wizard concerning Black-No-More, Incorporated; that several truckloads of letters condemning the corporation had been received at the White House and were now being answered by a special corps of clerks; that several Senators had talked over the matter with him, and that the country could expect him to take some action within the next fortnight.

At the end of a fortnight, the President announced that he had decided to appoint a commission of leading citizens to study the whole question thoroughly and to make recommendations. He asked Congress for an appropriation of $100,000 to cover the expenses of the commission.

The House of Representatives approved a resolution to that effect a week later. The Senate, which was then engaged in a spirited debate on the World Court and the League of Nations, postponed consideration of the resolution for three weeks. When it came to vote before that august body, it was passed, after long argument, with amendments and returned to the House.

Six weeks after President Goosie had made his request of Congress, the resolution was passed in its final form. He then announced that inside of a week he would name the members of the commission.

The President kept his word. He named the commission, consisting of seven members, five Republicans and two Democrats. They were mostly politicians temporarily out of a job.

In a private car the commission toured the entire country, visiting all of the Black-No-More sanitariums, the Crookman Lying-in Hospitals and the former Black Belts. They took hundreds of depositions, examined hundreds of witnesses and drank large quantities of liquor.

Two months later they issued a preliminary report in which they pointed out that the Black-No-More sanitariums and Lying-in Hospitals were being operated within the law; that only one million Negroes remained in the country; that it was illegal in most of the states for pure whites and persons of Negro ancestry to intermarry but that it was difficult to detect fraud because of collusion. As a remedy the Commission recommended stricter observance of the law, minor changes in the marriage laws, the organization of special matrimonial courts with trained genealogists attached to each, better equipped judges, more competent district attorneys, the strengthening of the Mann Act, the abolition of the road house, the closer supervision of dance halls, a stricter censorship on books and moving pictures and government control of cabarets. The commission promised to publish the complete report of its activities in about six weeks.

Two months later, when practically everyone had forgotten that there had ever been such an investigation, the complete report of the commission, comprising 1789 pages in fine print came off the press. Copies were sent broadcast to prominent citizens and organizations. Exactly nine people in the United States read it: the warden of a county jail, the proofreader at the Government Printing Office, the janitor of the City Hall in Ashtabula, Ohio, the city editor of the Helena (Ark.) *Bugle*, a stenographer in the Department of Health of Spokane, Wash., a dishwasher in a Bowery restaurant, a flunky in the office of the Research Director of Black-No-More, Incorporated, a life termer in Clinton Prison at Dannemora, N.Y., and a gag writer on the staff of a humorous weekly in Chicago.

Matthew received fulsome praise from the members of his organization and the higher-ups in the Southern Democracy. He had, they said, forced the government to take action, and they began to talk of him for public office.

The Grand Exalted Giraw was jubilant. Everything, he told Bunny, had gone as he had planned. Now he was ready to turn the next trick.

"What's that?" asked his assistant, looking up from the morning comic section.

"Ever hear of the Anglo-Saxon Association of America?" Matthew queried.

"No, what's their graft?"

"It isn't a graft, you crook. The Anglo-Saxon Association of America is an organization located in Virginia. The headquarters are in Richmond. It's a group of rich highbrows who can trace their ancestry back almost two hundred years. You see they believe in white supremacy the same as our outfit but they claim that the Anglo-Saxons are the cream of the white race and should maintain the leadership in American social, economic and political life."

"You sound like a college professor," sneered Bunny.

"Don't insult me, you tripe. Listen now: This crowd thinks they're too highbrow to come in with the Knights of Nordica. They say our bunch are morons."

"That about makes it unanimous," commented Bunny, biting off the end of a cigar.

"Well, what I'm trying to do now is to bring these two organizations together. We've got numbers but not enough money to win an election; they have the jack. If I can get them to see the light we'll win the next Presidential election hands down."

"What'll I be: Secretary of the Treasury?" laughed Bunny.

"Over my dead body!" Matthew replied, reaching for his flask. "But seriously, Old Top, if I can succeed in putting this deal over we'll have the White House in a bag. No fooling!"

"When do we get busy?"

"Next week this Anglo-Saxon Association has its annual meeting in Richmond. You and I'll go up there and give them a spiel. We may take Givens along to add weight."

"You don't mean intellectual weight, do you?"
"Will you never stop kidding?"

* * *

Mr. Arthur Snobbcraft, President of the Anglo-Saxon Association, an F.F.V. and a man suspiciously swarthy for an Anglo-Saxon, had devoted his entire life to fighting for two things: white racial integrity and Anglo-Saxon supremacy. It had been very largely a losing fight. The farther he got from his goal, the more desperate he became. He had been the genius that thought up the numerous racial integrity laws adopted in Virginia and many of the other Southern states. He was strong for sterilization of the unfit: meaning Negroes, aliens, Jews and other riff raff, and he had an abiding hatred of democracy.

Snobbcraft's pet scheme now was to get a genealogical law passed disfranchising all people of Negro or unknown ancestry. He argued that good citizens could not be made out of such material. His organization had money but it needed popularity – numbers.

His joy then knew no bounds when he received Matthew's communication. While he had no love for the Knights of Nordica which, he held, contained just the sort of people he wanted to legislate into impotency, social, economic and physical, he believed he could use them to gain his point. He wired Matthew at once, saying the Association would be delighted to have him address them, as well as the Imperial Grand Wizard.

The Grand Exalted Giraw had long known of Snobbcraft's obsession, the genealogical law. He also knew that there was no chance of ever getting such a law adopted but in order to even try to pass such a law it would be necessary to win the whole country in a national election. Together, his organization and Snobbcraft's could turn the trick; singly neither one could do it.

In an old pre-Civil War mansion on a broad, tree-shaded boulevard, the directors of the Anglo-Saxon Association gathered in their annual meeting. They listened first to Rev. Givens and next to Matthew. The matter was referred to a committee which in an hour or two reported favorably. Most of these men had dreamed from youth of holding high political office at the national capital as had so many eminent Virginians but none of them was Republican, of course, and the Democrats never won anything nationally. By swallowing their pride for a season and joining with the riff raff of the Knights of Nordica, they saw an opportunity, for the first time in years to get into power; and they took it. They would furnish plenty of money, they said, if the other group would furnish the numbers.

Givens and Matthew returned to Atlanta in high spirits.

"I tell you, Brother Fisher," croaked Givens, "our star is ascending. I can see no way for us to fail, with God's help. We'll surely defeat our enemy. Victory is in the air."

"It sure looks that way," the Grand Giraw agreed. "With their money and ours, we can certainly get together a larger campaign fund than the Republicans."

Back in Richmond Mr. Snobbcraft and his friends were in conference with the statistician of a great New York insurance company. This man, Dr. Samuel Buggerie, was highly respected among members of his profession and well known by the reading public. He was the author of several books and wrote frequently for the heavier periodicals. His well-known work, *The Fluctuation of the Sizes of Left Feet among the Assyrians during the Ninth Century before Christ* had been favorably commented upon by several reviewers, one of whom had actually read it. An even more learned work of his was entitled *Putting Wasted Energy to Work*, in which he called attention, by elaborate charts and graphs, to the possibilities of harnessing the power generated by the leaves of trees rubbing together on windy days. In several brilliant monographs he had proved that rich people have smaller families than the poor; that imprisonment does not stop crime; that laborers usually migrate in the wake of high wages. His most recent article in a very intellectual magazine read largely by those who loafed for a living, he had proved statistically that unemployment and poverty are principally a state of mind. This contribution was enthusiastically hailed by scholars and especially by business men as an outstanding contribution to contemporary thought.

Dr. Buggerie was a ponderous, nervous, entirely bald specimen of humanity, with thick moist hands, a receding double chin and very prominent eyes that were constantly shifting about and bearing an expression of seemingly perpetual wonderment behind their big horn-rimmed spectacles. He seemed about to burst out of his clothes and his pockets were always bulging with papers and notes.

Dr. Buggerie, like Mr. Snobbcraft, was a professional Anglo-Saxon as well as a descendant of one of the First Families of Virginia. He held that the only way to tell the pure whites from the imitation whites, was to study their family trees. He claimed that such a nationwide investigation would disclose the various non-Nordic strains in the population. Laws, said he, should then be passed forbidding these strains from mixing or marrying with the pure strains that had produced such fine specimens of mankind as Mr. Snobbcraft and himself.

In high falsetto voice he eagerly related to the directors of the Anglo-Saxon Association the results of some of his preliminary researches. These tended to show, he claimed, that there must be as many as twenty million people in the United States who possessed some slight non-Nordic strain and were thus unfit for both citizenship and procreation. If the organization would put up the money for the research on a national scale, he declared that he could produce statistics before election that would be so shocking that the Republicans would lose the country unless they adopted the Democratic plank on genealogical examinations. After a long and eloquent talk by Mr. Snobbcraft in support of Dr. Buggerie's proposition, the directors voted to appropriate the money, on condition that the work be kept as secret as possible. The statistician agreed although it hurt him to the heart to forego any publicity. The very next morning he began quietly to assemble his staff.

Chapter X

Hank Johnson, Chuck Foster, Dr. Crookman and Gorman Gay, National Chairman of the Republican National Committee, sat in the physician's hotel suite conversing in low tones.

"We're having a tough time getting ready for the Fall campaign," said Gay. "Unfortunately our friends are not contributing with their accustomed liberality."

"Can't complain about us, can you?" asked Foster.

"No, no," the politician denied quickly. "You have been most liberal in the past two years, but then we have done many favors for you, too."

"Yuh sho right, Gay," Hank remarked. "Dem crackahs mighta put us outa business efen it hadn' bin fo' th' admin'strations suppo't."

"I'm quite sure we deeply appreciate the many favors we've received from the present administration," added Dr. Crookman.

"We won't need it much longer, though," said Chuck Foster.

"How's that?" asked Gay, opening his half-closed eyes.

"Well, we've done about all the business we can do in this country. Practically all of the Negroes are white except a couple of thousand diehards and those in institutions," Chuck informed him.

"Dat's right," said Hank. "An' it sho makes dis heah country lonesome. Ah ain't seen a brown-skin ooman in so long Ah doan know whut Ah'd do if Ah seen one."

"That's right, Gay," added Dr. Crookman. "We've about cleaned up the Negro problem in this country. Next week we're closing all except five of our sanitariums."

"Well, what about your Lying-In hospitals?" asked Gay.

"Of course we'll have to continue operating them," Crookman replied. "The women would be in an awful fix if we didn't."

"Now look here," proposed Gay, drawing closer to them and lowering his voice. "This coming campaign is going to be one of the bitterest in the history of this country. I fear there will be rioting, shooting and killing. Those hospitals cannot be closed without tremendous mental suffering to the womanhood of the country. We want to avoid that and you want to avoid it, too. Yet, these hospitals will constantly be in danger. It ought to be worth something to you to have them especially protected by the forces of the government."

"You would do that anyway, wouldn't you Gay?" asked Crookman.

"Well, it's going to cost us millions of votes to do it, and the members of the National Executive Committee seem to feel that you ought to make a very liberal donation to the campaign fund to make up for the votes we'll lose."

"What would you call a liberal donation?" Crookman inquired.

"A successful campaign cannot be fought this year," Gay replied, "under twenty millions."

"Man," shouted Hank, "yuh ain't talkin' 'bout dollahs, is yuh?"

"You got it right, Hank," answered the National Chairman. "It'll cost that much and maybe more."

"Where do you expect to get all of that money?" queried Foster.

"That's just what's worrying us," Gay replied, "and that's why I'm here. You fellows are rolling in wealth and we need your help. In the past two years you've collected around ninety million dollars from the Negro public. Why not give us a good break? You won't miss five million, and it ought to be worth it to you fellows to defeat the Democrats."

"Five millions! Great Day," Hank exploded. "Man, is you los' yo' min'?"

"Not at all," Gay denied. "Might as well own up that if we don't get a contribution of about that size from you we're liable to lose this election... Come on, fellows, don't be so tight. Of course, you're setting pretty and all you've got to do is change your residence to Europe or some other place if things don't run smoothly in America, but you want to think of those poor women with their black babies. What will they do if you fellows leave the country or if the Democrats win and you have to close all of your places?"

"That's right, Chief," Foster observed. "You can't let the women down."

"Yeah," said Johnson. "Give 'im th' jack."

"Well, suppose we do?" concluded Crookman, smiling.

The National Chairman was delighted. "When can we collect?" he asked, "and how?"

"Tomorrow, if yuh really wants it then," Johnson observed.

"Now remember," warned Gay. "We cannot afford to let it be known that we are getting such a large sum from any one person or corporation."

"That's your lookout," said the physician, indifferently. "You know *we* won't say anything."

Mr. Gay, shortly afterward, departed to carry the happy news to the National Executive Committee, then in session right there in New York City.

* * *

The Republicans certainly needed plenty of money to re-elect President Goosie. The frequent radio addresses of Rev. Givens, the growing numbers of the Knights of Nordica, the inexplicable affluence of the Democratic Party and the vitriolic articles in *The Warning*, had not failed to rouse much Democratic sentiment. People were not exactly for the Democrats but they were against the Republicans. As early as May it did not seem possible for the Republicans to carry a single Southern state and many of the Northern and Eastern strongholds were in doubt. The Democrats seemed to have everything their way. Indeed, they were so confident of success that they were already counting the spoils.

When the Democratic Convention met in Jackson, Mississippi, on July 1, 1936, political wise-acres claimed that for the first time in history the whole program was cut and dried and would be run off smoothly and swiftly. Such, however, was not the case. The unusually hot sun, coupled with the enormous quantities of liquor vended, besides the many conflicting interests present, soon brought dissension.

Shortly after the keynote speech had been delivered by Senator Kretin, the Anglo-Saxon crowd let it be known that they wanted some distinguished Southerner like Arthur Snobbcraft nominated for the Presidency. The Knights of Nordica were intent on nominating Imperial Grand Wizard Givens. The Northern faction of the party, now reduced to a small minority in party councils, was holding out for former Governor Grogan of Massachusetts who as head of the League of Catholic Voters had a great following.

Through twenty ballots the voting proceeded, and it remained deadlocked. No faction would yield. Leaders saw that there had to be a compromise. They retired to a suite on the top floor of the Judge Lynch Hotel. There, in their shirt sleeves, with collars open, mint juleps on the table and electric fans stirring up the hot air, they got down to business. Twelve hours later they were still there.

Matthew, wilted, worn but determined, fought for his chief. Simeon Dump of the Anglo-Saxon Association swore he would not withdraw the name of Arthur Snobbcraft. Rev. John Whiffle, a power in the party, gulped drink after drink, kept dabbing a damp handkerchief at the shining surface of his skull, and held out for one Bishop Belch. Moses Lejewski of New York argued obstinately for the nomination of Governor Grogan.

In the meantime the delegates, having left the oven-like convention hall, either lay panting and drinking in their rooms, sat in the hotel lobbies discussing the deadlock or cruised the streets in automobiles confidently seeking the dens of iniquity which they had been told were eager to lure them into sin.

When the clock struck three, Matthew rose and suggested that since the Knights of Nordica and the Anglo-Saxon Association were the two most powerful organizations in the party, Givens should get the presidential nomination, Snobbcraft the vice-presidential and the other candidates be assured of cabinet positions. This suggested compromise appealed to no one except Matthew.

"You people forget," said Simeon Dump, "that the Anglo-Saxon Association is putting up half the money to finance this campaign."

"And you forget," declared Moses Lejewski, "that we're supporting your crazy scheme to disfranchise anybody possessing Negro ancestry when we get into office. That's going to cost us millions of votes in the North. You fellows can't expect to hog everything."

"Why not?" challenged Dump. "How could you win without money?"

"And how," added Matthew, "can you get anywhere without the Knights of Nordica behind you?"

"And how," Rev. Whiffle chimed in, "can you get anywhere without the Fundamentalists and the Drys?"

At four o'clock they had got no farther than they had been at three. They tried to pick some one not before mentioned, and went over and over the list of eligibles. None was satisfactory. One was too radical, another was too conservative, a third was an atheist, a fourth had once rifled a city treasury, the fifth was of immigrant extraction once removed, a sixth had married a Jewess, a seventh was an intellectual, an eighth had spent too long at Hot Springs trying to cure the syphilis, a ninth was rumored to be part Mexican and a tenth had at one time in his early youth been a Socialist.

At five o'clock they were desperate, drunk and disgusted. The stuffy room was a litter of discarded collars, cigarette and cigar butts, match stems, heaped ash trays and empty bottles. Matthew drank little and kept insisting on the selection of Rev. Givens. To the sodden and nodding men he painted marvelous pictures of the spoils of office and their excellent chance of getting there, and then suddenly declared that the Knights of Nordica would withdraw unless Givens was nominated. The threat aroused them. They cursed and called it a holdup, but Matthew was adamant. As a last stroke, he rose and pretended to be ready to bolt the caucus. They remonstrated with him and finally gave in to him.

Orders went out to the delegates. They assembled in the convention hall. The shepherds of the various state flocks cracked the whip and the delegates voted accordingly. Late that afternoon the news went out to a waiting world that the Democrats had nominated Henry Givens for President and Arthur Snobbcraft for Vice-President. Mr. Snobbcraft didn't like that at all, but it was better than nothing.

* * *

A few days later the Republican convention opened in Chicago. Better disciplined, as usual, than the Democrats, its business proceeded like clockwork. President Goosie was nominated for reelection on the first ballot and Vice-President Gump was again selected as his running mate. A platform was adopted whose chief characteristic was vagueness. As was customary, it stressed the party's record in office, except that which was criminal; it denounced fanaticism without being specific, and it emphasized the rights of the individual and the trusts in the same paragraph. As the Democratic slogan was White Supremacy and its platform dwelt largely on the necessity of genealogical investigation, the Republicans adopted the slogan: Personal Liberty and Ancestral Sanctity.

Dr. Crookman and his associates, listening in on the radio in his suite in the Robin Hood Hotel in New York City, laughed softly as they heard the President deliver his speech of acceptance which ended in the following original manner:

"And finally, my friends, I can only say that we shall continue in the path of rugged individualism, free from the influence of sinister interests, upholding the finest ideals of honesty, independence and integrity, so that, to quote Abraham Lincoln, 'This nation of the people, for the people and by the people shall not perish from the earth.'"

"That," said Foster, as the President ceased barking, "sounds almost like the speech of acceptance of Brother Givens that we heard the other day."

Dr. Crookman smiled and brushed the ashes off his cigar. "It may even be the same speech," he suggested.

* * *

Through the hot days of July and August the campaign slowly got under way. Innumerable photographs appeared in the newspapers depicting the rival candidates among the simple folk of some village, helping youngsters to pick cherries, assisting an old woman up a stairway, bathing in the old swimming hole, eating at a barbecue and posing on the rear platforms of special trains.

Long articles appeared in the Sunday newspapers extolling the simple virtues of the two great men. Both, it seemed, had come from poor but honest families; both were hailed as tried and true friends of the great, common people; both were declared to be ready to give their strength and intellect to America for the next four years. One writer suggested that Givens resembled Lincoln, while another declared that President Goosie's character was not unlike that of Roosevelt, believing he was paying the former a compliment.

Rev. Givens told the reporters: "It is my intention, if elected, to carry out the traditional tariff policy of the Democratic Party" (neither he or anyone else knew what that was).

President Goosie averred again and again, "I intend to make my second term as honest and efficient as my first." Though a dire threat, this statement was supposed to be a fine promise.

* * *

Meanwhile, Dr. Samuel Buggerie and his operatives were making great headway examining birth and marriage records throughout the United States. Around the middle of September the Board of Directors held a conference at which the learned man presented a partial report.

"I am now prepared to prove," gloated the obese statistician, "that fully one-quarter of the people of one Virginia county possess non-white ancestry, Indian or Negro; and we can further prove that all of the Indians on the Atlantic Coast are part Negro. In several counties in widely separated parts of the country, we have found that the ancestry of a considerable percentage of the people is in doubt. There is reason to believe that there are countless numbers of people who ought not to be classed with whites and should not mix with Anglo-Saxons."

It was decided that the statistician should get his data in simple form that anyone could read and understand, and have it ready to release just a few days before election. When the people saw how great was the danger from black blood, it was reasoned, they would flock to the Democratic standard and it would be too late for the Republicans to halt the stampede.

* * *

No political campaign in the history of the country had ever been so bitter. On one side were those who were fanatically positive of their pure Caucasian ancestry; on the other side were those who knew themselves to be "impure" white or had reason to suspect it. The former were principally Democratic, the latter Republican. There was another group which was Republican because it felt that a victory for the Democrats might cause another Civil War. The campaign roused acrimonious dispute even within families. Often behind these family rifts lurked the knowledge or suspicion of a dark past.

As the campaign grew more bitter, denunciations of Dr. Crookman and his activities grew more violent. A move was started to close all of his hospitals. Some wanted them to be closed for all time; others advised their closing for the duration of the campaign. The majority of thinking people (which wasn't so many) strenuously objected to the proposal.

"No good purpose will be served by closing these hospitals," declared the New York *Morning Earth*. "On the contrary such a step might have tragic results. The Negroes have disappeared into the body of our citizenry, large numbers have intermarried with the whites and the offspring of these marriages are appearing in increasing numbers. Without these hospitals, think how many couples would be estranged; how many homes wrecked! Instead of taking precipitate action, we should be patient and move slowly."

Other Northern newspapers assumed an even more friendly attitude, but the press generally followed the crowd, or led it, and in slightly veiled language urged the opponents of Black-No-More to take the law into their hands.

Finally, emboldened and inflamed by fiery editorials, radio addresses, pamphlets, posters and platform speeches, a mob seeking to protect white womanhood in Cincinnati attacked a Crookman hospital, drove several women into the streets and set fire to the building. A dozen babies were burned to death and others, hastily removed by their mothers, were recognized as mulattoes. The newspapers published names and addresses. Many of the women were very prominent socially either in their own right or because of their husbands.

The nation was shocked as never before. Republican sentiment began to dwindle. The Republican Executive Committee met and discussed ways and means of combating the trend. Gorman Gay was at his wits' end. Nothing, he thought, could save them except a miracle.

Two flights below in a spacious office sat two of the Republican campaigners, Walter Williams and Joseph Bonds, busily engaged in leading the other workers (who knew better) to believe that they were earning the ten dollars a day they were receiving. The former had passed for a Negro for years on the strength of a part-Negro grandparent and then gone back to the white race when the National Social Equality League was forced to cease operations at the insistence of both the sheriff and the landlord. Joseph Bonds, former head of the Negro Data League who had once been a Negro but thanks to Dr. Crookman was now Caucasian and proud of it, had but recently returned to the North from Atlanta, accompanied by Santop Licorice. Both Mr. Williams and Mr. Bonds had been unable to stomach the Democratic crowd and so had fallen in with the Republicans, who were as different from them as one billiard ball from another. The two gentlemen were in low tones discussing the dilemma of the Republicans, while rustling papers to appear busy.

"Jo, if we could figure out something to turn the tables on these Democrats, we wouldn't have to work for the rest of our lives," Williams observed, blowing a cloud of cigarette smoke out of the other corner of his mouth.

"Yes, that's right, Walt, but there ain't a chance in the world. Old Gay is almost crazy, you know. Came in here slamming doors and snapping at everybody this morning," Bonds remarked.

Williams leaned closer to him, lowered his flame-thatched head and then looking to the right and left whispered, "Listen here, do you know where Beard is?"

"No," answered Bonds, starting and looking around to see if anyone was listening. "Where is he?"

"Well, I got a letter from him the other day. He's down there in Richmond doing research work for the Anglo-Saxon Association under that Dr. Buggerie."

"Do they know who he is?"

"Of course they don't. He's been white quite a while now, you know, and of course they'd never connect him with the Dr. Shakespeare A. Beard who used to be one of their most outspoken enemies."

"Well, what about it?" persisted Bonds, eagerly. "Do you think he might know something on the Democrats that might help?"

"He might. We could try him out anyway. If he knows anything he'll spill it because he hates that crowd."

"How will you get in touch with him quickly? Write to him?"

"Certainly not," growled Williams. "I'll get expenses from Gay for the trip. He'll fall for anything now."

He rose and made for the elevator. Five minutes later he was standing before his boss, the National Chairman, a worried, gray little man with an aldermanic paunch and a convict's mouth.

"What is it, Williams?" snapped the Chairman.

"I'd like to get expenses to Richmond," said Williams. "I have a friend down there in Snobbcraft's office and he might have some dope we can use to our advantage."

"Scandal?" asked Mr. Gay, brightening.

"Well, I don't know right now, of course, but this fellow is a very shrewd observer and in six months' time he ought to have grabbed something that'll help us out of this jam."

"Is he a Republican or a Democrat?"

"Neither. He's a highly trained and competent social student. You couldn't expect him to be either," Williams observed. "But I happen to know that he hasn't got any money to speak of, so for a consideration I'm sure he'll spill everything he knows, if anything."

"Well, it's a gamble," said Gay, doubtfully, "but any port in a storm."

Williams left Washington immediately for Richmond. That night he sat in a cramped little room of the former champion of the darker races.

"What are you doing down there, Beard?" asked Williams, referring to the headquarters of the Anglo-Saxon Association.

"Oh, I'm getting, or helping to get, that data of Buggerie's into shape."

"What data? You told me you were doing research work. Now you say you're arranging data. Have they finished collecting it?"

"Yes, we finished that job some time ago. Now we're trying to get the material in shape for easy digestion."

"What do you mean: easy digestion?" queried Williams. "What are you fellows trying to find out and why must it be so easily digested. You fellows usually try to make your stuff unintelligible to the herd."

"This is different," said Beard, lowering his voice to almost a whisper. "We're under a pledge of secrecy. We have been investigating the family trees of the nation and so far, believe me, we certainly have uncovered astounding facts. When I'm finally discharged, which will probably be after election, I'm going to peddle some of that information. Snobbcraft and even Buggerie are not aware of the inflammatory character of the facts we've assembled." He narrowed his foxy eyes greedily.

"Is it because they've been planning to release some of it that they want it in easily digestible form, as you say?" pressed Williams.

"That's it exactly," declared Beard, stroking his now clean-shaven face. "I overheard Buggerie and Snobbcraft chuckling about it only a day or two ago."

"Well, there must be a whole lot of it," insinuated Williams, "if they've had all of you fellows working for six months. Where all did you work?"

"Oh, all over. North as well as South. We've got a whole basement vault full of index cards."

"I guess they're keeping close watch over it, aren't they?" asked Williams.

"Sure. It would take an army to get in that vault."

"Well, I guess they don't want anything to happen to the stuff before they spring it," observed the man from Republican headquarters.

Soon afterward Williams left Dr. Beard, took a stroll around the Anglo-Saxon Association's stately headquarters building, noted the half-dozen tough looking guards about it and then caught the last train for the capital city. The next morning he had a long talk with Gorman Gay.

"It's okeh, Jo," he whispered to Bonds, later, as he passed his desk.

Chapter XI

"What's the matter with you, Matt?" asked Bunny one morning about a month before election. "Ain't everything going okeh? You look as if we'd lost the election and failed to elect that brilliant intellectual, Henry Givens, President of the United States."

"Well, we might just as well lose it as far as I'm concerned," said Matthew, "if I don't find a way out of this jam I'm in."

"What jam?"

"Well, Helen got in the family way last winter again. I sent her to Palm Beach and the other resorts, thinking the travel and exercise might bring on another miscarriage."

"Did it?"

"Not a chance in the world. Then, to make matters worse, she miscalculates. At first she thought she would be confined in December; now she tells me she's only got about three weeks to go."

"Say not so!"

"I'm preaching gospel."

"Well, hush my mouth! Waddya gonna do? You can't send her to one o' Crookman's hospitals, it would be too dangerous right now."

"That's just it. You see, I figured she wouldn't be ready until about a month after election when everything had calmed down, and I could send her then."

"Would she have gone?"

"She couldn't afford not to with her old man the President of the United States."

"Well, whaddya gonna do, Big Boy? Think fast! Think fast! Them three weeks will get away from here in no time."

"Don't I know it?"

"What about an abortion?" suggested Bunny, hopefully.

"Nothing doing. First place, she's too frail, and second place she's got some fool idea about that being a sin."

"About the only thing for you to do, then," said Bunny, "is to get ready to pull out when that kid is born."

"Oh, Bunny, I'd hate to leave Helen. She's really the only woman I ever loved, you know. Course she's got her prejudices and queer notions like everybody else but she's really a little queen. She's been an inspiration to me, too, Bunny. Every time I talk about pulling out of this game when things don't go just right, she makes me stick it out. I guess I'd have been gone after I cleaned up that first million if it hadn't been for her."

"You'd have been better off if you had," Bunny commented.

"Oh, I don't know. She's hot for me to become Secretary of State or Ambassador to England or something like that; and the way things are going it looks like I will be. That is, if I can get out of this fix."

"If you can get out o' this jam, Matt, I'll sure take my hat off to you. An' I know how you feel about scuttling out and leaving her. I had a broad like that once in Harlem. 'Twas through her I got that job in th' bank. She was crazy about me, Boy, until she caught me two-timin'. Then she tried to shoot me.

"Squaws are funny that way," Bunny continued, philosophically. "Since I've been white I've found out they're all the same, white or black. Kipling was right. They'll fight to get you, fight to keep you and fight you when they catch you playin' around. But th' kinda woman that won't fight for a man ain't worth havin'."

"So you think I ought to pull out, eh Bunny?" asked the worried Matthew, returning to the subject.

"Well, what I'd suggest is this:" his plump friend advised, "about time you think Helen's gonna be confined, get together as much cash as you can and keep your plane ready. Then, when the baby's born, go to her, tell her everything an' offer to take her away with you. If she won't go, you beat it; if she will, why everything's hotsy totsy." Bunny extended his soft pink hands expressively.

"Well, that sounds pretty good, Bunny."

"It's your best bet, Big Boy," said his friend and secretary.

* * *

Two days before election the situation was unchanged. There was joy in the Democratic camp, gloom among the Republicans. For the first time in American history it seemed that money was not going to decide an election. The propagandists and publicity men of the Democrats had so played upon the fears and prejudices of the public that even the bulk of Jews and Catholics were wavering and many had been won over to the support of a candidate who had denounced them but a few months before. In this they were but running true to form, however, as they had usually been on the side of white supremacy in the old days when there was a Negro population observable to the eye. The Republicans sought to dig up some scandal against Givens and Snobbcraft but were dissuaded by their Committee on Strategy which feared to set so dangerous a precedent. There were also politicians in their ranks who were guilty of adulteries, drunkenness and grafting.

The Republicans, Goosie and Gump, and the Democrats, Givens and Snobbcraft, had ended their swings around the country and were resting from their labors. There were parades in every city and country town. Minor orators beat the lectern from the Atlantic to the Pacific extolling the imaginary virtues of the candidates of the party that hired them. Dr. Crookman was burned a hundred times in effigy. Several Lying-In hospitals were attacked. Two hundred citizens who knew nothing about either candidate were arrested for fighting over which was the better man.

The air was electric with expectancy. People stood around in knots. Small boys scattered leaflets on ten million doorsteps. Police were on the alert to suppress disorder, except what they created.

* * *

Arthur Snobbcraft, jovial and confident that he would soon assume a position befitting a member of one of the First Families of Virginia, was holding a brilliant pre-election party in his palatial residence. Strolling in and out amongst his guests, the master of the house accepted their premature congratulations in good humor. It was fine to hear oneself already addressed as Mr. Vice-President.

The tall English butler hastily edged his way through the throng surrounding the President of the Anglo-Saxon Association and whispered, "Dr. Buggerie is in the study upstairs. He says he must see you at once; that it is very, very important."

Puzzled, Snobbcraft went up to find out what in the world could be the trouble. As he entered, the massive statistician was striding back and forth, mopping his brow, his eyes starting from his head, a sheaf of typewritten sheets trembling in his hand.

"What's wrong, Buggerie?" asked Snobbcraft, perturbed.

"Everything! Everything!" shrilled the statistician.

"Be specific, please."

"Well," shaking the sheaf of papers in Snobbcraft's face, "we can't release any of this stuff! It's too damaging! It's too inclusive! We'll have to suppress it, Snobbcraft. You hear me? We musn't let anyone get hold of it." The big man's flabby jowls worked excitedly.

"What do you mean?" snarled the F.F.V. "Do you mean to tell me that all of that money and work is wasted?"

"That's exactly what I mean," squeaked Buggerie. "It would be suicidal to publish it."

"Why? Get down to brass tacks, man, for God's sake. You get my goat."

"Now listen here, Snobbcraft," replied the statistician soberly, dropping heavily into a chair. "Sit down and listen to me. I started this investigation on the theory that the data gathered would prove that around twenty million people, mostly of the lower classes, were of Negro ancestry, recent and remote, while about half that number would be of uncertain or unknown ancestry."

"Well, what have you found?" insisted Snobbcraft, impatiently.

"I have found," continued Buggerie, "that over half the population has no record of its ancestry beyond five generations!"

"That's fine!" chortled Snobbcraft. "I've always maintained that there were only a few people of good blood in this country."

"But those figures include all classes," protested the larger man. "Your class as well as the lower classes."

"Don't insult me, Buggerie!" shouted the head of the Anglo-Saxons, half rising from his seat on the sofa.

"Be calm! Be calm!" cried Buggerie excitedly, "You haven't heard anything yet."

"What else, in the name of God, could be a worse libel on the aristocracy of this state?" Snobbcraft mopped his dark and haughty countenance.

"Well, these statistics we've gathered prove that most of our social leaders, especially of Anglo-Saxon lineage, are descendants of colonial stock that came here in bondage. They associated with slaves, in many cases worked and slept with them. They intermixed with the blacks and the women were sexually exploited by their masters. Then, even more than today, the illegitimate birth rate was very high in America."

Snobbcraft's face was working with suppressed rage. He started to rise but reconsidered. "Go on," he commanded.

"There was so much of this mixing between whites and blacks of the various classes that very early the colonies took steps to put a halt to it. They managed to prevent intermarriage but they couldn't stop intermixture. You know the old records don't lie. They're right there for everybody to see...

"A certain percentage of these Negroes," continued Buggerie, quite at ease now and seemingly enjoying his dissertation, "in time lightened sufficiently to be able to pass for white. They then merged with the general population. Assuming that there were one thousand such cases fifteen generations ago – and we have proof that there were more – their descendants now number close to fifty million souls. Now I maintain that we dare not risk publishing this information. Too many of our very first families are touched right here in Richmond!"

"Buggerie!" gasped the F.F.V., "Are you mad?"

"Quite sane, sir," squeaked the ponderous man, somewhat proudly, "and I know what I know." He winked a watery eye.

"Well, go on. Is there any more?"

"Plenty," proceeded the statistician, amiably. "Take your own family, for instance. (Now don't get mad, Snobbcraft). Take your own family. It is true that your people descended from King Alfred, but he has scores, perhaps hundreds of thousands of descendants. Some are, of course, honored and respected citizens, cultured aristocrats who are a credit to the country; but most of them, my dear, dear Snobbcraft, are in what you call the lower orders: that is to say, laboring people, convicts, prostitutes, and that sort. One of your maternal ancestors in the late seventeenth century was the offspring of an English serving maid and a black slave. This woman in turn had a daughter by the plantation owner. This daughter was married to a former indentured slave. Their children were all white and you are one of their direct descendants!" Buggerie beamed.

"Stop!" shouted Snobbcraft, the veins standing out on his narrow forehead and his voice trembling with rage. "You can't sit there and insult my family that way, suh."

"Now that outburst just goes to prove my earlier assertion," the large man continued, blandly. "If you get so excited about the truth, what do you think will be the reaction of other people? There's no use getting angry at me. I'm not responsible for your ancestry! Nor, for that matter, are you. You're no worse off than I am, Snobbcraft. My great, great grandfather had his ears cropped for non-payment of debts and was later jailed for thievery. His illegitimate daughter married a free Negro who fought in the Revolutionary War." Buggerie wagged his head almost gleefully.

"How can you admit it?" asked the scandalized Snobbcraft.

"Why not?" demanded Buggerie. "I have plenty of company. There's Givens, who is quite a fanatic on the race question and white supremacy, and yet he's only four generations removed from a mulatto ancestor."

"Givens too?"

"Yes, and also the proud Senator Kretin. He boasts, you know, of being descended from Pocahontas and Captain John Smith, but so are thousands of Negroes. Incidentally, there hasn't been an Indian unmixed with Negro on the Atlantic coastal plain for over a century and a half."

"What about Matthew Fisher?"

"We can find no record whatever of Fisher, which is true of about twenty million others, and so," he lowered his voice dramatically, "I have reason to suspect that he is one of those Negroes who have been whitened."

"And to think that I entertained him in my home!" Snobbcraft muttered to himself. And then aloud: "Well, what are we to do about it?"

"We must destroy the whole shooting match," the big man announced as emphatically as possible for one with a soprano voice, "and we'd better do it at once. The sooner we get through with it the better."

"But I can't leave my guests," protested Snobbcraft. Then turning angrily upon his friend, he growled, "Why in the devil didn't you find all of this out before?"

"Well," said Buggerie, meekly, "I found out as soon as I could. We had to arrange and correlate the data, you know."

"How do you imagine we're going to get rid of that mountain of paper at this hour?" asked Snobbcraft, as they started down stairs.

"We'll get the guards to help us," said Buggerie, hopefully. "And we'll have the cards burned in the furnace."

"All right, then," snapped the F.F.V., "let's go and get it over with."

In five minutes they were speeding down the broad avenue to the headquarters of the Anglo-Saxon Association of America. They parked the car in front of the gate and walked up the cinder road to the front door. It was a balmy, moonlight night, almost as bright as day. They looked around but saw no one.

"I don't see any of the guards around," Snobbcraft remarked, craning his neck. "I wonder where they are?"

"Probably they're inside," Buggerie suggested, "although I remember telling them to patrol the outside of the building."

"Well, we'll go in, anyhow," remarked Snobbcraft. "Maybe they're down stairs."

He unlocked the door, swung it open and they entered. The hall was pitch dark. Both men felt along the wall for the button for the light. Suddenly there was a thud and Snobbcraft cursed.

"What's the matter?" wailed the frightened Buggerie, frantically feeling for a match.

"Turn on that God damned light!" roared Snobbcraft. "I just stumbled over a man... Hurry up, will you?"

Dr. Buggerie finally found a match, struck it, located the wall button and pressed it. The hall was flooded with light. There arranged in a row on the floor and neatly trussed up and gagged were the six special guards.

"What the hell does this mean?" yelled Snobbcraft at the mute men prone before them. Buggerie quickly removed the gags.

They had been suddenly set upon, the head watchman explained, about an hour before, just after Dr. Buggerie left, by a crowd of gunmen who had blackjacked them into unconsciousness and carried them into the building. The watchman displayed the lumps on their heads as evidence and looked quite aggrieved. Not one of them could remember what transpired after the sleep-producing buffet.

"The vault!" shrilled Buggerie. "Let's have a look at the vault."

Down the stairs they rushed, Buggerie wheezing in the lead, Snobbcraft following and the six tousled watchmen bringing up the rear. The lights in the basement were still burning brightly. The doors of the vault were open, sagging on their hinges. There was a litter of trash in front of the vault. They all clustered around the opening and peered inside. The vault was absolutely empty.

"My God!" exclaimed Snobbcraft and Buggerie in unison, turning two shades paler.

For a second or two they just gazed at each other. Then suddenly Buggerie smiled.

"That stuff won't do them any good," he remarked triumphantly.

"Why not?" demanded Snobbcraft, in his tone a mixture of eagerness, hope and doubt.

"Well, it will take them as long to get anything out of that mass of cards as it took our staff, and by that time you and Givens will be elected and no one will dare publish anything like that," the statistician explained. "I have in my possession the only summary – those papers I showed you at your house. As long as I've got that document and they haven't, we're all right!" he grinned in obese joy.

"That sounds good," sighed Snobbcraft, contentedly. "By the way, where is that summary?"

Buggerie jumped as if stuck by a pin and looked first into his empty hands, then into his coat pockets and finally his trousers pockets. He turned and dashed out to the car, followed by the grim-looking Snobbcraft and the six uniformed watchmen with their tousled hair and sore bumps. They searched the car in vain, Snobbcraft loudly cursing Buggerie's stupidity.

"I – I must have left it in your study," wept Buggerie, meekly and hopefully. "In fact I think I remember leaving it right there on the table."

The enraged Snobbcraft ordered him into the car and they drove off leaving the six uniformed watchmen gaping at the entrance to the grounds, the moonbeams playing through their tousled hair.

The two men hit the ground almost as soon as the car crunched to a stop, dashed up the steps, into the house, through the crowd of bewildered guests, up the winding colonial stairs, down the hallway and into the study.

Buggerie switched on the light and looked wildly, hopefully around. Simultaneously the two men made a grab for a sheaf of white paper lying on the sofa. The statistician reached it first and gazed hungrily, gratefully at it. Then his eyes started from his head and his hand trembled.

"Look!" he shrieked dolefully, thrusting the sheaf of paper under Snobbcraft's eyes.

All of the sheets were blank except the one on top. On that was scribbled:

> *Thanks very much for leaving that report where I could get hold of it. Am leaving this paper so you'll have something on which to write another summary.*
>
> *Happy dreams, Little One.*
>
> *G.O.P.*

"Great God!" gasped Snobbcraft, sinking into a chair.

Chapter XII

The afternoon before election Matthew and Bunny sat in the latter's hotel suite sipping cocktails, smoking and awaiting the inevitable. They had been waiting ever since the day before. Matthew, tall and tense; Bunny, rotund and apprehensive, trying ever so often to cheer up his chief with poor attempts at jocosity. Every time they heard a bell ring both jumped for the telephone, thinking it might be an announcement from Helen's bedside that an heir, and a dark one, had been born. When they could no longer stay around the office, they had come down to the hotel. In just a few moments they were planning to go back to the office again.

The hard campaign and the worry over the outcome of Helen's confinement had left traces on Matthew's face. The satanic lines were accentuated, the eyes seemed sunken farther back in the head, his well-manicured hand trembled a little as he reached for his glass again and again.

He wondered how it would all come out. He hated to leave. He had had such a good time since he'd been white: plenty of money, almost unlimited power, a beautiful wife, good liquor and the pick of damsels within reach. Must he leave all that? Must he cut and run just at the time when he was about to score his greatest victory? Just think: from an underpaid insurance agent to a millionaire commanding millions of people – and then oblivion. He shuddered slightly and reached again for his glass.

"I got everything fixed," Bunny remarked, shifting around in the overstuffed chair. "The plane's all ready with tanks full and I've got Ruggles right there in the hangar. The money's in that little steel box: all in thousand dollar bills."

"You're going with me, aren't you, Bunny?" asked Matthew in almost pleading tones.

"I'm not stayin' here!" his secretary replied.

"Gee, Bunny, you're a brick!" said Matthew leaning over and placing his hand on his plump little friend's knee. "You sure have been a good pal."

"Aw, cut th' comedy," exclaimed Bunny, reddening and turning his head swiftly away.

Suddenly the telephone rang, loud, clear, staccato. Both men sprang for it, eagerly, open-eyed, apprehensive. Matthew was first.

"Hello!" he shouted. "What's that! Yes, I'll be right up.

"Well, it's happened," he announced resignedly, hanging up the receiver. And then, brightening a bit, he boasted, "It's a boy!"

In the midst of her pain Helen was jubilant. What a present to give her Matthew on the eve of his greatest triumph! How good the Lord was to her; to doubly bless her in this way. The nurse wiped the tears of joy away from the young mother's eyes.

"You must stay quiet, Ma'am," she warned.

Outside in the hall, squirming uneasily on the window seat, was Matthew, his fists clenched, his teeth biting into his thin lower lip. At another window stood Bunny looking vacantly out into the street, feeling useless and out of place in such a situation, and yet convinced that it was his duty to stay here by his best friend during this great crisis.

Matthew felt like a young soldier about to leave his trench to face a baptism of machine gun fire or a gambler risking his last dollar on a roll of the dice. It seemed to him that he would go mad if something didn't happen quickly. He rose and paced the hall, hands in pockets, his tall shadow following him on the opposite wall. Why didn't the doctor come out and tell him something? What was the cause of the delay? What would Helen say? What would the baby look like? Maybe it might be miraculously light! Stranger things had happened in this world. But no, nothing like that could happen. Well, he'd had his lucky break; now the vacation was over.

A nurse, immaculate in white uniform, came out of Helen's bedroom, passed them hurriedly, smiling, and entered the bathroom. She returned with a basin of warm water in her hands, smiled again reassuringly and reentered the natal chamber. Bunny and Matthew, in unison, sighed heavily.

"Boy!" exclaimed Bunny, wiping the perspiration from his brow. "If somethin' don't happen pretty soon, here, I'm gonna do a Brodie out o' that window."

"The both of us," said Matthew. "I never knew it took these doctors so damn long to get through."

Helen's door opened and the physician came out looking quite grave and concerned. Matthew pounced upon him. The man held his finger to his lips and motioned to the room across the hall. Matthew entered.

"Well," said Matthew, guiltily, "what's the news?"

"I'm very sorry to have to tell you, Mr. Fisher, that something terrible has happened. Your son is very, very dark. Either you or Mrs. Fisher must possess some Negro blood. It might be called reversion to type if any such thing had ever been proved. Now I want to know what you want done. If you say so I can get rid of this child and it will save everybody concerned a lot of trouble and disgrace. Nobody except the nurse knows anything about this and she'll keep her mouth shut for a consideration. Of course, it's all in the day's work for me, you know. I've had plenty of cases like this in Atlanta, even before the disappearance of the Negroes. Come now, what shall I do?" he wailed.

"Yes," thought Matthew to himself, "what should he do?" The doctor had suggested an excellent way out of the dilemma. They could just say that the child had died. But what of the future? Must he go on forever in this way? Helen was young and fecund. Surely one couldn't go on murdering one's children, especially when one loved and wanted children. Wouldn't it be better to settle the matter once and for all? Or should he let the doctor murder the boy and then hope for a better situation the next time? An angel of frankness beckoned him to be done with this life of pretense; to take his wife and son and flee far away from everything, but a devil of ambition whispered seductively about wealth, power and prestige.

In almost as many seconds the pageant of the past three years passed in review on the screen of his tortured memory: the New Year's Eve at the Honky Tonk Club, the first glimpse of the marvelously beautiful Helen, the ordeal of getting white, the first, sweet days of freedom from the petty insults and cheap discriminations to which as a black man he had always been subjected, then the search for Helen around Atlanta, the organization of the Knights of Nordica, the stream of successes, the coming of Bunny, the campaign planned and executed by him: and now, the end. Must it be the end?

"Well?" came the insistent voice of the physician.

Matthew opened his mouth to reply when the butler burst into the room waving a newspaper.

"Excuse me, sir," he blurted, excitedly, "but Mister Brown said to bring this right to you."

The lurid headlines seemed to leap from the paper and strike Matthew between the eyes:

> *DEMOCRATIC LEADERS PROVED OF*
> *NEGRO DESCENT*
> *Givens, Snobbcraft, Buggerie, Kretin and Others*
> *of Negro Ancestry, According to Old*
> *Records Unearthed by Them.*

Matthew and the physician, standing side by side, read the long account in awed silence. Bunny entered the door.

"Can I speak to you a minute, Matt?" he asked casually. Almost reluctant to move, Matthew followed him into the hall.

"Keep your shirt on, Big Boy," Bunny advised, almost jovially. "They ain't got nothin' on you yet. That changing your name threw them off. You're not even mentioned."

Matthew braced up, threw back his shoulders and drew a long, deep breath. It seemed as if a mountain had been taken off his shoulders. He actually grinned as his confidence returned. He reached for Bunny's hand and they shook, silently jubilant.

"Well, doctor," said Matthew, arching his left eyebrow in his familiar Mephistophelian manner, "it sort of looks as if there is something to that reversion to type business. I used to think it was all boloney myself. Well, it's as I always say: you never can tell."

"Yes, it seems as if this is a very authentic case," agreed the physician, glancing sharply at the bland and blond countenance of Matthew. "Well, what now?"

"I'll have to see Givens," said Matthew as they turned to leave the room.

"Here he comes now," Bunny announced.

Sure enough, the little gray-faced, bald-headed man, came leaping up the stairs like a goat, his face haggard, his eyes bulging in mingled rage and terror, his necktie askew. He was waving a newspaper in his hand and opened his mouth without speaking as he shot past them and dashed into Helen's room. The old fellow was evidently out of his head.

They followed him into the room in time to see him with his face buried in the covers of Helen's bed and she, horrified, glancing at the six-inch-tall headline. Matthew rushed to her side as she slumped back on the pillow in a dead faint. The physician and nurse dashed to revive her. The old man on his knees sobbed hoarsely. Mrs. Givens looking fifteen years older appeared in the doorway. Bunny glanced at Matthew who slightly lowered his left eyelid and with difficulty suppressed a smile.

"We've got to get out o' this!" shouted the Imperial Grand Wizard. "We've got to get out o' this. Oh, it's terrible… I never knew it myself, for sure… Oh, Matthew, get us out of this, I tell you. They almost mobbed me at the office… Came in just as I went out the back way… Almost ten thousand of them… We can't lose a minute. Quick, I tell you! They'll murder us all."

"I'll look out for everything," Matthew soothed condescendingly. "I'll stick by you." Then turning swiftly to his partner he commanded, "Bunny, order both cars out at once. We'll beat it for the airport… Doctor Brocker, will you go with us to look out for Helen and the baby? We've got to get out right now. I'll pay you your price."

"Sure I'll go, Mr. Fisher," said the physician, quietly. "I wouldn't leave Mrs. Fisher now."

The nurse had succeeded in bringing Helen to consciousness. She was weeping bitterly, denouncing fate and her father. With that logicality that frequently causes people to accept as truth circumstantial evidence that is not necessarily conclusive, she was assuming that the suspiciously brown color of her new-born son was due to some hidden Negro drop of blood in her veins. She looked up at her husband beseechingly.

"Oh, Matthew, darling," she cried, her long red-gold hair framing her face, "I'm so sorry about all this. If I'd only known, I'd never have let you in for it. I would have spared you this disgrace and humiliation. Oh, Matthew, Honey, please forgive me. I love you, my husband. Please don't leave me, please don't leave me!" She reached out and grasped the tail of his coat as if he were going to leave that very minute.

"Now, now, little girl," said Matthew soothingly, touched by her words, "You haven't disgraced me; you've honored me by presenting me with a beautiful son."

He looked down worshipfully at the chubby, ball of brownness in the nurse's arms.

"You needn't worry about me, Helen. I'll stick by you as long as you'll have me and without you life wouldn't be worth a dime. You're not responsible for the color of our baby, my dear. I'm the guilty one."

Dr. Brocker smiled knowingly, Givens rose up indignantly, Bunny opened his mouth in surprise, Mrs. Givens folded her arms and her mouth changed to a slit and the nurse said "Oh!"

"You?" cried Helen in astonishment.

"Yes, me," Matthew repeated, a great load lifting from his soul. Then for a few minutes he poured out his secret to the astonished little audience.

Helen felt a wave of relief go over her. There was no feeling of revulsion at the thought that her husband was a Negro. There once would have been but that was seemingly centuries ago when she had been unaware of her remoter Negro ancestry. She felt proud of her Matthew. She loved him more than ever. They had money and a beautiful, brown baby. What more did they need? To hell with the world! To hell with society! Compared to what she possessed, thought Helen, all talk of race and color was damned foolishness. She would probably have been surprised to learn that countless Americans at that moment were thinking the same thing.

"Well," said Bunny, grinning, "it sure is good to be able to admit that you're a jigwalk once more."

"Yes, Bunny," said old man Givens, "I guess we're all niggers now."

"Negroes, Mr. Givens, Negroes," corrected Dr. Brocker, entering the room. "I'm in the same boat with the rest of you, only my dark ancestors are not so far back. I sure hope the Republicans win."

"Don't worry, Doc," said Bunny. "They'll win all right. And how! Gee whiz! I bet Sherlock Holmes, Nick Carter and all the Pinkertons couldn't find old Senator Kretin and Arthur Snobbcraft now."

"Come on," shouted the apprehensive Givens, "let's get out o' here before that mob comes."

"Whut mob, Daddy?" asked Mrs. Givens.

"You'll find out damn quick if you don't shake it up," replied her husband.

* * *

Through the crisp, autumn night air sped Fisher's big tri-motored plane, headed southwest to the safety of Mexico. Reclining in a large, comfortable deck chair was Helen Fisher, calm and at peace with the world. In a hammock near her was her little brown son, Matthew, Junior. Beside her, holding her hand, was Matthew. Up front near the pilot, Bunny and Givens were playing Conquian. Behind them sat the nurse and Dr. Brocker, silently gazing out of the window at the twinkling lights of the Gulf Coast. Old lady Givens snored in the rear of the ship.

"Damn!" muttered Givens, as Bunny threw down his last spread and won the third consecutive game. "I sure wish I'd had time to grab some jack before we pulled out o' Atlanta. Ain't got but five dollars and fifty-three cents to my name."

"Don't worry about that, Old Timer," Bunny laughed. "I don't think we left over a thousand bucks in the treasury. See that steel box over there? Well, that ain't got nothin' in it but bucks and more bucks. Not a bill smaller than a grand."

"Well, I'm a son-of-a-gun," blurted the Imperial Grand Wizard. "That boy thinks o' everything."

But Givens was greatly depressed, much more so than the others. He had really believed all that he had preached about white supremacy, race purity and the menace of the alien, the Catholic, the Modernist and the Jew. He had always been sincere in his prejudices.

When they arrived at the Valbuena Air Field outside Mexico City, a messenger brought Bunny a telegram.

"You better thank your stars you got away from there, Matt," he grinned, handing his friend the telegram. "See what my gal says?"

Matthew glanced over the message and handed it to Givens without comment. It read:

> *Hope you arrive safely Senator Kretin lynched in Union Station Stop Snobbcraft and Buggerie reported in flight Stop Goosie and Gump almost unanimously reelected Stop Government has declared martial law until disturbances stop Stop When can I come?*
>
> *Madeline Scranton.*

"Who's this Scranton broad?" queried Matthew in a whisper, cutting a precautionary glance at his wife.

"A sweet Georgia brown," exclaimed Bunny enthusiastically.

"No!" gasped Matthew, incredulous.

"She ain't no Caucasian!" Bunny replied.

"She must be the last black gal in the country," Matthew remarked, glancing enviously at his friend. "How come she didn't get white, too?"

"Well," Bunny replied, a slight hint of pride in his voice. "She's a race patriot. She's funny that way."

"Well, for cryin' out loud!" exclaimed Matthew, scratching his head and sort of half grinning in a bewildered way. "*What* kind o' *sheba* is that?"

Old man Givens came over to where they were standing, the telegram in his hand and an expression of serenity now on his face.

"Boys," he announced, "it looks like it's healthier down here right now than it is back there in Georgia."

"*Looks* like it's healthier?" mocked Bunny. "Brother, you know damn *well* it's healthier!"

Chapter XIII

Toward eleven o'clock on the evening before election day, a long, low roadster swept up to the door of a stately country home near Richmond, Va., crunched to a stop, the lights were extinguished and two men, one tall and angular, the other huge and stout, catapulted from the car. Without wasting words, they raced around the house and down a small driveway to a rambling shed in a level field about three hundred yards to the rear. Breathless, they halted before the door and beat upon it excitedly.

"Open up there, Frazier!" ordered Snobbcraft, for it was he. "Open that door." There was no answer. The only reply was the chirping of crickets and the rustle of branches.

"He must not be here," said Dr. Buggerie, glancing fearfully over his shoulder and wiping a perspiring brow with a damp handkerchief.

"The damned rascal had better be here," thundered the Democratic candidate for Vice-President, beating again on the door. "I telephoned him two hours ago to be ready."

As he spoke someone unlocked the door and rolled it aside an inch or two.

"Is that you, Mr. Snobbcraft?" asked a sleepy voice from the darkness within.

"Open that damned door, you fool," barked Snobbcraft. "Didn't I tell you to have that plane ready when we got here? Why don't you do as you're told?" He and Dr. Buggerie helped slide the great doors back. The man Frazier snapped on the lights, revealing within a big, three-motored plane with an automobile nestling under each of its wings.

"I-I kinda fell asleep waitin' for you, Mr. Snobbcraft," Frazier apologized, "but everything's ready."

"All right, man," shouted the president of the Anglo-Saxon Association, "let's get away from here then. This is a matter of life and death. You ought to have had the plane outside and all warmed up to go."

"Yes sir," the man mumbled meekly, busying himself.

"These damned, stupid, poor white trash!" growled Snobbcraft, glaring balefully at the departing aviator.

"D-D-Don't antagonize him," muttered Buggerie. "He's our only chance to get away."

"Shut up, fool! If it hadn't been for you and your damned fool statistics we wouldn't be in this fix."

"You wanted them, didn't you?" whined the statistician in defense.

"Well, I didn't tell you to leave that damned summary where anybody could get hold of it," Snobbcraft replied, reproachfully. "That was the most stupid thing I ever heard of."

Buggerie opened his mouth to reply but said nothing. He just glared at Snobbcraft who glared back at him. The two men presented a disheveled appearance. The Vice-Presidential candidate was haggard, hatless, collarless and still wore his smoking jacket. The eminent statistician and author of *The Incidence of Psittacosis among the Hiphopa Indians of the Amazon Valley and Its Relation to Life Insurance Rates in the United States*, looked far from dignified with no necktie, canvas breeches, no socks and wearing a shooting jacket he had snatched from a closet on his way out of the house. He had forgotten his thick spectacles and his bulging eyes were red and watery. They paced impatiently back and forth, glancing first at the swiftly working Frazier and then down the long driveway toward the glowing city.

Ten minutes they waited while Frazier went over the plane to see that all was well. Then they helped him roll the huge metal bird out of the hangar and on to the field. Gratefully they climbed inside and fell exhausted on the soft-cushioned seats.

"Well, that sure is a relief," gasped the ponderous Buggerie, mopping his brow.

"Wait until we get in the air," growled Snobbcraft. "Anything's liable to happen after that mob tonight. I was never so humiliated in my life. The idea of that gang of poor white trash crowding up my steps and yelling nigger. It was disgraceful."

"Yes, it was terrible," agreed Buggerie. "It's a good thing they didn't go in the rear where your car was. We wouldn't have been able to get away."

"I thought there would be a demonstration," said Snobbcraft, some of his old sureness returning, "that's why I 'phoned Frazier to get ready... Oh, it's a damned shame to be run out of your own home in this way!"

He glared balefully at the statistician who averted his gaze.

"All ready, sir," announced Frazier, "where are we headed?"

"To my ranch in Chihuahua, and hurry up," snapped Snobbcraft.

"But – But we ain't got enough gas to go that far," said Frazier. "I-I-You didn't say you wanted to go to Mexico, Boss."

Snobbcraft stared incredulously at the man. His rage was so great that he could not speak for a moment or two. Then he launched into a stream of curses that would have delighted a pirate captain, while the unfortunate aviator gaped indecisively.

In the midst of this diatribe, the sound of automobile horns and klaxons rent the air, punctuated by shouts and pistol shots. The three men in the plane saw coming down the road from the city a bobbing stream of headlights. Already the cavalcade was almost to the gate of the Snobbcraft country estate.

"Come on, get out of here," gasped Snobbcraft. "We'll get some gas farther down the line. Hurry up!"

Dr. Buggerie, speechless and purple with fear, pushed the aviator out of the plane. The fellow gave the propeller a whirl, jumped back into the cabin, took the controls and the great machine rolled out across the field.

They had started none too soon. The automobile cavalcade was already coming up the driveway. The drone of the motor drowned out the sound of the approaching mob but the two fearful men saw several flashes that betokened pistol shots. Several of the automobiles took out across the field in the wake of the plane. They seemed to gain on it. Snobbcraft and Buggerie gazed nervously ahead. They were almost at the end of the field and the plane had not yet taken to the air. The pursuing automobiles drew closer. There were several more flashes from firearms. A bullet tore through the side of the cabin. Simultaneously Snobbcraft and Buggerie fell to the floor.

At last the ship rose, cleared the trees at the end of the field and began to attain altitude. The two men took deep breaths of relief, rose and flung themselves on the richly upholstered seats.

A terrible stench suddenly became noticeable to the two passengers and the aviator. The latter looked inquiringly over his shoulder; Snobbcraft and Buggerie, their noses wrinkled and their foreheads corrugated, glanced suspiciously at each other. Both moved uneasily in their seats and looks of guilt succeeded those of accusation. Snobbcraft retreated precipitously to the rear cabin while the statistician flung open several windows and then followed the Vice-Presidential candidate.

Fifteen minutes later two bundles were tossed out of the window of the rear cabin and the two passengers, looking sheepish but much relieved, resumed their seats. Snobbcraft was wearing a suit of brown dungarees belonging to Frazier while his scientific friend had wedged himself into a pair of white trousers usually worn by Snobbcraft's valet. Frazier turned, saw them, and grinned.

Hour after hour the plane winged its way through the night. Going a hundred miles an hour it passed town after town. About dawn, as they were passing over Meridian, Mississippi, the motor began to miss.

"What's the matter there?" Snobbcraft inquired nervously into the pilot's ear.

"The gas is runnin' low," Frazier replied grimly. "We'll have to land pretty soon."

"No, no, not in Mississippi!" gasped Buggerie, growing purple with apprehension. "They'll lynch us if they find out who we are."

"Well, we can't stay up here much longer," the pilot warned.

Snobbcraft bit his lip and thought furiously. It was true they would be taking a chance by landing anywhere in the South, let alone in Mississippi, but what could they do? The motor was missing more frequently and Frazier had cut down their speed to save gasoline. They were just idling along. The pilot looked back at Snobbcraft inquiringly.

"By God, we're in a fix now," said the president of the Anglo-Saxon Association. Then he brightened with a sudden idea. "We could hide in the rear cabin while Frazier gets gasoline," he suggested.

"Suppose somebody looks in the rear cabin?" queried Buggerie, dolefully, thrusting his hands into the pockets of his white trousers. "There's bound to be a lot of curious people about when a big plane like this lands in a farming district."

As he spoke his left hand encountered something hard in the pocket. It felt like a box of salve. He withdrew it curiously. It was a box of shoe polish which the valet doubtless used on Snobbcraft's footgear. He looked at it aimlessly and was about to thrust it back into the pocket when he had a brilliant idea.

"Look here, Snobbcraft," he cried excitedly, his rheumy eyes popping out of his head farther than usual. "This is just the thing."

"What do you mean?" asked his friend, eyeing the little tin box.

"Well," explained the scientist, "you know real niggers are scarce now and nobody would think of bothering a couple of them, even in Mississippi. They'd probably be a curiosity."

"What are you getting at, man?"

"This: we can put this blacking on our head, face, neck and hands, and no one will take us for Snobbcraft and Buggerie. Frazier can tell anybody that inquires that we're two darkies he's taking out of the country, or something like that. Then, after we get our gas and start off again, we can wash the stuff off with gasoline. It's our only chance, Arthur. If we go down like we are, they'll kill us sure."

Snobbcraft pursed his lips and pondered the proposition for a moment. It was indeed, he saw, their only chance to effectively escape detection.

"All right," he agreed, "let's hurry up. This ship Won't stay up much longer."

Industriously they daubed each other's head, neck, face, chest, hands and arms with the shoe polish. In five minutes they closely resembled a brace of mammy singers. Snobbcraft hurriedly instructed Frazier.

The plane slowly circled to the ground. The region was slightly rolling and there was no good landing place. There could be no delay, however, so Frazier did his best. The big ship bumped over logs and through weeds, heading straight for a clump of trees. Quickly the pilot steered it to the left only to send it head first into a ditch. The plane turned completely over, one wing was entirely smashed and Frazier, caught in the wreckage under the engine, cried feebly for help for a few moments and then lay still.

Shaken up and bruised, the two passengers managed to crawl out of the cabin window to safety. Dolefully they stood in the Mississippi sunlight, surveying the wreckage and looking questioningly at each other.

"Well," whined Dr. Buggerie, rubbing one large sore buttock, "what now?"

"Shut up," growled Snobbcraft. "If it hadn't been for you, we wouldn't be here."

* * *

Happy Hill, Mississippi, was all aflutter. For some days it had been preparing for the great, open-air revival of the True Faith Christ Lovers' Church. The faithful for miles around were expected to attend the services scheduled for the afternoon of Election Day and which all hoped would last well into the night.

This section of the state had been untouched by the troubles through which the rest of the South had gone as a result of the activities of Black-No-More, Incorporated. The people for miles around were with very few exceptions old residents and thence known to be genuine blue-blooded Caucasians for as far back as any resident could remember which was at least fifty years. The people were proud of this fact. They were more proud, however, of the fact that Happy Hill was the home and birthplace of the True Faith Christ Lovers' Church, which made the prodigious boast of being the most truly Fundamentalist of all the Christian sects in the United States. Other things of which the community might have boasted were its inordinately high illiteracy rate and its lynching record – but these things were seldom mentioned, although no one was ashamed of them. Certain things are taken for granted everywhere.

Long before the United States had rid themselves of their Negroes through the good but unsolicited offices of Dr. Junius Crookman, Happy Hill had not only rid itself of what few Negroes had resided in its vicinity but of all itinerant blackamoors who lucklessly came through the place. Ever since the Civil War when the proud and courageous forefathers of the Caucasian inhabitants had vigorously resisted all efforts to draft them into the Confederate Army, there had been a sign nailed over the general store and post office reading, "NIGER REDE & RUN. IF U CAN'T REDE, RUN ENEYHOWE." The literate denizens of Happy Hill would sometimes stand off and spell out the words with the pride that usually accompanies erudition.

The method by which Happy Hill discouraged blackamoors who sought the hospitality of the place, was simple: the offending Ethiopian was either hung or shot and then broiled. Across from the general store and post office was a large iron post about five feet high. On it all blacks were burned. Down one side of it was a long line of nicks made with hammer and chisel. Each nick stood for a Negro dispatched. This post was one of the landmarks of the community and was pointed out to visitors with pardonable civic pride by local boosters. Sage old fellows frequently remarked between expectorations of tobacco juice that the only Negro problem in Happy Hill was the difficulty of getting hold of a sufficient number of the Sons or Daughters of Ham to lighten the dullness of the place.

Quite naturally the news that all Negroes had disappeared, not only from their state but from the entire country, had been received with sincere regret by the inhabitants of Happy Hill. They envisioned the passing of an old, established custom. Now there was nothing left to stimulate them but the old time religion and the clandestine sex orgies that invariably and immediately followed the great revival meetings.

So the simple country folk had turned to religion with renewed ardor. There were several churches in the county, Methodist, Baptist, Campbellite and, of course, Holy Roller. The latter, indeed, had the largest membership. But the people, eager for something new, found all of the old churches too tame. They wanted a faith with more punch to it; a faith that would fittingly accompany the fierce corn liquor which all consumed, albeit they were all confirmed Prohibitionists.

Whenever and wherever there is a social need, some agency arises to supply it. The needs of Happy Hill were no exception. One day, several weeks previously, there had come to the community one Rev. Alex McPhule who claimed to be the founder of a new faith, a true faith, that would save all from the machinations of the Evil One. The other churches, he averred, had failed. The other churches had grown soft and were flirting with atheism and Modernism which, according to Rev. McPhule, were the same thing. An angel of God had visited him one summer evening in Meridian, he told them, when he was down sick in bed as the result of his sinning ways, and had told him to reform and go forth into the world and preach the true faith of Christ's love. He had promised to do so, of course, and then the angel had placed the palm of his right hand on Rev. McPhule's forehead and all of the sickness and misery had departed.

The residents of Happy Hill and vicinity listened with rapt attention and respect. The man was sincere, eloquent and obviously a Nordic. He was tall, thin, slightly knock-kneed, with a shock of unkempt red hair, wild blue eyes, hollow cheeks, lantern jaw and long ape-like arms that looked very impressive when he waved them up and down during a harangue. His story sounded logical to the country people and they flocked in droves to his first revival held in a picturesque natural amphitheater about a mile from town.

No one had any difficulty in understanding the new faith. No music was allowed besides singing and thumping the bottom of a wooden tub. There were no chairs. Everybody sat on the ground in a circle with Rev. McPhule in the center. The holy man would begin an extemporaneous song and would soon have the faithful singing it after him and swinging from side to side in unison. Then he would break off abruptly and launch into an old fashion hellfire-and-damnation sermon in which demons, brimstone, adultery, rum, and other evils prominently figured. At the height of his remarks, he would roll his eyes heavenward, froth at the mouth, run around on all fours and embrace in turn each member of the congregation, especially the buxom ladies. This would be the signal for others to follow his example. The sisters and brothers osculated, embraced and rolled, shouting meanwhile: "Christ is Love!...Love Christ!...Oh, be happy in the arms of Jesus!...Oh, Jesus, my Sweetheart!...Heavenly Father!" Frequently these revivals took place on the darkest nights with the place of worship dimly illuminated by pine torches. As these torches always seemed to conveniently burn out about the time the embracing and rolling started, the new faith rapidly became popular.

In a very short time nothing in Happy Hill was too good for Rev. Alex McPhule. Every latch-string hung out for him. As usual with gentlemen of the cloth, he was especially popular with the ladies. When the men were at work in the fields, the Man of God would visit house after house and comfort the womenfolk with his Christian message. Being a bachelor, he made these professional calls with great frequency.

The Rev. Alex McPhule also held private audiences with the sick, sinful and neurotic in his little cabin. There he had erected an altar covered with the white marble top from an old bureau. Around this altar were painted some grotesque figures, evidently the handiwork of the evangelist, while on the wall in back of the altar hung a large square of white oilcloth upon which was painted a huge eye. The sinner seeking surcease was commanded to gaze upon the eye while making confessions and requests. On the altar reposed a crudely-bound manuscript about three inches thick. This was the "Bible" of the Christ Lovers which the Rev. McPhule declared he had written at the command of Jesus Christ Himself. The majority of his visitors were middle-aged wives and adenoidal and neurotic young girls. None departed unsatisfied.

With all the good fortune that had come to the Rev. McPhule as a result of engaging in the Lord's work, he was still dissatisfied. He never passed a Baptist, Methodist or Holy Roller church without jealousy and ambition surging up within him. He wanted everybody in the county in his flock. He wanted to do God's work so effectually that the other churches would be put out of business. He could only do this, he knew, with the aid of a message straight from Heaven. That alone would impress them.

He began to talk in his meetings about a sign coming down from Heaven to convince all doubters and infidels like Methodists and Baptists. His flock was soon on the nervous edge of expectancy but the Lord failed, for some reason, to answer the prayer of his right-hand man.

Rev. McPhule began to wonder what he had done to offend the Almighty. He prayed long and fervently in the quiet of his bedchamber, except when he didn't have company, but no sign appeared. Possibly, thought the evangelist, some big demonstration might attract the attention of Jesus; something bigger than the revivals he had been staging. Then one day somebody brought him a copy of *The Warning* and upon reading it he got an idea. If the Lord would only send him a nigger for his congregation to lynch! That would, indeed, be marked evidence of the power of Rev. Alex McPhule.

He prayed with increased fervency but no African put in an appearance. Two nights later as he sat before his altar, his "Bible" clutched in his hands, a bat flew in the window. It rapidly circled the room and flew out again. Rev. McPhule could feel the wind from its wings. He stood erect with a wild look in his watery blue eyes and screamed, "A sign! A sign! Oh, Glory be! The Lord has answered my prayer! Oh, thank you, God! A sign! A sign!" Then he grew dizzy, his eyes dimmed and he fell twitching across the altar, unconscious.

Next day he went around Happy Hill telling of his experience of the night before. An angel of the Lord, he told the gaping villagers, had flown through the window, alighted on his "Bible" and, kissing him on his forehead, had declared that the Lord would answer his prayer and send a sign. As proof of his tale, Rev. McPhule exhibited a red spot on his forehead which he had received when his head struck the marble altar top but which he claimed marked the place where the messenger of the Lord had kissed him.

The simple folk of Happy Hill were, with few exceptions, convinced that the Rev. McPhule stood in well with the celestial authorities. Nervous and expectant they talked of nothing but The Sign. They were on edge for the great revival scheduled for Election Day at which time they fervently hoped the Lord would make good.

At last the great day had arrived. From far and near came the good people of the countryside on horseback, in farm wagons and battered mud-caked flivvers. Many paused to cast their ballots for Givens and Snobbcraft, not having heard of the developments of the past twenty-four hours, but the bulk of the folk repaired immediately to the sacred grove where the preaching would take place.

Rev. Alex McPhule gloated inwardly at the many concentric circles of upturned faces. They were eager, he saw, to drink in his words of wisdom and be elevated. He noted with satisfaction that there were many strange people in the congregation. It showed that his power was growing. He glanced up apprehensively at the blue heavens. Would The Sign come? Would the Lord answer his prayers? He muttered another prayer and then proceeded to business.

He was an impressive figure today. He had draped himself in a long, white robe with a great red cross on the left breast and he looked not unlike one of the Prophets of old. He walked back and forth in the little circle surrounded by close-packed humanity, bending backward and forward, swinging his arms, shaking his head and rolling his eyes while he retold for the fiftieth time the story of the angel's visit. The man was a natural actor and his voice had that sepulchral tone universally associated with Men of God, court criers and Independence Day orators. In the first row squatted the Happy Hill True Faith Choir of eight young women with grizzled old man Yawbrew, the tub-thumper, among them. They groaned, amened and Yes-Lorded at irregular intervals.

Then, having concluded his story, the evangelist launched into song in a harsh, nasal voice:

I done come to Happy Hill to save you from Sin,
Salvation's door is open and you'd better come in,
Oh, Glory Hallelujah! you'd better come in.
Jesus Christ has called me to save this white race,
And with His Help I'll save you from awful disgrace.
Oh, Glory Hallelujah! We must save this race.

Old man Yawbrew beat on his tub while the sisters swayed and accompanied their pastor. The congregation joined in.

Suddenly Rev. McPhule stopped, glared at the rows of strained, upturned faces and extending his long arms to the sun, he shouted:

"It'll come I tell yuh. Yes Lord, the sign will come – ugh. I know that my Lord liveth and the sign will come – ugh. If – ugh – you just have faith – ugh. Oh, Jesus – ugh. Brothers and Sisters – ugh. Just have faith – ugh – and the Lord – ugh – will answer your prayers… Oh, Christ – ugh. Oh, Little Jesus – ugh… Oh, God – ugh – answer our prayers… Save us – ugh. Send us the Sign…"

The congregation shouted after him "Send us the Sign!" Then he again launched into a hymn composed on the spot:

"He will send the Sign,
Oh, He will send the Sign
Loving Little Jesus Christ
He will send the Sign."

Over and over he sang the verse. The people joined him until the volume of sound was tremendous. Then with a piercing scream, Rev. McPhule fell on all fours and running among the people hugged one after the other, crying "Christ is Love!…He'll send the Sign!…Oh, Jesus! send us The Sign!" The cries of the others mingled with his and there was a general kissing, embracing and rolling there in the green-walled grove under the midday sun.

* * *

As the sun approached its zenith, Mr. Arthur Snobbcraft and Dr. Samuel Buggerie, grotesque in their nondescript clothing and their blackened skins, trudged along the dusty road in what they hoped was the direction of a town. For three hours, now, they had been on the way, skirting isolated farmhouses and cabins, hoping to get to a place where they could catch a train. They had fiddled aimlessly around the wrecked plane for two or three hours before getting up courage enough to take to the highroad. Suddenly they both thrilled with pleasure somewhat dampened by apprehension as they espied from a rise in the road, a considerable collection of houses.

"There's a town," exclaimed Snobbcraft. "Now let's get this damned stuff off our faces. There's probably a telegraph office there."

"Oh, don't be crazy," Buggerie pleaded. "If we take off this blacking we're lost. The whole country has heard the news about us by this time, even in Mississippi. Let's go right in as we are, pretending we're niggers, and I'll bet we'll be treated all right. We won't have to stay long. With our pictures all over the country, it would be suicidal to turn up here in one of these hotbeds of bigotry and ignorance."

"Well, maybe you're right," Snobbcraft grudgingly admitted. He was eager to get the shoe polish off his skin. Both men had perspired freely during their hike and the sweat had mixed with the blacking much to their discomfort.

As they started toward the little settlement, they heard shouts and singing on their left.

"What's that?" cried Dr. Buggerie, stopping to listen.

"Sounds like a camp meeting," Snobbcraft replied. "Hope it is. We can be sure those folks will treat us right. One thing about these people down here they are real, sincere Christians."

"I don't think it will be wise to go where there's any crowds," warned the statistician. "You never can tell what a crowd will do."

"Oh, shut up, and come on!" Snobbcraft snapped. "I've listened to you long enough. If it hadn't been for you we would never have had all of this trouble. Statistics! Bah!"

They struck off over the fields toward the sound of the singing. Soon they reached the edge of the ravine and looked down on the assemblage. At about the same time, some of the people facing in that direction saw them and started yelling "The Sign! Look! Niggers! Praise God! The Sign! Lynch 'em!" Others joined in the cry. Rev. McPhule turned loose a buxom sister and stood wide-eyed and erect. His prayers had come true! "Lynch 'em!" he roared.

"We'd better get out of here," said Buggerie, quaking.

"Yes," agreed Snobbcraft, as the assemblage started to move toward them.

Over fences, through bushes, across ditches sped the two men, puffing and wheezing at the unaccustomed exertion, while in hot pursuit came Rev. McPhule followed by his enthusiastic flock.

Slowly the mob gained on the two Virginia aristocrats. Dr. Buggerie stumbled and sprawled on the ground. A dozen men and women fell upon him while he yelled to the speeding Snobbcraft for help. The angular Snobbcraft kept on but Rev. McPhule and several others soon overtook him.

The two men were marched protesting to Happy Hill. The enthused villagers pinched them, pulled them, playfully punched and kicked them during their triumphant march. No one paid the slightest attention to their pleas. Too long had Happy Hill waited for a Negro to lynch. Could the good people hesitate now that the Lord had answered their prayers?

Buggerie wept and Snobbcraft offered large sums of money for their freedom. The money was taken and distributed but the two men were not liberated. They insisted that they were not Negroes but they were only cudgeled for their pains.

At last the gay procession arrived at the long-unused iron post in front of the general store and post office in Happy Hill. As soon as Mr. Snobbcraft saw the post he guessed its significance. Something must be done quickly.

"We're not niggers," he yelled to the mob. "Take off our clothes and look at us. See for yourself. My God! don't lynch white men. We're white the same as you are."

"Yes, gentlemen," bleated Dr. Buggerie, "we're really white men. We just came from a masquerade ball over at Meridian and our plane wrecked. You can't do a thing like this. We're white men, I tell you."

The crowd paused. Even Rev. McPhule seemed convinced. Eager hands tore off the men's garments and revealed their pale white skins underneath. Immediately apology took the place of hatred. The two men were taken over to the general store and permitted to wash off the shoe polish while the crowd, a little disappointed, stood around wondering what to do. They felt cheated. Somebody must be to blame for depriving them of their fun. They began to eye Rev. McPhule. He glanced around nervously.

Suddenly, in the midst of this growing tenseness, an ancient Ford drove up to the outskirts of the crowd and a young man jumped out waving a newspaper.

"Looky here!" he yelled. "They've found out th' damned Demmycratic candidates is niggers. See here: Givens and Snobbcraft. Them's their pictures. They pulled out in airplanes last night or th' mobs wouldda lynched 'em." Men, women and children crowded around the newcomer while he read the account of the flight of the Democratic standard bearers. They gazed at each other bewildered and hurled imprecations upon the heads of the vanished candidates.

Washed and refreshed, Mr. Arthur Snobbcraft and Dr. Samuel Buggerie, each puffing a five-cent cigar (the most expensive sold in the store) appeared again on the porch of the general store. They felt greatly relieved after their narrow escape.

"I told you they wouldn't know who we were," said Snobbcraft disdainfully but softly.

"Who are you folks, anyway?" asked Rev. McPhule, suddenly at their elbow. He was holding the newspaper in his hand. The crowd was watching breathlessly.

"Why-why-y I'm-a-er-a that is…" spluttered Snobbcraft.

"Ain't that your pichure?" thundered the evangelist, pointing to the likeness on the front page of the newspaper.

"Why no," Snobbcraft lied, "but – but it looks like me, doesn't it?"

"You're mighty right it does!" said Rev. McPhule, sternly, "and it *is* you, too!"

"No, no, no, that's not me," cried the president of the Anglo-Saxon Association.

"Yes it is," roared McPhule, as the crowd closed in on the two hapless men. "It's you and you're a nigger, accordin' to this here paper, an' a newspaper wouldn't lie." Turning to his followers he commanded, "Take 'em. They're niggers just as I thought. The Lord's will be done. Idea of niggers runnin' on th' Demmycratic ticket!"

The crowd came closer. Buggerie protested that he was really white but it was of no avail. The crowd had sufficient excuse for doing what they had wanted to do at first. They shook their fists in the two men's faces, kicked them, tore off their nondescript garments, searched their pockets and found cards and papers proving their identity, and but for the calmness and presence of mind of the Rev. McPhule, the True Faith Christ Lovers would have torn the unfortunate men limb from limb. The evangelist restrained the more hot-headed individuals and insisted that the ceremonies proceed according to time-honored custom.

So the impetuous yielded to wiser counsel. The two men, vociferously protesting, were stripped naked, held down by husky and willing farm hands and their ears and genitals cut off with jack knives amid the fiendish cries of men and women. When this crude surgery was completed, some wag sewed their ears to their backs and they were released and told to run. Eagerly, in spite of their pain, both men tried to avail themselves of the opportunity. Anything was better than this. Staggering forward through an opening made in the crowd, they attempted to run down the dusty road, blood streaming down their bodies. They had only gone a few feet when, at a signal from the militant evangelist, a half-dozen revolvers cracked and the two Virginians pitched forward into the dust amid the uproarious laughter of the congregation.

The preliminaries ended, the two victims, not yet dead, were picked up, dragged to the stake and bound to it, back to back. Little boys and girls gaily gathered excelsior, scrap paper, twigs and small branches while their proud parents fetched logs, boxes, kerosene and the staves from a cider barrel. The fuel was piled up around the groaning men until only their heads were visible.

When all was in readiness, the people fell back and the Rev. McPhule, as master of ceremonies, ignited the pyre. As the flames shot upward, the dazed men, roused by the flames, strained vainly at the chains that held them. Buggerie found his voice and let out yelp after yelp as the flames licked at his fat flesh. The crowd whooped with glee and Rev. McPhule beamed with satisfaction. The flames rose higher and completely hid the victims from view. The fire crackled merrily and the intense heat drove the spectators back. The odor of cooking meat permeated the clear, country air and many a nostril was guiltily distended. The flames subsided to reveal a red-hot stake supporting two charred hulks.

There were in the assemblage two or three whitened Negroes, who, remembering what their race had suffered in the past, would fain have gone to the assistance of the two men but fear for their own lives restrained them. Even so they were looked at rather sharply by some of the Christ Lovers because they did not appear to be enjoying the spectacle as thoroughly as the rest. Noticing these questioning glances, the whitened Negroes began to yell and prod the burning bodies with sticks and cast stones at them. This exhibition restored them to favor and banished any suspicion that they might not be one-hundred-per-cent Americans.

When the roasting was over and the embers had cooled, the more adventurous members of Rev. McPhule's flock rushed to the stake and groped in the two bodies for skeletal souvenirs such as forefingers, toes and teeth. Proudly their pastor looked on. This was the crowning of a life's ambition. Tomorrow his name would be in every newspaper in the United States. God had indeed answered his prayers. He breathed again his thanks as he thrust his hand into his pocket and felt the soothing touch of the hundred-dollar bill he had extracted from Snobbcraft's pocket. He was supremely happy.

AND SO ON AND SO ON

In the last days of the Goosie administration, the Surgeon-General of the United States, Dr. Junius Crookman, published a monograph on the differences in skin pigmentation of the real whites and those he had made white by the Black-No-More process. In it he declared, to the consternation of many Americans, that in practically every instance the new Caucasians were from two to three shades lighter than the old Caucasians, and that approximately one-sixth of the population were in the first group. The old Caucasians had never been really white but rather were a pale pink shading down to a sand color and a red. Even when an old Caucasian contracted vitiligo, he pointed out, the skin became much lighter.

To a society that had been taught to venerate whiteness for over three hundred years, this announcement was rather staggering. What was the world coming to, if the blacks were whiter than the whites? Many people in the upper class began to look askance at their very pale complexions. If it were true that extreme whiteness was evidence of the possession of Negro blood, of having once been a member of a pariah class, then surely it were well not to be so white!

Dr. Crookman's amazing brochure started the entire country to examining shades of skin color again. Sunday magazine supplements carried long articles on the subject from the pens of hack writers who knew nothing whatever of pigmentation. Pale people who did not have blue eyes began to be whispered about. The comic weeklies devoted special numbers to the question that was on everyone's lips. Senator Bosh of Mississippi, about to run again for office, referred several times to it in the Congressional Record, his remarks interspersed with "Applauses." A popular song, "Whiter Than White" was being whistled by the entire nation. Among the working classes, in the next few months, there grew up a certain prejudice against all fellow workers who were exceedingly pale.

The new Caucasians began to grow self-conscious and resent the curious gazes bestowed upon their lily-white countenances in all public places. They wrote indignant letters to the newspapers about the insults and discriminations to which they were increasingly becoming subjected. They protested vehemently against the effort on the part of employers to pay them less and on the part of the management of public institutions to segregate them. A delegation that waited upon President Goosie firmly denounced the social trend and called upon the government to do something about it. The Down-With-White-Prejudice-League was founded by one Karl von Beerde, whom some accused of being the same Doctor Beard who had, as a Negro, once headed the National Social Equality League. Offices were established in the Times Square district of New York and the mails were soon laden with releases attempting to prove that those of exceedingly pale skin were just as good as anybody else and should not, therefore, be oppressed. A Dr. Cutten Prodd wrote a book proving that all enduring gifts to society came from those races whose skin color was not exceedingly pale, pointing out that the Norwegians and other Nordic peoples had been in savagery when Egypt and Crete were at the height of their development. Prof. Handen Moutthe, the eminent anthropologist (who was well known for his popular work on *The Sex Life of Left-Handed Morons among the Ainus*) announced that as a result of his long research among the palest citizens, he was convinced they were mentally inferior and that their children should be segregated from the others in school. Professor Moutthe's findings were considered authoritative because he had spent three entire weeks of hard work assembling his data. Four state legislatures immediately began to consider bills calling for separate schools for pale children.

Those of the upper class began to look around for ways to get darker. It became the fashion for them to spend hours at the seashore basking naked in the sunshine and then to dash back, heavily bronzed, to their homes, and, preening themselves in their dusky skins, lord it over their paler, and thus less fortunate, associates. Beauty shops began to sell face powders named *Poudre Nègre*, *Poudre le Egyptienne* and *L'Afrique*.

Mrs. Sari Blandine (formerly Mme. Sisseretta Blandish of Harlem), who had been working on a steam table in a Broadway Automat, saw her opportunity and began to study skin stains. She stayed away from work one week to read up on the subject at the Public Library and came back to find a recent arrival from Czecho-Slovakia holding down her job.

Mrs. Blandine, however, was not downhearted. She had the information and in three or four weeks time she had a skin stain that would impart a long-wearing light-brown tinge to the pigment. It worked successfully on her young daughter; so successfully, in fact, that the damsel received a proposal of marriage from a young millionaire within a month after applying it.

Free applications were given to all of the young women of the neighborhood. Mrs. Blandine's stain became most popular and her fame grew in her locality. She opened a shop in her front room and soon had it crowded from morning till night. The concoction was patented as Blandine's Egyptienne Stain.

By the time President-Elect Hornbill was inaugurated, her Egyptienne Stain Shoppes dotted the country and she had won three suits for infringement of patent. Everybody that was anybody had a stained skin. A girl without one was avoided by the young men; a young man without one was at a decided disadvantage, economically and socially. A white face became startlingly rare. America was definitely, enthusiastically mulatto-minded.

Imitations of Mrs. Blandine's invention sprang up like weeds in a cemetery. In two years there were fifteen companies manufacturing different kinds of stains and artificial tans. At last, even the Zulu Tan became the vogue among the smart set and it was a common thing to see a sweet young miss stop before a show window and dab her face with charcoal. Enterprising resort keepers in Florida and California, intent on attracting the *haute monde*, hired naturally black bathing girls from Africa until the white women protested against the practice on the ground that it was a menace to family life.

One Sunday morning Surgeon-General Crookman, in looking over the rotogravure section of his favorite newspaper, saw a photograph of a happy crowd of Americans arrayed in the latest abbreviated bathing suits on the sands at Cannes. In the group he recognized Hank Johnson, Chuck Foster, Bunny Brown and his real Negro wife, former Imperial Grand Wizard and Mrs. Givens and Matthew and Helen Fisher. All of them, he noticed, were quite as dusky as little Matthew Crookman Fisher who played in a sandpile at their feet.

Dr. Crookman smiled wearily and passed the section to his wife.

New Action

Nisi Shawl

LOOSING HER HOLD on the knotted strands of the message, its recipient sighed and tilted back her head. Above, the cloudless heavens flickered with light: the sun's reflection off the thousand high-altitude balloons flying over her even here, at the continent's edge.

The message was trouble. A request for connection. She couldn't accept it. She couldn't turn it down, either. She couldn't afford to be known to have read or received it, so she certainly couldn't afford to keep it. But the message carriers' passage was logged on Balloonnet's individual balloons' platforms. Loss, destruction – built-in redundancy handled a certain amount of that, and she'd stayed within statistical bounds when dealing with other such requests. But too many missing drones and there'd be attention, follow-up… She needed to try something different this time.

* * *

Excerpts from the Wikipedia article *The Five Petals of Thought*, accessed April 5, 2028:

> *The Five Petals of Thought, aka the New Bedford Rose, refers to a philosophical system dating back to the late-eighteenth and early-nineteenth centuries widely adopted by activists in Anglophone countries, primarily the US and UK.[1]…*
>
> ***Elements and Structures:*** *The Five Petals of the New Bedford Rose represent Thought, Action (also called "pre-action" and "pro-action"), Observation, Integration, and New Action (also called "re-action"). Thought is the first step in any course. The first petal is thus associated with visualizations, dreams, and all other methods of forming concepts. Action is next; its alternative names of pre-action and pro-action refer to the idea that any action taken will serve as a prequel or prologue to another action. Observation occurs both during and after Action, and provides material for Integration into the original concept. Integration then leads to New Action.[2]*
>
> *Many followers of the New Bedford Rose stipulate its application as cyclical in nature, saying that New Action should be followed again by Observation, Integration, and further New Action.[citation needed]…*
>
> ***Rediscovery:*** *The immensely successful [under review] popular psychology book* The Five Petals of Thought *by Melissa Skye is undoubtedly responsible [under review] for the resurgence of the activist philosophy for which it was named… Translated into twenty languages and also offered in multiple audiobook formats,* The Five Petals of Thought *focuses on personal applications of the philosophy. A brief history section relies heavily on quotations from the works of Elvira Coker and other first-hand participants, and a short chapter speculates on the philosophy's ontological roots in the remnants of its first proponents' African belief systems.[9]*

To date more than 100 million copies of The Five Petals of Thought *have been sold worldwide.*[10]

* * *

Received July 24 2025:
OxfordEgret463326Ninja16072025(EggPearl)(Almond)(MumboSyrup)(forward)

"She found out about us somehow." Willis shook his crinkly chestnut curls back from his sweaty face. July was hot and humid, even here in the Appalachian mountain valleys, even in the shade of the old growth.

Madison nodded. "Yeah! Do I care how? Do you know who Melissa Skye even *is*?"

"She—"

"She wrote the *book*! *Five Petals of Thought*? She brought the Five Petals back – she's why we're *here*!" In her excitement Madison grabbed his arm and Willis had to pry her hand off. "That's the template we used to form our *dopkwe*" – Madison, though white, used the Dahomean word – "for collecting these wild herbs. *Hers*!"

"All I'm sayin' is, if our security's compromised—"

"*Fuck* our security! Drug it and fuck it on the permafrost!"

"You don't really mean that," Junie's voice interrupted. It held half a question. Her small, plump hands held their lunch: tubes of peanut butter and plastic tubs of sliced peaches. Willis took his share and Madison took hers.

"I guess I don't." The white girl slumped down onto her sit-upon. "Just – I'm tired of the Antitrust butting in. They don't own the balloons. They have no right to tell us how many friends to make or seize harvests when someone won't co-operate. Didn't our parents fight for us being able to organize how we wanted?" She opened her tub and set the top aside, unscrewed the tube's cap and set it on its side on the sloping plastic.

Willis reached over and caught the peanut butter cylinder before it rolled off into the dirt. "Sure they fought. Same as their parents, and their parents' parents before them." He stood the cap on its bottom and it stayed on the tub top. Then he opened his own tub and tube. "Fighting ain't winning. Antitrust took last year's sang crop cause they wanted. Cause they could. How we gonna stop it?"

Junie hunkered down beside them. She waved off Willis's offer of a peach slice. "Thanks. I ate while we walked here. So you worried about that message?"

"I am." He tucked his chin to his chest. "The message itself is innocuous enough, but if we're charged with conspiracy to network across state lines we'll need lawyers. No, not if; *when*."

Madison frowned and unhooked her water bottle from her belt. "How would they get conspiracy from an unsolicited message about a care collective in Washington supporting the Rose?" She swallowed a judicious amount of cold water. Too much would cause cramps.

Junie laughed through her nose. "They'd get it by pulling it out their asses. Same as they get everything against us."

She unfolded from her hunker, smooth and graceful as a scissor lift. "And also they'd be talkin' about how Skye had got our internal address."

"That's the big problem," Willis agreed.

"So besides freakin' because we don't know—"

"The simplest solution, that we gave it to her? That, Madison, is what the Antitrust Authority will assume when we file our report with them tonight. That's what they'll use to accuse us of illegal, overextended organizing. Maybe resurrect the charge of harboring 'peripatetic' travelers who keep us in touch. Maybe add it to their list of excuses for shutting down the high-altitude balloon networks."

"Some of those balloon people rich."

"Get ready to make a recommendation back at camp tonight. Last time we all get to be with each other for a while; tomorrow we fan out in small groups till next Gathering Day." Junie moved off in the direction of the rest of the dopkwe, leaving Willis and Madison to eat in silence.

The Five Petals of the New Bedford Rose were Thought, Action, Observation, Integration, and New Action. Meals were a good time for Thought.

Presently Madison spoke. "If Melissa Skye messaged our co-ordinates by chance, there won't be any record of us sending them to her."

"Notoriously difficult to prove a negative such as us *not* sending them, though. In fact, it's impossible." Willis poured water in the peach tub and swirled it around to rinse it, then drank. "Besides, why we have to bring that up? Let's shift the focus. She only forwarded what someone else wrote, right? Maybe by mistake? Maybe she got it by mistake, too – I say we recommend returning the message to the original sender and Observe."

* * *

Excerpts from the Wikipedia article *Balloonnet*, accessed April 5, 2028:

> *Balloonnet refers to the redundant distributed communications system developed by hobbyists and activists primarily in the Northern Hemisphere. High-altitude balloons launch and dock drones carrying occasionally subversive*[citation needed] *messages recorded in a modern dialect of the Incan knot-based language known as khipu or quipu. New Bedford Rose adherents teach khipu encoding and deciphering free of charge… Wealthy amateurs built Balloonnet by expanding on the schedules and experimental practices of pre-existing educational groups, extending balloon flights' durations with superior materials till they became indistinguishable from permanent installations.*[citation needed] *The first khipu payload was recovered on August 25, 2021 (presumably launched shortly before), but subsequently disappeared from the NOAA facility where it was stored.* [citation needed]

* * *

Received July 28 2025:
OxfordEgret463326Ninja16072025(EggPearl)(Almond)(MumboSyrup)(forward)(HappyDust)(forward)

and

Received August 4 2025: StellarRobin880581Cat25072025(EggPearl)(Alto)

"Glitch?"

Donna shook her head no. "The system's too redundant. And we got the pingback twice. There's another East Pomona Care Collective way over in Washington State, and they're who sent this in the first place. So—"

"But they don't have our same co-ordinates – or username!" Spots protested. He slammed the washer door shut and jammed in the start button.

"True!" Donna shouted above the water rushing into the industrial washing machine. "And Washington puts them just about as far away from here in Florida as they could be on the continent."

"Get up. I gotta clean the dryer's lint trap behind where you're sittin'. Don't you think it's kinda coincidental they sent a message how they decided to join the Rose, and it's the very issue we've been talking about?"

"Coincidences happen. Us communications engineers know all about that."

"Sure." Spots balled up the maroon-and-grey lint wad he had scraped from the trap's screen. "But some people here are, I guess you could call 'em superstitious. That's why they scheduled a meeting for a vote on the topic this afternoon, a week ahead of time. Because we got that message last Monday. A week ahead, a week after. You goin'?"

"Of course! A 'yes' decision could put us on the wrong side of the Authority for good. Maybe force them to try to shut us down and seize the building. Which could be a heavy straw placed exactly right on the back of their camel of a regime. You're coming too, yeah?"

Spots shrugged. "I dunno."

"Why not? You use the Five Petals yourself, don't you? Scared that the monitors Antitrust is sending will see you?"

"Not really. And yeah, I use the Petals. Mostly. Look, let's say I'm like Slattery and Prine and Greta and Schrodinger and all them, and I expect the universe to conform to certain laws. I expect if I shoot this lint ball off the ceiling vent and it bounces straight in the wastebasket—" He twirled and executed the bank as he described it. "—that means I'm in tune with the music of the spheres. And *that* means my support of the New Bedford Rose is good and correct, and everything will wind up for the best."

"So?"

Spots opened the dryer door and shoveled warm clothes onto the steel-topped counter opposite. "Help me fold these, please."

"It's my break," Donna complained. But she picked up a pale pink gown and shook its static-y front and back apart.

"Thanks. So I don't think like that. Don't think we're basically one-up on the Antitrust without tryin'. I use the Rose, but I don't *believe* in it. If you get the difference."

"I do. Though I'm not sure an Antitrust officer would. They tend to set it off first, figure out what they're targeting later." She smoothed the tamed gown's fabric, squared its bottom fold with its shoulders and picked a dozen brightly-colored bandanas from the work pile to do next. Simple. But in the time those pieces took her, Spots demolished most of the rest of the pile.

Then her Fitbit chimed. Donna sighed. "Break's over. Incoming."

"Help me finish and I'll go up with you to collect."

One bedsheet left. They danced a minuet with it. Spots loaded their neat stacks of laundry into a basket, bra-and-panty sets on top. Scooping up the basket in his long, skinny arms, he walked it to the dumbwaiter by the steps to the ground floor and started the automatic pulleys that lifted it to the dressing room. "Now let's see what you got."

Their climb up the East Pomona Care Facility's open staircase turned into a race. Running off their nervousness. Breathless and giggling, they spilled out of the door on the roof.

The message drone waited on the far side of the drooping catchnet. Donna retrieved it and reset the notification trigger attached to the net's outermost strand. The practiced motions kept her calm. "This message's fletching's from Stellar Robin 880581 Cat's flock," Donna pronounced. "I like them. They've circumnavigated the globe sixteen times now."

"Why's that good? They learn from experience?"

"Hah. Like they're AIs. No, I guess not."

She read the message. "As I thought. It's about us and the Five Petals again. But I didn't expect..." Long seconds passed.

"Didn't expect what?" Spots peered over Donna's shoulder as if he, too, could read the coded text. Shimmering knots ran up and down its grid, their shifting shapes matching sigils Donna had memorized in her sleep. Her specialty, but Spots could have taken the course too; anyone at the care facility could have, as part of preparing to join the New Bedford Rose. Rumor was Antitrust Authority officers were regular participants.

"It's from the other East Pomona."

"In Washington?!"

"Yeah. Them. The same ones who sent that first message we got 'returned' this morning." She backed up to lean against the wall at the roof's edge. "They – Here, I'll read it.

"'We promise Integration after you incorporate. Help us unfurl the Petals. We will assist you, too, in any way we can. Any way you want. A program to exchange personnel? Recipes? Persecution avoidance? Look for advantages in our mirror-bias geographics.'"

Spots slid from where he'd been leaning beside Donna to sit on the mat of purslane growing beneath the catchnet and out to the wall. "What's all that mean?"

Their feet bruised the purslane's fat, rosy stems and freshened the hot afternoon air with their green smell. "Pretty much what it says. We'd have to axe an existing connection maybe, but no biggie. What's surprising is they decided they had to specifically say it, specifically to us."

"Well, if it's gonna affect our decision to join we got till the meeting at four to share it. If we'd rather the monitors the Authority sends don't get in on the discussion."

"Shouldn't affect anything." Donna scowled. "It's nothing new."

"Maybe they put a secret message inside?"

"Why? Reading messages is a skill taught by the Rose and nobody else."

"Taught to whoever wants to find out how. Plus if texts are cast from one flock to the next they can be intercepted."

"You're talking about what they do with radio waves?" Donna peered down at him, a peculiar but nice sensation. Usually he was looking down at her. "I suppose so. Which is why the idea of secrets is ridiculous. Messages go so many different places. Like they did on the internet before all those businesses took over, back before Neutrality ended.

"If there's anything hidden, anything to what they sent besides the words, it's in the words' context." Donna held out her hands. Spots grabbed them in his and hauled himself upright. "Let's ask some of the residents. They have the best perspective, the most experience."

"Start without me? I should unload the dumbwaiter and check to make sure the washer's gonna stay balanced through the spin cycle. We need to act normal, finish our chores in case Antitrust sends officers early, right?"

"I'll meet you on the second floor. First won't take long."

Fifteen minutes later the two slipped aside her soundproofing curtain and stepped together into Bridie Raymond's room. The resident's thin white plaits hung limply on her substantial bosom. She smiled in their direction. "Miss Donna. With the latest message? And who's that accompanying you? Mr. Spottiswoode?"

"Good guess." Spots cleared his throat. This client was partially blind, which the other staff knew made him uneasy. "I brought you a new spray-on odor remover to try. An experiment." He took the spritzer out of his apron pocket.

Her mouth twitched; smiling or frowning? Both? "Set it on my table. No, the big one by the door."

"Why are you really here?" The black eyes had turned towards Donna. "It isn't class time. Meeting's not for another hour and a half, couple hours."

"We're not actually sure," said Donna. "Could be something in this message?" She read it aloud.

The old woman rearranged herself on her pillows and tilted her head reflectively. "Seems normal. Which is weird, true. Why spend any effort sendin' a message when it's not sayin' anything you ain't already know?"

"What I was wonderin' myself. Want to hear it again?"

"No, no. Nothin' wrong with my memory. You mind me touchin' it?"

Donna handed over the message. Examining it visually and with her fingers, Bridie clucked her tongue. "They tell me these descended from them knotted cords the Incans carried around?"

"Incas and a bunch of people. The way these ones' figures move keep 'em from making sense if you haven't had the latest training. But I *have* had it, and I still don't get more outta this than I read you."

"And you think it's there. Under the surface…" The old woman's fingers combed apart the strands' twisted ends and stopped. "What's this?" Her voice cut sharp as a box knife.

"What's what?" Spots left the wall he'd been ostentatiously lounging against.

"These s'posed to come in pieces like this?" In Bridie's palm lay the straw-like segment of a hollow thread.

A moment of stunned-sounding silence. "No," said Donna. "No, they're not."

They found five other easily removable segments, all on the message's address edge. East Pomona's proper co-ordinates marked the old openings. But the new openings were inscribed with different marks. No one who'd received any version of the New Bedford Rose's reading lessons – recent or obsolete – could decipher them. Clandestine co-ordinates.

None of the rest of the residents they visited saw anything wrong – practically, ethically, or even legally – with what the overt message proposed.

Antitrust sent four officers to monitor the meeting. They arrived a quarter of an hour early, lotioned up with their standard first-line protectant against the sedative gas they always carried. Oily-faced and impassive, they occupied the comfortable seats reserved for them near the common room's exhaust vent and didn't appear to notice Spots hovering by the kitchen's serving hatch, despite performing their usual random credential checks for "peripatetics."

When they left two hours later East Pomona had officially voted to join the New Bedford Rose. When they'd been gone another two hours the meeting reconvened to consider another issue. Arguments took hardly any time. The conclusion reached had two elements: use the strange new inscriptions directing the drone instead of the original ones, and append to the drone's text lattice an affirmative response to the other East Pomona's offer.

* * *

Excerpt from the Wikipedia article *Antitrust Authority*, accessed April 5, 2028:

> ***History:*** *Following the suppression of so-called "freecycle"[3] and "Buy Nothing"[4] associations as competing against them unfairly, retail arms of many for-profit corporations sought further protection from social media-advantaged peer-to-peer distribution modes. Originating as an arm of the Federal Trade Commission's Bureau of Competition, establishment of the Antitrust Authority facilitated regulation of multiple kinds of "overconnectedness," ranging from commercial to cultural to aesthetic linkages.*

* * *

Sent August 4 2025: OxfordEgret463326Ninja04082025(EggPearl)(Amber-Zoo)

"Good. Because we don't know what Antitrust will try next."

Shyreesha shook her head "No" vigorously. "We never do. This way we're prepared when they shut our other addresses down. We can use these clandestine coordinates to communicate. That way we help the rich balloon hobbyists sow confusion."

"Pre-action," Melvin Wembley agreed, standing below the scaffolding where she knelt. "Pro-action. But what about the message to Melissa Skye?"

"Went wrong, I guess." The hopvines mostly curled in tight, clockwise spirals around the poles where they were planted. Then there were these rebels. "Nothing ever came back from her." They ought to just clip them off.

"You sure?"

From kneeling on the scaffold plank with her arms stretched overhead and hips straight, Shyreesha sank back on her heels. There was no reason for her to feel insulted. She reminded herself firmly that Melvin was woke. Softly, without force or rancor, she threw the ball of twine she'd used to tie back a wayward green bine down to where he waited on the ground. "Drones fail. Hawks and other predators—"

"I know, I know." Melvin caught the twine and rewound the loose end. "Anything ready to harvest yet?"

Shyreesha picked a promisingly dry cone and opened it. Golden powder filled the pale cups of its bracteoles. "Yes. Do you have a bag?"

"In a minute." The sound of Melvin brushing along the thickly planted row of hops receded towards the residence. Shyreesha continued to sit on her heels a moment, then began gathering ripe cones from the bines within the scaffold's reach.

Would it work? East Pomona had created four separate identities and joined the Rose under each, serially. Enough false leads? Too many? Each identity had reached its Antitrust Authority-mandated networking limit soon after its creation. The existence of a care facility with the same name clear across the continent was fortuitous – or was it? Distraction or clue? Especially now they'd contacted it directly and issued that invitation.

Melvin returned with a brown paper grocery bag and Shyreesha put the hop cones inside. Then she climbed down and they wheeled the scaffold further out the row.

"Careful of the spuds," Melvin warned her as she drifted too near the neighboring potato hills.

"All right." But Shyreesha's attention was on the road bordering their property. A skimmer stirred dust and light gravel as it approached. It crossed the old cattle guard, turning in. Yellow grass grown up between the road's ruts bent beneath the wind of its lift engines. It was headed for the residence. This was naptime. The kids. She dropped her hold on the scaffold's guide bar and moved to intercept the intruder. Fast.

In front of the ranch-exterior, the building's main elevation, the skimmer came to a stop and lowered itself gently to the ground. Crimson gull-wing doors lifted and twin-clad bureaucrats stepped out. Male-presenting. Tan complexions glowing with protective lotion. "May we speak with the person in charge?" said the one on the left.

"No."

"No such person," Melvin explained, breathing hard from catching up with her. "We're a collective, consensus-ruled."

The officers nodded. Probably they'd known all along there was no use asking. "We're from the Antitrust Authority." That was the one on the left again. "I'm Officer Stitt, and this is my partner, Officer Chumley."

An awkward silence. Neither Shyreesha nor Melvin offered their names.

"Shyreesha Dinan and Melvin Wembley, yes?" No hesitation. Antitrust had easy access to population registers. "We're here to investigate a possible infraction of the citizen connection laws." A shorter silence. "May we come in?"

"No."

Melvin once more explained her answer. "Our kids are lying down right now; it's quiet time. Questioning us might disturb them." And the gas in the canisters Antitrust officers carried was worse for minors than adults.

"All right," said Chumley. "Suit yourself. We can request a warrant."

Shyreesha's smile made no effort to look sincere. "And when you get it back and downloaded and printed you won't need it; we only have them sack out an hour. Twenty minutes left. Whynchou come sit with us by the duck pond till then?"

"I'll get us some lemonade," Melvin volunteered, heading for the front door at top speed.

Exchanging a loaded look, Stitt and Chumley followed Shyreesha around the house's far side to the fenced-in pond. Steps led up from the top of a stile to a gated balcony jutting from the roof of a low structure smelling of grain, mud, and duck shit. An awning provided shade to the balcony, and alders provided it to the water below. Plastic barrels and wooden crates topped with cushions were scattered around on the balcony's bare boards; Shyreesha gestured to the officers to have seats on them.

"So what can I tell you that you don't already know?" she asked, lowering herself to balance lightly on an empty olive barrel.

Officer Stitt tilted his head and gazed downward, body language evocative of self-deprecation. "Start with the basics, I guess. What do you call this place?"

Shyreesha stared at him warily. "We got a few names. Cause we does a few things."

"Let's cut the crap." Chumley pulled aside his tunic's top lapel and grabbed a fist of hardcopy. "We have you listed in our files three times." They'd missed an iteration. "Each listing admits to lateral connections with six suppliers, six outlets, six promotional associates, six financial affiliates, and one uncategorized organization. No replication. That's seventy-five total, making this location a real danger."

Shyreesha frowned and tucked her chin in like she was refusing a plate of spoiled food. "Danger to what?"

Stitt replied, "To the inherent hierarchy of government. You want to fight human nature."

He licked his thumbnail screen awake and read a quote from *The Five Petals of Thought*: "'Widespread lateral networks are able to prove that equality is stronger, overall, than inequality.' We're not giving you that chance."

Leaning forward, she said, "Could be just a misunderstanding. We call this here East Pomona Care Facility on most forms, but there's near as many names as we got members."

"But you're registered—"

"Hey! Anybody wanna help me?" Melvin's shouting interrupted the interrogation. "My hands are full and the gate swung shut." Shyreesha rose from her barrel, but Chumley beat her to the head of the steps. When he came back he bore a glass jar of sugar cookies lifted off the tray of mugs Melvin brought up behind him.

"'Scuse me." Melvin set the tray on a crate and picked up two sweating, near-full mugs by their handles.

"Oh, no." Chumley pursed his lips and Stitt pressed his together tight. "We couldn't. Not while we're working."

"Why? It ain't alcohol." He thrust them in the officers' faces. They took them, but didn't drink.

Melvin and Shyreesha took up theirs. "Cheers." Both swallowed big gulps and let out satisfied-sounding sighs. Melvin scooted a crate closer in from the rickety-looking railing and sat.

"Human nature." Shyreesha lifted her mug again, this time taking a mere sip. "It's complicated. You got lots of components. Some of 'em contradictory." She broke apart a sugar cookie and pointed at the pond below with its white crescent. "Society determines which parts of your nature get the most play."

"Ummm…" Stitt and Chumley exchanged another glance. "Right. So are you saying you deliberately subverted the law?" Stitt asked.

"'You're certainly at liberty to consider me a virgin if you like; I've been corn-holed.'"

Again Melvin translated. "That's a line from her favorite porno. Means she doesn't care for the question's root assumptions."

"Well she's not going to care for anything else we're asking either." Chumley inhaled the sweetly acid aroma of the lemonade but still held off from tasting it. He set it down on an empty barrel top, distancing the temptation. "'Root assumptions'? Got 'em. We assume the law's right. We assume we get to enforce it. We assume you owe us some answers." His voice hardened with each statement. "We assume you're going to give them to us whether you—"

"Now Herman," Stitt interrupted. "You catch more flies with honey than vinegar, as my aunt always said."

"What's that supposed to—"

Loud quacks burst from the pond like farts, drowning the officer out. The ducks contended against one another for some invisible advantage. Wings beat, beaks stabbed, water spouted up and splashed back down. Then the waves and noise subsided, leaving the ducks swimming cordially together as if nothing had happened.

"Very hierarchical animals, ducks," Melvin observed. "Humans, not so much."

"You think so?" Officer Stitt set his untouched mug next to Chumley's. "Why?"

Shyreesha finished her mug and slammed it down on the balcony's floor. "Ever hear of a concept called '*mudita*'?"

"No, can't say we have."

"Google it. Sort of the opposite idea of schadenfreude, which you guys keep in wide circulation. It's like a particular kind of empathy – joy in another's pleasure." She grinned. "According to the copy of your interning script I read, I am going to *mudita* the hell out of what happens next."

Scooping up the mug she'd just deposited Shyreesha leapt to her feet. She crouched, knees bent, arms wide, and sprang over the intervening space at Officer Stitt. They crashed together against the balcony's rail – which held.

"Reesha!" cried Melvin. He rose too. Tried to.

"Sit! Hands up!" Chumley ordered him. He pushed him back down to make him obey. "And you – Ms Dinan – stop! You're under arrest!"

Shyreesha looked up from her embrace of the other officer, eyes wide and angelic. She drew back the fist with the mug in it and smashed it against Stitt's head. Got in two more blows before Chumley ripped the top off of his gas canister.

Soundlessly, stainlessly, the nitrous oxide derivative it contained expanded outward. This sedative's contact vector was quick-absorbing – Officer Chumley barely had time to pull on his mask. Stitt's only protection was the chemical in the lotion Antitrust made them rub on their skin before field assignments. The injured officer inhaled the gas helplessly; Chumley accepted that was probably for the best. The aerosol component worked more slowly, but its analgesic properties would combat any pain from Stitt's wounds. And there'd be no permanent harm; as the woman had alluded, part of Antitrust Authority officers' training involved exposing themselves to this stuff. NewNight, which was what its manufacturers called the gas, wore off in a couple of hours.

Not this fast, though. Not so fast Shyreesha should be sitting up clear-eyed. Not so fast that Melvin remained erect on his crate rather than sliding off half-conscious.

"You oughta had some lemonade." The impervious man pointed at the officers' abandoned mugs. "If you hadn't suspected poison you'd be full of our antidote."

Officer Chumley protested the impossibility of an effective antidote to NewNight the best he could with his mask muffling his mouth. "Here, lemme help you." The woman snatched it off and tossed it to the ducks. Chumley scrambled to the balcony's edge but it was gone, a floating smudge in the pond's shining black-and-algae-green surface, dully translucent and drifting deeper, deeper, deeper, deeper.

"You hurt?" Melvin asked Shyreesha.

"Couple of splinters. I barely feel 'em. Messages sent?"

"I think the drones needed brushin' up, raise their charges so they reach the right berths. Kids are still workin' on them – they'll get 'em away before this wears off, though." He tapped Officer Chumley politely on one shoulder. "You want to stand up."

"Yes." NewNight made its recipients amazingly suggestible.

"You want to check how your buddy's doing." It helped if the suggestions matched the recipients' own desires.

Chumley walked to Stitt's side and knelt. No blood. The prone officer rolled over at his colleague's prodding. His eyes stayed closed. Chumley slapped weakly at his cheeks. "I'd better bring him to a medic."

"You hit him that hard?" Melvin asked Shyreesha.

"Hell no! With *this*?" She showed him the mug she'd used. Half of it had crumbled apart. "Papier mâché, remember? I did pound him with it, though, just like we practiced. Maybe the dose we coated it in was too high? But, you know, I'm feelin' good on about the same amount."

Melvin returned his attention to the fallen officer. "You want to wake up." Stitt's eyes opened and he levered himself from the floor.

"You found what you were looking for. Now you want to leave."

* * *

Excerpts from the Wikipedia article *Message drones*, accessed April 5, 2028:

Technical developments: *The ability to store kinetic power and derive it from human manipulation ("stroking" and "petting") were added almost simultaneously. Most credit these innovations to the same cohort of Five Petals followers that helped configure the original enthusiasts' haphazard high-altitude balloon flights into the current Balloonnet... Early and middle period address protocols relied on idiosyncratic impressions on freshly exposed string-end-sockets made by hand-cast tools. These tools, created by scattered artists, never conformed to a set standard. However, their individuality helped protect information subject to unwelcome government scrutiny, particularly important during the period in which tracking programs were monitored. Along with the frequent revisions of knot codes and the institution of multiple clandestine addresses, these highly interpretable sigils helped disseminate the practical lessons of the New Bedford Rose more widely even than Skye's bestselling book.*

* * *

Received August 1 2025: StellarRobin880581Cat25072025(EggPearl)(Beaver)

and

Sent August 11 2025: DancingPeacock907019Eel11082025(MumboSyrup)(Antler-Zinc)

Melissa sighed. That worrisome message from East Pomona had gone back to them by way of her attempt at giving it an imaginary address. The recipients it reached had been real. They'd forwarded it to a different East Pomona, which may have been what triggered an even more problematic message to that second East Pomona than the first one. How did she know the new message was even more problematic? Because she had a copy on her lap. They'd sent it to her complete with secret co-ordinate sets, and she'd read it, and kept it for the last ten days—

She sank her forehead onto her clenched fists, then knuckled her tightly closed eyes. She had *tried*. Writing *The Five Petals of Thought* was just supposed to make her rich. Yes, the New Bedford Rose was revolutionary and yes, she cared about it. Yes, in the past it had changed lives, spread around the world, probably changed the course of history: hard to imagine women's suffrage succeeding, or the civil rights movement, or the defeat of Belgium's Leopold, without it. Those, though, had all been before her time.

And yes, the Rose challenged the current government's fundamental precepts. But.

But she had her place in the scheme of things. She couldn't afford to lose it. She had her wins: this school, her home, her favorite charities. Health care providers who paid attention to her complaints.

Another sigh escaped her. Here on the hillside where she always lunched and breakfasted, always examined the latest messages, Melissa's view of New Ramblin's precincts fell before her like a rumpled tapestry: the red horse barn, the white goathouse, the chicken coop, dronecote, bath, woodshed, and workshops connected by flagstone paths; the pool and boathouse; the commissary. The clinic being built down near the main entrance. All those neat and oddly assorted visions: the commissary like a Black Forest cottage, dripping with faux gingerbread and windowed with sugary panes; the circular dorm with its circus tent roofline; and all the eccentric rest. Born of Thought, Action, Observation, and Integration. Persisting via Pro- or Pre-action, on her part or on the part of some other member of the Rose. Now for something New. She set aside the message that had meant another round of trouble.

Would the school go on without her? Could it?

One way to find out. One deliberately provocative way. Accept an illicitly high number of connections.

Shaking her head at what she was doing, Melissa turned and lifted the top drone off the fifty-plus crated beside her. Now where?...she found and opened the pen cushion compartment of the message kit on the wooden table beside her. Running her fingers over her pen's heads she selected the right one and thrust its point into a hollow thread's opening. Repeated the sequence for each of the other address threads. Then she stroked the wings on either side of the drone's body till she felt sure they were charged with enough kinetics to make it to the nearest balloon with a drone booster berth. And lifted it up and released it on the wind.

Ten Pieces

Ran Walker

Scenes in Afrosurrealism

I AM THAT OFF-KILTER SCENE from the movie where you know some weird shit is about to go down 'cause you can hear the swelling horns of Minnie Riperton's "Les Fleurs" building up in the background like a nut about to get busted, and those of us who like that Twilight Zone shit sit up in our seats and say, "Yes!" or "Bring it, Lakeith!" and Blerds glow like freshly shaved domes, and the celebration of being seen and felt resonates like light from a star a billion miles away.

Black Matter, or a Moment in Time

He misses her in the quiet moments of night, when the city sleeps just beyond his window sill. The electric glow of downtown hums the melody of her moans, and he smiles, remembering her like he would a favorite song playing on the radio at the most unexpected moment.

Does she think of him anymore, or has the world shrunk her memories of him into a footnote of her heart?

The only thing they now share is yesterday, a yesterday that struggles to echo into the present, except, at least for him, when the night, like a cinematic screen, beckons him, city soundtrack pulsing in the background, reminding him of when only the two of them mattered.

Astronaut: A Tanka

He is lost in the space between them, galaxies and stars and black holes. He longs to get home to her, breathe her atmosphere again.

Planet 4 C

Pick and pat. Pick and pat.

Doneisha's hands moved about Imani's seven-year-old head, taking the beautiful chaos of coiled hair and shaping it as the Creator might have once crafted the universe, her brown fingers moving like those of her mother and her mother's mother, liberating every strand to stand at its full potential.

"Mommy, is it done?"

"Almost."

"Please make it perfect."

The sphere gradually emerged, a celestial body born into their tiny sliver of the universe.

"Done."

Doneisha lifted the mirror to Imani's face, watching the reflection of her daughter's eyes, twin spheres filled with constellations of joy.

The Girl in Vernon Park

She vaguely remembered meeting the woman when she was eight. She was sitting on a swing in Vernon Park, staring up into the dusky sky, when the woman had approached. She couldn't remember what the woman had said, though.

Now, thirty years later, she found herself walking back towards Vernon Park, where the younger version of herself sat on a swing, staring up into the dusky sky. She had to warn the little girl about the impending danger, how humans would have to leave Earth or jump through time to avoid its fate.

She hoped she wouldn't forget this time.

Apocalyptic Ambivalence

Each day the horrors they woke to grew exponentially: the community water jugs had been stolen by marauders, food had grown scarcer, and some of them were now too sick to move.

McKafree had considered running away and taking his chances in the Desert of Death, beyond the Fellowship Walls, but the thought of facing the horrors out there by himself was scarier than the horrors themselves.

He'd stay put, nursing the sick, praying for the gods to release the rains and to strike down their enemies. He'd do what he'd always done, what he'd been trained to do: nothing.

Light Speed

She stared at him, admiring his physique and his dark complexion. She knew, without question, she would take him home with her.

He, on the other hand, knew if she ever asked him, he would go anywhere she wanted to go.

After all, he'd never been on a spaceship before.

The View From Here

Dusk wears many colors: violet, magenta, cyan, navy, orange, and even midnight. Above this blanket, stars settle like diamonds spread across a picnic blanket. Anita has no desire to be any closer to heaven than she already is. She has learned that sometimes the closer you get to something, the less impressive it is. She doesn't want to know the trick of it all, where the rabbit rests, awaiting the magician to lift it by its ears from a top hat. She plants her feet firmly on earth, anchoring herself to the place where everything can be beautiful and surreal.

Finity

She stares into the night, as if anticipating that a comet might streak the sky, always aware of the moon's phase. Some nights she can see only darkness above, the clouds seemingly erasing the universe's majesty in a single stroke. Other nights she can see nearly every constellation, the sky so clear it feels there is nothing separating her from space.

He sits next to her, holding her hand, wanting to say something so grand that it measures up to the miracles overhead, but he is left with English's twenty-six lowly letters, which can only be arranged in finite ways.

Afrofutura

Your lips are the dreamy synths of a 70s Stevie Wonder song. Your tongue sends me out into a galaxy contained within a single drop of dew, pooled along the vein of a leaf. You can tell me anything, and I will follow you. I breathe you like an intoxicant, your body pulling me towards the heavens, and there you electrify every cell of my being with your touch, ecstasy rolling in waves, crashing against moon rocks, beating our souls against these sinful shores.

But we are not making love on the ceiling.

The house is simply upside down.

Biographies & Sources

Nisi Shawl
Foreword
New Action
(Originally published in *e-flux Journal*, Issue 93, September 2018)
Nisi Shawl (they/them) is the multiple award-winning author and editor of over a dozen books of speculative fiction and related nonfiction. They co-wrote *Writing the Other: A Practical Approach*, a basis for classes taught with K. Tempest Bradford. Shawl's best-known fiction is the Nebula Award finalist *Everfair*. Recent books include Middle Grade historical fantasy *Speculation* (2023), *Everfair* sequel *Kinning*, Beat-era fantasy novella *The Day and Night Books of Mardou Fox*, and space opera novel-in-stories *Making Amends*. Editing credits include the acclaimed anthologies *New Suns* and *New Suns 2*. They've spoken at Duke University, Spelman College, and many other institutions.

Dr. Sandra M. Grayson
Associate Editor and Introduction
Dr. Sandra M. Grayson is a tenured Full Professor in the English Department at University of Wisconsin-Milwaukee. Her numerous publications include the books *Visions of the Third Millennium*; *Symbolizing the Past*; *A Literary Revolution*; and *Sparks of Resistance, Flames of Change*.

Isis Asare
Contributing Editor
Isis Asare is the CEO/Founder of Sistah Scifi, the first Black-owned US bookstore focused on science fiction and fantasy in the US as validated by the American Booksellers Association. Concurrently, Asare serves as the Executive Director of Aunt Lute Books, an intersectional, non-profit feminist press. Asare holds degrees from Stanford, Harvard and Columbia. Asare's hometown is Harlem, New York, she resides in Oakland, CA, in the San Francisco Bay Area, and has an extensive community in Seattle, WA, Washington, DC, and Atlanta, GA.

Abíọ̀dún Abdul
Forward Agenda
(Originally published in *Writers Space Africa*, 2023)
Abíọ́dún (pronounced A-byaw-doon) is a Yorùbá-Nigerian writer and UNESCO Global Poetry Slam Champion 2022. She also writes life essays and memoir-polemic series 'Stained Glass Eyes: Race, Family and Multiculturalism' encompassing her schooling across Yorùbá-Nigeria, Scots-Britain and Japan (achieved through a Japanese Government scholarship). Book 1 is nearing publication and Book 2 comprises her PhD research funded by a UoN Faculty of Arts Scholarship. She posts diasporic travel stories on her web platform Yorùbá Yonder, through which she also conceived her event series focusing on cultural and social themes of Yorùbá/Nigeria/Africa/Diaspora: YNAD Talks. Her other educational projects include 'What Colour Are Your Senses? (WCAYS)' and 'The Scottish Racism Project (ScRaP)'. She has been published in anthologies; writes/podcasts for literary magazines; performs at literary festivals/events;

delivers writing workshops; and presents at academic conferences. More at: yorubayonder.com and instagram.com/abiodunoa.

Linda D. Addison
Twice, At Once, Separated
(Originally published in *Dark Matter*. Copyright © Linda D. Addison 2000. Reprinted by permission of the author.)
Linda D. Addison is a five-time recipient of the HWA Bram Stoker Award®, including for *The Place of Broken Things* and *How To Recognize A Demon Has Become Your Friend*, recipient of HWA Lifetime Achievement Award, HWA Mentor of the Year and SFPA Grand Master of Fantastic Poetry. Her site: LindaAddisonWriter.com.

Aishatu Ado
Revolution in the Soil
(First Publication)
The Grief Pilgrim
(First Publication)
Aishatu Ado is an Afro-German author, poet, and peace technologist, who advocates for social justice. She is the 2025 winner of the 68th Jerry Jazz Musician Short Fiction Contest and a 2025 Clarion West fellow. Her work has earned support from fellowships with Tin House, VONA, Voodoonauts, Roots Words Wounds, and the Hurston/Wright Foundation. Her work is published or forthcoming in *Obsidian*, Kelp Books' 2025 *Ocean Poetry Anthology*, and *Liminal Spaces*. More at: aishatu.carrd.co.

John Akomfrah
The Last Angel of History
(Originally released in 1995 as a 45-minute documentary film. Copyright © Smoking Dogs Films.)
Sir John Akomfrah (b. 1957) is a director, screenwriter, artist, curator, teacher and a founder of the Black Audio Film Collective (1982–98). Born in Ghana, he moved with his mother to the UK to escape the aftermath of the military coup that led to the death of his father, a supporter of the ousted independent leader. This helped shaped his work, which deals with post-colonial politics, race and identity in radical, pioneering and poetic ways. He has received awards, honours and a knighthood in recognition of his contribution to film and art. His work is held in major collections, and notable pieces include *Handsworth Songs* (1986), *The Last Angel of History* (1996; written and researched by co-founder of the BAFC Edward George) and *The Unfinished Conversation* (2013).

Azure Arther
Flight Pattern
(Originally published in *Uncharted*, March 2024)
The Adoration of Random Strangers
(Originally Published in *Nightlight*, September 2023)
When she's not bumbling through a mystical realm, Azure Arther is a mom, playwright, author, poet, and, occasionally, a dryad. Her short stories and poems have appeared or are forthcoming in dozens of publications, including *midnight & indigo*, *Aurealis*, and *Zooscape*. She is an editor for Augur Literary Society and has been a resident artist or scholarship recipient for numerous organizations. You can keep up with her at azurearther.com.

Eugen Bacon
The Water Runner
(Originally published in *Danged Black Thing*, 2021, Transit Lounge Publishing)
Eugen Bacon is an African Australian author. She's a Solstice, British Fantasy and Foreword Book of the Year Award winner, a twice World Fantasy Award finalist, and a finalist in the Shirley Jackson, Philip K. Dick Award, and the Nommo Awards for speculative fiction by Africans. Eugen is an Otherwise Fellow, and was also announced in the honor list for 'doing exciting work in gender and speculative fiction'. *Danged Black Thing* made the Otherwise Award Honor List as a 'sharp collection of Afro-Surrealist work'. Visit her at eugenbacon.com.

Steven Barnes
Danakil
(First Publication)
Steven Barnes is an award-winning, *New York Times* bestselling author of over 35 novels, including his most recent, the Star Wars novel *The Glass Abyss*. He is also a stress performance counselor holding black belts in three different martial arts, and husband of *Los Angeles Times* book-award-winning novelist Tananarive Due. They live in Southern California with their son Jason.

Kayla Baskins
Easel Isle
(First Publication)
Kayla Baskins is a budding new author who lives in South Carolina with her incredible husband, Jeffrey, their three inspiring children, and their delightfully awkward cat. She works as a substitute teacher in a charming small town, and lives a fairly typical life with a wildly atypical mind. She is currently working to finish *Malena and the Isles*, a novella that begins with 'Easel Isle'. In short, she can be described as a mother that creates, a wife that reads, and a writer who is just getting started.

Maurice Broaddus
The Migration Suite: A Study in C Sharp Minor
(Originally published in *Uncanny Magazine*, 2019)
A librarian, editor, and community Afrofuturist, Maurice Broaddus's work has appeared in places like *Lightspeed Magazine*, *Magazine of F&SF*, *Asimov's Magazine*, *Uncanny Magazine*, Jordan Peele's *Out There Screaming*, *The End of the World As We Know It: New Tales of Stephen King's The Stand*, and *Black Panther: Tales from Wakanda*. His books include Marvel's *Black Panther: T'Challa Declassified*, *Sweep of Stars*, *Breath of Oblivion*, *A City Dreaming*, *Unfadeable*, *Pimp My Airship*, *Buffalo Soldier*, and *The Usual Suspects*. (MauriceBroaddus.com.)

Alan Ceaser
Kemi and the Sacred Amulet: Collected Patakí Vol. 1
(First Publication)
Dr. Alan Ceaser is a licensed clinical psychologist, cognitive neuroscientist, and writer based in Huchiun, the ancestral homeland of the Confederated Villages of Lisjan, now known as the East Bay, specifically in Oakland, California. His work explores the intersection of Black wellness, spirituality, and speculative futures. A descendant of Southern Black and German lineage, Alan weaves psychological insight with Afrofuturist imagination to challenge

dominant narratives and envision liberatory possibilities. When he is not writing or in session, he's often dreaming, tending to his sons, or paying respect to the ocean. This is his first fiction publication.

Tiffany M. Davis
Nikki's Rockin' Rocket Curls and Cuts
(First Publication)
Tiffany M. Davis is a Georgetown University alumna who has self-published four fiction novels in three genres and was a contributing author for three non-fiction anthologies. She was a panel participant at FIYAHCon and has served as a book reviewer for AALBC.com and QBR, where she also served as Senior Editor. Her coverage of the WNBA and NBA has been published in *Sports Illustrated* and *Ms. Magazine*. She is a member of Zeta Phi Beta Sorority, Inc, and the National Coalition of 100 Black Women. She lives on the east coast of the United States. You can read some of her other works on her Substack.

Samuel R. Delany
The Einstein Intersection
(First published in 1967 by Ace Books. In the present publication, the extract is reprinted from pages 1–63 of *The Einstein Intersection* © 1998 by Samuel R. Delany. Published by Wesleyan University Press. Used by permission.)
Delany (b. 1942) is a popular American writer and literary critic. His love for science fiction began early in his life – his first short story, 'Salt', was published in *Dynamo*, Bronx Science's literary magazine in 1960. His first novel, *The Jewels of Aptor*, was published in 1962, meaning he was a successfully published science fiction author by the time he was 20. This catapulted him into a successful and critically acclaimed career as a sci-fi author. Notable works include *Babel-17* (1966), *The Einstein Intersection* (1967), *Hogg* (1995) and *Nova* (1968).

Yazeed Dele-Azeez
Eyes of a Living Planet
(First Publication)
Yazeed Dele-Azeez is a Nigerian writer of Africanfuturism. His works have featured in three foreign translations of *Future Fiction* magazine and the EcoCast podcast anthology of ASLE (Association for the Study of Literature and Environment). His recent work has been published in Flame Tree's *Anansi* anthology. He was an inaugural finalist of the Analog Award for Emerging Black Voices. He lives in Abuja.

Tananarive Due
Like Daughter
(Originally published in *Dark Matter,* edited by Sheree R. Thomas. © 2000 by Tananarive Due. Reprinted by permission of the author.)
A leading voice in Black speculative fiction, Due has won an American Book Award, an NAACP Image Award and a British Fantasy Award. Her books include *The Reformatory* (winner of a Los Angeles Times Book Prize, Chautauqua Prize, Bram Stoker Award, World Fantasy Award, and a New York Times Notable Book), *The Wishing Pool and Other Stories*, *Ghost Summer: Stories, My Soul to Keep* and *The Good House*. She and her late mother, Patricia Stephens Due, co-authored *Freedom in the Family: A Mother-Daughter Memoir of the Fight for Civil Rights*.

Christian Emecheta
The Heartware Protocol
(First Publication)
Christian Emecheta is a multifaceted creator who blends writing, illustration, and computer science. His fiction and poetry grace prestigious publications including *Arts Lounge Magazine*, *Step Away Magazine*, and *The Decolonial Passage*. He is also a published contributor to *The Brussels Review*, FarmGirl Press, Cranked Anvil Press, Walden's Poetry and Reviews, and Mocking Owl Roost, among other publications too numerous to mention. Christian finds inspiration through reading, film, and the boundless landscapes of his imagination.

Naomi Eselojor
The Seventy-Year-Old Corpse Harvester
(Originally published in *Dark Matter Magazine*, March 2023)
Naomi Eselojor is a speculative fiction writer from Nigeria. She is the winner of the 2023 Utopian award for short fiction and the Wilson Okereke's Prize for short stories. Naomi's works have appeared in Flame Tree's *African Ghost* anthology, 2022 *Best of Utopian Science Fiction Anthology* by Android Press, *Omenana Magazine*, *Lolwe*, *Hexagon Magazine*, *Dark Matter Magazine* and elsewhere. A Nommo Award finalist, Naomi's works have been nominated for the Pushcart Prize, Ako Caine Prize and the Utopian Awards. Naomi is an alum of Milford Writer's Workshop and Voodoonauts Fellowship and was a Spring mentor in 2024.

Minister Faust
The Worth of a Nation
(Originally published in *E-Force*, 2013)
The critically acclaimed author of *The Alchemists of Kush* and the Kindred Award-winning and Philip K. Dick runner-up *Shrinking the Heroes*, Minister Faust first won accolades for his debut *The Coyote Kings of the Space-Age Bachelor Pad*, shortlisted for the Locus Best First Novel and Philip K. Dick awards. Minister Faust's short stories have appeared in *Cyber World*, *Edmonton on Location*, *Fiery Spirits*, *Griots: A Sword and Soul Anthology*, *Mothership: Tales from Afrofuturism and Beyond*, and elsewhere. *Adventure Rocketship*, *iO9, Canada 150: Stories of Reconciliation Connecting Us All*, *Engineer Magazine*, *The Globe & Mail*, Greg Tate's *Coon Bidness*, and more have published his articles. Minister Faust's Afritopianism (the term he created to replace 'Afrofuturism', a word coined by a non-African, because 'self-description is the first step of self-determination') draws from myriad ancient African civilizations, explores present realities, and imagines a future in which people struggle not only for justice, but for the stars.

Gabrielle Emem Harry
Familiar Planet
(Originally published in *Solarpunk Magazine*, 2023)
Gabrielle Emem Harry is a Nigerian speculative fiction writer. She won the 2024 Nommo Short Story Award, was shortlisted for the 2024 Writivism Short Story Prize, was longlisted for the 2025 BSFA award, selected as a 2024 Voodoonauts Fellow and a 2023 LLEAA Fellow. Her work has appeared or is forthcoming in *Strange Horizons*, *Logic(s)*, *The Year's Best African Speculative Fiction Volume 3*, *Afterlives: The Year's Best Death Fiction*, Flame Tree's *African Short Ghost Stories* anthology, *Omenana*, *Apparition*, *Isele* and more. Her favourite stories are the ones that feel like dreams.

Akua Lezli Hope
Invocations and Car Songs
(First Publication)
Timbuctoo
(First Publication)
Akua Lezli Hope, a Grand Master of Fantastic Poetry (SFPA), wisdom seeker, and paraplegic creator of poems, patterns, stories, music, and sculpture, has been in print since 1974. Her collections include *Embouchure: Poems on Jazz and Other Musics* (Writer's Digest Book Award), *THEM GONE, & Otherwheres* (Elgin Award). Her honors include NEA & NYFA fellowships; SFPA, Rhysling, CRITTER & IGNYTE awards; and NYSCA grants. She created the Speculative Sundays Poetry Reading Series & edited *NOMBONO: An Anthology of Speculative Poetry by BIPOC Creators*, the first of its kind. Her collection *Telepath* will be published by Gnashing Teeth Publishing in 2026. See more at akualezlihope.com.

Pauline E. Hopkins
The Mystery within Us
(Originally published in *The Colored American Magazine*, Vol. 1, May 1900)
Raised in Boston, Massachusetts, acclaimed African-American novelist and intellectual Pauline Elizabeth Hopkins (1859–1930) first rose to prominence as a playwright and performer before later turning to journalism and literature. Her use of the romantic novel as a medium by which to explore race and social issues, through works such as *Contending Forces: A Romance Illustrative of Negro Life North and South,* made her a pioneer of her time. As an editor and director of *Colored American Magazine*, she wielded significant literary and cultural influence, and went on to write stories and articles for a number of other magazines.

Melissa Jackson-Wagner
Hum
(Originally published in *The Dinesh Prize for Short Fiction 2023: Music Stories*)
Melissa Jackson-Wagner is a Guyanese-British retired academic who holds a PhD in Caribbean Literature. Her work has consistently centred the nuanced histories of Caribbean diasporas within academia and beyond. She has worked as a consultant on issues surrounding multiracial identities and was a guest on the *Mixed Up* podcast. Her poetry appears in *Wasafiri*, and *The Half of It: Exploring the Mixed-Race Experience*, 2024 and her first short story 'Soucouyant' appears in *Glimpse: An Anthology of Black British Speculative Fiction*, 2022. 'Hum', included in this anthology, was shortlisted for The Dinesh Allirajah Prize for Short Fiction, 2023.

Tenea D. Johnson
Foundling
(Originally published in *Sycorax's Daughters*, edited by Linda Addison, Kinitra Brooks, PhD and Susana Morris, PhD. Cedar Grove Publishing, 2017. Also published in *Broken Fevers*, Rosarium Publishing, 2021.)
Tenea D. Johnson is a multimedia storyteller, musician, editor, poet, arts and empowerment entrepreneur, and award-winning author of speculative fiction. Her work includes *Incandescence*, a sci fi/dance film collaboration; *Frequencies, a Fiction Album*; and *Broken Fevers*, of which *Publisher's Weekly* wrote "the hard-hitting, memorable short stories in this powerhouse collection…are astounding in their originality." *Smoketown*, her debut novel, won the Parallax Award while *R/evolution* earned an honorable mention

that year. She's performed at venues including the Public Theater. Follow what's next at teneadjohnson.com.

B.T. Karuma
Gilded Throne on a Mound of Ash
(First Publication)
The Devil's Metamorphosis
(First Publication)
B.T. Karuma is a Zimbabwean speculative fiction writer. One of his stories was published in the *African Ghost Short Stories* anthology (Flame Tree Publishing). Another story appeared in the *Ibua Journal* after it was longlisted in the Bold 2023 Continental Call: Climate Change. His story 'Demon of False Hope' was longlisted for the 2024 Afritondo Short Story Prize and published in the anthology *Travelling Men Don't Die*. Other stories have been published online in *Lolwe* and *Afritondo*. Before exploring writing, he worked in electrical power generation, distribution, and control. He has master's and bachelor's degrees in electrical and electronic engineering.

Astra Lee
Underground Railroad of Entanglement
(First Publication)
Astra is a Haitian-American storyteller who never misses a chance to lean in for a good story. Much of her work lives quietly on Google Drive or her trusted A. Plaud listening device, safeguarded by her reluctance to be so vulnerable with strangers. Her writing once appeared in the now-defunct *3Moon Magazine*. Astra's work is an invitation to witness her inner world: private thoughts, deepest fears, quiet insecurities, hidden madness, and hesitant hope. Her writing is deeply influenced by the works of Octavia Butler, R.F. Kuang, Tochi Onyebuchi, Rivers Solomon, and the expansive speculative worlds of *Star Trek*.

Kyoko M.
Comfort
(Originally published in *Cyberfunk*, 2021)
Kyoko M. is a *USA Today* bestselling author of *The Black Parade* urban fantasy series, the *Of Cinder and Bone* science-fiction series, and the *Starlight Contingency* space opera series with Falstaff Books. *The Black Parade* has been reviewed by *Publishers Weekly* and *New York Times* bestselling author Ilona Andrews. Kyoko M. has appeared as a guest and panelist at such conventions as Geek Girl Con, DragonCon, Blacktasticon, Momocon, JordanCon, ConCarolinas, and MultiverseCon. She is also a contributor to Marvel Comics' *Black Panther: Tales of Wakanda* anthology (2021) as well as the *Captain America: The Shield of Sam Wilson* (2025) anthology.

Kay Mabasa
Progenitor
(First Publication)
Kay Mabasa (she/her) is a Zimbabwean writer and poet who holds a BA in Publishing Studies from the National University of Science and Technology. She has had short stories and poems published in *Solarpunk Magazine, After Dinner Conversation Magazine, Brittle Paper, Deadlands Magazine* and *Maroko Magazine*, and published by Flame Tree and Inked in Gray Press. Kay is currently working on her debut short story collection. You can follow Kay on Twitter @kay_mabasa_ and Blue Sky @kaymabasa.bsky.social where she always follows back.

Oyedotun Damilola Muees
A Manual on Different Options of How to Bring a Loved One to Life
(Originally published in *Clarkesworld Magazine*, May 2022)
Damilola is a Nigerian writer of contemporary and speculative fiction, and non-fiction about pop culture. He was a winner in the 2022 PEN America Dau Prize for Emerging Writers, and a winner in the 2022 Utopia Award in the short story category. He has been published in *Reckoning*, *Clarkesworld*, *Our Move Next*, *Solarpunk*, Tor.com (*Africa Risen* anthology), *Lightspeed*, *Nightmare*, *Science Fiction World* and other places. You can find him on Twitter, @dhamlex99.

Masimba Musodza
Our Soil
(First Publication)
Masimba Musodza was born in Zimbabwe, but has lived much of his adult life in the UK, settling in the North East England town of Middlesbrough. His short fiction, mostly on the speculative fiction genre spectrum, has appeared in anthologies and periodicals around the world and online. He has published two novels and a novella in ChiShona, his native language, and a collection of short stories in English. He also writes for motion pictures.

Kortney Nash
The Long Way Home
(First Publication)
Kortney Nash is a writer, editor, and oral historian based in New Jersey. Her debut picture book is *Tell Me About Juneteenth* (Godwin Books), illustrated by Deandra Hodge, published in May 2025 and she has short stories featured in *The Black Girl Survives in this One* (Flatiron Books) and *What Rides at Night* (Microcosm publishing). When not writing, she can be found slurping ramen or losing games of online chess (or, occasionally, both at the same time). She can be found on Twitter at @quarrtknee.

Chinelo Onwualu
The Night Market
(Originally published online in *West Branch*, 2019; as an audio story by Realm.fm podcasts, 2020; and in *Omenana* magazine, 2024)
Chinelo Onwualu is a queer Nigerian writer and editor living in Toronto. She's the co-host of *Griots and Galaxies*, a podcast about African speculative fiction and the people who write it, and co-founder of *Omenana*, a magazine of African speculative fiction. Her writing has been featured in several anthologies and magazines, including *Slate*, *Uncanny* and *Strange Horizons*. She's been nominated for the Locus Awards, the British Science Fiction Awards, and the Nommo Awards for African Speculative Fiction. *Ex Marginalia*, her collection of essays by authors of colour, is available now.

J.V. Sadler
To Have Your Beans and Eat Them Too
(First Publication)
J.V. Sadler (she/her/hers) is a multi-genre writer and poet from Cincinnati, Ohio. She has an affinity for dark, avant-garde/weird, and macabre stories that have socio-political themes and commentary. Her work has been featured in *NIGHTLIGHT: A Black Horror Fiction Podcast* by

Ransom Media Productions LLC. She self-published a horror collection, *Licking*, and a poetry collection, *From My Eye to the Sky*. She is also an Oberlin College alum and currently studies Education at the University of Cincinnati. You can find all her socials and links at linktr.ee/JVSadler.

T.M. Sayed
Are We Yet Worthy
(First Publication)
T.M. Sayed is a sci-fi and fantasy obsessed nerd from the rural side of Egypt, and this story marks his debut published work. When not writing, or working as a physical therapist, he enjoys high adrenaline activities such as reading, crossword puzzles and occasionally even a walk. Many of his other rantings can be found at: @morgue-rat on tumblr.com.

George S. Schuyler
Black No More
(First published in 1931 by The Macaulay Company)
Schuyler (1895–1977) was a controversial, but successful journalist and novelist. He was an advocate for Black rights and a spokesperson for anti-racism in the United States. During the First World War, he enlisted in the U.S. Army in an all-Black division. After the war he moved to New York City, where his journalism career began. In the late 1920s he wrote for many publications, notably the *Pittsburgh Courier* – one of the largest Black newspapers in the United States at the time. Although his conservative views were problematic and unpopular at times, his work didn't go unnoticed. Notable works include *Black No More* (1931), *Black Empire* (1936) and *Slaves Today* (1931).

Ran Walker
Ten Pieces
('Scenes in Afrosurrealism', 'Black Matter, or a Moment in Time' and 'Astronaut: A Tanka' originally published in *Apollo's Toy Box*, 2024; 'Planet 4C' originally published in *Blind Corner Literary Magazine* and *The Library of Afro Curiosities: 100-Word Stories*, 2022; 'The Girl in Vernon Park' and 'Apocalyptic Ambivalence' originally published in *Keep It 100: 100-Word Stories*, 2021; 'Light Speed' originally published in *Spaceships Don't Come Equipped With Rearview Mirrors: 50-Word Stories*, 2023; 'A View From Here', 'Finity' and 'Afrofutura' origially published in *This Is Not a Poem/Story: 100-Word Stories*, 2023) Ran Walker (he/him) is an award-winning author and professor whose work spans novels, prose poetry and microfiction. He is the creator of the '100 x 100 micro novel', composed of 100 stories of exactly 100 words. His writing, translated into French, Arabic and Greek, has earned international acclaim, including honours from the Indie Author Project and the Black Caucus of the ALA. Ran teaches creative writing at Hampton University and lives in Virginia with his wife, Lauren, and their daughter, Zoë.

FLAME TREE PUBLISHING
Epic, Dark, Thrilling & Gothic

New & Classic Writing

Flame Tree's Gothic Fantasy books offer a carefully curated series of new titles, each with combinations of original and classic writing:

A Dying Planet • African Ghost • Afrofuturism • Agents & Spies • Alien Invasion Alternate History • American Gothic • Asian Ghost • Black Sci-Fi • Bodies in the Library • Chilling Crime Chilling Ghost • Chilling Horror • Christmas Gothic • Compelling Science Fiction • Cosy Crime Crime & Mystery • Detective Mysteries • Detective Thrillers • Dystopia Utopia • Endless Apocalypse Epic Fantasy • First Peoples Shared Stories • Footsteps in the Dark • Haunted House Heroic Fantasy • Hidden Realms • Immigrant Sci-Fi • Learning to be Human Lost Atlantis • Lost Souls • Lost Worlds • Lovecraft Mythos • Moon Falling • Murder Mayhem Pirates & Ghosts • Robots & AI • Robots Past & Future • Science Fiction • Shadows on the Water Spirits & Ghouls Strange Lands • Sun Rising • Supernatural Horror • Swords & Steam Terrifying Ghosts • Time Travel • Urban Crime • Weird Horror • Were Wolf

Also, new companion titles offer rich collections of classic fiction, myths and tales in the gothic fantasy tradition:

Charles Dickens Supernatural • George Orwell Visions of Dystopia • H.G. Wells • Lovecraft Sherlock Holmes • Edgar Allan Poe • Bram Stoker Horror Stories • Mary Shelley Horror Stories Sheridan Le Fanu Horror Stories • M.R. James Ghost Stories • Algernon Blackwood Horror Stories Arthur Machen Horror Stories • William Hope Hodgson Horror Stories • Robert Louis Stevenson The Age of Queen Victoria • Alice's Adventures in Wonderland • The Wonderful Wizard of Oz King Arthur & The Knights of the Round Table • Ramayana • The Odyssey and the Iliad • The Aeneid The Divine Comedy • Paradise Lost • The Decameron • One Thousand and One Arabian Nights Moby Dick • Don Quixote • Hans Christian Andersen Fairy Tales • Brothers Grimm Fairy Tales Babylon & Sumer Myths & Tales • Persian Myths & Tales • African Myths & Tales Greek Myths & Tales • Norse Myths & Tales • Chinese Myths & Tales • Japanese Myths & Tales Native American Myths & Tales • Aztec Myths & Tales • Egyptian Myths & Tales • Viking Folk & Fairy Tales Celtic Myths & Tales • Irish Fairy Tales • Scottish Folk & Fairy Tales • Heroes & Heroines Myths & Tales Quests & Journeys Myths & Tales • Gods & Monsters Myths & Tales • Titans & Giants Myths & Tales Beasts & Creatures Myths & Tales • Witches, Wizards, Seers & Healers Myths & Tales Origins & Endings Myths & Tales • Prophecies & Oracles Myths & Tales

Available from all good bookstores, worldwide, and online at
flametreepublishing.com

See our new fiction imprint
FLAME TREE PRESS | FICTION WITHOUT FRONTIERS
New and original writing in Horror, Crime, SF and Fantasy

And join our monthly newsletter with offers and more stories:
FLAME TREE FICTION NEWSLETTER
flametreepress.com

GOTHIC FANTASY